# WINTER OF THE WORLD

"GRIPPING...POWERFUL."
—*The New York Times*

"POLITICAL INTRIGUE, AMOROUS EPISODES,
SUSPENSE, AND DRAMA. HISTORY COMES TO LIFE."
—*The Louisville Courier-Journal*

"[FOLLETT] IS SO GOOD AT PLOTTING
A STORY, EVEN ONE THAT TAKES ON SUCH A COMPLEX
TOPIC AS THE WORLD WAR II ERA. THAT'S WHAT MAKES
*WINTER OF THE WORLD* SO HARD TO PUT DOWN. YOU
WANT TO KNOW WHAT HAPPENS NEXT."
—The Associated Press

"AN ENTERTAINING HISTORICAL SOAP OPERA."
—*Kirkus Reviews*

# WINTER *of the* WORLD

## EUROPEAN THEATER

BOOK TWO OF THE CENTURY TRILOGY

*CIRCA 1939–1945*

NORWAY

Bergen

SWEDE

SCOTLAND

*NORTH SEA*

Glasgow • Edinburgh

DENMARK

Copenhagen

Newcastle

Belfast

Hamburg

IRELAND Liverpool Manchester

Dublin

Berlin

ENGLAND

HOLLAND

Hanover

WALES Birmingham

GERMANY

Aberowen Cambridge

Cardiff London Dunkirk

Dresden

Southampton Calais BELGIUM

Frankfurt Pragu

Bournemouth

Brussels

*ENGLISH CHANNEL*

Amiens *SOMME RIVER*

Lemberg Königsber

Le Havre Rouen Sedan

*ALSACE-LORRAINE* *WÜRT-TEMBERG* BAVARIA

Versailles Paris *SEINE RIVER*

Brest

Belfort Basel Munich

FRANCE

Berne Innsbruck AUST

SWITZERLAND

*BAY OF BISCAY*

*LOIRE RIVER*

Geneva

Triest

Lyons

Milan Venice

Bordeaux

*RHÔNE RIVER*

Alessandria

A.

Toulouse

ITALY

Perpignan

Marseilles

Cerbère

Saragossa

Ro

*EBRO RIVER*

Barcelona

*ATLANTIC OCEAN*

SPAIN

ALGERIA

TUNISIA

## ALSO BY KEN FOLLETT

PRAISE FOR
*WINTER OF THE WORLD*

"It's hard not to like a Ken Follett book. . . . Follett does a masterful job of capturing the highs and lows of an extraordinarily bloody time. . . . He is so good at plotting a story, even one that takes on such a complex topic as the World War II era. That's what makes *Winter of the World* so hard to put down. You want to know what happens next."
—The Associated Press

"Follett's real gifts are those of a natural storyteller: swift, cinematic pacing, the ability to juggle multiple narratives coherently, and an eye for the telling detail. The result, as in *Fall of Giants*, is an honorable piece of popular entertainment and a consistently compelling portrait of a world in crisis."
—*The Washington Post*

"What [Follett] knows how to do is put readers' hearts in throats. . . . It would be surprising if this second installment did not prove to be the most powerful part of Mr. Follett's trilogy: because its naive characters improve over time, because its era is more approachable than the malaise-ridden later twentieth century, and because Mr. Follett is so reassuringly old-school."
—*The New York Times*

"Masterfully sweeping stories. . . . Although the two books of this trilogy are each upward of nine hundred pages, no fan says Ken Follett's work is too long. He is a huge critical and commercial success, entertaining with political intrigue, amorous episodes, suspense, and drama. History comes to life, and you will be advising your friends about this latest 'must read.'"
—*The Louisville Courier-Journal*

*continued . . .*

"*Winter of the World*, like its predecessor, should come with a warning label: 'Abandon your normal activities for a couple of days when you crack this one open, because you're likely to get hooked like a Copper River salmon.' . . . And, as in the previous book, Follett chooses his historical vignettes well, putting his major figures, essentially the children of the five international clusters of characters he created for *Fall of Giants*, in harm's way in the most spectacular and iconic fashion."

—*The Seattle Times*

"The man tells a story so well. . . . Follett can make things glow with some beautifully written episodes. . . . If you read Volume I, you'll have to read Volume II. And once you read Volume II, you'll be committed to reading Volume III. See you in a couple of years."

—*St. Louis Post-Dispatch*

"Follett's storytelling is unobtrusive and workmanlike, and he spins a reasonable and readable yarn that embraces dozens of characters and plenty of Big Picture history, with real historical figures bowing in now and then . . . an entertaining historical soap opera."  —*Kirkus Reviews*

"Clips along at a brisk pace. . . . He knows how to keep the pages turning and how to make the reader feel a kinship with the characters' struggles. . . . No matter the ultimate destination, readers can expect to savor the journey—and agonize while waiting for the final book to arrive."  —*The Christian Science Monitor*

### PRAISE FOR
### *FALL OF GIANTS*

"Follett is masterly in conveying so much drama and historical information so vividly . . . grippingly told."

—*The New York Times Book Review*

"*Fall of Giants*: Follett at his finest . . . sweeping epic that will thrill his fans for hours on end." —The Huffington Post

"Follett conjures the winds of war." —*The Washington Post*

"Tantalizing." —*Newsday*

"A good read. . . . It's a book that will suck you in, consume you for days or weeks, depending upon how quick a reader you are, then let you out the other side both entertained and educated. That's quite the feat."
—*USA Today*

"Follett apparently intends to give readers the sweeping history of that century in the form of a novel that follows five families—one American, two British, one German, and one Russian. That's a big job. But *Fall of Giants* suggests that Follett is up to the task." —*St. Louis Post-Dispatch*

"Follett entwines fiction and factual events well. . . . This is a dark novel, motivated by an unsparing view of human nature and a clear-eyed scrutiny of an ideal peace. It is not the least of Follett's feats that the reader finishes this near thousand-page book intrigued and wanting more." —*Chicago Sun-Times*

"Follett once again creates a world at once familiar and fantastic . . . A guiltless pleasure, the book is impossible to put down. . . . Empires fall. Heroes rise. Love conquers. After going through a war with these characters, you're left hoping that Follett gets moving with the next giant installment." —*Time Out New York*

"*Fall of Giants* grand in scope, scale, and story."
—The Associated Press

"Suspenseful, tightly constructed, sharply characterized, plot-driven."
—*The Seattle Times*

# KEN FOLLETT

# WINTER
*of the*
# WORLD

BOOK TWO OF THE CENTURY TRILOGY

 NEW AMERICAN LIBRARY

NEW AMERICAN LIBRARY
Published by the Penguin Group
Penguin Group (USA) Inc., 375 Hudson Street,
New York, New York 10014, USA

USA | Canada | UK | Ireland | Australia | New Zealand | India | South Africa | China

Penguin Books Ltd., Registered Offices: 80 Strand, London WC2R 0RL, England
For more information about the Penguin Group visit penguin.com.

Published by New American Library, a division of Penguin Group (USA) Inc.
Previously published in a Dutton edition.

First New American Library Printing, September 2013

REGISTERED TRADEMARK—MARCA REGISTRADA

New American Library Trade Paperback ISBN: 978-0-451-41924-8

THE LIBRARY OF CONGRESS HAS CATALOGED THE HARDCOVER
EDITION OF THIS TITLE AS FOLLOWS:
Follett, Ken.
p. cm.—(Century trilogy; bk. 2)
ISBN 978-0-525-95292-3
1. Twentieth century—Fiction.   2. World War, 1939–1945—Fiction.
3. Spain—History—Civil War, 1936–1939—Fiction.   I. Title
PR6056.O45W56 2012
823'.914—dc23        2012004653

Printed in the United States of America
1   3   5   7   9   10   8   6   4   2

Set in Warnock Pro
Designed by Amy Hill
Maps copyright © David Atkinson, Hand Made Maps Ltd.

PUBLISHER'S NOTE
This is a work of fiction. Names, characters, places, and incidents either are the product of the
author's imagination or are used fictitiously, and any resemblance to actual persons, living or dead,
business establishments, events, or locales is entirely coincidental.
    The publisher does not have any control over and does not assume any responsibility for author or
third-party Web sites or their content.

*To the memory of my grandparents,*

*Tom and Minnie Follett,*

*Arthur and Bessie Evans*

# CAST OF CHARACTERS

*American*

### DEWAR FAMILY

Senator Gus Dewar
Rosa Dewar, his wife
Woody Dewar, their elder son
Chuck Dewar, their younger son
Ursula Dewar, Gus's mother

### PESHKOV FAMILY

Lev Peshkov
Olga Peshkov, his wife
Daisy Peshkov, their daughter
Marga, Lev's mistress
Greg Peshkov, son of Lev and Marga
Gladys Angelus, film star, also Lev's mistress

### ROUZROKH FAMILY

Dave Rouzrokh
Joanne Rouzrokh, his daughter

### BUFFALO SOCIALITES

Dot Renshaw
Charlie Farquharson

OTHERS

Joe Brekhunov, a thug
Brian Hall, union organizer
Jacky Jakes, starlet
Eddie Parry, sailor, friend of Chuck
Captain Vandermeier, Chuck's superior
Margaret Cowdry, beautiful heiress

REAL HISTORICAL CHARACTERS

President Franklin D. Roosevelt
Marguerite "Missy" LeHand, his assistant
Vice President Harry Truman
Cordell Hull, Secretary of State
Sumner Welles, Under-Secretary of State
Colonel Leslie Groves, Army Corps of Engineers

## English

FITZHERBERT FAMILY

Earl Fitzherbert, called Fitz
Princess Bea, his wife
"Boy" Fitzherbert, Viscount Aberowen, their elder son
Andy, their younger son

LECKWITH-WILLIAMS FAMILY

Ethel Leckwith (née Williams), Member of Parliament for Aldgate
Bernie Leckwith, Ethel's husband
Lloyd Williams, Ethel's son, Bernie's stepson
Millie Leckwith, Ethel and Bernie's daughter

OTHERS

Ruby Carter, friend of Lloyd
Bing Westhampton, friend of Fitz
Lindy and Lizzie Westhampton, Bing's twin daughters
Jimmy Murray, son of General Murray
May Murray, his sister
Marquis of Lowther, called Lowthie

Naomi Avery, Millie's best friend
Abe Avery, Naomi's brother

REAL HISTORICAL CHARACTERS

Ernest Bevin, M.P., Foreign Secretary

## German and Austrian

VON ULRICH FAMILY

Walter von Ulrich
Maud, his wife (née Lady Maud Fitzherbert)
Erik, their son
Carla, their daughter
Ada Hempel, their maid
Kurt, Ada's illegitimate son
Robert von Ulrich, Walter's second cousin
Jörg Schleicher, Robert's partner
Rebecca Rosen, an orphan

FRANCK FAMILY

Ludwig Franck
Monika, his wife (née Monika von der Helbard)
Werner, their elder son
Frieda, their daughter
Axel, their younger son
Ritter, chauffeur
Count Konrad von der Helbard, Monika's father

ROTHMANN FAMILY

Dr. Isaac Rothmann
Hannelore Rothmann, his wife
Eva, their daughter
Rudi, their son

VON KESSEL FAMILY

Gottfried von Kessel
Heinrich von Kessel, his son

GESTAPO

Commissar Thomas Macke
Inspector Kringelein, Macke's boss
Reinhold Wagner
Klaus Richter
Günther Schneider

OTHERS

Hermann Braun, Erik's best friend
Sergeant Schwab, gardener
Wilhelm Frunze, scientist

## Russian

PESHKOV FAMILY

Grigori Peshkov
Katerina, his wife
Vladimir, always called Volodya, their son
Anya, their daughter

OTHERS

Zoya Vorotsyntsev, physicist
Ilya Dvorkin, officer of the secret police
Colonel Lemitov, Volodya's boss
Colonel Bobrov, Red Army officer in Spain

REAL HISTORICAL CHARACTERS

Lavrentiy Beria, head of the secret police
Vyacheslav Molotov, Foreign Minister

## Spanish

Teresa, literacy teacher

## *Welsh*

### WILLIAMS FAMILY

Dai Williams, "Granda"
Cara Williams, "Grandmam"
Billy Williams, M.P. for Aberowen
Dave, Billy's elder son
Keir, Billy's younger son

### GRIFFITHS FAMILY

Tommy Griffiths, Billy Williams's political agent
Lenny Griffiths, Tommy's son

# PART ONE

# THE OTHER CHEEK

# CHAPTER ONE

# 1933

C arla knew her parents were about to have a row. The second she walked into the kitchen, she felt the hostility, like the bone-deep cold of the wind that blew through the streets of Berlin before a February snowstorm. She almost turned and walked back out again.

It was unusual for them to fight. Mostly they were affectionate—too much so. Carla cringed when they kissed in front of other people. Her friends thought it was strange: their parents did not do that. She had said that to her mother, once. Mother had laughed in a pleased way and said: "The day after our wedding, your father and I were separated by the Great War." She had been born English, though you could hardly tell. "I stayed in London while he came home to Germany and joined the army." Carla had heard this story many times, but Mother never tired of telling it. "We thought the war would last three months, but I didn't see him again for five years. All that time I longed to touch him. Now I never tire of it."

Father was just as bad. "Your mother is the cleverest woman I ever met," he had said here in the kitchen just a few days ago. "That's why I married her. It had nothing to do with . . ." He had trailed off, and Mother and he had giggled conspiratorially, as if Carla at the age of eleven knew nothing about sex. It was so embarrassing.

But once in a while they had a quarrel. Carla knew the signs. And a new one was about to erupt.

They were sitting at opposite ends of the kitchen table. Father was somberly dressed in a dark gray suit, starched white shirt, and black satin tie. He looked dapper, as always, even though his hair was receding and his waistcoat bulged a little beneath the gold watch chain. His face was frozen in an expression of false calm. Carla knew that look. He wore it when one of the family had done something that angered him.

He held in his hand a copy of the weekly magazine for which Mother worked, *The Democrat*. She wrote a column of political and diplomatic gossip under the name of Lady Maud. Father began to read aloud. "'Our new chancellor, Herr Adolf Hitler, made his debut in diplomatic society at President Hindenburg's reception.'"

The president was the head of state, Carla knew. He was elected, but he stood above the squabbles of day-to-day politics, acting as referee. The chancellor was the premier. Although Hitler had been made chancellor, his Nazi Party did not have an overall majority in the Reichstag—the German parliament—so, for the present, the other parties could restrain Nazi excesses.

Father spoke with distaste, as if forced to mention something repellent, like sewage. "'He looked uncomfortable in a formal tailcoat.'"

Carla's mother sipped her coffee and looked out of the window to the street, as if interested in the people hurrying to work in scarves and gloves. She, too, was pretending to be calm, but Carla knew she was just waiting for her moment.

The maid, Ada, was standing at the counter in an apron, slicing cheese. She put a plate in front of Father, but he ignored it. "'Herr Hitler was evidently charmed by Elisabeth Cerruti, the cultured wife of the Italian ambassador, in a rose-pink velvet gown trimmed with sable.'"

Mother always wrote about what people were wearing. She said it helped the reader picture them. She herself had fine clothes, but times were hard and she had not bought anything new for years. This morning she looked slim and elegant in a navy blue cashmere dress that was probably as old as Carla.

"'Signora Cerruti, who is Jewish, is a passionate Fascist, and they talked for many minutes. Did she beg Hitler to stop whipping up hatred of Jews?'" Father put the magazine down on the table with a slap.

Here it comes, Carla thought.

"You realize that will infuriate the Nazis," he said.

"I hope so," Mother said coolly. "The day they're pleased with what I write, I shall give it up."

"They're dangerous when riled."

Mother's eyes flashed anger. "Don't you dare condescend to me, Walter. I know they're dangerous—that's why I oppose them."

"I just don't see the point of making them irate."

"You attack them in the Reichstag." Father was an elected parliamentary representative for the Social Democratic Party.

"I take part in a reasoned debate."

This is typical, Carla thought. Father was logical, cautious, law-abiding. Mother had style and humor. He got his way by quiet persistence, she with charm and cheek. They would never agree.

Father added: "I don't drive the Nazis mad with fury."

"Perhaps that's because you don't do them much harm."

Father was irritated by her quick wit. His voice became louder. "And you think you damage them with jokes?"

"I mock them."

"And that's your substitute for argument."

"I believe we need both."

Father became angrier. "But, Maud, don't you see how you're putting yourself and your family at risk?"

"On the contrary. The real danger is *not* to mock the Nazis. What would life be like for our children if Germany became a Fascist state?"

This kind of talk made Carla feel queasy. She could not bear to hear that the family was in danger. Life must go on as it always had. She wished she could sit in this kitchen for an eternity of mornings, with her parents at opposite ends of the pine table, Ada at the counter, and her brother, Erik, thumping around upstairs, late again. Why should anything change?

She had listened to political talk every breakfast-time of her life and she thought she understood what her parents did, and how they planned to make Germany a better place for everyone. But lately they had begun to talk in a different way. They seemed to think that a terrible danger loomed, but Carla could not quite imagine what it was.

Father said: "God knows I'm doing everything I can to hold back Hitler and his mob."

"And so am I. But when you do it, you believe you're following a sensible course." Mother's face hardened in resentment. "And when I do it, I'm accused of putting the family at risk."

"And with good reason," said Father. The row was only just getting started, but at that moment Erik came down, clattering like a horse on the stairs, and lurched into the kitchen with his school satchel swinging from his shoulder. He was thirteen, two years older than Carla, and there were unsightly black hairs sprouting from his upper lip. When they were small, Carla and Erik had played together all the time; but those days were over, and since he had grown so tall, he had pretended to think she was stupid and childish. In fact she was smarter than he, and knew about a lot of things he did not understand, such as women's monthly cycles.

"What was that last tune you were playing?" he said to Mother.

The piano often woke them in the morning. It was a Steinway grand—inherited, like the house itself, from Father's parents. Mother played in the morning because, she said, she was too busy the rest of the day and too tired in the evening. This morning she had performed a Mozart sonata, then a jazz tune. "It's called 'Tiger Rag,'" she told Erik. "Do you want some cheese?"

"Jazz is decadent," Erik said.

"Don't be silly."

Ada handed Erik a plate of cheese and sliced sausage, and he began to shovel it in. Carla thought his manners were dreadful.

Father looked severe. "Who's been teaching you this nonsense, Erik?"

"Hermann Braun says that jazz isn't music, just Negroes making a noise." Hermann was Erik's best friend; his father was a member of the Nazi Party.

"Hermann should try to play it." Father looked at Mother, and his face softened. She smiled at him. He went on: "Your mother tried to teach me ragtime, many years ago, but I couldn't master the rhythm."

Mother laughed. "It was like trying to get a giraffe to roller-skate."

The fight was over, Carla saw with relief. She began to feel better. She took some black bread and dipped it in milk.

But now Erik wanted an argument. "Negroes are an inferior race," he said defiantly.

"I doubt that," Father said patiently. "If a Negro boy were brought up in a nice house full of books and paintings, and sent to an expensive school with good teachers, he might turn out to be smarter than you."

"That's ridiculous!" Erik protested.

Mother put in: "Don't call your father ridiculous, you foolish boy." Her tone was mild: she had used up her anger on Father. Now she just sounded wearily disappointed. "You don't know what you're talking about, and neither does Hermann Braun."

Erik said: "But the Aryan race must be superior—we rule the world!"

"Your Nazi friends don't know any history," Father said. "The Ancient Egyptians built the pyramids when Germans were living in caves. Arabs ruled the world in the Middle Ages—the Muslims were doing algebra when German princes could not write their own names. It's nothing to do with race."

Carla frowned and said: "What is it to do with, then?"

Father looked at her fondly. "That's a very good question, and you're a bright girl to ask it." She glowed with pleasure at his praise. "Civilizations rise and fall—the Chinese, the Aztecs, the Romans—but no one really knows why."

"Eat up, everyone, and put your coats on," Mother said. "It's getting late."

Father pulled his watch out of his waistcoat pocket and looked at it with raised eyebrows. "It's not late."

"I've got to take Carla to the Francks' house," Mother said. "The girls' school is closed for a day—something about repairing the furnace—so Carla's going to spend today with Frieda."

Frieda Franck was Carla's best friend. Their mothers were best friends, too. In fact, when they were young, Frieda's mother, Monika, had been in love with Father—a hilarious fact that Frieda's grandmother had revealed one day after drinking too much Sekt.

Father said: "Why can't Ada look after Carla?"

"Ada has an appointment with the doctor."

"Ah."

Carla expected Father to ask what was wrong with Ada, but he nodded as if he already knew, and put his watch away. Carla wanted to ask, but something told her she should not. She made a mental note to ask Mother later. Then she immediately forgot about it.

Father left first, wearing a long black overcoat. Then Erik put on his cap—perching it as far back on his head as it would go without falling off, as was the fashion among his friends—and followed Father out of the door.

Carla and her mother helped Ada clear the table. Carla loved Ada almost as much as she loved her mother. When Carla was little, Ada had taken care of her full-time, until she was old enough to go to school, for Mother had always worked. Ada was not married yet. She was twenty-nine and homely-looking, though she had a lovely kind smile. Last summer she had had a romance with a policeman, Paul Huber, but it had not lasted.

Carla and her mother stood in front of the mirror in the hall and put on their hats. Mother took her time. She chose a dark blue felt, with a round crown and a narrow brim, the type all the women were wearing, but she tilted hers at a different angle, making it look chic. As Carla put on her knitted wool cap, she wondered whether she would ever have Mother's sense of style. Mother looked like a goddess of war, her long neck and chin and cheekbones carved out of white marble; beautiful, yes, but definitely not pretty. Carla had the same dark hair and green eyes, but looked more like a plump doll than a statue. Carla had once accidentally overheard her grandmother say to Mother: "Your ugly duckling will grow into a swan, you'll see." Carla was still waiting for it to happen.

When Mother was ready, they went out. Their home stood in a row of tall, gracious town houses in the Mitte district, the old center of the city, built for high-ranking ministers and army officers such as Carla's grandfather, who had worked at the nearby government buildings.

Carla and her mother rode a tram along Unter den Linden, then took the S train from Friedrich Strasse to the Zoo Station. The Francks lived in the southwestern suburb of Schöneberg.

Carla was hoping to see Frieda's brother Werner, who was fourteen. She liked him. Sometimes Carla and Frieda imagined they each married the other's brother, and were next-door neighbors, and their children were best friends. It was just a game to Frieda, but Carla was secretly serious. Werner was handsome and grown-up and not a bit silly like Erik. In the dollhouse in Carla's bedroom, the mother and father sleeping side by side in the miniature double bed were called Carla and Werner, but no one knew that, not even Frieda.

Frieda had another brother, Axel, seven, but he had been born with spina bifida, and had to have constant medical care. He lived in a special hospital on the outskirts of Berlin.

Mother was preoccupied on the journey. "I hope this is going to be all right," she muttered, half to herself, as they got off the train.

"Of course it will," Carla said. "I'll have a lovely time with Frieda."

"I didn't mean that. I'm talking about my paragraph about Hitler."

"Are we in danger? Was Father right?"

"Your father is usually right."

"What will happen to us if we've annoyed the Nazis?"

Mother stared at her strangely for a long moment, then said: "Dear God, what kind of a world did I bring you into?" Then she went quiet.

After a ten-minute walk they arrived at a grand villa in a big garden. The Francks were rich: Frieda's father, Ludwig, owned a factory making radio sets. Two cars stood in the driveway. The large shiny black one belonged to Herr Franck. The engine rumbled, and a cloud of blue vapor rose from the tailpipe. The chauffeur, Ritter, with uniform trousers tucked into high boots, stood cap in hand ready to open the door. He bowed and said: "Good morning, Frau von Ulrich."

The second car was a little green two-seater. A short man with a gray beard came out of the house carrying a leather case, and touched his hat to Mother as he got into the small car. "I wonder what Dr. Rothmann is doing here so early in the morning," Mother said anxiously.

They soon found out. Frieda's mother, Monika, came to the door, a tall woman with a mass of red hair. Anxiety showed on her pale face. Instead of welcoming them in, she stood squarely in the doorway as if to bar their entrance. "Frieda has measles!" she said.

"I'm so sorry!" said Mother. "How is she?"

"Miserable. She has a fever and a cough. But Rothmann says she'll be all right. However, she's quarantined."

"Of course. Have you had it?"

"Yes—when I was a girl."

"And Werner has, too—I remember he had a terrible rash all over. But what about your husband?" Mother asked.

"Ludi had it as a boy."

Both women looked at Carla. She had never had measles. She realized this meant she could not spend the day with Frieda.

Carla was disappointed, but Mother was quite shaken. "This week's magazine is our election issue—I *can't* be absent." She looked distraught. All the grown-ups were apprehensive about the general election to be held next Sunday. Mother and Father both feared the Nazis might do well enough to take full control of the government. "Plus my oldest friend is visiting from London. I wonder whether Walter could be persuaded to take a day off to look after Carla?"

Monika said: "Why don't you telephone him?"

Not many people had phones in their homes, but the Francks did, and Carla and her mother stepped into the hall. The instrument stood on a spindly-legged table near the door. Mother picked it up and gave the number of Father's office at the Reichstag, the parliament building. She got through to him and explained the situation. She listened for a minute, then looked angry. "My magazine will urge a hundred thousand readers to campaign for the Social Democratic Party," she said. "Do you really have something more important than that to do today?"

Carla could guess how this argument would end. Father loved her dearly, she knew, but in all her eleven years he had never looked after her for a whole day. All her friends' fathers were the same. Men did not do that sort of thing. But Mother sometimes pretended not to know the rules women lived by.

"I'll just have to take her to the office with me, then," Mother said into the phone. "I dread to think what Jochmann will say." Herr Jochmann was her boss. "He's not much of a feminist at the best of times." She replaced the handset without saying good-bye.

Carla hated it when they fought, and this was the second time in a day. It made the whole world seem unstable. She was much more scared of quarrels than of the Nazis.

"Come on, then," Mother said to her, and she moved to the door.

I'm not even going to see Werner, Carla thought unhappily.

Just then Frieda's father appeared in the hall, a pink-faced man with a small black mustache, energetic and cheerful. He greeted Mother pleasantly, and she paused to speak politely to him while Monika helped him into a black topcoat with a fur collar.

He went to the foot of the stairs. "Werner!" he shouted. "I'm going without you!" He put on a gray felt hat and went out.

"I'm ready, I'm ready!" Werner ran down the stairs like a dancer. He was as tall as his father and more handsome, with red-blond hair worn too long. Under his arm he had a leather satchel that appeared to be full of books; in the other hand he held a pair of ice skates and a hockey stick. He paused in his rush to say: "Good morning, Frau von Ulrich," very politely. Then in a more informal tone: "Hello, Carla. My sister's got the measles."

Carla felt herself blush, for no reason at all. "I know," she said. She tried to think of something charming and amusing to say, but came up with nothing. "I've never had it, so I can't see her."

"I had it when I was a kid," he said, as if that was ever such a long time ago. "I must hurry," he added apologetically.

Carla did not want to lose sight of him so quickly. She followed him outside. Ritter was holding the rear door open. "What kind of car is that?" Carla said. Boys always knew the makes of cars.

"A Mercedes-Benz W10 limousine."

"It looks very comfortable." She caught a look from her mother, half surprised and half amused.

Werner said: "Do you want a lift?"

"That would be nice."

"I'll ask my father." Werner put his head inside the car and said something.

Carla heard Herr Franck reply: "Very well, but hurry up!"

She turned to her mother. "We can go in the car!"

Mother hesitated for only a moment. She did not like Herr Franck's politics—he gave money to the Nazis—but she was not going to refuse a lift in a warm car on a cold morning. "How very kind of you, Ludwig," she said.

They got in. There was room for four in the back. Ritter pulled away smoothly. "I assume you're going to Koch Strasse?" said Herr Franck. Many newspapers and book publishers had their offices in the same street in the Kreuzberg district.

"Please don't go out of your way. Leipziger Strasse would be fine."

"I'd be happy to take you to the door—but I suppose you don't want your leftist colleagues to see you getting out of the car of a bloated plutocrat." His tone was somewhere between humorous and hostile.

Mother gave him a charming smile. "You're not bloated, Ludi—just a little plump." She patted the front of his coat.

He laughed. "I asked for that." The tension eased. Herr Franck picked up the speaking tube and gave instructions to Ritter.

Carla was thrilled to be in a car with Werner, and she wanted to make the most of it by talking to him, but at first she could not think what to speak about. She really wanted to say: "When you're older, do you think you might marry a girl with dark hair and green eyes, about three years younger than yourself, and clever?" Eventually she pointed to his skates and said: "Do you have a match today?"

"No, just practise after school."

"What position do you play in?" She knew nothing about ice hockey, but there were always positions in team games.

"Right wing."

"Isn't it a rather dangerous sport?"

"Not if you're quick."

"You must be ever such a good skater."

"Not bad," he said modestly.

Once again Carla caught her mother watching her with an enigmatic little smile. Had she guessed how Carla felt about Werner? Carla felt another blush coming.

Then the car came to a stop outside a school building, and Werner got out. "Good-bye, everyone!" he said, and ran through the gates into the yard.

Ritter drove on, following the south bank of the Landwehr Canal. Carla looked at the barges, their loads of coal topped with snow like mountains. She felt a sense of disappointment. She had contrived to spend longer with Werner, by hinting that she wanted a lift; then she had wasted the time talking about ice hockey.

What would she have liked to talk to him about? She did not know.

Herr Franck said to Mother: "I read your column in *The Democrat*."

"I hope you enjoyed it."

"I was sorry to see you writing disrespectfully about our chancellor."

"Do you think journalists should write respectfully about politicians?" Mother replied cheerfully. "That's radical. The Nazi press would have to be polite about my husband! They wouldn't like that."

"Not all politicians, obviously," Franck said irritably.

They crossed the teeming junction of Potsdamer Platz. Cars and trams vied with horse-drawn carts and pedestrians in a chaotic melee.

Mother said: "Isn't it better for the press to be able to criticize everyone equally?"

"A wonderful idea," he said. "But you socialists live in a dream world. We practical men know that Germany cannot live on ideas. People must have bread and shoes and coal."

"I quite agree," Mother said. "I could use more coal myself. But I want Carla and Erik to grow up as citizens of a free country."

"You overrate freedom. It doesn't make people happy. They prefer leadership. I want Werner and Frieda and poor Axel to grow up in a country that is proud, and disciplined, and united."

"And in order to be united, we need young thugs in brown shirts to beat up elderly Jewish shopkeepers?"

"Politics is rough. Nothing we can do about it."

"On the contrary. You and I are leaders, Ludwig, in our different ways. It's our responsibility to make politics less rough—more honest, more rational, less violent. If we do not do that, we fail in our patriotic duty."

Herr Franck bristled.

Carla did not know much about men, but she realized they did not like to be lectured on their duty by women. Mother must have forgotten to press her charm switch this morning. But everyone was tense. The coming election had them all on edge.

The car reached Leipziger Platz. "Where may I drop you?" Herr Franck said coldly.

"Just here will be fine," said Mother.

Franck tapped on the glass partition. Ritter stopped the car and hurried to open the door.

Mother said: "I do hope Frieda gets better soon."

"Thank you."

They got out and Ritter closed the door.

The office was several minutes' walk away, but Mother clearly had not wanted to stay any longer in the car. Carla hoped Mother was not going to quarrel permanently with Herr Franck. That might make it difficult for her to see Frieda and Werner. She would hate that.

They set off at a brisk pace. "Try not to make a nuisance of yourself at the office," Mother said. The note of genuine pleading in her voice touched Carla, making her feel ashamed of causing her mother worry. She resolved to behave perfectly.

Mother greeted several people on the way: she had been writing her column for as long as Carla could remember, and was well known in the press corps. They all called her "Lady Maud" in English.

Near the building in which *The Democrat* had its office, they saw someone they knew: Sergeant Schwab. He had fought with Father in the Great War, and still wore his hair brutally short in the military style. After the war he had worked as a gardener, first for Carla's grandfather and later for her father, but he had stolen money from Mother's purse and Father had sacked him. Now he was wearing the ugly military uniform of the storm troopers, the Brownshirts, who were not soldiers but Nazis who had been given the authority of auxiliary policemen.

Schwab said loudly: "Good morning, Frau von Ulrich!" as if he felt no shame at all about being a thief. He did not even touch his cap.

Mother nodded coldly and walked past him. "I wonder what he's doing here," she muttered uneasily as they went inside.

The magazine had the first floor of a modern office building. Carla knew a child would not be welcome, and she hoped they could reach Mother's office without being seen. But they met Herr Jochmann on the stairs. He was a heavy man with thick spectacles. "What's this?" he said brusquely, speaking around the cigarette in his mouth. "Are we running a kindergarten now?"

Mother did not react to his rudeness. "I was thinking over your comment the other day," she said. "About how young people imagine journalism is a glamorous profession, and don't understand how much hard work is necessary."

He frowned. "Did I say that? Well, it's certainly true."

"So I brought my daughter here to see the reality. I think it will be good for her education, especially if she becomes a writer. She will make a report on the visit to her class. I felt sure you would approve."

Mother was making this up as she went along, but it sounded convincing, Carla thought. She almost believed it herself. The charm switch had been turned to the On position at last.

Jochmann said: "Don't you have an important visitor from London coming today?"

"Yes, Ethel Leckwith, but she's an old friend—she knew Carla as a baby."

Jochmann was somewhat mollified. "Hmm. Well, we have an editorial meeting in five minutes, as soon as I've bought some cigarettes."

"Carla will get them for you." Mother turned to her. "There is a tobacconist three doors down. Herr Jochmann likes the Roth-Händle brand."

"Oh, that will save me a trip." Jochmann gave Carla a one-mark coin.

Mother said to her: "When you come back, you'll find me at the top of the stairs, next to the fire alarm." She turned away and took Jochmann's arm confidentially. "I thought last week's issue was possibly our best ever," she said as they went up.

Carla ran out into the street. Mother had got away with it, using her characteristic mixture of boldness and flirting. She sometimes said: "We women have to deploy every weapon we have." Thinking about it, Carla realized she had used Mother's tactics to get a lift from Herr Franck. Perhaps she was like her mother after all. That might be why Mother had given her that curious little smile: she was seeing herself thirty years ago.

There was a queue in the shop. Half the journalists in Berlin seemed to be buying their supplies for the day. At last Carla got a pack of Roth-Händles and returned to the *Democrat* building. She found the fire alarm easily—it was a big lever fixed to the wall—but Mother was not in her office. No doubt she had gone to that editorial meeting.

Carla walked along the corridor. All the doors were open, and most of the rooms were empty but for a few women who might have been typists and secretaries. At the back of the building, around a corner, was a closed door marked CONFERENCE ROOM. Carla could hear male voices raised in argument. She tapped on the door, but there was no response. She hesitated, then turned the handle and went in.

The room was full of tobacco smoke. Eight or ten people sat around a long table. Mother was the only woman. They fell silent, apparently surprised, when Carla went up to the head of the table and handed Jochmann the cigarettes and change. Their silence made her think she had done wrong to come in.

But Jochmann just said: "Thank you."

"You're welcome, sir," she said, and for some reason she gave a little bow.

The men laughed. One said: "New assistant, Jochmann?" Then she knew it was all right.

She left the room quickly and returned to Mother's office. She did not take off her coat—the place was cold. She looked around. On the desk were a phone, a typewriter, and stacks of paper and carbon paper.

Next to the phone was a photograph in a frame, showing Carla and Erik with Father. It had been taken a couple of years ago on a sunny day at the beach by the Wannsee lake, fifteen miles from the center of Berlin. Father was wearing shorts. They were all laughing. That was before Erik started to pretend to be a tough, serious man.

The only other picture, hanging on the wall, showed Mother with the Social Democratic hero Friedrich Ebert, who had been the first president of Germany after the war. It had been taken about ten years ago. Carla smiled at Mother's shapeless, low-waisted dress and boyish haircut; they must have been fashionable at the time.

The bookshelf held social directories, phone books, dictionaries in several languages, and atlases, but nothing to read. In the desk drawer were pencils, several new pairs of formal gloves still wrapped in tissue paper, a packet of sanitary towels, and a notebook with names and phone numbers.

Carla reset the desk calendar to today's date, Monday, February 27, 1933. Then she put a sheet of paper into the typewriter. She typed her full name, Heike Carla von Ulrich. At the age of five she had announced that she did not like the name Heike and she wanted everyone to use her second name, and somewhat to her surprise her family had complied.

Each key of the typewriter caused a metal rod to rise up and strike the paper through an inky ribbon, printing a letter. When by accident she pressed two keys, the rods got stuck. She tried to prize them apart but she could not. Pressing another key did not help: now there were three jammed rods. She groaned: she was in trouble already.

A noise from the street distracted her. She went to the window. A dozen Brownshirts were marching along the middle of the road, shouting slogans: "Death to all Jews! Jews, go to hell!" Carla could not understand why they got so angry about Jews, who seemed the same as everyone else, apart from their religion. She was startled to see Sergeant Schwab at the head of the troop. She had felt sorry for him when he was sacked, for she knew he would find it hard to get another job. There were millions of men looking for jobs in Germany; Father said it was a depression. But Mother had said: "How can we have a man in our house who steals?"

Their chant changed. "Smash Jew papers!" they said in unison. One of them threw something, and a rotten vegetable splashed on the door of a national newspaper. Then, to Carla's horror, they turned toward the building she was in.

She drew back and peeped around the edge of the window frame, hoping they could not see her. They stopped outside, still chanting. One threw a stone. It hit Carla's window without breaking it, but all the same she gave a little scream of fear. A moment later one of the typists came in, a young woman in a red beret. "What's the matter?" she said; then she looked out of the window. "Oh, hell."

The Brownshirts entered the building, and Carla heard boots on the stairs. She was scared: What were they going to do?

Sergeant Schwab came into Mother's office. He hesitated, seeing the two females, then seemed to screw up his nerve. He picked up the typewriter and threw it through the window, shattering the glass. Carla and the typist both screamed.

More Brownshirts passed the doorway, shouting their slogans.

Schwab grabbed the typist by the arm and said: "Now, darling, where's the office safe?"

"In the file room!" she said in a terrified voice.

"Show me."

"Yes, anything!"

He marched her out of the room.

Carla started to cry, then stopped herself.

She thought of hiding under the desk, but hesitated. She did not want to show them how scared she was. Something inside her wanted to defy them.

But what should she do? She decided to warn Mother.

She stepped to the doorway and looked along the corridor. The Brownshirts were going in and out of the offices but had not reached the far end. Carla did not know whether the people in the conference room could hear the commotion. She ran along the corridor as fast as she could, but a scream stopped her. She looked into a room and saw Schwab shaking the typist with the red beret, yelling: "Where's the key?"

"I don't know. I swear I'm telling the truth!" the typist cried.

Carla was outraged. Schwab had no right to treat a woman that way. She shouted: "Leave her alone, Schwab, you thief!"

Schwab looked at her with hatred in his eyes, and suddenly she was ten times more frightened. Then his gaze shifted to someone behind her, and he said: "Get the kid out of the damn way."

She was picked up from behind. "Are you a little Jew?" said a man's voice. "You look it, with all that dark hair."

That terrified her. "I'm not Jewish!" she screamed.

The Brownshirt carried her back along the corridor and put her down in Mother's office. She stumbled and fell to the floor. "Stay in here," he said, and he went away.

Carla got to her feet. She was not hurt. The corridor was full of Brownshirts now, and she could not get to her mother. But she had to summon help.

She looked out of the smashed window. A small crowd was gathering on the street. Two policemen stood among the onlookers, chatting. Carla shouted at them: "Help! Help, police!"

They saw her and laughed.

That infuriated her, and anger made her less frightened. She looked outside the office again. Her gaze lit on the fire alarm on the wall. She reached up and grasped the handle.

She hesitated. You were not supposed to sound the alarm unless there was a fire, and a notice on the wall warned of dire penalties.

She pulled the handle anyway.

For a moment nothing happened. Perhaps the mechanism was not working.

Then there came a loud, harsh klaxon sound, rising and falling, that filled the building.

Almost immediately the people from the conference room appeared at the far end of the corridor. Jochmann was first. "What the devil is going on?" he said angrily, shouting over the noise of the alarm.

One of the Brownshirts said: "This Jew Communist rag has insulted our leader, and we're closing it down."

"Get out of my office!"

The Brownshirt ignored him and went into a side room. A moment later there was a female scream and a crash that sounded like a steel desk being overturned.

Jochmann turned to one of his staff. "Schneider—call the police immediately!"

Carla knew that would be no good. The police were there already, doing nothing.

Mother pushed through the knot of people and came running along the corridor. "Are you all right?" she cried. She threw her arms around Carla.

Carla did not want to be comforted like a child. Pushing her mother away, she said: "I'm fine. Don't worry."

Mother looked around. "My typewriter!"

"They threw it through the window." Carla realized that now she would not get into trouble for jamming the mechanism.

"We must get out of here." Mother snatched up the desk photo, then took Carla's hand, and they hurried out of the room.

No one tried to stop them running down the stairs. Ahead of them, a well-built young man who might have been one of the reporters had a Brownshirt in a headlock and was dragging him out of the building. Carla and her mother followed the pair out. Another Brownshirt came up behind them.

The reporter approached the two policemen, still dragging the Brownshirt. "Arrest this man," he said. "I found him robbing the office. You will find a stolen jar of coffee in his pocket."

"Release him, please," said the older of the two policemen.

Reluctantly, the reporter let the Brownshirt go.

The second Brownshirt stood beside his colleague.

"What is your name, sir?" the policeman asked the reporter.

"I am Rudolf Schmidt, chief parliamentary correspondent of *The Democrat*."

"Rudolph Schmidt, I am arresting you on a charge of assaulting the police."

"Don't be ridiculous. I caught this man stealing!"

The policeman nodded to the two Brownshirts. "Take him to the station house."

They grabbed Schmidt by the arms. He seemed about to struggle, then changed his mind. "Every detail of this incident will appear in the next edition of *The Democrat*!" he said.

"There will never be another edition," the policeman said. "Take him away."

A fire engine arrived and half a dozen firemen jumped out. Their leader spoke brusquely to the police. "We need to clear the building," he said.

"Go back to your fire station—there's no fire," said the older policeman. "It's just the storm troopers closing down a Communist magazine."

"That's no concern of mine," the fireman said. "The alarm has been sounded, and our first task is to get everyone out, storm troopers and all. We'll manage without your help." He led his men inside.

Carla heard her mother say: "Oh, no!" She turned and saw that Mother was staring at her typewriter, which lay on the pavement where it had fallen. The metal casing had dropped away, exposing the links between keys and rods. The keyboard was twisted out of shape, one end of the roller had become detached, and the bell that sounded for the end of a line lay forlornly on the ground. A typewriter was not a precious object, but Mother looked as if she might cry.

The Brownshirts and the staff of the magazine came out of the building, herded by firemen. Sergeant Schwab was resisting, shouting angrily: "There's no fire!" The firemen just shoved him on.

Jochmann came out and said to Mother: "They didn't have time to do much damage—the firemen stopped them. Whoever sounded the alarm did us a great service!"

Carla had been worried that she would be reprimanded for causing a false alarm. Now she realized she had done exactly the right thing.

She took her mother's hand. That seemed to jerk Mother out of her momentary fit of grief. She wiped her eyes with her sleeve, an unusual act that revealed how badly shaken she was: if Carla had done that, she would have been told to use her handkerchief. "What do we do now?" Mother never said that—she always knew what to do next.

Carla became aware of two people standing nearby. She looked up. One was a woman about the same age as Mother, very pretty, with an air of authority. Carla knew her, but could not place her. Beside her was a man young enough to be her son. He was slim, and not very tall, but he looked like a movie star. He had a handsome face that would have been almost too pretty except that his nose was flattened and misshapen. Both newcomers looked shocked, and the young man was white with anger.

The woman spoke first, and she used the English language. "Hello, Maud," she said, and the voice was distantly familiar to Carla. "Don't you recognize me?" she went on. "I'm Eth Leckwith, and this is Lloyd."

## ii

Lloyd Williams found a boxing club in Berlin where he could do an hour's training for a few pennies. It was in a working-class district called Wedding, north of the city center. He exercised with the Indian clubs and the medicine ball, skipped rope, hit the punch bag, and then put on a helmet and did five rounds in the ring. The club coach found him a sparring partner, a German his own age and size—Lloyd was a welterweight. The German boy had a nice fast jab that came from nowhere and hurt Lloyd several times, until Lloyd hit him with a left hook and knocked him down.

Lloyd had been raised in a rough neighborhood, the East End of London. At the age of twelve he had been bullied at school. "Same thing happened to me," his stepfather, Bernie Leckwith, had said. "Cleverest boy in school, and you get picked on by the class *shlammer*." Bernie, whom he called "Dad," was Jewish—his mother spoke only Yiddish. He had taken Lloyd to the Aldgate Boxing Club. Ethel had been against it, but Bernie had overruled her, something that did not happen often.

Lloyd had learned to move fast and punch hard, and the bullying had stopped. He had also got the broken nose that made him look less of a pretty boy. And he discovered a talent. He had quick reflexes and a combative streak, and he had won prizes in the ring. The coach was disappointed that he wanted to go to Cambridge University instead of turning professional.

He showered and put his suit back on, then went to a workingmen's bar, bought a glass of draft beer, and sat down to write to his half sister, Millie, about the incident with the Brownshirts. Millie was envious of his taking this trip with their mother, and he had promised to send her frequent bulletins.

Lloyd had been shaken by this morning's fracas. Politics was part of everyday life for him: his mother had been a member of Parliament, his father was a local councilor in London, and he himself was London chairman of the Labour League of Youth. But it had always been a matter of debating and voting—until today. He had never before seen an office trashed by uniformed thugs while the police looked on, smiling. It was politics with the gloves off, and it had shocked him.

"Could this happen in London, Millie?" he wrote. His first instinct was to think it could not. But Hitler had admirers among British industrialists and newspaper proprietors. Only a few months ago the rogue M.P. Sir Oswald Mosley had started the British Union of Fascists. Like the Nazis, they liked to strut up and down in military-style uniforms. What next?

He finished his letter and folded it, then caught the S train back into the city center. He and his mother were going to meet Walter and Maud von Ulrich for dinner. Lloyd had been hearing about Maud all his life. She and his mother were unlikely friends: Ethel had started her working life as a maid in a grand house owned by Maud's family. Later they had been suffragettes together, campaigning for votes for women. During the war they had produced a feminist newspaper, *The Soldier's Wife*. Then they had quarreled over political tactics and become estranged.

Lloyd could remember vividly the von Ulrich family's trip to London in 1925. He had been ten, old enough to feel embarrassed that he spoke no German while Erik and Carla, aged five and three, were bilingual. That was when Ethel and Maud had patched up their quarrel.

He made his way to the restaurant, Bistro Robert. The interior was art deco, with unforgivingly rectangular chairs and tables, and elaborate iron lamp stands with colored glass shades; but he liked the starched white napkins standing at attention beside the plates.

The other three were already there. The women were striking, he realized as he approached the table: both poised, well dressed, attractive, and confident. They were getting admiring glances from other diners. He wondered how much of his mother's modish dress sense had been picked up from her aristocratic friend.

When they had ordered, Ethel explained her trip. "I lost my parliamentary seat in 1931," she said. "I hope to win it back at the next election, but meanwhile I have to make a living. Fortunately, Maud, you taught me to be a journalist."

"I didn't teach you much," Maud said. "You had a natural talent."

"I'm writing a series of articles about the Nazis for the *News Chronicle*, and I have a contract to write a book for a publisher called Victor Gollancz. I brought Lloyd as my interpreter—he's studying French and German."

Lloyd observed her proud smile and felt he did not deserve it. "My translation skills have not been much tested," he said. "So far we've mostly met people like you, who speak perfect English."

Lloyd had ordered breaded veal, a dish he had never even seen in England. He found it delicious. While they were eating, Walter said to him: "Shouldn't you be at school?"

"Mam thought I would learn more German this way, and the school agreed."

"Why don't you come and work for me in the Reichstag for a while? Unpaid, I'm afraid, but you'd be speaking German all day."

Lloyd was thrilled. "I'd love to. What a marvelous opportunity!"

"If Ethel can spare you," Walter added.

She smiled. "Perhaps I can have him back now and again, when I really need him?"

"Of course."

Ethel reached across the table and touched Walter's hand. It was an intimate gesture, and Lloyd realized that the bond between these three was very close. "How kind you are, Walter," she said.

"Not really. I can always use a bright young assistant who understands politics."

Ethel said: "I'm not sure I understand politics anymore. What on earth is happening here in Germany?"

Maud said: "We were doing all right in the midtwenties. We had a democratic government and a growing economy. But everything was ruined by the Wall Street crash of 1929. Now we're in the depths of a depression." Her voice shook with an emotion that seemed close to grief. "You can see a hundred men standing in line for one advertised job. I look at their faces. They're desperate. They don't know how they're going to feed their children. Then the Nazis offer them hope, and they ask themselves: What have I got to lose?"

Walter seemed to think she might be overstating the case. In a more cheerful tone he said: "The good news is that Hitler has failed to win over a majority of Germans. In the last election the Nazis got a third of the votes. Nevertheless they were the largest party, but fortunately Hitler only leads a minority government."

"That's why he demanded another election," Maud put in. "He needs an overall majority to turn Germany into the brutal dictatorship he wants."

"Will he get it?" Ethel asked.

"No," said Walter.

"Yes," said Maud.

Walter said: "I don't believe the German people will ever actually vote for a dictatorship."

"But it won't be a fair election!" Maud said angrily. "Look what happened to my magazine today. Anyone who criticizes the Nazis is in danger. Meanwhile, their propaganda is everywhere."

Lloyd said: "Nobody seems to fight back!" He wished he had arrived a few minutes earlier at the *Democrat* office this morning, so that he could have punched a few Brownshirts. He realized he was making a fist, and forced himself to open his hand. But the indignation did not go away. "Why don't left-wingers raid the offices of Nazi magazines? Give them a taste of their own medicine!"

"We must not meet violence with violence!" Maud said emphatically. "Hitler is looking for an excuse to crack down—to declare a national emergency, sweep away civil rights, and put his opponents in jail." Her voice took on a pleading note. "We must avoid giving him that pretext—no matter how hard it is."

They finished their meal. The restaurant began to empty out. As their coffee was served, they were joined by the owner, Walter's second cousin Robert von Ulrich, and the chef, Jörg. Robert had been a diplomat at the Austrian embassy in London before the Great War, while Walter was doing the same thing at the German embassy there—and falling in love with Maud.

Robert resembled Walter, but was more fussily dressed, with a gold pin in his tie, seals on his watch chain, and heavily slicked hair. Jörg was younger, a blond man with delicate features and a cheerful smile. The two had been prisoners of war together in Russia. Now they lived in an apartment over the restaurant.

They reminisced about the wedding of Walter and Maud, held in great secrecy on the eve of the war. There had been no guests, but Robert and Ethel had been best man and bridesmaid. Ethel said: "We had champagne at the hotel. Then I tactfully said that Robert and I would leave, and Walter—" She suppressed a fit of giggles. "Walter said: 'Oh, I assumed we would all have dinner together!'"

Maud chuckled. "You can imagine how pleased I was about that!"

Lloyd looked into his coffee, feeling embarrassed. He was eighteen and a virgin, and honeymoon jokes made him uncomfortable.

More somberly, Ethel asked Maud: "Do you ever hear from Fitz these days?"

Lloyd knew that the secret wedding had caused a terrible rift between Maud and her brother, Earl Fitzherbert. Fitz had disowned her because she had not gone to him, as head of the family, and asked his permission to marry.

Maud shook her head sadly. "I wrote to him that time we went to London, but he refused even to see me. I hurt his pride by marrying Walter without telling him. My brother is an unforgiving man, I'm afraid."

Ethel paid the bill. Everything in Germany was cheap if you had foreign currency. They were about to get up and leave when a stranger came to the table and, uninvited, pulled up a chair. He was a heavy man with a small mustache in the middle of a round face.

He wore a Brownshirt uniform.

Robert said coldly: "What may I do for you, sir?"

"My name is Criminal Commissar Thomas Macke." He grabbed a passing waiter by the arm and said: "Bring me a coffee."

The waiter looked inquiringly at Robert, who nodded.

"I work in the political department of the Prussian police," Macke went on. "I am in charge of the Berlin intelligence section."

Lloyd translated for his mother in a low voice.

"However," said Macke, "I wish to speak to the proprietor of the restaurant about a personal matter."

Robert said: "Where did you work a month ago?"

The unexpected question startled Macke, and he replied immediately: "At the police station in Kreuzberg."

"And what was your job there?"

"I was in charge of records. Why do you ask?"

Robert nodded as if he had expected something like this. "So you have gone from a job as a filing clerk to head of the Berlin intelligence section. Congratulations on your rapid promotion." He turned to Ethel. "When Hitler became chancellor at the end of January, his henchman Hermann Göring took the role of interior minister of Prussia—in charge of the largest police force in the world. Since then, Göring has been firing policemen wholesale and replacing them with Nazis." He turned back to Macke and said sarcastically: "However, in the case of our surprise guest I'm sure the promotion was purely on merit."

Macke flushed, but kept his temper. "As I said, I wish to speak to the proprietor about something personal."

"Please come and see me in the morning. Would ten o'clock suit you?"

Macke ignored this suggestion. "My brother is in the restaurant business," he plowed on.

"Ah! Perhaps I know him. Macke is the name? What kind of establishment does he run?"

"A small place for workingmen in Friedrichshain."

"Ah. Then it isn't likely that I have met him."

Lloyd was not sure it was wise for Robert to be so waspish. Macke was rude, and did not deserve kindness, but he could probably make serious trouble.

Macke went on: "My brother would like to buy this restaurant."

"Your brother wants to move up in the world, as you have."

"We are prepared to offer you twenty thousand marks, payable over two years."

Jörg burst out laughing.

Robert said: "Permit me to explain something to you, Commissar. I am an Austrian count. Twenty years ago I had a castle and a large country estate in Hungary where my mother and sister lived. In the war I lost my family, my castle, my lands, and even my country, which was . . . miniaturized." His tone of amused sarcasm had gone, and his voice became gruff with emotion. "I came to Berlin with nothing but the address of Walter von Ulrich, my second cousin. Nevertheless I managed to open this restaurant." He swallowed. "It is all I have." He paused, and drank some coffee. The others around the table were silent. He regained his poise, and something of his superior tone of voice.

"Even if you offered a generous price—which you have not—I would still refuse, because I would be selling my whole life. I have no wish to be rude to you, even though you have behaved unpleasantly. But my restaurant is not for sale at any price." He stood up and held out his hand to shake. "Good night, Commissar Macke."

Macke automatically shook hands, then looked as if he regretted it. He stood up, clearly angry. His fat face was a purplish color. "We will talk again," he said, and he walked out.

"What an oaf," said Jörg.

Walter said to Ethel: "You see what we have to put up with? Just because he wears that uniform, he can do anything he likes!"

What had bothered Lloyd was Macke's confidence. He had seemed to feel sure he could buy the restaurant at the price he named. He reacted to Robert's refusal as if it were no more than a temporary setback. Were the Nazis already so powerful?

This was the kind of thing Oswald Mosley and his British Fascists wanted—a country in which the rule of law was replaced by bullying and beating. How could people be so damn stupid?

They put on their coats and hats and said good night to Robert and Jörg. As soon as they stepped outside, Lloyd smelled smoke—not tobacco, but something else. The four of them got into Walter's car, a BMW Dixi 3/15, which Lloyd knew was a German-manufactured Austin Seven.

As they drove through the Tiergarten park, two fire engines overtook them, bells clanging. "I wonder where the fire is," said Walter.

A moment later they saw the glow of flames through the trees. Maud said: "It seems to be near the Reichstag."

Walter's tone changed. "We'd better take a look," he said worriedly, and he made a sudden turn.

The smell of smoke grew stronger. Over the tops of the trees Lloyd could see flames shooting skyward. "It's a *big* fire," he said.

They emerged from the park onto the Königs Platz, the broad plaza between the Reichstag building and the Kroll Opera House opposite. The Reichstag was ablaze. Red and yellow light danced behind the classical rows of windows. Flame and smoke jetted up through the central dome. "Oh, no!" said Walter, and to Lloyd he sounded stricken with grief. "Oh, God in heaven, no."

He stopped the car and they all got out.

"This is a catastrophe," said Walter.

Ethel said: "Such a beautiful old building."

"I don't care about the building," Walter said surprisingly. "It's our democracy that's on fire."

A small crowd watched from a distance of about fifty yards. In front of the building, fire engines were lined up, their hoses already playing on the flames, water jetting in through broken windows. A handful of policemen stood around doing nothing. Walter spoke to one of them. "I am a Reichstag deputy," he said. "When did this start?"

"An hour ago," the policeman said. "We've got one of them that did it—a man with nothing on but his trousers! He used his clothes to start the fire."

"You should put up a rope cordon," Walter said with authority. "Keep people at a safe distance."

"Yes, sir," said the policeman, and went off.

Lloyd slipped away from the others and moved nearer to the building. The firemen were bringing the blaze under control: there was less flame and more smoke. He walked past the fire engines and approached a window. It did not seem very dangerous, and anyway his curiosity overcame his sense of self-protection—as usual.

When he peered through a window, he saw that the destruction was severe: walls and ceilings had collapsed into piles of rubble. As well as firemen he saw civilians in coats—presumably Reichstag officials—moving around in the debris, assessing the damage. Lloyd went to the entrance and climbed the steps.

Two black Mercedes cars roared up just as the police were erecting their cordon. Lloyd looked on with interest. Out of the second car jumped a man in a light-colored trench coat and a floppy black hat. He had a narrow mustache under his nose. Lloyd realized he was looking at the new chancellor, Adolf Hitler.

Behind Hitler followed a taller man in the black uniform of the Schutzstaffel, the SS, his personal bodyguard. Limping after them came the Jew-hating propaganda chief, Joseph Goebbels. Lloyd recognized them from newspaper photographs. He was so fascinated to see them close up that he forgot to be horrified.

Hitler ran up the steps two at a time, heading directly toward Lloyd. On impulse, Lloyd pushed open the big door and held it wide for the chancellor. With a nod to him, Hitler walked in, and his entourage followed.

Lloyd joined them. No one spoke to him. Hitler's people seemed to assume he was one of the Reichstag staff, and vice versa.

There was a foul smell of wet ashes. Hitler and his party stepped over charred beams and hosepipes, treading in mucky puddles. In the entrance hall stood Hermann Göring, a camel-hair coat covering his huge belly, his hat turned up in front Potsdam-fashion. This was the man who was packing the police force with Nazis, Lloyd thought, recalling the conversation in the restaurant.

As soon as Göring saw Hitler, he shouted: "This is the beginning of the Communist uprising! Now they'll strike out! There's not a minute to waste!"

Lloyd felt weirdly as if he were in the audience at the theater, and these powerful men were being played by actors.

Hitler was even more histrionic than Göring. "There will be no mercy now!" he shrieked. He sounded as if he were addressing a stadium. "Anyone who stands in our way will be butchered." He trembled as he worked himself up into a fury. "Every Communist functionary will be shot where he is found. The Communist deputies to the Reichstag must be hanged this very night." He looked as if he would burst.

But there was something artificial about it all. Hitler's hatred seemed real, but the outburst was also a performance, put on for the benefit of those around him, his own people and others. He was an actor, feeling a genuine emotion but amplifying it for the audience. And it was working, Lloyd saw: everyone within earshot was staring, mesmerized.

Göring said: "My Führer, this is my chief of political police, Rudolf

Diels." He indicated a slim, dark-haired man at his side. "He has already arrested one of the perpetrators."

Diels was not hysterical. Calmly he said: "Marinus van der Lubbe, a Dutch construction worker."

"And a Communist!" Göring said triumphantly.

Diels said: "Expelled from the Dutch Communist Party for starting fires."

"I knew it!" said Hitler.

Lloyd saw that Hitler was determined to blame the Communists, regardless of the facts.

Diels said deferentially: "From my first interrogation of the man, I have to say it is clear he is a lunatic, working alone."

"Nonsense!" Hitler cried. "This was planned long in advance. But they miscalculated! They don't understand that the people are on our side."

Göring turned to Diels. "The police are on emergency footing from this moment," he said. "We have lists of Communists—Reichstag deputies, local government elected representatives, Communist Party organizers and activists. Arrest them all—tonight! Firearms should be used ruthlessly. Interrogate them without mercy."

"Yes, Minister," said Diels.

Lloyd realized that Walter had been right to worry. This was the pretext the Nazis had been looking for. They were not going to listen to anyone who said the fire had been started by a lone madman. They wanted a Communist plot so that they could announce a crackdown.

Göring looked down with distaste at the muck on his shoes. "My official residence is only a minute away, but is fortunately unaffected by the fire, my Führer," he said. "Perhaps we should adjourn there?"

"Yes. We have much to discuss."

Lloyd held the door and they all went out. As they drove away, he stepped over the police cordon and rejoined his mother and the von Ulrichs.

Ethel said: "Lloyd! Where have you been? I was worried sick!"

"I went inside," he said.

"What? How?"

"No one stopped me. It's all chaos and confusion."

His mother threw her hands in the air. "He has no sense of danger," she said.

"I met Adolf Hitler."

Walter said: "Did he say anything?"

"He's blaming the Communists for the fire. There's going to be a purge."

"God help us," said Walter.

## iii

Thomas Macke was still smarting from the sarcasm of Robert von Ulrich. "Your brother wants to move up in the world, as you have," von Ulrich had said.

Macke wished he had thought to reply: "And why should we not? We are as good as you, you arrogant popinjay." Now he yearned for revenge. But for a few days he was too busy to do anything about it.

The headquarters of the Prussian secret police were in a large, elegant building of classical architecture at no. 8 Prinz Albrecht Strasse in the government quarter. Macke felt proud every time he walked through the door.

It was a hectic time. Four thousand Communists had been arrested within twenty-four hours of the Reichstag fire, and more were being rounded up every hour. Germany was being cleansed of a plague, and to Macke the Berlin air already tasted purer.

But the police files were not up-to-date. People had moved house, elections had been lost and won, old men had died and young men had taken their places. Macke was in charge of a group updating the records, finding new names and addresses.

He was good at this. He liked registers, directories, street maps, news clippings, any kind of list. His talents had not been valued at the

Kreuzberg police station, where criminal intelligence was simply beating up suspects until they named names. He was hoping to be better appreciated here.

Not that he had any problem with beating up suspects. In his office at the back of the building he could hear the screams of men and women being tortured in the basement, but it did not bother him. They were traitors, subversives, and revolutionaries. They had ruined Germany with their strikes, and they would do worse if they got the chance. He had no sympathy for them. He only wished Robert von Ulrich was among them, groaning in agony and begging for mercy.

It was eight o'clock in the evening on Thursday, March 2, before he got a chance to check on Robert.

He sent his team home, and took a sheaf of updated lists upstairs to his boss, Criminal Inspector Kringelein. Then he returned to the files.

He was in no hurry to go home. He lived alone. His wife, an undisciplined woman, had gone off with a waiter from his brother's restaurant, saying she wanted to be free. There were no children.

He began to comb the files.

He had already established that Robert von Ulrich had joined the Nazi Party in 1923 and had left two years later. That in itself did not mean much. Macke needed more.

The filing system was not as logical as he would have liked. All in all, he was disappointed in the Prussian police. The rumor was that Göring was equally unimpressed, and planned to detach the political and intelligence departments from the regular force and form them into a new, more efficient secret police force. Macke thought that was a good idea.

Meanwhile, he failed to find Robert von Ulrich in any of the regular files. Perhaps that was not merely a sign of inefficiency. The man might be blameless. As an Austrian count, he was unlikely to be a Communist or a Jew. It seemed the worst that could be said of him was that his cousin Walter was a Social Democrat. That was not a crime—not yet.

Macke now realized he should have done this research before approaching the man. But he had gone ahead without full information.

He might have known that was a mistake. In consequence he had been forced to submit to condescension and sarcasm. He had felt humiliated. But he would get his own back.

He began to go through miscellaneous papers in a dusty cupboard at the back of the room.

The name of von Ulrich did not appear here either, but there was one document missing.

According to the list pinned to the inside of the cupboard door, there should have been a file of 117 pages entitled "Vice Establishments." It sounded like a survey of Berlin's nightclubs. Macke could guess why it was not here. It must have been in use recently: all the more decadent night spots had been closed down when Hitler became chancellor.

Macke went back upstairs. Kringelein was briefing uniformed police who were to raid the updated addresses Macke had provided for Communists and their allies.

Macke did not hesitate to interrupt his boss. Kringelein was not a Nazi, and would therefore be afraid to reprimand a storm trooper. Macke said: "I'm looking for the 'Vice Establishments' file."

Kringelein looked annoyed but made no protest. "On the side table," he said. "Help yourself."

Macke took the file and returned to his own room.

The survey was five years old. It detailed the clubs then in existence and stated what activities went on in them: gambling, indecent displays, prostitution, sale of drugs, homosexuality, and other depravities. The file named owners and investors, club members and employees. Macke patiently read each entry: perhaps Robert von Ulrich was a drug addict or a user of whores.

Berlin was famous for its homosexual clubs. Macke plowed through the dreary entry on the Pink Slipper, where men danced with men and the floor show featured transvestite singers. Sometimes, he thought, his work was disgusting.

He ran his finger down the list of members, and found Robert von Ulrich.

He gave a sigh of satisfaction.

Looking farther down, he saw the name of Jörg Schleicher.

"Well, well," he said. "Let's see how sarcastic you are now."

## iv

The next time Lloyd saw Walter and Maud he found them angrier—and more scared.

It was the following Saturday, March 4, the day before the election. Lloyd and Ethel were planning to attend a Social Democratic Party rally organized by Walter, and they went to the von Ulrichs' home in Mitte for lunch beforehand.

It was a nineteenth-century house with spacious rooms and large windows, though much of the furniture was worn. The lunch was plain, pork chops with potatoes and cabbage, but there was good wine with it. Walter and Maud talked as if they were poor, and no doubt they were living more simply than their parents had, but all the same they were not going hungry.

However, they were frightened.

Hitler had persuaded Germany's aging president, Paul von Hindenburg, to approve the Reichstag Fire Decree, which gave the Nazis authority for what they were already doing, beating and torturing their political opponents. "Twenty thousand people have been arrested since Monday night!" Walter said, his voice shaking. "Not just Communists, but people the Nazis call 'Communist sympathizers.'"

"Which means anyone they dislike," said Maud.

Ethel said: "How can there be a democratic election now?"

"We must do our best," Walter said. "If we don't campaign, it will only help the Nazis."

Lloyd said impatiently: "When will you stop accepting this and start to fight back? Do you still believe it would be wrong to meet violence with violence?"

"Absolutely," said Maud. "Peaceful resistance is our only hope."

Walter said: "The Social Democratic Party has a paramilitary wing, the Reichsbanner, but it's weak. A small group of Social Democrats proposed a violent response to the Nazis, but they were outvoted."

Maud said: "Remember, Lloyd, the Nazis have the police and the army on their side."

Walter looked at his pocket watch. "We must get going."

Maud said suddenly: "Walter, why don't you cancel?"

He stared at her in surprise. "Seven hundred tickets have been sold."

"Oh, to blazes with the tickets," Maud said. "I'm worried about *you*."

"Don't worry. Seats have been carefully allocated, so there should be no troublemakers in the hall."

Lloyd was not sure Walter was as confident as he pretended.

Walter went on: "Anyway, I cannot let down people who are still willing to come to a democratic political meeting. They are all the hope that remains to us."

"You're right," Maud said. She looked at Ethel. "Perhaps you and Lloyd should stay home. It's dangerous, no matter what Walter says, and this isn't your country, after all."

"Socialism is international," Ethel said stoutly. "Like your husband, I appreciate your concern, but I'm here to witness German politics firsthand, and I'm not going to miss this."

"Well, the children can't go," Maud said.

Erik, the son, said: "I don't even want to go."

Carla looked disappointed but said nothing.

Walter, Maud, Ethel, and Lloyd got into Walter's little car. Lloyd was nervous but excited, too. He was getting a perspective on politics superior to anything his friends back home had. And if there was going to be a fight, he was not afraid.

They drove east, crossing Alexander Platz, into a neighborhood of poor houses and small shops, some of which had signs in Hebrew letters. The Social Democratic Party was working-class, but like the British Labour Party it had a few affluent supporters. Walter von Ulrich was in a small upper-class minority.

The car pulled up outside a marquee that said PEOPLE'S THEATER. A line had already formed outside. Walter crossed the pavement to the door, waving to the waiting crowd, who cheered. Lloyd and the others followed him inside.

Walter shook hands with a solemn young man of about eighteen. "This is Wilhelm Frunze, secretary of the local branch of our party." Frunze was one of those boys who looked as if they had been born middle-aged. He wore a blazer with buttoned pockets that had been fashionable ten years ago.

Frunze showed Walter how the theater doors could be barred from the inside. "When the audience is seated, we will lock up, so that no troublemakers can get in," he said.

"Very good," said Walter. "Well done."

Frunze ushered them into the auditorium. Walter went up onstage and greeted some other candidates who were already there. The public began to come in and take their seats. Frunze showed Maud, Ethel, and Lloyd to reserved places in the front row.

Two boys approached. The younger, who looked about fourteen but was taller than Lloyd, greeted Maud with careful good manners and made a little bow. Maud turned to Ethel and said: "This is Werner Franck, the son of my friend Monika." Then she said to Werner: "Does your father know you're here?"

"Yes—he said I should find out about Social Democracy myself."

"He's broad-minded, for a Nazi."

Lloyd thought this was a rather tough line to take with a fourteen-year-old, but Werner was a match for her. "My father doesn't really believe in Nazism, but he thinks Hitler is good for German business."

Wilhelm Frunze said indignantly: "How can it be good for business to throw thousands of people into jail? Apart from the injustice, they can't work!"

Werner said: "I agree with you. And yet Hitler's crackdown is popular."

"People think they're being saved from a Bolshevik revolution," Frunze said. "The Nazi press has them convinced that the Communists were about to launch a campaign of murder, arson, and poison in every town and village."

The boy with Werner, who was shorter but older, said: "And yet it is the Brownshirts, not the Communists, who drag people into basements and break their bones with clubs." He spoke German fluently with a slight accent that Lloyd could not place.

Werner said: "Forgive me. I forgot to introduce Vladimir Peshkov. He goes to the Berlin Boys' Academy, my school, and he's always called Volodya."

Lloyd stood up to shake hands. Volodya was about Lloyd's age, a striking young man with a frank blue-eyed gaze.

Frunze said: "I know Volodya Peshkov. I go to the Berlin Boys' Academy, too."

Volodya said: "Wilhelm Frunze is the school genius—top marks in physics and chemistry and math."

"It's true," said Werner.

Maud looked hard at Volodya and said: "Peshkov? Is your father Grigori?"

"Yes, Frau von Ulrich. He is a military attaché at the Soviet embassy."

So Volodya is Russian. He speaks German effortlessly, Lloyd thought with a touch of envy. No doubt that comes from living here.

"I know your parents well," Maud said to Volodya. She knew all the diplomats in Berlin, Lloyd had already gathered. It was part of her job.

Frunze checked his watch and said: "Time to begin." He went up onstage and called for order.

The theater went quiet.

Frunze announced that the candidates would make speeches and then take questions from the audience. Tickets had been issued only to Social Democratic Party members, he added, and the doors were now closed, so everyone could speak freely, knowing they were among friends.

It was like being a member of a secret society, Lloyd thought. This was not what he called democracy.

Walter spoke first. He was no demagogue, Lloyd observed. He had no rhetorical flourishes. But he flattered his audience, telling them they were intelligent and well-informed men and women who understood the complexity of political issues.

He had been speaking for only a few minutes when a Brownshirt walked onstage.

Lloyd cursed. How had he got in? He came from the wings: someone must have opened the stage door.

He was a huge brute with an army haircut. He stepped to the front of the stage and shouted: "This is a seditious gathering. Communists and subversives are not wanted in today's Germany. The meeting is closed."

The confident arrogance of the man outraged Lloyd. He wished he could get this great oaf in a boxing ring.

Wilhelm Frunze leaped to his feet, stood in front of the intruder, and yelled furiously: "Get out of here, you thug!"

The man shoved him in the chest powerfully. Frunze staggered back, stumbled, and fell over backward.

The audience were on their feet, some shouting in angry protest, some screaming in fear.

More Brownshirts appeared from the wings.

Lloyd realized with dismay that the bastards had planned this well.

The man who had shoved Frunze shouted: "Out!" The other Brownshirts took up the cry: "Out! Out! Out!" There were about twenty of them now, and more appearing all the time. Some carried police nightsticks or improvised clubs. Lloyd saw a hockey stick, a wooden sledgehammer, even a chair leg. They strutted up and down the stage, grinning fiendishly and waving their weapons as they chanted, and Lloyd had no doubt they were itching to start hitting people.

He was on his feet. Without thinking, he, Werner, and Volodya had formed a protective line in front of Ethel and Maud.

Half the audience were trying to leave, the other half shouting and shaking their fists at the intruders. Those attempting to get out were shoving others, and minor scuffles had broken out. Many of the women were crying.

Onstage, Walter grasped the lectern and shouted: "Everyone try to keep calm, please! There is no need for disorder!" Most people could not hear and the rest ignored him.

The Brownshirts began to jump off the stage and wade into the audience. Lloyd took his mother's arm, and Werner did the same with Maud. They moved toward the nearest exit in a group. But all the doors were already jammed with knots of panicking people trying to leave. That made no difference to the Brownshirts, who kept yelling at people to get out.

The attackers were mostly able-bodied, whereas the audience included women and old men. Lloyd wanted to fight back, but it was not a good idea.

A man in a Great War steel helmet shouldered Lloyd, and he lurched forward and bumped into his mother. He resisted the temptation to turn and confront the man. His priority was to protect Mam.

A spotty-faced boy carrying a truncheon put a hand on Werner's back and shoved energetically, yelling: "Get out, get out!" Werner turned quickly and took a step toward him. "Don't touch me, you Fascist pig," he said. The Brownshirt suddenly stopped dead and looked scared, as if he had not been expecting resistance.

Werner turned away again, concentrating like Lloyd on getting the two women to safety. But the huge man had heard the exchange and yelled: "Who are you calling a pig?" He lashed out at Werner, hitting the back of his head with his fist. His aim was poor and it was a glancing blow, but all the same Werner cried out and staggered forward.

Volodya stepped between them and hit the big man in the face, twice. Lloyd admired Volodya's rapid one-two, but turned his attention back to his task. Seconds later the four of them reached the doorway. Lloyd and Werner managed to help the women out into the theater foyer. Here the crush eased and the violence stopped—there were no Brownshirts.

Seeing the women safe, Lloyd and Werner looked back into the auditorium.

Volodya was fighting the big man bravely, but he was in trouble. He kept punching the man's face and body, but his blows had little effect, and the man shook his head as if pestered by an insect. The Brownshirt was heavy-footed and slow-moving, but he hit Volodya in the chest and then the head, and Volodya staggered. The big man drew back his fist for a massive punch. Lloyd was afraid it could kill Volodya.

Then Walter took a flying leap off the stage and landed on the big man's back. Lloyd wanted to cheer. They fell to the floor in a blur of arms and legs, and Volodya was saved, for the moment.

The spotty youth who had shoved Werner was now harassing the people trying to leave, hitting their backs and heads with his truncheon. "You fucking coward!" Lloyd yelled, stepping forward. But Werner was ahead of him. He shoved past Lloyd and grabbed the truncheon, trying to wrestle it away from the youth.

The older man in the steel helmet joined in and hit Werner with a pickax handle. Lloyd stepped forward and hit the older man with a straight right. The blow landed perfectly, next to the man's left eye.

But he was a war veteran, and not easily discouraged. He swung around and lashed out at Lloyd with his club. Lloyd dodged the blow easily and hit him twice more. He connected in the same area, around the man's eyes, breaking the skin. But the helmet protected the man's head, and Lloyd could not land a left hook, his knockout punch. He ducked a swing of the pickax handle and hit the man's face again, and the man backed away, blood pouring from cuts around his eyes.

Lloyd looked around. He saw that the Social Democrats were fighting back now, and he got a jolt of savage pleasure. Most of the audience had passed through the doors, leaving mainly young men in the auditorium, and they were coming forward, clambering over the theater seats to get at the Brownshirts; there were dozens of them.

Something hard struck his head from behind. It was so painful that he roared. He turned to see a boy of his own age holding a length of timber, raising it to strike again. Lloyd closed in on him and hit him hard in the stomach twice, first with his right fist, then with his left. The boy gasped for breath and dropped the wood. Lloyd hit him with an uppercut to the chin and he passed out.

Lloyd rubbed the back of his head. It hurt like hell but there was no blood.

The skin on his knuckles was raw and bleeding, he saw. He bent down and picked up the length of timber dropped by the boy.

When he looked around again, he was thrilled to see some of the Brownshirts retreating, clambering up onto the stage and disappearing into the wings, presumably aiming to leave through the stage door by which they had entered.

The big man who had started it all was on the floor, groaning and holding his knee as if he had dislocated something. Wilhelm Frunze stood over him, hitting him with a wooden shovel again and again, repeating at the top of his voice the words the man had used to start the riot: "Not! Wanted! In! Today's! Germany!" Helpless, the big man tried to roll away from the blows, but Frunze went after him, until two more Brownshirts grabbed the man's arms and dragged him away.

Frunze let them go.

Did we beat them? Lloyd thought with growing exultation. Maybe we did!

Several of the younger men chased their opponents up onto the stage, but they stopped there and contented themselves with shouting insults as the Brownshirts disappeared.

Lloyd looked at the others. Volodya had a swollen face and one closed eye. Werner's jacket was ripped, a big square of cloth dangling. Walter was sitting on a front-row seat, breathing hard and rubbing his elbow, but he was smiling. Frunze threw his shovel away, sailing it across the rows of empty seats to the back.

Werner, who was only fourteen, was exultant. "We gave them hell, didn't we?"

Lloyd grinned. "Yes, we certainly did."

Volodya put his arm around Frunze's shoulders. "Not bad for a bunch of schoolboys, eh?"

Walter said: "But they stopped our meeting."

The youngsters stared resentfully at him for spoiling their triumph.

Walter looked angry. "Be realistic, boys. Our audience has fled in terror. How long will it be before those people have the nerve to go to a political meeting again? The Nazis have made their point. It's dangerous even to listen to any party other than theirs. The big loser today is Germany."

Werner said to Volodya: "I hate those fucking Brownshirts. I think I might join you Communists."

Volodya looked at him hard with those intense blue eyes and spoke in a low voice. "If you're serious about fighting the Nazis, there might be something more effective you could do."

Lloyd wondered what Volodya meant.

Then Maud and Ethel came running back into the auditorium, both speaking at the same time, crying and laughing with relief, and Lloyd forgot Volodya's words and never thought of them again.

## V

Four days later, Erik von Ulrich came home in a Hitler Youth uniform.

He felt like a prince.

He had a brown shirt just like the one worn by storm troopers, with various patches and a swastika armband. He also had the regulation black tie and black shorts. He was a patriotic soldier dedicated to the service of his country. At last he was one of the gang.

This was even better than supporting Hertha, Berlin's favorite soccer team. Erik was taken to matches occasionally, on Saturdays when his father did not have a political meeting to attend. That gave him the same sense of belonging to a great big crowd of people all feeling the same emotions.

But Hertha sometimes lost, and he came home disconsolate.

The Nazis were winners.

He was terrified of what his father was going to say.

His parents infuriated him by insisting on marching out of step. All the boys were joining the Hitler Youth. They had sports and singing and adventures in the fields and forests outside the city. They were smart and fit and loyal and efficient.

Erik was deeply troubled by the thought that he might have to fight in battle someday—his father and grandfather had—and he wanted to be ready for that, trained and hardened, disciplined and aggressive.

The Nazis hated Communists, but so did Mother and Father. So what if the Nazis hated Jews as well? The von Ulrichs were not Jewish; why should they care? But Mother and Father stubbornly refused to join in. Well, Erik was fed up with being left out, and he had decided to defy them.

He was scared stiff.

As usual, neither Mother nor Father was at the house when Erik and Carla came home from school. Ada pursed her lips disapprovingly as she served their tea, but she said: "You'll have to clear the table yourselves today—I've got a terrible backache. I'm going to lie down."

Carla looked concerned. "Is that what you had to see the doctor about?"

Ada hesitated before replying: "Yes, that's right."

She was obviously hiding something. The thought of Ada being ill—and lying about it—made Erik uneasy. He would never go as far as Carla and say he loved Ada, but she had been a kindly presence all his life, and he was more fond of her than he liked to say.

Carla was just as concerned. "I hope it gets better."

Lately Carla had become more grown-up, somewhat to Erik's bewilderment. Although he was two years older, he still felt like a kid, but she acted like an adult half the time.

Ada said reassuringly: "I'll be fine after a rest."

Erik ate some bread. When Ada left the room, he swallowed and said: "I'm only in the junior section, but as soon as I'm fourteen, I can move up."

Carla said: "Father's going to hit the roof! Are you mad?"

"Herr Lippmann said Father will be in trouble if he tries to make me leave."

"Oh, brilliant," said Carla. She had developed a streak of withering sarcasm that sometimes stung Erik. "So you'll get Father into a row with the Nazis," she said scornfully. "What a great idea. So good for the whole family."

Erik was taken aback. He had not thought of it that way. "But all the boys in my class are members," he said indignantly. "Except for Frenchy Fontaine and Jewboy Rothmann."

Carla spread fish paste on her bread. "Why do you have to be the same as the others?" she said. "Most of them are stupid. You told me Rudi Rothmann was the cleverest boy in the class."

"I don't want to be with Frenchy and Rudi!" Erik cried, and to his mortification he felt tears come to his eyes. "Why should I have to play with the boys no one likes?" This was what had given him the courage to defy his father: he could no longer bear to walk out of school with the Jews and the foreigners while all the German boys marched around the playing field in their uniforms.

They both heard a cry.

Erik looked at Carla and said: "What was that?"

Carla frowned. "It was Ada, I think."

Then, more distinctly, they heard: "Help!"

Erik got to his feet, but Carla was ahead of him. He went after her. Ada's room was in the basement. They ran down the stairs and into the small bedroom.

There was a narrow single bed up against the wall. Ada was lying there, her face screwed up in pain. Her skirt was wet and there was a puddle on the floor. Erik could hardly believe what he was seeing. Had she pissed herself? It was scary. There were no other grown-ups in the house. He did not know what to do.

Carla was scared, too—Erik could see it in her face—but she was not panicked. She said: "Ada, what's wrong?" Her voice sounded strangely calm.

"My waters broke," Ada said.

Erik had no idea what that meant.

Nor did Carla. "I don't understand," she said.

"It means my baby is coming."

"You're pregnant?" Carla said in astonishment.

Erik said: "But you're not married!"

Carla said furiously: "Shut up, Erik—don't you know anything?"

He did know, of course, that women could have babies when they were not married—but surely not Ada!

"That's why you went to the doctor last week," Carla said to Ada.
Ada nodded.

Erik was still trying to get used to the idea. "Do you think Mother and Father know?"

"Of course they do. They just didn't tell us. Fetch a towel."

"Where from?"

"The airing cupboard on the upstairs landing."

"A clean one?"

"Of course a clean one!"

Erik ran up the stairs, took a small white towel from the cupboard, and ran down again.

"That's not much good," Carla said, but she took it and dried Ada's legs.

Ada said: "The baby's coming soon. I can feel it. But I don't know what to do." She started to cry.

Erik was watching Carla. She was in charge now. It did not matter that he was the older one: he looked to her for leadership. She was being practical and staying calm, but he could tell that she was terrified, and her composure was fragile. She could crack at any minute, he thought.

Carla turned to Erik again. "Go and fetch Dr. Rothmann," she said. "You know where his office is."

Erik was hugely relieved to have been given a task he could manage. Then he thought of a snag. "What if he's out?"

"Then ask Frau Rothmann what you should do, you idiot!" Carla said. "Get going—run!"

Erik was glad to get out of the room. What was happening there was mysterious and frightening. He went up the stairs three at a time and flew out of the front door. Running was one thing he did know how to do.

The doctor's surgery was half a mile away. He settled into a fast trot. As he ran, he thought about Ada. Who was the father of her baby? He recalled that she had gone to the movies with Paul Huber a couple of times last summer. Had they had sexual intercourse? They must have! Erik and his friends talked about sex a lot, but they did not really know anything about it. Where had Ada and Paul done it? Not in a movie theater, surely? Didn't people have to lie down? He was baffled.

Dr. Rothmann's place was in a poorer street. He was a good doctor, Erik had heard Mother say, but he treated a lot of working-class people who could not pay high fees. The doctor's house had a consulting room and a waiting room on the ground floor, and the family lived upstairs.

Outside was parked a green Opel 4, an ugly little two-seater unofficially called the Tree Frog.

The front door of the house was unlatched. Erik walked in, breathing hard, and entered the waiting room. There was an old man coughing in a corner and a young woman with a baby. "Hello!" Erik called. "Dr. Rothmann?"

The doctor's wife stepped out of the consulting room. Hannelore Rothmann was a tall, fair woman with strong features, and she gave Erik a look like thunder. "How dare you come to this house in that uniform?" she said.

Erik was petrified. Frau Rothmann was not Jewish, but her husband was; Erik had forgotten that in his excitement. "Our maid is having a baby!" he said.

"And so you want a Jewish doctor to help you?"

Erik was taken completely by surprise. It had never occurred to him that the Nazis' attacks might cause the Jews to retaliate. But suddenly he saw that Frau Rothmann made total sense. The Brownshirts went around shouting, "Death to Jews!" Why should a Jewish doctor help such people?

Now he did not know what to do. There were other doctors, of course, plenty of them, but he did not know where, nor whether they would come out to see a total stranger. "My sister sent me," he said feebly.

"Carla's got a lot more sense than you."

"Ada said the waters have broken." Erik was not sure what that meant, but it sounded significant.

With a disgusted look, Frau Rothmann went back into the consulting room.

The old man in the corner cackled. "We're all dirty Jews until you need our help!" he said. "Then it's: 'Please come, Dr. Rothmann,' and 'What's your advice, Lawyer Koch?' and 'Lend me a hundred marks, Herr Goldman,' and—" He was overcome by a fit of coughing.

A girl of about sixteen came in from the hall. Erik thought she must be the Rothmanns' daughter, Eva. He had not seen her for years. She had breasts now, but she was still plain and dumpy. She said: "Did your father let you join the Hitler Youth?"

"He doesn't know," said Erik.

"Oh, boy," said Eva. "You're in trouble."

He looked from her to the consulting room door. "Do you think your father's going to come?" he said. "Your mother was awfully cross with me."

"Of course he'll come," Eva said. "If people are sick, he helps them." Her voice became scornful. "He doesn't check their race or politics first. We're not Nazis." She went out again.

Erik felt bewildered. He had not expected this uniform to get him into so much trouble. At school everyone thought it was wonderful.

A moment later Dr. Rothmann appeared. Speaking to the two waiting patients, he said: "I'll be back as soon as I can. I'm sorry, but a baby won't wait to be born." He looked at Erik. "Come on, young man, you'd better ride with me, despite that uniform."

Erik followed him out and got into the passenger seat of the Tree Frog. He loved cars and was desperate to be old enough to drive, and normally he enjoyed riding in any vehicle, watching the dials and studying the driver's technique. But now he felt as if he were on display, sitting beside a Jewish doctor in his brown shirt. What if Herr Lippmann should see him? The trip was agony.

Fortunately it was short: in a couple of minutes they were at the von Ulrich house.

"What's the young woman's name?" Rothmann said.

"Ada Hempel."

"Ah, yes, she came to see me last week. The baby's early. All right, take me to her."

Erik led the way into the house. He heard a baby cry. It had come already! He hurried down to the basement, the doctor following.

Ada lay on her back. The bed was soaked with blood and something else. Carla stood holding a tiny baby in her arms. The baby was covered in slime. Something that looked like thick string ran from the baby up Ada's skirt. Carla was wide-eyed with terror. "What must I do?" she cried.

"You're doing exactly the right thing," Dr. Rothmann reassured her. "Just hold that baby close a minute longer." He sat beside Ada. He listened to her heart, took her pulse, and said: "How do you feel, my dear?"

"I'm so tired," she said.

Rothmann gave a satisfied nod. He stood up again and looked at the baby in Carla's arms. "A little boy," he said.

Erik watched with a mixture of fascination and revulsion as the doctor opened his bag, took out some thread, and tied two knots in the cord. While he was doing so, he spoke to Carla in a soft voice. "Why are you crying? You've done a marvelous job. You've delivered a baby all on your own. You hardly needed me! You'd better be a doctor when you grow up."

Carla became calmer. Then she whispered: "Look at his head." The doctor had to lean toward her to hear. "I think there's something wrong with him."

"I know." The doctor took out a pair of sharp scissors and cut the cord between the two knots. Then he took the naked baby from Carla and held him at arm's length, studying him. Erik could not see anything wrong, but the baby was so red and wrinkled and slimy that it was hard to tell. However, after a thoughtful moment the doctor said: "Oh, dear."

Looking more carefully, Erik could see that there was something wrong. The baby's face was lopsided. One side was normal, but on the other the head seemed dented and there was something strange about the eye.

Rothmann handed the baby back to Carla.

Ada groaned again, and seemed to strain.

When she relaxed, Rothmann reached under her skirt and drew out a lump of something that looked disgustingly like meat. "Erik," he said. "Fetch me a newspaper."

Erik said: "Which one?" His parents took all the main papers every day.

"Any one, lad," said Rothmann gently. "I don't want to read it."

Erik ran upstairs and found yesterday's *Vossische Zeitung.* When he returned, the doctor wrapped the meaty thing in the paper and put it on the floor. "It's what we call the afterbirth," he said to Carla. "Best to burn it, later."

Then he sat on the edge of the bed again. "Ada, my dear girl, you must be very brave," he said. "Your baby is alive, but there may be something wrong with him. We're going to wash him and wrap him up warmly. Then we must take him to the hospital."

Ada looked frightened. "What's the matter?"

"I don't know. We need to have him checked."

"Will he be all right?"

"The hospital doctors will do everything they can. The rest we must leave to God."

Erik remembered that Jews worshipped the same God as Christians. It was easy to forget that.

Rothmann said: "Do you think you could get up and come to the hospital with me, Ada? Baby needs you to feed him."

"I'm so tired," she said again.

"Take a minute or two to rest, then. But not much more, because Baby needs to be looked at soon. Carla will help you get dressed. I'll wait upstairs." He addressed Erik with gentle irony. "Come with me, little Nazi."

Erik wanted to squirm. Dr. Rothmann's forbearance was even worse than Frau Rothmann's scorn.

As they were leaving, Ada said: "Doctor?"

"Yes, my dear."

"His name is Kurt."

"A very good name," said Dr. Rothmann. He went out, and Erik followed.

## vi

Lloyd Williams's first day working as assistant to Walter von Ulrich was also the first day of the new parliament.

Walter and Maud were struggling frantically to save Germany's fragile democracy. Lloyd shared their desperation, partly because they were good people whom he had known off and on all his life, and partly because he feared that Britain could follow Germany down the road to hell.

The election had resolved nothing. The Nazis got 44 percent, an increase but still short of the 51 percent they craved.

Walter saw hope. Driving to the opening of the parliament, he said: "Even with massive intimidation, they failed to win the votes of most Germans." He banged his fist on the steering wheel. "Despite everything they say, they are *not* popular. And the longer they stay in government, the better people will get to know their wickedness."

Lloyd was not so sure. "They've closed opposition newspapers, thrown Reichstag deputies in jail, and corrupted the police," he said. "And yet forty-four percent of Germans approve? I don't find that reassuring."

The Reichstag building was badly fire-damaged and quite unusable, so the parliament assembled in the Kroll Opera House, on the opposite side of the Königs Platz. It was a vast complex with three concert halls and fourteen smaller auditoria, plus restaurants and bars.

When they arrived, they had a shock. The place was surrounded by Brownshirts. Deputies and their aides crowded around the entrances, trying to get in. Walter said furiously: "Is this how Hitler plans to get his way—by preventing us from entering the chamber?"

Lloyd saw that the doors were barred by Brownshirts. They admitted those in Nazi uniform without question, but everyone else had to produce credentials. A boy younger than Lloyd looked him up and down contemptuously before grudgingly letting him in. This was intimidation, pure and simple.

Lloyd felt his temper beginning to simmer. He hated to be bullied. He knew he could knock the Brownshirt boy down with one good left hook. He forced himself to remain calm, turn away, and walk through the door.

After the fight in the People's Theater, his mother had examined the egg-shaped lump on his head and ordered him to go home to England. He had talked her round, but it had been a close thing.

She said he had no sense of danger, but that was not quite right. He did get scared sometimes, but it always made him feel combative. His instinct was to go on the attack, not to retreat. This scared his mother.

Ironically, she was just the same. She was not going home. She was frightened, but she was also thrilled to be here in Berlin at this turning point in German history, and outraged by the violence and repression she was witnessing. She felt sure she could write a book that would forewarn democrats in other countries about Fascist tactics. "You're worse than me," Lloyd had said to her, and she had had no answer.

Inside, the opera house was swarming with Brownshirts and SS men, many of them armed. They guarded every door and showed, with looks and gestures, their hatred and contempt for anyone not supporting the Nazis.

Walter was late for a Social Democratic Party group meeting. Lloyd hurried around the building looking for the right room. Glancing into the debating chamber, he saw that a giant swastika hung from the ceiling, dominating the room.

The first matter to be discussed, when proceedings began that afternoon, was to be the Enabling Act, which would permit Hitler's cabinet to pass laws without the approval of the Reichstag.

The act offered a dreadful prospect. It would make Hitler a dictator. The repression, intimidation, violence, torture, and murder that

Germany had seen in the past few weeks would become permanent. It was unthinkable.

But Lloyd could not imagine that any parliament in the world would pass such a law. They would be voting themselves out of power. It was political suicide.

He found the Social Democrats in a small auditorium. Their meeting had already begun. Lloyd hurried Walter to the room; then he was sent for coffee.

Waiting in the queue, he found himself behind a pale, intense-looking young man dressed in funereal black. Lloyd's German had become more fluent and colloquial, and he now had the confidence to strike up a conversation with a stranger. The man in black was Heinrich von Kessel, he learned. He was doing the same sort of job as Lloyd, working as an unpaid aide to his father, Gottfried von Kessel, a deputy for the Centre Party, which was Catholic.

"My father knows Walter von Ulrich very well," Heinrich said. "They were both attachés at the German embassy in London in 1914."

The world of international politics and diplomacy was quite small, Lloyd reflected.

Heinrich told Lloyd that a return to the Christian faith was the answer to Germany's problems.

"I'm not much of a Christian," Lloyd said candidly. "I hope you don't mind my saying so. My grandparents are Welsh Bible-punchers, but my mother is indifferent and my stepfather's Jewish. Occasionally we go to the Calvary Gospel Hall in Aldgate, mainly because the pastor is a Labour Party member."

Heinrich smiled and said: "I'll pray for you."

Catholics were not proselytizers, Lloyd remembered. What a contrast with his dogmatic grandparents in Aberowen, who thought that people who did not believe as they did were willfully blinding themselves to the Gospel, and would be condemned to eternal damnation.

When Lloyd reentered the Social Democratic Party meeting, Walter was speaking. "It can't happen!" he said. "The Enabling Act is a constitutional amendment. Two-thirds of the representatives must be present, which would be 432 out of a possible 647. And two-thirds of those present must approve."

Lloyd added up the numbers in his head as he put the tray down on the table. The Nazis had 288 seats, and the Nationalists, who were their close allies, had 52, making 340—nearly 100 short. Walter was right. The act could not be passed. Lloyd was comforted, and sat down to listen to the discussion and improve his German.

But his relief was short-lived. "Don't be so sure," said a man with a working-class Berlin accent. "The Nazis are caucusing with the Centre Party." That was Heinrich's lot, Lloyd recalled. "That could give them another 74," the man finished.

Lloyd frowned. Why would the Centre Party support a measure that would take away all its power?

Walter voiced the same thought more bluntly. "How could the Catholics be so stupid?"

Lloyd wished he had known about this before he went for coffee— then he could have discussed it with Heinrich. He might have learned something useful. Damn.

The man with the Berlin accent said: "In Italy, the Catholics made a deal with Mussolini—a concordat to protect the Church. Why not here?"

Lloyd calculated that the Centre Party's support would bring the Nazis' votes up to 414. "It's still not two-thirds," he said to Walter with relief.

Another young aide heard him and said: "But that doesn't take into account the Reichstag president's latest announcement." The Reichstag president was Hermann Göring, Hitler's closest associate. Lloyd had not heard about an announcement. Nor had anyone else, it seemed. The deputies went quiet. The aide went on: "He has ruled that Communist deputies who are absent because they are in jail don't count."

There was an outburst of indignant protest all around the room. Lloyd saw Walter go red in the face. "He can't do that!" Walter said.

"It's completely illegal," said the aide. "But he has done it."

Lloyd was dismayed. Surely the law could not be passed by a trick? He did some more arithmetic. The Communists had 81 seats. If they were discounted, the Nazis needed only two-thirds of 566, which was 378. Even with the Nationalists they still did not have enough—but if they won the support of the Catholics, they could swing it.

Someone said: "This is all completely illegal. We should walk out in protest."

"No, no!" said Walter emphatically. "They would pass the act in our absence. We've got to talk the Catholics out of it. Wels must speak to Kaas immediately." Otto Wels was the leader of the Social Democratic Party, prelate Ludwig Kaas the head of the Centre Party.

There was a murmur of agreement around the room.

Lloyd took a deep breath and spoke up. "Herr von Ulrich, why don't you take Gottfried von Kessel to lunch? I believe you two worked together in London before the war."

Walter laughed mirthlessly. "That creep!" he said.

Maybe the lunch was not such a good idea. Lloyd said: "I didn't realize you disliked the man."

Walter looked thoughtful. "I hate him—but I'll try anything, by God."

Lloyd said: "Shall I find him and extend the invitation?"

"All right, give it a try. If he accepts, tell him to meet me at the Herrenklub at one."

"Very good."

Lloyd hurried back to the room into which Heinrich had disappeared. He stepped inside. A meeting was going on similar to the one he had left. He scanned the room, spotted the black-clad Heinrich, met his gaze, and beckoned him urgently.

They both stepped outside; then Lloyd said: "They're saying your party is going to support the Enabling Act!"

"It's not certain," said Heinrich. "They're divided."

"Who's against the Nazis?"

"Brüning and some others." Brüning was a former chancellor and a leading figure.

Lloyd felt more hopeful. "Which others?"

"Did you call me out of the room to pump me for information?"

"Sorry. No, I didn't. Walter von Ulrich wants to have lunch with your father."

Heinrich looked dubious. "They don't like each other—you know that, don't you?"

"I gathered as much. But they'll put their differences aside today!"

Heinrich did not seem sure. "I'll ask him. Wait here." He went back inside.

Lloyd wondered whether there was any chance this would work. It was a shame Walter and Gottfried were not bosom buddies. But he could hardly believe the Catholics would vote with the Nazis.

What bothered him most was the thought that if it could happen in Germany, it could happen in Britain. This grim prospect made him shiver with dread. He had his whole life in front of him, and he did not want to live it in a repressive dictatorship. He wanted to work in politics, like his parents, and make his country a better place for people such as the Aberowen coal miners. For that he needed political meetings where people could speak their minds, and newspapers that could attack the government, and pubs where men could have arguments without looking over their shoulders to see who was listening.

Fascism threatened all that. But perhaps Fascism would fail. Walter might be able to talk Gottfried around, and prevent the Centre Party supporting the Nazis.

Heinrich came out. "He'll do it."

"Great! Herr von Ulrich suggested the Herrenklub at one o'clock."

"Really? Is he a member?"

"I assume so—why?"

"It's a conservative institution. I suppose he is Walter *von* Ulrich, so he must come from a noble family, even if he is a socialist."

"I should probably book a table. Do you know where it is?"

"Just around the corner." Heinrich gave Lloyd directions.

"Shall I book for four?"

Heinrich grinned. "Why not? If they don't want you and me there, they can just ask us to leave." He went back into the room.

Lloyd left the building and walked quickly across the plaza, passing the burned-out Reichstag building, and made his way to the Herrenklub.

There were gentlemen's clubs in London, but Lloyd had never been inside one. This place was a cross between a restaurant and a funeral parlor, he thought. Waiters in full evening dress padded about, laying silent cutlery on tables shrouded in white. A headwaiter took his reservation and wrote down the name "von Ulrich" as solemnly as if he were making an entry in the Book of the Dead.

He returned to the opera house. The place was getting busier and noisier, and the tension seemed higher. Lloyd heard someone say excitedly that Hitler himself would open the proceedings this afternoon by proposing the act.

A few minutes before one, Lloyd and Walter walked across the plaza. Lloyd said: "Heinrich von Kessel was surprised to learn that you are a member of the Herrenklub."

Walter nodded. "I was one of the founders, a decade or more ago. In those days it was the Juniklub. We got together to campaign against the Versailles Treaty. It's become a right-wing bastion, and I'm probably the only Social Democrat, but I remain a member because it's a useful place to meet with the enemy."

Inside the club Walter pointed to a sleek-looking man at the bar. "That's Ludwig Franck, the father of young Werner, who fought alongside us at the People's Theater," Walter said. "I'm sure he's not a member here—he isn't even German-born—but it seems he's having lunch with his father-in-law, Count von der Helbard, the elderly man beside him. Come with me."

They went to the bar and Walter performed introductions. Franck said to Lloyd: "You and my son got into quite a scrap a couple of weeks back."

Lloyd touched the back of his head reflexively: the swelling had gone down, but the place was still painful to touch. "We had women to protect, sir," he said.

"Nothing wrong with a bit of a punch-up," Franck said. "Does you lads good."

Walter cut in impatiently: "Come on, Ludi. Busting up election meetings is bad enough, but your leader wants to completely destroy our democracy!"

"Perhaps democracy is not the right form of government for us," said Franck. "After all, we're not like the French or the Americans— thank God."

"Don't you care about losing your freedom? Be serious!"

Franck suddenly dropped his facetious air. "All right, Walter," he said coldly. "I will be serious, if you insist. My mother and I arrived here from Russia more than ten years ago. My father was not able to come with us. He had been found to be in possession of subversive literature, specifically a book called *Robinson Crusoe*, apparently a novel that promotes bourgeois individualism, whatever the hell that might be. He was sent to a prison camp somewhere in the Arctic. He may—" Franck's voice broke for a moment, and he paused, swallowed, and at last finished quietly: "He may still be there."

There was a moment of silence. Lloyd was shocked by the story. He knew that the Russian Communist government could be cruel, in general, but it was quite another thing to hear a personal account, told simply by a man who was clearly still grieving.

Walter said: "Ludi, we all hate the Bolsheviks—but the Nazis could be worse!"

"I'm willing to take that risk," said Franck.

Count von der Helbard said: "We'd better go in for lunch. I've got an afternoon appointment. Excuse us." The two men left.

"It's what they always say!" Walter raged. "The Bolsheviks! As if they were the only alternative to the Nazis! I could weep."

Heinrich walked in with an older man who was obviously his father: they had the same thick dark hair combed with a parting, except that Gottfried's was shorter and tweeded with silver. Although their features were similar, Gottfried looked like a fussy bureaucrat in an old-fashioned collar, whereas Heinrich was more like a romantic poet than a political aide.

The four of them went into the dining room. Walter wasted no time.

As soon as they had ordered, he said: "I can't understand what your party hopes to gain by supporting this Enabling Act, Gottfried."

Von Kessel was equally direct. "We are a Catholic party, and our first duty is to protect the position of the Church in Germany. That's what people hope for when they vote for us."

Lloyd frowned in disapproval. His mother had been a member of Parliament, and she always said it was her duty to serve the people who did *not* vote for her, as well as those who did.

Walter employed a different argument. "A democratic parliament is the best protection for all our churches—yet you're about to throw that away!"

"Wake up, Walter," Gottfried said testily. "Hitler won the election. He has come to power. Whatever we do, he's going to rule Germany for the foreseeable future. We have to protect ourselves."

"His promises are worth nothing!"

"We have asked for specific assurances in writing: the Catholic Church to be independent of the state, Catholic schools to operate unmolested, no discrimination against Catholics in the civil service." He looked inquiringly at his son.

Heinrich said: "They promised the agreement would be with us first thing this afternoon."

Walter said: "Weigh the options! A scrap of paper signed by a tyrant, against a democratic parliament—which is better?"

"The greatest power of all is God."

Walter rolled his eyes. "Then God save Germany," he said.

The Germans had not had time to develop faith in democracy, Lloyd reflected as the argument surged back and forth between Walter and Gottfried. The Reichstag had been sovereign for only fourteen years. They had lost a war, seen their currency devalued to nothing, and suffered mass unemployment: to them, the right to vote seemed inadequate protection.

Gottfried proved immovable. At the end of lunch his position was as firm as ever. His responsibility was to protect the Catholic Church. It made Lloyd want to scream.

They returned to the opera house and the deputies took their seats in the auditorium. Lloyd and Heinrich sat in a box looking down.

Lloyd could see the Social Democratic Party members in a group on the far left. As the hour approached, he noticed Brownshirts and SS men placing themselves at the exits and around the walls in a threatening arc behind the Social Democrats. It was almost as if they planned to prevent the deputies leaving the building until they had passed the act. Lloyd found it powerfully sinister. He wondered, with a shiver of fear, whether he, too, might find himself imprisoned here.

There was a roar of cheering and applause, and Hitler walked in, wearing a Brownshirt uniform. The Nazi deputies, most of them similarly dressed, rose to their feet in ecstasy as he mounted the rostrum. Only the Social Democrats remained seated, but Lloyd noticed that one or two looked uneasily over their shoulders at the armed guards. How could they speak and vote freely if they were nervous even about not joining in the standing ovation for their opponent?

When at last they became quiet, Hitler began to speak. He stood straight, his left arm at his side, gesturing only with his right. His voice was harsh and grating but powerful, reminding Lloyd of both a machine gun and a barking dog. His tone thrilled with feeling as he spoke of the "November traitors" of 1918 who had surrendered when Germany was about to win the war. He was not pretending: Lloyd felt he sincerely believed every stupid, ignorant word he spoke.

The November traitors were a well-worn topic for Hitler, but then he took a new tack. He spoke of the churches, and the important place of the Christian religion in the German state. This was an unusual theme for him, and his words were clearly aimed at the Centre Party, whose votes would determine today's result. He said that he saw the two main denominations, Protestant and Catholic, as the most important factors for upholding nationhood. Their rights would not be touched by the Nazi government.

Heinrich shot a triumphant look at Lloyd.

"I'd still get it in writing, if I were you," Lloyd muttered.

It was two and a half hours before Hitler reached his peroration.

He ended with an unmistakable threat of violence. "The government of the nationalist uprising is determined and ready to deal with the announcement that the act has been rejected—and with it, that resistance has been declared." He paused dramatically, letting the message sink in: voting against the act would be a declaration of resistance. Then he reinforced it. "May you, gentlemen, now take the decision yourselves as to whether it is to be peace or war!"

He sat down to roars of approval from the Nazi delegates, and the session was adjourned.

Heinrich was elated, Lloyd depressed. They went off in different directions: their parties would now hold desperate last-minute discussions.

The Social Democrats were gloomy. Their leader, Wels, had to speak in the chamber, but what could he say? Several deputies said that if he criticized Hitler he might not leave the building alive. They feared for their own lives, too. If the deputies were killed, Lloyd thought in a moment of cold dread, what would happen to their aides?

Wels revealed that he had a cyanide capsule in his waistcoat pocket. If arrested, he would commit suicide to avoid torture. Lloyd was horrified. Wels was an elected representative, yet he was forced to behave like some kind of saboteur.

Lloyd had started the day with false expectations. He had thought the Enabling Act a crazy idea that had no chance of becoming reality. Now he saw that most people expected the act to become a reality today. He had misjudged the situation badly.

Was he equally wrong to believe that something like this could not happen in his own country? Was he fooling himself?

Someone asked if the Catholics had made a final decision. Lloyd stood up. "I'll find out," he said. He left and ran to the Centre Party's meeting room. As before, he put his head around the door and beckoned Heinrich outside.

"Brüning and Ersing are wavering," Heinrich said.

Lloyd's heart sank. Ersing was a Catholic union leader. "How can a trade unionist even think about voting for this bill?" he said.

"Kaas says the Fatherland is in danger. They all think there will be bloody anarchy if we reject this act."

"There'll be bloody tyranny if you pass it."

"What about your lot?"

"They think they will all be shot if they vote against. But they're going to do it anyway."

Heinrich went back inside and Lloyd returned to the Social Democrats. "The diehards are weakening," Lloyd told Walter and his colleagues. "They're afraid of a civil war if the act is rejected."

The gloom deepened.

They all returned to the debating chamber at six o'clock.

Wels spoke first. He was calm, reasonable, and unemotional. He pointed out that life in a democratic republic had been good for Germans, overall, bringing freedom of opportunity and social welfare, and reinstating Germany as a normal member of the international community.

Lloyd noticed Hitler making notes.

At the end Wels bravely professed allegiance to humanity and justice, freedom and socialism. "No Enabling Law gives you the power to annihilate ideas that are eternal and indestructible," he said, gaining courage as the Nazis began to laugh and jeer.

The Social Democrats applauded, but they were drowned out.

"We greet the persecuted and oppressed!" Wels shouted. "We greet our friends in the Reich. Their steadfastness and loyalty deserve admiration."

Lloyd could just make out his words over the hooting and booing of the Nazis.

"The courage of their convictions and their unbroken optimism guarantee a brighter future!"

He sat down amid raucous heckling.

Would the speech make any difference? Lloyd could not tell.

After Wels, Hitler spoke again. This time his tone was quite different. Lloyd realized that in his earlier speech the chancellor had only been warming up. His voice was louder now, his phrases more intemperate, his tone full of contempt. He used his right arm constantly to make aggressive gestures—pointing, hammering, clenching his fist, putting his hand on his heart, and sweeping the air in a motion that seemed to brush all opposition aside. Every impassioned phrase was cheered uproariously by his supporters. Every sentence expressed the same emotion: a savage, all-consuming, murderous rage.

Hitler was also confident. He claimed he had not needed to propose the Enabling Act. "We appeal in this hour to the German Reichstag to grant us something we would have taken anyway!" he jeered.

Heinrich looked worried, and left the box. A minute later Lloyd saw him on the floor of the auditorium, whispering in his father's ear.

When he returned to the box, he looked stricken.

Lloyd said: "Have you got your written assurances?"

Heinrich could not meet Lloyd's eye. "The document is being typed up," he replied.

Hitler finished by scorning the Social Democrats. He did not want their votes. "Germany shall be free!" he screamed. "But not through you!"

The leaders of the other parties spoke briefly. Every one appeared crushed. Prelate Kaas said the Centre Party would support the bill. The rest followed suit. Everyone but the Social Democrats was in favor.

The result of the vote was announced, and the Nazis cheered wildly.

Lloyd was awestruck. He had seen naked power brutally wielded, and it was an ugly sight.

He left the box without speaking to Heinrich.

He found Walter in the entrance lobby, weeping. He was using a large white handkerchief to wipe his face, but the tears kept coming. Lloyd had not seen men cry like that except at funerals.

Lloyd did not know what to say or do.

"My life has been a failure," Walter said. "This is the end of all hope. German democracy is dead."

## vii

Saturday, April 1, was Boycott Jews Day. Lloyd and Ethel walked around Berlin, staring in incredulity, Ethel making notes for her book. The Star of David was crudely daubed on the windows of Jewish-owned shops. Brownshirts stood at the doors of Jewish-owned department stores, intimidating people who wanted to go in. Jewish lawyers and doctors were picketed. Lloyd happened to see a couple of Brownshirts stopping patients going in to see the von Ulrichs' family physician, Dr. Rothmann, but then a hard-handed coal-heaver with a sprained ankle told the Brownshirts to fuck off out of it, and they went in search of easier prey. "How can people be so mean to each other?" Ethel said.

Lloyd was thinking of the stepfather he loved. Bernie Leckwith was Jewish. If Fascism came to Britain, Bernie would be the target of this kind of hatred. The thought made Lloyd shudder.

A sort of wake was held at Bistro Robert that evening. Apparently no one had organized it, but by eight o'clock the place was full of Social Democrats, Maud's journalistic colleagues, and Robert's theatrical friends. The more optimistic among them said that liberty had merely gone into hibernation for the duration of the economic slump, and one day it would awaken. The rest just mourned.

Lloyd drank little. He did not enjoy the effect of alcohol on his brain. It blurred his thinking. He was asking himself what German left-wingers could have done to prevent this catastrophe, and he did not have an answer.

Maud told them about Ada's baby, Kurt. "She's brought him home from the hospital, and he seems to be happy enough for now. But his brain is damaged and he will never be normal. When he's older, he will have to live in an institution, poor mite."

Lloyd had heard how the baby had been delivered by eleven-year-old Carla. That little girl had grit.

Commissar Thomas Macke arrived at half past nine, wearing his Brownshirt uniform.

Last time he was here, Robert had treated him as a figure of fun, but

Lloyd had sensed the menace of the man. He looked foolish, with the little mustache in the middle of the fat face, but there was a glint of cruelty in his eyes that made Lloyd nervous.

Robert had refused to sell the restaurant. What did Macke want now?

Macke stood in the middle of the dining area and shouted: "This restaurant is being used to promote degenerate behavior!"

The patrons went quiet, wondering what this was about.

Macke raised a finger in a gesture that meant *You'd better listen!* Lloyd felt there was something horribly familiar about the action, and realized Macke was mimicking Hitler.

Macke said: "Homosexuality is incompatible with the masculine character of the German nation!"

Lloyd frowned. Was he saying that Robert was queer?

Jörg came into the restaurant from the kitchen, wearing his tall chef's hat. He stood by the door, glaring at Macke.

Lloyd was struck by a shocking thought. Maybe Robert *was* queer.

After all, he and Jörg had been living together since the war.

Looking around at their theatrical friends, Lloyd noticed that they were all men in pairs, except for two women with short hair . . .

Lloyd felt bewildered. He knew that queers existed, and as a broad-minded person he believed they should not be persecuted but helped. However, he thought of them as perverts and creeps. Robert and Jörg seemed like normal men, running a business and living quietly—almost like a married couple!

He turned to his mother and said quietly: "Are Robert and Jörg really . . ."

"Yes, dear," she said.

Maud, sitting next to her, said: "Robert in his youth was a menace to footmen."

Both women giggled.

Lloyd was doubly shocked: not only was Robert queer, but Ethel and Maud thought it a matter for lighthearted banter.

Macke said: "This establishment is now closed!"

Robert said: "You have no right!"

Macke could not close the place on his own, Lloyd thought; then he remembered how the Brownshirts had crowded onto the stage at the People's Theater. He looked toward the entrance—and was aghast to see Brownshirts pushing through the door.

They went around the tables knocking over bottles and glasses. Some customers sat motionless and watched; others got to their feet. Several men shouted and a woman screamed.

Walter stood up and spoke loudly but calmly. "We should all leave quietly," he said. "There's no need for any rough stuff. Everybody just get your coats and hats and go home."

The customers began to leave, some trying to get their coats, others just fleeing. Walter and Lloyd ushered Maud and Ethel toward the door. The till was near the exit, and Lloyd saw a Brownshirt open it and begin stuffing money into his pockets.

Until then Robert had been standing still, watching miserably as a night's business hurried out of the door, but this was too much. He gave a shout of protest and shoved the Brownshirt away from the till.

The Brownshirt punched him, knocking him to the floor, and began to kick him as he lay there. Another Brownshirt joined in.

Lloyd leaped to Robert's rescue. He heard his mother shout, "No!" as he shoved the Brownshirts aside. Jörg was almost as quick, and the two of them bent to help Robert up.

They were immediately attacked by several more Brownshirts. Lloyd was punched and kicked, and something heavy hit him over the head, and as he cried out in pain, he thought: No, not again.

He turned on his attackers, punching with his left and right, making every blow connect hard, trying to punch *through* the target as he had been taught. He knocked two men down; then he was grabbed from behind and thrown off balance. A moment later he was on the floor with two men holding him down while a third kicked him.

Then he was rolled over onto his front, his arms were pulled behind his back, and he felt metal on his wrists. He had been handcuffed for the first time in his life. He felt a new kind of fear. This was not just another roughhouse. He had been beaten and kicked, but worse was in store.

"Get up," someone told him in German.

He struggled to his feet. His head hurt. Robert and Jörg were also in handcuffs, he saw. Robert's mouth was bleeding and Jörg had one closed eye. Half a dozen Brownshirts were guarding them. The rest were drinking from the glasses and bottles left on the tables, or standing at the dessert cart stuffing their faces with pastries.

All the customers seemed to have gone. Lloyd felt relieved that his mother had got away.

The restaurant door opened and Walter came back in. "Commissar Macke," he said, displaying a typical politician's facility for remembering names. With as much authority as he could muster he said: "What is the meaning of this outrage?"

Macke pointed to Robert and Jörg. "These two men are homosexuals," he said. "And that boy attacked an auxiliary policeman who was arresting them."

Walter pointed to the till, which was open, its drawer sticking out and empty except for a few small coins. "Do police officers commit robbery nowadays?"

"A customer must have taken advantage of the confusion created by those resisting arrest."

Some of the Brownshirts laughed knowingly.

Walter said: "You used to be a law enforcement officer, didn't you, Macke? You might have been proud of yourself, once. But what are you now?"

Macke was stung. "We enforce order, to protect the Fatherland."

"Where are you planning to take your prisoners, I wonder?" Walter persisted. "Will it be a properly constituted place of detention? Or some half-hidden unofficial basement?"

"They will be taken to the Friedrich Strasse Barracks," Macke said indignantly.

Lloyd saw a look of satisfaction pass briefly across Walter's face, and realized Walter had cleverly manipulated Macke, playing on whatever was left of his professional pride in order to get him to reveal his intentions. Now, at least, Walter knew where Lloyd and the others were being taken.

But what would happen at the barracks?

Lloyd had never been arrested. However, he lived in the East End of London, so he knew plenty of people who got into trouble with the police. Most of his life he had played street football with boys whose fathers were arrested frequently. He knew the reputation of Leman Street police station in Aldgate. Few men came out of that building uninjured. People said there was blood all over the walls. Was it likely the Friedrich Strasse Barracks would be any better?

Walter said: "This is an international incident, Commissar." Lloyd guessed he was using the title in the hope of making Macke behave more like an officer and less like a thug. "You have arrested three foreign citizens—two Austrians and one Englishman." He held up a hand as if to fend off a protest. "It is too late to back out now. Both embassies are being informed, and I have no doubt that their representatives will be knocking on the door of our Foreign Office in Wilhelm Strasse within the hour."

Lloyd wondered whether that was true.

Macke grinned unpleasantly. "The Foreign Office will not hasten to defend two queers and a young hooligan."

"Our foreign minister, von Neurath, is not a member of your party," Walter said. "He may well put the interests of the Fatherland first."

"I think you will find that he does what he's told. And now you are obstructing me in the course of my duty."

"I warn you!" Walter said bravely. "You had better follow procedure by the book—or there will be trouble."

"Get out of my sight," said Macke.

Walter left.

Lloyd, Robert, and Jörg were marched outside and bundled into the back of some kind of truck. They were forced to lie on the floor while Brownshirts sat on benches, guarding them. The vehicle moved off. It was painful being handcuffed, Lloyd discovered. He felt constantly that his shoulder was about to become dislocated.

The trip was mercifully short. They were shoved out of the truck and into a building. It was dark, and Lloyd saw little. At a desk, his name was written in a book and his passport was taken away. Robert lost his gold tiepin and watch chain. At last the handcuffs were removed and they were pushed into a room with dim lights and barred windows. About forty other prisoners were there already.

Lloyd hurt all over. He had a pain in his chest that felt like a cracked rib. His face was bruised and he had a blinding headache. He wanted an aspirin, a cup of tea, and a pillow. He had a feeling it might be some hours before he got any of those things.

The three of them sat on the floor near the door. Lloyd held his head in his hands while Robert and Jörg discussed how soon help would come. No doubt Walter would phone a lawyer. But all the usual rules had been suspended by the Reichstag Fire Decree, so they had no proper protection under the law. Walter would also contact the embassies: political influence was their main hope now. Lloyd thought his mother would probably try to place an international phone call to the British Foreign Office in London. If she could get through, the government would surely have something to say about the arrest of a British schoolboy. It would all take time—an hour at least, probably two or three.

But four hours passed, then five, and the door did not open.

Civilized countries had a law about how long the police could keep someone in custody without formalities: a charge, a lawyer, a court. Lloyd now realized that such a rule was no mere technicality. He could be here forever.

The other prisoners in the room were all political, he discovered: Communists, Social Democrats, trade union organizers, and one priest.

The night passed slowly. None of the three slept. To Lloyd sleep seemed unthinkable. The gray light of morning was coming through the barred windows when at last the cell door opened. But no lawyers or diplomats came in, just two men in aprons pushing a trolley on which stood a large urn. They ladled out a thin oatmeal. Lloyd did not eat any, but he drank a tin mug of coffee that tasted of burned barley.

He surmised that the staff on duty overnight at the British embassy were junior diplomats who carried little weight. This morning, as soon as the ambassador himself got up, action would be taken.

An hour after breakfast the door opened again, but this time only Brownshirts stood there. They marched all the prisoners out and loaded them onto a truck, forty or fifty men in one canvas-sided vehicle, packed so tightly that they had to remain standing. Lloyd managed to stay close to Robert and Jörg.

Perhaps they were going to court, even though it was Sunday. He hoped so. At least there would be lawyers, and some semblance of due process. He thought he was fluent enough to state his simple case in German, and he practised his speech in his head. He had been dining in a restaurant with his mother; he had seen someone robbing the till; he had intervened in the resulting fracas. He imagined his cross-examination. He would be asked if the man he attacked was a Brownshirt. He would answer: "I didn't notice his clothing—I just saw a thief." There would be laughter in court, and the prosecutor would look foolish.

They were driven out of town.

They could see through gaps in the canvas sides of the truck. It seemed to Lloyd that they had gone about twenty miles when Robert said: "We're in Oranienburg," naming a small town north of Berlin.

The truck came to a halt outside a wooden gate between brick pillars. Two Brownshirts with rifles stood guard.

Lloyd's fear rose a notch. Where was the court? This looked more like a prison camp. How could they put people in prison without a judge?

After a short wait, the truck drove in and stopped at a group of derelict buildings.

Lloyd was becoming even more anxious. Last night he at least had the consolation that Walter knew where he was. Today it was possible no one would know. What if the police simply said he was not in custody and they had no record of his arrest? How could he be rescued?

They got out of the truck and shuffled into what looked like a factory of some sort. The place smelled like a pub. Perhaps it had been a brewery.

Once again all their names were taken. Lloyd was glad there was some record of his movements. They were not tied up or handcuffed, but they were constantly watched by Brownshirts with rifles, and Lloyd had a grim feeling that those young men were only too eager for an excuse to shoot.

They were each given a canvas mattress filled with straw and a thin blanket. They were herded into a tumbledown building that might once have been a warehouse. Then the waiting began.

No one came for Lloyd all that day.

In the evening there was another trolley and another urn, this one containing a stew of carrots and turnips. Each man got a bowlful and a piece of bread. Lloyd was now ravenous, not having eaten for twenty-four hours, and he wolfed his meager supper and wished for more.

Somewhere in the camp there were three or four dogs that howled all night.

Lloyd felt dirty. This was the second night he had spent in the same clothes. He needed a bath and a shave and a clean shirt. The toilet facilities, two barrels in the corner, were absolutely disgusting.

But tomorrow was Monday. Then there would be some action.

Lloyd fell asleep around four. At six they were awakened by a Brownshirt bawling: "Schleicher! Jörg Schleicher! Which one is Schleicher?"

Maybe they were going to be released.

Jörg stood up and said: "Me, I'm Schleicher."

"Come with me," said the Brownshirt.

Robert said in a frightened voice: "Why? What do you want him for? Where is he going?"

"What are you, his mother?" said the Brownshirt. "Lie down and shut your mouth." He poked Jörg with his rifle. "Outside, you."

Watching them go, Lloyd asked himself why he had not punched the Brownshirt and snatched the rifle. He might have escaped. And if he had failed, what would they do to him—throw him in jail? But at the crucial moment the thought of escape had not even occurred to him. Was he already taking on the mentality of the prisoner?

He was even looking forward to the oatmeal.

Before breakfast, they were all taken outside.

They stood around a small wire-fenced area a quarter the size of a tennis court. It looked as if it might have been used to store something not very valuable, timber or tires perhaps. Lloyd shivered in the cold morning air: his overcoat was still at Bistro Robert.

Then he saw Thomas Macke approaching.

The police detective wore a black coat over his Brownshirt uniform. He had a heavy, flat-footed stride, Lloyd noticed.

Behind Macke were two Brownshirts holding the arms of a naked man with a bucket over his head.

Lloyd stared in horror. The prisoner's hands were tied behind his back, and the bucket was tightly tied with string under his chin so that it would not fall off.

He was a slight, youngish man with blond pubic hair.

Robert groaned: "Oh, sweet Jesus, it's Jörg."

All the Brownshirts in the camp had gathered. Lloyd frowned. What was this, some kind of cruel game?

Jörg was led into the fenced compound and left there, shivering. His two escorts withdrew. They disappeared for a few minutes, then returned, each of them leading two Alsatian dogs.

That explained the all-night barking.

The dogs were thin, with unhealthy bald patches in their tan fur. They looked starved.

The Brownshirts led them to the fenced compound.

Lloyd had a vague but dreadful premonition of what was to come.

Robert screamed: "No!" He ran forward. "No, no, no!" He tried to open the gate of the compound. Three or four Brownshirts pulled him away roughly. He struggled, but they were strong young thugs, and Robert was approaching fifty years old: he could not resist them. They threw him contemptuously to the ground.

"No," said Macke to his men. "Make him watch."

They lifted Robert to his feet and held him facing the wire fence.

The dogs were led into the compound. They were excited, barking and slavering. The two Brownshirts handled them expertly and without fear, clearly experienced. Lloyd wondered dismally how many times they had done this before.

The handlers released the dogs and hurried out of the compound.

The dogs dashed for Jörg. One bit his calf, another his arm, a third his thigh. From behind the metal bucket there was a muffled scream of agony and terror. The Brownshirts cheered and applauded. The prisoners looked on in mute horror.

After the first shock, Jörg tried to defend himself. His hands were tied and he was unable to see, but he could kick out randomly. However, his bare feet made little impact on the starving dogs. They dodged and came again, ripping his flesh with their sharp teeth.

He tried running. With the dogs at his heels he ran blindly in a straight line until he crashed into the wire fence. The Brownshirts cheered raucously. Jörg ran in a different direction with the same result. A dog took a chunk out of Jörg's behind, and they hooted with laughter.

A Brownshirt standing next to Lloyd was shouting: "His tail! Bite his tail!" Lloyd guessed that *tail* in German—der Schwanz—was slang for *penis*. The man was hysterical with excitement.

Jörg's white body was now running with blood from multiple wounds. He pressed himself up against the wire, face-first, protecting his genitals, kicking out backward and sideways. But he was weakening. His kicks became feeble. He was having trouble staying upright. The dogs became bolder, tearing at him and swallowing bloody chunks.

At last Jörg slid to the ground.

The dogs settled down to feed.

The handlers reentered the compound. With practised motions they reattached the dogs' leashes, pulled them off Jörg, and led them away.

The show was over, and the Brownshirts began to move away, chattering excitedly.

Robert ran into the compound, and this time no one stopped him. He bent over Jörg, moaning.

Lloyd helped him untie Jörg's hands and remove the bucket. Jörg was unconscious but breathing. Lloyd said: "Let's get him indoors. You take his legs." Lloyd grasped Jörg under the arms and the two of them carried him into the building where they had slept. They put him on a mattress. The other prisoners gathered around, frightened and subdued. Lloyd hoped one of them might announce that he was a doctor, but no one did.

Robert stripped off his jacket and waistcoat, then took off his shirt and used it to wipe the blood. "We need clean water," he said.

There was a standpipe in the yard. Lloyd went out, but he had no container. He returned to the compound. The bucket was still there on the ground. He washed it out, then filled it with water.

When he returned, the mattress was soaked in blood.

Robert dipped his shirt in the bucket and continued to wash Jörg's wounds, kneeling beside the mattress. Soon the white shirt was red.

Jörg stirred.

Robert spoke to him in a low voice. "Be calm, my beloved," he said. "It's over now, and I'm here." But Jörg seemed not to hear.

Then Macke came in, with four or five Brownshirts following. He grabbed Robert's arm and pulled him. "So!" he said. "Now you know what we think of homosexual perverts."

Lloyd pointed at Jörg and said angrily: "The pervert is the one who caused this to happen." Mustering all his rage and contempt, he said: "Commissar Macke."

Macke gave a slight nod to one of the Brownshirts. In a movement that was deceptively casual, the man reversed his rifle and hit Lloyd over the head with the butt.

Lloyd fell to the ground, holding his head in agony.

He heard Robert say: "Please, just let me look after Jörg."

"Perhaps," said Macke. "First come over here."

Despite his pain, Lloyd opened his eyes to see what was happening.

Macke pulled Robert across the room to a rough wooden table. From his pocket he drew a document and a fountain pen. "Your restaurant is now worth half of what I last offered you—ten thousand marks."

"Anything," said Robert, weeping. "Leave me to be with Jörg."

"Sign here," said Macke. "Then the three of you can go home."

Robert signed.

"This gentleman can be a witness," Macke said. He gave the pen to one of the Brownshirts. He looked across the room and met Lloyd's eye. "And perhaps our foolhardy English guest can be the second witness."

Robert said: "Just do what he wants, Lloyd."

Lloyd struggled to his feet, rubbed his sore head, took the pen, and signed.

Macke pocketed the contract triumphantly and went out.

Robert and Lloyd returned to Jörg.

But Jörg was dead.

## viii

Walter and Maud came to the Lehrte Station, just north of the burned-out Reichstag, to see Ethel and Lloyd off. The station building was in the neo-Renaissance style and looked like a French palace. They were early, and they sat in a station café while they waited for the train.

Lloyd was glad to be leaving. In six weeks he had learned a lot, about the German language and about politics, but now he wanted to get home, tell people what he had seen, and warn them against the same thing happening to them.

All the same he felt strangely guilty about departing. He was going to a place where the law ruled, the press was free, and it was not a crime to be a Social Democrat. He was leaving the von Ulrich family to live on in a cruel dictatorship where an innocent man could be torn to pieces by dogs and no one would ever be brought to justice for the crime.

The von Ulrichs looked crushed, Walter even more than Maud. They were like people who have heard bad news, or suffered a death in the family. They seemed unable to think much about anything other than the catastrophe that had happened to them.

Lloyd had been released with profuse apologies from the German Foreign Ministry, and an explanatory statement that was abject yet at the same time mendacious, implying that he had got into a brawl through his own foolishness and then been held prisoner by an administrative error for which the authorities were deeply sorry.

Walter said: "I've had a telegram from Robert. He's arrived safely in London."

As an Austrian citizen Robert had been able to leave Germany without much difficulty. Getting his money out had been more tricky. Walter had demanded that Macke pay the money to a bank in Switzerland. At first Macke had said that was impossible, but Walter had put pressure on him, threatening to challenge the sale in court, saying that Lloyd was prepared to testify that the contract had been signed under duress, and in the end Macke had pulled some strings.

"I'm glad Robert got out," Lloyd said. He would be even happier when he himself was safe in London. His head was still tender and he got a pain in his ribs every time he turned over in bed.

Ethel said to Maud: "Why don't you come to London? Both of you. The whole family, I mean."

Walter looked at Maud. "Perhaps we should," he said. But Lloyd could tell that he did not really mean it.

"You've done your best," Ethel said. "You've fought bravely. But the other side won."

Maud said: "It's not over yet."

"But you're in danger."

"So is Germany."

"If you came to live in London, Fitz might soften his attitude, and help you."

Earl Fitzherbert was one of the wealthiest men in Britain, Lloyd knew, because of the coal mines beneath his land in South Wales.

"He wouldn't help me," Maud said. "Fitz doesn't relent. I know that, and so do you."

"You're right," Ethel said. Lloyd wondered how she could be so sure, but he did not get a chance to ask. Ethel went on: "Well, you could easily get a job on a London newspaper, with your experience."

Walter said: "And what would I do in London?"

"I don't know," Ethel said. "What are you going to do here? There's not much point in being an elected representative in an impotent parliament." She was being brutally frank, Lloyd felt, but characteristically she was saying what had to be said.

Lloyd sympathized, but felt the von Ulrichs should stay. "I know it will be hard," Walter said. "But if decent people flee from Fascism, it will spread all the faster."

"It's spreading anyway," Ethel rejoined.

Maud startled them all by saying vehemently: "I will not go. I absolutely refuse to leave Germany."

They all stared at her.

"I'm German, and have been for fourteen years," she said. "This is my country now."

"But you were born English," said Ethel.

"A country is mostly the people in it," Maud said. "I don't love England. My parents died a long time ago, and my brother has disowned me. I love Germany. For me, Germany is my wonderful husband, Walter; my misguided son, Erik; my alarmingly capable daughter, Carla; our maid, Ada, and her disabled son; my friend Monika and her family; my journalistic colleagues . . . I'm staying, to fight the Nazis."

"You've already done more than your share," Ethel said gently.

Maud's tone became emotional. "My husband has dedicated himself, his life, his entire being to making this country free and prosperous. I will not be the cause of his giving up his life's work. If he loses that, he loses his soul."

Ethel pushed the point in a way that only an old friend could. "Still," she said, "there must be a temptation to take your children to safety."

"A temptation? You mean a longing, a yearning, a desperate desire!" She began to cry. "Carla has nightmares about Brownshirts, and Erik puts on that shit-colored uniform every chance he gets." Lloyd was startled by her fervor. He had never heard a respectable woman say *shit*. She went on: "Of course I want to take them away." Lloyd could see how torn she was. She rubbed her hands together as if washing them, turned her head from side to side in distraction, and spoke in a voice that shook violently with her inner conflict. "But it's the wrong thing to do, for them as well as for us. I will not give in to it! Better to suffer evil than stand by and do nothing."

Ethel touched Maud's arm. "I'm sorry I asked. Perhaps it was silly of me. I might have known you wouldn't run away."

"I'm glad you asked," Walter said. He reached out and took Maud's slim hands in his own. "The question has been hanging in the air between Maud and me, unspoken. It was time we faced it." Their joined hands rested on the café table. Lloyd rarely thought about the emotional lives of his mother's generation—they were middle-aged and married, and that seemed to say it all—but now he saw that between Walter and Maud there was a powerful connection that was much more than the familiar habit of a mature marriage. They were under no illusions: they knew that by staying here they were risking their lives and the lives of their children. But they had a shared commitment that defied death.

Lloyd wondered whether he would ever have such a love.

Ethel looked at the clock. "Oh, my goodness!" she said. "We're going to miss the train!"

Lloyd picked up their bags and they hurried across the platform. A whistle blew. They boarded the train just in time. They both leaned out of the window as it pulled out of the station.

Walter and Maud stood on the platform, waving, getting smaller and smaller in the distance, until finally they disappeared.

# CHAPTER TWO

# 1935

"Two things you need to know about girls in Buffalo," said Daisy Peshkov. "They drink like fish, and they're all snobs."

Eva Rothmann giggled. "I don't believe you," she said. Her German accent had almost completely vanished.

"Oh, it's true," said Daisy. They were in her pink-and-white bedroom, trying on clothes in front of a full-length three-way mirror. "Navy and white might look good on you," Daisy said. "What do you think?" She held a blouse up to Eva's face and studied the effect. The contrasting colors seemed to suit her.

Daisy was looking through her closet for an outfit Eva could wear to the beach picnic. Eva was not a pretty girl, and the frills and bows that decorated many of Daisy's clothes only made Eva look frumpy. Stripes better suited her strong features.

Eva's hair was dark, and her eyes deep brown. "You can wear bright colors," Daisy told her.

Eva had few clothes of her own. Her father, a Jewish doctor in Berlin, had spent his life savings to send her to America, and she had arrived a year ago with nothing. A charity paid for her to go to Daisy's boarding school—they were the same age, nineteen. But Eva had nowhere to go in the summer vacation, so Daisy had impulsively invited her home.

At first Daisy's mother, Olga, had resisted. "Oh, but you're away at school all year—I so look forward to having you to myself in the summer."

"She's really great, Mother," Daisy had said. "She's charming and easygoing and a loyal friend."

"I suppose you feel sorry for her because she's a refugee from the Nazis."

"I don't care about the Nazis. I just like her."

"That's fine, but does she have to live with us?"

"Mother, she has nowhere else to go!"

As usual, Olga let Daisy have her way in the end.

Now Eva said: "Snobs? No one would be snobby to you!"

"Oh, yes, they would."

"But you're so pretty and vivacious."

Daisy did not bother to deny it. "They hate that about me."

"And you're rich."

It was true. Daisy's father was wealthy, her mother had inherited a fortune, and Daisy herself would come into money when she was twenty-one. "It doesn't mean a thing. In this town it's about how long you've been rich. You're nobody if you work. The superior people are those who live on the millions left by their great-grandparents." She spoke in a tone of gay mockery to hide the resentment she felt.

Eva said: "And your father is famous!"

"They think he's a gangster."

Daisy's grandfather, Josef Vyalov, had owned bars and hotels. Her father, Lev Peshkov, had used the profits to buy ailing vaudeville theaters and convert them into cinemas. Now he owned a Hollywood studio, too.

Eva was indignant on Daisy's behalf. "How can they say such a thing?"

"They believe he was a bootlegger. They're probably right. I can't see how else he made money out of bars during Prohibition. Anyway, that's why Mother will never be invited to join the Buffalo Ladies' Society."

They both looked at Olga, sitting on Daisy's bed, reading the *Buffalo Sentinel.* In photographs taken when she was young, Olga was a willowy beauty. Now she was dumpy and drab. She had lost interest in her appearance, though she shopped energetically with Daisy, never caring how much she spent to make her daughter look fabulous.

Olga looked up from the newspaper to say: "I'm not sure they mind your father being a bootlegger, dear. But he's a Russian immigrant, and on the rare occasions he decides to attend divine service he goes to the Russian Orthodox Church on Ideal Street. That's almost as bad as being Catholic."

Eva said: "It's so unfair."

"I might as well warn you that they're not too fond of Jews, either," Daisy said. Eva was in fact half-Jewish. "Sorry to be blunt."

"Be as blunt as you like—after Germany, this country feels like the promised land."

"Don't get too comfortable," Olga warned her. "According to this paper, plenty of American business leaders hate President Roosevelt and admire Adolf Hitler. I know that's true, because Daisy's father is one of them."

"Politics is boring," said Daisy. "Isn't there something interesting in the *Sentinel*?"

"Yes, there is. Muffie Dixon is to be presented at the British court."

"Good for her," Daisy said sourly, failing to conceal her envy.

Olga read: "'Miss Muriel Dixon, daughter of the late Charles "Chuck" Dixon, who was killed in France during the war, will be presented at Buckingham Palace next Tuesday by the wife of the United States ambassador, Mrs. Robert W. Bingham.'"

Daisy had heard enough about Muffie Dixon. "I've been to Paris, but never London," she said to Eva. "What about you?"

"Neither," said Eva. "The first time I left Germany was when I sailed to America."

Olga suddenly said: "Oh, dear!"

"What's happened?" Daisy said.

Her mother crumpled the paper. "Your father took Gladys Angelus to the White House."

"Oh!" Daisy felt as if she had been slapped. "But he said he would take me!"

President Roosevelt had invited a hundred businessmen to a reception in an attempt to win them over to his New Deal. Lev Peshkov thought Franklin D. Roosevelt was the next thing to a Communist, but he had been flattered to be asked to the White House. However, Olga had refused to accompany him, saying angrily: "I'm not willing to pretend to the president that we have a normal marriage."

Lev officially lived here, in the stylish prewar prairie home built by Grandfather Vyalov, but he spent more nights at the swanky downtown apartment where he kept his mistress of many years, Marga. On top of that, everyone assumed he was having an affair with his studio's biggest star, Gladys Angelus. Daisy understood why her mother felt spurned. Daisy, too, felt rejected when Lev drove off to spend his evenings with his other family.

She had been thrilled when he asked her to accompany him to the White House instead of her mother. She had told everyone she was going. None of her friends had met the president except the Dewar boys, whose father was a senator.

Lev had not told her the exact date, and she assumed he would let her know at the last minute, which was his usual style. But he had changed his mind, or perhaps just forgotten. Either way, he had rejected Daisy again.

"I'm sorry, honey," said her mother. "But promises never did mean much to your father."

Eva was looking sympathetic. Her pity stung Daisy. Eva's father was thousands of miles away, and she might never see him again, but she felt sorry for Daisy, as if Daisy's plight were worse.

It made Daisy feel defiant. She would not let this ruin her day. "Well, I'll be the only girl in Buffalo who has been stood up for Gladys Angelus," she said. "Now, what shall I wear?"

Skirts were dramatically short this year in Paris, but the conservative Buffalo set followed fashion at a distance. However, Daisy had a knee-length tennis dress in a shade of baby blue the same as her eyes. Maybe today was the day to bring it out. She slipped off her dress and put on the new one. "What do you think?" she said.

Eva said: "Oh, Daisy, it's beautiful, but . . ."

Olga said: "That'll make their eyes pop." Olga liked it when Daisy dressed to kill. Perhaps it reminded her of her youth.

Eva said: "Daisy, if they're all so snobbish, why do you want to go to the party?"

"Charlie Farquharson will be there, and I'm thinking of marrying him," Daisy said.

"Are you serious?"

Olga said emphatically: "He's a great catch."

Eva said: "What's he like?"

"Absolutely adorable," Daisy said. "Not the handsomest boy in Buffalo, but sweet and kind, and rather shy."

"He sounds very different from you."

"It's the attraction of opposites."

Olga spoke again. "The Farquharsons are among the oldest families in Buffalo."

Eva raised her dark eyebrows. "Snobby?"

"Very," Daisy said. "But Charlie's father lost all his money in the Wall Street crash, then died—killed himself, some say—so they need to restore the family fortunes."

Eva looked shocked. "You're hoping he'll marry you for your money?"

"No. He'll marry me because I will bewitch him. But his mother will accept me for my money."

"You say you *will* bewitch him. Does he know about any of this?"

"Not yet. But I think I might make a start this afternoon. Yes, this is definitely the right dress."

Daisy wore the baby blue and Eva the navy-and-white stripes. By the time they got ready, they were late.

Daisy's mother would not have a chauffeur. "I married my father's chauffeur, and it ruined my life," she sometimes said. She was terrified Daisy might do something similar—that was why she was so keen on

Charlie Farquharson. If she needed to go anywhere in her creaking 1925 Stutz, she made Henry, the gardener, take off his rubber boots and put on a black suit. But Daisy had her own car, a red Chevrolet Sport Coupe.

Daisy liked driving, loved the power and speed of it. They headed south out of the city. She was almost sorry it was only five or six miles to the beach.

As she drove, she thought about life as Charlie's wife. With her money and his status they would become the leading couple in Buffalo society. At their dinner parties the table settings would be so elegant that people would gasp in delight. They would have the biggest yacht in the harbor, and throw onboard parties for other wealthy, fun-loving couples. People would yearn for an invitation from Mrs. Charles Farquharson. No charity function would be a success without Daisy and Charlie at the top table. In her head she watched a movie of herself, in a ravishing Paris gown, walking through a crowd of admiring men and women, smiling graciously at their compliments.

She was still daydreaming when they reached their destination.

The city of Buffalo was in upstate New York, near the Canadian border. Woodlawn Beach was a mile of sand on the shore of Lake Erie. Daisy parked and they walked across the dunes.

Fifty or sixty people were already there. These were the adolescent children of the Buffalo elite, a privileged group who spent their summers sailing and water-skiing in the daytime and going to parties and dances at night. Daisy greeted the people she knew, which was just about everyone, and introduced Eva around. They got glasses of punch. Daisy tasted it cautiously: some of the boys would think it hilarious to spike the drink with a couple of bottles of gin.

The party was for Dot Renshaw, a sharp-tongued girl whom no one wanted to marry. The Renshaws were an old Buffalo family, like the Farquharsons, but their fortune had survived the crash. Daisy made sure to approach the host, Dot's father, and thank him. "I'm sorry we're late," she said. "I lost track of time!"

Philip Renshaw looked her up and down. "That's a very short skirt." Disapproval vied with lasciviousness in his expression.

"I'm so glad you like it," Daisy replied, pretending he had paid her a straightforward compliment.

"Anyway, it's good that you're here at last," he went on. "A photographer from the *Sentinel* is coming and we must have some pretty girls in the picture."

Daisy muttered to Eva: "So that's why I was invited. How kind of him to let me know."

Dot came up. She had a thin face with a pointed nose. Daisy always thought she looked as if she might peck you. "I thought you were going with your father to meet the president," she said.

Daisy felt mortified. She wished she had not boasted to everyone about this.

"I see he took his, ahem, leading lady," Dot went on. "Unusual, that sort of thing, in the White House."

Daisy said: "I guess the president likes to meet movie stars occasionally. He deserves a little glamour, don't you think?"

"I can't imagine Eleanor Roosevelt approved. According to the *Sentinel,* all the other men took their wives."

"How thoughtful of them." Daisy turned away, desperate to escape.

She spotted Charlie Farquharson, trying to erect a net for beach tennis. He was too good-natured to mock her about Gladys Angelus. "How are you, Charlie?" she said brightly.

"Fine, I guess." He stood up, a tall man of about twenty-five, a little overweight, stooping slightly as if he feared his height might be intimidating.

Daisy introduced Eva. Charlie was sweetly awkward in company, especially with girls, but he made an effort and asked Eva how she liked America, and what she heard from her family back in Berlin.

Eva asked him if he was enjoying the picnic.

"Not much," he said candidly. "I'd rather be at home with my dogs."

No doubt he found pets easier to deal with than girls, Daisy thought. But the mention of dogs was interesting. "What kind of dogs do you have?" she asked.

"Jack Russell terriers."

Daisy made a mental note.

An angular woman of about fifty approached. "For goodness' sake, Charlie, haven't you got that net up yet?"

"Almost there, Mom," he said.

Nora Farquharson was wearing a gold tennis bracelet, diamond ear studs, and a Tiffany necklace—more jewelry than she really needed for a picnic. The Farquharsons' poverty was relative, Daisy reflected. They said they had lost everything, but Mrs. Farquharson still had a maid and a chauffeur and a couple of horses for riding in the park.

Daisy said: "Good afternoon, Mrs. Farquharson. This is my friend Eva Rothmann from Berlin."

"How do you do," said Nora Farquharson without offering her hand. She felt no need to be friendly toward arriviste Russians, much less their Jewish guests.

Then she seemed to be struck by a thought. "Ah, Daisy, you could go round and find out who wants to play tennis."

Daisy knew she was being treated somewhat as a servant, but she decided to be compliant. "Of course," she said. "Mixed doubles, I suggest."

"Good idea." Mrs. Farquharson held out a pencil stub and a scrap of paper. "Write the names down."

Daisy smiled sweetly and took a gold pen and a little beige leather notebook from her bag. "I'm equipped."

She knew who the tennis players were, good and bad. She belonged to the Racquet Club, which was not as exclusive as the Yacht Club. She paired Eva with Chuck Dewar, the fourteen-year-old son of Senator Dewar. She put Joanne Rouzrokh with the older Dewar boy, Woody, only fifteen but already as tall as his beanpole father. Naturally she herself would be Charlie's partner.

Daisy was startled to come across a somewhat familiar face and recognize her half brother, Greg, the son of Marga. They did not meet often, and she had not seen him for a year. In that time he seemed to have become a man. He was six inches taller, and although still only fifteen he had the dark shadow of a beard. As a child he had been disheveled, and that had not changed. He wore his expensive clothes carelessly: the sleeves of the blazer rolled up, the striped tie loose at the neck, the linen pants sea-wet and sandy at the cuffs.

Daisy was always embarrassed to run into Greg. He was a living reminder of how their father had rejected Daisy and her mother in favor of Greg and Marga. Many married men had affairs, she knew, but *her* father's indiscretion showed up at parties for everyone to see. Father should have moved Marga and Greg to New York, where nobody knew anybody, or to California, where no one saw anything wrong with adultery. Here they were a permanent scandal, and Greg was part of the reason people looked down on Daisy.

He asked her politely how she was, and she answered: "Angry as heck, if you want to know. Father's let me down—again."

Greg said guardedly: "What did he do?"

"Asked me to go to the White House with him—then took that tart Gladys Angelus. Now everyone's laughing at me."

"It must have been good publicity for *Passion,* her new film."

"You always take his side because he prefers you to me."

Greg looked irritated. "Maybe that's because I admire him instead of complaining about him all the time."

"I don't—" Daisy was about to deny complaining all the time when she realized it was true. "Well, maybe I do complain, but he should keep his promises, shouldn't he?"

"He has so much on his mind."

"Maybe he shouldn't have two mistresses as well as a wife."

Greg shrugged. "It's a lot to handle."

They both noticed the unintentional double entendre, and after a moment they giggled.

Daisy said: "Well, I guess I shouldn't blame you. You didn't ask to be born."

"And I should probably forgive you for taking my father away from me three nights a week—no matter how I cried and begged him to stay."

Daisy had never thought of it that way. In her mind Greg was the usurper, the illegitimate child who kept stealing her father. But now she realized he felt as hurt as she did.

She stared at him. Some girls might find him attractive, she guessed. He was too young for Eva, though. And he would probably turn out as selfish and unreliable as their father.

"Anyway," she said, "do you play tennis?"

He shook his head. "They don't let people like me into the Racquet Club." He forced an insouciant grin, and Daisy realized that, like her, Greg felt rejected by Buffalo society. "Ice hockey's my sport," he said.

"Too bad." She moved on.

When she had enough names, she returned to Charlie, who had finally got the net up. She sent Eva to round up the first foursome. Then she said to Charlie: "Help me make a competition tree."

They knelt side by side and drew a diagram in the sand with heats, semifinals, and a final. While they were entering the names, Charlie said: "Do you like the movies?"

Daisy wondered if he was about to ask her for a date. "Sure," she said.

"Have you seen *Passion,* by any chance?"

"No, Charlie, I haven't seen it," she said in a tone of exasperation. "It stars my father's mistress."

He was shocked. "The papers say they're just good friends."

"And why do you think Miss Angelus, who is barely twenty, is so *friendly* with my forty-year-old father?" Daisy asked sarcastically. "Do you think she likes his receding hairline? Or his little paunch? Or his fifty million dollars?"

"Oh, I see," said Charlie, looking abashed. "Sorry."

"You shouldn't be sorry. I'm being kind of bitchy. You're not like everyone else—you don't automatically think the worst of people."

"I guess I'm just dumb."

"No. You're just nice."

Charlie looked embarrassed, but pleased.

"Let's get on with this," Daisy said. "We have to rig it so the best players get through to the final."

Nora Farquharson reappeared. She looked at Charlie and Daisy kneeling side by side in the sand, then studied their drawing.

Charlie said: "Pretty good, Mom, don't you think?" He longed for approval from her; that was obvious.

"Very good." She gave Daisy an appraising look, like a mother dog seeing a stranger approach her puppies.

"Charlie did most of it," Daisy said.

"No, he didn't," Mrs. Farquharson said bluntly. Her gaze went to Charlie and back. "You're a smart girl," she said. She looked as if she were about to add something, but hesitated.

"What?" said Daisy.

"Nothing." She turned away.

Daisy stood up. "I know what she was thinking," she murmured to Eva.

"What?"

"You're a smart girl—almost good enough for my son, if you came from a better family."

Eva was skeptical. "You can't know that."

"I sure can. And I'll marry him if only to prove his mother wrong."

"Oh, Daisy, why do you care so much what these people think?"

"Let's watch the tennis."

Daisy sat on the sand beside Charlie. He might not have been handsome, but he would worship his wife and do anything for her. The mother-in-law would be a problem, but Daisy thought she could handle her.

Tall Joanne Rouzrokh was serving, in a white skirt that flattered her long legs. Her partner, Woody Dewar, who was even taller, handed her a tennis ball. Something in the way he looked at Joanne made Daisy think he was attracted to her, maybe even in love with her. But he was fifteen and she eighteen, so there was no future in that.

She turned to Charlie. "Maybe I should see *Passion* after all," she said.

He did not take the hint. "Maybe you should," he said indifferently. The moment had passed.

Daisy turned to Eva. "I wonder where I could buy a Jack Russell terrier."

## ii

Lev Peshkov was the best father a guy could have—or, at least, he would have been, if he had been around more. He was rich and generous, he was smarter than anybody, he was even well dressed. He had probably been handsome when younger, and even now women threw themselves at him. Greg Peshkov adored him, and his only complaint was that he did not see enough of him.

"I should have sold this fucking foundry when I had the chance," Lev said as they walked around the silent, deserted factory. "It was losing money even before the goddamn strike. I should stick to cinemas and bars." He wagged a didactic finger. "People always buy booze, in good times and bad. And they go to the movies even when they can't afford to. Never forget that."

Greg was pretty sure his father did not often make mistakes in business. "So why did you keep it?" he said.

"Sentiment," Lev replied. "When I was your age, I worked in a place like this, the Putilov Machine Works in St. Petersburg." He looked around at the furnaces, molds, hoists, lathes, and workbenches. "Actually, it was a lot worse."

The Buffalo Metal Works made fans of all sizes, including huge propellers for ships. Greg was fascinated by the mathematics of the curved blades. He was top of his class in math. "Were you an engineer?" he asked.

Lev grinned. "I tell people that, if I need to impress them," he said. "But the truth is I looked after the horses. I was a stable boy. I was never good with machines. That was my brother Grigori's talent. You take after him. All the same, never buy a foundry."

"I won't."

Greg was to spend the summer shadowing his father, learning the business. Lev had just got back from Los Angeles, and Greg's lessons had begun today. But he did not want to know about the foundry. He was good at math but he was interested in power. He wished his father would take him on one of his frequent trips to Washington to lobby for the movie industry. That was where the real decisions were made.

He was looking forward to lunch. He and his father were to meet Senator Gus Dewar. Greg wanted to ask a favor of Senator Dewar. However, he had not yet cleared this with his father. He was nervous about asking, and instead he said: "Do you ever hear of your brother in Leningrad?"

Lev shook his head. "Not since the war. I wouldn't be surprised if he's dead. A lot of old Bolsheviks have disappeared."

"Speaking of family, I saw my half sister on Saturday. She was at the beach picnic."

"Did you have a good time?"

"She's mad at you—did you know that?"

"What have I done now?"

"You said you'd take her to the White House. Then you took Gladys Angelus."

"That's true. I forgot. But I wanted the publicity for *Passion*."

They were approached by a tall man whose striped suit was loud even by current fashions. He touched the brim of his fedora and said: "Morning, boss."

Lev said to Greg: "Joe Brekhunov is in charge of security here. Joe, this is my son Greg."

"Pleased to meet ya," said Brekhunov.

Greg shook his hand. Like most factories, the foundry had its own police force. But Brekhunov looked more like a hoodlum than a cop.

"All quiet?" Lev asked.

"A little incident in the night," Brekhunov said. "Two machinists tried to heist a length of fifteen-inch steel bar, aircraft quality. We caught them trying to manhandle it over the fence."

Greg said: "Did you call the police?"

"It wasn't necessary." Brekhunov grinned. "We gave them a little talk about the concept of private property, and sent them to the hospital to think about it."

Greg was not surprised to learn that his father's security men beat thieves so badly that they had to go to hospital. Although Lev had never struck him or his mother, Greg felt that violence was never far below his father's charming surface. It was because of Lev's youth in the slums of Leningrad, he guessed.

A portly man wearing a blue suit with a workingman's cap appeared from behind a furnace. "This is the union leader, Brian Hall," said Lev. "Morning, Hall."

"Morning, Peshkov."

Greg raised his eyebrows. People usually called his father Mr. Peshkov.

Lev stood with his feet apart and his hands on his hips. "Well, have you got an answer for me?"

Hall's face took on a stubborn expression. "The men won't come back to work with a pay cut, if that's what you mean."

"But I've improved my offer!"

"It's still a pay cut."

Greg began to feel nervous. His father did not like opposition, and he might explode.

"The manager tells me we aren't getting any orders, because he can't tender a competitive price at these wage levels."

"That's because you've got outdated machinery, Peshkov. Some of these lathes were here before the war! You need to reequip."

"In the middle of a depression? Are you out of your mind? I'm not going to throw away more money."

"That's how your men feel," said Hall, with the air of one who plays a trump card. "They're not going to give money to you when they haven't got enough for themselves."

Greg thought workers were stupid to strike during a depression, and he was angered by Hall's nerve. The man spoke as if he were Lev's equal, not an employee.

Lev said: "Well, as things are, we're all losing money. Where's the sense in that?"

"It's out of my hands now," said Hall. Greg thought he sounded smug. "The union is sending a team from headquarters to take over." He pulled a large steel watch out of his waistcoat pocket. "Their train should be here in an hour."

Lev's face darkened. "We don't need outsiders stirring up trouble."

"If you don't want trouble, you shouldn't provoke it."

Lev clenched a fist, but Hall walked away.

Lev turned to Brekhunov. "Did you know about these men from headquarters?" he said angrily.

Brekhunov looked nervous. "I'll get on it right away, boss."

"Find out who they are and where they're staying."

"Won't be difficult."

"Then send them back to New York in a fucking ambulance."

"Leave it to me, boss."

Lev turned away, and Greg followed him. Now, that was power, Greg thought with a touch of awe. His father gave the word, and union officials would be beaten up.

They walked outside and got into Lev's car, a Cadillac five-passenger sedan in the new streamlined style. Its long curving fenders made Greg think of a girl's hips.

Lev drove along Porter Avenue to the waterfront and parked at the Buffalo Yacht Club. Sunlight played prettily on the boats in the marina. Greg was pretty sure his father did not belong to this elite club. Gus Dewar must have been a member.

They walked onto the pier. The clubhouse was built on pilings over the water. Lev and Greg went inside and checked their hats. Greg immediately felt uneasy, knowing he was a guest in a club that would not have him as a member. The people here probably thought he must feel privileged to be allowed in. He put his hands in his pockets and slouched, so they would know he was not impressed.

"I used to belong to this club," Lev said. "But in 1921 the chairman told me I had to resign because I was a bootlegger. Then he asked me to sell him a case of Scotch."

"Why does Senator Dewar want to have lunch with you?" Greg asked.

"We're about to find out."

"Would you mind if I asked him a favor?"

Lev frowned. "I guess not. What are you after?"

But before Greg could answer, Lev greeted a man of about sixty. "This is Dave Rouzrokh," he said to Greg. "He's my main rival."

"You flatter me," the man said.

Roseroque Theatres was a chain of dilapidated movie houses in New York State. The owner was anything but decrepit. He had a patrician air: he was tall and white-haired, with a nose like a curved blade. He wore a blue cashmere blazer with the badge of the club on the breast pocket. Greg said: "I had the pleasure of watching your daughter, Joanne, play tennis on Saturday."

Dave was pleased. "Pretty good, isn't she?"

"Very."

Lev said: "I'm glad I ran into you, Dave—I was planning to call you."

"Why?"

"Your theaters need remodeling. They're very old-fashioned."

Dave looked amused. "You were planning to call me to give me this news?"

"Why don't you do something about it?"

He shrugged elegantly. "Why bother? I'm making enough money. At my age I don't want the strain."

"You could double your profits."

"By raising ticket prices. No, thanks."

"You're crazy."

"Not everyone is obsessed with money," Dave said with a touch of disdain.

"Then sell to me," Lev said.

Greg was surprised. He had not seen that coming.

"I'll give you a good price," Lev added.

Dave shook his head. "I like owning cinemas," he said. "They give people pleasure."

"Eight million dollars," Lev said.

Greg felt bemused. He thought: Did I just hear Father offer Dave eight million dollars?

"That is a fair price," Dave admitted. "But I'm not selling."

"No one else will give you as much," Lev said with exasperation.

"I know." Dave looked as if he had taken enough browbeating. He swallowed the rest of his drink. "Nice to see you both," he said, and he strolled out of the bar into the dining room.

Lev looked disgusted. "'Not everyone is obsessed with money,'" he quoted. "Dave's great-grandfather arrived here from Persia a hundred years ago with nothing but the clothes he wore and six rugs. He wouldn't have turned down eight million dollars."

"I didn't know you had that much money," Greg said.

"I don't, not in ready cash. That's what banks are for."

"So you'd take out a loan to pay Dave?"

Lev raised his forefinger again. "Never use your own money when you can spend someone else's."

Gus Dewar walked in, a tall figure with a large head. He was in his midforties, and his light brown hair was salted with silver. He greeted them with cool courtesy, shaking hands and offering them a drink. Greg saw immediately that Gus and Lev did not like one another. He feared that would mean Gus would not grant the favor Greg wanted to beg. Maybe he should give up the thought.

Gus was a big shot. His father had been a senator before him, a dynastic succession that Greg thought was un-American. Gus had helped Franklin Roosevelt become governor of New York and then president. Now he was on the powerful Senate Foreign Relations Committee.

His sons, Woody and Chuck, went to the same school as Greg. Woody was brainy; Chuck was a sportsman.

Lev said: "Has the president told you to settle my strike, Senator?"

Gus smiled. "No—not yet, anyway."

Lev turned to Greg. "Last time the foundry was on strike, twenty years ago, President Wilson sent Gus to strong-arm me into giving the men a raise."

"I saved you money," Gus said mildly. "They were asking for a dollar—I made them take half that."

"Which was exactly fifty cents more than I intended to give."

Gus smiled and shrugged. "Shall we have lunch?"

They went into the dining room. When they had ordered, Gus said: "The president was glad you could make it to the reception at the White House."

"I probably shouldn't have taken Gladys," Lev said. "Mrs. Roosevelt was a bit frosty with her. I guess she doesn't approve of movie stars."

She probably doesn't approve of movie stars who sleep with married men, Greg thought, but he kept his mouth shut.

Gus made small talk while they ate. Greg looked for an opportunity to ask his favor. He wanted to work in Washington one summer, to learn the ropes and make contacts. His father might have been able to get him an internship, but it would have been with a Republican, and they were out of power. Greg wanted to work in the office of the influential and respected Senator Dewar, personal friend and ally of the president.

He asked himself why he was nervous about asking. The worst that could happen was that Dewar would say no.

When the dessert was finished, Gus got down to business. "The president has asked me to speak to you about the Liberty League," he said.

Greg had heard of this organization, a right-wing group opposed to the New Deal.

Lev lit a cigarette and blew out smoke. "We have to guard against creeping socialism."

"The New Deal is all that is saving us from the kind of nightmare they're having in Germany."

"The Liberty League aren't Nazis."

"Aren't they? They have a plan for an armed insurrection to overthrow the president. It's not realistic, of course—not yet, anyway."

"I believe I have a right to my opinions."

"Then you're supporting the wrong people. The league is nothing to do with liberty, you know."

"Don't talk to me about liberty," Lev said with a touch of anger. "When I was twelve years old, I was flogged by the Leningrad police because my parents were on strike."

Greg was not sure why his father had said that. The brutality of the tsar's regime seemed like an argument for socialism, not against.

Gus said: "Roosevelt knows you give money to the league, and he wants you to stop."

"How does he know who I give money to?"

"The FBI told him. They investigate such people."

"We're living in a police state! You're supposed to be a liberal."

There was not much logic to Lev's arguments, Greg perceived. Lev was just trying everything he could think of to wrong-foot Gus, and he did not care if he contradicted himself in the process.

Gus remained cool. "I'm trying to make sure this doesn't become a matter for the police," he said.

Lev grinned. "Does the president know I stole your fiancée?"

This was news to Greg—but it had to be true, for Lev had at last succeeded in throwing Gus off balance. Gus looked shocked, turned his gaze aside, and reddened. Score one for our team, Greg thought.

Lev explained to Greg: "Gus was engaged to Olga, back in 1915," he said. "Then she changed her mind and married me."

Gus recovered his composure. "We were all terribly young."

Lev said: "You certainly got over Olga quickly enough."

Gus gave Lev a cool look and said: "So did you."

Greg saw that his father was embarrassed now. Gus's shot had hit home.

There was a moment of awkward silence; then Gus said: "You and I fought in a war, Lev. I was in a machine-gun battalion with my school friend Chuck Dixon. In a little French town called Château-Thierry he was blown to pieces in front of my eyes." Gus was speaking in a conversational tone, but Greg found himself holding his breath. Gus went on: "My ambition for my sons is that they should never have to go through what we went through. That's why groups such as the Liberty League have to be nipped in the bud."

Greg saw his chance. "I'm interested in politics, too, Senator, and I'd like to learn more. Might you be able to take me as an intern one summer?" He held his breath.

Gus looked surprised, but said: "I can always use a bright young man who's willing to work in a team."

That was neither a yes nor a no. "I'm top in math, and captain of ice hockey," Greg persisted, selling himself. "Ask Woody about me."

"I will." Gus turned to Lev. "And will you consider the president's request? It's really very important."

It almost seemed as if Gus was suggesting an exchange of favors. But would Lev agree?

Lev hesitated a long moment, then stubbed out his cigarette and said: "I guess we have a deal."

Gus stood up. "Good," he said. "The president will be pleased."

Greg thought: I did it!

They walked out of the club to their cars.

As they drove out of the parking lot, Greg said: "Thank you, Father. I really appreciate what you did."

"You chose your moment well," Lev said. "I'm glad to see you're so smart."

The compliment pleased Greg. In some ways he was smarter than his father—he certainly understood science and math better—but he feared he was not as shrewd and cunning as his old man.

"I want you to be a wise guy," Lev went on. "Not like some of these dummies." Greg had no idea who the dummies were. "You got to stay ahead of the curve, all the time. That's the way to get on."

Lev drove to his office, in a modern block downtown. As they walked through the marble lobby, Lev said: "Now I'm going to teach a lesson to that fool Dave Rouzrokh."

Going up in the elevator, Greg wondered how Lev would do that.

Peshkov Pictures occupied the top floor. Greg followed Lev along a broad corridor and through an outer office with two attractive young secretaries. "Get Sol Starr on the phone, will you?" Lev said as they walked into the inner office.

Lev sat behind the desk. "Solly owns one of the biggest studios in Hollywood," he explained.

The phone on the desk rang and Lev picked it up. "Sol!" he said.

"How are they hanging?" Greg listened to a minute or two of masculine joshing; then Lev got down to business. "Little piece of advice," he said. "Here in New York State we have a crappy chain of fleapits called Roseroque Theatres . . . Yeah, that's the one . . . Take my tip, don't send them your top-of-the-line first-run pictures this summer—you may not get paid." Greg realized that would hit Dave hard: without exciting new movies to show, his takings would tumble. "A word to the wise, right? Solly, don't thank me—you'd do the same for me . . . Bye."

Once again Greg was awestruck by his father's power. He could have people beaten up. He could offer eight million dollars of other people's money. He could scare a president. He could seduce another man's fiancée. And he could ruin a business with a single phone call.

"You wait and see," said his father. "In a month's time, Dave Rouzrokh will be begging me to buy him out—at half the price I offered him today."

## iii

"I don't know what's wrong with this puppy," Daisy said. "He won't do anything I tell him. I'm going crazy." There was a shake in her voice and a tear in her eye, and she was exaggerating only a little.

Charlie Farquharson studied the dog. "There's nothing wrong with him," he said. "He's a lovely little fellow. What's his name?"

"Jack."

"Hmm."

They were sitting on lawn chairs in the well-kept two-acre garden of Daisy's home. Eva had greeted Charlie, then tactfully retired to write a letter home. The gardener, Henry, was hoeing a bed of purple and yellow pansies in the distance. His wife, Ella, the maid, brought a pitcher of lemonade and some glasses, and set them on a folding table.

The puppy was a tiny Jack Russell terrier, small and strong, white with tan patches. He had an intelligent look, as if he understood every word, but he seemed to have no inclination to obey. Daisy held him on her lap and stroked his nose with dainty fingers in a way that she hoped Charlie would find strangely disturbing. "Don't you like the name?"

"A bit obvious, perhaps?" Charlie stared at her white hand on the dog's nose and shifted uneasily in his chair.

Daisy did not want to overdo it. If she inflamed Charlie too much, he would just go home. This was why he was still single at twenty-five: several Buffalo girls, including Dot Renshaw and Muffie Dixon, had found it impossible to nail his foot to the floor. But Daisy was different. "Then you shall name him," she said.

"It's good to have two syllables, as in Bonzo, to make it easier for him to recognize the name."

Daisy had no idea how to name dogs. "How about Rover?"

"Too common. Rusty might be better."

"Perfect!" she said. "Rusty he shall be."

The dog wriggled effortlessly out of her grasp and jumped to the ground.

Charlie picked him up. Daisy noticed he had big hands. "You must show Rusty you're the boss," Charlie said. "Hold him tight, and don't let him jump down until you say so." He put the dog back on her lap.

"But he's so strong! And I'm afraid of hurting him."

Charlie smiled condescendingly. "You probably couldn't hurt him if you tried. Hold his collar tightly—twist it a bit if you need to—then put your other hand firmly on his back."

Daisy followed Charlie's orders. The dog sensed the increased pressure in her touch and became still, as if waiting to see what would happen next.

"Tell him to sit. Then press down on his rear end."

"Sit," she said.

"Say it louder, and pronounce the letter *T* very clearly. Then press down hard."

"Sit, Rusty!" she said, and pushed him down. He sat.

"There you are," said Charlie.

"You're so clever!" Daisy gushed.

Charlie looked pleased. "It's just a matter of knowing what to do," he said modestly. "You must always be emphatic and decisive with dogs. You have to almost bark at them." He sat back, looking content. He was quite heavy, and filled the chair. Talking about the subject in which he was expert had relaxed him, as Daisy had hoped.

She had called him that morning. "I'm in despair!" she had said. "I have a new puppy and I can't manage him at all. Can you give me any advice?"

"What breed of puppy?"

"It's a Jack Russell."

"Why, that's the kind of dog I like best—I have three!"

"What a coincidence!"

As Daisy had hoped, Charlie volunteered to come over and help her train the dog.

Eva had said doubtfully: "Do you really think Charlie is right for you?"

"Are you kidding?" Daisy had replied. "He's one of the most eligible bachelors in Buffalo!"

Now she said: "I bet you'd be really good with children, too."

"Oh, I don't know about that."

"You love dogs, but you're firm with them. I'm sure that works with children, too."

"I have no idea." He changed the subject. "Are you intending to go to college in September?"

"I might go to Oakdale. It's a two-year finishing college for ladies. Unless . . ."

"Unless what?"

Unless I get married, she meant, but she said: "I don't know. Unless something else happens."

"Such as what?"

"I'd like to see England. My father went to London and met the Prince of Wales. What about you? Any plans?"

"It was always assumed I would take over Father's bank, but now there is no bank. Mother has a little money from her family, and I manage that, but otherwise I'm kind of a loose wheel."

"You should raise horses," Daisy said. "I know you'd be good at it." She was a good rider and had won prizes when younger. She pictured herself and Charlie in the park on matching grays, with two children on ponies following behind. The vision gave her a warm glow.

"I love horses," Charlie said.

"So do I! I want to breed racehorses." Daisy did not have to feign this enthusiasm. It was her dream to raise a string of champions. She saw racehorse owners as the ultimate international elite.

"Thoroughbreds cost a lot of money," Charlie said lugubriously.

Daisy had plenty. If Charlie married her, he would never have to worry about money again. She naturally did not say so, but she guessed Charlie was thinking it, and she let the thought hang unspoken in the air for as long as possible.

Eventually Charlie said: "Did your father really have those two union organizers beaten up?"

"What a strange idea!" Daisy did not know whether Lev Peshkov had done any such thing, but in truth it would not have surprised her.

"The men who came from New York to take over the strike," Charlie persisted. "They were hospitalized. The *Sentinel* says they quarreled with local union leaders, but everyone thinks your father was responsible."

"I never talk about politics," Daisy said gaily. "When did you get your first dog?"

Charlie began a long reminiscence. Daisy considered what to do next. I've got him here, she thought, and put him at ease; now I have to get him aroused. But stroking the dog suggestively had unnerved him. What they needed was some casual physical contact.

"What should I do next with Rusty?" she asked when Charlie had finished his story.

"Teach him to walk to heel," Charlie said promptly.

"How do you do that?"

"Do you have some dog biscuits?"

"Sure." The kitchen windows were open, and Daisy raised her voice so that the maid could hear her. "Ella, would you kindly bring me that box of Milk-Bones?"

Charlie broke up one of the biscuits, then took the dog on his lap. He held a piece of biscuit in his closed fist, letting Rusty sniff it, then opened his hand and allowed the dog to eat the morsel. He took another piece, making sure the dog knew he had it. Then he stood up and put the dog at his feet. Rusty kept an alert gaze on Charlie's closed fist. "Walk to heel!" Charlie said, and walked a few steps.

The dog followed him.

"Good boy!" Charlie said, and gave Rusty the biscuit.

"That's amazing!" Daisy said.

"After a while you won't need the biscuit—he'll do it for a pat. Then eventually he'll do it automatically."

"Charlie, you are a genius!"

Charlie looked pleased. He had nice brown eyes, just like the dog, she observed. "Now you try," he said to Daisy.

She copied what Charlie had done, and achieved the same result.

"See?" said Charlie. "It's not so hard."

Daisy laughed with delight. "We should go into business," she said. "Farquharson and Peshkov, dog trainers."

"What a nice idea," he said, and he seemed to mean it.

This is going very well, Daisy thought.

She went to the table and poured two glasses of lemonade.

Standing beside her, he said: "I'm usually a bit shy with girls."

No kidding, she thought, but she kept her mouth firmly closed.

"But you're so easy to talk to," he went on. He imagined that was a happy accident.

As she handed a glass to him, she fumbled, spilling lemonade on him. "Oh, how clumsy!" she cried.

"It's nothing," he said, but the drink had wetted his linen blazer and his white cotton trousers. He pulled out a handkerchief and began to mop it.

"Here, let me," said Daisy, and she took the handkerchief from his large hand.

She moved intimately close to pat his lapel. He went still, and she knew he could smell her Jean Naté perfume—lavender notes on top, musk underneath. She brushed the handkerchief caressingly over the front of his jacket, though there was no spill there. "Almost done," she said as if she regretted having to stop soon.

Then she went down on one knee as if worshipping him. She began to blot the wet patches on his pants with butterfly lightness. As she stroked his thigh, she put on a look of alluring innocence and glanced up. He was staring down at her, breathing hard through his open mouth, mesmerized.

## iv

Woody Dewar impatiently inspected the yacht *Sprinter,* checking that the kids had made everything shipshape. She was a forty-eight-foot racing ketch, long and slender like a knife. Dave Rouzrokh had loaned her to the Shipmates, a club Woody belonged to that took the sons of Buffalo's unemployed out on Lake Erie and taught them the rudiments of sailing. Woody was glad to see that the dock lines and fenders were set, the sails furled, the halyards tied off, and all the other lines neatly coiled.

His brother, Chuck, a year younger at fourteen, was on the dock already, joshing with a couple of colored kids. Chuck had an easygoing manner that enabled him to get on with everyone. Woody, who wanted to go into politics like their father, envied Chuck's effortless charm.

The boys wore nothing but shorts and sandals, and the three on the dock looked a picture of youthful strength and vitality. Woody would have liked to take a photograph, if he had had his camera with him. He was a keen photographer and had built a darkroom at home so that he could develop and print his own pictures.

Satisfied that the *Sprinter* was being left as they had found her that morning, Woody jumped onto the dock. A group of a dozen youngsters left the boatyard together, windswept and sunburned, aching pleasantly from their exertions, laughing as they relived the day's blunders and pratfalls and jokes.

The gap between the two rich brothers and the crowd of poor boys had vanished when they were out on the water, working together to control the yacht, but now it reappeared in the parking lot of the Buffalo Yacht Club. Two vehicles stood side by side: Senator Dewar's Chrysler Airflow, with a uniformed chauffeur at the wheel, for Woody and Chuck, and a Chevrolet Roadster pickup truck with two wooden benches in the back for the others. Woody felt embarrassed, saying good-bye as the chauffeur held the door for him, but the boys did not seem to care, thanking him and saying: "See you next Saturday!"

As they drove up Delaware Avenue, Woody said: "That was fun, though I'm not sure how much good it does."

Chuck was surprised. "Why?"

"Well, we're not helping their fathers find jobs, and that's the only thing that really counts."

"It might help the sons get work in a few years' time." Buffalo was a port city: in normal times there were thousands of jobs on merchant ships plying the Great Lakes and the Erie Canal, as well as on pleasure craft.

"Provided the president can get the economy moving again."

Chuck shrugged. "So go work for Roosevelt."

"Why not? Papa worked for Woodrow Wilson."

"I'll stick with the sailing."

Woody checked his wristwatch. "We've got time to change for the ball—just." They were going to a dinner-dance at the Racquet Club. Anticipation made his heart beat faster. "I want to be with humans that have soft skin, speak with high voices, and wear pink dresses."

"Huh," Chuck said derisively. "Joanne Rouzrokh never wore pink in her life."

Woody was taken aback. He had been dreaming about Joanne all day and half the night for a couple of weeks, but how did his brother know that? "What makes you think—"

"Oh, come on," Chuck said scornfully. "When she arrived at the beach party in a tennis skirt, you practically fainted. Everyone could see you were crazy about her. Fortunately *she* didn't seem to notice."

"Why was that fortunate?"

"For God's sake—you're fifteen, and she's eighteen. It's embarrassing! She's looking for a husband, not a schoolboy."

"Oh, gee, thanks. I forgot what an expert you are on women."

Chuck flushed. He had never had a girlfriend. "You don't have to be an expert to see what's under your goddamn nose."

They talked like this all the time. There was no malice in it: they were just brutally frank with each other. They were brothers, so there was no need to be nice.

They reached home, a mock-Gothic mansion built by their late grandfather, Senator Cam Dewar. They ran inside to shower and change.

Woody was now the same height as his father, and he put on one of Papa's old dress suits. It was a bit worn, but that was all right. The younger boys would be wearing school suits or blazers, but the college men would have tuxedos, and Woody was keen to look older. Tonight he would dance with her, he thought as he slicked his hair with brilliantine. He would be allowed to hold her in his arms. The palms of his hands would feel the warmth of her skin. He would look into her eyes as she smiled. Her breasts would brush against his jacket as they danced.

When he came down, his parents were waiting in the drawing room, Papa drinking a cocktail, Mama smoking a cigarette. Papa was long and thin, and looked like a coat hanger in his double-breasted tuxedo. Mama was beautiful, despite having only one eye, the other being permanently closed—she had been born that way. Tonight she looked stunning in a floor-length dress, black lace over red silk, and a short black velvet evening jacket.

Woody's grandmother was the last to arrive. At sixty-eight she was poised and elegant, as thin as her son but petite. She studied Mama's dress and said: "Rosa, dear, you look wonderful." She was always kind to her daughter-in-law. To everyone else she was waspish.

Gus made her a cocktail without being asked. Woody hid his impatience while she took her time drinking it. Grandmama could never be hurried. She assumed no social event would begin before she arrived: she was the grand old lady of Buffalo society, widow of a senator and mother of another, matriarch of one of the city's oldest and most distinguished families.

Woody asked himself when he had fallen for Joanne. He had known her most of his life, but he had always regarded girls as uninteresting spectators to the exciting adventures of boys—until two or three years ago, when girls had suddenly become even more fascinating than cars and speedboats. Even then he had been more interested in girls his own age or a little younger. Joanne for her part had always treated him as a kid—a bright kid, worth talking to now and again, but certainly not a possible boyfriend. But this summer, for no reason he could put a finger on, he had suddenly begun to see her as the most alluring girl in the world. Sadly, her feelings for him had not undergone a similar transformation.

Not yet.

Grandmama addressed a question to his brother. "How is school, Chuck?"

"Terrible, Grandmama, as you know perfectly well. I'm the family cretin, a throwback to our chimpanzee forbears."

"Cretins don't use phrases such as 'our chimpanzee forbears,' in my experience. Are you quite sure laziness plays no part?"

Rosa butted in. "Chuck's teachers say he works pretty hard at school, Mama."

Gus added: "And he beats me at chess."

"Then I ask what the problem is," Grandmama persisted. "If this goes on, he won't get into Harvard."

Chuck said: "I'm a slow reader, that's all."

"Curious," she said. "My father-in-law, your paternal great-grandfather, was the most successful banker of his generation, yet he could barely read or write."

Chuck said: "I didn't know that."

"It's true," she said. "But don't use it as an excuse. Work harder."

Gus looked at his watch. "If you're ready, Mama, we'd better go."

At last they got into the car and drove to the club. Papa had taken a table for the dinner and invited the Renshaws and their offspring, Dot and George. Woody looked around, but to his disappointment, he did not see Joanne. He checked the table plan, on an easel in the lobby, and was dismayed to see that there was no Rouzrokh table. Were they not coming? That would ruin his evening.

The talk over the lobster and steak was of events in Germany. Philip Renshaw thought Hitler was doing a good job. Woody's father said: "According to today's *Sentinel*, they jailed a Catholic priest for criticizing the Nazis."

"Are you Catholic?" said Mr. Renshaw in surprise.

"No, Episcopalian."

"It's not about religion, Philip," said Rosa crisply. "It's about freedom." Woody's mother had been an anarchist in her youth, and she was still a libertarian at heart.

Some people skipped the dinner and came later for the dancing, and more revelers appeared as the Dewars were served dessert. Woody kept his eyes peeled for Joanne. In the next room a band started to play "The Continental," a hit from last year.

He could not say what it was about Joanne that had so captivated him. Most people would not call her a great beauty, though she was certainly striking. She looked like an Aztec queen, with high cheekbones and the same knife-blade nose as her father, Dave. Her hair was dark and thick and her skin an olive shade, no doubt because of her Persian ancestry. There was a brooding intensity about her that made Woody long to know her better, to make her relax and hear her murmur softly about nothing in particular. He felt that her formidable presence must signify a capacity for deep passion. Then he thought: Now who's pretending to be an expert on women?

"Are you looking out for someone, Woody?" said Grandmama, who did not miss much.

Chuck sniggered knowingly.

"Just wondering who's coming to the dance," Woody replied casually, but he could not help blushing.

He still had not spotted her when his mother stood up and they all left the table. Disconsolate, he wandered into the ballroom to the strains of Benny Goodman's "Moonglow"—and there Joanne was: she must have come in when he was not looking. His spirits lifted.

Tonight she wore a dramatically simple silver-gray silk dress with a deep V-neck that showed off her figure. She had looked sensational in a tennis skirt that revealed her long brown legs, but this was even more arousing. As she glided across the room, graceful and confident, she made Woody's throat go dry.

He moved toward her, but the ballroom had filled up, and suddenly he was irritatingly popular: everyone wanted to talk to him. During his progress through the crowd he was surprised to see dull old Charlie Farquharson dancing with the vivacious Daisy Peshkov. He could not recall seeing Charlie dance with anyone, let alone a tootsie like Daisy. What had she done to bring him out of his shell?

By the time he reached Joanne, she was at the end of the room farthest from the band, and to his chagrin she was deep in discussion with a group of boys four or five years older than he. Fortunately he was taller than most of them, so the difference was not too obvious. They were all holding Coke glasses, but Woody could smell Scotch: one of them must have had a bottle in his pocket.

As he joined them, he heard Victor Dixon say: "No one's in favor of lynching, but you have to understand the problems they have in the South."

Woody knew that Senator Wagner had proposed a law to punish sheriffs who permitted lynchings—but President Roosevelt had refused to back the bill.

Joanne was outraged. "How can you say that, Victor? Lynching is murder! We don't have to understand their problems. We have to stop them killing people!"

Woody was pleased to learn how much Joanne shared his political values. But clearly this was not a good time to ask her to dance, which was unfortunate.

"You don't get it, Joanne, honey," said Victor. "Those Southern Negroes are not really civilized."

I might be young and inexperienced, Woody thought, but I wouldn't have made the mistake of speaking so condescendingly to Joanne.

"It's the people who carry out lynchings who are uncivilized!" she said.

Woody decided this was the moment to make his contribution to the argument. "Joanne is right," he said. He made his voice lower in pitch, to sound older. "There was a lynching in the hometown of our help, Joe and Betty, who have looked after me and my brother since we were babies. Betty's cousin was stripped naked and burned with a blowtorch, while a crowd watched. Then he was hanged." Victor glared at him, resentful of this kid who was taking Joanne's attention away, but the others in the group listened with horrified interest. "I don't care what his crime was," Woody said. "The white people who did that to him are savages."

Victor said: "Your beloved President Roosevelt didn't support the anti-lynch bill, though, did he?"

"No, and that was very disappointing," said Woody. "I know why he made that decision: he was afraid that angry Southern congressmen would retaliate by sabotaging the New Deal. All the same, I would have liked him to tell them to go to hell."

Victor said: "What do you know? You're just a kid." He took a silver flask from his jacket pocket and topped up his drink.

Joanne said: "Woody's political ideas are more grown-up than yours, Victor."

Woody glowed. "Politics is kind of the family business," he said. Then he was irritated by a tug at his elbow. Too polite to ignore it, he turned to see Charlie Farquharson, perspiring from his exertions on the dance floor.

"Can I talk to you for a minute?" said Charlie.

Woody resisted the temptation to tell him to buzz off. Charlie was a likable guy who did no harm to anyone. You had to feel sorry for a man with a mother like that. "What is it, Charlie?" he said with as much good grace as he could muster.

"It's about Daisy."

"I saw you dancing with her."

"Isn't she a great dancer?"

Woody had not noticed but, to be nice, he said: "You bet she is!"

"She's great at everything."

"Charlie," said Woody, trying to suppress a tone of incredulity, "are you and Daisy courting?"

Charlie looked bashful. "We've been horse riding in the park a couple of times, and so on."

"So you *are* courting." Woody was surprised. They seemed an unlikely pair. Charlie was such a lump, and Daisy was a poppet.

Charlie added: "She's not like other girls. She's so easy to talk to! And she loves dogs and horses. But people think her father is a gangster."

"I guess he is a gangster, Charlie. Everyone bought their liquor from him during Prohibition."

"That's what my mother says."

"So your mother doesn't like Daisy." Woody was not surprised.

"She likes Daisy fine. It's Daisy's family she objects to."

An even more surprising thought occurred to Woody. "Are you thinking of *marrying* Daisy?"

"Oh, God, yes," said Charlie. "And I think she might say yes, if I asked her."

Well, Woody thought, Charlie had class but no money, and Daisy was the opposite, so maybe they would complement one another. "Stranger things have happened," he said. This was kind of fascinating, but he wanted to concentrate on his own romantic life. He looked around, checking that Joanne was still there. "Why are you telling me this?" he asked Charlie. It was not as if they were great friends.

"My mother might change her mind if Mrs. Peshkov were invited to join the Buffalo Ladies' Society."

Woody had not been expecting that. "Why, it's the snobbiest club in town!"

"Exactly. If Olga Peshkov were a member, how could Mom object to Daisy?"

Woody did not know whether this scheme would work or not, but there was no doubting the earnest warmth of Charlie's feelings. "Maybe you're right," Woody said.

"Would you approach your grandmother for me?"

"Whoa! Wait a minute. Grandmama Dewar is a dragon. I wouldn't ask her for a favor for myself, let alone for you."

"Woody, listen to me. You know she's really the boss of that little clique. If she wants someone, they're in—and if she doesn't, they're out."

That was true. The society had a chairwoman and a secretary and a treasurer, but Ursula Dewar ran the club as if it belonged to her. All the same, Woody was reluctant to petition her. She might bite his head off. "I don't know," he said apologetically.

"Oh, come on, Woody, please. You don't understand." Charlie lowered his voice. "You don't know what it's like to love someone this much."

Yes, I do, Woody thought, and that changed his mind. If Charlie feels as bad as I do, how can I refuse him? I hope someone else would do the same for me, if it meant I had a better chance with Joanne. "Okay, Charlie," he said. "I'll talk to her."

"Thanks! Say—she's here, isn't she? Could you do it tonight?"

"Hell, no. I've got other things on my mind."

"Okay, sure . . . but when?"

Woody shrugged. "I'll do it tomorrow."

"You're a pal!"

"Don't thank me yet. She'll probably say no."

Woody turned back to speak to Joanne, but she had gone.

He began to look for her, then stopped himself. He must not appear desperate. A needy man was not sexy; he knew that much.

He danced dutifully with several girls: Dot Renshaw, Daisy Peshkov, and Daisy's German friend Eva. He got a Coke and went outside to where some of the boys were smoking cigarettes. George Renshaw poured some Scotch into Woody's Coke, which improved the taste, but he did not want to get drunk. He had done it before and he did not like it.

Joanne would want a man who shared her intellectual interests,

Woody believed—and that would rule out Victor Dixon. Woody had heard Joanne mention Karl Marx and Sigmund Freud. In the public library he had read *The Communist Manifesto,* but it just seemed like a political rant. He had had more fun with Freud's *Studies in Hysteria,* which made a kind of detective story out of mental illness. He was looking forward to letting Joanne know, in a casual way, that he had read these books.

He was determined to dance with Joanne at least once tonight, and after a while he went in search of her. She was not in the ballroom or the bar. Had he missed his chance? In trying not to show his desperation, had he been too passive? It was unbearable to think that the ball could end without his even having touched her shoulder.

He stepped outside again. It was dark, but he saw her almost immediately. She was walking away from Greg Peshkov, looking a little flushed, as if she had been arguing with him. "You might be the only person here who isn't a goddamn conservative," she said to Woody. She sounded a little drunk.

Woody smiled. "Thanks for the compliment—I think."

"Do you know about the march tomorrow?" she asked abruptly.

He did. Strikers from the Buffalo Metal Works planned a demonstration to protest against the beating up of union men from New York. Woody guessed that was the subject of her argument with Greg: his father owned the factory. "I was planning to go," he said. "I might take some photographs."

"Bless you," she said, and she kissed him.

He was so surprised that he almost failed to respond. For a second he stood there passively as she crushed her mouth to his, and he tasted whisky on her lips.

Then he recovered his composure. He put his arms around her and pressed her body to his, feeling her breasts and her thighs press delightfully against him. Part of him feared she would be offended, push him away, and angrily accuse him of treating her disrespectfully, but a deeper instinct told him he was on safe ground.

He had little experience of kissing girls—and none of kissing mature

women of eighteen—but he liked the feel of her soft mouth so much
that he moved his lips against hers in little nibbling motions that gave
him exquisite pleasure, and he was rewarded by hearing her moan
quietly.

He was vaguely aware that if one of the older generation should walk
by there might be an embarrassing scene, but he was too aroused to
care.

Joanne's mouth opened and he felt her tongue. This was new to him:
the few girls he had kissed had not done that. But he figured she must
know what she was doing, and anyway he really liked it. He imitated the
motions of her tongue with his own. It was shockingly intimate and
highly exciting. It must have been the right thing to do, because she
moaned again.

Summoning his nerve, he put his right hand on her left breast. It was
wonderfully soft and heavy under the silk of her dress. As he caressed
it, he felt a small protuberance and thought, with a thrill of discovery,
that it must be her nipple. He rubbed it with his thumb.

She pulled away from him abruptly. "Good God," she said. "What
am I doing?"

"You're kissing me," Woody said happily. He rested his hands on her
round hips. He could feel the heat of her skin through the silk dress.
"Let's do it some more."

She pushed his hands away. "I must be out of my mind. This is the
Racquet Club, for Christ's sake."

Woody could see that the spell had been broken, and sadly there
would be no more kissing tonight. He looked around. "Don't worry," he
said. "No one saw." He felt enjoyably conspiratorial.

"I'd better go home, before I do something even more stupid."

He tried not to be offended. "May I escort you to your car?"

"Are you crazy? If we walk in there together, everyone will guess
what we've been doing—especially with that dumb grin all over your
face."

Woody tried to stop grinning. "Then why don't you go inside and I'll
wait out here for a minute?"

"Good idea." She walked away.

"See you tomorrow," he called after her.

She did not look back.

## V

Ursula Dewar had her own small suite of rooms in the old Victorian mansion on Delaware Avenue. There was a bedroom, a bathroom, and a dressing room, and after her husband died, she had converted his dressing room into a little parlor. Most of the time she had the whole house to herself: Gus and Rosa spent a lot of time in Washington, and Woody and Chuck went to a boarding school. But when they came home, she spent a good deal of the day in her own quarters.

Woody went to talk to her on Sunday morning. He was still walking on air after Joanne's kiss, though he had spent half the night trying to figure out what it meant. It could signify anything from true love to true drunkenness. All he knew was that he could hardly wait to see Joanne again.

He walked into his grandmother's room behind the maid, Betty, as she took in the breakfast tray. He liked it that Joanne got angry about the way Betty's Southern relations were treated. In politics, dispassionate argument was overrated, he felt. People *should* get angry about cruelty and injustice.

Grandmama was already sitting up in bed, wearing a lace shawl over a mushroom-colored silk nightgown. "Good morning, Woodrow!" she said, surprised.

"I'd like to have a cup of coffee with you, Grandmama, if I may." He had already asked Betty to bring two cups.

"This is an honor," Ursula said.

Betty was a gray-haired woman of about fifty with the kind of figure that was sometimes called comfortable. She set the tray in front of Ursula, and Woody poured coffee into Meissen cups.

He had given some thought to what he would say, and had marshaled his arguments. Prohibition was over, and Lev Peshkov was now a legitimate businessman, he would contend. Furthermore, it was not fair to punish Daisy because her father had been a criminal—especially since most of the respectable families in Buffalo had bought his illegal booze.

"Do you know Charlie Farquharson?" he began.

"Yes."

Of course she did. She knew every family in *The Buffalo Blue Book*.

She said: "Would you like a piece of this toast?"

"No, thank you, I've had breakfast."

"Boys of your age never have enough to eat." She looked at him shrewdly. "Unless they're in love."

She was in good form this morning.

Woody said: "Charlie is kind of under the thumb of his mother."

"She kept her husband there, too," Ursula said drily. "Dying was the only way he could get free." She drank some coffee and started to eat her grapefruit with a fork.

"Charlie came to me last night and asked me to ask you a favor."

She raised an eyebrow, but said nothing.

Woody took a breath. "He wants you to invite Mrs. Peshkov to join the Buffalo Ladies' Society."

Ursula dropped her fork, and there was a chime of silver on fine porcelain. As if covering her discomposure, she said: "Pour me some more coffee, please, Woody."

He did her bidding, saying nothing for the moment. He could not recall ever seeing her discombobulated.

She sipped the coffee and said: "Why in the name of heaven would Charles Farquharson, or anyone else for that matter, want Olga Peshkov in the society?"

"He wants to marry Daisy."

"Does he?"

"And he's afraid his mother will object."

"He's got that part right."

"But he thinks he might be able to talk her around . . ."

"If I let Olga into the society."

"Then people might forget that her father was a gangster."

"A gangster?"

"Well, a bootlegger at least."

"Oh, that," Ursula said dismissively. "That's not it."

"Really?" It was Woody's turn to be surprised. "What is it, then?"

Ursula looked thoughtful. She was silent for such a long time that Woody wondered if she had forgotten he was there. Then she said: "Your father was in love with Olga Peshkov."

"Jesus!"

"Don't be vulgar."

"Sorry, Grandmama. You surprised me."

"They were engaged to be married."

"Engaged?" he said, astonished. He thought for a minute, then said: "I suppose I'm the only person in Buffalo who doesn't know about this."

She smiled at him. "There is a special mixture of wisdom and innocence that comes only to adolescents. I remember it so clearly in your father, and I see it in you. Yes, everyone in Buffalo knows, though your generation undoubtedly regard it as boring ancient history."

"Well, what happened?" Woody said. "I mean, who broke it off?"

"She did, when she got pregnant."

Woody's mouth fell open. "By Papa?"

"No, by her chauffeur—Lev Peshkov."

"He was the chauffeur?" This was one shock after another. Woody was silent, trying to take it in. "My goodness, Papa must have felt such a fool."

"Your Papa was never a fool," Ursula said sharply. "The only foolish thing he did in his life was propose to Olga."

Woody remembered his mission. "All the same, Grandmama, it was an awful long time ago."

"*Awfully.* You require an adverb, not an adjective. But your judgment is better than your grammar. It *is* a long time."

That sounded hopeful. "So you'll do it?"

"How do you think your father would feel?"

Woody considered. He could not bullshit Ursula—she would see through it in a heartbeat. "Would he care? I guess he might be embarrassed, if Olga were around as a constant reminder of a humiliating episode in his youth."

"You guess right."

"On the other hand, he's very committed to the ideal of behaving fairly to the people around him. He hates injustice. He wouldn't want to punish Daisy for something her mother did. Even less to punish Charlie. Papa has a pretty big heart."

"Bigger than mine, you mean," said Ursula.

"I didn't mean that, Grandmama. But I bet if you asked him, he wouldn't object to Olga joining the society."

Ursula nodded. "I agree. But I wonder whether you've worked out who is the real originator of this request."

Woody saw what she was driving at. "Oh, you're saying Daisy put Charlie up to it? I wouldn't be surprised. Does it make any difference to the rights and wrongs of the situation?"

"I guess not."

"So, will you do it?"

"I'm glad to have a grandson with a kind heart—even if I do suspect he's being used by a clever and ambitious girl."

Woody smiled. "Is that a yes, Grandmama?"

"You know I can't guarantee anything. I'll suggest it to the committee."

Ursula's suggestions were regarded by everyone else as royal commands, but Woody did not say so. "Thank you. You're very kind."

"Now give me a kiss and get ready for church."

Woody made his escape.

He quickly forgot about Charlie and Daisy. Sitting in the Cathedral of St. Paul in Shelton Square, he ignored the sermon—about Noah and the Flood—and thought about Joanne Rouzrokh. Her parents were in church, but she was not. Would she really show up at the demonstration? If she did, he was going to ask her for a date. But would she accept?

She was too smart to care about the age difference, he reckoned. She must have known she had more in common with Woody than with boneheads such as Victor Dixon. And that kiss! He was still tingling from it. What she had done with her tongue—did other girls do that? He wanted to try it again, as soon as he could.

Thinking ahead, if she did agree to date him, what would happen in September? She was going to Vassar College, in the town of Poughkeepsie; he knew that. He would return to school and not see her until Christmas. Vassar was for girls only but there must be men in Poughkeepsie. Would she date other guys? He was jealous already.

Outside the church he told his parents he was not coming home for lunch, but was going on the protest march.

"Good for you," his mother said. When young she had been the editor of the *Buffalo Anarchist*. She turned to her husband. "You should go, too, Gus."

"The union has brought charges," Papa said. "You know I can't prejudge the result of a court case."

She turned back to Woody. "Just don't get beaten up by Lev Peshkov's goons."

Woody got his camera out of the trunk of his father's car. It was a Leica III, so small he could carry it on a strap around his neck, yet it had shutter speeds as fast as one-five-hundredth of a second.

He walked a few blocks to Niagara Square, where the march was to begin. Lev Peshkov had tried to persuade the city to ban the demonstration on the grounds that it would lead to violence, but the union had insisted it would be peaceful. The union seemed to have won that argument, for several hundred people were milling around outside city hall. Many carried lovingly embroidered banners, red flags, and placards reading SAY NO TO BOSS THUGS. Woody looked around for Joanne but did not see her.

The weather was fine and the mood was sunny, and he took a few shots: workmen in their Sunday suits and hats; a car festooned with banners; a young cop biting his nails. There was still no sign of Joanne, and he began to think she would not appear. She might have a headache this morning, he guessed.

The march was due to move off at noon. It finally got going a few minutes before one. There was a heavy police presence along the route, Woody noted. He found himself near the middle of the procession.

As they walked south on Washington Street, heading for the city's industrial heartland, he saw Joanne join the march a few yards ahead, and his heart leaped. She was wearing tailored pants that flattered her figure. He hurried to catch up with her. "Good afternoon!" he said happily.

"Good grief, you're cheerful," she said.

It was an understatement. He was delirious with happiness. "Are you hungover?"

"Either that or I've contracted the Black Death. Which do you think it is?"

"If you have a rash, it's the Black Death. Are there any spots?" Woody hardly knew what he was saying. "I'm not a doctor, but I'd be happy to check you over."

"Stop being irrepressible. I know it's charming, but I'm not in the mood."

Woody tried to calm down. "We missed you in church," he said. "The sermon was about Noah."

To his consternation she burst out laughing. "Oh, Woody," she said. "I like you so much when you're funny, but please don't make me laugh today."

He thought this remark was probably favorable, but he was far from certain.

He spotted an open grocery store on a side street. "You need fluids," he said. "I'll be right back." He ran into the store and bought two bottles of Coke, ice-cold from the refrigerator. He got the clerk to open them, then returned to the march. When he handed a bottle to Joanne, she said: "Oh, boy, you're a lifesaver." She put the bottle to her lips and drank a long draft.

Woody felt he was ahead, so far.

The march was good-humored, despite the grim incident they were protesting about. A group of older men were singing political anthems and traditional songs. There were even a few families with children. And there was not a cloud in the sky.

"Have you read *Studies in Hysteria*?" Woody asked as they walked along.

"Never heard of it."

"Oh! It's by Sigmund Freud. I thought you were a fan of his."

"I'm interested in his ideas. I've never read one of his books."

"You should. *Studies in Hysteria* is amazing."

She looked curiously at him. "What made you read a book such as that? I bet they don't teach psychology at your expensively old-fashioned school."

"Oh, I don't know. I guess I heard you talking about psychoanalysis and thought it sounded really extraordinary. And it is."

"In what way?"

Woody had the feeling she was testing him, to see whether he had really understood the book or was merely pretending. "The idea that a crazy act, such as obsessively spilling ink on a tablecloth, can have a kind of hidden logic."

She nodded. "Yeah," she said. "That's it."

Woody knew instinctively that she did not understand what he was talking about. He had already overtaken her in his knowledge of Freud, but she was embarrassed to admit it.

"What's your favorite thing to do?" he asked her. "Theater? Classical music? I guess going to a film is no big treat to someone whose father owns about a hundred movie houses."

"Why do you ask?"

"Well . . ." He decided to be honest. "I want to ask you out, and I'd like to tempt you with something you really love to do. So name it, and we'll do it."

She smiled at him, but it was not the smile he was hoping for. It was friendly but sympathetic, and it told him that bad news was coming. "Woody, I'd like to, but you're fifteen."

"As you said last night, I'm more mature than Victor Dixon."

"I wouldn't go out with him, either."

Woody's throat seemed to constrict, and his voice came out hoarse. "Are you turning me down?"

"Yes, very firmly. I don't want to date a boy three years younger."

"Can I ask you again in three years? We'll be the same age then."

She laughed, then said: "Stop being witty. It hurts my head."

Woody decided not to hide his pain. What did he have to lose? Feeling anguished, he said: "So what was that kiss about?"

"It was nothing."

He shook his head miserably. "It was something to me. It was the best kiss I've ever had."

"Oh, God, I knew it was a mistake. Look, it was just a bit of fun. Yes, I enjoyed it—be flattered, you're entitled. You're a cute kid, and smart as a whip, but a kiss is not a declaration of love, Woody, no matter how much you enjoy it."

They were near the front of the march, and Woody saw their destination up ahead: the high wall around the Buffalo Metal Works. The gate was closed and guarded by a dozen or more factory police, thuggish men in light blue shirts that mimicked police uniforms.

"And I was drunk," Joanne added.

"Yeah, I was drunk, too," Woody said.

It was a pathetic attempt to salvage his dignity, but Joanne had the grace to pretend to believe him. "Then we both did something a little foolish, and we should just forget it," she said.

"Yeah," said Woody, looking away.

They were outside the factory now. Those at the head of the march stopped at the gates, and someone began to make a speech through a bullhorn. Looking more closely, Woody saw that the speaker was a local union organizer, Brian Hall. Woody's father knew and liked the man: at some time in the dim past they had worked together to resolve a strike.

The rear of the procession kept coming forward, and a crush developed across the width of the street. The factory police were keeping the entrance clear, though the gates were shut. Woody now saw that they were armed with police-type nightsticks. One of them was shouting: "Stay away from the gate! This is private property!" Woody lifted his camera and took a picture.

But the people at the front were being pushed forward by those behind. Woody took Joanne's arm and tried to steer her away from the focus of tension. However, it was difficult: the crowd was dense now, and no one wanted to move out of the way. Against his will, Woody found himself edging closer to the factory gate and the guards with nightsticks. "This is not a good situation," he said to Joanne.

But she was flushed with excitement. "Those bastards can't keep us back!" she cried.

A man next to her shouted: "Right! Damn right!"

The crowd was still ten yards or more from the gate, but just the same the guards unnecessarily began to push demonstrators away. Woody took a photograph.

Brian Hall had been yelling into his bullhorn about boss thugs and pointing an accusing finger at the factory police. Now he changed his tune and began to call for calm. "Move away from the gates, please, brothers," he said. "Move back, no rough stuff."

Woody saw a woman pushed by a guard hard enough to make her stumble. She did not fall over, but she cried out, and the man with her said to the guard: "Hey, buddy, take it easy, will you?"

"Are you trying to start something?" the guard said challengingly.

The woman yelled: "Just stop shoving!"

"Move back, move back!" the guard shouted. He raised his nightstick. The woman screamed.

As the nightstick came down, Woody took a picture.

Joanne said: "The son of a bitch hit that woman!" She stepped forward.

But most of the crowd began to move in the opposite direction, away from the factory. As they turned, the guards came after them, shoving, kicking, and lashing out with their truncheons.

Brian Hall said: "There is no need for violence! Factory police, step back! Do not use your clubs!" Then his bullhorn was knocked out of his hands by a guard.

Some of the younger men fought back. Half a dozen real policemen moved into the crowd. They did nothing to restrain the factory police, but began to arrest anyone fighting back.

The guard who had started the fracas fell to the ground, and two demonstrators started kicking him.

Woody took a picture.

Joanne was screaming with fury. She threw herself at a guard and scratched his face. He put out a hand to shove her away. Accidentally or otherwise, the heel of his hand connected sharply with her nose. She fell back with blood coming from her nostrils. The guard raised his nightstick. Woody grabbed her by the waist and jerked her back. The stick missed her. "Come on!" Woody yelled at her. "We have to get out of here!"

The blow to her face had deflated her fury, and she offered no resistance as he half-pulled, half-carried her away from the gates as fast as he could, his camera swinging on the strap around his neck. The crowd was panicking now, people falling over and others trampling them as everyone tried to flee.

Woody was taller than most and he managed to keep himself and Joanne upright. They fought their way through the crush, staying just ahead of the nightsticks. At last the crowd thinned out. Joanne detached herself from his grasp and they both began to run.

The noise of the fight receded behind them. They turned a couple of corners and, a minute later, found themselves on a deserted street of factories and warehouses, all closed on Sunday. They slowed to a walk, catching their breath. Joanne began to laugh. "That was so exciting!" she said.

Woody could not share her enthusiasm. "It was nasty," he said. "And it could have gotten worse." He had rescued her, and he half hoped that might cause her to change her mind about dating him.

But she did not feel she owed him much. "Oh, come on," she said in a tone of disparagement. "Nobody died."

"Those guards deliberately provoked a riot!"

"Of course they did! Peshkov wants to make union members look bad."

"Well, we know the truth." Woody tapped his camera. "And I can prove it."

They walked half a mile; then Woody saw a cruising cab and hailed it. He gave the driver the address of the Rouzrokh family home.

Sitting in the back of the taxi, he took a handkerchief from his pocket. "I don't want to bring you home to your father looking like this," he said. He unfolded the white cotton square and gently dabbed at the blood on her upper lip.

It was an intimate act, and he found it sexy, but she did not indulge him for long. After a second she said: "I've got it." She took the handkerchief from his grasp and cleaned herself up. "How's that?"

"You've missed a bit," he lied. He took the handkerchief back. Her mouth was wide, she had even white teeth, and her lips were enchantingly full. He pretended there was something under her lower lip. He wiped it gently, then said: "Better."

"Thanks." She looked at him with an odd expression, half fond, half annoyed. She knew he had been lying about the blood on her chin, he guessed, and she was not sure whether to be cross with him or not.

The cab halted outside her house. "Don't come in," she said. "I'm going to lie to my parents about where I've been, and I don't want you blabbing the truth."

Woody reckoned he was probably the more discreet of the two of them, but he did not say so. "I'll call you later."

"Okay." She got out of the taxi and walked up the driveway with a perfunctory wave.

"She's a doll," said the driver. "Too old for you, though."

"Take me to Delaware Avenue," Woody said. He gave the number and the cross street. He was not going to talk about Joanne to a goddamn cabby.

He pondered his rejection. He should not have been surprised: everyone from his brother to the taxi driver said he was too young for her. All the same it hurt. He felt as if he did not know what to do with his life now. How would he get through the rest of the day?

Back at home, his parents were taking their ritual Sunday afternoon nap. Chuck believed that was when they had sex. Chuck himself had gone swimming with a bunch of friends, according to Betty.

Woody went into the darkroom and developed the film from his camera. He ran warm water into the basin to bring the chemicals to the ideal temperature, then put the film into a black bag to transfer it into a light-trap tank.

It was a lengthy process that required patience, but he was happy to sit in the dark and think about Joanne. Their being together during a riot had not made her fall in love with him, but it had certainly brought them closer. He felt sure she was at least growing to like him more and more. Maybe her rejection was not final. Perhaps he should keep trying. He certainly had no interest in any other girls.

When his timer rang, he transferred the film into a stop bath to halt the chemical reaction, then to a bath of fixer to make the image permanent. Finally he washed and dried his film and looked at the negative black-and-white images on the reel.

He thought they were pretty good.

He cut the film into frames, then put the first into the enlarger. He laid a sheet of ten-by-eight photographic paper on the base of the enlarger, turned on the light, and exposed the paper to the negative image while he counted seconds. Then he put the paper into an open bath of developer.

This was the best part of the process. Slowly the white paper began to show patches of gray, and the image he had photographed began to appear. It always seemed to him like a miracle. The first print showed a Negro and a white man, both in Sunday suits and hats, holding a banner that said BROTHERHOOD in large letters. When the image was clear, he moved the paper to a bath of fixer, then washed it and dried it.

He printed all the shots he had taken, took them out into the light, and laid them out on the dining room table. He was pleased: they were vivid, active pictures that clearly showed a sequence of events. When he heard his parents moving about upstairs, he called his mother. She had been a journalist before she married, and she still wrote books and magazine articles. "What do you think?" he asked her.

She studied them thoughtfully with her one eye. After a while she said: "I think they're good. You should take them to a newspaper."

"Really?" he said. He began to feel excited. "Which paper?"

"They're all conservative, unfortunately. Maybe the *Buffalo Sentinel.* The editor is Peter Hoyle—he's been there since God was a boy. He knows your father well; he'll probably see you."

"When should I show him the photos?"

"Now. The march is hot news. It will be in all tomorrow's papers. They need the pictures tonight."

Woody was energized. "All right," he said. He picked up the glossy sheets and shuffled them into a neat stack. His mother produced a cardboard folder from Papa's study. Woody kissed her and left the house.

He caught a bus downtown.

The front entrance of the *Sentinel* office was closed, and he suffered a moment of dismay, but he reasoned that reporters must be able to get in and out today if they were to produce a Monday morning paper, and sure enough he found a side entrance. "I have some photographs for Mr. Hoyle," he said to a man sitting inside the door, and he was directed upstairs.

He found the editor's office, a secretary took his name, and a minute later he was shaking hands with Peter Hoyle. The editor was a tall, imposing man with white hair and a black mustache. He appeared to be finishing a meeting with a younger colleague. He spoke loudly, as if shouting over the noise of a printing press. "The hit-and-run-drivers story is fine, but the intro stinks, Jack," he said with a dismissive hand on the man's shoulder, moving him to the door. "Put a new nose on it. Move the mayor's statement to later and start with crippled children." Jack left, and Hoyle turned to Woody. "What have you got, kid?" he said without preamble.

"I was at the march today."

"You mean the riot."

"It wasn't a riot until the factory guards started hitting women with their clubs."

"I hear the marchers tried to break into the factory, and the guards repelled them."

"It's not true, sir, and the photos prove it."

"Show me."

Woody had arranged them in order while sitting on the bus. He put the first down on the editor's desk. "It started peacefully."

Hoyle pushed the photograph aside. "That's nothing," he said.

Woody brought out a picture taken at the factory. "The guards were waiting at the gate. You can see their nightsticks." His next picture had been taken when the shoving started. "The marchers were at least ten yards from the gate, so there was no need for the guards to try to move them back. It was a deliberate provocation."

"Okay," said Hoyle, and he did not push the pictures aside.

Woody brought out his best shot: a guard using a truncheon to beat a woman. "I saw this whole incident," Woody said. "All the woman did was tell him to stop shoving her, and he hit her like this."

"Good picture," said Hoyle. "Any more?"

"One," said Woody. "Most of the marchers ran away as soon as the fighting began, but a few fought back." He showed Hoyle the photograph of two demonstrators kicking a guard on the ground. "These men retaliated against the guard who hit the woman."

"You did a good job, young Dewar," said Hoyle. He sat at his desk and pulled a form from a tray. "Twenty bucks okay?"

"You mean you're going to print my photographs?"

"I assume that's why you brought them here."

"Yes, sir, thank you. Twenty dollars is okay. I mean fine. I mean plenty."

Hoyle scribbled on the form and signed it. "Take this to the cashier. My secretary will tell you where to go."

The phone on the desk rang. The editor picked it up and barked: "Hoyle." Woody gathered he was dismissed, and left the room.

He was elated. The payment was amazing, but he was more thrilled that the newspaper would use his photos. He followed the secretary's directions to a little room with a counter and a teller's window, and got his twenty bucks. Then he went home in a taxi.

His parents were delighted by his coup, and even his brother seemed pleased. Over dinner, Grandmama said: "As long as you don't consider journalism as a career. That would be lowering."

In fact Woody had been thinking that he might take up news photography instead of politics, and he was surprised to learn that his grandmother disapproved.

His mother smiled and said: "But, Ursula dear, I was a journalist."

"That's different—you're a girl," Grandmama replied. "Woodrow must become a man of distinction, like his father and grandfather before him."

Mother did not take offense at this. She was fond of Grandmama and listened with amused tolerance to her pronouncements of orthodoxy.

However, Chuck resented the traditional focus on the elder son. He said: "And what must I become, chopped liver?"

"Don't be vulgar, Charles," said Grandmama, having the last word as usual.

That night Woody lay awake a long time. He could hardly wait to see his photos in the paper. He felt the way he had as a kid on Christmas Eve: his longing for the morning kept him from sleep.

He thought about Joanne. She was wrong to think him too young. He was right for her. She liked him, they had a lot in common, and she had enjoyed the kiss. He still thought he might win her heart.

He fell asleep at last, and when he woke, it was daylight. He put on a dressing gown over his pajamas and ran downstairs. Joe, the butler, always went out early to buy the newspapers, and they were already laid out on the side table in the breakfast room. Woody's parents were there, his father eating scrambled eggs, his mother sipping coffee.

Woody picked up the *Sentinel*. His work was on the front page.

But it was not what he expected.

They had used only one of his shots—the last. It showed a factory guard lying on the ground being kicked by two workers. The headline WAS: METAL STRIKERS RIOT.

"Oh, no!" he said.

He read the report with incredulity. It said that marchers had attempted to break into the factory and had been bravely repelled by the factory police, several of whom had suffered minor injuries. The behavior of the workers was condemned by the mayor, the chief of police, and Lev Peshkov. At the foot of the article, like an afterthought, union spokesman Brian Hall was quoted as denying the story and blaming the guards for the violence.

Woody put the newspaper in front of his mother. "I told Hoyle that the guards started the riot—and I gave him the pictures to prove it!" he said angrily. "Why would he print the opposite of the truth?"

"Because he's a conservative," she said.

"Newspapers are supposed to tell the truth!" Woody said, his voice rising with furious indignation. "They can't just make up lies!"

"Yes, they can," she said.

"But it's not fair!"

"Welcome to the real world," said his mother.

＊

## vi

Greg Peshkov and his father were in the lobby of the Ritz-Carlton hotel in Washington, D.C., when they ran into Dave Rouzrokh.

Dave was wearing a white suit and a straw hat. He glared at them with hatred. Lev greeted him, but he turned away contemptuously without answering.

Greg knew why. Dave had been losing money all summer, because Roseroque Theatres was not able to get first-run hit movies. And Dave must have guessed that Lev was somehow responsible.

Last week Lev had offered Dave four million dollars for his movie houses—half the original bid—and Dave had again refused. "The price is dropping, Dave," Lev had warned him.

Now Greg said: "I wonder what he's doing here?"

"He's meeting with Sol Starr. He's going to ask why Sol won't give him good movies." Lev obviously knew all about it.

"What will Mr. Starr do?"

"String him along."

Greg marveled at his father's ability to know everything and stay on top of a changing situation. He was always ahead of the game.

They rode up in the elevator. This was the first time Greg had visited his father's permanent suite at the hotel. His mother, Marga, had never been here.

Lev spent a lot of time in Washington because the government was forever interfering with the movie business. Men who considered themselves to be moral leaders got very agitated about what was shown on the big screen, and they put pressure on the government to censor pictures. Lev saw this as a negotiation—he saw life as a negotiation—and his constant aim was to avoid formal censorship by adhering to a voluntary code, a strategy backed by Sol Starr and most other Hollywood big shots.

They entered a living room that was extremely fancy, much more so than the spacious apartment in Buffalo where Greg and his mother lived, and which Greg had always thought to be luxurious. This room had spindly-legged furniture that Greg imagined to be French, rich chestnut-brown velvet drapes at the windows, and a large phonograph.

In the middle of the room he was stunned to see, sitting on a yellow silk sofa, the movie star Gladys Angelus.

People said she was the most beautiful woman in the world.

Greg could see why. She radiated sex appeal, from her dark blue inviting eyes to the long legs crossed under her clinging skirt. As she put out a hand to shake, her red lips smiled and her round breasts moved alluringly inside a soft sweater.

He hesitated a split second before shaking her hand. He felt disloyal to his mother, Marga. She never mentioned the name of Gladys Angelus, a sure sign that she knew what people were saying about Gladys and Lev. Greg felt he was making friends with his mother's enemy. If Mom knew about this, she would cry, he thought.

But he had been taken by surprise. If he had been forewarned, if he had had time to think about his reaction, he might have prepared, and rehearsed a gracious withdrawal. But he could not bring himself to be clumsily rude to this overwhelmingly lovely woman.

So he took her hand, looked into her amazing eyes, and gave what people called a shit-eating grin.

She kept hold of his hand as she said: "I'm so happy to meet you at long last. Your father has told me all about you—but he didn't say how handsome you are!"

There was something unpleasantly proprietorial about this, as if she were a member of the family, rather than a whore who had usurped his mother. All the same he found himself falling under her spell. "I love your films," he said awkwardly.

"Oh, stop it—you don't have to say that," she said, but Greg thought she liked to hear it all the same. "Come and sit by me," she went on. "I want to get to know you."

He did as he was told. He could not help himself. Gladys asked him what school he attended, and while he was telling her, the phone rang. He vaguely heard his father say into the phone: "It was supposed to be tomorrow . . . Okay, if we have to, we can rush it . . . Leave it with me. I'll handle it."

Lev hung up and interrupted Gladys. "Your room is down the hall, Greg," he said. He handed over a key. "And you'll find a gift from me. Settle in and enjoy yourself. We'll meet for dinner at seven."

This was abrupt, and Gladys looked put out, but Lev could be peremptory sometimes, and it was best just to obey. Greg took the key and left.

In the corridor was a broad-shouldered man in a cheap suit. He reminded Greg of Joe Brekhunov, head of security at the Buffalo Metal Works. Greg nodded, and the man said: "Good afternoon, sir." Presumably he was a hotel employee.

Greg entered his room. It was pleasant enough, though not as swanky as his father's suite. He did not see the gift his father had mentioned, but his suitcase was there, and he began to unpack, thinking about Gladys. Was he being disloyal to his mother by shaking hands with his father's mistress? Of course, Gladys was only doing what Marga herself had done, sleeping with a married man. All the same he felt painfully uncomfortable. Was he going to tell his mother that he had met Gladys? Hell, no.

As he was hanging up his shirts, he heard a knock. It came from a door that looked as if it might lead to the neighboring room. Next moment the door opened and a girl walked through.

She was older than Greg, but not much. Her skin was the color of dark chocolate, and she wore a polka-dot dress and carried a clutch bag. She smiled broadly, showing white teeth, and said: "Hello, I've got the room next door."

"I figured that out," he said. "Who are you?"

"Jacky Jakes." She held out her hand. "I'm an actress."

Greg shook hands with the second beautiful actress in an hour. Jacky had a playful look that Greg found more attractive than Gladys's overpowering magnetism. Her mouth was a dark pink bow. He said: "My dad said he got me a gift—are you it?"

She giggled. "I guess I am. He said I would like you. He's going to get me into the movies."

Greg got the picture. His father had guessed he might feel bad about being friendly with Gladys. Jacky was his reward for not making a fuss. He thought he probably ought to reject such a bribe, but he could not resist. "You're a very nice gift," he said.

"Your father's real good to you."

"He's wonderful," Greg said. "And so are you."

"Aren't you sweet?" She put her purse down on the dresser, stepped closer to Greg, stood on tiptoe, and kissed his mouth. Her lips were soft and warm. "I like you," she said. She felt his shoulders. "You're strong."

"I play ice hockey."

"Makes a girl feel safe." She put both hands on his cheeks and kissed him again, longer; then she sighed and said: "Oh, boy, I think we're going to have fun."

"Are we?" Washington was a Southern city, still largely segregated. In Buffalo, white and black people could eat in the same restaurants and drink in the same bars, mostly, but here it was different. Greg was not sure what the laws were, but he felt certain that in practise a white man with a black woman would cause trouble. It was surprising to find Jacky occupying a room in this hotel; Lev must have fixed it. But there was certainly no question of Greg and Jacky swanning around town with Lev and Gladys in a foursome. So what did Jacky think they were going to do to have fun together? The amazing notion crossed his mind that she might be willing to go to bed with him.

He put his hands on her waist, to draw her to him for another kiss, but she pulled back. "I need to take a shower," she said. "Give me a few minutes." She turned and disappeared through the communicating door, closing it behind her.

He sat on the bed, trying to take it all in. Jacky wanted to act in movies, and it seemed she was willing to use sex to advance her career. She certainly was not the first actress, black or white, to use that strategy. Gladys was doing the same by sleeping with Lev. Greg and his father were the lucky beneficiaries.

He saw that she had left her clutch bag behind. He picked it up and tried the door. It was not locked. He stepped through.

She was on the phone, wearing a pink bathrobe. She said: "Yes, hunky-dory, no problem." Her voice seemed different, more mature, and he realized that with him she had been using a sexy little-girl tone that was not natural. Then she saw him, smiled, and reverted to the girly voice as she said into the phone: "Please hold my calls. I don't want to be disturbed. Thank you. Good-bye."

"You left this," said Greg, and handed her the purse.

"You just wanted to see me in my bathrobe," she said coquettishly. The front of the robe did not entirely hide her breasts, and he could see an enchanting curve of flawless brown skin.

He grinned. "No, but I'm glad I did."

"Go back to your room. I have to shower. I might let you see more later."

"Oh, my God," he said.

He returned to his room. This was astonishing. "I might let you see more later," he repeated to himself aloud. What a thing for a girl to say!

He had a hard-on, but he did not want to jerk off when the real thing seemed so close. To take his mind off it, he went on unpacking. He had an expensive shaving kit, a razor and brush with pearl handles, a present from his mother. He laid the things out in the bathroom, wondering whether they would impress Jacky if she saw them.

The walls were thin, and he heard the sound of running water from the next room. The thought of her body naked and wet possessed him. He tried to concentrate on arranging his underwear and socks in a drawer.

Then he heard her scream.

He froze. For a moment he was too surprised to move. What did it mean? Why would she yell out like that? Then she screamed again, and he was shocked into action. He threw open the communicating door and stepped into her room.

She was naked. He had never seen a naked woman in real life. She had pointed breasts with dark brown tips. At her groin was a thatch of wiry black hair. She was cowering back against the wall, trying ineffectually to cover her nakedness with her hands.

Standing in front of her was Dave Rouzrokh, with twin scratches down his aristocratic cheek, presumably caused by Jacky's pink-varnished nails. There was blood on the broad lapel of Dave's double-breasted white jacket.

Jacky screamed: "Get him away from me!"

Greg swung a fist. Dave was an inch taller, but he was an old man, and Greg was an athletic teenager. The blow connected with Dave's chin—more by luck than by judgment—and Dave staggered back, then fell to the floor.

The room door opened.

The broad-shouldered hotel employee Greg had seen earlier came in.

He must have a master key, Greg thought. "I'm Tom Cranmer, house detective," the man said. "What's going on here?"

Greg said: "I heard her scream and came in to find him here."

Jacky said: "He tried to rape me!"

Dave struggled to his feet. "That's not true," he said. "I was asked to come to this room for a meeting with Sol Starr."

Jacky began to sob. "Oh, now he's going to lie about it!"

Cranmer said: "Put something on, please, miss."

Jacky put on her pink bathrobe.

The detective picked up the room phone, dialed a number, and said: "There's usually a cop on the corner. Get him into the lobby, right now."

Dave was staring at Greg. "You're Peshkov's bastard, aren't you?"

Greg was about to hit him again.

Dave said: "Oh, my God, this is a setup."

Greg was thrown by this remark. He felt intuitively that Dave was telling the truth. He dropped his fist. This whole scene must have been scripted by Lev, he realized. Dave Rouzrokh was no rapist. Jacky was faking. And Greg himself was just an actor in the movie. He felt dazed.

"Please come with me, sir," said Cranmer, taking Dave firmly by the arm. "You two as well."

"You can't arrest me," said Dave.

"Yes, sir, I can," said Cranmer. "And I'm going to hand you over to a police officer."

Greg said to Jacky: "Do you want to get dressed?"

She shook her head quickly and decisively. Greg realized it was part of the plan that she would appear in her robe.

He took Jacky's arm and they followed Cranmer and Dave along the corridor and into the elevator. A cop was waiting in the lobby. Both he and the hotel detective must be in on the plot, Greg surmised.

Cranmer said: "I heard a scream from her room, found the old guy in there. She says he tried to rape her. The kid is a witness."

Dave looked bewildered, as if he thought this might be a bad dream. Greg found himself feeling sorry for Dave. He had been cruelly trapped. Lev was more pitiless than Greg had imagined. Half of him admired his father; the other half wondered if such ruthlessness was really necessary.

The cop snapped handcuffs on Dave and said: "All right, let's go."

"Go where?" Dave said.

"Downtown," said the cop.

Greg said: "Do we all have to go?"

"Yeah."

Cranmer spoke to Greg in a low voice. "Don't worry, son," he said. "You did a great job. We'll go to the precinct house and make our statements, and after that you can fuck her from here to Christmastime."

The cop led Dave to the door, and the others followed.

As they stepped outside, a photographer popped a flashgun.

### vii

Woody Dewar got a copy of Freud's *Studies in Hysteria* mailed to him by a bookseller in New York. On the night of the Yacht Club ball—the climactic social event of the summer season in Buffalo—he wrapped it neatly in brown paper and tied a red ribbon around it. "Chocolates for a lucky girl?" said his mother, passing him in the hall. She had only one eye but she saw everything.

"A book," he said. "For Joanne Rouzrokh."

"She won't be at the ball."

"I know."

Mama stopped and gave him a searching look. After a moment she said: "You're serious about her."

"I guess. But she thinks I'm too young."

"Her pride is probably involved. Her friends would ask why she can't find a guy her own age to go out with. Girls are cruel like that."

"I'm planning to persist until she grows more mature."

Mama smiled. "I bet you make her laugh."

"I do. It's the best card I hold."

"Well, heck, I waited long enough for your father."

"Did you?"

"I loved him from the first time I met him. I pined for years. I had to watch him fall for that shallow cow Olga Vyalov, who wasn't worthy of him but had two working eyes. Thank God she got knocked up by her chauffeur." Mother's language could be a little coarse, especially when Grandmama was not around. She had picked up bad habits during the years she spent working on newspapers. "Then he went off to war. I had to follow him to France before I could nail his foot to the goddamn floor."

Nostalgia was mixed with pain in her reminiscence, Woody could tell. "But he realized you were the right girl for him."

"In the end, yes."

"Maybe that'll happen to me."

Mama kissed him. "Good luck, my son," she said.

The Rouzrokh house was less than a mile away and Woody walked there. None of the Rouzrokhs would be at the Yacht Club tonight. Dave had been all over the papers after a mysterious incident at the Ritz-Carlton hotel in Washington. A typical headline had read CINEMA MOGUL ACCUSED BY STARLET. Woody had recently learned to mistrust newspapers. However, gullible people said there must be something in it; otherwise, why would the police have arrested Dave?

None of the family had been seen at any social event since.

Outside the house an armed guard stopped Woody. "The family isn't seeing callers," he said brusquely.

Woody guessed the man had spent a lot of time repelling reporters, and he forgave the discourteous tone. He recalled the name of the Rouzrokhs' maid. "Please ask Miss Estella to tell Joanne that Woody Dewar has a book for her."

"You can leave it with me," said the guard, holding out his hand.

Woody held on firmly to the book. "Thanks, but no."

The guard looked annoyed, but he walked Woody up the drive and rang the doorbell. Estella opened it and said at once: "Hello, Mr. Woody, come in—Joanne will be so glad to see you!" Woody permitted himself a triumphant glance at the guard as he stepped inside.

Estella showed him into an empty drawing room. She offered him milk and cookies, as if he were still a kid, and he declined politely. Joanne came in a minute later. Her face was drawn and her olive skin looked washed out, but she smiled pleasantly at him and sat down to chat.

She was pleased with the book. "Now I'll have to read Dr. Freud instead of just gabbing about him," she said. "You're a good influence on me, Woody."

"I wish I could be a bad influence."

She let that pass. "Aren't you going to the ball?"

"I have a ticket, but if you're not there, I'm not interested. Would you like to go to a movie instead?"

"No, thanks, really."

"Or we could just get dinner. Somewhere really quiet. If you don't mind taking the bus."

"Oh, Woody, of course I don't mind the bus, but you're too young for me. Anyway, the summer's almost over. You'll be back at school soon, and I'm going to Vassar."

"Where you'll go on dates, I guess."

"I sure hope so!"

Woody stood up. "Okay, well, I'm going to take a vow of celibacy and enter a monastery. Please don't come and visit me—you'll distract the other brethren."

She laughed. "Thank you for taking my mind off my family's troubles."

It was the first time she had mentioned what had happened to her father. He had not been planning to raise the subject, but now that she had, he said: "You know we're all on your side. Nobody believes that actress's story. Everyone in town realizes it was a setup by that swine Lev Peshkov, and we're furious about it."

"I know," she said. "But the accusation alone is too shameful for my father to bear. I think my parents are going to move to Florida."

"I'm so sorry."

"Thank you. Now go to the ball."

"Maybe I will."

She walked him to the door.

"May I kiss you good-bye?" he said.

She leaned forward and kissed his lips. This was not like the last kiss, and he knew instinctively not to grab her and press his mouth to hers. It was a gentle kiss, her lips on his for a sweet moment that was over in a breath. Then she pulled away and opened the front door.

"Good night," Woody said as he stepped out.

"Good-bye," said Joanne.


## viii

Greg Peshkov was in love.

He knew that Jacky Jakes had been bought for him by his father, as his reward for helping to entrap Dave Rouzrokh, but despite that it was real love.

He had lost his virginity a few minutes after they returned from the precinct house, and the two of them had then spent most of a week in bed at the Ritz-Carlton. Greg did not need to use birth control, she told him, because she was already "fixed up." He had only the vaguest idea what that meant, but he took her at her word.

He had never been so happy in his life, and he adored her, especially when she dropped the little-girl act and revealed a shrewd intelligence and a mordant sense of humor. She admitted she had seduced Greg on his father's orders, but confessed that against her will she had fallen in love. Her real name was Mabel Jakes and, although she pretended to be nineteen, she was in fact just sixteen, only a few months older than Greg.

Lev had promised her a part in a movie but, he said, he was still looking for just the right role. In a perfect imitation of Lev's vestigial Russian accent she said: "But I don't guess he's lookin' too fuckin' hard."

"I guess there aren't many parts written for Negro actors," Greg said.

"I know, I'll end up playing the maid, rolling my eyes and saying *lawdy*. There are Africans in plays and films—Cleopatra, Hannibal, Othello—but they're usually played by white actors." Her father, now dead, had been a professor in a Negro college, and she knew more about literature than Greg did. "Anyway, why should Negroes only play black people? If Cleopatra can be played by a white actress, why can't Juliet be black?"

"People would find it strange."

"People would get used to it. They get used to anything. Does Jesus have to be played by a Jew? Nobody cares."

She was right, Greg thought, but all the same it was never going to happen.

When Lev had announced their return to Buffalo—leaving it until the last minute, as usual—Greg had been devastated. He had asked his father if Jacky could come to Buffalo, but Lev had laughed and said: "Son, you don't shit where you eat. You can see her next time you come to Washington."

Despite that, Jacky had followed him to Buffalo a day later and moved into a cheap apartment near Canal Street.

Lev and Greg had been busy for the next couple of weeks with the takeover of Roseroque Theatres. Dave had sold for two million in the end, a quarter of the original offer, and Greg's admiration for his father went up another notch. Jacky had withdrawn her charges and hinted to the newspapers that she had accepted a cash settlement. Greg was awestruck by his father's callous nerve.

And he had Jacky. He told his mother he was out every night with male friends, but in fact he spent all his spare time with Jacky. He showed her around town, picnicked with her at the beach, even managed to take her out in a borrowed speedboat. No one connected her with the rather blurred newspaper photograph of a girl walking out of the Ritz-Carlton hotel in a bathrobe. But mostly they spent the warm summer evenings having sweaty, deliriously happy sex, tangling the worn sheets on the narrow bed in her small apartment. They decided to get married as soon as they were old enough.

Tonight he was taking her to the Yacht Club Ball.

It had been extraordinarily difficult to get tickets, but Greg had bribed a school friend.

He had bought Jacky a new dress, pink satin. He got a generous allowance from Marga, and Lev loved to slip him fifty bucks now and again, so he always had more money than he needed.

In the back of his mind a warning was sounding. Jacky would be the only Negro at the ball not serving drinks. She was very reluctant to go, but Greg had talked her around. The young men would envy him but the older ones might be hostile, he knew. There would be some muttering. Jacky's beauty and charm would overcome much prejudice, he felt: How could anyone resist her? But if some fool got drunk and insulted her, Greg would teach him a lesson with both fists.

Even as he thought this, he heard his mother telling him not to be a love-struck fool. But a man could not go through life listening to his mother.

As he walked along Canal Street in white tie and tails, he looked forward to seeing her in the new dress, and maybe kneeling to lift the hem up until he could see her panties and garter belt.

He entered her building, an old house now subdivided. There was a threadbare red carpet on the stairs and a smell of spicy cooking. He let himself into the apartment with his own key.

The place was empty.

That was odd. Where would she go without him?

With fear in his heart, he opened the closet. The pink satin ball dress hung there on its own. Her other clothes were gone.

"No!" he said aloud. How could this happen?

On the rickety pine table was an envelope. He picked it up and saw his name on the front in Jacky's neat, schoolgirl handwriting. A feeling of dread came over him.

He tore open the envelope with shaky hands and read the short message.

My darling Greg,
The last three weeks have been the happiest time of my entire life.

I knew in my heart that we couldn't ever get married but it was nice to pretend.

You are a lovely boy and will grow into a fine man, if you don't take after your father too much.

Had Lev found out that Jacky was living here, and somehow made her leave? He would not do that—would he?

Good-bye and don't forget me.

Your Gift,

Jacky

Greg crumpled the paper and wept.

## ix

"You look wonderful," Eva Rothmann said to Daisy Peshkov. "If I was a boy, I'd fall in love with you in a minute."

Daisy smiled. Eva was already a little bit in love with her. And Daisy did look wonderful, in an ice-blue silk organdy ball gown that deepened the blue of her eyes. The skirt of the dress had a frilled hem that was ankle length in front but rose playfully to midcalf behind, giving a tantalizing glimpse of Daisy's legs in sheer stockings.

She wore a sapphire necklace of her mother's. "Your father bought me that, back in the days when he was still occasionally nice to me," Olga said. "But hurry up, Daisy, you're making us all late."

Olga was wearing matronly navy blue, and Eva was in red, which suited her dark coloring.

Daisy walked down the stairs on a cloud of happiness.

They stepped out of the house. Henry, the gardener, doubling as chauffeur tonight, opened the doors of the shiny old black Stutz.

This was Daisy's big night. Tonight Charlie Farquharson would formally propose to her. He would offer her a diamond ring that was a family heirloom—she had seen and approved it, and it had been altered to fit her. She would accept his proposal, and then they would announce their engagement to everyone at the ball.

She got into the car feeling like Cinderella.

Only Eva had expressed doubts. "I thought you'd go for someone who was more of a match for you," she had said.

"You mean a man who won't let me boss him around," Daisy had replied.

"No, but someone more like you, good-looking and charming and sexy."

This was unusually sharp for Eva: it implied that Charlie was homely and charmless and unglamorous. Daisy had been taken aback, and did not know how to reply.

Her mother had saved her. Olga had said: "I married a man who was good-looking and charming and sexy, and he made me utterly miserable."

Eva had said no more.

As the car approached the Yacht Club, Daisy vowed to restrain herself. She must not show how triumphant she felt. She must act as if there were nothing unexpected about her mother being asked to join the Buffalo Ladies' Society. As she showed the other girls her enormous diamond, she would be so gracious as to declare that she did not deserve someone as wonderful as Charlie.

She had plans to make him even more wonderful. As soon as the honeymoon was over, she and Charlie would start building their stable of racehorses. In five years they would be entering the most prestigious races around the world: Saratoga Springs, Longchamps, Royal Ascot.

Summer was turning to fall, and it was dusk when the car drew up at the pier. "I'm afraid we may be very late tonight, Henry," Daisy said gaily.

"Quite all right, Miss Daisy," he replied. He adored her. "You have a wonderful time, now."

At the door, Daisy noticed Victor Dixon following them in. Feeling well disposed toward everyone, she said: "So, Victor, your sister met the king of England. Congratulations!"

"Mm, yes," he said, looking embarrassed.

They entered the club. The first person they saw was Ursula Dewar, who had agreed to accept Olga into her snobby club. Daisy smiled warmly at her and said: "Good evening, Mrs. Dewar."

Ursula seemed distracted. "Excuse me just a moment," she said, and moved away across the lobby. She thought herself a queen, Daisy reflected, but did that mean she had no need of good manners? One day Daisy would rule over Buffalo society, but she would be unfailingly gracious to all, she vowed.

The three women went into the ladies' room, where they checked their appearance in the mirrors, in case anything had gone wrong in the twenty minutes since they left home. Dot Renshaw came in, looked at them, and went out again. "Stupid girl," Daisy said.

But her mother looked worried. "What's happening?" she said. "We've been here five minutes, and already three people have snubbed us!"

"Jealousy," Daisy said. "Dot would like to marry Charlie herself."

Olga said: "At this point Dot Renshaw would like to marry more or less anybody, I guess."

"Come on, let's enjoy ourselves," said Daisy, and she led the way out.

As she entered the ballroom, Woody Dewar greeted her. "At last, a gentleman!" Daisy said.

In a lowered voice he said: "I just want to say that I think it's wrong of people to blame you for anything your father might have done."

"Especially when they all bought their booze from him!" she replied.

Then she saw her future mother-in-law, in a ruched pink gown that did nothing for her angular figure. Nora Farquharson was not ecstatic about her son's choice of bride, but she had accepted Daisy and had been charming to Olga when they had exchanged visits. "Mrs. Farquharson!" Daisy said. "What a lovely dress!"

Nora Farquharson turned her back and walked away.

Eva gasped.

A feeling of horror came over Daisy. She turned back to Woody. "This isn't about bootlegging, is it?"

"No."

"What, then?"

"You must ask Charlie. Here he comes."

Charlie was perspiring, though it was not warm. "What's going on?" Daisy asked him. "Everyone's giving me the cold shoulder!"

He was terribly nervous. "People are so angry at your family," he said.

"What for?" she cried.

Several people nearby heard her raised voice and looked around. She did not care.

Charlie said: "Your father ruined Dave Rouzrokh."

"Are you talking about that incident in the Ritz-Carlton? What has that got to do with me?"

"Everyone likes Dave, even though he's Persian or something. And they don't believe he would rape anybody."

"I never said he did!"

"I know," Charlie said. He was clearly in agony.

People were frankly staring, now: Victor Dixon, Dot Renshaw, Chuck Dewar.

Daisy said to Charlie: "But I'm going to be blamed. Is that so?"

"Your father did a terrible thing."

Daisy was cold with fear. Surely she could not lose her triumph at the last minute? "Charlie," she said. "What are you telling me? Talk straight, for the love of God."

Eva put her arm around Daisy's waist in a gesture of support.

Charlie replied: "Mother says it's unforgivable."

"What does that mean, unforgivable?"

He stared miserably at her. He could not bring himself to speak.

But there was no need. She knew what he was going to say. "It's over, isn't it?" she said. "You're jilting me."

He nodded.

Olga said: "Daisy, we must leave." She was in tears.

Daisy looked around. She tilted her chin as she stared them all down: Dot Renshaw looking maliciously pleased, Victor Dixon admiring, Chuck Dewar with his mouth open in adolescent shock, and his brother, Woody, looking sympathetic.

"To hell with you all," Daisy said loudly. "I'm going to London to dance with the king!"

CHAPTER THREE

# 1936

It was a sunny Saturday afternoon in May 1936, and Lloyd
Williams was at the end of his second year at Cambridge, when
Fascism reared its vile head among the white stone cloisters of
the ancient university.

Lloyd was at Emmanuel College—known as "Emma"—
doing modern languages. He was studying French and German, but he
preferred German. As he immersed himself in the glories of German
culture, reading Goethe, Schiller, Heine, and Thomas Mann, he looked
up occasionally from his desk in the quiet library to watch with sadness
as today's Germany descended into barbarism.

Then the local branch of the British Union of Fascists announced
that their leader, Sir Oswald Mosley, would address a meeting in
Cambridge. The news took Lloyd back to Berlin three years earlier. He
saw again the Brownshirt thugs wrecking Maud von Ulrich's magazine
office; heard again the grating sound of Hitler's hate-filled voice as
he stood in the parliament and poured scorn on democracy; shuddered
anew at the memory of the dogs' bloody muzzles savaging Jörg with a
bucket over his head.

Now Lloyd stood on the platform at Cambridge railway station, waiting to meet his mother off the train from London. With him was Ruby Carter, a fellow activist in the local Labour Party. She had helped him organize today's meeting on the subject of "the Truth about Fascism." Lloyd's mother, Eth Leckwith, was to speak. Her book about Germany had been a big success, she had stood for Parliament again in the 1935 election, and she was once again the member for Aldgate.

Lloyd was tense about the meeting. Mosley's new political party had gained many thousands of members, due in part to the enthusiastic support of the *Daily Mail,* which had run the infamous headline HURRAH FOR THE BLACKSHIRTS! Mosley was a charismatic speaker, and would undoubtedly recruit new members today. It was vital that there should be a bright beacon of reason to contrast with his seductive lies.

However, Ruby was chatty. She was complaining about the social life of Cambridge. "I'm so bored with local boys," she said. "All they want to do is go to a pub and get drunk."

Lloyd was surprised. He had imagined that Ruby had a well-developed social life. She wore inexpensive clothes that were always a bit tight, showing off her plump curves. Most men would find her attractive, he thought. "What do you like to do?" he asked. "Apart from organize Labour Party meetings."

"I love dancing."

"You can't be short of partners. There are twelve men for every woman at the university."

"No offense intended, but most of the university men are pansies."

There were a lot of homosexual men in Cambridge University, Lloyd knew, but it startled him to hear her mention the subject. Ruby was famously blunt, but this was shocking even from her. He had no idea how to respond, so he said nothing.

Ruby said: "You're not one of them, are you?"

"No! Don't be ridiculous."

"No need to be insulted. You're handsome enough for a pansy, except for that squashed nose."

He laughed. "That's what they call a backhanded compliment."

"You are, though. You look like Douglas Fairbanks Junior."

"Well, thanks, but I'm not a pansy."

"Have you got a girlfriend?"

This was becoming embarrassing. "No, not at the moment." He made a show of checking his watch and looking for the train.

"Why not?"

"I just haven't met Miss Right."

"Oh, thank you very much, I'm sure."

He looked at her. She was only half joking. He felt mortified that she had taken his remark personally. "I didn't mean . . ."

"Yes, you did. But never mind. Here's the train."

The locomotive drew into the station and came to a halt in a cloud of steam. The doors opened and passengers stepped out onto the platform: students in tweed jackets, farmers' wives going shopping, workingmen in flat caps. Lloyd scanned the crowd for his mother. "She'll be in a third-class carriage," he said. "Matter of principle."

Ruby said: "Would you come to my twenty-first-birthday party?"

"Of course."

"My friend's got a little flat in Market Street, and a deaf landlady."

Lloyd was not comfortable about this invitation, and hesitated over his reply; then his mother appeared, as pretty as a songbird in a red summer coat and a jaunty little hat. She hugged and kissed him. "You look very well, my lovely," she said. "But I must buy you a new suit for next term."

"This one is fine, Mam." He had a scholarship that paid his university fees and basic living expenses, but it did not run to suits. When he started at Cambridge, his mother had dipped into her savings and bought him a tweed suit for daytime and an evening suit for formal dinners. He had worn the tweed every day for two years, and it showed. He was particular about his appearance, and made sure he always had a clean white shirt, a perfectly knotted tie, and a folded white handkerchief in his breast pocket: there had to be a dandy somewhere in his ancestry. The suit was carefully pressed, but it was beginning to look shabby, and in truth he longed for a new one, but he did not want his mother to spend her savings.

"We'll see," she said. She turned to Ruby, smiled warmly, and held out her hand. "I'm Eth Leckwith," she said with the easy grace of a visiting duchess.

"Pleased to meet you. I'm Ruby Carter."

"Are you a student, too, Ruby?"

"No, I'm a maid at Chimbleigh, a big country house." Ruby looked a bit ashamed as she made this confession. "It's five miles out of town, but I can usually borrow a bike."

"Fancy that!" said Ethel. "When I was your age, I was a maid at a country house in Wales."

Ruby was amazed. "You, a housemaid? And now you're a member of Parliament!"

"That's what democracy means."

Lloyd said: "Ruby and I organized today's meeting together."

His mother said: "And how is it going?"

"Sold out. In fact we had to move to a bigger hall."

"I told you it would work."

The meeting was Ethel's idea. Ruby Carter and many others in the Labour Party had wanted to mount a protest demonstration, marching through the town. Lloyd had agreed at first. "Fascism must be publicly opposed at every opportunity," he had said.

Ethel had counseled otherwise. "If we march and shout slogans, we look just like them," she had said. "Show that we're different. Hold a quiet, intelligent meeting to discuss the reality of Fascism." Lloyd had been dubious. "I'll come and speak, if you like," she had said.

Lloyd had put that to the Cambridge party. There had been a lively discussion, with Ruby leading the opposition to Ethel's plan, but in the end the prospect of having an M.P. and famous feminist to speak had clinched it.

Lloyd was still not sure it had been the right decision. He recalled Maud von Ulrich in Berlin saying: "We must not meet violence with violence." That had been the policy of the German Social Democratic Party. For the von Ulrich family, and for Germany, the policy had been a catastrophe.

They walked out through the yellow-brick Romanesque arches of the station and hurried along leafy Station Road, a street of smug middle-class houses made of the same yellow brick. Ethel put her arm through Lloyd's. "How's my little undergraduate, then?" she said.

He smiled at the word *little*. He was four inches taller than she, and muscular because of his training with the university boxing team: he could have picked her up with one hand. She was bursting with pride, he knew. Few things in life had pleased her as much as his coming to this place. That was probably why she wanted to buy him suits.

"I love it here, you know that," he said. "I'll love it more when it's full of working-class boys."

"And girls," Ruby put in.

They turned into Hills Road, the main thoroughfare leading to the town center. Since the coming of the railway, the town had expanded south toward the station, and churches had been built along Hills Road to serve the new suburb. Their destination was a Baptist chapel whose left-wing pastor had agreed to loan it free of charge.

"I made a bargain with the Fascists," Lloyd said. "I said we'd refrain from marching if they would promise to do the same."

"I'm surprised they agreed," said Ethel. "Fascists love marching."

"They were reluctant. But I told the university authorities and the police what I was proposing, and the Fascists pretty much had to go along with it."

"That was clever."

"But, Mam, guess who is their local leader? Viscount Aberowen, otherwise known as Boy Fitzherbert, the son of your former employer Earl Fitzherbert!" Boy was twenty-one, the same age as Lloyd. He was at Trinity, the aristocratic college.

"What? My God!"

She seemed more shaken than he had expected, and he glanced at her. She had gone pale. "Are you shocked?"

"Yes!" She seemed to recover her composure. "His father is a junior minister in the Foreign Office." The government was a Conservative-dominated coalition. "Fitz must be embarrassed."

"Most Conservatives are soft on Fascism, I imagine. They see little wrong with killing Communists and persecuting Jews."

"Some of them, perhaps, but you exaggerate." She gave Lloyd a sideways look. "So, you went to see Boy?"

"Yes." Lloyd thought this seemed to have special significance for Ethel, but he could not imagine why. "I thought him perfectly frightful. In his room at Trinity he had a whole case of Scotch—twelve bottles!"

"You met him once before—do you remember?"

"No. When was that?"

"You were nine years old. I took you to the Palace of Westminster, shortly after I was elected. We met Fitz and Boy on the stairs."

Lloyd did vaguely remember. Then as now, the incident seemed to be mysteriously important to his mother. "That was him? How funny."

Ruby put in: "I know him. He's a pig. He paws maids."

Lloyd was shocked, but his mother seemed unsurprised. "Very unpleasant, but it happens all the time." Her grim acceptance made it more horrifying to him.

They reached the chapel and went in through the back door. There, in a kind of vestry, was Robert von Ulrich, looking startlingly British in a bold green-and-brown check suit and a striped tie. He stood up and Ethel hugged him. In faultless English Robert said: "My dear Ethel, what a perfectly charming hat."

Lloyd introduced his mother to the local Labour Party women who were preparing urns of tea and plates of biscuits to be served after the meeting. Having heard Ethel complain, many times, that people who organized political events seemed to think an M.P. never needed to go to the toilet, he said: "Ruby, before we start, would you show my mother where the ladies' facilities are?" The two women went off.

Lloyd sat down next to Robert and said conversationally: "How's business?"

Robert was now the proprietor of a restaurant much favored by the homosexuals about whom Ruby had been complaining. Somehow he had known that Cambridge in the 1930s was congenial to such men, just as Berlin had been in the 1920s. His new place had the same name as the old, Bistro Robert. "Business is good," he answered. A shadow crossed his face, a brief but intense look of real fear. "This time, I hope I can keep what I've built up."

"We're doing our best to fight off the Fascists, and meetings such as this are the way to do it," Lloyd said. "Your talk will be a big help—it will open people's eyes." Robert was going to speak about his personal experience of life under Fascism. "A lot of them say it couldn't happen here, but they're wrong."

Robert nodded in grim agreement. "Fascism is a lie, but an alluring one."

Lloyd's visit to Berlin three years ago was vivid in his mind. "I often wonder what happened to the old Bistro Robert," he said.

"I had a letter from a friend," Robert said in a voice full of sadness. "None of the old crowd go there anymore. The Macke brothers auctioned off the wine cellar. Now the clientele is mostly middle-ranking cops and bureaucrats." He looked even more pained as he added: "They no longer use tablecloths." He changed the subject abruptly. "Do you want to go to the Trinity Ball?"

Most of the colleges held summer dances to celebrate the end of exams. The balls, plus associated parties and picnics, constituted May Week, which illogically took place in June. The Trinity Ball was famously lavish. "I'd love to go, but I can't afford it," Lloyd said. "Tickets are two guineas, aren't they?"

"I've been given one. But you can have it. Several hundred drunk students dancing to a jazz band is actually my idea of hell."

Lloyd was tempted. "But I haven't got a tailcoat." College balls required white tie and tails.

"Borrow mine. It'll be too big at the waist, but we're the same height."

"Then I will. Thank you!"

Ruby reappeared. "Your mother is wonderful," she said to Lloyd. "I can't believe she used to be a maid!"

Robert said: "I have known Ethel for more than twenty years. She is truly extraordinary."

"I can see why you haven't met Miss Right," Ruby said to Lloyd. "You're looking for someone like her, and there aren't many."

"You're right about the last part, anyway," Lloyd said. "There's no one like her."

Ruby winced, as if in pain.

Lloyd said: "What's wrong?"

"Toothache."

"You must go to the dentist."

She looked at him as if he had said something stupid, and he realized that on a housemaid's wage she could not afford to pay a dentist. He felt foolish.

He went to the door and peeped through to the main hall. Like many nonconformist churches, this was a plain rectangular room with walls painted white. It was a warm day, and the clear glass windows were open. The rows of chairs were full and the audience was waiting expectantly.

When Ethel reappeared, Lloyd said: "If it's all right with everyone, I'll open the meeting. Then Robert will tell his personal story, and my mother will draw out the political lessons."

They all agreed.

"Ruby, will you keep an eye on the Fascists? Let me know if anything happens."

Ethel frowned. "Is that really necessary?"

"We probably shouldn't trust them to keep their promise."

Ruby said: "They're meeting a quarter of a mile up the road. I don't mind running in and out."

She left by the back door, and Lloyd led the others into the church. There was no stage, but a table and three chairs stood at the near end, with a lectern to one side. As Ethel and Robert took their seats, Lloyd went to the lectern. There was a brief round of subdued applause.

"Fascism is on the march," Lloyd began. "And it is dangerously attractive. It gives false hope to the unemployed. It wears a spurious patriotism, as the Fascists themselves wear imitation military uniforms."

The British government was keen to appease Fascist regimes, to

Lloyd's dismay. It was a coalition dominated by Conservatives, with a few Liberals and a sprinkling of renegade Labour ministers who had split with their party. Only a few days after it was reelected last November, the Foreign Secretary had proposed to yield much of Abyssinia to the conquering Italians and their Fascist leader Benito Mussolini.

Worse still, Germany was rearming and aggressive. Just a couple of months ago, Hitler had violated the Versailles Treaty by sending troops into the demilitarized Rhineland—and Lloyd had been horrified to see that no country had been willing to stop him.

Any hope he had that Fascism might be a temporary aberration had now vanished. Lloyd believed that democratic countries such as France and Britain must get ready to fight. But he did not say so in his speech today, for his mother and most of the Labour party opposed a buildup in British armaments and hoped the League of Nations would be able to deal with the dictators. They wanted at all costs to avoid repeating the dreadful slaughter of the Great War. Lloyd sympathized with that hope, but feared it was not realistic.

He was preparing himself for war. He had been an officer cadet at school and, when he came up to Cambridge, he had joined the Officer Training Corps—the only working-class boy and certainly the only Labour Party member to do so.

He sat down to muted applause. He was a clear and logical speaker, but he did not have his mother's ability to touch hearts—not yet, anyway.

Robert stepped to the lectern. "I am Austrian," he said. "In the war I was wounded, captured by the Russians, and sent to a prison camp in Siberia. After the Bolsheviks made peace with the Central Powers, the guards opened the gates and told us we were free to go. Getting home was our problem, not theirs. It is a long way from Siberia to Austria— more than three thousand miles. There was no bus, so I walked."

Surprised laughter rippled around the room, with a few appreciative hand-claps. Robert had already charmed them, Lloyd saw.

Ruby came up to him, looking annoyed, and spoke in his ear. "The

Fascists just went by. Boy Fitzherbert was driving Mosley to the railway station, and a bunch of hotheads in black shirts were running after the car, cheering."

Lloyd frowned. "They promised they wouldn't march. I suppose they'll say that running behind a car doesn't count."

"What's the difference, I'd like to know?"

"Any violence?"

"No."

"Keep a lookout."

Ruby retired. Lloyd was bothered. The Fascists had certainly broken the spirit of the agreement, if not the letter. They had appeared on the street in their uniforms—and there had been no counterdemonstration. The socialists were here, inside the church, invisible. All there was to show for their stand was a banner outside the church saying THE TRUTH ABOUT FASCISM in large red letters.

Robert was saying: "I am pleased to be here, honored to have been invited to address you, and delighted to see several patrons of Bistro Robert in the audience. However, I must warn you that the story I have to tell is most unpleasant, and indeed gruesome."

He related how he and Jörg had been arrested after refusing to sell the Berlin restaurant to a Nazi. He described Jörg as his chef and longtime business partner, saying nothing of their sexual relationship, though the more knowing people in the church probably guessed.

The audience became very quiet as he began to describe events in the concentration camp. Lloyd heard gasps of horror when he got to the part where the starving dogs appeared. Robert described the torture of Jörg in a low, clear voice that carried across the room. By the time he came to Jörg's death, several people were weeping.

Lloyd himself relived the cruelty and anguish of those moments, and he was possessed by rage against such fools as Boy Fitzherbert whose infatuation with marching songs and smart uniforms threatened to bring the same torment to England.

Robert sat down and Ethel went to the lectern. As she began to speak, Ruby reappeared, looking furious. "I told you this wouldn't work!" she hissed in Lloyd's ear. "Mosley has gone, but the boys are singing 'Rule, Britannia!' outside the station."

That certainly was a breach of the agreement, Lloyd thought angrily. Boy had broken his promise. So much for the word of an English gentleman.

Ethel was explaining how Fascism offered false solutions, simplistically blaming groups such as Jews and Communists for complex problems such as unemployment and crime. She made merciless fun of the concept of the triumph of the will, likening the Führer and the Duce to playground bullies. They claimed popular support, but banned all opposition.

Lloyd realized that when the Fascists returned from the railway station to the center of town they would have to pass this church. He began to listen to the sounds coming through the open windows. He could hear cars and lorries growling along Hills Road, punctuated now and again by the trill of a bicycle bell or the cry of a child. He thought he heard a distant shout, and it sounded ominously like the noise made by rowdy boys young enough still to be proud of their deep new voices. He tensed, straining to hear, and there were more shouts. The Fascists were marching.

Ethel raised her own voice as the bellowing outside got louder. She argued that working people of all kinds needed to band together in trade unions and the Labour Party to build a fairer society step by democratic step, not through the kind of violent upheaval that had gone so badly wrong in Communist Russia and Nazi Germany.

Ruby reentered. "They're marching up Hills Road now," she said in a low, urgent murmur. "We have to go out there and confront them!"

"No!" Lloyd whispered. "The party made a collective decision— no demonstration. We must stick to that. We must be a disciplined movement!" He knew the reference to party discipline would carry weight with her.

The Fascists were nearby now, raucously chanting. Lloyd guessed there must be fifty or sixty. He itched to go out there and face them. Two young men near the back stood up and went to the windows to look out. Ethel urged caution. "Don't react to hooliganism by becoming a hooligan," she said. "That will only give the newspapers an excuse to say that one side is as bad as the other."

There was a crash of breaking glass, and a stone came through the window. A woman screamed, and several people got to their feet. "Please remain seated," Ethel said. "I expect they will go away in a minute." She talked on in a calm and reassuring voice. Few people attended to her speech. Everyone was looking backward toward the church door, and listening to the hoots and jeers of the ruffians outside. Lloyd had to struggle to sit still. He looked toward his mother with a neutral expression fixed like a mask on his face. Every bone in his body wanted to rush outside and punch heads.

After a minute the audience quietened somewhat. They returned their attention to Ethel, though still fidgeting and looking back over their shoulders. Ruby muttered: "We're like a pack of rabbits, shaking in our burrow while the fox barks outside." Her tone was contemptuous, and Lloyd felt she was right.

But his mother's forecast proved true, and no more stones were thrown. The chanting receded.

"Why do the Fascists want violence?" Ethel asked rhetorically. "Those out there in Hills Road may be mere hooligans, but someone is directing them, and their tactics have a purpose. When there is fighting in the streets, they can claim that public order has broken down, and drastic measures are needed to restore the rule of law. Those emergency measures will include banning democratic political parties such as Labour, prohibiting trade union action, and jailing people without trial—people such as us, peaceful men and women whose only crime is to disagree with the government. Does this sound fantastic to you, unlikely, something that could never happen? Well, they used exactly those tactics in Germany—and it worked."

She went on to talk about how Fascism should be opposed: in discussion groups, at meetings such as this one, by writing letters to the newspapers, by using every opportunity to alert others to the danger. But even Ethel had trouble making this sound courageous and decisive.

Lloyd was cut to the quick by Ruby's talk of rabbits. He felt like a coward. He was so frustrated that he could hardly sit still.

Slowly the atmosphere in the hall returned to normal. Lloyd turned to Ruby. "The rabbits are safe, anyhow," he said.

"For now," she said. "But the fox will be back."

## ii

"If you like a boy, you can let him kiss you on the mouth," said Lindy Westhampton, sitting on the lawn in the sunshine.

"And if you really like him, he can feel your breasts," said her twin sister, Lizzie.

"But nothing below the waist."

"Not until you're engaged."

Daisy was intrigued. She had expected English girls to be inhibited, but she had been wrong. The Westhampton twins were sex mad.

Daisy was thrilled to be a guest at Chimbleigh, the country house of Sir Bartholomew "Bing" Westhampton. It made her feel she had been accepted into English society. But she still had not met the king.

She recalled her humiliation at the Buffalo Yacht Club with a sense of shame that was still like a burn on her skin, continuing to give her agonizing pain long after the flame had gone away. But whenever she felt that pain, she thought about how she was going to dance with the king, and she imagined them all—Dot Renshaw, Nora Farquharson, Ursula Dewar—poring over her picture in the *Buffalo Sentinel,* reading every word of the report, envying her, and wishing they could honestly say they had always been her friends.

Things had been difficult at first. Daisy had arrived three months ago with her mother and her friend Eva. Her father had given them a handful of introductions to people who turned out not to be the crème de la crème of London's social scene. Daisy had begun to regret her overconfident exit from the Yacht Club Ball: What if it all came to nothing?

But Daisy was determined and resourceful, and she needed no more than a foot in the door. Even at entertainments that were more or less public, such as horse races and operas, she met high-ranking people. She flirted with the men, and she piqued the curiosity of the matrons by letting them know she was rich and single. Many aristocratic English families had been ruined by the Depression, and an American heiress would have been welcome even if she were not pretty and charming. They liked her accent, they tolerated her holding her fork in her right hand, and they were amused that she could drive a car—in England men did the driving. Many English girls could ride a horse as well as Daisy, but few looked so pertly assured in the saddle. Some older women still viewed Daisy with suspicion, but she would win them around eventually, she felt sure.

Bing Westhampton had been easy to flirt with. An elfin man with a winning smile, he had an eye for a pretty girl, and Daisy knew instinctively that more than his eye would be involved if he got the chance of a twilight fumble in the garden. Clearly his daughters took after him.

The Westhamptons' house party was one of several in Cambridgeshire held to coincide with May Week. The guests included Earl Fitzherbert, known as Fitz, and his wife, Bea. She was Countess Fitzherbert, of course, but she preferred her Russian title of princess. Their elder son, Boy, was at Trinity College.

Princess Bea was one of the social matriarchs who were doubtful about Daisy. Without actually telling a lie, Daisy had let people assume that her father was a Russian nobleman who had lost everything in the revolution, rather than a factory worker who had fled to America one step ahead of the police. But Bea was not taken in. "I can't recall a family called Peshkov in St. Petersburg or Moscow," she had said, hardly pretending to be puzzled, and Daisy had forced herself to smile as if it were of no consequence what the princess could remember.

There were three girls the same age as Daisy and Eva: the Westhampton twins plus May Murray, the daughter of a general. The balls went on all night, so everyone slept until midday, but the afternoons were dull. The five girls lazed in the garden or strolled in the woods. Now, sitting up in her hammock, Daisy said: "What can you do *after* you're engaged?"

Lindy said: "You can rub his thing."

"Until it squirts," said her sister.

May Murray, who was not as daring as the twins, said: "Oh, disgusting!"

That only encouraged the twins. "Or you can suck it," said Lindy. "They like that best of all."

"Stop it!" May protested. "You're just making this up."

They stopped, having teased May enough. "I'm bored," said Lindy. "What shall we do?"

An imp of mischief seized Daisy, and she said: "Let's come down to dinner in men's clothes."

She regretted it immediately. A stunt like that could ruin her social career when it had only just got started.

Eva's German sense of propriety was upset. "Daisy, you don't mean it!"

"No," she said. "Silly notion."

The twins had their mother's fine blond hair, not their father's dark curls, but they had inherited his streak of naughtiness, and they both loved the idea. "They'll all be in tailcoats tonight, so we can steal their dinner jackets," said Lindy.

"Yes!" said her twin. "We'll do it while they're having tea."

Daisy saw that it was too late to back out.

May Murray said: "We couldn't go to the ball like that!" The whole party was to attend the Trinity Ball after dinner.

"We'll change again before leaving," said Lizzie.

May was a timid creature, probably cowed by her military father, and she always went along with whatever the other girls decided. Eva as the only dissident was overruled, and the plan went ahead.

When the time came to dress for dinner, a maid brought two evening suits into the bedroom Daisy was sharing with Eva. The maid's name was Ruby. Yesterday she had been miserable with a toothache, so

Daisy had given her the money for a dentist, and she had had the tooth pulled out. Now Ruby was bright-eyed with excitement, toothache forgotten. "Here you are, ladies!" she said. "Sir Bartholomew's should be small enough for you, Miss Peshkov, and Mr. Andrew Fitzherbert's for Miss Rothmann."

Daisy took off her dress and put on the shirt. Ruby helped her with the unfamiliar studs and cuff links. Then she climbed into Bing Westhampton's trousers, black with a satin stripe. She tucked her slip in and pulled the suspenders over her shoulders. She felt a bit daring as she buttoned the fly.

None of the girls knew how to knot a tie, so the results were distinctly limp. But Daisy came up with the winning touch. Using an eyebrow pencil, she gave herself a mustache. "It's marvelous!" said Eva. "You look even prettier!" Daisy drew side-whiskers on Eva's cheeks.

The five girls met up in the twins' bedroom. Daisy walked in with a mannish swagger that made the others giggle hysterically.

May voiced the concern that remained in the back of Daisy's mind. "I hope we're not going to get into trouble over this."

Lindy said: "Oh, who cares if we do?"

Daisy decided to forget her misgivings and enjoy herself, and she led the way down to the drawing room.

They were the first to arrive, and the room was empty. Repeating something she had heard Boy Fitzherbert say to the butler, Daisy put on a man's voice and drawled: "Pour me a whisky, Grimshaw, there's a good chap—this champagne tastes like piss." The others squealed with shocked laughter.

Bing and Fitz came in together. Bing in his white waistcoat made Daisy think of a pied wagtail, a cheeky black-and-white bird. Fitz was a good-looking middle-aged man, his dark hair touched with gray. As a result of war wounds he walked with a slight limp, and one eyelid drooped, but this evidence of his courage in battle only made him more dashing.

Fitz saw the girls, looked twice, and said: "Good God!" His tone was sternly disapproving.

Daisy suffered a moment of sheer panic. Had she spoiled everything? The English could be frightfully straightlaced; everyone knew that. Would she be asked to leave the house? How terrible that would be. Dot Renshaw and Nora Farquharson would crow if she went home in disgrace. She would rather die.

But Bing burst out laughing. "I say, that's terribly good," he said. "Look at this, Grimshaw."

The elderly butler, coming in with a bottle of champagne in a silver ice bucket, observed them bleakly. In a tone of withering insincerity he said: "Most amusing, Sir Bartholomew."

Bing continued to regard them all with a delight mingled with lasciviousness, and Daisy realized—too late—that dressing like the opposite sex might misleadingly suggest, to some men, a degree of sexual freedom and a willingness to experiment—a suggestion that could obviously lead to trouble.

As the party assembled for dinner, most of the other guests followed the lead of their host in treating the girls' prank as an amusing piece of tomfoolery, though Daisy could tell they were not all equally charmed. Daisy's mother went pale with fright when she saw them, and sat down quickly as if she felt shaky. Princess Bea, a heavily corseted woman in her forties who might once have been pretty, wrinkled her powdered brow in a censorious frown. But Lady Westhampton was a jolly woman who reacted to life, as to her wayward husband, with a tolerant smile: she laughed heartily and congratulated Daisy on her mustache.

The boys, coming last, were also delighted. General Murray's son, Lieutenant Jimmy Murray, not as straightlaced as his father, roared with pleased laughter. The Fitzherbert sons, Boy and Andy, came in together, and it was Boy's reaction that was the most interesting of all. He stared at the girls with mesmeric fascination. He tried to cover up with jollity, haw-hawing like the other men, but it was clear he was weirdly captivated.

At dinner the twins picked up Daisy's joke and talked like men, in deep voices and hearty tones, making the others laugh. Lindy held up her wineglass and said: "How do you like this claret, Liz?"

Lizzie replied: "I think it's a bit thin, old boy. I've a notion Bing's been watering it, don't you know."

All through dinner Daisy kept catching Boy staring at her. He did not resemble his handsome father, but all the same he was good-looking, with his mother's blue eyes. She began to feel embarrassed, as if he was ogling her breasts. To break the spell she said: "And have you been taking exams, Boy?"

"Good Lord, no," he said.

His father said: "Too busy flying his plane to study much." This was phrased as a criticism, but it sounded as if Fitz was actually proud of his elder son.

Boy pretended to be outraged. "A slander!" he said.

Eva was mystified. "Why are you at the university if you don't wish to study?"

Lindy explained: "Some of the boys don't bother to graduate, especially if they're not academic types."

Lizzie added: "Especially if they're rich and lazy."

"I do study!" Boy protested. "But I don't intend actually to sit the exams. It's not as if I'm hoping to make a living as a doctor, or something." Boy would inherit one of the largest fortunes in England when Fitz died.

And his lucky wife would be Countess Fitzherbert.

Daisy said: "Wait a minute. Do you really have your own airplane?"

"Yes, I do. A Hornet Moth. I belong to the University Aero Club. We use a little airfield outside the town."

"But that's wonderful! You must take me up!"

Daisy's mother said: "Oh, dear, no!"

Boy said to Daisy: "Wouldn't you be nervous?"

"Not a bit!"

"Then I will take you." He turned to Olga. "It's perfectly safe, Mrs. Peshkov. I promise I'll bring her back in one piece."

Daisy was thrilled.

The conversation moved on to this summer's favorite topic: England's stylish new king, Edward VIII, and his romance with Wallis Simpson, an American woman separated from her second husband.

The London newspapers said nothing about it, except to include Mrs. Simpson on lists of guests at royal events, but Daisy's mother got the American papers sent over, and they were full of speculation that Wallis would divorce Mr. Simpson and marry the king.

"Completely out of the question," said Fitz severely. "The king is the head of the Church of England. He cannot possibly marry a divorcée."

When the ladies retired, leaving the men to port and cigars, the girls hurried to change. Daisy decided to emphasize how very feminine she really was, and chose a ball dress of pink silk patterned with tiny flowers that had a matching jacket with puffed short sleeves.

Eva wore a dramatically simple black silk gown with no sleeves. In the past year she had lost weight, changed her hair, and learned—under Daisy's tuition—to dress in an unfussy tailored style that flattered her. Eva had become like one of the family, and Olga delighted in buying clothes for her. Daisy regarded her as the sister she never had.

It was still light when they all climbed into cars and carriages and drove the five miles into the town center.

Daisy thought Cambridge was the quaintest place she had ever seen, with its winding little streets and elegant college buildings. They got out at Trinity and Daisy gazed up at the statue of its founder, King Henry VIII. When they passed through the sixteenth-century brick gatehouse, Daisy gasped with pleasure at the sight that met her eyes: a large quadrangle, its trimmed green lawn crossed by cobbled paths, with an elaborate architectural fountain in the middle. On all four sides, timeworn buildings of golden stone formed the backdrop against which young men in tailcoats danced with gorgeously dressed girls, and dozens of waiters in evening dress offered trays crowded with glasses of champagne. Daisy clapped her hands with joy: this was just the kind of thing she loved.

She danced with Boy, then Jimmy Murray, then Bing, who held her close and let his right hand drift from the small of her back down to the swell of her hips. She decided not to protest. The English band played a watery imitation of American jazz, but they were loud and fast, and they knew all the latest hits.

Night fell, and the quadrangle was illuminated with blazing torches.

Daisy took a break to check on Eva, who was not so self-confident and sometimes needed to be introduced around. However, she need not have worried: she found Eva talking to a strikingly handsome student in a suit too big for him. Eva introduced him as Lloyd Williams. "We've been talking about Fascism in Germany," Lloyd said, as if Daisy might want to join in the discussion.

"How extraordinarily dull of you," Daisy said.

Lloyd seemed not to hear that. "I was in Berlin three years ago, when Hitler came to power. I didn't meet Eva then, but it turns out we have some acquaintances in common."

Jimmy Murray appeared and asked Eva to dance. Lloyd was visibly disappointed to see her go, but summoned his manners and graciously asked Daisy, and they moved closer to the band. "What an interesting person your friend Eva is," he said.

"Why, Mr. Williams, that's what every girl longs to hear from her dancing partner," Daisy replied. As soon as the words were out of her mouth, she regretted sounding shrewish.

But he was amused. He grinned and said: "Dear me, you're so right. I am justly reproved. I must try to be more gallant."

She immediately liked him better for being able to laugh at himself. It showed confidence.

He said: "Are you staying at Chimbleigh, like Eva?"

"Yes."

"Then you must be the American who gave Ruby Carter the money for the dentist."

"How on earth do you know about that?"

"She's a friend of mine."

Daisy was surprised. "Do many undergraduates befriend housemaids?"

"My goodness, what a snobbish thing to say! My mother was a housemaid, before she became a member of Parliament."

Daisy felt herself blush. She hated snobbery and often accused others of it, especially in Buffalo. She thought she was totally innocent of such unworthy attitudes. "I've got off on the wrong foot with you, haven't I?" she said as the dance came to an end.

"Not really," he said. "You think it's dull to talk about Fascism, yet you take a German refugee into your home and even invite her to travel to England with you. You think housemaids have no right to be friends with undergraduates, yet you pay for Ruby to see the dentist. I don't suppose I'll meet another girl half as intriguing as you tonight."

"I'll take that as a compliment."

"Here comes your Fascist friend, Boy Fitzherbert. Do you want me to scare him off?"

Daisy sensed that Lloyd would relish the chance of a quarrel with Boy. "Certainly not!" she said, and turned to smile at Boy.

Boy nodded curtly to Lloyd. "Evening, Williams."

"Good evening," said Lloyd. "I was disappointed that your Fascists marched along Hills Road last Saturday."

"Ah, yes," Boy said. "They got a bit overenthusiastic."

"It surprised me, when you had given your word they would not." Daisy saw that Lloyd was angry about this, underneath his mask of cool courtesy.

Boy refused to take it seriously. "Sorry about that," he said lightly. He turned to Daisy. "Come and see the library," he said to her. "It's by Christopher Wren."

"With pleasure!" Daisy said. She waved good-bye to Lloyd and let Boy take her arm. Lloyd looked disappointed to see her go, which pleased her.

On the west side of the quadrangle a passage led to a courtyard with a single elegant building at the far end. Daisy admired the cloisters on the ground floor. Boy explained that the books were on the upper floor, because the river Cam was liable to flood. "Let's go and look at the river," he said. "It's pretty at night."

Daisy was twenty years old and, though she was inexperienced, she knew that Boy did not really care for gazing on rivers at night. But she wondered, after his reaction to seeing her in men's clothing, whether he might really prefer boys to girls. She guessed she was about to find out.

"Do you actually know the king?" she asked as he led her across a second courtyard.

"Yes. He's more my father's friend, obviously, but he comes to our house sometimes. And he's jolly keen on some of my political ideas, I can tell you."

"I'd love to meet him." She was sounding naïve, she knew, but this was her chance and she was not going to miss it.

They passed through a gateway and emerged onto a smooth lawn sloping down to a narrow walled-in river. "This area is called the Backs," Boy said. "Most of the older colleges own the fields on the other side of the water." He put his arm around her waist as they approached a little bridge. His hand moved up, as if accidentally, until his forefinger lay along the underside of her breast.

At the far end of the little bridge two college servants in uniform stood guard, presumably to repel gatecrashers. One of the men murmured: "Good evening, Viscount Aberowen," and the other smothered a grin. Boy responded with a barely perceptible nod. Daisy wondered how many other girls he had led across this bridge.

She knew Boy had a motive for giving her this tour, and sure enough, he stopped in the darkness and put his hands on her shoulders. "I say, you looked jolly fetching in that outfit at dinner." His voice was throaty with excitement.

"I'm glad you thought so." She knew the kiss was coming, and she felt aroused at the prospect, but she was not quite ready. She put a hand on his shirtfront, palm flat, holding him at a distance. "I really want to be presented at the royal court," she said. "Is it difficult to arrange?"

"Not difficult at all," he said. "Not for my family, at least. And not for someone as pretty as you." He dipped his head eagerly toward hers.

She leaned away. "Would you do that for me? Will you fix it for me to be presented?"

"Of course."

She moved in closer, and felt the erection bulging at the front of his trousers. No, she thought, he doesn't prefer boys. "Promise?" she said.

"I promise," he said breathlessly.

"Thank you," she said; then she let him kiss her.

## iii

The little house in Wellington Row, Aberowen, South Wales, was crowded at one o'clock on Saturday afternoon. Lloyd's grandfather sat at the kitchen table looking proud. On one side he had his son, Billy Williams, a coal miner who had become member of Parliament for Aberowen. On the other was his grandson, Lloyd, the Cambridge University student. Absent was his daughter, also a member of Parliament. It was the Williams dynasty. No one here would ever say that—the notion of a dynasty was undemocratic, and these people believed in democracy the way the pope believed in God—but just the same Lloyd suspected Granda was thinking it.

Also at the table was Uncle Billy's lifelong friend and agent, Tom Griffiths. Lloyd was honored to sit with such men. Granda was a veteran of the miners' union; Uncle Billy had been court-martialed in 1919 for revealing Britain's secret war against the Bolsheviks; Tom had fought alongside Billy at the Battle of the Somme. This was more impressive than dining with royalty.

Lloyd's grandmother, Cara Williams, had served them stewed beef with homemade bread, and now they sat drinking tea and smoking. Friends and neighbors had come in, as they always did when Billy was here, and half a dozen of them stood leaning against the walls, smoking pipes and hand-rolled cigarettes, filling the little kitchen with the smell of men and tobacco.

Billy had the short stature and broad shoulders of many miners but, unlike the others, he was well dressed, in a navy blue suit with a clean white shirt and a red tie. Lloyd noticed that they all used his first name often, as if to emphasize that he was one of them, empowered by their votes. They called Lloyd "boyo," making it clear they were not overimpressed by a university student. But they addressed Granda as Mr. Williams: he was the one they truly respected.

Through the open back door Lloyd could see the slag heap from the mine, an ever-growing mountain that had now reached the lane behind the house.

Lloyd was spending the summer vacation as a low-paid organizer at a camp for unemployed colliers. Their project was to refurbish the Miners' Institute Library. Lloyd found the physical work of sanding and painting and building shelves a refreshing change from reading Schiller in German and Molière in French. He enjoyed the banter among the men: he had inherited from his mother a love of the Welsh sense of humor.

It was great, but it was not fighting Fascism. He winced every time he remembered how he had skulked in the Baptist chapel while Boy Fitzherbert and the other bullies chanted in the street and threw stones through the window. He wished he had gone outside and punched someone. It might have been stupid but he would have felt better. He thought about it every night before falling asleep.

He also thought about Daisy Peshkov in a pink silk jacket with puffed sleeves.

He had seen Daisy a second time in May Week. He had gone to a recital in the chapel of King's College, because the student in the room next to his at Emmanuel was playing the cello, and Daisy had been in the audience with the Westhamptons. She had been wearing a straw hat with a turned-up brim that made her look like a naughty schoolgirl. He had sought her out afterward, and asked her questions about America, where he had never been. He wanted to know about President Roosevelt's administration, and whether it had any lessons to teach Britain, but all Daisy talked about was tennis parties and polo matches and yacht clubs. Despite that, he had been captivated by her all over again. He liked her gay chatter all the more because it was punctuated, now and again, by unexpected darts of sarcastic wit. He had said: "I don't want to keep you from your friends—I just wanted to ask about the New Deal," and she had replied: "Oh, boy, you really know how to flatter a girl." But then, as they parted, she had said: "Call me when you come to London—Mayfair two four three four."

Today he had come to his grandparents' house for the midday meal, on his way to the railway station. He had a few days off from the work camp, and he was taking the train to London for a short break. He was vaguely hoping he might run into Daisy, as if London were a little town like Aberowen.

At the camp he was in charge of political education, and he told his grandfather he had organized a series of lectures by left-wing dons from Cambridge. "I tell them it's their chance to get out of the ivory tower and meet the working class, and they find it hard to refuse me."

Granda's pale blue eyes looked down his long, sharp nose. "I hope our lads teach them a thing or two about the real world."

Lloyd pointed to Tom Griffiths' son, standing in the open back door and listening. At sixteen Lenny already had the characteristic Griffiths shadow of a black beard that never went away even when his cheeks were freshly shaved. "Lenny had an argument with a Marxist lecturer."

"Good for you, Len," said Granda. Marxism was popular in South Wales, which was sometimes jokingly called Little Moscow, but Granda had always been fiercely anti-Communist.

Lloyd said: "Tell Granda what you said, Lenny."

Lenny grinned and said: "'In 1872 the anarchist leader Mikhail Bakunin warned Karl Marx that Communists in power would be as oppressive as the aristocracy they replaced. After what has happened in Russia, can you honestly say Bakunin was wrong?'"

Granda clapped his hands. A good debating point had always been relished around his kitchen table.

Lloyd's grandmother poured him a fresh cup of tea. Cara Williams was gray, lined, and bent, like all the women of her age in Aberowen. She asked Lloyd: "Are you courting yet, my lovely?"

The men grinned and winked.

Lloyd blushed. "Too busy studying, Grandmam." But an image of Daisy Peshkov came into his mind, together with the phone number: Mayfair two four three four.

His grandmother said: "Who's this Ruby Carter, then?"

The men laughed, and Uncle Billy said: "Caught out, boyo!"

Lloyd's mother had obviously been talking. "Ruby is membership officer of my local Labour Party in Cambridge, that's all," Lloyd protested.

Billy said sarcastically: "Oh, aye, very convincing," and the men laughed again.

"You wouldn't want me to go out with Ruby, Grandmam," Lloyd said. "You'd think she wears her clothes too tight."

"She doesn't sound very suitable," Cara said. "You're a university man, now. You must set your sights higher."

She was just as snobbish as Daisy, Lloyd perceived. "There's nothing wrong with Ruby Carter," he said. "But I'm not in love with her."

"You must marry an educated woman, a schoolteacher or a trained nurse."

The trouble was that she was right. Lloyd liked Ruby, but he would never love her. She was pretty enough, and intelligent, too, and Lloyd was as vulnerable as the next man to a curvy figure, but still he knew she was not right for him. Worse, Grandmam had put her wrinkled old finger precisely on the reason: Ruby's outlook was restricted, her horizons narrow. She was not exciting. Not like Daisy.

"That's enough women's chatter," Granda said. "Billy, tell us the news from Spain."

"It's bad," said Billy.

All Europe was watching Spain. The left-wing government elected last February had suffered an attempted military coup backed by Fascists and conservatives. The rebel general Franco had won support from the Catholic Church. The news had struck the rest of the continent like an earthquake. After Germany and Italy would Spain, too, fall under the curse of Fascism?

"The revolt was botched, as you probably know, and it almost failed," Billy went on. "But Hitler and Mussolini came to the rescue, and saved the insurrection by airlifting thousands of rebel troops from North Africa as reinforcements."

Lenny put in: "And the unions saved the government!"

"That's true," Billy said. "The government was slow to react, but the trade unions led the way in organizing workers and arming them with weapons they seized from military arsenals, ships, gun shops, and anywhere else they could find them."

Granda said: "At least someone is fighting back. Until now the Fascists have had it all their own way. In the Rhineland and Abyssinia, they just walked in and took what they wanted. Thank God for the Spanish people, I say. They've got the guts to say no."

There was a murmur of agreement from the men around the walls.

Lloyd again recalled that Saturday afternoon in Cambridge. He, too, had let the Fascists have it all their own way. He seethed with frustration.

"But can they win?" said Granda. "Weapons seem to be the issue now, aren't they?"

"Aye," said Billy. "The Germans and the Italians are supplying the rebels with guns and ammunition, as well as fighter planes and pilots. But no one is helping the elected Spanish government."

"And why the bloody hell not?" said Lenny angrily.

Cara looked up from the cooking range. Her dark Mediterranean eyes flashed disapproval, and Lloyd thought he glimpsed the beautiful girl she had once been. "None of that language in my kitchen!" she said.

"Sorry, Mrs. Williams."

"I can tell you the inside story," Billy said, and the men went quiet, listening. "The French prime minister, Léon Blum—a socialist, as you know—was all set to help. He's already got one Fascist neighbor, Germany, and the last thing he wants is a Fascist regime on his southern border, too. Sending arms to the Spanish government would enrage the French right wing, and French Catholic socialists, too, but Blum could withstand that, especially if he had British support and could say that arming the government was an international initiative."

Granda said: "So what went wrong?"

"Our government talked him out of it. Blum came to London and our foreign secretary, Anthony Eden, told him we would not support him."

Granda was angered. "Why does he need support? How can a socialist prime minister let himself be bullied by the conservative government of another country?"

"Because there's a danger of a military coup in France, too," said Billy. "The press there is rabidly right-wing, and they're whipping their own Fascists into a frenzy. Blum can fight them off with British support—but perhaps not without."

"So it's our Conservative government being soft on Fascism again!"

"All those Tories have investments in Spain—wine, textiles, coal, steel—and they're afraid the left-wing government will expropriate them."

"What about America? They believe in democracy. Surely they'll sell guns to Spain?"

"You'd think so, wouldn't you? But there's a well-financed Catholic lobby, led by a millionaire called Joseph Kennedy, opposing any help to the Spanish government. And a Democratic president needs Catholic support. Roosevelt won't do anything to jeopardize his New Deal."

"Well, there's something we can do," said Lenny Griffiths, and a look of adolescent defiance came over his face.

"What's that, Len boy?" said Billy.

"We can go to Spain and fight."

His father said: "Don't talk daft, Lenny."

"Lots of people are talking about going, all over the world, even in America. They want to form volunteer units to fight alongside the regular army."

Lloyd sat upright. "Do they?" This was the first he had heard of it. "How do you know?"

"I read about it in the *Daily Herald*."

Lloyd was electrified. Volunteers going to Spain to fight the Fascists!

Tom Griffiths said to Lenny: "Well, you're not going, and that's that."

Billy said: "Remember those boys who lied about their age to fight in the Great War? Thousands of them."

"And totally useless, most of them," Tom said. "I recall that kid who cried before the Somme. What was his name, Billy?"

"Owen Bevin. He ran away, didn't he?"

"Aye—to a firing squad. The bastards shot him for desertion. Fifteen, he was, poor little tyke."

Lenny said: "I'm sixteen."

"Aye," said his father. "Big difference, that."

Granda said: "Lloyd here is going to miss the train to London in about ten minutes."

Lloyd had been so struck by Lenny's revelation that he had not kept an eye on the clock. He jumped up, kissed his grandmother, and picked up his small suitcase.

Lenny said: "I'll walk with you to the station."

Lloyd said his good-byes and hurried down the hill. Lenny said nothing, seeming preoccupied. Lloyd was glad not to have to talk: his mind was in turmoil.

The train was in. Lloyd bought a third-class ticket to London. As he was about to board, Lenny said: "Tell me, now, Lloyd, how do you get a passport?"

"You're serious about going to Spain, aren't you?"

"Come on, man, don't muck about. I want to know."

The whistle blew. Lloyd climbed aboard, closed the door, and let down the window. "You go to the post office and ask for a form," he said.

Lenny said despondently: "If I went to the Aberowen Post Office and asked for a passport form, my mother would hear of it about thirty seconds later."

"Then go to Cardiff," said Lloyd, and the train pulled away.

He settled in his seat and took from his pocket a copy of *Le Rouge et le Noir* by Stendhal in French. He stared at the page without taking anything in. He could think of only one idea: going to Spain.

He knew he should be scared, but all he felt was excitement at the prospect of fighting—really fighting, not just holding meetings—against the kind of men who had set the dogs on Jörg. No doubt fear would come later. Before a boxing match he was not scared in the dressing room. But when he entered the ring and saw the man who wanted to beat him unconscious, looked at the muscular shoulders and the hard fists and the vicious face, then his mouth went dry and his heart pounded and he had to suppress the impulse to turn and run away.

Right now he was mainly worried about his parents. Bernie was so proud of having a stepson at Cambridge—he had told half the East End—and he would be devastated if Lloyd left before getting his degree.

Ethel would be frightened that her son might be wounded or killed. They would both be terribly upset.

There were other issues. How would he get to Spain? What city would he go to? How would he pay the fare? But only one snag really gave him pause.

Daisy Peshkov.

He told himself not to be ridiculous. He had met her twice. She was not even very interested in him. That was smart of her, because they were ill-suited. She was a millionaire's daughter and a shallow socialite who thought talking about politics was dull. She liked men such as Boy Fitzherbert; that alone proved she was wrong for Lloyd. Yet he could not get her out of his mind, and the thought of going to Spain and losing all chance of seeing her again filled him with sadness.

Mayfair two four three four.

He felt ashamed of his hesitation, especially when he recalled Lenny's simple determination. Lloyd had been talking about fighting Fascism for years. Now there was a chance to do it. How could he not go?

He reached London's Paddington station, took the Tube to Aldgate, and walked to the row house in Nutley Street where he had been born. He let himself in with his own key. The place had not changed much since he was a child, but one innovation was the telephone on a little table next to the hat stand. It was the only phone on the street, and the neighbors treated it as public property. Beside the phone was a box in which they placed the money for their calls.

His mother was in the kitchen. She had her hat on, ready to go out to address a Labour Party meeting—what else?—but she put the kettle on and made him tea. "How are they all in Aberowen?" she asked.

"Uncle Billy is there this weekend," he said. "All the neighbors came into Granda's kitchen. It's like a medieval court."

"Are your grandparents well?"

"Granda is the same as ever. Grandmam looks older." He paused. "Lenny Griffiths wants to go to Spain, to fight the Fascists."

She pursed her lips in disapproval. "Does he, now?"

"I'm considering going with him. What do you think?"

He was expecting opposition, but even so her reaction surprised him. "Don't you bloody dare," she said savagely. She did not share her mother's aversion to swear words. "Don't even speak of it!" She slammed the teapot down on the kitchen table. "I bore you in pain and suffering, and raised you, and put shoes on your feet and sent you to school, and I didn't go through all that for you to throw your life away in a bloody war!"

He was taken aback. "I wasn't thinking of throwing my life away," he said. "But I might risk it in a cause you brought me up to believe in."

To his astonishment she began to sob. She rarely cried—in fact Lloyd could not remember the last time.

"Mother, don't." He put his arm around her shaking shoulders. "It hasn't happened yet."

Bernie came into the kitchen, a stocky middle-aged man with a bald dome. "What's all this?" he said. He looked a bit scared.

Lloyd said: "I'm sorry, Dad. I've upset her." He stepped back and let Bernie put his arms around Ethel.

She wailed: "He's going to Spain! He'll be killed!"

"Let's all calm down and discuss it sensibly," Bernie said. He was a sensible man wearing a sensible dark suit and much-repaired shoes with sensible thick soles. No doubt that was why people voted for him: he was a local politician, representing Aldgate on the London County Council. Lloyd had never known his own father, but he could not imagine loving a real father more than he loved Bernie, who had been a gentle stepfather, quick to comfort and advise, slow to command or punish. He treated Lloyd no differently from his daughter, Millie.

Bernie persuaded Ethel to sit at the kitchen table, and Lloyd poured her a cup of tea.

"I thought my brother was dead, once," Ethel said, her tears still flowing. "The telegrams came to Wellington Row, and the wretched boy from the post office had to go from one house to the next, giving men and women the bits of paper that said their sons and husbands were dead. Poor lad, what was his name? Geraint, I think. But he didn't have a telegram for our house and, wicked woman that I am, I thanked God it was others that had died and not our Billy!"

"You're not a wicked woman," Bernie said, patting her.

Lloyd's half sister, Millie, appeared from upstairs. She was sixteen, but looked older, especially dressed as she was this evening, in a stylish black outfit and small gold earrings. For two years she had worked in a women's-wear shop in Aldgate, but she was bright and ambitious, and in the last few days she had got a job in a swanky West End department store. She looked at Ethel and said: "Mam, what's the matter?" She spoke with a cockney accent.

"Your brother wants to go to Spain and get himself killed!" Ethel cried.

Millie looked accusingly at Lloyd. "What have you been saying to her?" Millie was always quick to find fault with her older brother, who she felt was undeservedly adored.

Lloyd responded with fond tolerance. "Lenny Griffiths from Aberowen is going to fight the Fascists, and I told Mam I was thinking about going with him."

"Trust you," Millie said disgustedly.

"I doubt if you can get there," said Bernie, ever practical. "After all, the country is in the middle of a civil war."

"I can get a train to Marseilles. Barcelona's not far from the French border."

"Eighty or ninety miles. And it's a cold walk over the Pyrenees."

"There must be ships going from Marseilles to Barcelona. It's not so far by sea."

"True."

"Stop it, Bernie!" Ethel cried. "You sound as if you're discussing the quickest way to Piccadilly Circus. He's talking about going to war! I won't allow it."

"He's twenty-one, you know," Bernie said. "We can't stop him."

"I know how bloody old he is!"

Bernie looked at his watch. "We need to get to the meeting. You're the main speaker. And Lloyd's not going to Spain tonight."

"How do you know?" she said. "We might get home and find a note saying he's caught the boat train to Paris!"

"I tell you what," said Bernie. "Lloyd, promise your mother you won't go for a month at least. It's not a bad idea anyway—you need to check the lie of the land before you rush off. Set her mind at ease, just temporarily. Then we can talk about it again."

It was a typical Bernie compromise, calculated to let everyone back off without backing down, but Lloyd was reluctant to make a commitment. On the other hand he probably could not simply jump on a train. He had to find out what arrangements the Spanish government might be making to receive volunteers. Ideally he would go in company with Lenny and others. He would need visas, foreign currency, a pair of boots . . . "All right," he said. "I won't go for a month."

"Promise," his mother said.

"I promise."

Ethel became calm. After a minute she powdered her face and looked more normal. She drank her tea.

Then she put her coat on, and she and Bernie left.

"Right, I'm off, too," said Millie.

"Where are you going?" Lloyd asked her.

"The Gaiety."

It was a music hall in the East End. "Do they let sixteen-year-olds in?"

She gave him an arch look. "Who's sixteen? Not me. Anyway, Dave's going and he's only fifteen." She was speaking of their cousin David Williams, son of Uncle Billy and Aunt Mildred.

"Well, enjoy yourselves."

She went to the door and came back. "Just don't get killed in Spain, you stupid sod." She put her arms around him and hugged him hard, then went out without saying any more.

When he heard the front door slam, he went to the phone.

He did not have to think to recall the number. He could see Daisy in his mind's eye, turning as she left him, smiling winningly under the straw hat, saying: "Mayfair two four three four."

He picked up the phone and dialed.

What was he going to say? "You told me to phone, so here I am." That was feeble. The truth? "I don't admire you at all, but I can't get you off my mind." He should invite her to something, but what? A Labour Party meeting?

A man answered. "This is Mrs. Peshkov's residence. Good evening." The deferential tone made Lloyd think he was a butler. No doubt Daisy's mother had rented a London house complete with staff.

"This is Lloyd Williams . . ." He wanted to say something that would explain or justify his call, and he added the first thing that came to mind: ". . . of Emmanuel College." It meant nothing but he hoped it sounded impressive. "May I speak to Miss Daisy Peshkov?"

"No, I'm sorry, Professor Williams," said the butler, assuming Lloyd must be a don. "They've all gone to the opera."

Of course, Lloyd thought with disappointment. No socialite was home at this time of the evening, especially on a Saturday. "I remember," he lied. "She told me she was going, and I forgot. Covent Garden, isn't it?" He held his breath.

But the butler was not suspicious. "Yes, sir. *The Magic Flute*, I believe."

"Thank you." Lloyd hung up.

He went to his room and changed. In the West End most people wore evening dress, even to go to the cinema. But what would he do when he got there? He could not afford a ticket to the opera, and anyway it would be over soon.

He took the Tube. The Royal Opera House was incongruously located next to Covent Garden, London's wholesale fruit and vegetable market. The two institutions got along well because they kept different hours: the market opened for business at three or four o'clock in the morning, when London's most determined revelers were beginning to head for home, and it closed before the matinee.

Lloyd walked past the shuttered stalls of the market and looked through glazed doors into the opera house. Its bright lobby was empty, and he could hear muffled Mozart. He stepped inside. Adopting a careless upper-class manner, he said to an attendant: "What time does the curtain come down?"

If he had been wearing his tweed suit, he would probably have been told it was none of his business, but the dinner jacket was the uniform of authority, and the attendant said: "In about five minutes, sir."

Lloyd nodded curtly. To say "Thank you" would have given him away.

He left the building and walked around the block. It was a moment of quiet. In the restaurants, people were ordering coffee; in the cinemas, the big feature was approaching its melodramatic climax. Everything would change soon, and the streets would be thronged with people shouting for taxis, heading to nightclubs, kissing good-bye at bus stops, and hurrying for the last train back to the suburbs.

He returned to the opera house and went inside. The orchestra was silent, and the audience was just beginning to emerge. Released from long imprisonment in their seats, they were talking animatedly, praising the singers, criticizing the costumes, and making plans for late suppers.

He saw Daisy almost immediately.

She was wearing a lavender dress with a little cape of champagne-colored mink over her bare shoulders, and she looked ravishing. She emerged from the auditorium at the head of a small clutch of people her own age. Lloyd was sorry to recognize Boy Fitzherbert beside her, and to see her laugh gaily at something he murmured to her as they stepped down the red-carpeted stairs. Behind her was the interesting German girl, Eva Rothmann, escorted by a tall young man in the kind of military evening dress known as a mess kit.

Eva recognized Lloyd and smiled, and he spoke to her in German. "Good evening, Fräulein Rothmann, I hope you enjoyed the opera."

"Very much, thank you," she replied in the same language. "I didn't realize you were in the audience."

Boy said amiably: "I say, speak English, you lot." He sounded slightly drunk. He was good-looking in a dissipated way, like a sulkily handsome adolescent, or a pedigree dog that is fed too many scraps. He had a pleasant manner, and probably could be devastatingly charming when he chose.

Eva said in English: "Viscount Aberowen, this is Mr. Williams."

"We know each other," said Boy. "He's at Emma."

Daisy said: "Hello, Lloyd. We're going slumming."

Lloyd had heard this word before. It meant going to the East End to visit low pubs and watch working-class entertainment such as dogfights.

Boy said: "I bet Williams knows some places."

Lloyd hesitated only a fraction of a second. Was he willing to put up with Boy in order to be with Daisy? Of course he was. "As a matter of fact, I do," he said. "Do you want me to show you?"

"Splendid!"

An older woman appeared and wagged a finger at Boy. "You must have these girls home by midnight," she said in an American accent. "Not a second later, please." Lloyd guessed she must be Daisy's mother.

The tall man in the military outfit replied: "Leave it to the army, Mrs. Peshkov. We'll be on time."

Behind Mrs. Peshkov came Earl Fitzherbert with a fat woman who must have been his wife. Lloyd would have liked to question the earl about his government's policy on Spain.

Two cars were waiting for them outside. The earl, his wife, and Daisy's mother got into a black-and-cream Rolls-Royce Phantom III. Boy and his group piled into the other car, a dark blue Daimler E20 limousine, the royal family's favorite car. There were seven young people including Lloyd. Eva seemed to be with the soldier, who introduced himself to Lloyd as Lieutenant Jimmy Murray. The third girl was his sister, May, and the other boy—a slimmer, quieter version of Boy— turned out to be Andy Fitzherbert.

Lloyd gave the chauffeur directions to the Gaiety.

He noticed that Jimmy Murray discreetly slipped his arm around Eva's waist. Her reaction was to move slightly closer to him: obviously they were courting. Lloyd was happy for her. She was not a pretty girl, but she was intelligent and charming. He liked her, and he was glad she had found herself a tall soldier. He wondered, though, how others in this upper-class social set would react if Jimmy announced he was going to marry a half-Jewish German girl.

It occurred to him that the others formed two more couples: Andy and May, and—annoyingly—Boy and Daisy. Lloyd was the odd one out.

Not wanting to stare at them, he studied the polished mahogany window surrounds.

The car went up Ludgate Hill to St. Paul's Cathedral. "Take Cheapside," Lloyd said to the driver.

Boy took a long pull from a silver hip flask. Wiping his mouth, he said: "You know your way around, Williams."

"I live here," said Lloyd. "I was born in the East End."

"How splendid," said Boy, and Lloyd was not sure whether he was being thoughtlessly polite or unpleasantly sarcastic.

All the seats were taken at the Gaiety, but there was plenty of standing room, and the audience moved around constantly, greeting friends and going to the bar. They were dressed up, the women in brightly colored frocks, the men in their best suits. The air was warm and smoky, and there was a powerful odor of spilled beer. Lloyd found a place for his group near the back. Their clothes identified them as visitors from the West End, but they were not the only ones: music halls were popular with all classes.

Onstage a middle-aged performer in a red dress and blond wig was doing a double-entendre routine. "I said to him, 'I'm not letting you into my passage.'" The audience roared with laughter. "He said to me, 'I can see it from here, love.' I told him, 'You keep your nose out.'" She was pretending indignation. "He said, 'It looks to me like it needs a good clean-out.' Well! I ask you."

Lloyd saw that Daisy was grinning widely. He leaned over and murmured in her ear: "Do you realize it's a man?"

"No!" she said.

"Look at the hands."

"Oh, my God!" she said. "She's a man!"

Lloyd's cousin David walked past, spotted Lloyd, and came back. "What are you all dressed up for?" he said in a cockney accent. He was wearing a knotted scarf and a cloth cap.

"Hello, Dave, how's life?"

"I'm going to Spain with you and Lenny Griffiths," Dave said.

"No, you're not," said Lloyd. "You're fifteen."

"Boys my age fought in the Great War."

"But they were no use—ask your father. Anyway, who says I'm going?"

"Your sister, Millie," Dave said, and he walked on.

Boy said: "What do people usually drink in this place, Williams?"

Lloyd thought Boy did not need any more alcohol, but he replied: "Pints of best bitter for the men and port-and-lemon for the girls."

"Port-and-lemon?"

"It's port diluted with lemonade."

"How perfectly ghastly." Boy disappeared.

The comedian reached the climax of the act. "I said to him, 'You fool, *that's the wrong passage!*'" She, or he, went off to gales of applause.

Millie appeared in front of Lloyd. "Hello," she said. She looked at Daisy. "Who's your friend?"

Lloyd was glad Millie looked so pretty, in her sophisticated black dress, with a row of fake pearls and a discreet touch of makeup. He said: "Miss Peshkov, allow me to present my sister, Miss Leckwith. Millie, this is Daisy."

They shook hands. Daisy said: "I'm very glad to meet Lloyd's sister."

"Half sister, to be exact," said Millie.

Lloyd explained: "My father was killed in the Great War. I never knew him. My mother married again when I was still a baby."

"Enjoy the show," Millie said, turning away; then, as she left, she murmured to Lloyd: "Now I see why Ruby Carter has no chance."

Lloyd groaned inwardly. His mother had obviously told the whole family that he was romancing Ruby.

Daisy said: "Who's Ruby Carter?"

"She's a maid at Chimbleigh. You gave her the money to see a dentist."

"I remember. So her name is being romantically linked with yours."

"In the imagination of my mother, yes."

Daisy laughed at his discomfiture. "So you're not going to marry a housemaid."

"I'm not going to marry Ruby."

"She might suit you very well."

Lloyd gave her a direct look. "We don't always fall in love with the most suitable people, do we?"

She looked at the stage. The show was approaching its end, and the entire cast was beginning a familiar song. The audience joined in enthusiastically. The standing customers at the back linked arms and swayed in time, and Boy's party did likewise.

When the curtain came down, Boy still had not reappeared. "I'll look for him," Lloyd said. "I think I know where he might be." The Gaiety had a ladies' toilet, but the men's was a backyard with an earth closet and several halved oil drums. Lloyd found Boy puking into one of the drums.

He gave Boy a handkerchief to wipe his mouth, then took his arm and led him through the emptying theater and outside to the Daimler limousine. The others were waiting. They all got in and Boy immediately fell asleep.

When they got back to the West End, Andy Fitzherbert told the driver to go first to the Murray house, in a modest street near Trafalgar Square. Getting out of the car with May, he said: "You lot go on. I'll see May to her door, then walk home." Lloyd presumed that Andy was planning a romantic good night on May's doorstep.

They drove on to Mayfair. As the car was approaching Grosvenor Square, where Daisy and Eva were living, Jimmy told the chauffeur: "Just stop at the corner, please." Then he said quietly to Lloyd: "I say, Williams, would you mind taking Miss Peshkov to the door, and I'll follow with Fräulein Rothmann in half a minute?"

"Of course." Jimmy wanted to kiss Eva good night in the car, obviously. Boy would know nothing about it: he was snoring. The chauffeur would pretend to be oblivious in the expectation of a tip.

Lloyd got out of the car and handed Daisy out. When she grasped his hand, he got a thrill like a mild electric shock. He took her arm and they walked slowly along the pavement. At the midpoint between two streetlamps, where the light was dimmest, Daisy stopped. "Let's give them time," she said.

Lloyd said: "I'm so glad Eva has a paramour."

"Me, too."

He took a breath. "I can't say the same about you and Boy Fitzherbert."

"He got me presented at court!" Daisy said. "And I danced with the king in a nightclub—it was in all the American newspapers."

"And that's why you're courting him?" Lloyd said incredulously.

"Not only. He likes all the things I do—parties and racehorses and beautiful clothes. He's such fun! He even has his own airplane."

"None of that means anything," Lloyd said. "Give him up. Be my girlfriend instead."

She looked pleased, but she laughed. "You're crazy," she said. "But I like you."

"I mean it," he said desperately. "I can't stop thinking about you, even though you're the last person in the world I should marry."

She laughed again. "You say the rudest things! I don't know why I talk to you. I guess I think you're nice under your clumsy manners."

"I'm not really clumsy—only with you."

"I believe you. But I'm not going to marry a penniless socialist."

Lloyd had opened his heart only to be charmingly rejected, and now he felt miserable. He looked back at the Daimler. "I wonder how long they're going to be," he said disconsolately.

Daisy said: "I might kiss a socialist, though, just to see what it's like."

For a moment he did not react. He assumed she was speaking theoretically. But a girl would never say something like that theoretically. It was an invitation. He had almost been stupid enough to miss it.

He moved closer, putting his hands on her small waist. She tilted her face up, and her beauty took his breath away. He bent his head and kissed her mouth softly. She did not close her eyes, and neither did he. He felt tremendously aroused, staring into her blue eyes as he moved his lips against hers. She opened her mouth slightly, and he touched her parted lips with the tip of his tongue. A moment later he felt her tongue respond. She was still looking at him. He was in paradise, and he wanted to stay locked in this embrace for all eternity. She pressed her body to his. He had an erection, and he was embarrassed in case she might feel it, so he eased back—but she pushed forward again, and he understood, looking into her eyes, that she wanted to feel his penis pressed against her soft body. The realization heated him unbearably. He felt as if he was going to ejaculate, and it occurred to him that she might even want him to.

Then he heard the door of the Daimler open, and Jimmy Murray speaking with slightly unnatural loudness, as if giving a warning. Lloyd broke the embrace with Daisy.

"Well," she murmured in a surprised tone, "that was an unexpected pleasure."

Lloyd said hoarsely: "More than a pleasure."

Then Jimmy and Eva were beside them, and they all walked to the door of Mrs. Peshkov's house. It was a grand building with steps up to a covered porch. Lloyd wondered if the porch might give shelter enough for another kiss, but as they climbed the steps, the door was opened from the inside by a man in evening dress, probably the butler Lloyd had spoken to earlier. How glad he was that he had made that phone call!

The two girls said good night demurely, giving no hint that only seconds ago they had both been locked in passionate embraces; then the door closed and they were gone.

Lloyd and Jimmy went back down the steps.

"I'm going to walk from here," Jimmy said. "Shall I tell the chauffeur to drive you back to the East End? You must be three or four miles from home. And Boy won't care—he'll sleep until breakfast time, I should think."

"That's thoughtful of you, Murray, and I appreciate it; but, believe it or not, I feel like walking. Lots to think about."

"As you wish. Good night, then."

"Good night," said Lloyd, and, with his mind in a whirl and his erection slowly deflating, he turned east and headed for home.

## iv

London's social season ended in the middle of August, and still Boy Fitzherbert had not proposed marriage to Daisy Peshkov.

Daisy was hurt and puzzled. Everyone knew they were courting. They saw one another almost every day. Earl Fitzherbert talked to Daisy like a daughter, and even the suspicious Princess Bea had warmed to her. Boy kissed her whenever he got the chance, but said nothing about the future.

The long series of lavish lunches and dinners, glittering parties and balls, traditional sporting events and champagne picnics that made up the London season came to an abrupt end. Many of the new friends Daisy had made suddenly left town. Most of them went to country houses where, as far as she could gather, they would spend their time hunting foxes, stalking deer, and shooting birds.

Daisy and Olga stayed for Eva Rothmann's wedding. Unlike Boy, Jimmy Murray was in a rush to marry the woman he loved. The ceremony was held at his parents' parish church in Chelsea.

Daisy felt she had done a great job with Eva. She had taught her friend how to choose clothes that suited her, smart styles without frills, in plain strong colors that flattered her dark hair and brown eyes. Gaining in confidence, Eva had learned how to use her natural warmth and quick intelligence to charm men and women. And Jimmy had fallen in love with her. He was no movie star, but he was tall and craggily attractive. He came from a military family with a modest fortune, so Eva would be comfortable, though not rich.

The British were as prejudiced as anyone else, and at first General Murray and Mrs. Murray had not been thrilled at the prospect of their son marrying a half-Jewish German refugee. Eva had won them over quickly, but many of their friends still expressed coded doubts. At the wedding Daisy had been told that Eva was "exotic," Jimmy was "courageous," and the Murrays were "marvelously broad-minded," all ways of making the best of an unsuitable match.

Jimmy had written formally to Dr. Rothmann in Berlin, and received permission to ask Eva for her hand in marriage, but the German authorities had refused to let the Rothmann family come to the wedding. Eva had said tearfully: "They hate Jews so much, you'd think they'd be happy to see them leave the country!"

Boy's father, Fitz, had heard this remark, and had later spoken to Daisy about it. "Tell your friend Eva not to say too much about Jews, if she can avoid it," he had said, in the tone of one who gives a friendly warning. "Having a half-Jewish wife is not going to help Jimmy's army career, you know." Daisy had not passed on this unpleasant counsel.

The happy couple went off to Nice for their honeymoon. Daisy realized with a pang of guilt that she was relieved to get Eva off her hands. Boy and his political pals disliked Jews so much that Eva was becoming a problem. Already the friendship between Boy and Jimmy had ended—Boy had refused to be Jimmy's best man.

After the wedding Daisy and Olga were invited by the Fitzherberts to a shooting party at their country house in Wales. Daisy's hopes rose. Now that Eva was out of the way, there was nothing to stop Boy proposing. The earl and princess must surely assume he was on the point of it. Perhaps they planned for him to do so this weekend.

Daisy and Olga went to Paddington station on a Friday morning and took a train west. They crossed the heart of England, rich rolling farmland dotted with hamlets, each with its stone church spire rising from a stand of ancient trees. They had a first-class carriage to themselves, and Olga asked Daisy what she thought Boy might do. "He must know I like him," Daisy said. "I've let him kiss me enough times."

"Have you shown any interest in anyone else?" her mother asked shrewdly.

Daisy suppressed the guilty memory of that brief moment of foolishness with Lloyd Williams. Boy could not possibly know about that, and anyway she had not seen Lloyd again, nor had she replied to the three letters he had sent her. "No one," she said.

"Then it's because of Eva," said Olga. "And now she's gone."

The train went through a long tunnel under the estuary of the river Severn, and when it emerged, they were in Wales. Bedraggled sheep grazed the hills, and in the cleft of each valley was a small mining town, its pithead winding gear rising from a scatter of ugly industrial buildings.

Earl Fitzherbert's black-and-cream Rolls-Royce was waiting for them at Aberowen station. The town was dismal, Daisy thought, with small gray stone houses in rows along the steep hillsides. They drove a mile or so out of town to the house, Tŷ Gwyn.

Daisy gasped with pleasure as they passed through the gates. Tŷ Gwyn was enormous and elegant, with long rows of tall windows in a perfectly classical façade. It was set in elaborate gardens of flowers, shrubs, and specimen trees that clearly were the pride of the earl himself. What a joy it would be to be mistress of this house, she thought. The British aristocracy might no longer rule the world, but they had perfected the art of living, and Daisy longed to be one of them.

*Tŷ Gwyn* meant "White House," but the place was actually gray, and Daisy learned why when she touched the stonework with her hand and got coal dust on her fingertips.

She was given a room called the Gardenia Suite.

That evening she and Boy sat on the terrace before dinner and watched the sun go down over the purple mountaintop, Boy smoking a cigar and Daisy sipping champagne. They were alone for a while, but Boy said nothing about marriage.

Over the weekend her anxiety grew. Boy had plenty more chances to speak to her alone—she made sure of that. On Saturday the men went shooting, but Daisy went out to meet them at the end of the afternoon, and she and Boy walked back through the woods together. On Sunday morning the Fitzherberts and most of their guests went to the Anglican church in the town. After the service, Boy took Daisy to a pub called the Two Crowns, where squat, broad-shouldered miners in flat caps stared at her in her lavender cashmere coat as if Boy had brought in a leopard on a leash.

She told him that she and her mother would soon have to go back to Buffalo, but he did not take the hint.

Could it simply be that he liked her, but not enough to marry her?

By lunch on Sunday she was desperate. Tomorrow she and her

mother were to return to London. If Boy had not proposed by then, his parents would begin to think he was not serious, and there would be no more invitations to Tŷ Gwyn.

That prospect frightened Daisy. She had made up her mind to marry Boy. She wanted to be Viscountess Aberowen, and then one day Countess Fitzherbert. She had always been rich, but she craved the respect and deference that went with social status. She longed to be addressed as "Your Ladyship." She coveted Princess Bea's diamond tiara. She wanted to count royalty among her friends.

She knew Boy liked her, and there was no doubt about his desire when he kissed her. "He needs something to spur him on," Olga murmured to Daisy as they drank their after-lunch coffee with the other ladies in the morning room.

"But what?"

"There is one thing that never fails with men."

Daisy raised her eyebrows. "Sex?" She and her mother talked about most things, but generally skirted around this subject.

"Pregnancy would do it," Olga said. "But that only happens for sure when you *don't* want it."

"What, then?"

"You need to give him a glimpse of the promised land, but not let him in."

Daisy shook her head. "I'm not certain, but I think he may have already been to the promised land with someone else."

"Who?"

"I don't know—a maid, an actress, a widow . . . I'm guessing, but he just doesn't have that virginal air."

"You're right. He doesn't. That means you have to offer him something he can't get from the others. Something he'd do anything for."

Daisy wondered briefly where her mother got this wisdom, having spent her life in a cold marriage. Perhaps she had done a lot of thinking about how her husband, Lev, had been stolen from her by his mistress Marga. Anyway, there was nothing Daisy could offer Boy that he couldn't get from another girl, was there?

The women were finishing their coffee and heading to their

bedrooms for the afternoon nap. The men were still in the dining room, smoking their cigars, but they would follow in a quarter of an hour. Daisy stood up.

Olga said: "What are you going to do?"

"I'm not sure," she said. "I'll think of something."

She left the room. She was going to go to Boy's room, she had decided, but she did not want to say so in case her mother objected. She would be waiting for him when he came for his nap. The servants also took a break at that time of day, so it was unlikely anyone would come into the room.

She would have Boy on his own then. But what would she say or do? She did not know. She would have to improvise.

She went to the Gardenia Suite, brushed her teeth, dabbed Jean Naté perfume on her neck, and walked quietly along the corridor to Boy's room.

No one saw her go in.

He had a spacious bedroom with a view of misty mountaintops. It felt as if it might have been his for many years. There were masculine leather chairs, pictures of airplanes and racehorses on the wall, a cedarwood humidor full of fragrant cigars, and a side table with decanters of whisky and brandy and a tray of crystal glasses.

She pulled open a drawer and saw Tŷ Gwyn writing paper, a bottle of ink, and pens and pencils. The paper was blue with the Fitzherbert crest. Would that one day be her crest?

She wondered what Boy would say when he found her here. Would he be pleased, take her in his arms, and kiss her? Or would he be angry that his privacy had been invaded, and accuse her of snooping? She had to take the risk.

She went into the adjoining dressing room. There was a small washbasin with a mirror over it. His shaving tackle was on the marble surround. Daisy thought she would like to learn to shave her husband. How intimate that would be.

She opened the wardrobe doors and looked at his clothes: formal morning dress, tweed suits, riding clothes, a leather pilot's jacket with a fur lining, and two evening suits.

That gave her an idea.

She recalled how aroused Boy had been, at Bing Westhampton's house back in June, by the sight of her and the other girls dressed as men. That evening had been the first time he kissed her. She was not sure why he had been so excited—such things were generally inexplicable. Lizzie Westhampton said some men liked women to spank their bottoms; how could you account for that?

Perhaps she should dress in his clothes now.

*Something he'd do anything for,* her mother had said. Was this it?

She stared at the row of suits on hangers, the stack of folded white shirts, the polished leather shoes each with its wooden tree inside. Would it work? Did she have time?

Did she have anything to lose?

She could pick the clothes she needed, take them to the Gardenia Suite, change there, and then hurry back, hoping no one saw her on the way . . .

No. There was no time for that. His cigar was not long enough. She had to change here, and fast—or not at all.

She made up her mind.

She pulled her dress off.

She was in danger now. Until this moment, she might have explained her presence here, just about plausibly, by pretending she had lost her bearings in Tŷ Gwyn's miles of corridors and gone into the wrong room by mistake. But no girl's reputation could survive being found in a man's room in her underwear.

She took the top shirt off the pile. The collar had to be attached with a stud, she saw with a groan. She found a dozen starched collars in a drawer with a box of studs, and fixed one to the shirt, then pulled the shirt over her head.

She heard a man's heavy footsteps in the corridor outside, and froze, her heart beating like a big drum, but the steps went by.

She decided to wear formal morning dress. The striped trousers had no suspenders attached, but she found some in another drawer. She figured out how to button the suspenders to the trousers, then pulled the trousers on. The waist was big enough for two of her.

She pushed her stockinged feet into a pair of shiny black shoes and laced them.

She buttoned the shirt and put on a silver tie. The knot was wrong, but it did not matter, and anyway she did not know the correct way to tie it, so she left it as it was.

She put on a fawn double-breasted waistcoat and a black tailcoat; then she looked in the full-length mirror on the inside of the wardrobe door.

The clothes were baggy but she looked cute anyway.

Now that she had time, she put gold links in the shirt cuffs and a white handkerchief in the breast pocket of the coat.

Something was missing. She stared at herself in the mirror until she figured out what else she needed.

A hat.

She opened another cupboard and saw a row of hatboxes on a high shelf. She found a gray top hat and perched it on the back of her head.

She remembered the mustache.

She did not have an eyebrow pencil with her. She returned to Boy's bedroom and bent over the fireplace. It was still summer, and there was no fire. She got some soot on her fingertip, returned to the mirror, and carefully drew a mustache on her upper lip.

She was ready.

She sat in one of the leather armchairs to wait for him.

Her instinct told her she was doing the right thing, but rationally it seemed bizarre. However, there was no accounting for arousal. She herself had got wet inside when he took her up in his plane. It had been impossible for them to canoodle while he was concentrating on flying the little aircraft, and that was just as well, for soaring through the air had been so exciting that she probably would have let him do anything he wanted.

However, boys could be unpredictable, and she feared he might be angry. When that happened, his handsome face would twist into an unattractive grimace, he would tap his foot very quickly, and he could become quite cruel. Once when a waiter with a limp had brought him the wrong drink, he had said: "Just hobble back to the bar and bring me the Scotch I ordered—being a cripple doesn't make you deaf, does it?" The wretched man had flushed with shame.

She wondered what Boy would say to her if he was angered by her being in his room.

He arrived five minutes later.

She heard his tread outside, and realized she already knew him well enough to recognize his step.

The door opened and he came in without seeing her.

She put on a deep voice and said: "Hello, old chap, how are you?"

He started and said: "Good God!" Then he looked again. "Daisy?"

She stood up. "The same," she said in her normal voice. He was still staring at her in surprise. She doffed the top hat, gave a little bow, and said: "At your service." She replaced the hat on her head at an angle.

After a long moment, he recovered from the shock and grinned.

Thank God, she thought.

He said: "I say, that topper does suit you."

She came closer. "I put it on to please you."

"Jolly nice of you, I must say."

She turned her face up invitingly. She liked kissing him. In truth, she liked kissing most men. She was secretly embarrassed by how much she liked it. She had even enjoyed kissing girls, at her boarding school where they did not see a boy for weeks on end.

He bent his head and touched his lips to hers. Her hat fell off, and they both giggled. Quickly he thrust his tongue into her mouth. She relaxed and enjoyed it. He was enthusiastic about all sensual pleasures, and she was excited by his eagerness.

She reminded herself that she had a purpose. Things were progressing nicely, but she wanted him to propose. Would he be satisfied with just a kiss? She needed him to want more. Often, if they had more than a few hasty moments, he would fondle her breasts.

A lot depended on how much wine he had drunk with lunch. He had a large capacity, but there came a point when he lost the urge.

She moved her body, pressing herself to him. He put a hand on her chest, but she was wearing a baggy waistcoat of woolen cloth and he could not find her small breasts. He grunted in frustration.

Then his hand roamed across her stomach and inside the waistband of the loose-fitting trousers.

She had never before let him touch her down there.

She still had on a silk petticoat and substantial cotton underdrawers, so he surely could not feel much, but his hand went to the fork of her thighs and pressed firmly against her through the layers. She felt a twinge of pleasure.

She pulled away from him.

Panting, he said: "Have I gone too far?"

"Lock the door," she said.

"Oh, my goodness." He went to the door, turned the key in the lock, and came back. They embraced again, and he resumed where he had left off. She touched the front of his trousers, found his erect penis through the cloth, and grasped it firmly. He groaned with pleasure.

She pulled away again.

The shadow of anger crossed his face. An unpleasant memory came back to her. Once, when she had made a boy called Theo Coffman take his hand off her breasts, he had turned nasty and called her a prick-teaser. She had never seen that boy again, but the insult had made her feel irrationally ashamed. Momentarily she feared that Boy might be about to make a similar accusation.

Then his face softened and he said: "I am dreadfully keen on you, y'know."

This was her moment. Sink or swim, she told herself. "We shouldn't be doing this," she said with a regret that was not greatly exaggerated.

"Why not?"

"We're not even engaged."

The word hung in the air for a long moment. For a girl to say that was tantamount to a proposal. She watched his face, terrified that he would take fright, turn away, mumble excuses, and ask her to leave.

He said nothing.

"I want to make you happy," she said. "But . . ."

"I do love you, Daisy," he said.

That was not enough. She smiled at him and said: "Do you?"

"Ever such a lot."

She said nothing, but looked at him expectantly.

At last he said: "Will you marry me?"

"Oh, yes," she said, and she kissed him again. With her mouth pressed to his she unbuttoned his fly, burrowed through his underclothing, found his penis, and took it out. The skin was silky and hot. She stroked it, remembering a conversation with the Westhampton twins. "You can rub his thing," Lindy had said, and Lizzie had added: "Until it squirts." Daisy was intrigued and excited by the idea of making a man do that. She grasped a bit harder.

Then she remembered Lindy's next remark. "Or you can suck it— they like that best of all."

She moved her lips away from Boy's and spoke into his ear. "I'll do anything for my husband," she said.

Then she knelt down.

## v

It was the wedding of the year. Daisy and Boy were married at St. Margaret's Church, Westminster, on Saturday, October 3, 1936. Daisy was disappointed it was not Westminster Abbey, but she was told that was for the royal family only.

Coco Chanel made her wedding dress. Depression fashion was for simple lines and minimal extravagance. Daisy's floor-length bias-cut satin gown had pretty butterfly sleeves and a short train that could be carried by one page boy.

Her father, Lev Peshkov, came across the Atlantic for the ceremony. Her mother, Olga, agreed for the sake of appearances to sit beside him in church and generally pretend that they were a more or less happily married couple. Daisy's nightmare was that at some point Marga would show up with Lev's illegitimate son, Greg, on her arm, but it did not happen.

The Westhampton twins and May Murray were bridesmaids, and Eva Murray was matron of honor. Boy had been grumpy about Eva's being half-Jewish—he had not wanted to invite her at all—but Daisy had insisted.

She stood in the ancient church, conscious that she looked heartbreakingly beautiful, and happily gave herself to Boy Fitzherbert body and soul.

She signed the register "Daisy Fitzherbert, Viscountess Aberowen." She had been practising that signature for weeks, carefully tearing the paper into unreadable shreds afterward. Now she was entitled to it. It was her name.

Processing out of the church, Fitz took Olga's arm amiably, but Princess Bea put a yard of empty space between herself and Lev.

Princess Bea was not a nice person. She was friendly enough toward Daisy's mother, and if there was a heavy strain of condescension in her tone, Olga did not notice it, so relations were amiable. But Bea did not like Lev.

Daisy now realized that Lev lacked the veneer of social respectability. He walked and talked, ate and drank, smoked and laughed and scratched like a gangster, and he did not care what people thought. He did what he liked because he was an American millionaire, just as Fitz did what he liked because he was an English earl. Daisy had always known this, but it struck her with extra force when she saw her father with all these upper-class English people, at the wedding breakfast in the grand ballroom of the Dorchester Hotel.

But it did not matter now. She was Lady Aberowen, and that could not be taken away from her.

Nevertheless, Bea's constant hostility to Lev was an irritant, like a slightly bad smell or a distant buzzing noise, giving Daisy a feeling of dissatisfaction. Sitting beside Lev at the top table, Bea always turned slightly away. When he spoke to her, she replied briefly without meeting his eye. He seemed not to notice, smiling and drinking champagne, but

Daisy, seated on Lev's other side, knew he had not failed to read the signs. He was uncouth, not stupid.

When the toasts were over and the men began to smoke, Lev, who as the father of the bride was paying the bill, looked along the table and said: "Well, Fitz, I hope you enjoyed your meal. Were the wines up to your standards?"

"Very good, thank you."

"I must say, I thought it was a damn fine spread."

Bea tutted audibly. Men were not supposed to say *damn* in her hearing.

Lev turned to her. He was smiling, but Daisy knew the dangerous look in his eye. "Why, Princess, have I offended you?"

She did not want to reply, but he looked expectantly at her, and did not turn his gaze aside. At last she spoke. "I prefer not to hear coarse language," she said.

Lev took a cigar from his case. He did not light it at once, but sniffed it and rolled it between his fingers. "Let me tell you a story," he said, and he looked up and down the table to make sure they were all listening: Fitz, Olga, Boy, Daisy, and Bea. "When I was a kid, my father was accused of grazing livestock on someone else's land. No big deal, you might think, even if he was guilty. But he was arrested, and the land agent built a scaffold in the north meadow. Then the soldiers came and grabbed me and my brother and our mother and took us there. My father was on the scaffold with a noose around his neck. Then the landlord arrived."

Daisy had never heard this story. She looked at her mother. Olga seemed equally surprised.

The little group at the table were all very silent now.

"We were forced to watch while my father was hanged," Lev said. He turned to Bea. "And you know something strange? The landlord's sister was there as well." He put the cigar in his mouth, wetting the end, and took it out again.

Daisy saw that Bea had turned pale. Was this about her?

"The sister was about nineteen years old, and she was a princess,"

Lev said, looking at his cigar. Daisy heard Bea let out a small cry, and realized this story *was* about her. "She stood there and watched the hanging, cold as ice," Lev said.

Then he looked directly at Bea. "Now that's what I call coarse," he said.

There was a long moment of silence.

Then Lev put the cigar back in his mouth and said: "Has anyone got a light?"

## vi

Lloyd Williams sat at the table in the kitchen of his mother's house in Aldgate, anxiously studying a map.

It was Sunday, October 4, 1936, and today there was going to be a riot.

The old Roman town of London, built on a hill beside the river Thames, was now the financial district, called the City. West of this hill were the palaces of the rich, and the theaters and shops and cathedrals that catered to them. The house in which Lloyd sat was to the east of the hill, near the docks and the slums. Here for centuries waves of immigrants had landed, determined to work their fingers to the bone so that their grandchildren could one day move from the East End to the West End.

The map Lloyd was looking at so intently was in a special edition of the *Daily Worker*, the Communist Party newspaper, and it showed the route of today's march by the British Union of Fascists. They planned to assemble outside the Tower of London, on the border between the City and the East End, then march east—

Straight into the overwhelmingly Jewish borough of Stepney.

Unless Lloyd and people who thought as he did could stop them.

There were 330,000 Jews in Britain, according to the newspaper, and half of them lived in the East End. Most were refugees from Russia, Poland, and Germany, where they had lived in fear that on any day the police, the army, or the Cossacks might ride into town, robbing families, beating old men and outraging young women, lining fathers and brothers up against the wall to be shot.

Here in the London slums those Jews had found a place where they had as much right to live as anyone else. How would they feel if they looked out of their windows to see, marching down their own streets, a gang of uniformed thugs sworn to wipe them all out? Lloyd felt that it just could not be allowed to happen.

The *Worker* pointed out that from the Tower there were really only two routes the marchers could take. One went through Gardiner's Corner, a five-way junction known as the Gateway to the East End; the other led along Royal Mint Street and the narrow Cable Street. There were a dozen other routes for an individual using side streets, but not for a march. St. George Street led to Catholic Wapping rather than Jewish Stepney, and was therefore no use to the Fascists.

The *Worker* called for a human wall to block Gardiner's Corner and Cable Street, and stop the march.

The paper often called for things that did not happen: strikes, revolutions, or—most recently—an alliance of all left parties to form a People's Front. The human wall might be just another fantasy. It would take many thousands of people to effectively close off the East End. Lloyd did not know whether enough would show up.

All he knew for sure was that there would be trouble.

At the table with Lloyd were his parents, Bernie and Ethel; his sister, Millie; and sixteen-year-old Lenny Griffiths from Aberowen, in his Sunday suit. Lenny was part of a small army of Welsh miners who had come to London to join the counterdemonstration.

Bernie looked up from his newspaper and said to Lenny: "The Fascists claim that the train fares for all you Welshmen to come to London have been paid by the big Jews."

Lenny swallowed a mouthful of fried egg. "I don't know any big Jews," he said. "Unless you count Mrs. Levy Sweetshop; she's quite big. Anyway, I came to London on the back of a lorry with sixty Welsh lambs going to Smithfield meat market."

Millie said: "That accounts for the smell."

Ethel said: "Millie! How rude."

Lenny was sharing Lloyd's bedroom, and he had confided that after the demonstration he was not planning to return to Aberowen. He and Dave Williams were going to Spain to join the International Brigades being formed to fight the Fascist insurrection.

"Did you get a passport?" Lloyd had asked. Getting a passport was not difficult, but the applicant did have to provide a reference from a clergyman, doctor, lawyer, or other person of status, so a young person could not easily keep it secret.

"No need," Lenny said. "We go to Victoria station and get a weekend return ticket to Paris. You can do that without a passport."

Lloyd had vaguely known that. It was a loophole intended for the convenience of the prosperous middle class. Now the anti-Fascists were taking advantage of it. "How much is the ticket?"

"Three pounds fifteen shillings."

Lloyd had raised his eyebrows. That was more money than an unemployed coal miner was likely to have.

Lenny had added: "But the Independent Labour Party is paying for my ticket, and the Communist Party for Dave's."

They must have lied about their ages. "Then what happens when you get to Paris?" Lloyd had asked.

"We'll be met by the French Communists at the Gare du Nord." He pronounced it *gair duh nord.* He did not speak a word of French. "From there we'll be escorted to the Spanish border."

Lloyd had delayed his own departure. He told people he wanted to soothe his parents' worries, but the truth was he could not give up on Daisy. He still dreamed of her throwing Boy over. It was hopeless—she did not even answer his letters—but he could not forget her.

Meanwhile Britain, France, and the USA had agreed with Germany and Italy to adopt a policy of nonintervention in Spain, which meant none of them would supply weapons to either side. This in itself was infuriating to Lloyd: surely the democracies should support the elected government? But what was worse, Germany and Italy were breaching the agreement every day, as Lloyd's mother and Uncle Billy pointed out at many public meetings held that autumn in Britain to discuss Spain. Earl Fitzherbert, as the government minister responsible, defended the policy stoutly, saying the Spanish government should not be armed for fear it would go Communist.

This was a self-fulfilling prophecy, as Ethel had argued in a scathing speech. The one nation willing to support the government of Spain was the Soviet Union, and the Spaniards would naturally gravitate toward the only country in the world that helped them.

The truth was that the Conservatives felt Spain had elected people who were dangerously left-wing. Men such as Fitzherbert would not be unhappy if the Spanish government was violently overthrown and replaced by right-wing extremists. Lloyd seethed with frustration.

Then had come this chance to fight Fascism at home.

"It's ridiculous," Bernie had said a week ago, when the march had been announced. "The Metropolitan Police must force them to change the route. They have the right to march, of course, but not in Stepney." However, the police said they did not have the power to interfere with a perfectly legal demonstration.

Bernie and Ethel and the mayors of eight London boroughs had been in a delegation that begged the home secretary, Sir John Simon, to ban the march or at least divert it, but he, too, claimed he had no power to act.

The question of what to do next had split the Labour Party, the Jewish community, and the Williams family.

The Jewish People's Council Against Fascism and Anti-Semitism, founded by Bernie and others three months ago, had called for a massive counterdemonstration that would keep the Fascists out of Jewish streets. Their slogan was the Spanish phrase *"No pasaran,"* meaning "They shall not pass," the cry of the anti-Fascist defenders of Madrid. The council was a small organization with a grand name. It occupied two upstairs rooms in a building on Commercial Road, and it owned a Gestetner duplicating machine and a couple of old typewriters. But it commanded huge support in the East End. In forty-eight hours it had collected an incredible one hundred thousand signatures on a petition calling for the march to be banned. Still the government did nothing.

Only one major political party supported the counterdemonstration, and that was the Communists. The protest was also backed by the fringe Independent Labour Party, to which Lenny belonged. The other parties were against.

Ethel said: "I see *The Jewish Chronicle* has advised its readers to stay off the streets today."

This was the problem, in Lloyd's opinion. A lot of people were taking the view that it was best to keep out of trouble. But that would give the Fascists a free hand.

Bernie, who was Jewish though not religious, said to Ethel: "How can you quote *The Jewish Chronicle* at me? It believes Jews should not be against Fascism, just anti-Semitism. What kind of political sense does that make?"

"I hear that the Board of Deputies of British Jews says the same as the *Chronicle*," Ethel persisted. "Apparently there was an announcement yesterday in all the synagogues."

"Those so-called deputies are alrightniks from Golders Green," Bernie said with contempt. "They've never been insulted on the streets by Fascist hooligans."

"You're in the Labour Party," Ethel said accusingly. "Our policy is not to confront the Fascists on the streets. Where's your solidarity?"

Bernie said: "What about solidarity with my fellow Jews?"

"You're only Jewish when it suits you. And you've never been abused on the street."

"All the same, the Labour Party has made a political mistake."

"Just remember, if you allow the Fascists to provoke violence, the press will blame the left for it, regardless of who really started it."

Lenny said rashly: "If Mosley's boys start a fight, they'll get what's coming to them."

Ethel sighed. "Think about it, Lenny: in this country, who's got the most guns—you and Lloyd and the Labour Party, or the Conservatives with the army and the police on their side?"

"Oh," said Lenny. Clearly he had not considered that.

Lloyd said angrily to his mother: "How can you talk like that? You were in Berlin three years ago—you saw how it was. The German left tried to oppose Fascism peacefully, and look what happened to them."

Bernie put in: "The German Social Democrats failed to form a popular front with the Communists. That allowed them to be picked off separately. Together they might have won." Bernie had been angry when the local Labour Party branch had refused an offer from the Communists to form a coalition against the march.

Ethel said: "An alliance with Communists is a dangerous thing."

She and Bernie disagreed on this. In fact it was an issue that split the Labour Party. Lloyd thought that Bernie was right and Ethel wrong. "We have to use every resource we've got to defeat Fascism," he said; then he added diplomatically: "But Mam's right, it will be best for us if today goes off without violence."

"It will be best if you all stay home, and oppose the Fascists through the normal channels of democratic politics," Ethel said.

"You tried to get equal pay for women through the normal channels of democratic politics," Lloyd said. "You failed." Only last April women Labour M.P.s had promoted a parliamentary bill to guarantee female government employees equal pay for equal work. It had been voted down by the male-dominated House of Commons.

"You don't give up on democracy every time you lose a vote," Ethel said crisply.

The trouble was, Lloyd knew, that these divisions could fatally weaken the anti-Fascist forces, as had happened in Germany. Today would be a harsh test. Political parties could try to lead, but the people would choose whom to follow. Would they stay at home, as urged by the timid Labour Party and *The Jewish Chronicle*? Or would they come out onto the streets in their thousands and say no to Fascism? By the end of the day he would know the answer.

There was a knock at the back door and their neighbor Sean Dolan came in dressed in his churchgoing suit. "I'll be joining you after Mass," he said to Bernie. "Where should we meet up?"

"Gardiner's Corner, not later than two o'clock," said Bernie. "We're hoping to have enough people to stop the Fascists there."

"You'll have every dockworker in the East End with you," said Sean enthusiastically.

Millie asked: "Why is that? The Fascists don't hate you, do they?"

"You're too young to remember, you darlin' girl, but the Jews have always supported us," Sean explained. "In the dock strike of 1912, when I was only nine years old, my father couldn't feed us, and me and my brother were taken in by Mrs. Isaacs the baker's wife in New Road, may God bless her great big heart. Hundreds of dockers' children were looked after by Jewish families then. It was the same in 1926. We're not going to let the bloody Fascists come down our streets—excuse my language, Mrs. Leckwith."

Lloyd was heartened. There were thousands of dockers in the East End: if they showed up en masse, it would hugely swell the ranks.

From outside the house came the sound of a loudspeaker. "Keep Mosley out of Stepney," said a man's voice. "Assemble at Gardiner's Corner at two o'clock."

Lloyd drank his tea and stood up. His role today was to be a spy, checking the position of the Fascists and calling in updates to Bernie's Jewish People's Council. His pockets were heavy with big brown pennies for public phones. "I'd better get started," he said. "The Fascists are probably assembling already."

His mother got up and followed him to the door. "Don't get into a fight," she said. "Remember what happened in Berlin."

"I'll be careful," Lloyd said.

She tried a light tone. "Your rich American girl won't like you with no teeth."

"She doesn't like me anyway."

"I don't believe it. What girl could resist you?"

"I'll be all right, Mam," Lloyd said. "Really I will."

"I suppose I should be glad you're not going to bloody Spain."

"Not today, anyway." Lloyd kissed his mother and went out.

It was a bright autumn morning, the sun unseasonably warm. In the middle of Nutley Street a temporary platform had been set up by a group of men, one of whom was speaking through a megaphone. "People of the East End, we do not have to stand quiet while a crowd of strutting anti-Semites insult us!" Lloyd recognized the speaker as a local official of the National Unemployed Workers' Movement. Because of the Depression there were thousands of unemployed Jewish tailors. They signed on every day at the Settle Street Labor Exchange.

Before Lloyd had gone ten yards, Bernie came after him and handed him a paper bag of the little glass balls that children called marbles. "I've been in a lot of demonstrations," he said. "If the mounted police charge the crowd, throw these under the horses' hooves."

Lloyd smiled. His stepfather was a peacemaker, almost all the time, but he was no softie.

All the same, Lloyd was dubious about the marbles. He had never had much to do with horses, but they seemed to him to be patient, harmless beasts, and he did not like the idea of causing them to crash to the ground.

Bernie read the look on his face and said: "Better a horse should fall than my boy should be trampled."

Lloyd put the marbles in his pocket, thinking that it did not commit him to using them.

He was pleased to see many people already on the streets. He noted other encouraging signs. The slogan "They shall not pass" in English and Spanish had been chalked on walls everywhere he looked. The Communists were out in force, handing out leaflets. Red flags draped many windowsills. A group of men wearing medals from the Great War carried a banner that read JEWISH EX-SERVICEMEN'S ASSOCIATION. Fascists hated to be reminded how many Jews had fought for Britain. Five Jewish soldiers had won the country's highest medal for bravery, the Victoria Cross.

Lloyd began to think that perhaps there would be enough people to stop the march after all.

Gardiner's Corner was a broad five-way junction, named for the Scottish clothing store, Gardiner and Company, that occupied a corner building with a distinctive clock tower. Lloyd saw when he got there that trouble was expected. There were several first-aid stations and hundreds of St. John Ambulance volunteers in their uniforms. Ambulances were parked in every side street. Lloyd hoped there would be no fighting, but better to risk violence, he thought, than to let the Fascists march unhindered.

He took a roundabout route and came toward the Tower of London from the northwest, in order not to be identified as an East Ender. Some minutes before he got there, he could hear the brass bands.

The Tower was a riverside palace that had symbolized authority and repression for eight hundred years. It was surrounded by a long wall of pale old stone that looked as if the color had been washed out of it by centuries of London rain. Outside the walls, on the landward side, was a park called Tower Gardens, and here the Fascists were assembling. He estimated there were already a couple of thousand of them, in a line that stretched back westward into the financial district. Every now and again they broke into a rhythmic chant:

> One, two, three, four,
> We're gonna get rid of the Yids!
> The Yids! The Yids!
> We're gonna get rid of the Yids!

They carried Union Jack flags. Why was it, Lloyd wondered, that the people who wanted to destroy everything good about their country were the quickest to wave the national flag?

They looked impressively military, in their wide black leather belts and black shirts, as they formed neat columns across the grass. Their officers wore a smart uniform: a black military-cut jacket, gray riding breeches, jackboots, a black cap with a shiny peak, and a red-and-white armband. Several motorcyclists in uniform roared around ostentatiously, delivering messages with Fascist salutes. More marchers were arriving, some of them in armored vans with wire mesh at the windows.

This was not a political party. It was an army.

The purpose of the display, Lloyd figured, was to give them false authority. They wanted to look as if they had the right to close meetings and empty buildings, to burst into homes and offices and arrest people, to drag them to jails and camps and beat them up, interrogate and torture them, as the Brownshirts did in Germany under the Nazi regime so admired by Mosley and the *Daily Mail*'s proprietor, Lord Rothermere.

They would terrify the people of the East End, people whose parents and grandparents had fled from repression and pogroms in Ireland and Poland and Russia.

Would East Enders come out on the streets and fight them? If not—if today's march went ahead as planned—what might the Fascists dare tomorrow?

He walked around the edge of the park, pretending to be one of the hundred or so casual onlookers. Side streets radiated from the hub like spokes. In one of them he noticed a familiar-looking black-and-cream Rolls-Royce drawing up. The chauffeur opened the rear door and, to Lloyd's shock and dismay, Daisy Peshkov got out.

There was no doubt why she was here. She was wearing a beautifully tailored female version of the uniform, with a long gray skirt instead of the breeches, her fair curls escaping from under the black cap. Much as he hated the outfit, Lloyd could not help finding her irresistibly alluring.

He stopped and stared. He should not have been surprised: Daisy had told him she liked Boy Fitzherbert, and Boy's politics clearly made no difference to that. But to see her obviously supporting the Fascists in their attack on Jewish Londoners rammed home to him how utterly alien she was from everything that mattered in his life.

He should simply have turned away, but he could not. As she hurried along the pavement, he blocked her way. "What the devil are you doing here?" he said brusquely.

She was cool. "I might ask you the same question, Mr. Williams," she said. "I don't suppose you're intending to march with us."

"Don't you understand what these people are like? They break up peaceful political meetings, they bully journalists, they imprison their political rivals. You're an American—how can you be against democracy?"

"Democracy is not necessarily the most appropriate political system for every country in all times." She was quoting Mosley's propaganda, Lloyd guessed.

He said: "But these people torture and kill everyone who disagrees with them!" He thought of Jörg. "I've seen it for myself, in Berlin. I was in one of their camps, briefly. I was forced to watch while a naked man was savaged to death by starving dogs. That's the kind of thing your Fascist friends do."

She was unintimidated. "And who, exactly, has been killed by Fascists here in England recently?"

"The British Fascists haven't got the power yet—but your Mosley admires Hitler. If they ever get the chance, they'll do exactly the same as the Nazis."

"You mean they will eliminate unemployment and give the people pride and hope."

Lloyd was drawn to her so powerfully that it broke his heart to hear her spouting this rubbish. "You know what the Nazis have done to the family of your friend Eva."

"Eva got married, did you know?" Daisy said, in the determinedly cheerful tone of one who tries to switch a dinner-table conversation to a more agreeable topic. "To nice Jimmy Murray. She's an English wife now."

"And her parents?"

Daisy looked away. "I don't know them."

"But you know what the Nazis have done to them." Eva had told Lloyd all about it at the Trinity Ball. "Her father is no longer allowed to practise medicine—he's working as an assistant in a pharmacy. He can't enter a park or a public library. *His* father's name has been scraped off the war memorial in his home village!" Lloyd realized he had raised his voice. More quietly he said: "How can you possibly stand side by side with people who do such things?"

She looked troubled, but she did not answer his question. Instead she said: "I'm late already. Please excuse me."

"What you're doing can't be excused."

The chauffeur said: "All right, sonny, that's enough."

He was a heavy middle-aged man who evidently took little exercise, and Lloyd was not in the least intimidated, but he did not want to start a fight. "I'm leaving," he said in a mild tone. "But don't call me sonny."

The chauffeur took his arm.

Lloyd said: "You'd better take your hand off me, or I'll knock you down before I go." He looked into the chauffeur's face.

The chauffeur hesitated. Lloyd tensed, preparing to react, watching for warning signs, as he would in the boxing ring. If the chauffeur tried to hit him, it would be a great swinging haymaker of a blow, easily dodged.

But the man either sensed Lloyd's readiness or felt the well-developed muscle in the arm he was holding; for one reason or the other he backed off and released his grip, saying: "No need for threats."

Daisy walked away.

Lloyd looked at her back in the perfectly fitting uniform as she hurried toward the ranks of the Fascists. With a deep sigh of frustration he turned and went in the other direction.

He tried to concentrate on the job at hand. What a fool he had been to threaten the chauffeur. If he had got into a fight, he would probably have been arrested; then he would have spent the day in a police cell—and how would that have helped defeat Fascism?

It was now half past twelve. He left Tower Hill, found a telephone box, called the Jewish People's Council, and spoke to Bernie. After he reported what he had seen, Bernie told him to make an estimate of the number of policemen in the streets between the Tower and Gardiner's Corner.

He crossed to the east side of the park and explored the radiating side streets. What he saw astonished him.

He had expected a hundred or so police. In fact there were thousands. They stood lining the pavements, waited in dozens of parked buses, and sat astride huge horses in remarkably neat rows. Only a narrow gap was left for people who wanted to walk along the streets. There were more police than Fascists.

From inside one of the buses, a uniformed constable gave him the Hitler salute.

Lloyd was dismayed. If all these policemen sided with the Fascists, how could the counterdemonstrators resist them?

This was worse than a Fascist march: it was a Fascist march with police authority. What kind of message did that send to the Jews of the East End?

In Mansell Street he saw a beat policeman he knew, Henry Clarke. "Hello, Nobby," he said. For some reason all Clarkes were called Nobby. "A copper just gave me the Hitler salute."

"They're not from round here," Nobby said quietly, as if revealing a confidence. "They don't live with Jews like I do. I tell them Jews are the same as everyone else, mostly decent law-abiding people, a few villains and troublemakers. But they don't believe me."

"All the same . . . the Hitler salute?"

"Might have been a joke."

Lloyd did not think so.

He left Nobby and moved on. The police were forming cordons where the side streets entered the area around Gardiner's Corner, he saw.

He went into a pub with a phone—he had scouted all the available telephones the day before—and told Bernie there were at least five thousand policemen in the neighborhood. "We can't resist that many coppers," he said gloomily.

"Don't be so sure," Bernie said. "Have a look at Gardiner's Corner."

Lloyd found a way around the police cordon and joined the counterdemonstration. It was not until he got into the middle of the street outside Gardiner's that he could appreciate the full extent of the crowd.

It was the largest gathering of people he had ever seen.

The five-way junction was jammed, but that was the least of it. The crowd stretched east along Whitechapel High Street as far as the eye could see. Commercial Road, which ran southeast, was also crammed. Leman Street, where the police station stood, was impenetrable.

There must be a hundred thousand people here, Lloyd thought. He wanted to throw his hat in the air and cheer. East Enders had come out in force to repel the Fascists. There could be no doubt about their feelings now.

In the middle of the junction stood a stationary tram, abandoned by its driver and passengers.

Nothing could pass through this crowd, Lloyd realized with mounting optimism.

He saw his neighbor Sean Dolan climb a lamppost and fix a red flag to its top. The Jewish Lads' Brigade brass band was playing—probably without the knowledge of the respectable conservative organizers of the club. A police aircraft flew overhead, an autogyro of some kind, Lloyd thought.

Near the windows of Gardiner's he ran into his sister, Millie, and her friend Naomi Avery. He did not want Millie to become involved in any rough stuff; the thought chilled his heart. "Does Dad know you've come?" he said in a tone of reproof.

She was insouciant. "Don't be daft," she replied.

He was surprised she was there at all. "You're not usually very political," he said. "I thought you were more interested in making money."

"I am," she said. "But this is special."

Lloyd could imagine how upset Bernie would be if Millie got hurt. "I think you should go home."

"Why?"

He looked around. The crowd was amiable and peaceful. The police were some distance away, the Fascists nowhere to be seen. There would be no march today: that was clear. Mosley's people could not force their way through a crowd of a hundred thousand people determined to stop them, and the police would be insane to let them try. Millie was probably quite safe.

Just as he was thinking this, everything changed.

Several whistles shrilled. Looking in the direction of the sound, Lloyd saw the mounted police drawn up in an ominous line. The horses were stamping and blowing in agitation. The police had drawn long clubs shaped like swords.

They seemed to be getting ready to attack—but surely that could not be so.

Next moment, they charged.

There were angry shouts and terrified screams from the people. Everyone scrambled to get out of the way of the giant horses. The crowd made a path, but those at the edge fell under the pounding hooves. The police lashed out left and right with their long clubs. Lloyd was pushed helplessly backward.

He felt furious: What did the police think they were doing? Were they stupid enough to believe they could clear a path for Mosley to march along? Did they really imagine that two or three thousand Fascists chanting insults could pass through a crowd of a hundred thousand of their victims without starting a riot? Were the police led by idiots, or out of control? He was not sure which would be worse.

They backed away, wheeling their panting horses, and regrouped, forming a ragged line; then a whistle blew and they heeled the flanks of their mounts, urging them into another reckless charge.

Millie was scared now. She was only sixteen, and her bravado had gone. She screamed with fear as the crowd squeezed her up against the plate-glass window of Gardiner and Company. Tailor's dummies in cheap suits and winter coats stared out at the horrified crowd and the warlike riders. Lloyd was deafened by the roar of thousands of voices yelling in fearful protest. He got in front of Millie and pushed against the press with all his might, trying to protect her, but it was in vain. Despite his efforts he was crushed against her. Forty or fifty screaming people had their backs to the window, and the pressure was building dangerously.

Lloyd realized with rage that the police were determined to make a pathway through the crowd regardless of the cost.

A moment later there was a terrific crash of breaking glass and the window gave way. Lloyd fell on top of Millie, and Naomi fell on him. Dozens of people cried out in pain and panic.

Lloyd struggled to his feet. Miraculously, he was unhurt. He looked around frantically for his sister. It was maddeningly difficult to distinguish the people from the tailor's dummies. Then he spotted Millie lying in a mess of broken glass. He grasped her arms and pulled her to her feet. She was crying. "My back!" she said.

He turned her around. Her coat was cut to ribbons and there was blood all over her. He felt sick with anguish. He put his arm around her shoulders protectively. "There's an ambulance just around the corner," he said. "Can you walk?"

They had gone only a few yards when the police whistles blew again. Lloyd was terrified that he and Millie would be shoved back into Gardiner's window. Then he remembered what Bernie had given him. He took the paper bag of marbles from his pocket.

The police charged.

Drawing back his arm, Lloyd threw the paper bag over the heads of the crowd to land in front of the horses. He was not the only one so equipped, and several other people threw marbles. As the horses came at them, there was the sound of firecrackers. A police horse slipped on marbles and went down. Others stopped and reared at the banging of the fireworks. The police charge turned into chaos. Naomi Avery had somehow pushed to the front of the crowd, and he saw her burst a bag of pepper under the nose of a horse, causing it to veer away, shaking its head frantically.

The crush eased, and Lloyd led Millie around the corner. She was still in pain, but she had stopped crying.

A line of people were waiting for attention from the St. John Ambulance volunteers: a weeping girl whose hand appeared to have been crushed; several young men with bleeding heads and faces; a middle-aged woman sitting on the ground nursing a swollen knee. As Lloyd and Millie arrived, Sean Dolan walked away with a bandage around his head and went straight back into the crowd.

A nurse looked at Millie's back. "This is bad," she said. "You need to go to the London Hospital. We'll take you in an ambulance." She looked at Lloyd. "Do you want to go with her?"

Lloyd did, but he was supposed to be phoning in reports, and he hesitated.

Millie solved the dilemma for him with characteristic spunk. "Don't you dare come," she said. "You can't do anything for me, and you've got important work to do here."

She was right. He helped her into a parked ambulance. "Are you sure—?"

"Yes, I'm sure. Try not to end up in hospital yourself."

He was leaving her in the best hands, he decided. He kissed her cheek and returned to the fray.

The police had changed their tactics. The people had repelled the horse charges, but the police were still determined to make a path through the crowd. As Lloyd pushed his way to the front, they charged on foot, attacking with their batons. The unarmed demonstrators cowered back from them, like piled leaves in a wind, then surged forward in a different part of the line.

The police started to arrest people, perhaps hoping to weaken the crowd's determination by taking ringleaders away. In the East End, being arrested was no legal formality. Few people came back without a black eye or a few gaps in their teeth. Leman Street police station had a particularly bad reputation.

Lloyd found himself behind a vociferous young woman carrying a red flag. He recognized Olive Bishop, a neighbor in Nutley Street. A policeman hit her over the head with his truncheon, screaming: "Jewish whore!" She was not Jewish, and she certainly was not a whore; in fact she played the piano at the Calvary Gospel Hall. But she had forgotten the admonition of Jesus to turn the other cheek, and she scratched the cop's face, drawing parallel red lines on his skin. Two more officers grabbed her arms and held her while the scratched man hit her on the head again.

The sight of three strong men attacking one girl maddened Lloyd. He stepped forward and hit the woman's assailant with a right hook that had all of his rage behind it. The blow landed on the policeman's temple. Dazed, the man stumbled and fell.

More officers converged on the scene, lashing out randomly with their clubs, hitting arms and legs and heads and hands. Four of them picked up Olive, each taking an arm or a leg. She screamed and wriggled desperately but she could not get free.

But the bystanders were not passive. They attacked the police carrying the girl off, trying to pull the uniformed men away from her. The police turned on their attackers, yelling: "Jew bastards!" even though not all their assailants were Jews and one was a black-skinned Somali sailor.

The police let go of Olive, dropping her to the road, and began to defend themselves. Olive pushed through the crowd and vanished. The cops retreated, hitting out at anyone within reach as they backed away.

Lloyd saw with a thrill of triumph that the police strategy was not working. For all their brutality, the attacks had completely failed to make a way through the crowd. Another baton charge began, but the angry crowd surged forward to meet it, eager now for combat.

Lloyd decided it was time for another report. He worked his way backward through the crush and found a phone box. "I don't think they're going to succeed, Dad," he told Bernie excitedly. "They're trying to beat a path through us but they're making no progress. We're too many."

"We're redirecting people to Cable Street," Bernie said. "The police may be about to switch their thrust, thinking they have more chance there, so we're sending reinforcements. Go along there, see what's happening, and let me know."

"Right," said Lloyd, and he hung up before realizing he had not told his stepfather that Millie had been taken to hospital. But perhaps it was better not to worry him right now.

Getting to Cable Street was not going to be easy. From Gardiner's Corner, Leman Street led directly south to the near end of Cable Street, a distance of less than half a mile, but the road was jammed by demonstrators fighting with police. Lloyd had to take a less direct route.

He struggled eastward through the crowd into Commercial Road. Once there, further progress was not much easier. There were no police, therefore there was no violence, but the crowd was almost as dense. It was frustrating, but Lloyd was consoled for his difficulties by the reflection that the police would never force a way through so many.

He wondered what Daisy Peshkov was doing. Probably she was sitting in the car, waiting for the march to begin, tapping the toe of her expensive shoe impatiently on the Rolls-Royce's carpet. The thought that he was helping to frustrate her purpose gave him an oddly spiteful sense of satisfaction.

With persistence and a slightly ruthless attitude to those in his way, Lloyd pushed through the throng. The railway that ran along the north side of Cable Street obstructed his route, and he had to walk some distance before reaching a side road that tunneled beneath the line. He passed under the tracks and entered Cable Street.

The crowd here was not so close packed, but the street was narrow, and passage was still difficult. That was a good thing: it would be even more difficult for the police to get through. But there was another obstruction, he saw. A lorry had been parked across the road and turned on its side. At either end of the vehicle, the barricade had been extended the full width of the street with old tables and chairs, odd lengths of timber, and other assorted rubbish piled high.

A barricade! It made Lloyd think of the French Revolution. But this was no revolution. The people of the East End did not want to overthrow the British government. On the contrary, they were deeply attached to their elections and their borough councils and their Houses of Parliament. They liked their system of government so much that they were determined to defend it against Fascism even if it would not defend itself.

He had emerged behind the barrier, and now he moved toward it to see what was happening. He stood on a wall to get a better view. He saw a lively scene. On the far side, police were trying to dismantle the blockage, picking up broken furniture and dragging old mattresses away. But they were not having an easy time of it. A hail of missiles fell on their helmets, some hurled from behind the barricade, some thrown from the upstairs windows of the houses packed closely on either side of the street: stones, milk bottles, broken pots, and bricks that came, Lloyd saw, from a nearby builder's yard. A few daring young men stood on top of the barricade, lashing out at the police with sticks, and occasionally a fight would break out as the police tried to pull one down and give him a kicking. With a start Lloyd recognized two of the figures standing on the barricade as Dave Williams, his cousin, and Lenny Griffiths, from Aberowen. Side by side they were fighting policemen off with shovels.

But as the minutes passed, Lloyd saw that the police were winning. They were working systematically, picking up the components of the barricade and taking them away. On this side a few people reinforced the wall, replacing what the police removed, but they were less organized and did not have an infinite supply of materials. It looked to Lloyd as if the police would soon prevail. And if they could clear Cable Street, they would let the Fascists march down here, past one Jewish shop after another.

Then, looking behind him, he saw that whoever was organizing the defense of Cable Street was thinking ahead. Even while the police dismantled the barricade, another was going up a few hundred yards farther along the street.

Lloyd retreated and began enthusiastically to help build the second wall. Dockers with pickaxes were prizing up paving stones, housewives dragged dustbins from their yards, and shopkeepers brought empty crates and boxes. Lloyd helped carry a park bench, then pulled down a notice board from outside a municipal building. Learning from experience, the builders did a better job this time, using their materials economically and making sure the structure was sturdy.

Looking behind him again, Lloyd saw that a third barricade was beginning to rise farther east.

The people began to retreat from the first one and regroup behind the second. A few minutes later the police at last made a gap in the first barricade and poured through it. The first of them went after the few young men remaining, and Lloyd saw Dave and Lenny chased down an alley. The houses on either side were swiftly shut up, doors slamming and windows closing.

Then, Lloyd saw, the police did not know what to do next. They had broken through the barricade only to be confronted with another, stronger one. They seemed not to have the heart to begin dismantling the second. They milled around in the middle of Cable Street, talking desultorily, looking resentfully at the residents watching them from upstairs windows.

It was too early to proclaim victory, but all the same, Lloyd could not suppress a happy feeling of success. It was beginning to look as if the anti-Fascists were going to win the day.

He remained at his post for another quarter of an hour, but the police did nothing more, so he left the scene, found a telephone kiosk, and called in.

Bernie was cautious. "We don't know what's happening," he said. "There seems to be a lull everywhere, but we need to find out what the Fascists are up to. Can you get back to the Tower?"

Lloyd certainly could not fight his way through the massed police, but perhaps there was another way. "I could try going via St. George Street," he said doubtfully.

"Do the best you can. I want to know their next move."

Lloyd worked his way south through a maze of alleys. He hoped he was right about St. George Street. It was outside the contested area, but the crowds might have spilled over.

However, as he had hoped, there were no crowds there, even though he was still within earshot of the counterdemonstration, and could hear shouting and police whistles. A few women stood in the street talking, and a gaggle of little girls skipped a rope in the middle of the road. Lloyd headed west, breaking into a jog-trot, expecting to see crowds of demonstrators or police around every bend. He came across a few people who had strayed from the fracas—two men with bandaged heads, a woman in a ripped coat, a bemedaled veteran with his arm in a sling—but no crowds. He ran all the way to where the street ended at the Tower. He was able to walk unhindered into Tower Gardens.

The Fascists were still there.

That in itself was an achievement, Lloyd felt. It was now half past three: the marchers had been kept waiting here, not marching, for hours. He saw that their high spirits had evaporated. They were no longer singing or chanting but stood quiet and listless, lined up but not so neatly, their banners drooping, their bands silent. They already looked beaten.

However, there was a change a few minutes later. An open car emerged from a side street and drove alongside the Fascist lines. Cheers went up. The lines straightened, the officers saluted, the Fascists stood at attention. In the backseat of the car sat their leader, Sir Oswald Mosley, a handsome man with a mustache, wearing the uniform complete with cap. Rigidly straight-backed, he saluted repeatedly as his car went by at walking pace, as if he were a monarch inspecting his troops.

His presence reinvigorated his forces and worried Lloyd. This probably meant they were going to march as planned—otherwise why was he here? The car followed the Fascist line along a side street into the financial district. Lloyd waited. Half an hour later Mosley returned, this time on foot, again saluting and acknowledging cheers.

When he reached the head of the line, he turned and, accompanied by one of his officers, entered a side street.

Lloyd followed.

Mosley approached a group of older men standing in a huddle on the pavement. Lloyd was surprised to recognize Sir Philip Game, the commissioner of police, in a bow tie and trilby hat. The two men began an intense conversation. Sir Philip must surely be telling Sir Oswald that the crowd of counterdemonstrators was too huge to be dispersed. But what then would be his advice to the Fascists? Lloyd longed to get close enough to eavesdrop, but he decided not to risk arrest, and remained at a discreet distance.

The police commissioner did most of the talking. The Fascist leader nodded briskly several times and asked a few questions. Then the two men shook hands and Mosley walked away.

He returned to the park and conferred with his officers. Among them Lloyd recognized Boy Fitzherbert, wearing the same uniform as Mosley. Boy did not look so well in it: the trim military outfit did not suit his soft body and the lazy sensuality of his stance.

Mosley seemed to be giving orders. The other men saluted and moved away, no doubt to carry out his commands. What had he told them to do? Their only sensible option was to give up and go home. But if they had been sensible, they would not have been Fascists.

Whistles blew, orders were shouted, bands began to play, and the men stood to attention. They were going to march, Lloyd realized. The police must have assigned them a route. But what route?

Then the march began—and they went in the opposite direction. Instead of heading into the East End, they went west, into the financial district, deserted on a Sunday afternoon.

Lloyd could hardly believe it. "They've given up!" he said aloud, and a man standing near him said: "Looks like it, don't it?"

He watched for five minutes as the columns slowly moved off. When there was absolutely no doubt what was happening, he ran to a phone box and called Bernie. "They're marching away!" he said.

"What, into the East End?"

"No, the other way! They're going west, into the City. We've won!"

"Good God!" Bernie spoke to the other people with him. "Everybody! The Fascists are marching west. They've given up!"

Lloyd heard a burst of wild cheering in the room.

After a minute Bernie said: "Keep an eye on them. Let us know when they've all left Tower Gardens."

"Absolutely." Lloyd hung up.

He walked around the perimeter of the park in high spirits. It became clearer every minute that the Fascists were defeated. Their bands played, and they marched in time, but there was no spring in their step, and they no longer chanted that they were going to get rid of the Yids. The Yids had got rid of them.

As he passed the end of Byward Street, he saw Daisy again.

She was heading toward the distinctive black-and-cream Rolls-Royce, and she had to walk past Lloyd. He could not resist the temptation to gloat. "The people of the East End have rejected you and your filthy ideas," he said.

She stopped and looked at him, cool as ever. "We've been obstructed by a gang of thugs," she said with disdain.

"Still, you're marching in the other direction now."

"One battle doesn't make a war."

That might be true, Lloyd thought, but it was a pretty big battle. "You're not marching home with your boyfriend?"

"I prefer to drive," she said. "And he's not my boyfriend."

Lloyd's heart leaped in hope.

Then she said: "He's my husband."

Lloyd stared at her. He had never really believed she would be so stupid. He was speechless.

"It's true," she said, reading the disbelief in his face. "Didn't you see our engagement reported in the newspapers?"

"I don't read the society pages."

She showed him her left hand, with a diamond engagement ring and a gold wedding band. "We were married yesterday. We postponed our honeymoon to join the march today. Tomorrow we're flying to Deauville in Boy's plane."

She walked the few steps to the car and the chauffeur opened the door. "Home, please," she said.

"Yes, my lady."

Lloyd was so angry he wanted to hit someone.

Daisy looked back over her shoulder. "Good-bye, Mr. Williams."

He found his voice. "Good-bye, Miss Peshkov."

"Oh, no," she said. "I'm Viscountess Aberowen now."

She just loved saying it, Lloyd could tell. She was a titled lady, and it meant the world to her.

She got into the car and the chauffeur closed the door.

Lloyd turned away. He was ashamed to realize he had tears in his eyes. "Hell," he said aloud.

He sniffed, swallowing tears. He squared his shoulders and headed back toward the East End at a brisk walk. Today's triumph had been soured. He knew he was a fool to care about Daisy—clearly she did not care about him—but all the same it broke his heart that she was throwing herself away on Boy Fitzherbert.

He tried to put her out of his mind.

The police were getting back into their buses and leaving the scene. Lloyd had not been surprised by their brutality—he had lived in the East End all his life, and it was a rough neighborhood—but their anti-Semitism had shocked him. They had called every woman a Jewish whore, every man a Jew bastard. In Germany the police had supported the Nazis and sided with the Brownshirts. Would they do the same here? Surely not!

The crowd at Gardiner's Corner had begun to rejoice. The Jewish Lads' Brigade band was playing a jazz tune for men and women to dance to, and bottles of whisky and gin were passed from hand to hand. Lloyd decided to go to the London Hospital and check on Millie. Then he decided he should probably go to the Jewish Council headquarters and break the news to Bernie that Millie had been hurt.

Before he got any farther, he ran into Lenny Griffiths. "We sent the buggers packing!" Lenny said excitedly.

"We did, too." Lloyd grinned.

Lenny lowered his voice. "We beat the Fascists here, and we're going to beat them in Spain, too."

"When are you leaving?"

"Tomorrow. Me and Dave are catching a train to Paris in the morning."

Lloyd put his arm around Lenny's shoulders. "I'll come with you," he said.

# CHAPTER FOUR

# 1937

**V**olodya Peshkov bent his head against the driving snow as he walked across the bridge over the Moscow River. He wore a heavy greatcoat, a fur hat, and a stout pair of leather boots. Few Muscovites were so well dressed. Volodya was lucky.

He always had good boots. His father, Grigori, was an army commander. Grigori was not a high flyer: although he was a hero of the Bolshevik revolution and a personal acquaintance of Stalin, his career had stalled at some point in the twenties. All the same, the family had always lived comfortably.

Volodya himself *was* a high flyer. After university he had got into the prestigious Military Intelligence Academy. A year later he had been posted to Red Army Intelligence headquarters.

His greatest piece of luck had been meeting Werner Franck in Berlin, while his father was a military attaché at the Soviet embassy there. Werner had been at the same school in a more junior class. Learning that young Werner hated Fascism, Volodya had suggested to him that he could best oppose the Nazis by spying for the Russians.

Werner had been only fourteen years old then, but now he was eighteen, he worked at the Air Ministry, he hated the Nazis even more, and he had a powerful radio transmitter and a codebook. He was resourceful and courageous, taking dreadful risks and gathering priceless information. And Volodya was his contact.

Volodya had not seen Werner for four years, but he remembered him vividly. Tall with striking red-blond hair, Werner looked and acted older than he was, and even at fourteen he had been enviably successful with women.

Werner had recently tipped him off about Markus, a diplomat at the German embassy in Moscow who was secretly a Communist. Volodya had sought Markus out and recruited him as a spy. For some months now Markus had been supplying a stream of reports that Volodya translated into Russian and passed to his boss. The latest was a fascinating account of how pro-Nazi American business leaders were supplying the right-wing Spanish rebels with trucks, tires, and oil. Texaco's chairman, the Hitler-admiring Torkild Rieber, was using the company's tankers to smuggle oil to the rebels in defiance of a specific request from President Roosevelt.

Volodya was on his way to meet Markus now.

He walked along Kutuzovsky Prospekt and turned toward the Kiev Station. Their rendezvous today was a workingmen's bar near the station. They never used the same place twice, but finished each meeting by arranging the next one: Volodya was meticulous about tradecraft. They always used cheap bars or cafés where Markus's diplomatic colleagues would never dream of going. If somehow Markus were to fall under suspicion and be followed by a German counterespionage agent, Volodya would know, for such a man would stand out from the other customers.

This place was called the Ukraine Bar. Like most buildings in Moscow, it was a timber structure. The windows were steamed up, so at least it would be warm inside. But Volodya did not go in immediately. There were further precautions to be taken. He crossed the street and ducked into the entrance of an apartment house. He stood in the cold hallway, looking out through a small window, watching the bar.

He wondered if Markus would show up. He always had, in the past, but Volodya could not feel sure. If he did show up, what information would he bring? Spain was the hot issue in international politics, but Red Army Intelligence was also passionately interested in German armaments. How many tanks were they producing per month? How many Mauser M34 machine guns per day? How good was the new Heinkel He 111 bomber? Volodya longed for such information to pass to his boss, Major Lemitov.

Half an hour went by, and Markus did not come.

Volodya began to worry. Had Markus been found out? He worked as assistant to the ambassador, and therefore saw everything that crossed the ambassador's desk, but Volodya had been urging him to seek access to other documents, especially the correspondence of military attachés. Had that been a mistake? Had someone noticed Markus sneaking a peek at cables that were none of his business?

Then Markus came along the street, a professorial figure in spectacles and an Austrian-style loden coat, white snowflakes spotting the green felt cloth. He turned into the Ukraine Bar. Volodya waited, watching. Another man followed Markus in, and Volodya frowned anxiously, but the second man was obviously a Russian worker, not a German counterespionage agent. He was a small, rat-faced man in a threadbare coat, his boots wrapped in rags, and he wiped the wet end of his pointed nose with his sleeve.

Volodya crossed the street and went into the bar.

It was a smoky place, none too clean, and it smelled of men who did not often bathe. On the walls were fading watercolors of Ukrainian scenery in cheap frames. It was midafternoon, and there were not many customers. The only woman in the place looked like an aging prostitute recovering from a hangover.

Markus was at the back of the room, hunched over an untasted glass of beer. He was in his thirties but looked older, with a neat fair beard and mustache. He had thrown open his coat, revealing a fur lining. The rat-faced Russian sat two tables away, rolling a cigarette.

As Volodya approached, Markus stood up and punched him in the mouth.

"You cowfucker!" he screamed in German. "You pig's cunt!"

Volodya was so shocked that for a moment he did nothing. His lips hurt and he tasted blood. Reflexively, he raised his arm to hit back. But he restrained himself.

Markus swung at him again, but this time Volodya was ready, and he easily dodged the wild blow.

"Why did you do it?" Markus yelled. "Why?"

Then, just as suddenly, he crumpled, falling back into his chair, burying his face in his hands, and beginning to sob.

Volodya spoke through bleeding lips. "Shut up, you fool," he said. He turned around and spoke to the other customers, who were all staring. "It's nothing—he's upset."

They all looked away, and one man left. Muscovites never voluntarily got involved in trouble. It was dangerous even to separate two scrapping drunks, in case one of them was powerful in the party. And they knew that Volodya was such a man: they could tell by his good coat.

Volodya turned back to Markus. In a lowered voice he said angrily: "What the hell was that for?" He spoke German; Markus's Russian was poor.

"You arrested Irina," the man replied, weeping. "You fucking bastard, you burned her nipples with a cigarette."

Volodya winced. Irina was Markus's Russian girlfriend. Volodya began to see what this might be about and he had a bad feeling. He sat down opposite Markus. "I didn't arrest Irina," he said. "And I'm sorry if she's been hurt. Just tell me what happened."

"They came for her in the middle of the night. Her mother told me. They wouldn't say who they were, but they weren't regular police detectives—they had better clothes. She doesn't know where they took her. They questioned her about me and accused her of being a spy. They tortured her and raped her. Then they threw her out."

"Fuck," said Volodya. "I'm really sorry."

"You're sorry? It must have been you that did it—who else?"

"This is nothing to do with Army Intelligence, I swear."

"Makes no difference," Markus said. "I'm finished with you, and I'm finished with Communism."

"There are sometimes casualties in the war against capitalism." It sounded glib even to Volodya as he said it.

"You young fool," Markus said savagely. "Don't you understand that socialism means freedom from this kind of shit?"

Volodya glanced up and saw a burly man in a leather coat come through the door. He was not here for a drink, Volodya knew instinctively.

Something was going on, and Volodya did not know what it was. He was new to this game, and right now he felt his lack of experience like a missing limb. He thought he might be in danger but he did not know what to do.

The newcomer approached the table where Volodya sat with Markus.

Then the rat-faced man stood up. He was about the same age as Volodya. Surprisingly, he spoke with an educated accent. "You two are under arrest."

Volodya cursed.

Markus jumped to his feet. "I am commercial attaché at German embassy!" he screamed in ungrammatical Russian. "You cannot arrest! I have diplomatic immunity!"

The other customers left the bar in a rush, shoving at each other as they squeezed through the door. Only two people remained: the bartender, nervously swiping at the counter with a filthy rag, and the prostitute, smoking a cigarette and staring into an empty vodka glass.

"You can't arrest me, either," Volodya said calmly. He took his identification card from his pocket. "I'm Lieutenant Peshkov, Army Intelligence. Who the fuck are you?"

"Dvorkin, NKVD."

The man in the leather coat said: "Berezovsky, NKVD."

The secret police. Volodya groaned; he might have known. The NKVD overlapped with Army Intelligence. He had been warned that the two organizations were always treading on each other's toes, but this was his first experience of it. He said to Dvorkin: "I suppose it was you who tortured this man's girlfriend."

Dvorkin wiped his nose on his sleeve; apparently that unpleasant habit was not part of his disguise. "She had no information."

"So you burned her nipples for nothing."

"Lucky for her. If she had been a spy, it would have been worse."

"It didn't occur to you to check with us first?"

"When did you ever check with us?"

Markus said: "I'm leaving."

Volodya felt desperate. He was about to lose a valuable asset. "Don't go," he pleaded. "We'll make this up to Irina somehow. We'll get her the best hospital treatment—"

"Fuck you," said Markus. "You'll never see me again." He walked out of the bar.

Dvorkin evidently did not know what to do. He did not want to let Markus go, but clearly he could not arrest him without looking foolish. In the end he said to Volodya: "You shouldn't let people speak to you that way. It makes you look weak. They should respect you."

"You prick," Volodya said. "Can't you see what you've done? That man was a good source of reliable intelligence—but now he'll never work for us again, thanks to your blundering."

Dvorkin shrugged. "As you said to him, sometimes there are casualties."

"God spare me," Volodya said, and he went out.

He felt vaguely nauseated as he walked back across the river. He was sickened by what the NKVD had done to an innocent woman, and downcast by the loss of his source. He boarded a tram; he was too junior to have a car. He brooded as the vehicle trundled through the snow to his place of work. He had to report to Major Lemitov, but he hesitated, wondering how to tell the story. He needed to make it clear that he was not to blame, yet avoid seeming to make excuses.

Army Intelligence headquarters stood on one edge of the Khodynka airfield, where a patient snowplow crawled up and down, keeping the runway clear. The architecture was peculiar: a two-story building with no windows in its outer walls surrounded a courtyard in which stood the nine-story head office, sticking up like a pointed finger out of a brick fist. Cigarette lighters and fountain pens could not be brought in, as they might set off the metal detectors at the entrance, so the army provided its staff with one of each inside. Belt buckles were a problem, too, so most people wore suspenders. The security was superfluous, of course. Muscovites would do anything to stay out of such a building; no one was mad enough to want to sneak inside.

Volodya shared an office with three other subalterns, their steel desks side by side on opposite walls. There was so little space that Volodya's desk prevented the door from opening fully. The office wit, Kamen, looked at his swollen lips and said: "Let me guess—her husband came home early."

"Don't ask," said Volodya.

On his desk was a decrypt from the radio section, the German words penciled letter by letter under the code groups.

The message was from Werner.

Volodya's first reaction was fear. Had Markus already reported what had happened to Irina, and persuaded Werner, too, to withdraw from espionage? Today seemed a sufficiently unlucky day for such a disaster.

But the message was the opposite of disastrous.

Volodya read with growing amazement. Werner explained that the German military had decided to send spies to Spain posing as anti-Fascist volunteers wanting to fight for the government side in the civil war. They would report clandestinely from behind the lines to German-manned listening stations in the rebel camp.

That in itself was red-hot information.

But there was more.

Werner had the names.

Volodya had to restrain himself from whooping with joy. A coup like this could happen only once in the lifetime of an intelligence man, he thought. It more than made up for losing Markus. Werner was solid gold. Volodya dreaded to think what risks he must have taken to purloin this list of names and smuggle it out of Air Ministry headquarters in Berlin.

He was tempted to run upstairs to Lemitov's office right away, but he restrained himself.

The four subalterns shared a typewriter. Volodya lifted the heavy old machine off Kamen's desk and put it on his own. Using the forefinger of each hand, he typed out a Russian translation of the message from Werner. While he was doing so, the daylight faded and powerful security lights came on outside the building.

Leaving a carbon copy in his desk drawer, he took the top copy and went upstairs. Lemitov was in. A good-looking man of about forty, he had dark hair slicked down with brilliantine. He was shrewd, and had a knack of thinking one step ahead of Volodya, who strove to emulate his forethought. He did not subscribe to the orthodox military view that army organization was about shouting and bullying, yet he was merciless with incompetent people. Volodya respected him and feared him.

"This might be tremendously useful information," Lemitov said when he had read the translation.

"Might be?" Volodya did not see any reason for doubt.

"It could be disinformation," Lemitov pointed out.

Volodya did not want to believe that, but he realized with a surge of disappointment that he had to acknowledge the possibility that Werner had been caught and turned into a double agent. "What kind of disinformation?" he asked dispiritedly. "Are these false names, to send us on a wild goose chase?"

"Perhaps. Or they might be the real names of genuine volunteers, Communists and socialists who have escaped from Nazi Germany and gone to Spain to fight for freedom. We could end up arresting real anti-Fascists."

"Hell."

Lemitov smiled. "Don't look so miserable! The information is still very good. We have our own spies in Spain—young Russian soldiers and officers who have 'volunteered' to join the International Brigades. They can investigate." He picked up a red pencil and wrote on the sheet of paper in small, neat handwriting. "Well done," he said.

Volodya took that for dismissal and went to the door.

Lemitov said: "Did you meet Markus today?"

Volodya turned back. "There was a problem."

"I guessed, by your mouth."

Volodya told the story. "So I lost a good source," he finished. "But I don't know what I could have done differently. Should I have told the NKVD about Markus and warned them off?"

"Fuck, no," said Lemitov. "They're completely untrustworthy. Never tell them anything. But don't worry—you haven't lost Markus. You can get him back easily."

"How?" Volodya said uncomprehendingly. "He hates us all now."

"Arrest Irina again."

"What?" Volodya was horrified. Had she not suffered enough? "Then he'll hate us even more."

"Tell him that if he doesn't continue to cooperate with us, we'll interrogate her all over again."

Volodya tried desperately to hide his revulsion. It was important not to appear squeamish. And he could see that Lemitov's plan would work. "Yes," he managed to say.

"Only this time," Lemitov went on, "tell him we'll put the lighted cigarettes up her cunt."

Volodya felt as if he might vomit. He swallowed hard and said: "Good idea. I'll pick her up now."

"Tomorrow is soon enough," said Lemitov. "Four in the morning. Maximum shock."

"Yes, sir." Volodya went out and closed the door behind him.

He stood in the corridor for a moment, feeling unsteady. Then a passing clerk looked strangely at him and he forced himself to walk away.

He was going to have to do this. He would not torture Irina, of course: the threat would be enough. But she would surely *think* she was going to be tortured all over again, and that would terrify her out of her wits. Volodya felt that in her place he might go insane. He had never imagined, when he joined the Red Army, that he might have to do such things. Of course the army was about killing people—he knew that—but torturing girls?

The building was emptying, lights being switched off in offices, men with hats on in the corridors. It was time to go home. Returning to his office, Volodya called the military police and arranged to meet a squad at three thirty in the morning to arrest Irina. Then he put on his coat and went to catch a tram home.

Volodya lived with his parents, Grigori and Katerina, and his sister, Anya, nineteen, who was still at university. On the tram he wondered if he could talk to his father about this. He imagined saying: "Do we have to torture people in a Communist society?" But he knew what the answer would be. It was a temporary necessity, essential to defend the revolution against spies and subversives in the pay of the capitalist imperialists. Perhaps he could ask: "How long will it be until we can abandon such dreadful practises?" Of course his father would not know, nor would anyone else.

On their return from Berlin, the Peshkov family had moved into Government House, sometimes called the House on the Embankment, an apartment block across the river from the Kremlin, occupied by members of the Soviet elite. It was a huge building in the Constructivist style, with more than five hundred flats.

Volodya nodded at the military policeman at the door, then passed through the grand lobby—so large that some evenings there was dancing to a jazz band—and went up in the elevator. The apartment was luxurious by Soviet standards, with constant hot water and a phone, but it was not as pleasant as their home in Berlin.

His mother was in the kitchen. Katerina was an indifferent cook and an unenthusiastic housekeeper, but Volodya's father adored her. Back in 1914, in St. Petersburg, he had rescued her from the unwelcome attentions of a bullying policeman, and he had been in love with her ever since. She was still attractive at forty-three, Volodya guessed, and while the family had been on the diplomatic circuit, she had learned how to dress more stylishly than most Russian women—though she was careful not to look Western, a serious offense in Moscow.

"Did you hurt your mouth?" she said to him after he kissed her hello.

"It's nothing." Volodya smelled chicken. "Special dinner?"

"Anya is bringing a boyfriend home."

"Ah! A fellow student?"

"I don't think so. I'm not sure what he does."

Volodya was pleased. He was fond of his sister, but he knew she was not beautiful. She was short and stumpy, and wore dull clothes in drab colors. She had not had many boyfriends, and it was good news that one liked her enough to come home with her.

He went to his room, took off his jacket, and washed his face and hands. His lips were almost back to normal: Markus had not hit him very hard. While he was drying his hands, he heard voices, and gathered that Anya and her boyfriend had arrived.

He put on a knitted cardigan, for comfort, and left his room. He went into the kitchen. Anya was sitting at the table with a small, rat-faced man Volodya recognized. "Oh, no!" Volodya said. "You!"

It was Ilya Dvorkin, the NKVD agent who had arrested Irina. His disguise had gone, and he was dressed in a normal dark suit and decent boots. He stared at Volodya in surprise. "Of course—Peshkov!" he said. "I didn't make the connection."

Volodya turned to his sister. "Don't tell me this is your boyfriend."

Anya said in dismay: "What's the matter?"

Volodya said: "We met earlier today. He screwed up an important army operation by sticking his nose in where it didn't belong."

"I was doing my job," said Dvorkin. He wiped the end of his nose on his sleeve.

"Some job!"

Katerina stepped in to rescue the situation. "Don't bring your work home," she said. "Volodya, please pour a glass of vodka for our guest."

Volodya said: "Really?"

His mother's eyes flashed anger. "Really!"

"Okay." Reluctantly, he took the bottle from the shelf. Anya got glasses from a cupboard and Volodya poured.

Katerina took a glass and said: "Now, let's start again. Ilya, this is my son, Vladimir, who we always call Volodya. Volodya, this is Anya's friend Ilya, who has come to dinner. Why don't you shake hands."

Volodya had no option but to shake the man's hand.

Katerina put snacks on the table: smoked fish, pickled cucumber, sliced sausage. "In summer we have salad that I grow at the dacha, but at this time of year of course there is nothing," she said apologetically. Volodya realized she was keen to impress Ilya. Did his mother really want Anya to marry this creep? He supposed she must.

Grigori came in, wearing his army uniform, all smiles, sniffing the chicken and rubbing his hands together. At forty-eight he was red-faced and corpulent: it was hard to imagine him storming the Winter Palace as he had in 1917. He must have been thinner then.

He kissed his wife with relish. Volodya thought his mother was thankful for his father's unabashed lust without actually returning it. She would smile when he patted her bottom, hug him when he embraced her, and kiss him as often as he wanted, but she was never the initiator. She liked him, respected him, and seemed happy being married to him; but clearly she did not burn with desire. Volodya would want more than that from marriage.

The matter was purely hypothetical: Volodya had had a dozen or so short-term girlfriends but had not yet met a woman he wanted to marry.

Volodya poured his father a shot of vodka, and Grigori tossed it back with relish, then took some smoked fish. "So, Ilya, what work do you do?"

"I'm with the NKVD," Ilya said proudly.

"Ah! A very good organization to belong to!"

Grigori did not really think this, Volodya suspected; he was just trying to be friendly. Volodya thought the family should be unfriendly, in the hope that they could drive Ilya away. He said: "I suppose, Father, that when the rest of the world follows the Soviet Union in adopting the Communist system, there will no longer be a need for the secret police, and the NKVD can then be abolished."

Grigori chose to treat the question lightly. "No police at all!" he said jovially. "No criminal trials, no prisons. No counterespionage department, as there will be no spies. No army, either, since we will have no enemies! What will we all do for a living?" He laughed heartily. "This, however, may still be some distance in the future."

Ilya looked suspicious, as if he felt something subversive was being said but could not put his finger on it.

Katerina brought to the table a plate of black bread and five bowls of hot borscht, and they all began to eat. "When I was a boy in the countryside," Grigori said, "all winter long my mother would save vegetable peelings, apple cores, the discarded outer leaves of cabbages, the hairy part of the onion, anything like that, in a big old barrel outside the house, where it all froze. Then, in the spring, when the snow melted, she would use it to make borscht. That's what borscht really is, you know—soup made from peelings. You youngsters have no idea how well off you are."

There was a knock at the door. Grigori frowned, not expecting anyone, but Katerina said: "Oh, I forgot! Konstantin's daughter is coming."

Grigori said: "You mean Zoya Vorotsyntsev? The daughter of Magda the midwife?"

"I remember Zoya," said Volodya. "Skinny kid with blond ringlets."

"She's not a kid anymore," Katerina said. "She's twenty-four and a scientist." She stood up to go to the door.

Grigori frowned. "We haven't seen her since her mother died. Why has she suddenly made contact?"

"She wants to talk to you," Katerina replied.

"To me? About what?"

"Physics." Katerina went out.

Grigori said proudly: "Her father, Konstantin, and I were delegates to the Petrograd Soviet in 1917. We issued the famous Order Number One." His face darkened. "He died, sadly, after the Civil War."

Volodya said: "He must have been young—what did he die of?"

Grigori glanced at Ilya and quickly looked away. "Pneumonia," he said, and Volodya knew he was lying.

Katerina returned, followed by a woman who took Volodya's breath away.

She was a classic Russian beauty, tall and slim, with light blond hair, blue eyes so pale they were almost colorless, and perfect white skin. She wore a simple Nile-green dress whose plainness only drew attention to her slender figure.

She was introduced all around; then she sat at the table and accepted a bowl of borscht. Grigori said: "So, Zoya, you're a scientist."

"I'm a graduate student, doing my doctorate, and I teach undergraduate classes," she said.

"Volodya here works in Red Army Intelligence," Grigori said proudly.

"How interesting," she said, obviously meaning the opposite.

Volodya realized that Grigori saw Zoya as a potential daughter-in-law. He hoped his father would not hint at this too heavily. He had already made up his mind to ask her for a date before the end of the evening. But he could manage that by himself. He did not need his father's help. On the contrary: unsubtle parental boasting might put her off.

"How is the soup?" Katerina asked Zoya.

"Delicious, thank you."

Volodya was already getting the impression of a matter-of-fact personality behind the gorgeous exterior. It was an intriguing combination: a beautiful woman who made no attempt to charm.

Anya cleared away the soup bowls while Katerina brought the main course, chicken and potatoes cooked in a pot. Zoya tucked in, stuffing the food into her mouth, chewing and swallowing and eating more. Like most Russians, she did not often see food this good.

Volodya said: "What kind of science do you do, Zoya?"

With evident regret she stopped eating to answer. "I'm a physicist," she said. "We're trying to understand the atom: what its components are, what holds them together."

"Is that interesting?"

"Completely fascinating." She put down her fork. "We're finding out what the universe is really made of. There's nothing so exciting." Her eyes lit up. Apparently physics was the one thing that could distract her from her dinner.

Ilya spoke up for the first time. "Ah, but how does all this theoretical stuff help the revolution?"

Zoya's eyes blazed anger, and Volodya liked her even more. "Some comrades make the mistake of undervaluing pure science, preferring practical research," she said. "But technical developments, such as improved aircraft, are ultimately based on theoretical advances."

Volodya concealed a grin. Ilya had been demolished with one casual swipe.

But Zoya had not finished. "This is why I wanted to talk to you, sir," she said to Grigori. "We physicists read all the scientific journals published in the West—they foolishly reveal their results to the whole world. And we have lately realized that they are making alarming forward leaps in their understanding of atomic physics. Soviet science is in grave danger of falling behind. I wonder if Comrade Stalin is aware of this."

The room went quiet. The merest hint of a criticism of Stalin was dangerous. "He knows most things," Grigori said.

"Of course," Zoya said automatically. "But perhaps there are times when loyal comrades such as yourself need to draw important matters to his attention."

"Yes, that's true."

Ilya said: "Undoubtedly Comrade Stalin believes that science should be consistent with Marxist-Leninist ideology."

Volodya saw a flash of defiance in Zoya's eyes, but she dropped her gaze and said humbly: "There can be no question that he is right. We scientists must clearly redouble our efforts."

This was horseshit, and everyone in the room knew it, but no one would say so. The proprieties had to be observed.

"Indeed," said Grigori. "Nevertheless, I will mention it next time I get a chance to talk to the comrade general secretary of the party. He may wish to look into it further."

"I hope so," said Zoya. "We want to be ahead of the West."

"And how about after work, Zoya?" said Grigori cheerily. "Do you have a boyfriend, a fiancé perhaps?"

Anya protested: "Dad! That's none of our business."

Zoya did not seem to mind. "No fiancé," she said mildly. "No boyfriend."

"As bad as my son, Volodya! He, too, is single. He is twenty-three years old, well educated, tall, and handsome—yet he has no fiancée!"

Volodya squirmed at the heavy-handedness of this hint.

"Hard to believe," Zoya said, and as she glanced at Volodya, he saw a gleam of humor in her eyes.

Katerina put a hand on her husband's arm. "Enough," she said. "Stop embarrassing the poor girl."

The doorbell rang.

"Again?" said Grigori.

"This time I have no idea who it might be," said Katerina as she left the kitchen.

She returned with Volodya's boss, Major Lemitov.

Startled, Volodya jumped to his feet. "Good evening, sir," he said. "This is my father, Grigori Peshkov. Dad, may I present Major Lemitov?"

Lemitov saluted smartly.

Grigori said: "At ease, Lemitov. Sit down and have some chicken. Has my son done something wrong?"

That was precisely the thought that was making Volodya's hands shake.

"No, sir—rather the contrary. But . . . I was hoping for a private word with you and him."

Volodya relaxed a little. Perhaps he was not in trouble after all.

"Well, we've just about finished dinner," Grigori said, standing up. "Let's go into my study."

Lemitov looked at Ilya. "Aren't you with the NKVD?" he said.

"And proud of it. Dvorkin is the name."

"Oh! You tried to arrest Volodya this afternoon."

"I thought he was behaving like a spy. I was right, wasn't I?"

"You must learn to arrest enemy spies, not our own." Lemitov went out.

Volodya grinned. That was the second time Dvorkin had been put down.

Volodya, Grigori, and Lemitov crossed the hallway. The study was a small room, sparsely furnished. Grigori took the only easy chair.

Lemitov sat at a small table. Volodya closed the door and remained standing.

Lemitov said to Volodya: "Does your comrade father know about this afternoon's message from Berlin?"

"No, sir."

"You'd better tell him."

Volodya related the story of the spies in Spain. His father was delighted. "Well done!" he said. "Of course this might be disinformation, but I doubt it; the Nazis aren't that imaginative. However, we are. We can arrest the spies and use their radios to send misleading messages to the right-wing rebels."

Volodya had not thought of that. Dad may play the fool with Zoya, he thought, but he still has a sharp mind for intelligence work.

"Exactly," said Lemitov.

Grigori said to Volodya: "Your school friend Werner is a brave man." He turned back to Lemitov. "How do you plan to handle this?"

"We'll need some good intelligence men in Spain to investigate these Germans. It shouldn't be too difficult. If they really are spies, there will be evidence: codebooks, wireless sets, and so on." He hesitated. "I've come here to suggest we send your son."

Volodya was astonished. He had not seen that coming.

Grigori's face fell. "Ah," he said thoughtfully. "I must confess, the prospect fills me with dismay. We would miss him so much." Then a look of resignation came over his face, as if he realized he did not really have a choice. "The defense of the revolution must come first, of course."

"An intelligence man needs field experience," Lemitov said. "You and I have seen action, sir, but the younger generation have never been on the battlefield."

"True, true. How soon would he go?"

"In three days' time."

Volodya could see that his father was trying desperately to think of a reason to keep him at home, but finding none. Volodya himself was excited. Spain! He thought of bloodred wine, black-haired girls with strong brown legs, and hot sunshine instead of Moscow snow. It would be dangerous, of course, but he had not joined the army to be safe.

Grigori said: "Well, Volodya, what do you think?"

Volodya knew his father wanted him to come up with an objection. The only drawback he could think of was that he would not have time to get to know the stunning Zoya. "It is a wonderful opportunity," he said. "I'm honored to have been chosen."

"Very well," said his father.

"There is one small problem," Lemitov said. "It has been decided that Army Intelligence will investigate but not actually carry out the arrests. That will be the prerogative of the NKVD." His smile was humorless. "I'm afraid you will be working with your friend Dvorkin."

## ii

It was amazing, Lloyd Williams thought, how quickly you could come to love a place. He had been in Spain for only ten months, but already his passion for the country was almost as strong as his attachment to Wales. He loved to see a rare flower blooming in the scorched landscape; he enjoyed sleeping in the afternoon; he liked the way there was wine to drink even when there was nothing to eat. He had experienced flavors he had never tasted before: olives, paprika, chorizo, and the fiery spirit they called *orujo*.

He stood on a rise, staring across a heat-hazed landscape with a map in his hand. There were a few meadows beside a river, and some trees on distant mountainsides, but in between was a barren, featureless desert of dusty soil and rock. "Not much cover for our advance," he said anxiously.

Beside him, Lenny Griffiths said: "It's going to be a bloody hard battle."

Lloyd looked at his map. Saragossa straddled the Ebro River about a hundred miles from its Mediterranean end. The town dominated communications in the Aragon region. It was a major crossroads, a rail junction, and the meeting of three rivers. Here the Spanish army confronted the antidemocratic rebels across an arid no-man's-land.

Some people called the government forces Republicans and the rebels Nationalists, but these were misleading names. Many people on both sides were republicans, in that they did not want to be ruled by a king. And they were all nationalist, in that they loved their country and were willing to die for it. Lloyd thought of them as the government and the rebels.

Right now Saragossa was held by Franco's rebels, and Lloyd was looking toward the town from a vantage point fifty miles south. "Still, if we can take the town, the enemy will be bottled up in the north for another winter," he said.

"If," said Lenny.

It was a grim prognosis, Lloyd thought gloomily, when the best he could wish for was that the rebel advance might be halted. But no victory was in sight this year for the government.

All the same, a part of Lloyd was looking forward to the fight. He had been in Spain for ten months, and this would be his first taste of action. Until now he had been an instructor in a base camp. As soon as the Spaniards discovered he had been in Britain's Officer Training Corps, they had speeded him through his induction, made him a lieutenant, and put him in charge of new arrivals. He had to drill them until obeying orders became a reflex, march them until their feet stopped bleeding and their blisters turned to calluses, and show them how to strip down and clean what few rifles were available.

But the flood of volunteers had now slowed to a trickle, and the instructors had been moved to fighting battalions.

Lloyd wore a beret, a zipped blouson with his badge of rank roughly hand-sewn to the sleeve, and corduroy breeches. He carried a short Spanish Mauser rifle, firing seven-millimeter ammunition that had presumably been stolen from some Civil Guard arsenal.

Lloyd, Lenny, and Dave had been split up for a while, but the three had been reunited in the British battalion of the Fifteenth International

Brigade for the coming battle. Lenny now had a black beard and looked a decade older than his seventeen years. He had been made a sergeant, though he had no uniform, just blue dungarees and a striped bandana. He looked more like a pirate than a soldier.

Now Lenny said: "Anyway, this attack has nothing to do with bottling up the rebels. It's political. This region has always been dominated by the anarchists."

Lloyd had seen anarchism in action during a brief spell in Barcelona. It was a cheerfully fundamentalist form of Communism. Officers and men got the same pay. The dining rooms of the grand hotels had been turned into canteens for the workers. Waiters would hand back a tip, explaining amiably that the practise of tipping was demeaning. Posters everywhere condemned prostitution as exploitation of female comrades. There had been a wonderful atmosphere of liberation and camaraderie. The Russians hated it.

Lenny went on: "Now the government has brought Communist troops from the Madrid area and amalgamated us all into the new Army of the East—under overall Communist command, of course."

This kind of talk made Lloyd despair. The only way to win was for all the left-wing factions to work together, as they had—in the end, at least—at the Battle of Cable Street. But anarchists and Communists had been fighting each other in the streets of Barcelona. He said: "Prime Minister Negrín isn't a Communist."

"He might as well be."

"He understands that without the support of the Soviet Union we're finished."

"But does that mean we abandon democracy and let the Communists take over?"

Lloyd nodded. Every discussion about the government ended the same way: Do we have to do everything the Soviets want just because they are the only people who will sell us guns?

They walked down the hill. Lenny said: "We'll have a nice cup of tea, now, is it?"

"Yes, please. Two lumps of sugar in mine."

It was a standing joke. Neither of them had had tea for months.

They came to their camp by the river. Lenny's platoon had taken over a little cluster of crude stone buildings that had probably been cowsheds until the war drove the farmers away. A few yards upriver a boathouse had been occupied by some Germans from the Eleventh International Brigade.

Lloyd and Lenny were met by Lloyd's cousin Dave Williams. Like Lenny, Dave had aged ten years in one. He looked thin and hard, his skin tanned and dusty, his eyes wrinkled with squinting into the sun. He wore the khaki tunic and trousers, leather belt pouches, and ankle-buckled boots that formed the standard-issue uniform—though few soldiers had a complete set. He had a red cotton scarf around his neck. He carried a Russian Mosin-Nagant rifle with the old-fashioned spike bayonet reversed, making the weapon less clumsy. At his belt he had a German nine-millimeter Luger that he must have taken from the corpse of a rebel officer. Apparently he was very accurate with rifle or pistol.

"We've got a visitor," he said excitedly.

"Who is he?"

"She!" said Dave, and pointed.

In the shade of a misshapen black poplar tree, a dozen British and German soldiers were talking to a startlingly beautiful woman.

"Oh, *Duw*," said Lenny, using the Welsh word for *God*. "She's a sight for sore eyes."

She looked about twenty-five, Lloyd thought, and she was petite, with big eyes and a mass of black hair pinned up and topped by a fore-and-aft army cap. Somehow her baggy uniform seemed to cling to her like an evening gown.

A volunteer called Heinz who knew that Lloyd understood German spoke to him in that language. "This is Teresa, sir. She has come to teach us to read."

Lloyd nodded understanding. The International Brigades consisted of foreign volunteers mixed with Spanish soldiers, and literacy was a problem with the Spanish. They had spent their childhood chanting the catechism in village schools run by the Catholic Church. Many priests did not teach the children to read, for fear that in later life they would get hold of socialist books. As a result, only about half the population had been literate under the monarchy. The republican government elected in 1931 had improved education, but there remained millions of Spaniards who could not read or write, and classes for soldiers continued even in the front line.

"I'm illiterate," said Dave, who was not.

"Me, too," said Joe Eli, who taught Spanish literature at Columbia University in New York.

Teresa spoke in Spanish. Her voice was low and calm and very sexy. "How many times do you think I have heard this joke?" she said, but she did not seem very cross.

Lenny moved closer. "I'm Sergeant Griffiths," he said. "I'll do anything I can to help you, of course." His words were practical, but his tone of voice made them sound like an amorous invitation.

She gave him a dazzling smile. "That would be most helpful," she said.

Lloyd spoke formally to her in his best Spanish. "I'm so very glad you're here, señorita." He had spent much of the last ten months studying the language. "I am Lieutenant Williams. I can tell you exactly which members of the group require lessons . . . and which do not."

Lenny said dismissively: "But the lieutenant has to go to Bujaraloz to get our orders." Bujaraloz was the small town where government forces had set up headquarters. "Perhaps you and I should look around here for a suitable place to hold classes." He might have been suggesting a walk in the moonlight.

Lloyd smiled and nodded agreement. He was happy to let Lenny romance Teresa. He himself was in no mood for flirting, whereas Lenny seemed already in love. In Lloyd's opinion Lenny's chances were close to zero. Teresa was an educated twenty-five-year-old who probably got a dozen propositions a day, and Lenny was a seventeen-year-old coal miner who had not taken a bath for a month. But he said nothing: Teresa seemed capable of looking after herself.

A new figure appeared, a man of Lloyd's age who looked vaguely familiar. He was dressed better than the soldiers, in wool breeches and a cotton shirt, and had a handgun in a buttoned holster. His hair was cut so short it looked like stubble, a style favored by Russians. He was only a lieutenant, but had an air of authority, even power. He said in fluent German: "I am looking for Lieutenant Garcia."

"He's not here," said Lloyd in the same language. "Where have you and I met before?"

The Russian seemed shocked and irritated at the same time, like one who finds a snake in his bedroll. "We have never met," he said firmly. "You are mistaken."

Lloyd snapped his fingers. "Berlin," he said. "Nineteen thirty-three. We were attacked by Brownshirts."

A look of relief came briefly over the man's face, as if he had been expecting something worse. "Yes, I was there," he said. "My name is Vladimir Peshkov."

"But we called you Volodya."

"Yes."

"At that scrap in Berlin you were with a boy called Werner Franck."

Volodya looked panicked for a moment, then hid his feelings with an effort. "I know no one of that name."

Lloyd decided not to press the point. He could guess why Volodya was jumpy. The Russians were as terrified as everyone else of their secret police, the NKVD, who were operating in Spain and had a reputation for brutality. To them, any Russian who was friendly with foreigners might be a traitor. "I'm Lloyd Williams."

"I do remember." Volodya looked at him with a penetrating blue-eyed stare. "How strange that we should meet again here."

"Not so strange, really," Lloyd said. "We fight the Fascists wherever we can."

"Can I have a quiet word?"

"Of course."

They walked a few yards away from the others. Peshkov said: "There is a spy in Garcia's platoon."

Lloyd was astonished. "A spy? Who?"

"A German called Heinz Bauer."

"Why, that's him in the red shirt. A spy? Are you sure?"

Peshkov did not bother to answer that question. "I'd like you to summon him to your dugout, if you have one, or some other private place." Peshkov looked at his wristwatch. "In one hour, an arrest unit will be here to pick him up."

"I'm using that little shed as my office," said Lloyd, pointing. "But I need to speak to my commanding officer about this." The CO was a Communist, and unlikely to interfere, but Lloyd wanted time to think.

"If you wish." Volodya clearly did not care what Lloyd's commanding officer thought. "I want the spy taken quietly, without any fuss. I have explained to the arrest unit the importance of discretion." He sounded as if he was not sure his wishes would be obeyed. "The fewer people who know, the better."

"Why?" said Lloyd, but before Volodya could reply, he figured out the answer for himself. "You're hoping to turn him into a double agent, sending misleading reports to the enemy. But if too many people know he has been caught, then other spies may warn the rebels, and they will not believe the disinformation."

"It is better not to speculate about such matters," Peshkov said severely. "Now let us go to your shed."

"Wait a minute," said Lloyd. "How do you know he is a spy?"

"I can't tell you without compromising security."

"That's a bit unsatisfactory."

Peshkov looked exasperated. Clearly he was not used to being told that his explanations were unsatisfactory. Discussion of orders was a feature of the Spanish Civil War that the Russians particularly detested.

Before Peshkov could say anything further, two more men appeared and approached the group under the tree. One of the newcomers wore a leather jacket despite the heat. The other, who seemed to be in charge, was a scrawny man with a long nose and a receding chin.

Peshkov let out an exclamation of anger. "Too early!" he said; then he called out something indignant in Russian.

The scrawny man made a dismissive gesture. In rough Spanish he said: "Which one is Heinz Bauer?"

No one answered. The scrawny man wiped the end of his nose with his sleeve.

Then Heinz moved. He did not immediately flee, but cannoned into the man in the leather jacket, knocking him down. Then he dashed away—but the scrawny man stuck out a leg and tripped him up.

Heinz fell hard, his body skidding on the dry soil. He lay stunned—only for a moment, but it was a moment too long. As he got to his knees, the two men pounced on him and knocked him down again.

He lay still, but all the same they started to beat him up. They drew wooden clubs. Standing either side of him they took turns to hit his head and body, raising their arms above their heads and striking down in a vicious ballet. In a few seconds there was blood all over Heinz's face. He tried desperately to escape, but when he got to his knees, they pushed him down again. Then he curled up in a ball, whimpering. He was clearly finished, but they were not. They clubbed the helpless man again and again.

Lloyd found himself shouting a protest and pulling the scrawny man off. Lenny did the same to the other one. Lloyd grabbed his man in a bear hug and lifted him; Lenny knocked his man to the ground. Then Lloyd heard Volodya say in English: "Stand still, or I'll shoot!"

Lloyd let go of his man and turned, incredulous. Volodya had drawn his sidearm, a standard-issue Russian Nagant M1895 revolver, and cocked it. "Threatening an officer with a weapon is a court-martial offense in every army in the world," Lloyd said. "You're in deep trouble, Volodya."

"Don't be a fool," said Volodya. "When was the last time a Russian was in trouble in this army?" But he lowered the gun.

The man in the leather jacket raised his club as if to hit Lenny, but Volodya barked: "Back off, Berezovsky!" and the man obeyed.

Other soldiers appeared, drawn by the mysterious magnetism that attracts men to a fight, and in seconds there were twenty of them.

The scrawny man pointed a finger at Lloyd. Speaking English with a heavy accent, he said: "You have interfered in matters that do not concern you!"

Lloyd helped Heinz to his feet. He was groaning in pain and covered in blood.

"You people can't just march in and start beating people up!" Lloyd said to the scrawny man. "Where's your authority?"

"This German is a Trotsky-Fascist spy!" the man screeched.

Volodya said: "Shut up, Ilya."

Ilya took no notice. "He has been photographing documents!" he said.

"Where is your evidence?" Lloyd said calmly.

Ilya clearly did not know or care about the evidence. But Volodya sighed and said: "Look in his kit bag."

Lloyd nodded to Mario Rivera, a corporal. "Go and check," he said.

Corporal Rivera ran to the boathouse and disappeared inside.

But Lloyd had a dreadful feeling Volodya was telling the truth. He said: "Even if you're right, Ilya, you could use a little courtesy."

Ilya said: "Courtesy? This is a war, not an English tea party."

"It might save you from getting into unnecessary fights."

Ilya said something contemptuous in Russian.

Rivera emerged from the building carrying a small, expensive-looking camera and a sheaf of official papers. He showed them to Lloyd. The top document was yesterday's general order for deployment of troops ahead of the coming assault. The paper bore a wine stain of familiar shape, and Lloyd realized with a shock that it was his own copy, and must have been purloined from his shed.

He looked at Heinz, who straightened, gave the Fascist salute, and said: "*Heil* Hitler!"

Ilya looked triumphant.

Volodya said: "Well, Ilya, you have now ruined the prisoner's value as a double agent. Another coup for the NKVD. Congratulations." And he walked off.

### iii

Lloyd went into battle for the first time on Tuesday, August 24.

His side, the elected government, had eighty thousand men. The antidemocratic rebels had fewer than half that. The government also had two hundred aircraft against the rebels' fifteen.

To make the most of this superiority, the government advanced over a wide front, a north-south line sixty miles long, so that the rebels could not concentrate their limited numbers.

It was a good plan—so why, Lloyd asked himself two days later, was it not working?

It had started well enough. On the first day the government had taken two villages north of Saragossa and two to the south. Lloyd's group, in the south, had overcome fierce resistance to take a village called Codo. The only failure was the central push, up the river valley, which had stalled at a place called Fuentes de Ebro.

Lloyd had been scared, before the battle, and spent the night awake, imagining what was to come, as he sometimes did before a boxing match. But once the fighting started, he was too busy to worry. The worst moment was advancing across the barren scrubland, with no cover but stunted bushes, while the defenders fired from inside stone buildings. Even then, what he had felt was not fear but a kind of desperate cunning, zigzagging as he ran, crawling and rolling when the bullets came too near, then getting up and running, bent double, a few more yards. The main problem was shortage of ammunition: they had to make every shot count. They took Codo by force of numbers, and Lloyd, Lenny, and Dave ended the day unhurt.

The rebels were tough and brave—but so were the government forces. The foreign brigades were made up of idealistic volunteers who had come to Spain knowing they might have to give their lives. Because of their reputation for courage they were often chosen to spearhead attacks.

The assault began to go wrong on the second day. The northern forces had stayed put, reluctant to advance because of lack of intelligence about rebel defenses—a feeble excuse, Lloyd thought. The central group still could not take Fuentes de Ebro, despite being reinforced on the third day, and Lloyd was appalled to hear that they had lost nearly all their tanks to devastating defensive fire. In the south Lloyd's group, instead of pushing forward, was directed to make a sideways move, to the riverside village of Quinto. Once again they had to overcome determined defenders in house-to-house fighting. When the enemy surrendered, Lloyd's group took a thousand prisoners.

Now Lloyd sat in the evening light outside a church that had been wrecked by artillery fire, surrounded by the smoking ruins of houses and the strangely still bodies of the recently dead. A group of exhausted men gathered around him: Lenny, Dave, Joe Eli, Corporal Rivera, and a Welshman called Muggsy Morgan. There were so many Welshmen in Spain that someone had made up a limerick poking fun at the similarity in their names:

> There was a young fellow named Price
> And another young fellow named Price
> And a fellow named Roberts
> And a fellow named Roberts
> And another young fellow named Price.

The men were smoking, waiting quietly to see whether there would be any dinner, too weary even to banter with Teresa, who was, remarkably, still with them, as the transport due to take her to the rear had failed to appear. They could hear occasional bursts of shooting as mopping up continued a few streets away.

"What have we gained?" Lloyd said to Dave. "We used scarce ammunition, we lost a lot of men, and we're no farther forward. Worse, we've given the Fascists time to bring up reinforcements."

"I can tell you the fucking reason," Dave said in his East End accent. His soul had hardened even more than his body, and he had become cynical and contemptuous. "Our officers are more afraid of their commissars than of the fucking enemy. At the least excuse they can be branded as Trotsky-Fascist spies and tortured to death, so they're terrified of sticking their necks out. They'd rather sit still than move, they won't do anything on their own initiative, and they never take risks. I bet they don't shit without an order in writing."

Lloyd wondered whether Dave's scornful analysis was right. The Communists never ceased to talk about the need for a disciplined army with a clear chain of command. By that they meant an army following Russian orders, but all the same Lloyd saw their point. However, too much discipline could stifle thinking. Was that what was going wrong?

Lloyd did not want to believe it. Surely Social Democrats and Communists and anarchists could fight in their common cause without one group tyrannizing the others; they all hated Fascism, and they all believed in a future society that was fairer to everyone.

He wondered what Lenny thought, but Lenny was sitting next to Teresa, talking to her in a low voice. She giggled at something he said, and Lloyd guessed he must be making progress. It was a good sign when you could make a girl laugh. Then she touched his arm, said a few words, and stood up. Lenny said: "Hurry back." She smiled over her shoulder.

Lucky Lenny, thought Lloyd, but he felt no envy. A passing romance held no appeal for him: he did not see the point. He was an all or nothing man, he supposed. The only girl he had ever really wanted had been Daisy. She was now Boy Fitzherbert's wife, and Lloyd still had not met the girl who might take her place in his heart. He would, one day, he felt sure, but, meanwhile, he was not much attracted to temporary substitutes even when they were as alluring as Teresa.

Someone said: "Here come the Russians." The speaker was Jasper Johnson, a black American electrician from Chicago. Lloyd looked up to see a dozen or so military advisers walking through the village like conquerors. The Russians were recognizable by their leather jackets and buttoned holsters. "Strange thing, I didn't see them while we were fighting," Jasper went on sarcastically. "I guess they must have been in a different part of the battlefield."

Lloyd looked around, making sure that no political commissars were nearby to hear this subversive talk.

As the Russians passed through the graveyard of the ruined church, Lloyd spotted Ilya Dvorkin, the weaselly secret policeman he had clashed with a week ago. The Russian crossed paths with Teresa and stopped to speak to her. Lloyd heard him say something in bad Spanish about dinner.

She replied, he spoke again, and she shook her head, evidently refusing. She turned to walk away, but he took hold of her arm, detaining her.

Lloyd saw Lenny sit upright, looking alertly at the tableau, the two figures framed by a stone archway that no longer led anywhere.

"Oh, shit," said Lloyd.

Teresa tried again to move away, and Ilya seemed to tighten his grip.

Lenny moved to get up, but Lloyd put a hand on his shoulder and pushed him down. "Let me deal with this," he said.

Dave murmured a low warning. "Careful, mate—he's in the NKVD. Best not to mess with those fucking bastards."

Lloyd walked over to Teresa and Ilya.

The Russian saw him and said in Spanish: "Get lost."

Lloyd said: "Hello, Teresa."

She said: "I can handle this. Don't worry."

Ilya looked more closely at Lloyd. "I know you," he said. "You tried to prevent the arrest of a dangerous Trotsky-Fascist spy last week."

Lloyd said: "And is this young lady also a dangerous Trotsky-Fascist spy? I thought I just heard you ask her to have dinner with you."

Ilya's sidekick Berezovsky appeared and stood aggressively close to Lloyd.

Out of the corner of his eye, Lloyd saw Dave draw the Luger from his belt.

This was getting out of control.

Lloyd said: "I came to tell you, señorita, that Colonel Bobrov wants to see you in his headquarters immediately. Please follow me and I'll take you to him." Bobrov was a senior Russian military "adviser." He had not invited Teresa, but it was a plausible story, and Ilya did not know it was a lie.

For a frozen moment Lloyd could not tell which way it was going to go. Then the bang of a nearby gunshot was heard, perhaps from the next street. It seemed to return the Russians to reality. Teresa again moved away from Ilya, and this time he let her go.

Ilya pointed a finger aggressively at Lloyd's face. "I'll see you again," he said, and he made a dramatic exit, followed doglike by Berezovsky.

Dave said: "Stupid prick."

Ilya pretended not to hear.

They all sat down. Dave said: "You've made a bad enemy, Lloyd."

"I didn't have much choice."

"All the same, watch your back from now on."

"An argument about a girl," Lloyd said dismissively. "Happens a thousand times a day."

As darkness fell, a handbell summoned them to a field kitchen. Lloyd got a bowl of thin stew, a slab of dry bread, and a big cup of red wine so harsh tasting that he imagined it taking the enamel off his teeth. He dipped his bread in the wine, improving both.

When the food was gone, he was still hungry, as usual. He said. "We'll have a nice cup of tea, shall we?"

"Aye," said Lenny. "Two lumps of sugar, please."

They unrolled their thin blankets and prepared to sleep. Lloyd went in search of a latrine, found none, and relieved himself in a small orchard on the edge of the village. There was a three-quarter moon, and he could see the dusty leaves on olive trees that had survived the shelling.

As he buttoned up, he heard a footstep. He turned around slowly— too slowly. By the time he saw Ilya's face, the club was coming down on his head. He felt an agonizing pain and fell to the ground. Dazed, he looked up. Berezovsky held a short-barreled revolver pointed at his head. Beside him, Ilya said: "Don't move or you'll be dead."

Lloyd was terrified. Desperately he shook his head to clear it. This was insane. "Dead?" he said incredulously. "And how will you explain the murder of a lieutenant?"

"Murder?" said Ilya. He smiled. "This is the front line. A stray bullet got you." He switched to English. "Jolly bad luck."

Lloyd realized with despair that Ilya was right. When his body was found, it would look as if he had been killed in the battle.

What a way to die.

Ilya said to Berezovsky: "Finish him off."

There was a bang.

Lloyd felt nothing. Was this death? Then Berezovsky crumpled and fell to the ground. At the same moment Lloyd realized that the shot had come from behind him. He turned, incredulous, to look. In the moonlight he saw Dave holding his stolen Luger. Relief swamped him like a tidal wave. He was alive!

Ilya, too, had seen Dave, and he ran like a startled rabbit.

Dave tracked him with the pistol for several seconds, and Lloyd willed him to shoot, but Ilya dodged frantically between the olive trees, like a rat in a maze, then disappeared into the darkness.

Dave lowered the gun.

Lloyd looked down at Berezovsky. He was not breathing. Lloyd said: "Thanks, Dave."

"I told you to watch your back."

"You watched it for me. But it's a pity you didn't get Ilya, too. Now you're in trouble with the NKVD."

"I wonder," said Dave. "Will Ilya want people to know that he got his sidekick killed in a squabble over a woman? Even the NKVD people are frightened of the NKVD. I think he'll keep it quiet."

Lloyd looked again at the body. "How do we explain this?"

"You heard the man," Dave said. "This is the front line. No explanation needed."

Lloyd nodded. Dave and Ilya were both right. No one would ask how Berezovsky had died. A stray bullet got him.

They walked away, leaving the body where it lay.

"Jolly bad luck," said Dave.

## iv

Lloyd and Lenny spoke to Colonel Bobrov and complained that the attack on Saragossa was stalemated.

Bobrov was an older Russian with a cropped fuzz of white hair, nearing retirement and rigidly orthodox. In theory he was there only to help and advise the Spanish commanders. In practise the Russians called the shots.

"We're wasting time and energy on these little villages," Lloyd said, translating into German what Lenny and all the experienced men were saying. "Tanks are supposed to be armored fists, used for deep penetration, striking far into enemy territory. The infantry should follow, mopping up and securing after the enemy has been scattered."

Volodya was standing nearby, listening, and seemed by his expression to agree, though he said nothing.

"Small strongpoints like this wretched one-horse town should not be allowed to delay the advance, but should be bypassed and dealt with later by a second line," Lloyd finished.

Bobrov looked shocked. "This is the theory of the discredited Marshal Tuchachevsky!" he said in hushed tones. It was as if Lloyd had told a bishop to pray to Buddha.

"So what?" said Lloyd.

"He has confessed to treason and espionage, and has been executed."

Lloyd stared incredulously. "Are you telling me that the Spanish government cannot use modern tank tactics because some general has been purged in Moscow?"

"Lieutenant Williams, you are becoming disrespectful."

Lloyd said: "Even if the charges against Tuchachevsky are true, that doesn't mean his methods are wrong."

"That will do!" Bobrov thundered. "This conversation is over."

Any hope Lloyd might have had remaining was crushed when his battalion was moved from Quinto back in the direction they had come, another sideways maneuver. On September 1 they were part of the attack on Belchite, a well-defended but strategically worthless small town twenty-five miles wide of their objective.

It was another hard battle.

Some seven thousand defenders were well dug in at the town's largest church, San Agustin, and atop a nearby hill, with trenches and earthworks. Lloyd and his platoon reached the outskirts of town without casualties, but then came under withering fire from windows and rooftops.

Six days later they were still there.

The corpses were stinking in the heat. As well as humans, there were dead animals, for the town's water supply had been cut off and livestock were dying of thirst. Whenever they could, the engineers stacked the bodies up, doused them with gasoline, and set fire to them, but the smell of roasting humans was worse than the stink of corruption. It seemed hard to breathe, and some of the men wore their gas masks.

The narrow streets around the church were killing fields, but Lloyd had devised a way to make progress without going outside. Lenny had found some tools in a workshop. Now two men were making a hole in the wall of the house in which they were sheltering. Joe Eli was using a pickax, sweat gleaming on his bald head. Corporal Rivera, who wore a striped shirt in the anarchist colors of red and black, wielded a sledgehammer. The wall was made of flat, yellow local bricks, roughly mortared. Lenny directed the operation to make sure they did not bring the entire house down: as a miner, he had an instinct for the trustworthiness of a roof.

When the hole was big enough for a man to pass through, Lenny nodded to Jasper, also a corporal. Jasper took one of his few remaining grenades from his belt pouch, drew the pin, and threw it into the next house, just in case there was an ambush. As soon as it had exploded, Lloyd crawled quickly through the hole, rifle at the ready.

He found himself in another poor Spanish home, with whitewashed walls and a floor of beaten earth. There was no one here, dead or alive.

The thirty-five men of his platoon followed him through the hole and ran through the place to flush out any defenders. The house was small and empty.

In this way they were moving slowly but safely through a row of cottages toward the church.

They started work on the next hole, but before they broke through, they were halted by a major called Marquez who came along the row of houses by the route they had made through the walls. "Forget all that," he said in Spanish-accented English. "We're going to rush the church."

Lloyd went cold. It was suicidal. He said: "Is that Colonel Bobrov's idea?"

"Yes," said Major Marquez noncommittally. "Wait for the signal: three sharp blows on the whistle."

"Can we get more ammunition?" Lloyd said. "We're low, especially for this kind of action."

"No time," said the major, and he went away.

Lloyd was horrified. He had learned a lot in a few days of battle, and he knew that the only way to rush a well-defended position was under a hail of covering fire. Otherwise the defenders would just mow the attackers down.

The men looked mutinous, and Corporal Rivera said: "It is impossible."

Lloyd was responsible for maintaining their morale. "No complaints, you lot," he said breezily. "You're all volunteers. Did you think war wasn't dangerous? If it was safe, your sisters could do it for you." They laughed, and the moment of danger passed, for now.

He moved to the front of the house, opened the door a crack, and peeped out. The sun glared down on a narrow street with houses and shops on both sides. The buildings and the ground were the same pale tan color, like undercooked bread, except where shelling had gouged up red earth. Right outside the door a militiaman lay dead, a cloud of flies feasting on the hole in his chest. Looking toward the square, Lloyd saw that the street widened toward the church. The gunmen in the high twin towers had a clear view and an easy shot at anyone approaching. On the ground there was only minimal cover: some rubble, a dead horse, a wheelbarrow.

We're all going to die, he thought.

But why else did we come here?

He turned back to his men, wondering what to say. He had to keep them thinking positively. "Just hug the sides of the street, close to the houses," he said. "Remember, the slower you go, the longer you're exposed—so wait for the whistle, then run like fuck."

Sooner than expected, he heard the three sharp chirrups of Major Marquez's whistle.

"Lenny, you're last out," he said.

"Who's first?" said Lenny.

"I am, of course."

Good-bye, world, Lloyd thought. At least I'll die fighting Fascists.

He threw the door wide. "Let's go!" he yelled, and he ran out.

Surprise gave him a few seconds' grace, and he ran freely along the street toward the church. He felt the scorch of the midday sun on his face and heard the pounding of his men's boots behind him, and noted with a weird sentiment of gratitude that such sensations meant he was still alive. Then gunfire broke out like a hailstorm. For a few more heartbeats he ran, hearing the zip and thwack of bullets, then there was a feeling in his left arm as if he had banged it against something, and inexplicably he fell down.

He realized he had been hit. There was no pain, but his arm was numb and hung lifeless. He managed to roll sideways until he hit the wall of the nearest building. Shots continued to fly, and he was terribly vulnerable, but a few feet ahead he saw a dead body. It was a rebel soldier, propped against the house. He looked as if he had been sitting on the ground, resting with his back against the wall, and had gone to sleep, except that there was a bullet wound in his neck.

Lloyd wriggled forward, moving awkwardly, rifle in his right hand, left arm dragging behind, then crouched behind the body, trying to make himself small.

He rested his rifle barrel on the dead man's shoulder and took aim at a high window in the church tower. He fired all five rounds in his magazine in rapid succession. He could not tell whether he had hit anyone.

He looked back. To his horror he saw the street littered with the corpses of his platoon. The still body of Mario Rivera in his red-and-black shirt looked like a crumpled anarchist flag. Next to Mario was

Jasper Johnson, his black curls soaked in blood. All the way from a factory in Chicago, Lloyd thought, to die on the street in a small town in Spain, because he believed in a better world.

Worse were those who still lived, moaning and crying on the ground. Somewhere a man was screaming in agony, but Lloyd could not see who or where. A few of his men were still running, but as he watched, more fell and others threw themselves down. Seconds later no one was moving except the writhing wounded.

What a slaughter, he thought, and a bile of anger and sorrow rose chokingly in his throat.

Where were the other units? Surely Lloyd's platoon was not the only one involved in the attack? Perhaps others were advancing along parallel streets leading to the square. But a rush required overwhelming numbers. Lloyd and his thirty-five were obviously too few. The defenders had been able to kill and wound nearly all of them, and the few who remained of Lloyd's platoon had been forced to take cover before reaching the church.

He caught the eye of Lenny, peering from behind the dead horse. At least he was still alive. Lenny held up his rifle and made a helpless gesture, pantomiming "no ammunition." Lloyd was out, too. In the next minute, firing from the street died away as the others also ran out of bullets.

That was the end of the attack on the church. It had been impossible anyway. With no ammunition it would have been pointless suicide.

The hail of fire from the church had lessened as the easier targets were eliminated, but sporadic sniping continued at those remaining behind cover. Lloyd realized that all his men would be killed eventually. They had to withdraw.

They would probably all be killed in the retreat.

He caught Lenny's eye again and waved emphatically toward the rear, away from the church. Lenny looked around, repeating the gesture to the few others left alive. They would have a better chance if they all moved at the same time.

When as many as possible had been forewarned, Lloyd struggled to his feet.

"Retreat!" he yelled at the top of his voice.

Then he began to run.

It was no more than two hundred yards, but it was the longest journey of his life.

The rebels in the church opened fire as soon as they saw the government troops move. Out of the corner of his eye Lloyd thought he saw five or six of his men retreating. He ran with a ragged gait, his wounded arm putting him off balance. Lenny was ahead of him, apparently unhurt. Bullets scored the masonry of the buildings that Lloyd staggered past. Lenny made it to the house they had come from, dashed in, and held the door open. Lloyd ran in, panting hoarsely, and collapsed on the floor. Three more followed them in.

Lloyd stared at the survivors: Lenny, Dave, Muggsy Morgan, and Joe Eli. "Is that all?" he said.

Lenny said: "Yes."

"Jesus. Five of us left, out of thirty-six."

"What a great military adviser Colonel Bobrov is."

They stood panting, catching their breath. The feeling returned to Lloyd's arm and it hurt like hell. He found he could move it, painfully, so perhaps it was not broken. Looking down, he saw that his sleeve was soaked with blood. Dave took off his red scarf and improvised a sling.

Lenny had a head wound. There was blood on his face, but he said it was a scratch, and he seemed all right.

Dave, Muggsy, and Joe were miraculously unhurt.

"We'd better go back for fresh orders," Lloyd said when they had lain down a few minutes. "We can't accomplish anything without ammunition anyway."

"Let's have a nice cup of tea first, is it?" said Lenny.

Lloyd said: "We can't. We haven't got teaspoons."

"Oh, all right, then."

Dave said: "Can't we rest here a bit longer?"

"We'll rest in the rear," Lloyd said. "It's safer."

They made their way back along the row of houses, using the holes they had made in the walls. The repeated bending made Lloyd dizzy. He wondered if he was weak from loss of blood.

They emerged out of sight of the church of San Agustin, and hurried along a side street. Lloyd's relief at still being alive was rapidly giving way to a feeling of rage at the waste of the lives of his men.

They came to the barn on the outskirts where the government forces had made their headquarters. Lloyd saw Major Marquez behind a stack of crates, giving out ammunition. "Why couldn't we have had some of that?" he said furiously.

Marquez just shrugged.

"I'm reporting this to Bobrov," Lloyd said.

Colonel Bobrov was outside the barn, sitting on a chair at a table, both of which looked as if they had been taken from a village house. His face was reddened with sunburn. He was talking to Volodya Peshkov. Lloyd went straight up to them. "We rushed the church, but we had no support," he said. "And we ran out of ammunition because Marquez refused to supply us!"

Bobrov looked coldly at Lloyd. "What are you doing here?" he said.

Lloyd was puzzled. He expected Bobrov to congratulate him for a brave effort and at least commiserate with him over the lack of support. "I just told you," he said. "There was no support. You can't rush a fortified building with one platoon. We did our best, but we were slaughtered. I've lost thirty-one of my thirty-six men." He pointed at his four companions. "This is all that's left of my platoon!"

"Who ordered you to retreat?"

Lloyd was fighting off dizziness. He felt close to collapse, but he had to explain to Bobrov how bravely his men had fought. "We came back for fresh orders. What else could we do?"

"You should have fought to the last man."

"What should we have fought with? We had no bullets!"

"Silence!" Bobrov barked. "Stand to attention!"

Automatically, they all stood to attention: Lloyd, Lenny, Dave, Muggsy, and Joe in a line. Lloyd feared he was about to faint.

"About-face!"

They turned their backs. Lloyd thought: What now?

"Those who are wounded, fall out."

Lloyd and Lenny stepped back.

Bobrov said: "The walking wounded are transferred to prisoner escort duty."

Dimly, Lloyd perceived that this meant he would probably be guarding prisoners of war on a train to Barcelona. He swayed on his feet. Right now I couldn't guard a flock of sheep, he thought.

Bobrov said: "Retreating under fire without orders is desertion."

Lloyd turned and looked at Bobrov. To his astonishment and horror he saw that Bobrov had drawn his revolver from its buttoned holster.

Bobrov stepped forward so that he was immediately behind the three men standing to attention. "You three are found guilty and sentenced to death." He raised the gun until the barrel was three inches from the back of Dave's head.

Then he fired.

There was a bang. A bullet hole appeared in Dave's head, and blood and brains exploded from his brow.

Lloyd could not believe what he was seeing.

Next to Dave, Muggsy began to turn, his mouth open to shout, but Bobrov was quicker. He swung the gun to Muggsy's neck and fired again. The bullet entered behind Muggsy's right ear and came out through his left eye, and he crumpled.

At last Lloyd's voice came, and he shouted: "No!"

Joe Eli turned, roaring with shock and rage, and raised his hands to grab Bobrov. The gun banged again and Joe got a bullet in the throat. Blood spurted like a fountain from his neck and splashed Bobrov's Red Army uniform, causing the colonel to curse and jump back a pace. Joe fell to the ground but did not die immediately. Lloyd watched, helpless, as the blood pumped out of Joe's carotid artery into the parched Spanish earth. Joe seemed to try to speak, but no words came, and then his eyes closed and he went limp.

"There's no mercy for cowards," Bobrov said, and he walked away.

Lloyd looked at Dave on the ground: thin, grimy, brave as a lion, sixteen years old, and dead. Killed not by the Fascists but by a stupid and brutal Soviet officer. What a waste, Lloyd thought, and tears came to his eyes.

A sergeant came running out of the barn. "They've given up!" he shouted joyfully. "The town hall has surrendered—they've raised the white flag. We've taken Belchite!"

The dizziness overwhelmed Lloyd at last, and he fainted.

**v**

London was cold and wet. Lloyd walked along Nutley Street in the rain, heading for his mother's house. He still wore his zipped Spanish army blouson and corduroy breeches, and boots with no socks. He carried a small backpack containing his spare underwear, a shirt, and a tin cup. Around his neck he had the red scarf Dave had turned into an improvised sling for his wounded arm. The arm still hurt, but he no longer needed the sling.

It was late on an October afternoon.

As expected, he had been put on a supply train returning to Barcelona crammed with rebel prisoners. The journey was not much more than a hundred miles, but it had taken three days. In Barcelona he had been separated from Lenny and lost contact. He had got a lift in a lorry going north. After the trucker dropped him off, he had walked, hitchhiked, and ridden in railway wagons full of coal or gravel or—on one lucky occasion—cases of wine. He had slipped across the border into France at night. He had slept rough, begged food, done odd jobs for a few coins, and, for two glorious weeks, earned his cross-channel boat fare picking grapes in a Bordeaux vineyard. Now he was home.

He inhaled the damp, soot-smelling Aldgate air as if it were perfume. He stopped at the garden gate and looked up at the terraced house in which he had been born more than twenty-two years ago. Lights glowed behind the rain-streaked windows: someone was at home. He walked up to the front door. He still had his key: he had kept it with his passport. He let himself in.

He dropped his backpack on the floor in the hall, by the hat stand.

From the kitchen he heard: "Who's that?" It was the voice of his stepfather, Bernie.

Lloyd found he could not speak.

Bernie came into the hall. "Who . . . ?" Then he recognized Lloyd. "My life!" he said. "It's you."

Lloyd said: "Hello, Dad."

"My boy," said Bernie. He put his arms around Lloyd. "Alive," Bernie said. Lloyd could feel him shaking with sobs.

After a minute Bernie rubbed his eyes with the sleeve of his cardigan, then went to the bottom of the stairs. "Eth!" he called.

"What?"

"Someone to see you."

"Just a minute."

She came down the stairs a few seconds later, pretty as ever in a blue dress. Halfway down she saw his face and turned pale. "Oh, *Duw*," she said. "It's Lloyd." She came down the rest of the stairs in a rush and threw her arms around him. "You're alive!" she said.

"I wrote to you from Barcelona—"

"We never got that letter."

"Then you don't know . . ."

"What?"

"Dave Williams died."

"Oh, no!"

"Killed at the Battle of Belchite." Lloyd had decided not to tell the truth about how Dave died.

"What about Lenny Griffiths?"

"I don't know. I lost touch with him. I was hoping he might have got home before me."

"No, there's no word."

Bernie said: "What was it like over there?"

"The Fascists are winning. And it's mainly the fault of the Communists, who are more interested in attacking the other left parties."

Bernie was shocked. "Surely not."

"It's true. If I've learned one thing in Spain, it's that we have to fight the Communists just as hard as the Fascists. They're both evil."

His mother smiled wryly. "Well, just fancy that." She had figured out the same thing long ago, Lloyd realized.

"Enough politics," he said. "How are you, Mam?"

"Oh, I'm the same, but look at you—you're so thin!"

"Not much to eat in Spain."

"I'd better make you something."

"No rush. I've been hungry for twelve months—I can keep going a few more minutes. I tell you what would be nice, though."

"What? Anything!"

"I'd love a nice cup of tea."

# CHAPTER FIVE

# 1939

T homas Macke was watching the Soviet embassy in Berlin when Volodya Peshkov came out.

The Prussian secret police had been transformed into the new, more efficient Gestapo six years ago, but Commissar Macke was still in charge of the section that monitored traitors and subversives in the city of Berlin. The most dangerous of them were undoubtedly getting their orders from this building at 63–65 Unter den Linden. So Macke and his men watched everyone who went in and came out.

The embassy was an art deco fortress made of a white stone that painfully reflected the glare of the August sun. A pillared lantern stood watchful above the central block, and to either side the wings had rows of tall, narrow windows like guardsmen at attention.

Macke sat at a pavement café opposite. Berlin's most elegant boulevard was busy with cars and bicycles; the women shopped in their summer dresses and hats; the men walked briskly by in suits or smart uniforms. It was hard to believe there were still German Communists. How could anyone possibly be against the Nazis? Germany was transformed. Hitler had wiped out unemployment—something no other European leader had achieved. Strikes and demonstrations were a distant memory of the bad old days. The police had no-nonsense powers to stamp out crime. The country was prospering: many families had a radio, and soon they would have people's cars to drive on the new autobahns.

And that was not all. Germany was strong again. The military was well armed and powerful. In the last two years both Austria and Czechoslovakia had been absorbed into Greater Germany, which was now the dominant power in Europe. Mussolini's Italy was allied with Germany in the Pact of Steel. Earlier this year Madrid had at last fallen to Franco's rebels, and Spain now had a Fascist-friendly government. How could any German wish to undo all that and bring the country under the heel of the Bolsheviks?

In Macke's eyes such people were scum, vermin, filth that had to be ruthlessly sought out and utterly destroyed. As he thought about them, his face twisted into a scowl of anger, and he tapped his foot on the pavement as if preparing to stomp a Communist.

Then he saw Peshkov.

He was a young man in a blue serge suit, carrying a light coat over his arm as if expecting a change in the weather. His close-cropped hair and quick march indicated the army, despite his civilian clothes, and the way he scanned the street, deceptively casual but thorough, suggested either Red Army Intelligence or the NKVD, the Russian secret police.

Macke's pulse quickened. He and his men knew everyone at the embassy by sight, of course. Their passport photographs were on file and the team watched them all the time. But he did not know much about Peshkov. The man was young—twenty-five, according to his file, Macke recalled—so he might be a junior staffer of no importance. Or he could be good at seeming unimportant.

Peshkov crossed Unter den Linden and walked toward where Macke sat, near the corner of Friedrich Strasse. As Peshkov came closer, Macke noted that the Russian was quite tall, with the build of an athlete. He had an alert look and an intense gaze.

Macke looked away, suddenly nervous. He picked up his cup and sipped the cold dregs of his coffee, partly covering his face. He did not want to meet those blue eyes.

Peshkov turned onto Friedrich Strasse. Macke nodded to Reinhold Wagner, standing on the opposite corner, and Wagner followed Peshkov. Macke then got up from his table and followed Wagner.

Not everyone in Red Army Intelligence was a cloak-and-dagger spy, of course. They got most of their information legitimately, mainly by reading the German newspapers. They did not necessarily believe everything they read, but they took note of clues such as an advertisement by a gun factory needing to recruit ten skilled lathe operators. Furthermore, Russians were free to travel Germany and look around— unlike diplomats in the Soviet Union, who were not allowed to leave Moscow unescorted. The young man whom Macke and Wagner were now tailing might be the tame, newspaper-reading kind of intelligence gatherer; all that was required for such a job was fluent German and the ability to summarize.

They followed Peshkov past Macke's brother's restaurant. It was still called Bistro Robert, but it had a different clientele. Gone were the wealthy homosexuals, the Jewish businessmen with their mistresses, and the overpaid actresses calling for pink champagne. Such people kept their heads down nowadays, if they were not already in concentration camps. Some had left Germany—and good riddance, Macke thought, even if it did, unfortunately, mean that the restaurant no longer made much money.

He wondered idly what had become of the former owner, Robert von Ulrich. He vaguely remembered the man had gone to England. Perhaps he had opened a restaurant for perverts there.

Peshkov went into a bar.

Wagner followed him in a minute or two later, while Macke watched the outside. It was a popular place. While Macke waited for Peshkov to reappear, he saw a soldier and a girl enter, and a couple of well-dressed women and an old man in a grubby coat come out and walk away. Then Wagner came out alone, looked directly at Macke, and spread his arms in a gesture of bewilderment.

Macke crossed the street. Wagner was distressed. "He's not there!"

"Did you look everywhere?"

"Yes, including the toilets and the kitchen."

"Did you ask if anyone had gone out the back way?"

"They said not."

Wagner was scared, with reason. This was the new Germany, and errors were no longer dealt with by a slap on the wrist. He could be severely punished.

But not this time. "That's all right," said Macke.

Wagner could not hide his relief. "Is it?"

"We've learned something important," Macke said. "The fact that he shook us off so expertly tells us that he's a spy—and a very good one."


## ii

Volodya entered the Friedrich Strasse station and boarded a U-Bahn train. He took off the cap, glasses, and dirty raincoat that had helped him look like an old man. He sat down, took out a handkerchief, and wiped away the powder he had put on his shoes to make them appear shabby.

He had been unsure about the raincoat. It was such a sunny day that he feared the Gestapo might have noticed it and realized what he was up to. But they had not been that clever, and no one had followed him from the bar after he had done his quick change in the men's room.

He was about to do something highly dangerous. If they caught him contacting a German dissident, the best that he could expect was to be deported back to Moscow with his career in ruins. If he was less lucky, he and the dissident would both vanish into the basement of Gestapo headquarters in Prinz-Albrecht-Strasse, never to be seen again. The Soviets would complain that one of their diplomats had disappeared, and the German police would pretend to do a missing-persons search, then regretfully report no success.

Volodya had never been to Gestapo headquarters, of course, but he knew what it would be like. The NKVD had a similar facility in the Soviet Trade Mission at 11 Lietsenburger Strasse: steel doors, an interrogation room with tiled walls so that the blood could be washed off easily, a tub for cutting up the bodies, and an electrical furnace for burning the parts.

Volodya had been sent to Berlin to expand the network of Soviet spies there. Fascism was triumphant in Europe, and Germany was more of a threat to the USSR now than ever. Stalin had fired his foreign minister, Litvinov, and replaced him with Vyacheslav Molotov. But what could Molotov do? The Fascists seemed unstoppable. The Kremlin was haunted by the humiliating memory of the Great War, in which the Germans had defeated a Russian army of six million men. Stalin had taken steps to form a pact with France and Britain to restrain Germany, but the three powers had been unable to agree, and the talks had broken down in the last few days.

Sooner or later, war was expected between Germany and the Soviet Union, and it was Volodya's job to gather military intelligence that would help the Soviets win that war.

He got off the train in the poor working-class district of Wedding, north of Berlin's center. Outside the station he stood and waited, watching the other passengers as they left, pretending to study a timetable pasted on the wall. He did not move off until he was quite sure no one had followed him there.

Then he made his way to the cheap restaurant that was his chosen rendezvous. As was his regular practise, he did not go in, but stood at a bus stop on the other side of the road and watched the entrance. He was confident he had shaken off any tail, but now he needed to make sure Werner had not been followed.

He was not sure he would recognize Werner Franck, who had been a fourteen-year-old boy when Volodya last saw him, and was now twenty. Werner felt the same, so they had agreed they would both carry today's edition of the *Berliner Morgenpost* open to the sports page. Volodya read a preview of the new soccer season as he waited, glancing up every few seconds to look for Werner. Ever since he was a schoolboy in Berlin, Volodya had followed the city's top team, Hertha. He had often chanted: "Ha! Ho! He! Hertha B-S-C!" He was interested in the team's prospects, but anxiety spoiled his concentration, and he read the same report over and over again without taking anything in.

His two years in Spain had not boosted his career in the way he had hoped—rather the reverse. Volodya had uncovered numerous Nazi spies like Heinz Bauer among the German "volunteers." But then the NKVD had used that as an excuse to arrest genuine volunteers who had merely expressed mild disagreement with the Communist line. Hundreds of idealistic young men had been tortured and killed in the NKVD's prisons. At times it had seemed as if the Communists were more interested in fighting their anarchist allies than their Fascist enemies.

And all for nothing. Stalin's policy was a catastrophic failure. The upshot was a right-wing dictatorship, the worst imaginable outcome for the Soviet Union. But the blame was put on those Russians who had been in Spain, even though they had faithfully carried out Kremlin instructions. Some of them had disappeared soon after returning to Moscow.

Volodya had gone home in fear after the fall of Madrid. He had found many changes. In 1937 and 1938 Stalin had purged the Red Army. Thousands of commanders had disappeared, including many of the residents of Government House, where his parents lived. But previously neglected men such as Grigori Peshkov had been promoted to take the places of those purged, and Grigori's career had a new impetus. He was in charge of the defense of Moscow against air raids, and was frantically busy. His enhanced status was probably the reason why Volodya was not among those scapegoated for the failure of Stalin's Spanish policy.

The unpleasant Ilya Dvorkin had also somehow avoided punishment. He was back in Moscow and married to Volodya's sister, Anya, much to Volodya's regret. There was no accounting for women's choices in such matters. She was already pregnant, and Volodya could not repress a nightmare image of her nursing a baby with the head of a rat.

After a brief leave Volodya had been posted to Berlin, where he had to prove his worth all over again.

He looked up from his paper to see Werner walking along the street.

Werner had not changed much. He was a little taller and broader, but he had the same strawberry blond hair falling over his forehead in a way girls had found irresistible, the same look of tolerant amusement in his blue eyes. He wore an elegant light blue summer suit, and gold links glinted at his cuffs.

There was no one following him.

Volodya crossed the road and intercepted him before he reached the café. Werner smiled broadly, showing white teeth. "I wouldn't have recognized you with that army haircut," he said. "It's good to see you, after all these years."

He had not lost any of his warmth and charm, Volodya noted. "Let's go inside."

"You don't really want to go into that dump, do you?" Werner said. "It will be full of plumbers eating sausages with mustard."

"I want to get off the street. Here we could be seen by anyone passing."

"There's an alley three doors down."

"Good."

They walked a short distance and turned into a narrow passage between a coal yard and a grocery store. "What have you been doing?" Werner said.

"Fighting the Fascists, just like you." Volodya considered whether to tell him more. "I was in Spain." It was no secret.

"Where you had no more success than we did here in Germany."

"But it's not over yet."

"Let me ask you something," Werner said, leaning against the wall. "If you thought Bolshevism was wicked, would you be a spy working against the Soviet Union?"

Volodya's instinct was to say *No, absolutely not!* But before the words came out, he realized how tactless that would be—for the prospect that revolted him was precisely what Werner was doing, betraying his country for the sake of a higher cause. "I don't know," he said. "I think it must be very difficult for you to work against Germany, even though you hate the Nazis."

"You're right," Werner said. "And what happens if war breaks out? Am I going to help you kill our soldiers and bomb our cities?"

Volodya was worried. It seemed that Werner was weakening. "It's the only way to defeat the Nazis," he said. "You know that."

"I do. I made my decision a long time ago. And the Nazis have done nothing to change my mind. It's hard, that's all."

"I understand," Volodya said sympathetically.

Werner said: "You asked me to suggest other people who might do for you what I do."

Volodya nodded. "People like Willi Frunze. Remember him? Cleverest boy in school. He was a serious socialist—he chaired that meeting the Brownshirts broke up."

Werner shook his head. "He went to England."

Volodya's heart sank. "Why?"

"He's a brilliant physicist and he's studying in London."

"Shit."

"But I've thought of someone else."

"Good!"

"Did you ever know Heinrich von Kessel?"

"I don't think so. Was he at our school?"

"No, he went to a Catholic school. And in those days he didn't share our politics, either. His father was a big shot in the Centre Party—"

"Which put Hitler in power in 1933!"

"Correct. Heinrich was then working for his father. The father has now joined the Nazis, but the son is racked by guilt."

"How do you know?"

"He got drunk and told my sister, Frieda. She's seventeen. I think he fancies her."

This was promising. Volodya's spirits lifted. "Is he a Communist?"

"No."

"What makes you think he'll work for us?"

"I asked him, straight out. 'If you got a chance to fight against the Nazis by spying for the Soviet Union, would you do it?' He said he would."

"What's his job?"

"He's in the army, but he has a weak chest, so they made him a pen pusher—which is lucky for us, because now he works for the Supreme High Command in the economic planning and procurement department."

Volodya was impressed. Such a man would know exactly how many trucks and tanks and machine guns and submarines the German military was acquiring month by month—and where they were being deployed. He began to feel excited. "When can I meet him?"

"Now. I've arranged to have a drink with him in the Hotel Adlon after work."

Volodya groaned. The Adlon was Berlin's swankiest hotel. It was located on Unter den Linden. Because it was in the government and diplomatic district, the bar was a favorite haunt of journalists hoping to pick up gossip. It would not have been Volodya's choice of rendezvous. But he could not afford to miss this chance. "All right," he said. "But I'm not going to be seen talking to either of you in that place. I'll follow you in, identify Heinrich, then follow him out and accost him later."

"Okay. I'll drive you there. My car's around the corner."

As they walked to the other end of the alley, Werner told Volodya Heinrich's work and home addresses and phone numbers, and Volodya committed them to memory.

"Here we are," said Werner. "Jump in."

The car was a Mercedes 540K Autobahnkurier, a model that was head-turningly beautiful, with sensually curved fenders, a bonnet longer than an entire Ford Model T, and a sloping fastback rear end. It was so expensive that only a handful had ever been sold.

Volodya stared aghast. "Shouldn't you have a less ostentatious car?" he said incredulously.

"It's a double bluff," Werner said. "They think no real spy would be so flamboyant."

Volodya was going to ask how he could afford it, but then he recalled that Werner's father was a wealthy manufacturer.

"I'm not getting into that thing," Volodya said. "I'll go by train."

"As you wish."

"I'll see you at the Adlon, but don't acknowledge me."

"Of course."

Half an hour later Volodya saw Werner's car carelessly parked in front of the hotel. This cavalier attitude of Werner's seemed foolish to him, but now he wondered whether it was a necessary element of Werner's courage. Perhaps Werner had to pretend to be carefree in order to take the appalling risks required to spy on the Nazis. If he acknowledged the danger he was in, maybe he would not be able to carry on.

The bar of the Adlon was full of fashionable women and well-dressed men, many in smartly tailored uniforms. Volodya spotted Werner right away, at a table with another man who was presumably Heinrich von Kessel. Passing close to them, Volodya heard Heinrich say argumentatively: "Buck Clayton is a much better trumpeter than Hot Lips Page." He squeezed in at the counter, ordered a beer, and discreetly studied the new potential spy.

Heinrich had pale skin and thick dark hair that was long by army standards. Although they were talking about the relatively unimportant topic of jazz, he seemed very intense, arguing with gestures and repeatedly running his fingers through his hair. He had a book stuffed into the pocket of his uniform tunic, and Volodya would have bet it contained poetry.

Volodya drank two beers slowly and pretended to read the *Morgenpost* from cover to cover. He tried not to get too keyed up about Heinrich. The man was thrillingly promising, but there was no guarantee he would cooperate.

Recruiting informers was the hardest part of Volodya's work. Precautions were difficult to take because the target was not yet on his side. The proposition often had to be made in inappropriate places, usually somewhere public. It was impossible to know how the target would react: he might be angry and shout his refusal, or be terrified and literally run away. But there was not much the recruiter could do to control the situation. At some point he just had to ask the simple, blunt question: "Do you want to be a spy?"

He thought about how to approach Heinrich. Religion was probably the key to his personality. Volodya recalled his boss, Lemitov, saying: "Lapsed Catholics make good agents. They reject the total authority of the Church only to accept the total authority of the party." Heinrich might need to seek forgiveness for what he had done. But would he risk his life?

At last Werner paid the bill and the two men left. Volodya followed. Outside the hotel they parted company, Werner driving off with a squeal of tires and Heinrich going on foot across the park. Volodya went after Heinrich.

Night was falling, but the sky was clear and he could see well. There were many people strolling in the warm evening air, most of them in couples. Volodya looked back repeatedly, to make sure no one had followed him or Heinrich from the Adlon. When he was satisfied, he took a deep breath, steeled his nerve, and caught up with Heinrich.

Walking alongside him, Volodya said: "There is atonement for sin."

Heinrich looked at him warily, as at someone who might be mad. "Are you a priest?"

"You could strike back at the wicked regime you helped to create."

Heinrich kept walking, but he looked worried. "Who are you? What do you know about me?"

Volodya continued to ignore Heinrich's questions. "The Nazis will be defeated, one day. That day could come sooner, with your help."

"If you're a Gestapo agent hoping to entrap me, don't bother. I'm a loyal German."

"Do you notice my accent?"

"Yes—you sound Russian."

"How many Gestapo agents speak German with a Russian accent? Or have the imagination to fake it?"

Heinrich laughed nervously. "I know nothing about Gestapo

agents," he said. "I shouldn't have mentioned the subject—very foolish of me."

"Your office produces reports of the quantities of armaments and other supplies ordered by the military. Copies of those reports could be immeasurably useful to the enemies of the Nazis."

"To the Red Army, you mean."

"Who else is going to destroy this regime?"

"We keep careful track of all copies of such reports."

Volodya suppressed a surge of triumph. Heinrich was thinking about practical difficulties. That meant he was inclined to agree in principle. "Make an extra carbon," Volodya said. "Or write out a copy in longhand. Or take someone's file copy. There are ways."

"Of course there are. And any of them could get me killed."

"If we do nothing about the crimes that are being committed by this regime . . . is life worth living?"

Heinrich stopped and stared at Volodya. Volodya could not guess what the man was thinking, but instinct told him to remain quiet. After a long pause, Heinrich sighed and said: "I'll think about it."

I have him, Volodya thought exultantly.

Heinrich said: "How do I contact you?"

"You don't," Volodya said. "I will contact you." He touched the brim of his hat, then walked back the way he had come.

He felt exultant. If Heinrich had not meant to accept the proposition, he would have rejected it firmly. His promising to think about it was almost as good as acceptance. He would sleep on it. He would run over the dangers. But he would do it, eventually. Volodya felt almost certain.

He told himself not to be overconfident. A hundred things could go wrong.

All the same he was full of hope as he left the park and walked in bright lights past the shops and restaurants of Unter den Linden. He had had no dinner, but he could not afford to eat on this street.

He took a tram eastward into the low-rent neighborhood called Friedrichshain and made his way to a small apartment in a tenement. The door was opened by a short, pretty girl of eighteen with fair hair.

She wore a pink sweater and dark slacks, and her feet were bare. Although she was slim, she had delightfully generous breasts.

"I'm sorry to call unexpectedly," Volodya said. "Is it inconvenient?"

She smiled. "Not at all," she said. "Come in."

He stepped inside. She closed the door, then threw her arms around him. "I'm always happy to see you," she said, and kissed him eagerly.

Lili Markgraf was a girl with a lot of affection to give. Volodya had been taking her out about once a week since he got back to Berlin. He was not in love with her, and he knew that she dated other men, including Werner, but when they were together, she was passionate.

After a moment she said: "Have you heard the news? Is that why you've come?"

"What news?" Lili worked as a secretary in a press agency, and always heard things first.

"The Soviet Union has made a pact with Germany!" she said.

That made no sense. "You mean with Britain and France, against Germany."

"No, I don't! That's the surprise—Stalin and Hitler have made friends."

"But . . ." Volodya trailed off, baffled. Friends with Hitler? It seemed crazy. Was this the solution devised by the new Soviet foreign minister, Molotov? *We have failed to stop the tide of world Fascism—so we give up trying?*

*Did my father fight a revolution for that?*

### iii

Woody Dewar saw Joanne Rouzrokh again after four years.

No one who knew her father actually believed he had tried to rape a starlet in the Ritz-Carlton hotel. The girl had dropped the charges, but that was dull news, and the papers had given it little prominence. Consequently Dave was still a rapist in the eyes of Buffalo people. So Joanne's parents had moved to Palm Beach, and Woody lost touch.

Next time he saw her it was in the White House.

Woody was with his father, Senator Gus Dewar, and they were going to see the president. Woody had met Franklin D. Roosevelt several times. His father and the president had been friends for many years. But those had been social occasions, when FDR had shaken Woody's hand and asked him how he was getting along at school. This would be the first time Woody attended a real political meeting with the president.

They went in through the main entrance of the West Wing, passed through the entrance lobby, and stepped into a large waiting room— and there she was.

Woody stared at her in delight. She had hardly changed. With her narrow, haughty face and curved nose she still looked like the high priestess of an ancient religion. As ever, she wore simple clothes to dramatic effect: today she had on a dark blue suit of some cool fabric and a straw hat the same color with a big brim. Woody was glad he had put on a clean white shirt and his new striped tie this morning.

She seemed pleased to see him. "You look great!" she said. "Are you working in D.C. now?"

"Just helping out in my father's office for the summer," he replied. "I'm still at Harvard."

She turned to his father and said deferentially: "Good afternoon, Senator."

"Hello, Joanne."

Woody was thrilled to run into her. She was as alluring as ever. He wanted to keep the conversation going. "What are you doing here?" Woody said.

"I work at the State Department."

Woody nodded. That explained her deference to his father. She had joined a world in which people kowtowed to Senator Dewar. Woody said: "What's your job?"

"I'm assistant to an assistant. My boss is with the president now, but I'm too lowly to go in with him."

"You were always interested in politics. I recall an argument about lynching."

"I miss Buffalo. What fun we used to have!"

Woody remembered kissing her at the Racquet Club Ball, and he felt himself blush.

His father said: "Please give my best regards to your father," indicating that they needed to move on.

Woody considered asking for her phone number, but she preempted him. "I'd love to see you again, Woody," she said.

He was delighted. "Sure!"

"Are you free tonight? I'm having a few friends for cocktails."

"Sounds great!"

She gave him the address, an apartment building not far away; then his father hurried him out of the other end of the room.

A guard nodded familiarly to Gus, and they stepped into another waiting room.

Gus said: "Now, Woody, don't say anything unless the president addresses you directly."

Woody tried to concentrate on the imminent meeting. There had been a political earthquake in Europe: the Soviet Union had signed a peace pact with Nazi Germany, upsetting everyone's calculations. Woody's father was a key member of the Senate Foreign Relations Committee, and the president wanted to know what he thought.

Gus Dewar had another subject to discuss. He wanted to persuade Roosevelt to revive the League of Nations.

It would be a tough sell. The USA had never joined the league and Americans did not much like it. The league had failed dismally to deal with the crises of the 1930s: Japanese aggression in the Far East, Italian imperialism in Africa, Nazi takeovers in Europe, the ruin of democracy in Spain. But Gus was determined to try. It had always been his dream, Woody knew: a world council to resolve conflicts and prevent war.

Woody was 100 percent behind him. He had made a speech about this in a Harvard debate. When two nations had a quarrel, the worst possible procedure was for men to kill people on the other side. That seemed to him pretty obvious. "I understand why it happens, of course," he had said in the debate. "Just like I understand why drunks get into fistfights. But that doesn't make it any less irrational."

But now Woody found it hard to think about the threat of war in Europe. All his old feelings about Joanne came back in a rush. He wondered if she would kiss him again—maybe tonight. She had always liked him, and it seemed she still did—why else would she have invited him to her party? She had refused to date him, back in 1935, because he had been fifteen and she eighteen, which was understandable, though he had not thought so at the time. But now that they were both four years older, the age difference would not seem so stark—would it? He hoped not. He had dated girls in Buffalo and at Harvard, but he had not felt for any of them the overwhelming passion he had had for Joanne.

"Have you got that?" his father said.

Woody felt foolish. His father was about to make a proposal to the president that could bring world peace, and all Woody could think about was kissing Joanne. "Sure," he said. "I won't say anything unless he speaks to me first."

A tall, slim woman in her early forties came into the room, looking relaxed and confident, as if she owned the place, and Woody recognized Marguerite LeHand, nicknamed Missy, who managed Roosevelt's office. She had a long, masculine face with a big nose, and there was a touch of gray in her dark hair. She smiled warmly at Gus. "What a pleasure to see you again, Senator."

"How are you, Missy? You remember my son, Woodrow."

"I do. The president is ready for you both."

Missy's devotion to Roosevelt was famous. FDR was more fond of her than a married man was entitled to be, according to Washington gossip. Woody knew, from guarded but revealing remarks his parents made to one another, that Roosevelt's wife, Eleanor, had refused to sleep with him since she gave birth to their sixth child. The paralysis, which had struck him five years later, did not extend to his sexual equipment. Perhaps a man who had not slept with his wife for twenty years was entitled to an affectionate secretary.

She showed them through another door and across a narrow corridor; then they were in the Oval Office.

The president sat at a desk with his back to three tall windows in a curving bay. The blinds were drawn to filter the August sun coming through the south-facing glass. Roosevelt used an ordinary office chair, Woody saw, not his wheelchair. He wore a white suit and he was smoking a cigarette in a holder.

He was not really handsome. He had a receding hairline and a jutting chin, and he wore pince-nez glasses that made his eyes seem too close together. All the same there was something immediately attractive about his engaging smile, his hand extended to shake, and the amiable tone of voice in which he said: "Good to see you, Gus. Come on in."

"Mr. President, you remember my elder son, Woodrow."

"Of course. How's Harvard, Woody?"

"Just fine, sir, thank you. I'm on the debating team." He knew that politicians often had the knack of seeming to know everyone intimately. Either they had remarkable memories, or their secretaries reminded them efficiently.

"I was at Harvard myself. Sit down, sit down." Roosevelt removed the end of his cigarette from the holder and stubbed it in a full ashtray. "Gus, what the heck is happening in Europe?"

The president knew what was happening in Europe, of course, thought Woody. He had an entire State Department to tell him. But he wanted Gus Dewar's analysis.

Gus said: "Germany and Russia are still mortal enemies, in my opinion."

"That's what we all thought. But then why have they signed this pact?"

"Short-term convenience for both. Stalin needs time. He wants to build up the Red Army, so they can defeat the Germans if it comes to that."

"And the other guy?"

"Hitler is clearly on the point of doing something to Poland. The German press is full of ridiculous stories about how the Poles are mistreating their German-speaking population. Hitler doesn't stir up hatred without a purpose. Whatever he's planning, he doesn't want the Soviets to stand in his way. Hence the pact."

"That's pretty much what Hull says." Cordell Hull was secretary of state. "But he doesn't know what will happen next. Will Stalin let Hitler do anything he wants?"

"My guess is they'll carve up Poland between them in the next couple of weeks."

"And then what?"

"A few hours ago the British signed a new treaty with the Poles promising to come to their aid if they're attacked."

"But what can they do?"

"Nothing, sir. The British army, navy, and air force have no power to prevent the Germans overrunning Poland."

"What do you think we should do, Gus?" said the president.

Woody knew that this was his father's chance. He had the president's attention for a few minutes. It was a rare opportunity to make something happen. Woody discreetly crossed his fingers.

Gus leaned forward. "We don't want our sons to go to war as we did." Roosevelt had four boys in their twenties and thirties. Woody suddenly understood why he was here: he had been brought to the meeting to remind the president of his own sons. Gus said quietly: "We can't send American boys to be slaughtered in Europe again. The world needs a police force."

"What do you have in mind?" Roosevelt said noncommittally.

"The League of Nations isn't such a failure as people think. In the 1920s it resolved a border dispute between Finland and Sweden, and another between Turkey and Iraq." Gus was ticking items off on his fingers. "It stopped Greece and Yugoslavia from invading Albania, and persuaded Greece to pull out of Bulgaria. And it sent a peacekeeping force to keep Colombia and Peru from hostilities."

"All true. But in the thirties . . ."

"The league was not strong enough to deal with Fascist aggression. It's not surprising. The league was crippled from the start because Congress refused to ratify the covenant, so the United States was never a member. We need a new, American-led version, with teeth." Gus paused. "Mr. President, it's too soon to give up on a peaceful world."

Woody held his breath. Roosevelt nodded, but then he always nodded, Woody knew. It was rare for him to disagree openly. He hated confrontation. You had to be careful, Woody had heard his father say, not to take his silence for consent. Woody did not dare look at his father, sitting beside him, but he could sense the tension.

At last the president said: "I believe you're right."

Woody had to restrain himself from whooping aloud. The president had consented! He looked at his father. The normally imperturbable Gus was barely concealing his surprise. It had been such a quick victory.

Gus moved rapidly to consolidate it. "In that case, may I suggest that Cordell Hull and I draft a proposal for your consideration?"

"Hull has a lot on his plate. Talk to Welles."

Sumner Welles was under-secretary of state. He was both ambitious and flamboyant, and Woody knew he would not have been Gus's first choice. But he was a longtime friend of the Roosevelt family—he had been a page boy at FDR's wedding.

Anyway, Gus was not going to make difficulties at this point. "By all means," he said.

"Anything else?"

That was clearly a dismissal. Gus stood up, and Woody followed suit. Gus said: "What about Mrs. Roosevelt, your mother, sir? Last I heard she was in France."

"Her ship left yesterday, thank goodness."

"I'm glad to hear it."

"Thank you for coming in," Roosevelt said. "I really value your friendship, Gus."

Gus said: "Nothing could give me more pleasure, sir." He shook hands with the president, and Woody did the same.

Then they left.

Woody half-hoped that Joanne would still be hanging around, but she had gone.

As they made their way out of the building, Gus said: "Let's go for a celebratory drink."

Woody looked at his watch. It was five o'clock. "Sure," he said.

They went to Old Ebbitt, on Fifteenth Street near F: stained glass, green velvet, brass lamps, and hunting trophies. The place was full of congressmen, senators, and the people who followed them around: aides, lobbyists, and journalists. Gus ordered a dry martini straight up with a twist for himself and a beer for Woody. Woody smiled: maybe he would have liked a martini. In fact he would not—to him it just tasted like cold gin—but it would have been nice to be asked. However, he raised his glass and said: "Congratulations. You got what you wanted."

"What the world needs."

"You argued brilliantly."

"Roosevelt hardly needed convincing. He's a liberal, but a pragmatist. He knows you can't do everything—you have to pick the battles you can win. The New Deal is his number one priority—getting unemployed men back to work. He won't do anything that interferes with the main mission. If my plan becomes controversial enough to upset his supporters, he'll drop it."

"So we haven't won anything yet."

Gus smiled. "We've taken the important first step. But no, we haven't won anything."

"A pity he forced Welles on you."

"Not entirely. Sumner strengthens the project. He's closer to the president than I am. But he's unpredictable. He might pick it up and run in a different direction."

Woody looked across the room and saw a familiar face. "Guess who's here. I might have known."

His father looked in the same direction.

"Standing at the bar," Woody said. "With a couple of older guys in hats, and a blond girl. It's Greg Peshkov." As usual, Greg looked a mess despite his expensive clothes: his silk tie was awry, his shirt was coming out of his waistband, and there was a smear of cigarette ash on his ice-cream-colored trousers. Nevertheless the blonde was looking adoringly at him.

"So it is," said Gus. "Do you see much of him at Harvard?"

"He's a physics major, but he doesn't hang around with the

scientists—too dull for him, I guess. I run into him at the *Crimson*." *The Harvard Crimson* was the student newspaper. Woody took photographs for the paper and Greg wrote articles. "He's doing an internship at the State Department this summer—that's why he's here."

"In the press office, I imagine," said Gus. "The two men he's with are reporters, the one in the brown suit for the *Chicago Tribune* and the pipe smoker for the Cleveland *Plain Dealer*."

Woody saw that Greg was talking to the journalists as if they were old friends, taking the arm of one as he leaned forward to say something in a low voice, patting the other on the back in mock congratulation. They seemed to like him, Woody thought, as they laughed loudly at something he said. Woody envied that talent. It was useful to politicians—though perhaps not essential: his father did not have that hail-fellow-well-met quality, and he was one of the most senior statesmen in America.

Woody said: "I wonder how his half sister, Daisy, feels about the threat of war. She's over there in London. She married some English lord."

"To be exact, she married the elder son of Earl Fitzherbert, whom I used to know quite well."

"She's the envy of every girl in Buffalo. The king went to her wedding."

"I also knew Fitzherbert's sister, Maud—a wonderful woman. She married Walter von Ulrich, a German. I would have married her myself if Walter hadn't got to her first."

Woody raised his eyebrows. It was not like Papa to talk this way.

"That was before I fell in love with your mother, of course."

"Of course." Woody smothered a grin.

"Walter and Maud dropped out of sight after Hitler banned the Social Democrats. I hope they're all right. If there's a war . . ."

Woody saw that talk of war had put his father in a reminiscent mood. "At least America isn't involved."

"That's what we thought last time." Gus changed the subject. "What do you hear from your kid brother?"

Woody sighed. "He's not going to change his mind, Papa. He won't go to Harvard, or any other university."

This was a family crisis. Chuck had announced that as soon as he was eighteen he was going to join the navy. Without a college degree he would be an enlisted man, with no prospect of ever becoming an officer. This horrified his high-achieving parents.

"He's bright enough for college, damn it," said Gus.

"He beats me at chess."

"He beats me, too. So what's his problem?"

"He hates to study. And he loves boats. Sailing is the only thing he cares about." Woody looked at his wristwatch.

"You've got a party to go to," his father said.

"There's no hurry—"

"Sure there is. She's a very attractive girl. Get the hell out of here."

Woody grinned. His father could be surprisingly smart. "Thanks, Papa." He got up.

Greg Peshkov was leaving at the same time, and they went out together. "Hello, Woody, how are things?" Greg said amiably, turning in the same direction.

There had been a time when Woody wanted to punch Greg for his part in what had been done to Dave Rouzrokh. His feelings had cooled over the years, and in truth it was Lev Peshkov who had been responsible, not his son, who had then been only fifteen. All the same Woody was no more than polite. "I'm enjoying Washington," he said, walking along one of the city's wide Parisian boulevards. "How about you?"

"I like it. They soon get over their surprise at my name." Seeing Woody's inquiring look, Greg explained: "The State Department is all Smiths, Fabers, Jensens, and McAllisters. No one called Kozinsky or Cohen or Papadopoulos."

Woody realized it was true. Government was carried on by a rather exclusive little ethnic group. Why had he not noticed that before? Perhaps because it had been the same in school, in church, and at Harvard.

Greg went on: "But they're not narrow-minded. They'll make an exception for someone who speaks fluent Russian and comes from a wealthy family."

Greg was being flippant, but there was an undertone of real resentment, and Woody saw that the guy had a serious chip on his shoulder.

"They think my father is a gangster," Greg said. "But they don't really mind. Most rich people have a gangster somewhere in their ancestry."

"You sound as if you hate Washington."

"On the contrary! I wouldn't be anywhere else. The power is here."

Woody felt he was more high-minded. "I'm here because there are things I want to do, changes I want to make."

Greg grinned. "Same thing, I guess—power."

"Hmm." Woody had not thought of it that way.

Greg said: "Do you think there will be war in Europe?"

"You should know: you're in the State Department!"

"Yeah, but I'm in the press office. All I know is the fairy tales we tell reporters. I have no idea what the truth is."

"Heck, I don't know, either. I've just been with the president and I don't think even he knows."

"My sister, Daisy, is over there."

Greg's tone had changed. His worry was evidently genuine, and Woody warmed to him. "I know."

"If there's bombing, even women and children won't be safe. Do you think the Germans will bomb London?"

There was only one honest answer. "I guess they will."

"I wish she'd come home."

"Maybe there won't be a war. Chamberlain, the British premier, made a last-minute deal with Hitler over Czechoslovakia last year—"

"A last-minute sellout."

"Right. So perhaps he'll do the same over Poland—although time is running out."

Greg nodded glumly and changed the subject. "Where are you headed?"

"To Joanne Rouzrokh's apartment. She's giving a party."

"I heard about it. I know one of her roommates. But I'm not invited, as you could probably guess. Her building is—good God!" Greg stopped in midsentence.

Woody stopped, too. Greg was staring ahead. Following his gaze, Woody saw that he was looking at an attractive black woman walking toward them on E Street. She was about their age, and pretty, with wide pinky-brown lips that made Woody think about kissing. She had on a plain black dress that might have been part of a waitress uniform, but she wore it with a cute hat and fashionable shoes that gave her a stylish look.

She saw the two of them, caught Greg's eye, and looked away.

Greg said: "Jacky? Jacky Jakes?"

The girl ignored him and kept walking, but Woody thought she looked troubled.

Greg said: "Jacky, it's me, Greg Peshkov."

Jacky—if it were she—did not respond, but she looked as if she might be about to burst into tears.

"Jacky—real name Mabel. You know me!" Greg stood in the middle of the sidewalk with his arms spread in a gesture of appeal.

She deliberately went around him, not speaking or meeting his eye, and walked on.

Greg turned. "Wait a minute!" he called after her. "You ran out on me, four years ago—you owe me an explanation!"

This was uncharacteristic of Greg, Woody thought. He had always been such a smooth operator with girls, at school and at Harvard. Now he seemed genuinely upset: bewildered, hurt, almost desperate.

Four years ago, Woody reflected. Could this be the girl in the scandal? It had taken place here in Washington. No doubt she lived here.

Greg ran after her. A cab had stopped at the corner and the passenger, a man in a tuxedo, was standing at the curb paying the driver. Jacky jumped in, slamming the door.

Greg went to the window and shouted through it: "Talk to me, please!"

The man in the tuxedo said: "Keep the change," and walked away.

The cab moved off, leaving Greg staring after it.

He slowly returned to where Woody stood waiting, intrigued. "I don't understand it," Greg said.

Woody said: "She looked frightened."

"What of? I never did her any harm. I was crazy about her."

"Well, she was scared of something."

Greg seemed to shake himself. "Sorry," he said. "Not your problem anyway. My apologies."

"Not at all."

Greg pointed to an apartment block a few steps away. "That's Joanne's building," he said. "Have a good time." Then he walked away.

Somewhat bemused, Woody went to the entrance. But he soon forgot about Greg's romantic life and started to think about his own. Did Joanne really like him? She might not kiss him this evening, but maybe he could ask her for a date.

This was a modest apartment house, with no doorman or hall porter. A list in the lobby revealed that Rouzrokh shared her place with Stewart and Fisher, presumably two other girls. Woody went up in the elevator. He realized he was empty-handed: he should have brought candy or flowers. He thought about going back to buy something, then decided that would be taking good manners too far. He rang the bell.

A girl in her early twenties opened the door.

Woody said: "Hello, I'm—"

"Come on in," she said, not waiting to hear his name. "The drinks are in the kitchen, and there's food on the table in the living room, if there's any left." She turned away, clearly thinking she had given him sufficient welcome.

The small apartment was packed with people drinking, smoking, and shouting at one another over the noise of the phonograph. Joanne had said "a few friends" and Woody had imagined eight or ten young people sitting around a coffee table discussing the crisis in Europe. He was disappointed: this overcrowded bash would give him little opportunity to demonstrate to Joanne how much he had grown up.

He looked around for her. He was taller than most people and could see over the heads. She was not in sight. He pushed through the crowd, searching for her. A girl with plump breasts and nice brown eyes looked up at him as he squeezed past and said: "Hello, big guy. I'm Diana Taverner. What's your name?"

"I'm looking for Joanne," he said.

She shrugged. "Good luck with that." She turned away.

He made his way into the kitchen. The noise level dropped a fraction. Joanne was nowhere to be seen, but he decided to get a drink while he was there. A broad-shouldered man of about thirty was rattling a cocktail shaker. Well dressed in a tan suit, pale blue shirt, and dark blue tie, he clearly was not a barman, but was acting like a host. "Scotch is over there," he said to another guest. "Help yourself. I'm making martinis, for anyone who's interested."

Woody said: "Got any bourbon?"

"Right here." The man passed him a bottle. "I'm Bexforth Ross."

"Woody Dewar." Woody found a glass and poured bourbon.

"Ice in that bucket," said Bexforth. "Where are you from, Woody?"

"I'm an intern in the Senate. You?"

"I work in the State Department. I'm in charge of the Italy desk." He started passing martinis around.

Clearly a rising star, Woody thought. The man had so much self-confidence it was irritating. "I was looking for Joanne."

"She's somewhere around. How do you know her?"

Here Woody felt he could show clear superiority. "Oh, we're old friends," he said airily. "In fact I've known her all my life. We were kids together in Buffalo. How about you?"

Bexforth took a long sip of martini and gave a satisfied sigh. Then he looked speculatively at Woody. "I haven't known Joanne as long as you have," he said. "But I guess I know her better."

"How so?"

"I'm planning to marry her."

Woody felt as if he had been slapped. "Marry her?"

"Yes. Isn't that great?"

Woody could not hide his dismay. "Does she know about this?"

Bexforth laughed, and patted Woody's shoulder condescendingly. "She sure does, and she's all for it. I'm the luckiest guy in the world."

Clearly Bexforth had divined that Woody was attracted to Joanne. Woody felt a fool. "Congratulations," he said dispiritedly.

"Thank you. And now I must circulate. Good talking to you, Woody."

"My pleasure."

Bexforth moved away.

Woody put his drink down untasted. "Fuck it," he said quietly. Then he left.

## iv

The first day of September was sultry in Berlin. Carla von Ulrich woke up sweaty and uncomfortable, her bedsheets thrown off during the warm night. She looked out of her bedroom window to see low gray clouds hanging over the city, keeping heat in like a saucepan lid.

Today was a big day for her. In fact it would determine the course of her life.

She stood in front of the mirror. She had her mother's coloring, the dark hair and green eyes of the Fitzherberts. She was prettier than Maud, who had an angular face, striking rather than beautiful. Yet there was a bigger difference. Her mother attracted just about every man she met. Carla, by contrast, could not flirt. She watched other eighteen-year-old girls doing it—simpering, pulling their sweaters tight over their breasts, tossing their hair, and batting their eyelashes—and she just felt embarrassed. Her mother was more subtle, of course, so that men hardly knew they were being enchanted, but it was essentially the same game.

Today, however, Carla did not want to appear sexy. On the contrary, she needed to look practical, sensible, and capable. She put on a plain stone-colored cotton dress that came to midcalf, stepped into her flat unglamorous school sandals, and wove her hair into two plaits in the approved German-maiden fashion. The mirror showed her an ideal girl student: conservative, dull, sexless.

She was up and dressed before the rest of the family. The maid, Ada, was in the kitchen, and Carla helped her set out the breakfast things.

Her brother appeared next. Erik, nineteen and sporting a clipped black mustache, supported the Nazis, infuriating the rest of his family. He was a student at the Charité, the medical school of the University of Berlin, as was his best friend and fellow Nazi, Hermann Braun. The von Ulrichs could not afford tuition fees, of course, but Erik had won a scholarship.

Carla had applied for the same scholarship to study at the same institution. Her interview was today. If she was successful, she would study and become a doctor. If not . . .

She had no idea what else she would do.

The coming to power of the Nazis had ruined her parents' lives. Her father was no longer a deputy in the Reichstag, having lost his job when the Social Democratic Party became illegal, along with all other parties except for the Nazis. There was no work her father could do that would use his expertise as a politician and a diplomat. He scraped a living translating German newspaper articles for the British embassy, where he still had a few friends. Mother had once been a famous left-wing journalist, but newspapers were no longer allowed to publish her articles.

Carla found it heartbreaking. She was deeply devoted to her family, which included Ada. She was saddened by the decline in her father, who in her childhood had been a hardworking and politically powerful man and was now simply defeated. Even worse was the brave face put on by her mother, a famous suffragette leader in England before the war, now scraping a few marks by giving piano lessons.

But they said they could bear anything as long as their children grew up to lead happy and fulfilled lives.

Carla had always taken it for granted that she would spend her life making the world a better place, as her parents had. She did not know whether she would have followed her father into politics or her mother into journalism, but both were out of the question now.

What else was she to do, under a government that prized ruthlessness and brutality above all else? Her brother had given her the clue. Doctors made the world a better place regardless of the government. So she had made it her ambition to go to medical school. She had studied harder than any other girl in her class, and she had passed every exam with top marks, especially the sciences. She was better qualified than her brother to win a scholarship.

"There are no girls at all in my year," Erik said. He sounded grumpy. Carla thought he disliked the idea of her following in his footsteps. Their parents were proud of his achievements, despite his repellent politics. Perhaps he was afraid of being outshone.

Carla said: "All my grades are better than yours: biology, chemistry, math—"

"All right, all right."

"And the scholarship is available to female students, in principle—I checked."

Their mother came in at the end of this exchange, dressed in a gray watered-silk bathrobe with the cord doubled around her narrow waist. "They should follow their own rules," she said. "This is Germany, after all." Mother said she loved her adopted country, and perhaps she did, but since the coming of the Nazis she had taken to making wearily ironic remarks.

Carla dipped bread into milky coffee. "How will you feel, Mother, if England attacks Germany?"

"Miserably unhappy, as I felt last time," she replied. "I was married to your father throughout the Great War, and every day for more than four years I was terrified that he would be killed."

Erik said in a challenging tone: "But whose side will you take?"

"I'm German," she said. "I married for better or worse. Of course, we never foresaw anything as wicked and oppressive as this Nazi regime. No one did." Erik grunted in protest and she ignored him. "But a vow is a vow, and anyway I love your father."

Carla said: "We're not at war yet."

"Not quite," said Mother. "If the Poles have any sense, they will back down and give Hitler what he asks for."

"They should," said Erik. "Germany is strong now. We can take what we want, whether they like it or not."

Mother rolled her eyes up. "God spare us."

A car horn sounded outside. Carla smiled. A minute later her friend Frieda Franck entered the kitchen. She was going to accompany Carla to the interview, just to give moral support. She, too, was dressed in sober-schoolgirl fashion, though she, unlike Carla, had a wardrobe full of stylish clothes.

She was followed in by her older brother. Carla thought Werner Franck was wonderful. Unlike so many handsome boys, he was kind and thoughtful and funny. He had once been very left-wing, but all that seemed to have faded away, and he was nonpolitical now. He had had a string of beautiful and stylish girlfriends. If Carla had known how to flirt, she would have started with him.

Mother said: "I'd offer you coffee, Werner, but ours is ersatz, and I know you have the real thing at home."

"Shall I steal some from our kitchen for you, Frau von Ulrich?" he said. "I think you deserve it."

Mother blushed slightly, and Carla realized, with a twinge of disapproval, that even at forty-eight Mother was susceptible to Werner's charm.

Werner glanced at a gold wristwatch. "I have to go," he said. "Life is completely frantic at the Air Ministry these days."

Frieda said: "Thank you for the lift."

Carla said to Frieda: "Wait a minute—if you came in Werner's car, where's your bike?"

"Outside. We strapped it to the back of the car."

The two girls belonged to the Mercury Cycling Club and went everywhere by bike.

Werner said: "Best wishes for the interview, Carla. Bye, everyone."

Carla swallowed the last of her bread. As she was about to leave, her father came down. He had not shaved or put on a tie. He had been quite plump, when Carla was a girl, but now he was thin. He kissed Carla affectionately.

Mother said: "We haven't listened to the news!" She turned on the radio that stood on the shelf.

While the set was warming up, Carla and Frieda left the house, so they did not hear the news.

The University Hospital was in Mitte, the central area of Berlin where the von Ulrichs lived, so Carla and Frieda had a short bicycle ride. Carla began to feel nervous. The fumes from car exhausts nauseated her, and she wished she had not eaten breakfast. They reached the hospital, a new building put up in the twenties, and found their way to the room of Professor Bayer, who had the job of recommending a student for the scholarship. A haughty secretary said they were early and told them to wait.

Carla wished she had worn a hat and gloves. That would have made her look older and more authoritative, like someone sick people would trust. The secretary might have been polite to a girl in a hat.

The wait was long, but Carla was sorry when it came to an end and the secretary said the professor was ready to see her.

Frieda whispered: "Good luck!"

Carla went in.

Bayer was a thin man in his forties with a small gray mustache. He sat behind a desk, wearing a tan linen jacket over the waistcoat of a gray business suit. On the wall was a photograph of him shaking hands with Hitler.

He did not greet Carla, but barked: "What is an imaginary number?"

She was taken aback by his abruptness, but at least it was an easy question. "The square root of a negative real number; for example, the square root of minus one," she said in a shaky voice. "It cannot be assigned a real numerical value but can, nevertheless, be used in calculations."

He seemed a bit surprised. Perhaps he had expected to floor her completely. "Correct," he said after a momentary hesitation.

She looked around. There was no chair for her. Was she to be interviewed standing up?

He asked her some questions in chemistry and biology, all of which she answered easily. She began to feel a bit less nervous. Then he suddenly said: "Do you faint at the sight of blood?"

"No, sir."

"Aha!" he said triumphantly. "How do you know?"

"I delivered a baby when I was eleven years old," she said. "That was quite bloody."

"You should have sent for a doctor!"

"I did," she said indignantly. "But babies don't wait for doctors."

"Hmm." Bayer stood up. "Wait there." He left the room.

Carla stayed where she was. She was being subjected to a harsh test, but so far she thought she was doing all right. Fortunately, she was used to give-and-take arguments with men and women of all ages: combative discussions were commonplace in the von Ulrich house, and she had been holding her own with her parents and brother for as long as she could remember.

Bayer was gone for several minutes. What was he doing? Had he gone to fetch a colleague to meet this unprecedentedly brilliant girl applicant? That seemed too much to hope for.

She was tempted to pick up one of the books on his shelf and read, but she was scared of offending him, so she stood still and did nothing.

He came back after ten minutes with a pack of cigarettes. Surely he had not kept her standing in the middle of the room all this time while he went to the tobacconist's shop? Or was that another test? She began to feel angry.

He took his time lighting up, as if he needed to collect his thoughts. He blew out smoke and said: "How would you, as a woman, deal with a man who had an infection of the penis?"

She was embarrassed, and felt herself blush. She had never discussed the penis with a man. But she knew she had to be robust about such things if she wanted to be a doctor. "In the same way that you, as a man, would deal with a vaginal infection," she said. He looked horrified, and she feared she had been insolent. Hastily she went on: "I would examine the infected area carefully, try to establish the nature of the infection, and probably treat it with sulfonamide, although I have to admit we did not cover this in my school biology course."

He said skeptically: "Have you ever seen a naked man?"

"Yes."

He affected to be outraged. "But you are a single girl!"

"When my grandfather was dying, he was bedridden and incontinent. I helped my mother keep him clean—she could not manage on her own. He was too heavy." She tried a smile. "Women do these things all the time, Professor, for the very young and the very old, the sick and the helpless. We're used to it. It's only men who find such tasks embarrassing."

He was looking more and more cross, even though she was answering well. What was going wrong? It was almost as if he would have been happier for her to be intimidated by his manner and to give stupid replies.

He put out his cigarette thoughtfully in the ashtray on his desk. "I'm afraid you are not suitable as a candidate for this scholarship," he said.

She was astonished. How had she failed? She had answered every question! "Why not?" she said. "My qualifications are irreproachable."

"You are unwomanly. You talk freely of the vagina and the penis."

"It was you who started that! I merely answered your question."

"You have clearly been brought up in a coarse environment where you saw the nakedness of your male relatives."

"Do you think old people's diapers should be changed by men? I'd like to see you do it!"

"Worst of all you are disrespectful and insolent."

"You asked me challenging questions. If I had given you timid replies, you would have said I wasn't tough enough to be a doctor—wouldn't you?"

He was momentarily speechless, and she realized that was exactly what he would have done.

"You've wasted my time," she said, and she went to the door.

"Get married," he said. "Produce children for the Führer. That's your role in life. Do your duty!"

She went out and slammed the door.

Frieda looked up in alarm. "What happened?"

Carla headed for the exit without replying. She caught the eye of the secretary, who looked pleased, clearly knowing what had happened. Carla said to her: "You can wipe that smirk off your face, you dried-up old bitch." She had the satisfaction of seeing the woman's shock and horror.

Outside the building she said to Frieda: "He had no intention of recommending me for the scholarship, because I'm a woman. My qualifications were irrelevant. I did all that work for nothing." Then she burst into tears.

Frieda put her arms around her.

After a minute she felt better. "I'm not going to raise children for the damned Führer," she muttered.

"What?"

"Let's go home. I'll tell you when we get there." They climbed onto their bikes.

There was a strange air in the streets, but Carla was too full of her own woes to wonder what was going on. People were gathering around the loudspeakers that sometimes broadcast Hitler's speeches from the Kroll Opera, the building that was being used instead of the burned-out Reichstag. Presumably he was about to speak.

When they got back to the von Ulrich town house, Mother and Father were still in the kitchen, Father sitting next to the radio with a frown of concentration.

"They turned me down," Carla said. "Regardless of what their rules say, they don't want to give a scholarship to a girl."

"Oh, Carla, I'm so sorry," said Mother.

"What's on the radio?"

"Haven't you heard?" said Mother. "We invaded Poland this morning. We're at war."

**V**

The London season was over, but most people were still in town because of the crisis. Parliament, normally in recess at this time of year, had been specially recalled. But there were no parties, no royal receptions, no balls. It was like being at a seaside resort in February, Daisy thought. Today was Saturday, and she was getting ready to go to dinner at the home of her father-in-law, Earl Fitzherbert. What could be more dull?

She sat at her dressing table wearing an evening gown in eau-de-nil silk with a V-neck and a pleated skirt. She had silk flowers in her hair and a fortune in diamonds around her neck.

Her husband, Boy, was getting ready in his dressing room. She was pleased he was here. He spent many nights elsewhere. Although they lived in the same Mayfair house, sometimes several days would go by without their meeting. But he was at home tonight.

She held in her hand a letter from her mother in Buffalo. Olga had divined that Daisy was discontented in her marriage. There must have been hints in Daisy's letters home. Mother had good intuition. "I only want you to be happy," she wrote. "So listen when I tell you not to give up too soon. You're going to be Countess Fitzherbert one day, and your son, if you have one, will be the earl. You might regret throwing all that away just because your husband didn't pay you enough attention."

She might be right. People had been addressing Daisy as "my lady" for almost three years, yet it still gave her a little jolt of pleasure every time, like a puff on a cigarette.

But Boy seemed to think that marriage need make no great difference to his life. He spent evenings with his men friends, traveled all over the country to go horse racing, and rarely told his wife what his plans were. Daisy found it embarrassing to go to a party and be surprised to meet her husband there. But if she wanted to know where he was going, she had to ask his valet, and that was too demeaning.

Would he gradually grow up, and start to behave as a husband should, or would he always be like this?

He put his head around her door. "Come on, Daisy, we're late."

She put Mother's letter in a drawer, locked it, and went out. Boy was waiting in the hall, wearing a tuxedo. Fitz had at last succumbed to fashion and permitted informal short dinner jackets for family dinners at home.

They could have walked to Fitz's house, but it was raining, so Boy had had the car brought around. It was a Bentley Airline saloon, cream-colored with whitewall tires. Boy shared his father's love of beautiful cars.

Boy drove. Daisy hoped he would let her drive back. She enjoyed it, and anyway he was not safe after dinner, especially on wet roads.

London was preparing for war. Barrage balloons floated over the city at a height of two thousand feet, to impede bombers. In case that failed, sandbags were stacked outside important buildings. Alternate curbstones had been painted white, for the benefit of drivers in the blackout, which had begun yesterday. There were white stripes on large trees, street statues, and other obstacles that might cause accidents.

Princess Bea welcomed Boy and Daisy. In her fifties she was quite fat, but she still dressed like a girl. Tonight she wore a pink gown embroidered with beads and sequins. She never spoke about the story Daisy's father had told at the wedding, but she had stopped hinting that Daisy was socially inferior, and now always spoke to Daisy with courtesy, if not warmth. Daisy was cautiously friendly, and treated Bea like a slightly dotty aunt.

Boy's younger brother, Andy, was there. He and May had two children and May looked, to Daisy's interested eye, as if she might be expecting a third.

Boy wanted a son, of course, to be heir to the Fitzherbert title and fortune, but so far Daisy had failed to get pregnant. It was a sore point, and the evident fecundity of Andy and May made it worse. Daisy would have had a better chance if Boy spent more nights at home.

She was delighted to see her friend Eva Murray there—but without her husband. Jimmy Murray, now a captain, was with his unit and had not been able to get away, for most troops were in barracks and their officers were with them. Eva was family now, because Jimmy was May's brother and therefore an in-law. So Boy had been forced to overcome his prejudice against Jews and be polite to Eva.

Eva adored Jimmy as much now as she had three years ago when she married him. They, too, had produced two children in three years. But Eva looked worried tonight, and Daisy could guess why. "How are your parents?" she said.

"They can't get out of Germany," Eva said miserably. "The government won't give them exit visas."

"Can't Fitz help?"

"He's tried."

"What have they done to deserve this?"

"It's not them, particularly. There are thousands of German Jews in the same position. Only a few get visas."

"I'm so sorry." Daisy was more than sorry. She squirmed with embarrassment when she recalled how she and Boy had supported the Fascists in the early days. Her doubts had grown rapidly as the brutality of Fascism at home and abroad had become more and more obvious, and in the end she had been relieved when Fitz had complained that they were embarrassing him and had begged them to leave Mosley's party. Now Daisy felt she had been an utter fool ever to join in the first place.

Boy was not quite so repentant. He still thought that upper-class white Europeans formed a superior species, chosen by God to rule the earth. But he no longer believed that was a practical political philosophy. He was often infuriated by British democracy, but he did not advocate abolishing it.

They sat down to dinner early. "Neville is making a statement in the House of Commons at half past seven," Fitz said. Neville Chamberlain was prime minister. "I want to see it—I shall sit in the peers' gallery. I may have to leave you before dessert."

Andy said: "What do you think will happen, Papa?"

"I really don't know," Fitz said with a touch of exasperation. "Of course we would all like to avoid a war, but it's important not to give an impression of indecision."

Daisy was surprised: Fitz believed in loyalty and rarely criticized his government colleagues, even as obliquely as this.

Princess Bea said: "If there is a war, I shall go and live in Tŷ Gwyn."

Fitz shook his head. "If there is a war, the government will ask owners of large country houses to put them at the disposal of the military for the duration. As a member of the government I must set an example. I shall have to lend Tŷ Gwyn to the Welsh Rifles for use as a training center, or possibly a hospital."

Bea was outraged. "But it is my country house!"

"We may reserve a small part of the premises for private use."

"I don't choose to live in a small part of the premises—I am a princess!"

"It might be cozy. We could use the butler's pantry as a kitchen, and the breakfast room as a dining room, plus three or four of the smaller bedrooms."

"Cozy!" Bea looked disgusted, as if something unpleasant had been set before her, but she said no more.

Andy said: "Presumably Boy and I will have to join the Welsh Rifles."

May made a noise in her throat like a sob.

Boy said: "I shall join the air force."

Fitz was shocked. "But you can't. The Viscount Aberowen has always been in the Welsh Rifles."

"They haven't got any planes. The next war will be an air war. The RAF will be desperate for pilots. And I've been flying for years."

Fitz was about to argue, but the butler came in and said: "The car is ready, my lord."

Fitz looked at the clock on the mantelpiece. "Dash it, I've got to go. Thank you, Grout." He looked at Boy. "Don't make a final decision until we've talked some more. This is not right."

"Very well, Papa."

Fitz looked at Bea. "Forgive me, my dear, for leaving in the middle of dinner."

"Of course," she said.

Fitz got up from the table and walked to the door. Daisy noticed his limp, a grim reminder of what the last war had done.

The rest of dinner was gloomy. They were all wondering whether the prime minister would declare war.

When the ladies got up to withdraw, May asked Andy to take her arm. He excused himself to the two remaining men, saying: "My wife is in a delicate condition." It was the usual euphemism for pregnancy.

Boy said: "I wish my wife were as quick to get delicate."

It was a cheap shot, and Daisy felt herself blush bright red. She repressed a retort, then asked herself why she should be silent. "You know what footballers say, Boy," she said loudly. "You have to shoot to score."

It was Boy's turn to blush. "How dare you!" he said furiously.

Andy laughed. "You asked for it, brother."

Bea said: "Stop it, both of you. I expect my sons to wait until the ladies are out of earshot before indulging in such disgusting talk." She swept out of the room.

Daisy followed, but she parted company from the other women on the landing and went on upstairs, still feeling angry, wanting to be alone. How could Boy say such a thing? Did he really believe it had to be her fault that she was not pregnant? It could just as easily be his! Perhaps he knew that, and tried to blame her because he was afraid people would think he was infertile. That was probably the truth, but it was no excuse for a public insult.

She went to his old room. After they got married, the two of them had lived here for three months while their own house was being redecorated. They had used Boy's old bedroom and the one next door, although in those days they had slept together every night.

She went in and turned on the light. To her surprise she saw that Boy appeared not to have completely moved out. There was a razor on the washstand and a copy of *Flight* magazine on the bedside table. She opened a drawer and found a tin of Leonard's Liver-Aid, which he took every morning before breakfast. Did he sleep here when he was too disgustingly drunk to face his wife?

The lower drawer was locked, but she knew he kept the key in a pot on the mantelpiece. She had no qualms about prying: in her view a husband should have no secrets from his wife. She opened the drawer.

The first thing she found was a book of photographs of naked women. In artistic paintings and photographs, the women generally posed to half-conceal their private parts, but these girls were doing the opposite: legs akimbo, buttocks held open, even the lips of their vaginas spread to show the inside. Daisy would pretend to be shocked if anyone caught her, but in truth she was fascinated. She looked through the entire book with great interest, comparing the women with herself: the size and shape of their breasts, the amount of hair, their sexual organs. What a wonderful variety there was in women's bodies!

Some of the girls were stimulating themselves, or pretending to, and some were photographed in pairs, doing it to each other. Daisy was not really surprised that men liked this sort of thing.

She felt like an eavesdropper. It reminded her of the time she had gone to his room at Tŷ Gwyn, before they were married. Then she had been desperate to learn more about him, to gain intimate knowledge of the man she loved, to find a way to make him her own. What was she doing now? Spying on a husband who seemed no longer to love her, trying to understand where she had failed.

Beneath the book was a brown paper bag. Inside were several small, square paper envelopes, white with red lettering on the front. She read:

"Prentif" Reg. Trade Mark
## SERVISPAK

**NOTICE**
Do not leave the envelope
or contents in public places
as this is likely to cause offense

BRITISH MADE
Latex rubber
*Withstands all climates*

None of it made any sense. Nowhere did it say what the package actually contained. So she opened it.

Inside was a piece of rubber. She unfolded it. It was shaped like a tube, closed at one end. She took a few seconds to figure out what it was.

She had never seen one, but she had heard people talk about such things. Americans called it a Trojan, the British a rubber johnny. The correct term was *condom*, and it was to stop you getting pregnant.

Why did her husband have a bag of them? There could be only one answer. They were to be used with another woman.

She felt like crying. She had given him everything he wanted. She had never told him she was too tired to make love—even when she was—nor had she refused anything he suggested in bed. She would even have posed like the women in the book of photographs, if he had asked her to.

What had she done wrong?

She decided to ask him.

Sorrow turned to anger. She stood up. She would take the paper packets down to the dining room and confront him with them. Why should she protect his feelings?

At that moment he walked in.

"I saw the light from the hall," he said. "What are you doing in here?" He looked at the open drawers of the bedside cupboard and said: "How dare you spy on me?"

"I suspected you of being unfaithful," she said. She held up the condom. "And I was right."

"Damn you for a sneak."

"Damn you for an adulterer."

He raised his hand. "I should beat you like a Victorian husband."

She snatched a heavy candlestick from the mantelpiece. "Try it, and I'll bop you like a twentieth-century wife."

"This is ridiculous." He sat down heavily on a chair by the door, looking defeated.

His evident unhappiness deflated Daisy's rage, and she just felt sad. She sat on the bed. But she had not lost her curiosity. "Who is she?"

He shook his head. "Never mind."

"I want to know!"

He shifted uncomfortably. "Does it matter?"

"It sure does." She knew she would get it out of him eventually.

He would not meet her eye. "Nobody you know, or would ever know."

"A prostitute?"

He was stung by this suggestion. "No!"

She goaded him further. "Do you pay her?"

"No. Yes." He was clearly ashamed enough to wish to deny it. "Well, an allowance. It's not the same thing."

"Why do you pay, if she's not a prostitute?"

"So they don't have to see anyone else."

"They? You have several mistresses?"

"No! Only two. They live in Aldgate. Mother and daughter."

"What? You can't be serious."

"Well, one day Joanie was . . . the French say *elle avait les fleurs.*"

"American girls call it the curse."

"So Pearl offered to . . ."

"Act as a substitute? This is the most sordid arrangement imaginable! So you go to bed with them both?"

"Yes."

She thought of the book of photographs, and an outrageous possibility occurred to her. She had to ask. "Not at the same time?"

"Occasionally."

"How utterly foul."

"You don't need to worry about disease." He pointed to the condom in her hand. "Those things prevent infection."

"I'm overwhelmed by your thoughtfulness."

"Look, most men do this sort of thing, you know. At least, most men of our class."

"No, they don't," she said, but she thought of her father, who had a wife and a longtime mistress and still felt the need to romance Gladys Angelus.

Boy said: "My father isn't a faithful husband. He has bastards all over the place."

"I don't believe you. I think he loves your mother."

"He has one bastard for certain."

"Where?"

"I don't know."

"Then you can't be sure."

"I heard him say something to Bing Westhampton once. You know what Bing is like."

"I do," said Daisy. This seemed a moment for telling the truth, so she added: "He feels my bottom every chance he gets."

"Dirty old man. Anyway, we were all a bit drunk, and Bing said: 'Most of us have got one or two bastards hidden away, haven't we?' and Papa said: 'I'm pretty sure I've only got one.' Then he seemed to realize what he'd said, and he coughed and looked foolish and changed the subject."

"Well, I don't care how many bastards your father has. I'm a modern American girl and I won't live with an unfaithful husband."

"What can you do about it?"

"I'll leave you." She put on a defiant expression, but she felt in pain, as if he had stabbed her.

"And go back to Buffalo with your tail between your legs?"

"Perhaps. Or I could do something else. I've got plenty of money." Her father's lawyers had made sure Boy did not get his hands on the Vyalov-Peshkov fortune when they married. "I could go to California. Act in one of Father's movies. Become a film star. I bet you I could." This was all pretense. She wanted to burst into tears.

"Leave me, then," he said. "Go to hell, for all I care." She wondered if that was true. Looking at his face, she thought not.

They heard a car. Daisy pulled the blackout curtain aside an inch and saw Fitz's black-and-cream Rolls-Royce outside, its headlights dimmed by slit masks. "Your father's back," she said. "I wonder if we're at war."

"We'd better go down."

"I'll follow you."

Boy went out and Daisy looked in the mirror. She was surprised to see that she looked no different from the woman who had walked in here half an hour ago. Her life had been turned upside down, but there was no sign of it on her face. She felt terribly sorry for herself, and wanted to cry, but she repressed the urge. Steeling herself, she went downstairs.

Fitz was in the dining room, with raindrops on the shoulders of his dinner jacket. Grout, the butler, had set out cheese and fruit, as Fitz had skipped dessert. The family sat around the table as Grout poured a glass of claret for Fitz. He drank some and said: "It was absolutely dreadful."

Andy said: "What on earth happened?"

Fitz ate a corner of cheddar cheese before answering. "Neville spoke for four minutes. It was the worst performance by a prime minister that I have ever seen. He mumbled and prevaricated and said Germany might withdraw from Poland, which no one believes. He said nothing about war, or even an ultimatum."

Andy said: "But why?"

"Privately, Neville says he's waiting for the French to stop dithering and declare war simultaneously with us. But a lot of people suspect that's just a cowardly excuse."

Fitz took another draft of wine. "Arthur Greenwood spoke next." Greenwood was deputy leader of the Labour Party. "As he stood up, Leo Amery—a Conservative member of Parliament, mind you—shouted out: 'Speak for England, Arthur!' To think that a damned socialist might speak for England where a Conservative prime minister has failed! Neville looked as sick as a dog."

Grout refilled Fitz's glass.

"Greenwood was quite mild, but he did say: 'I wonder how long we are prepared to vacillate?' and, at that, M.P.s on both sides of the house roared their approval. I should think Neville wanted the earth to swallow him up." Fitz took a peach and sliced it with a knife and fork.

Andy said: "How were things left?"

"Nothing is resolved! Neville has gone back to Number Ten Downing Street. But most of the cabinet is holed up in Simon's room at the Commons." Sir John Simon was Chancellor of the Exchequer. "They're saying they won't leave the room until Neville sends the Germans an ultimatum. Meanwhile, Labour's National Executive Committee is in session, and discontented backbenchers are meeting in Winston's flat."

Daisy had always said she did not like politics, but since becoming part of Fitz's family, and seeing everything from the inside, she had become interested, and she found this drama fascinating and scary. "Then the prime minister must act!" she said.

"Oh, certainly," said Fitz. "Before Parliament meets again—which should be at noon tomorrow—I think Neville must either declare war or resign."

The phone rang in the hall and Grout went out to answer it. A minute later he came back and said: "That was the Foreign Office, my lord. The gentleman would not wait for you to come to the telephone, but insisted on giving a message." The old butler looked disconcerted, as if he had been spoken to rather sharply. "The prime minister has called an immediate meeting of the cabinet."

"Movement!" said Fitz. "Good."

Grout went on. "The foreign secretary would like you to be in attendance, if convenient." Fitz was not in the cabinet, but junior ministers were sometimes asked to attend meetings on their area of specialization, sitting at the side of the room rather than at the central table, so that they could answer questions of detail.

Bea looked at the clock. "It's almost eleven. I suppose you must go."

"Indeed I must. The phrase 'if convenient' is an empty courtesy." He patted his lips with a snowy napkin and limped out again.

Princess Bea said: "Make some more coffee, Grout, and bring it to the drawing room. We may be up late tonight."

"Yes, Your Highness."

They all returned to the drawing room, talking animatedly. Eva was in favor of war: she wanted to see the Nazi regime destroyed. She would worry about Jimmy, of course, but she had married a soldier and had always known he would have to risk his life in battle. Bea was pro-war, too, now that the Germans were allied with the Bolsheviks she hated. May feared that Andy would be killed, and could not stop crying. Boy did not see why two great nations such as England and Germany should go to war over a half-barbaric wasteland such as Poland.

As soon as she could, Daisy got Eva to go with her to another room where they could talk privately. "Boy's got a mistress," she said immediately. She showed Eva the condoms. "I found these."

"Oh, Daisy, I'm so sorry," Eva said.

Daisy thought of giving Eva the grisly details—they normally told each other everything—but this time Daisy felt too humiliated, so she just said: "I confronted him, and he admitted it."

"Is he sorry?"

"Not very. He says all men of his class do it, including his father."

"Jimmy doesn't," Eva said decisively.

"No, I'm sure you're right."

"What will you do?"

"I'm going to leave him. We can get divorced. Then someone else can be the viscountess."

"But you can't if there's a war!"

"Why not?"

"It's too cruel, when he's on the battlefield."

"He should have thought of that before he slept with a pair of prostitutes in Aldgate."

"But it would be cowardly, as well. You can't dump a man who is risking his life to protect you."

Reluctantly, Daisy saw Eva's point. War would transform Boy from a despicable adulterer who deserved rejection into a hero defending his wife, his mother, and his country from the terror of invasion and conquest. It was not just that everyone in London and Buffalo would see Daisy as a coward for leaving him. She would feel that way herself. If there was a war, she wanted to be brave, even though she was not sure what that might involve.

"You're right," she said grudgingly. "I can't leave him if there's a war."

There was a clap of thunder. Daisy looked at the clock: it was midnight. The rain altered in sound as a torrential downpour began.

Daisy and Eva returned to the drawing room. Bea was asleep on a couch. Andy had his arm around May, who was still sniveling. Boy was smoking a cigar and drinking brandy. Daisy decided she would definitely be driving home.

Fitz came in at half past midnight, his evening suit soaking wet. "The dithering is over," he said. "Neville will send the Germans an ultimatum in the morning. If they do not begin to withdraw their troops from Poland by midday—eleven o'clock our time—we will be at war."

They all got up and prepared to leave. In the hall, Daisy said: "I'll drive," and Boy did not argue with her. They got into the cream Bentley and Daisy started the engine. Grout closed the door of Fitz's house. Daisy turned on the windscreen wipers but did not pull away.

"Boy," she said, "let's try again."

"What do you mean?"

"I don't really want to leave you."

"I certainly don't want you to go."

"Give up those women in Aldgate. Sleep with me every night. Let's really try for a baby. It's what you want, isn't it?"

"Yes."

"Then will you do as I ask?"

There was a long pause. Then he said: "All right."

"Thank you."

She looked at him, hoping for a kiss, but he sat still, looking straight ahead through the windscreen, as the rhythmic wipers swept away the relentless rain.

## vi

On Sunday the rain stopped and the sun came out. Lloyd Williams felt as if London had been washed clean.

During the course of the morning, the Williams family gathered in the kitchen of Ethel's house in Aldgate. There was no prior arrangement:

they turned up spontaneously. They wanted to be together, Lloyd guessed, if war was declared.

Lloyd longed for action against the Fascists, and at the same time dreaded the prospect of war. In Spain he had seen enough bloodshed and suffering for a lifetime. He wished never to take part in another battle. He had even given up boxing. Yet he hoped with all his heart that Chamberlain would not back down. He had seen for himself what Fascism meant in Germany, and the rumors coming out of Spain were equally nightmarish: the Franco regime was murdering former supporters of the elected government in their hundreds and thousands, and the priests were in control of the schools again.

This summer, after he graduated, he had immediately joined the Welsh Rifles, and as a former member of the Officer Training Corps he had been given the rank of lieutenant. The army was energetically preparing for combat: it was only with the greatest difficulty that he had got a twenty-four-hour pass to visit his mother this weekend. If the prime minister declared war today, Lloyd would be among the first to go.

Billy Williams came to the house in Nutley Street after breakfast on Sunday morning. Lloyd and Bernie were sitting by the radio, newspapers open on the kitchen table, while Ethel prepared a leg of pork for dinner. Uncle Billy almost wept when he saw Lloyd in uniform. "It makes me think of our Dave, that's all," he said. "He'd be a conscript now, if he'd come back from Spain."

Lloyd had never told Billy the truth about how Dave had died. He pretended he did not know the details, just that Dave had been killed in action at Belchite and was presumably buried there. Billy had been in the Great War and knew how haphazardly bodies were dealt with on the battlefield, and that probably made his grief worse. His great hope was to visit Belchite one day, when Spain was freed at last, and pay his respects to the son who died fighting in that great cause.

Lenny Griffiths was another who had never returned from Spain. No one had any idea where he might be buried. It was even possible he was still alive, in one of Franco's prison camps.

Now the radio reported Prime Minister Chamberlain's statement to the House of Commons last night, but nothing further.

"You'd never know what a stink there was afterwards," said Billy.

"The BBC doesn't report stinks," said Lloyd. "They like to sound reassuring."

Both Billy and Lloyd were members of the Labour Party's National Executive Committee—Lloyd as the representative of the party's youth section. After he came back from Spain, he had managed to gain readmission to Cambridge University, and while finishing his studies he had toured the country addressing Labour Party groups, telling people how the elected Spanish government had been betrayed by Britain's Fascist-friendly government. It had done no good—Franco's antidemocracy rebels had won anyway—but Lloyd had become a well-known figure, even something of a hero, especially among young left-wingers, hence his election to the Executive.

So both Lloyd and Uncle Billy had been at last night's committee meeting. They knew that Chamberlain had bowed to pressure from the cabinet and sent the ultimatum to Hitler. Now they were waiting on tenterhooks to see what would happen.

As far as they knew, no response had yet been received from Hitler.

Lloyd recalled his mother's friend Maud and her family in Berlin. Those two little children would be eighteen and nineteen now, he calculated. He wondered if they were sitting around a radio wondering whether they were going to war against England.

At ten o'clock Lloyd's half sister, Millie, arrived. She was now nineteen, and married to her friend Naomi Avery's brother Abe, a leather wholesaler. She earned good money as a salesgirl on commission in an expensive dress shop. She had ambitions to open her own shop, and Lloyd had no doubt that she would do it one day. Although it was not the career Bernie would have chosen for her, Lloyd could see how proud he was of her brains and ambition and smart appearance.

But today her poised self-assurance had collapsed. "It was awful when you were in Spain," she said tearfully to Lloyd. "And Dave and Lenny never did come back. Now it will be you and my Abie off somewhere, and us women waiting every day for news, wondering if you're dead yet."

Ethel put in: "And your cousin Keir. He's almost eighteen now."

Lloyd said to his mother: "Which regiment was my real father in?"

"Oh, does it matter?" She was never keen to talk about Lloyd's father, perhaps out of consideration for Bernie.

But Lloyd wanted to know. "It matters to me," he said.

She threw a peeled potato into a pan of water with unnecessary vigor. "He was in the Welsh Rifles."

"The same as me! Why didn't you tell me before?"

"The past is the past."

There might be another reason for her caginess, Lloyd knew. She had probably been pregnant when she married. This did not bother Lloyd, but to her generation it was shameful. All the same, he persisted. "Was my father Welsh?"

"Yes."

"From Aberowen?"

"No."

"Where, then?"

She sighed. "His parents moved around—something to do with his father's job—but I think they were from Swansea originally. Satisfied now?"

"Yes."

Lloyd's aunt Mildred came in from church, a stylish middle-aged woman, pretty except for protruding front teeth. She wore a fancy hat—she was a milliner with a small factory. Her two daughters by her first marriage, Enid and Lillian, both in their late twenties, were married with children of their own. Her elder son was the Dave who died in Spain. Her younger son, Keir, followed her into the kitchen. Mildred insisted on taking her children to church, even though her husband, Billy, would have nothing to do with religion. "I had a lifetime's worth of that when I was a child," he often said. "If I'm not saved, no one is."

Lloyd looked around. This was his family: mother, stepfather, half sister, uncle, aunt, cousin. He did not want to leave them and go away to die somewhere.

Lloyd looked at his watch, a stainless-steel model with a square face that Bernie had given him as a graduation present. It was eleven o'clock. On the radio, the fruity voice of newsreader Alvar Liddell said the prime minister was expected to make an announcement shortly. Then there was some solemn classical music.

"Hush, now, everyone," said Ethel. "I'll make you all a cup of tea after."

The kitchen went quiet.

Alvar Liddell announced the prime minister, Neville Chamberlain.

The appeaser of Fascism, Lloyd thought; the man who gave Czechoslovakia to Hitler; the man who had stubbornly refused to help the elected government of Spain even after it became indisputably obvious that the Germans and Italians were arming the rebels. Was he about to cave in yet again?

Lloyd noticed that his parents were holding hands, Ethel's small fingers digging into Bernie's palm.

He checked his watch again. It was a quarter past eleven.

Then they heard the prime minister say: "I am speaking to you from the Cabinet Room at Ten Downing Street."

Chamberlain's voice was reedy and overprecise. He sounded like a pedantic schoolmaster. What we need is a warrior, Lloyd thought.

"This morning the British ambassador in Berlin handed the German government a final note, stating that unless we heard from them by eleven o'clock that they were prepared at once to withdraw their troops from Poland, a state of war would exist between us."

Lloyd found himself feeling impatient with Chamberlain's verbiage. *A state of war would exist between us:* what a strange way to put it. Get on with it, he thought; get to the point. This is life and death.

Chamberlain's voice deepened and became more statesmanlike. Perhaps he was no longer looking at the microphone, but instead seeing millions of his countrymen in their homes, sitting by their radio sets, waiting for his fateful words. "I have to tell you now that no such undertaking has been received . . ."

Lloyd heard his mother say: "Oh, God, spare us." He looked at her. Her face was gray.

Chamberlain uttered his next, dreadful words quite slowly. ". . . and that, consequently, this country is at war with Germany."

Ethel began to cry.

# PART TWO

## A SEASON
## OF
## BLOOD

# CHAPTER SIX

# 1940 (I)

berowen had changed. There were cars, trucks, and buses on the streets. When Lloyd had come here as a child in the 1920s to visit his grandparents, a parked car had been a rarity that would draw a crowd.

But the town was still dominated by the twin towers of the pithead, with their majestically revolving wheels. There was nothing else: no factories, no office blocks, no industry other than coal. Almost every man in town worked down the pit. There were a few dozen exceptions: some shopkeepers, numerous clergymen of all denominations, a town clerk, a doctor. Whenever the demand for coal slumped, as it had in the thirties, and men were laid off, there was nothing else for them to do. That was why the Labour Party's most passionate demand was help for the unemployed, so that such men would never again suffer the agony and humiliation of being unable to feed their families.

Lieutenant Lloyd Williams arrived by train from Cardiff on a Sunday in April 1940. Carrying a small suitcase, he walked up the hill to Tŷ Gwyn. He had spent eight months training new recruits—the same work he had done in Spain—and coaching the Welsh Rifles boxing team, but the army had at last realized he spoke fluent German, transferred him to intelligence duties, and sent him on a training course.

Training was all the army had done so far. No British forces had yet fought the enemy in an engagement of any significance. Germany and the USSR had overrun Poland and divided it between them, and the Allied guarantee of Polish independence had proved worthless.

British people called it the Phoney War, and they were impatient for the real thing. Lloyd had no sentimental illusions about warfare—he had heard the piteous voices of dying men begging for water on the battlefields of Spain—but even so he was eager to get started on the final showdown with Fascism.

The army was expecting to send more forces to France, assuming the Germans would invade. It had not happened, and they remained at the ready, but meanwhile they did a lot of training.

Lloyd's initiation into the mysteries of military intelligence was to take place in the stately home that had featured in his family's destiny for so long. The wealthy and noble owners of many such palaces had loaned them to the armed forces, perhaps for fear that otherwise they might be confiscated permanently.

The army had certainly made Tŷ Gwyn look different. There were a dozen olive-drab vehicles parked on the lawn, and their tires had chewed up the earl's lush turf. The gracious entrance courtyard, with its curved granite steps, had become a supply dump, and giant cans of baked beans and cooking lard stood in teetering stacks where, formerly, bejeweled women and men in tailcoats had stepped out of their carriages. Lloyd grinned: he liked the leveling effect of war.

Lloyd entered the house. He was greeted by a podgy officer in a creased and stained uniform. "Here for the intelligence course, Lieutenant?"

"Yes, sir. My name is Lloyd Williams."

"I'm Major Lowther."

Lloyd had heard of him. He was the Marquis of Lowther, known to his pals as Lowthie.

Lloyd looked around. The paintings on the walls had been shrouded with huge dust sheets. The ornate carved marble fireplaces had been boxed in with rough planking, leaving only a small space for a grate. The dark old furniture that his mother sometimes mentioned fondly had all disappeared, to be replaced by steel desks and cheap chairs. "My goodness, the place looks different," he said.

Lowther smiled. "You've been here before. Do you know the family?"

"I was up at Cambridge with Boy Fitzherbert. I met the viscountess there, too, although they weren't married then. But I suppose they've moved out for the duration."

"Not entirely. A few rooms have been reserved for their private use. But they don't bother us at all. So you came here as a guest?"

"Goodness, no, I don't know them well. No, I was shown around the place as a boy, one day when the family weren't in residence. My mother worked here at one time."

"Really? What, looking after the earl's library, or something?"

"No, as a housemaid." As soon as the words were out of Lloyd's mouth, he knew he had made a mistake.

Lowther's face changed to an expression of distaste. "I see," he said. "How very interesting."

Lloyd knew he had instantly been pigeonholed as a proletarian upstart. He would now be treated as a second-class citizen throughout his time here. He should have kept quiet about his mother's past: he knew how snobbish the army was.

Lowthie said: "Show the lieutenant to his room, Sergeant. Attic floor."

Lloyd had been assigned a room in the old servants' quarters. He did not really mind. It was good enough for my mother, he thought.

As they walked up the back stairs, the sergeant told Lloyd he had no obligations until dinner in the mess. Lloyd asked whether any of the Fitzherberts happened to be in residence right now, but the man did not know.

It took Lloyd two minutes to unpack. He combed his hair, put on a clean uniform shirt, and went to visit his grandparents.

The house in Wellington Row seemed smaller and more drab than ever, though it now had hot water in the scullery and a flushing toilet in the outhouse. The decor had not altered within Lloyd's memory: same rag rug on the floor, same faded paisley curtains, same hard oak chairs in the single ground-floor room that served as living room and kitchen.

His grandparents had changed, though. Both were about seventy now, he guessed, and looking frail. Granda had pains in his legs, and had reluctantly retired from his job with the miners' union. Grandmam had a weak heart: Dr. Mortimer had told her to put her feet up for a quarter of an hour after meals.

They were pleased to see Lloyd in his uniform. "Lieutenant, is it?" said Grandmam. A class warrior all her life, she nevertheless could not conceal her pride that her grandson was an officer.

News traveled fast in Aberowen, and the fact that Dai Williams's grandson was visiting probably went halfway round the town before Lloyd had finished his first cup of Grandmam's strong tea. So he was not really surprised when Tommy Griffiths dropped in.

"I expect my Lenny would be a lieutenant, like you, if he'd come back from Spain," Tommy said.

"I should think so," Lloyd said. He had never met an officer who had been a coal miner in civilian life, but anything might happen once the war got going properly. "He was the best sergeant in Spain, I can tell you that."

"You two went through a lot together."

"We went through hell," Lloyd said. "And we lost. But the Fascists won't win this time."

"I'll drink to that," said Tommy, and emptied his mug of tea.

Lloyd went with his grandparents to the evening service at the Bethesda Chapel. Religion was not a big part of his life, and he certainly did not go along with Granda's dogmatism. The universe was mysterious, Lloyd thought, and people might as well admit it. But it pleased his grandparents that he sat with them in chapel.

The extempore prayers were eloquent, knitting biblical phrases seamlessly into colloquial language. The sermon was a bit tedious. But the singing thrilled Lloyd. Welsh chapelgoers automatically sang in four-part harmony, and when they were in the mood, they could raise the roof.

As he joined in, Lloyd felt this was the beating heart of Britain, here in this whitewashed chapel. The people around him were poorly dressed and ill-educated, and they lived lives of unending hard work, the men winning the coal underground, the women raising the next generation of miners. But they had strong backs and sharp minds, and all on their own they had created a culture that made life worth living. They gained hope from nonconformist Christianity and left-wing politics, they found joy in rugby football and male voice choirs, and they were bonded together by generosity in good times and solidarity in bad. This was what he would be fighting for, these people, this town. And if he had to give his life for them, it would be well spent.

Granda gave the closing prayer, standing up with his eyes shut, leaning on a walking stick. "You see among us, O Lord, your young servant Lloyd Williams, sitting by here in his uniform. We ask you, in your wisdom and grace, to spare his life in the conflict to come. Please, Lord, send him back home to us safe and whole. If it be your will, O Lord."

The congregation gave a heartfelt amen, and Lloyd wiped away a tear.

He walked the old folks home as the sun went down behind the mountain and an evening gloom settled on the rows of gray houses. He refused the offer of supper and hurried back to Tŷ Gwyn, arriving in time for dinner in the mess.

They had braised beef, boiled potatoes, and cabbage. It was no better or worse than most army food, and Lloyd tucked in, aware that it had been paid for by people such as his grandparents who were having bread-and-dripping for their supper. There was a bottle of whisky on the table, and Lloyd took some to be convivial. He studied his fellow trainees and tried to remember their names.

On his way up to bed he passed through the Sculpture Room, now empty of art and furnished with a blackboard and twelve cheap desks.

There he saw Major Lowther talking to a woman. At a second glance he saw that the woman was Daisy Fitzherbert.

He was so surprised that he stopped. Lowther looked around with an irritated expression. He saw Lloyd and reluctantly said: "Lady Aberowen, I believe you know Lieutenant Williams."

If she denies it, Lloyd thought, I shall remind her of the time she kissed me, long and hard, on a Mayfair street in the dark.

"How nice to see you again, Mr. Williams," she said, and put out her hand to shake.

Her skin was warm and soft to his touch. His heart beat faster.

Lowther said: "Williams tells me his mother worked at this house as a maid."

"I know," Daisy said. "He told me that at the Trinity Ball. He was reproving me for being a snob. I'm sorry to say that he was quite right."

"You're generous, Lady Aberowen," said Lloyd, feeling embarrassed. "I don't know what business I had to say such a thing to you." She seemed less brittle than he remembered; perhaps she had matured.

Daisy said to Lowther: "Mr. Williams's mother is a member of Parliament now, though."

Lowther was taken aback.

Lloyd said to Daisy: "And how is your Jewish friend Eva? I know she married Jimmy Murray."

"They have two children now."

"Did she get her parents out of Germany?"

"How kind of you to remember—but no, sadly, the Rothmanns can't get exit visas."

"I'm so sorry. It must be hell for her."

"It is."

Lowther was visibly impatient with this talk of housemaids and Jews. "To get back to what I was saying, Lady Aberowen . . ."

Lloyd said: "I'll bid you good night." He left the room and ran upstairs.

As he got ready for bed, he found himself singing the last hymn from the service:

*No storm can shake my inmost calm*
*While to that rock I'm clinging*
*Since Love is Lord of heaven and earth*
*How can I keep from singing?*

## ii

Three days later Daisy was finishing writing to her half brother, Greg. When war broke out, he had sent her a sweetly anxious letter, and since then they had corresponded every month or so. He had told her about seeing his old flame, Jacky Jakes, on E Street in Washington, and asked Daisy what would make a girl run away like that. Daisy had no idea. She said so, and wished him luck, then signed off.

She looked at the clock. It was an hour before the trainees' dinnertime, so lessons had ended and she had a good chance of catching Lloyd in his room.

She went up to the old servants' quarters on the attic floor. The young officers were sitting or lying on their beds, reading or writing. She found Lloyd in a narrow room with an old cheval glass, sitting by the window, studying an illustrated book. She said: "Reading something interesting?"

He sprang to his feet. "Hello, this is a surprise."

He was blushing. He probably still had a crush on her. It had been very cruel of her to kiss him, when she had no intention of letting the relationship go any further. But that was four years ago, and they had both been kids. He should have gotten over it by now.

She looked at the book in his hands. It was in German, and had color pictures of badges.

"We have to know German insignia," he explained. "A lot of military intelligence comes from interrogation of prisoners of war immediately after their capture. Some won't talk, of course; so the interrogator needs to be able to tell, just by looking at the prisoner's uniform, what his rank is, what army corps he belongs to, whether he is from infantry, cavalry, artillery, or a specialist unit such as veterinarian, and so on."

"That's what you're learning here?" she said skeptically. "The meanings of German badges?"

He laughed. "It's one of the things we're learning. One I can tell you about without giving away military secrets."

"Oh, I see."

"Why are you here in Wales? I'm surprised you're not doing something for the war effort."

"There you go again," she said. "Moral reproof. Did someone tell you this was a way to charm women?"

"Pardon me," he said stiffly. "I didn't mean to rebuke you."

"Anyway, there is no war effort. Barrage balloons float in the air as a hazard to German planes that never come."

"At least you'd have a social life in London."

"Do you know, that used to be the most important thing in the world, and now it's not?" she said. "I must be getting old."

There was another reason she had left London, but she was not going to tell him.

"I imagined you in a nurse's uniform," he said.

"Not likely. I hate sick people. But before you give me another of those disapproving frowns, take a look at this." She handed him the framed photograph she was carrying.

He studied it, frowning. "Where did you get it?"

"I was looking through a box of old pictures in the basement junk room."

It was a group photo taken on the east lawn of Tŷ Gwyn on a summer morning. In the center was the young Earl Fitzherbert, with a big white dog at his feet. The girl next to him was probably his sister, Maud, whom Daisy had never met. Lined up on either side of them were forty or fifty men and women in a variety of servants' uniforms.

"Look at the date," she said.

"Nineteen twelve," Lloyd read aloud.

She watched him, studying his reactions to the photo he was holding. "Is your mother in it?"

"Goodness! She might be." Lloyd looked closer. "I believe she is," he said after a minute.

"Show me."

Lloyd pointed. "I think that's her."

Daisy saw a slim, pretty girl of about nineteen, with curly black hair under a maid's white cap, and a smile that had more than a hint of mischief in it. "Why, she's enchanting!" she said.

"She was then, anyway," Lloyd said. "Nowadays people are more likely to call her formidable."

"Have you ever met Lady Maud? Do you think that's her next to Fitz?"

"I suppose I've known her all my life, off and on. She and my mother were suffragettes together. I haven't seen her since I left Berlin in 1933, but this is definitely her in the picture."

"She's not so pretty."

"Perhaps, but she's very poised, and wonderfully well dressed."

"Anyway, I thought you might like to have the picture."

"To keep?"

"Of course. No one else wants it—that's why it was in a box in the basement."

"Thank you!"

"You're welcome." Daisy went to the door. "Go back to your studies."

Going down the back stairs she hoped she had not flirted. She probably should not have gone to see him at all. She had succumbed to a generous impulse. Heaven forbid that he should misinterpret it.

She felt a sharp pain in her tummy, and stopped on the half landing. She had had a slight backache all day—which she attributed to the cheap mattress she was sleeping on—but this was different. She thought back over what she had eaten today, but could not identify anything that might have made her ill: no undercooked chicken, no unripe fruit. She had not eaten oysters—no such luck! The pain went as quickly as it had come and she told herself to forget about it.

She returned to her quarters in the basement. She was living in what had been the housekeeper's flat: a tiny bedroom, a sitting room, a small kitchen, and an adequate bathroom with a tub. An old footman called Morrison was acting as caretaker to the house, and a young woman from Aberowen was her maid. The girl was called Little Maisie Owen, although she was quite big. "My mother's Maisie, too, so I've always been Little Maisie, even though I'm taller than her now," she had explained.

The phone rang as Daisy entered. She picked it up and heard her husband's voice. "How are you?" he said.

"I'm fine. What time will you be here?" He had flown to RAF St. Athan, a large air base outside Cardiff, on some mission, and he had promised to visit her and spend the night.

"I'm not going to make it. I'm sorry."

"Oh, how disappointing!"

"There's a ceremonial dinner at the base that I'm required to attend."

He did not sound particularly dispirited that he would not see her, and she felt spurned. "How nice for you," she said.

"It will be boring, but I can't get out of it."

"Not half as boring as living here on my own."

"It must be dull. But you're better off there, in your condition."

Thousands of people had left London after war was declared, but most of them had drifted back when the expected bombing raids and gas attacks did not materialize. However, Bea and May and even Eva were agreed that Daisy's pregnancy meant she should live at Tŷ Gwyn. Many women gave birth safely every day in London, Daisy had pointed out, but of course the heir to the earldom was different.

In truth she did not mind as much as she had expected. Perhaps pregnancy had made her uncharacteristically passive. But there was a halfhearted quality about London social life since the declaration of war, as if people felt they did not have the right to enjoy themselves. They were like vicars in a pub, knowing it was supposed to be fun but unable to enter into the spirit.

"I wish I had my motorcycle here, though," she said. "Then at least I could explore Wales." Petrol was rationed, but not severely.

"Really, Daisy!" he said censoriously. "You can't ride a motorcycle— the doctor absolutely forbade it."

"Anyway, I've discovered literature," she said. "The library here is wonderful. A few rare and valuable editions have been packed away, but nearly all the books are still on the shelves. I'm getting the education I worked so hard to avoid at school."

"Excellent," he said. "Well, curl up with a good murder mystery and enjoy your evening."

"I had a slight tummy pain earlier."

"Probably indigestion."

"I expect you're right."

"Give my regards to that slob Lowthie."

"Don't drink too much port at your dinner."

Just as Daisy hung up, she got the tummy cramp again. This time it lasted longer. Maisie came in, saw her face, and said: "Are you all right, my lady?"

"Just a twinge."

"I have came to ask if you are ready for your supper."

"I don't feel hungry. I think I'll skip supper tonight."

"I done you a lovely cottage pie," Maisie said reproachfully.

"Cover it and put it in the larder. I'll eat it tomorrow."

"Shall I make you a nice cup of tea?"

Just to get rid of her Daisy said: "Yes, please." Even after four years she had not grown to like strong British tea with milk and sugar in it.

The pain went away, and she sat down and opened *The Mill on the Floss*. She forced herself to drink Maisie's tea and felt a little better. When she had finished the drink, and Maisie had washed the cup and saucer, she sent Maisie home. The girl had to walk a mile in the dark, but she carried a flashlight, and said she did not mind.

An hour later the pain returned, and this time it did not go away. Daisy went to the toilet, vaguely hoping to relieve pressure in her abdomen. She was surprised and worried to see spots of dark red blood in her underwear.

She put on clean panties, and, seriously worried now, she went to the phone. She got the number of RAF St. Athan and called the base. "I need to speak to Flight Lieutenant the Viscount Aberowen," she said.

"We can't connect personal calls to officers," said a pedantic Welshman.

"This is an emergency. I must speak to my husband."

"There are no phones in the rooms—this isn't the Dorchester Hotel." Perhaps it was her imagination, but he sounded quite pleased that he could not help her.

"My husband will be at the ceremonial banquet. Please send an orderly to bring him to the phone."

"I haven't got any orderlies, and anyway there's no banquet."

"No banquet?" Daisy was momentarily at a loss.

"Just the usual dinner in the mess," the operator said. "And that was finished an hour ago."

Daisy slammed the phone down. No banquet? Boy had distinctly said he had to attend a ceremonial dinner at the base. He must have lied. She wanted to cry. He had chosen not to see her, preferring to go drinking with his comrades, or perhaps to visit some woman. The reason did not matter. Daisy was not his priority.

She took a deep breath. She needed help. She did not know the phone number of the Aberowen doctor, if there was one. What was she to do?

Last time Boy had left he had said: "You'll have a hundred or more army officers to look after you if necessary." But she could not tell the Marquis of Lowther that she was bleeding from her vagina.

The pain was getting worse, and she could feel something warm and sticky between her legs. She went to the bathroom again and washed herself. There were clots in the blood, she saw. She did not have any sanitary towels—pregnant women did not need them, she had thought. She cut a length off a hand towel and stuffed it in her panties.

Then she thought of Lloyd Williams.

He was kind. He had been brought up by a strong-minded feminist woman. He adored Daisy. He would help her.

She went up to the hall. Where was he? The trainees would have finished their dinner by now. He might be upstairs. Her stomach hurt so much that she did not think she could make it all the way to the attic.

Perhaps he was in the library. The trainees used the room for quiet study. She went in. A sergeant was poring over an atlas. "Would you be very kind," she said to him, "and find Lieutenant Lloyd Williams for me?"

"Of course, my lady," said the man, closing the book. "What's the message?"

"Ask him if he would come down to the basement for a moment."

"Are you all right, ma'am? You look a bit pale."

"I'll be fine. Just fetch Williams as quickly as you can."

"Right away."

Daisy returned to her rooms. The effort of seeming normal had exhausted her, and she lay on the bed. Before long she felt the blood soaking through her dress, but she hurt too much to care. She looked at her watch. Why had Lloyd not come? Perhaps the sergeant could not find him. It was such a big house. Perhaps she would just die here.

There was a tap at the door, and then to her immense relief she heard his voice. "It's Lloyd Williams."

"Come in," she called. He was going to see her in a dreadful state. Perhaps it would put him off her for good.

She heard him enter the next room. "It took me a while to find your quarters," he said. "Where are you?"

"Through here."

He stepped into the bedroom. "Good God!" he exclaimed. "What on earth has happened?"

"Get help," she said. "Is there a doctor in this town?"

"Of course. Dr. Mortimer. He's been here for centuries. But there may not be time. Let me . . ." He hesitated. "You may be hemorrhaging, but I can't tell unless I look."

She closed her eyes. "Go ahead." She was almost too scared to be embarrassed.

She felt him raise the skirt of her dress. "Oh, dear," he said. "Poor you." Then he ripped her underpants. "I'm sorry," he said. "Is there some water . . . ?"

"Bathroom," she said, pointing.

He stepped into the bathroom and ran a tap. A moment later she felt a warm, damp cloth being used to clean her.

Then he said: "It's just a trickle. I've seen men bleed to death, and you're not in that danger." She opened her eyes to see him pulling her skirt back down. "Where's the phone?" he said.

"Sitting room."

She heard him say: "Put me through to Dr. Mortimer, quick as you can." There was a pause. "This is Lloyd Williams. I'm at Tŷ Gwyn. May I speak to the doctor? . . . Oh, hello, Mrs. Mortimer, when do you expect him back? . . . It's a woman with abdominal pain and vaginal bleeding . . . Yes, I do realize most women suffer that every month, but this is clearly abnormal . . . She's twenty-four . . . yes, married . . . no children . . . I'll ask." He raised his voice. "Could you be pregnant?"

"Yes," Daisy replied. "Three months."

He repeated her answer; then there was a long silence. Eventually he hung up the phone and returned to her.

He sat on the edge of the bed. "The doctor will come as soon as he can, but he's operating on a miner crushed by a runaway dram. However, his wife is quite sure that you've suffered a miscarriage." He took her hand. "I'm sorry, Daisy."

"Thank you," she whispered. The pain seemed less, but she felt terribly sad. The heir to the earldom was no more. Boy would be so upset.

Lloyd said: "Mrs. Mortimer says it's quite common, and most women suffer one or two miscarriages between pregnancies. There's no danger, provided the bleeding isn't copious."

"What if it gets worse?"

"Then I must drive you to Merthyr Hospital. But going ten miles in an army lorry would be quite bad for you, so it's to be avoided unless your life is in danger."

She was not frightened anymore. "I'm so glad you were here."

"May I make a suggestion?"

"Of course."

"Do you think you can walk a few steps?"

"I don't know."

"Let me run you a bath. If you can manage it, you'll feel so much better when you're clean."

"Yes."

"Then perhaps you can improvise a bandage of some kind."

"Yes."

He returned to the bathroom, and she heard water running. She sat upright. She felt dizzy, and rested for a minute; then her head cleared. She swung her feet to the floor. She was sitting in congealing blood, and felt disgusted with herself.

The taps were turned off. He came back in and took her arm. "If you feel faint, just tell me," he said. "I won't let you fall." He was surprisingly strong, and half-carried her as he walked her into the bathroom. At some point her ripped underwear fell to the floor. She stood beside the bath and let him undo the buttons at the back of her dress. "Can you manage the rest?" he said.

She nodded, and he went out.

Leaning on the linen basket, she took off her clothes slowly, leaving them on the floor in a bloodstained heap. Gingerly, she got into the bath. The water was just hot enough. The pain eased as she lay back and relaxed. She felt overwhelmed with gratitude to Lloyd. He was so kind that it made her want to cry.

After a few minutes, the door opened a crack and his hand appeared holding some clothes. "A nightdress, and so on," he said. He placed them on top of the linen basket and closed the door.

When the water began to cool, she stood up. She felt dizzy again, but only for a moment. She dried herself with a towel, then put on the nightdress and underwear he had brought. She placed a hand towel inside her panties to soak up the blood that continued to seep.

When she returned to the bedroom, her bed was made up with clean sheets and blankets. She climbed in and sat upright, pulling the covers to her neck.

He came in from the sitting room. "You must be feeling better," he said. "You look embarrassed."

"*Embarrassed* isn't the word," she said. "Mortified, perhaps, though even that seems understated." The truth was not so simple. She winced when she thought of how he had seen her—but, on the other hand, he had not seemed disgusted.

He went into the bathroom and picked up her discarded clothes. Apparently he was not squeamish about menstrual blood.

She said: "Where have you put the sheets?"

"I found a big sink in the flower room. I left them to soak in cold water. I'll do the same with your clothes, shall I?"

She nodded.

He disappeared again. Where had he learned to be so competent and self-sufficient? In the Spanish Civil War, she supposed.

She heard him moving around the kitchen. He reappeared with two cups of tea. "You probably hate this stuff, but it will make you feel better." She took the tea. He showed her two white pills in the palm of his hand. "Aspirin? May ease the stomach cramps a bit."

She took them and swallowed them with hot tea. He had always struck her as being mature beyond his years. She remembered how confidently he had gone off to find the drunken Boy at the Gaiety Theatre. "You've always been like this," she said. "A real grown-up, when the rest of us were just pretending."

She finished the tea and felt sleepy. He took the cups away. "I may just close my eyes for a moment," she said. "Will you stay here, if I go to sleep?"

"I'll stay as long as you like," he said. Then he said something else, but his voice seemed to fade away, and she slept.


## iii

After that Lloyd began to spend his evenings in the little housekeeper's flat.

He looked forward to it all day.

He would go downstairs a few minutes after eight, when dinner in the mess was over and Daisy's maid had left for the night. They would sit opposite one another in the two old armchairs. Lloyd would bring a book to study—there was always "homework," with tests in the morning—and Daisy would read a novel, but mostly they talked. They related what had happened during the day, discussed whatever they were reading, and told each other the story of their lives.

He recounted his experiences at the Battle of Cable Street. "Standing there in a peaceful crowd, we were charged by mounted policemen screaming about dirty Jews," he told her. "They beat us with their truncheons and pushed us through the plate-glass windows."

She had been quarantined with the Fascists in Tower Gardens, and had seen none of the fighting. "That wasn't the way it was reported," she said. She had believed the newspapers that said it had been a street riot organized by hooligans.

Lloyd was not surprised. "My mother watched the newsreel at the Aldgate Essoldo a week later," he recalled. "That plummy-voiced commentator said: 'From impartial observers the police received nothing but praise.' Mam said the entire audience burst out laughing."

Daisy was shocked by his skepticism about the news. He told her that most British papers had suppressed stories of atrocities by Franco's army in Spain, and exaggerated any report of bad behavior by government forces. She admitted she had swallowed Earl Fitzherbert's view that the rebels were high-minded Christians liberating Spain from the threat of Communism. She knew nothing of mass executions, rape, and looting by Franco's men.

It seemed never to have occurred to her that newspapers owned by capitalists might play down news that reflected badly on the Conservative government, the military, or businessmen, and would seize upon any incident of bad behavior by trade unionists or left-wing parties.

Lloyd and Daisy talked about the war. There was action at last. British and French troops had landed in Norway, and were contending for control with the Germans who had done the same. The newspapers could not quite conceal the fact that it was going badly for the Allies.

Her attitude to him had changed. She no longer flirted. She was always pleased to see him, and complained if he was late arriving in the evening, and she teased him sometimes, but she was never coquettish. She told him how disappointed everyone was about the baby she had lost: Boy, Fitz, Bea, her mother in Buffalo, even her father, Lev. She could not shake the irrational feeling that she had done something shameful, and she asked if he thought that was foolish. He did not. Nothing she did was foolish to him.

Their conversation was personal but they kept their distance from one another physically. He would not exploit the extraordinary intimacy of the night she miscarried. Of course the scene would live in his heart forever. Wiping the blood from her thighs and her belly had not been sexy—not in the least—but it had been unbearably tender. However, it had been a medical emergency, and it did not give him permission to take liberties later. He was so afraid of giving the wrong impression about this that he was careful never to touch her.

At ten o'clock she would make them cocoa, which he loved and she said she liked, though he wondered if she was just being nice. Then he would say good night and go upstairs to his attic bedroom.

They were like old friends. It was not what he wanted, but she was a married woman, and this was the best he was going to get.

He tended to forget Daisy's status. He was startled, one evening, when she announced that she was going to pay a visit to the earl's retired butler, Peel, who was living in a cottage just outside the grounds. "He's eighty!" she told Lloyd. "I'm sure Fitz has forgotten all about him. I should check on him."

Lloyd raised his eyebrows in surprise, and she added: "I need to make sure he's all right. It's my duty as a member of the Fitzherbert clan. Taking care of your old retainers is an obligation of wealthy families—didn't you know that?"

"It had slipped my mind."

"Will you come with me?"

"Of course."

The next day was a Sunday, and they went in the morning, when Lloyd had no lectures. They were both shocked by the state of the little house. The paint was flaking, the wallpaper was peeling, and the curtains were gray with coal dust. The only decoration was a row of photographs cut from magazines and tacked to the wall: the king and queen, Fitz and Bea, and other assorted members of the nobility. The place had not been properly cleaned for years, and there was a smell of urine and ash and decay. But Lloyd guessed it was not unusual for an old man on a small pension.

Peel had white eyebrows. He looked at Lloyd and said: "Good morning, my lord—I thought you were dead!"

Lloyd smiled. "I'm just a visitor."

"Are you, sir? My poor brain is scrambled eggs. The old earl died, what, thirty-five or forty years ago? Well, then, who are you, young sir?"

"I'm Lloyd Williams. You knew my mother, Ethel, years ago."

"You're Eth's boy? Well, in that case, of course . . ."

Daisy said: "In that case, what, Mr. Peel?"

"Oh, nothing. My brain's scrambled eggs!"

They asked him if he needed anything, and he insisted he had everything a man could want. "I don't eat much, and I rarely drink beer. I've got enough money to buy pipe tobacco, and the newspaper. Will Hitler invade us, do you think, young Lloyd? I hope I don't live to see that."

Daisy cleaned up his kitchen a bit, though housekeeping was not her forte. "I can't believe it," she said to Lloyd in a low voice. "Living here, like this, he says he's got everything—he thinks he's lucky!"

"Many men his age are worse off," Lloyd said.

They talked to Peel for an hour. Before they left, he thought of something he did want. He looked at the row of pictures on the wall. "At the funeral of the old earl, there was a photograph took," he said. "I was a mere footman, then, not the butler. We all lined up alongside the hearse. There was a big old camera with a black cloth over it, not like the little modern ones. That was in 1906."

"I bet I know where that photograph is," said Daisy. "We'll go and look."

They returned to the big house and went down to the basement. The junk room, next to the wine cellar, was quite large. It was full of boxes and chests and useless ornaments: a ship in a bottle, a model of Tŷ Gwyn made of matchsticks, a miniature chest of drawers, a sword in an ornate scabbard.

They began to sort through old photographs and paintings. The dust made Daisy sneeze, but she insisted on continuing.

They found the photograph Peel wanted. In the box with it was an even older photo of the previous earl. Lloyd stared at it in some astonishment. The sepia picture was five inches high and three inches wide, and showed a young man in the uniform of a Victorian army officer.

He looked exactly like Lloyd.

"Look at this," he said, handing the photo to Daisy.

"It could be you, if you had side-whiskers," she said.

"Perhaps the old earl had a romance with one of my ancestors," Lloyd said flippantly. "If she was a married woman, she might have passed off the earl's child as her husband's. I wouldn't be very pleased, I can tell you, to learn that I was illegitimately descended from the aristocracy—a red-hot socialist like me!"

Daisy said: "Lloyd, how stupid are you?"

He could not tell whether she was serious. Besides, she had a smear of dust on her nose that looked so sweet that he longed to kiss it. "Well," he said, "I've made a fool of myself more than once, but—"

"Listen to me. Your mother was a maid in this house. Suddenly in 1914 she went to London and married a man called Teddy whom no one knows anything about except that his surname was Williams, the same as hers, so she did not have to change her name. The mysterious Mr. Williams died before anyone met him and his life insurance bought her the house she still lives in."

"Exactly," he said. "What are you getting at?"

"Then, after Mr. Williams died, she gave birth to a son who happens to look remarkably like the late Earl Fitzherbert."

He began to get a glimmer of what she might be saying. "Go on."

"Has it never occurred to you that there might be a completely different explanation for this whole story?"

"Not until now . . ."

"What does an aristocratic family do when one of their daughters gets pregnant? It happens all the time, you know."

"I suppose it does, but I don't know how they handle it. You never hear about it."

"Exactly. The girl disappears for a few months—to Scotland, or Brittany, or Geneva—with her maid. When the two of them reappear, the maid has a little baby, which, she says, she gave birth to during the holiday. The family treat her surprisingly kindly, even though she has admitted fornication, and send her to live a safe distance away, with a small pension."

It seemed like a fairy story, nothing to do with real life, but all the same Lloyd was intrigued and troubled. "And you think I was the baby in some such pretense?"

"I think Lady Maud Fitzherbert had a love affair with a gardener, or a coal miner, or perhaps a charming rogue in London, and she got pregnant. She went away somewhere to give birth in secret. Your mother agreed to pretend the baby was hers, and in exchange she was given a house."

Lloyd was struck by a corroborating thought. "She's always been evasive whenever I've asked about my real father." That now seemed suspicious.

"There you are! There never was a Teddy Williams. To maintain her respectability, your mother said she was a widow. She called her fictional late husband Williams to avoid the problem of changing her name."

Lloyd shook his head in disbelief. "It seems too fantastic."

"She and Maud continued to be friends, and Maud helped raise you. In 1933 your mother took you to Berlin because your real mother wanted to see you again."

Lloyd felt as if he were either dreaming or just waking up. "You think I'm Maud's child?" he said incredulously.

Daisy tapped the frame of the picture she was still holding. "And you look just like your grandfather!"

Lloyd was bewildered. It could not be true—yet it made sense. "I'm used to Bernie not being my real father," he said. "Is Ethel not my real mother?"

Daisy must have seen a look of helplessness on his face, for she leaned forward and touched him—something she did not generally do—and said: "I'm sorry. Have I been brutal? I just want you to see what's in front of your eyes. If Peel suspects the truth, don't you think others may, too? It's the kind of news you want to hear from someone who . . . from a friend."

A gong sounded distantly. Lloyd said mechanically: "I'd better go to the mess for lunch." He took the photograph out of its frame and slipped it into a pocket of his uniform jacket.

"You're upset," Daisy said anxiously.

"No, no. Just . . . astonished."

"Men always deny that they're upset. Please come and see me later."

"All right."

"Don't go to bed without talking to me again."

"I won't."

He left the junk room and made his way upstairs to the grand dining room, now the mess. He ate his canned beef mince automatically, his mind in turmoil. He took no part in the discussion at the table about the battle raging in Norway.

"Having a daydream, Williams?" said Major Lowther.

"Sorry, sir," Lloyd said mechanically. He improvised an excuse. "I was trying to remember which was the higher German rank, *Generalleutnant* or *Generalmajor*."

Lowther said: "*Generalleutnant* is higher." Then he added quietly: "Just don't forget the difference between *meine Frau* and *deine Frau*."

Lloyd felt himself blush. So his friendship with Daisy was not as discreet as he had imagined. It had even come to Lowther's notice. He felt indignant: he and Daisy had done nothing improper. Yet he did not protest. He felt guilty, even though he was not. He could not put his hand on his heart and swear that his intentions were pure. He knew what Granda would say: "Whosoever looketh on a woman to lust after her hath committed adultery with her already in his heart."

That was the no-bullshit teaching of Jesus and there was a lot of truth in it.

Thinking of his grandparents led him to wonder if they knew about his real parents. Being in doubt about his real father and mother gave him a lost feeling, like a dream about falling from a height. If he had been told lies about that, he might have been misled about anything.

He decided he would question Granda and Grandmam. He could do it today, as it was Sunday. As soon as he could decently excuse himself from the mess, he walked downhill to Wellington Row.

It occurred to him that if he asked them outright whether he was Maud's son they might simply deny everything point-blank. Perhaps a more gradual approach would be more likely to elicit information.

He found them sitting in their kitchen. To them Sunday was the Lord's Day, devoted to religion, and they would not read newspapers or listen to the radio. But they were pleased to see him, and Grandmam made tea, as always.

Lloyd began: "I wish I knew more about my real father. Mam says that Teddy Williams was in the Welsh Rifles. Did you know that?"

Grandmam said: "Oh, why do you want to go digging up the past? Bernie's your father."

Lloyd did not contradict her. "Bernie Leckwith has been everything a father should be to me."

Granda nodded. "A Jew, but a good man, there's no doubt." He imagined he was being magnanimously tolerant.

Lloyd let it pass. "All the same, I'm curious. Did you meet Teddy Williams?"

Granda looked angry. "No," he said. "And it was a sorrow to us."

Grandmam said: "He came to Tŷ Gwyn as a valet to a guest. We never knew your mother was sweet on him till she went to London to marry him."

"Why didn't you go to the wedding?"

They were both silent. Then Granda said: "Tell him the truth, Cara. No good ever comes of lies."

"Your mother yielded to temptation," Grandmam said. "After the valet left Tŷ Gwyn, she found she was with child." Lloyd had suspected that, and thought it might account for her evasiveness. "Your Granda was very angry," Grandmam added.

"Too angry," Granda said. "I forgot that Jesus said: 'Judge not, that ye be not judged.' Her sin was lust, but mine was pride." Lloyd was astonished to see tears in his grandfather's pale blue eyes. "God forgave her, but I didn't, not for a long time. By then my son-in-law was dead, killed in France."

Lloyd was more bewildered than before. Here was another detailed story, somewhat different from what he had been told by his mother and completely different from Daisy's theory. Was Granda weeping for a son-in-law who had never existed?

He persisted. "And the family of Teddy Williams? Mam said he came from Swansea. He probably had parents, brothers and sisters . . ."

Grandmam said: "Your mother never talked about his family. I think she was ashamed. Whatever the reason, she didn't want to know them. And it wasn't our place to go against her in that."

"But I might have two more grandparents in Swansea. And uncles and aunts and cousins I've never met."

"Aye," said Granda. "But we don't know."

"My mother knows, though."

"I suppose she does."

"I'll ask her, then," said Lloyd.

### iv

Daisy was in love.

She knew now that she had never loved anyone before Lloyd. She had never truly loved Boy, though she had been excited by him. As for poor Charlie Farquharson, she had been at most fond of him. She had believed that love was something she could bestow upon whomever she liked, and that her main responsibility was to choose cleverly. Now she knew that was all wrong. Cleverness had nothing to do with it, and she had no choice. Love was an earthquake.

Life was empty but for the two hours she spent with Lloyd each evening. The rest of the day was anticipation; the night was recollection.

Lloyd was the pillow she put her cheek on. He was the towel with which she patted her breasts when she got out of the bathtub. He was the knuckle she put into her mouth and sucked thoughtfully.

How could she have ignored him for four years? The love of her life had appeared before her at the Trinity Ball, and she had noticed only that he appeared to be wearing someone else's dress clothes! Why had she not taken him in her arms and kissed him and insisted they get married immediately?

He had known all along, she surmised. He must have fallen in love with her from the start. He had begged her to throw Boy over. "Give him up," he had said the night they went to the Gaiety Theatre. "Be my girlfriend instead." And she had laughed at him. But he had seen the truth to which she had been blind.

However, some intuition deep within her had told her to kiss him, there on the Mayfair pavement in the darkness between two streetlights. At the time she had regarded it as a self-indulgent whim, but in fact it was the smartest thing she had ever done, for it had probably sealed his devotion.

Now, at Tŷ Gwyn, she refused to think about what would happen next. She was living from day to day, walking on air, smiling at nothing. She got an anxious letter from her mother in Buffalo, worrying about her health and her state of mind after the miscarriage, and she sent back a reassuring reply. Olga included tidbits of news: Dave Rouzrokh had died in Palm Beach; Muffie Dixon had married Philip Renshaw; Senator Dewar's wife, Rosa, had written a bestseller called *Behind the Scenes at the White House,* with photographs by Woody. A month ago this would have made her homesick; now she was just mildly interested.

She felt sad only when she thought of the baby she had lost. The pain had gone immediately, and the bleeding had stopped after a week, but the loss grieved her. She no longer cried about it, but occasionally she found herself staring into empty space, thinking about whether it would have been a girl or a boy, and what it would have looked like—and then realized with a shock that she had not moved for an hour.

Spring had come, and she walked on the windy mountainside, in waterproof boots and a raincoat. Sometimes, when she was sure there was no one to hear but the sheep, she shouted at the top of her voice: "I love him!"

She worried about his reaction to her questions about his parentage. Perhaps she had done wrong to raise the issue: it had only made him unhappy. Yet her excuse had been valid: sooner or later the truth would probably come out, and it was better to hear such things from someone who loves you. His pained bafflement touched her heart, and made her love him even more.

Then he told her he had arranged leave. He was going to a south-coast resort called Bournemouth for the Labour Party's annual conference on the second weekend in May, which was a British holiday called Whitsun.

His mother would also be at Bournemouth, he said, so he would have a chance to question her about his parentage; and Daisy thought he looked eager and afraid at the same time.

Lowther would certainly have refused to let him go, but Lloyd had spoken to Colonel Ellis-Jones back in March, when he had been assigned to this course, and the colonel either liked Lloyd or sympathized with the party, or both, and gave him permission that Lowther could not countermand. Of course, if the Germans invaded France, then nobody would be able to take leave.

Daisy was strangely frightened by the prospect of Lloyd's leaving Aberowen without knowing that she loved him. She was not sure why, but she had to tell him before he went.

Lloyd was to leave on Wednesday and return six days later. By coincidence, Boy had announced he would come to visit, arriving on Wednesday evening. Daisy was glad, for reasons she could not quite figure out, that the two men would not be there at the same time.

She decided to make her confession to Lloyd on Tuesday, the day before he left. She had no idea what she was going to say to her husband a day later.

Imagining the conversation she would have with Lloyd, she realized that he would surely kiss her, and when they kissed, they would be overwhelmed by their feelings, and they would make love. And then they would lie all night in each other's arms.

At this point in her thinking, the need for discretion intruded into her daydream. Lloyd must not be seen emerging from her quarters in the morning, for both their sakes. Lowthie already had his suspicions: she could tell by his attitude toward her, which was both disapproving and roguish, almost as if he felt that he rather than Lloyd should be the one she should fall for.

How much better it would be if she and Lloyd could meet somewhere else for their fateful conversation. She thought of the unused bedrooms in the west wing, and she felt breathless. He could leave at dawn, and if anyone saw him, they would not know he had been with her. She could emerge later, fully dressed, and pretend to be looking for some lost piece of family property, a painting perhaps. In fact, she thought, elaborating on the lie she would tell if necessary, she could take some object from the junk room and place it in the bedroom in advance, ready to be used as concrete evidence of her story.

At nine o'clock on Tuesday, when the students were all in classes, she walked along the upper floor, carrying a set of perfume vials with tarnished silver tops and a matching hand mirror. She felt guilty already. The carpet had been taken up, and her footsteps rang loud on the floorboards, as if announcing the approach of a scarlet woman. Fortunately there was no one in the bedrooms.

She went to the Gardenia Suite, which she vaguely thought was being used for storage of bed linen. There was no one in the corridor as she stepped inside. She closed the door quickly behind her. She was panting. I haven't done anything yet, she told herself.

She had remembered aright: all around the room, piled up against the gardenia-printed wallpaper, were neat stacks of sheets and blankets and pillows, wrapped in covers of coarse cotton and tied with string like large parcels.

The room smelled musty, and she opened a window. The original furniture was still here: a bed, a wardrobe, a chest of drawers, a writing table, and a kidney-shaped dressing table with three mirrors. She put the perfume vials on the dressing table; then she made the bed up with some of the stored linen. The sheets were cold to her touch.

Now I've done something, she thought. I've made a bed for my lover and me.

She looked at the white pillows and the pink blankets with their satin edging, and she saw herself and Lloyd, locked in a clinging embrace, kissing with mad desperation. The thought aroused her so much that she felt faint.

She heard footsteps outside, ringing on the floorboards as hers had. Who could that be? Morrison, perhaps, the old footman, on his way to look at a leaking gutter or a cracked windowpane. She waited, heart pounding with guilt, as the footsteps came nearer, then receded.

The scare calmed her excitement and cooled the heat she felt inside. She took one last look around the scene and left.

There was no one in the corridor.

She walked along, her shoes heralding her progress, but she looked perfectly innocent now, she told herself. She could go anywhere she wanted; she had more right to be here than anyone else; she was at home; her husband was heir to the whole place.

The husband she was carefully planning to betray.

She knew she should be paralyzed by guilt, but in fact she was eager to do it, consumed by longing.

Next she had to brief Lloyd. He had come to her apartment last night, as usual, but she could not have made this assignation with him then, for he would have expected her to explain herself and then, she knew, she would have told him everything and taken him to her bed and ruined the whole plan. So she had to speak to him briefly today.

She did not normally see him in the daytime, unless she ran into him by accident, in the hall or library. How could she make sure of meeting him? She went up the back stairs to the attic floor. The trainees were not in their rooms, but at any moment one of them might appear, returning to his room for something he had forgotten. So she had to be quick.

She went into Lloyd's room. It smelled of him. She could not say exactly what the fragrance was. She did not see a bottle of cologne in the room, but there was a jar of some kind of hair lotion beside his razor. She opened it and sniffed: yes, that was it, citrus and spice. Was he vain? she asked herself. Perhaps a little bit. He usually looked well dressed, even in his uniform.

She would leave him a note. On top of the dresser was a pad of cheap writing paper. She opened it and tore out a sheet. She looked around for something to write with. He had a black fountain pen with his name engraved on the barrel, she knew, but he would have that with him, for writing notes in class. She found a pencil in the top drawer.

What could she write? She had to be careful in case someone else should read the note. In the end she just wrote: "Library." She left the pad open on the dresser where he could hardly fail to see it. Then she left.

No one saw her.

He would probably come to his room at some point, she speculated, perhaps to fill his pen with ink from the bottle on the dresser. Then he would see the note and come to her.

She went to the library to wait.

The morning was long. She was reading Victorian authors—they seemed to understand how she felt right now—but today Mrs. Gaskell could not hold her attention, and she spent most of the time looking out of the window. It was May, and there would normally have been a brilliant display of spring flowers on the grounds of Tŷ Gwyn, but most of the gardeners had joined the armed forces, and the rest were growing vegetables, not flowers.

Several trainees came into the library just before eleven, and settled down in the green leather chairs with their notebooks, but Lloyd was not among them.

The last lecture of the morning ended at half past twelve, she knew. At that point the men got up and left the library, but Lloyd did not appear.

Surely he would go to his room now, she thought, just to put down his books and wash his hands in the nearby bathroom.

The minutes passed, and the gong sounded for lunch.

Then he came in, and her heart leaped.

He looked worried. "I just saw your note," he said. "Are you all right?"

His first concern was for her. A problem of hers was not a nuisance to him, but an opportunity to help her, and he would seize it eagerly. No man had cared for her this way, not even her father.

"Everything is all right," she said. "Do you know what a gardenia looks like?" She had rehearsed this speech all morning.

"I suppose so. A bit like a rose. Why?"

"In the west wing there's an apartment called the Gardenia Suite. It has a white gardenia painted on the door, and it's full of stored linen. Do you think you could find it?"

"Of course."

"Meet me there tonight, instead of coming to the flat. Usual time."

He stared at her, trying to figure out what was going on. "I will," he said. "But why?"

"I want to tell you something."

"How exciting," he said, but he looked puzzled.

She could guess what was going through his mind. He was electrified by the thought that she might intend a romantic assignation, and at the same time he was telling himself that was a hopeless dream.

"Go to lunch," she said.

He hesitated.

She said: "I'll see you tonight."

"I can't wait," he said, and went out.

She returned to her flat. Maisie, who was not much of a cook, had made her a sandwich with two slabs of bread and a slice of canned ham. Daisy's stomach was full of butterflies; she could not have eaten if it had been peach ice cream.

She lay down to rest. Her thoughts about the night to come were so explicit she felt embarrassed. She had learned a lot about sex from Boy, who clearly had much experience with other women, and she knew a great deal about what men liked. She wanted to do everything with Lloyd, to kiss every part of his body, to do what Boy called *soixante-neuf*, to swallow his semen. The thoughts were so arousing that it took all her willpower to resist the temptation to pleasure herself.

She had a cup of coffee at five, then washed her hair and took a long bath, shaving her underarms and trimming her pubic hair, which grew too abundantly. She dried herself and rubbed in a light body lotion all over. She perfumed herself and began to get dressed.

She put on new underwear. She tried on all her dresses. She liked the look of one with fine blue-and-white stripes, but all down the front it had little buttons that would take forever to undo, and she knew she would want to undress quickly. I'm thinking like a whore, she realized, and she did not know whether to be amused or ashamed. In the end she decided on a simple peppermint green cashmere knee-length that showed off her shapely legs.

She studied herself in the narrow mirror on the inside of the wardrobe door. She looked good.

She perched on the edge of the bed to put her stockings on, and Boy came in.

Daisy felt faint. If she had not been sitting, she would have fallen down. She stared at him in disbelief.

"Surprise!" he said with jollity. "I came a day early."

"Yes," she said when at last she was able to speak. "Surprise."

He bent down and kissed her. She had never much liked his tongue in her mouth, because he always tasted of booze and cigars. He did not mind her distaste; in fact he seemed to enjoy forcing the issue. But now, out of guilt, she tongued him back.

"Gosh!" he said when he ran out of breath. "You're frisky."

You have no idea, Daisy thought; at least, I hope you don't.

"The exercise was brought forward by a day," he explained. "No time to warn you."

"So you're here for the night," she said.

"Yes."

And Lloyd was leaving in the morning.

"You don't seem very pleased," Boy said. He looked at her dress. "Did you have something else planned?"

"Such as what?" she said. She had to regain her composure. "A night out at the Two Crowns pub, perhaps?" she asked sarcastically.

"Speaking of that, let's have a drink." He left the room in search of booze.

Daisy buried her face in her hands. How could this be? Her plan was ruined. She would have to find some way of alerting Lloyd. And she could not declare her love for him in a hurried whisper with Boy around the corner.

She told herself that the whole scheme would simply be postponed. It was only for a few days: he was due back next Tuesday. The delay would be agonizing, but she would survive, and so would her love. All the same, she almost cried with disappointment.

She finished putting on her stockings and shoes; then she went into the little sitting room.

Boy had found a bottle of Scotch and two glasses. She took some to be convivial. He said: "I see that girl is making a fish pie for supper. I'm starving. Is she a good cook?"

"Not really. Her food is edible, if you're hungry."

"Oh, well, there's always whisky," he said, and he poured himself another drink.

"What have you been doing?" She was desperate to get him to talk so that she would not have to. "Did you fly to Norway?" The Germans were winning the first land battle of the war there.

"No, thank God. It's a disaster. There's a big debate in the House of Commons tonight." He began to talk about the mistakes the British and French commanders had made.

When supper was ready, Boy went down to the cellar to get some wine. Daisy saw a chance to alert Lloyd. But where would he be? She looked at her wristwatch. It was half past seven. He would be having dinner in the mess. She could not walk into that room and whisper in his ear as he sat at the table with his fellow officers: it would be as good as telling everyone they were lovers. Was there some way she could get him out of there? She racked her brains, but before she could think of anything, Boy returned, triumphantly carrying a bottle of 1921 Dom Pérignon. "The first vintage they made," he said. "Historic."

They sat at the table and ate Maisie's fish pie. Daisy drank a glass of the champagne but she found it difficult to eat. She pushed her food around the plate in an attempt to look normal. Boy had a second helping.

For dessert Maisie served canned peaches with condensed milk. "War has been bad for British cuisine," Boy said.

"Not that it was great before," Daisy commented, still working on seeming normal.

By now Lloyd must be in the Gardenia Suite. What would he do if she were unable to get a message to him? Would he remain there all night, waiting and hoping for her to arrive? Would he give up at midnight and return to his own bed? Or would he come down here looking for her? That might be awkward.

Boy took out a large cigar and smoked it with satisfaction, occasionally dipping the unlit end into a glass of brandy. Daisy tried to think of an excuse to leave him and go upstairs, but nothing came. What pretext could she possibly cite for visiting the trainees' quarters at this time of night?

She still had done nothing when he put out his cigar and said: "Well, time for bed. Do you want to use the bathroom first?"

Not knowing what else to do, she got up and went into the bedroom. Slowly, she took off the clothes she had put on so carefully for Lloyd. She washed her face and put on her least alluring nightdress. Then she got into bed.

Boy was moderately drunk when he climbed in beside her, but he still wanted sex. The thought appalled her. "I'm sorry," she said. "Dr. Mortimer said no marital relations for three months." This was not true. Mortimer had said it would be all right when the bleeding stopped.

She felt horribly dishonest. She had been planning to do it with Lloyd tonight.

"What?" Boy said indignantly. "Why?"

Improvising, she said: "If we do it too soon, it might affect my chances of getting pregnant again, apparently."

That convinced him. He was desperate for an heir. "Ah, well," he said, and turned away.

In a minute he was asleep.

Daisy lay awake, her mind buzzing. Could she slip away now? She would have to get dressed—she certainly could not walk around the house in her nightdress. Boy slept heavily, but often woke to go to the bathroom. What if he did that while she was gone, and saw her return with her clothes on? What story could she tell that had a chance of being believed? Everyone knew there was only one reason why a woman went creeping around a country house at night.

Lloyd would have to suffer. And she suffered with him, thinking of him alone and disappointed in that musty room. Would he lie down in his uniform and fall asleep? He would be cold, unless he pulled a blanket around him. Would he assume some emergency, or just think she had carelessly stood him up? Perhaps he would feel let down, and be angry with her.

Tears rolled down her face. Boy was snoring, so he would never know.

She dozed off in the small hours, and dreamed she was catching a train, but silly things kept happening to delay her: the taxi took her to the wrong place, she had to walk unexpectedly far with her suitcase, she could not find her ticket, and when she reached the platform, she found waiting for her an old-fashioned stagecoach that would take days to get to London.

When she woke from the dream, Boy was in the bathroom, shaving.

She lost heart. She got up and dressed. Maisie prepared breakfast, and Boy had eggs and bacon and buttered toast. By the time they had finished, it was nine o'clock. Lloyd had said he was leaving at nine. He might be in the hall now, with his suitcase in his hand.

Boy got up from the table and went into the bathroom, taking the newspaper with him. Daisy knew his morning habits: he would be there five or ten minutes. Suddenly her apathy left her. She went out of the flat and ran up the stairs to the hall.

Lloyd was not there. He must already have left. Her heart sank.

But he would be walking to the railway station: only the wealthy and infirm took taxis to go a mile. Perhaps she could catch him up. She went out through the front door.

She saw him four hundred yards down the drive, walking smartly, carrying his case, and her heart leaped. Throwing caution to the wind, she ran after him.

A light army pickup truck of the kind they called a Tilly was bowling down the drive ahead of her. To her dismay it slowed alongside Lloyd. "No!" Daisy said, but Lloyd was too far away to hear her.

He threw his suitcase into the back and jumped into the cab beside the driver.

She kept running, but it was hopeless. The little truck pulled away and picked up speed.

Daisy stopped. She stood and watched as the Tilly passed through the gates of Tŷ Gwyn and disappeared from view. She tried not to cry.

After a moment she turned around and went back inside the house.

## v

On the way to Bournemouth Lloyd spent a night in London, and that evening, Wednesday, May 8, he was in the visitors' gallery of the House of Commons, watching the debate that would decide the fate of the prime minister, Neville Chamberlain.

It was like being in the gods at the theater: the seats were cramped and hard, and you looked vertiginously down on the drama unfolding below. The gallery was full tonight. Lloyd and his stepfather, Bernie, had got tickets only with difficulty, through the influence of his mother,

Ethel, who was now sitting with his uncle Billy among the Labour M.P.s down in the packed chamber.

Lloyd had had no chance yet to ask about his real father and mother: everyone was too preoccupied with the political crisis. Both Lloyd and Bernie wanted Chamberlain to resign. The appeaser of Fascism had little credibility as a war leader, and the debacle in Norway only underlined that.

The debate had begun the night before. Chamberlain had been furiously attacked, not just by Labour M.P.s but by his own side, Ethel had reported. The Conservative Leo Amery had quoted Cromwell at him: "You have sat too long here for any good you have been doing. Depart, I say, and let us have done with you. In the name of God, go!" It was a cruel speech to come from a colleague, and it was made more wounding by the chorus of "Hear, hear!" that arose from both sides of the chamber.

Lloyd's mother and the other female M.P.s had got together in their own room in the palace of Westminster and agreed to force a vote. The men could not stop them and so joined them instead. When this was announced on Wednesday, the debate was transformed into a ballot on Chamberlain. The prime minister accepted the challenge, and—in what Lloyd felt was a sign of weakness—appealed to his friends to stand by him.

The attacks continued tonight. Lloyd relished them. He hated Chamberlain for his policy on Spain. For two years, from 1937 to 1939, Chamberlain had continued to enforce "nonintervention" by Britain and France, while Germany and Italy poured arms and men into the rebel army, and American ultraconservatives sold oil and trucks to Franco. If any one British politician bore guilt for the mass murders now being carried out by Franco, it was Neville Chamberlain.

"And yet," said Bernie to Lloyd during a lull, "Chamberlain isn't really to blame for the fiasco in Norway. Winston Churchill is first lord of the Admiralty, and your mother says he was the one who pushed for this invasion. After all Chamberlain has done—Spain, Austria, Czechoslovakia—it will be ironic if he falls from power because of something that isn't really his fault."

"Everything is ultimately the prime minister's fault," said Lloyd. "That's what it means to be the leader."

Bernie smiled wryly, and Lloyd knew he was thinking that young people saw everything too simply, but to his credit Bernie did not say it.

It was a noisy debate, but the house went quiet when the former prime minister David Lloyd George stood up. Lloyd had been named after him. Seventy-seven years old now, a white-haired elder statesman, he spoke with the authority of the man who had won the Great War.

He was merciless. "It is not a question of who are the prime minister's friends," he said, stating the obvious with withering sarcasm. "It is a far bigger issue."

Once again, Lloyd was heartened to see that the chorus of approval came from the Conservative side as well as the opposition.

"He has appealed for sacrifices," Lloyd George said, his nasal North Wales accent seeming to sharpen the edge of his contempt. "There is nothing which can contribute more to victory, in this war, than that he should sacrifice the seals of office."

The opposition shouted their approval, and Lloyd could see his mother cheering.

Churchill closed the debate. As a speaker he was the equal of Lloyd George, and Lloyd feared that his oratory might rescue Chamberlain. But the House was against him, interrupting and jeering, sometimes so loudly that he could not be heard over the clamor.

He sat down at eleven P.M. and the vote was taken.

The voting system was cumbersome. Instead of raising their hands, or ticking slips of paper, M.P.s had to leave the chamber and be counted as they walked through one of two lobbies, for ayes or noes. The process took fifteen or twenty minutes. It could have been devised only by men who did not have enough to do, Ethel said. She felt sure it would be modernized soon.

Lloyd waited on tenterhooks. The fall of Chamberlain would give him profound satisfaction, but it was by no means certain.

To distract himself he thought about Daisy, always a pleasant occupation. How strange his last twenty-four hours at Tŷ Gwyn had been: first the one-word note, "Library"; then the rushed conversation, with her tantalizing summons to the Gardenia Suite; then a whole night of waiting, cold and bored and bewildered, for a woman who did not show up. He had stayed there until six o'clock in the morning, miserable but unwilling to give up hope until the moment when he was obliged to wash and shave and change his clothes and pack his suitcase for the trip.

Clearly something had gone wrong, or she had changed her mind, but what had she intended in the first place? She had said she wanted to tell him something. Had she planned to say something earth-shaking, to merit all that drama? Or something so trivial that she had forgotten all about it and the rendezvous? He would have to wait until next Tuesday to ask her.

He had not told his family that Daisy had been at Tŷ Gwyn. That would have required him to explain to them what his relationship with Daisy was now, and he could not do that, for he did not really understand it himself. Was he in love with a married woman? He did not know. How did she feel about him? He did not know. Most likely, he thought, Daisy and he were two good friends who had missed their chance at love. And somehow he did not want to admit that to anyone, for it seemed unbearably final.

He said to Bernie: "Who will take over, if Chamberlain goes?"

"The betting is on Halifax." Lord Halifax was currently the foreign secretary.

"No!" said Lloyd indignantly. "We can't have an earl for prime minister at a time like this. Anyway, he's an appeaser, just as bad as Chamberlain!"

"I agree," said Bernie. "But who else is there?"

"What about Churchill?"

"You know what Stanley Baldwin said about Churchill?" Baldwin, a Conservative, had been prime minister before Chamberlain. "When Winston was born, lots of fairies swooped down on his cradle with gifts— imagination, eloquence, industry, ability—and then came a fairy who said: 'No person has a right to so many gifts,' picked him up, and gave him such a shake and a twist that he was denied judgment and wisdom."

Lloyd smiled. "Very witty, but is it true?"

"There's something in it. In the last war he was responsible for the Dardanelles campaign, which was a terrible defeat for us. Now he's pushed us into the Norwegian adventure, another failure. He's a fine orator, but the evidence suggests he has a tendency to wishful thinking."

Lloyd said: "He was right about the need to rearm in the thirties—when everyone else was against it, including the Labour Party."

"Churchill will be calling for rearmament in paradise, when the lion lies down with the lamb."

"I think we need someone with an aggressive streak. We want a prime minister who will bark, not whimper."

"Well, you may get your wish. The tellers are coming back."

The votes were announced. The ayes had 280, the noes 200. Chamberlain had won. There was uproar in the chamber. The prime minister's supporters cheered, but others yelled at him to resign.

Lloyd was bitterly disappointed. "How can they want to keep him, after all that?"

"Don't jump to conclusions," said Bernie as the prime minister left and the noise subsided. Bernie was making calculations with a pencil in the margin of the *Evening News*. "The government usually has a majority of about two hundred and forty. That's dropped to eighty." He scribbled numbers, adding and subtracting. "Taking a rough guess at the number of M.P.s absent, I reckon about forty of the government's supporters voted against Chamberlain, and another sixty abstained. That's a terrible blow to a prime minister—a hundred of his colleagues don't have confidence in him."

"But is it enough to force him to resign?" Lloyd said impatiently.

Bernie spread his arms in a gesture of surrender. "I don't know," he said.

## vi

Next day Lloyd, Ethel, Bernie, and Billy went to Bournemouth by train.

The carriage was full of delegates from all over Britain. They all spent the entire journey discussing last night's debate and the future of the prime minister, in accents ranging from the harsh chop of Glasgow to the swerve and swoop of cockney. Once again Lloyd had no chance to raise with his mother the subject that was haunting him.

Like most delegates, they could not afford the swanky hotels on the cliff tops, so they stayed in a boardinghouse on the outskirts. That evening the four of them went to a pub and sat in a quiet corner, and Lloyd saw his chance.

Bernie bought a round of drinks. Ethel wondered aloud what was happening to her friend Maud in Berlin; she no longer got news, for the war had ended the postal service between Germany and Britain.

Lloyd sipped his pint of beer, then said firmly: "I'd like to know more about my real father."

Ethel said sharply: "Bernie is your father."

Evasion again! Lloyd suppressed the anger that immediately rose in him. "You don't need to tell me that," he said. "And I don't need to tell Bernie that I love him like a father, because he already knows."

Bernie patted him on the shoulder, an awkward but genuine gesture of affection.

Lloyd made his voice insistent. "But I'm curious about Teddy Williams."

Billy said: "We need to talk about the future, not the past—we're at war."

"Exactly," said Lloyd. "So I want answers to my questions *now*. I'm not willing to wait, because I will be going into battle soon, and I don't want to die in ignorance." He did not see how they could deny that argument.

Ethel said: "You know all there is to know," but she was not meeting his eye.

"No, I don't," he said, forcing himself to be patient. "Where are my other grandparents? Do I have uncles and aunts and cousins?"

"Teddy Williams was an orphan," Ethel said.

"Raised in what orphanage?"

She said irritably: "Why are you so stubborn?"

Lloyd allowed his voice to rise in reciprocal annoyance. "Because I'm like you!"

Bernie could not repress a grin. "That's true, anyway."

Lloyd was not amused. "What orphanage?"

"He might have told me, but I don't remember. In Cardiff, I think."

Billy intervened. "You're touching a sore place, now, Lloyd, boy. Drink your beer and drop the subject."

Lloyd said angrily: "I've got a bloody sore place, too, Uncle Billy, thank you very much, and I'm fed up with lies."

"Now, now," said Bernie. "Let's not have talk of lies."

"I'm sorry, Dad, but it's got to be said." Lloyd held up a hand to stave off interruption. "Last time I asked, Mam told me Teddy Williams's family came from Swansea but they moved around a lot because of his father's job. Now she says he was raised in an orphanage in Cardiff. One of those stories is a lie—if not both."

At last Ethel looked him in the eye. "Me and Bernie fed you and clothed you and sent you to school and university," she said indignantly. "You've got nothing to complain about."

"And I'll always be grateful to you, and I'll always love you," Lloyd said.

Billy said: "Why has this come up now, anyhow?"

"Because of something somebody said to me in Aberowen."

His mother did not respond, but there was a flash of fear in her eyes. Someone in Wales knows the truth, Lloyd thought.

He went on relentlessly: "I was told that perhaps Maud Fitzherbert fell pregnant in 1914, and her baby was passed off as yours, for which you were rewarded with the house in Nutley Street."

Ethel made a scornful noise.

Lloyd held up a hand. "That would explain two things," he said. "One, the unlikely friendship between you and Lady Maud." He reached into his jacket pocket. "Two, this picture of me in side-whiskers." He showed them the photograph.

Ethel stared at the picture without speaking.

Lloyd said: "It could be me, couldn't it?"

Billy said testily: "Yes, Lloyd, it could. But obviously it's not, so stop mucking about and tell us who it is."

"It's Earl Fitzherbert's father. Now *you* stop mucking about, Uncle Billy, and you, Mam. Am I Maud's son?"

Ethel said: "The friendship between me and Maud was a political alliance, foremost. It was broken off when we disagreed about strategy for suffragettes, then resumed later. I like her a lot, and she gave me important chances in life, but there is no secret bond. She doesn't know who your father is."

"All right, Mam," said Lloyd. "I could believe that. But this photo . . ."

"The explanation of that resemblance . . ." She choked up.

Lloyd was not going to let her escape. "Come on," he said remorselessly. "Tell me the truth."

Billy intervened again. "You're barking up the wrong tree, boyo," he said.

"Am I? Well, then, set me straight, why don't you?"

"It's not for me to do that."

That was as good as an admission. "So you *were* lying before."

Bernie looked gobsmacked. He said to Billy: "Are you saying the Teddy Williams story isn't true?" Clearly he had believed it all these years, just as Lloyd had.

Billy did not reply.

They all looked at Ethel.

"Oh, bugger it," she said. "My father would say: 'Be sure your sins will find you out.' Well, you've asked for the truth, so you shall have it, though you won't like it."

"Try me," Lloyd said recklessly.

"You're not Maud's child," she said. "You're Fitz's."

## vii

Next day, Friday, May 10, Germany invaded Holland, Belgium, and Luxembourg.

Lloyd heard the news on the radio as he sat down to breakfast with his parents and Uncle Billy in the boardinghouse. He was not surprised: everyone in the army had believed the invasion was imminent.

He was much more stunned by the revelations of the previous evening. Last night he had lain awake for hours, angry that he had been misled so long, dismayed that he was the son of a right-wing aristocratic appeaser who was also, weirdly, the father-in-law of the enchanting Daisy.

"How could you fall for him?" he had said to his mother in the pub.

Her reply had been sharp. "Don't be a hypocrite. You used to be crazy about your rich American girl, and she was so right-wing she married a Fascist."

Lloyd had wanted to argue that that was different, but quickly realized it was the same. Whatever his relationship with Daisy now, there was no doubt he had once felt in love with her. Love was not logical. If he could succumb to an irrational passion, so could his mother; indeed, they had been the same age, twenty-one, when it had happened.

He had said she should have told him the truth from the start, but she had an argument for that, too. "How would you have reacted, as a little boy, if I had told you that you were the son of a rich man, an earl? How long would it have been before you boasted to the other boys at school? Think how they would have mocked your childish fantasy. Think how they would have hated you for being superior to them."

"But later . . ."

"I don't know," she had said wearily. "There never seemed to be a good time."

Bernie had at first gone white with shock, but soon recovered and became his usual phlegmatic self. He said he understood why Ethel had not told him the truth. "A secret shared is a secret no more."

Lloyd wondered about his mother's relationship with the earl now. "I suppose you must see him all the time, in Westminster."

"Just occasionally. Peers have a separate section of the palace, with their own restaurants and bars, and when we see them, it's usually by arrangement."

That night Lloyd was too shocked and bewildered to know how he felt. His father was Fitz—the aristocrat, the Tory, the father of Boy, the father-in-law of Daisy. Should he be sad about it, angry, suicidal? The revelation was so devastating that he felt numbed. It was like an injury so grave that at first there was no pain.

The morning news gave him something else to think about.

In the early hours the German army had made a lightning westward strike. Although it was anticipated, Lloyd knew that the best efforts of Allied intelligence had been unable to discover the date in advance, and the armies of those small states had been taken by surprise. Nevertheless, they were fighting back bravely.

"That's probably true," said Uncle Billy, "but the BBC would say it anyway."

Prime Minister Chamberlain had called a cabinet meeting that was going on at that very moment. However, the French army, reinforced by ten British divisions already in France, had long ago agreed on a plan for dealing with such an invasion, and that plan had automatically gone into operation. Allied troops had crossed the French border into Holland and Belgium from the west and were rushing to meet the Germans.

With the momentous news heavy on their hearts, the Williams family caught the bus into the town center and made their way to Bournemouth Pavilion, where the party conference was being held.

There they heard the news from Westminster. Chamberlain was clinging to power. Billy learned that the prime minister had asked Labour Party leader Clement Attlee to become a cabinet minister, making the government a coalition of the three main parties.

All three of them were aghast at this prospect. Chamberlain the appeaser would remain prime minister, and the Labour Party would be obliged to support him in a coalition government. It did not bear thinking about.

"What did Attlee say?" asked Lloyd.

"That he would have to consult his National Executive Committee," Billy replied.

"That's us." Both Lloyd and Billy were members of the committee, which had a meeting scheduled for four o'clock that afternoon.

"Right," said Ethel. "Let's start canvassing, and find out how much support Chamberlain's plan might have on our Executive."

"None, I should think," said Lloyd.

"Don't be so sure," said his mother. "There will be some who want to keep Churchill out at any price."

Lloyd spent the next few hours in constant political activity, talking to members of the committee and their friends and assistants, in cafés and bars in the pavilion and along the seafront. He ate no lunch, but drank so much tea he felt he might have floated.

He was disappointed to find that not everyone shared his view of Chamberlain and Churchill. There were a few pacifists left over from the last war, who wanted peace at any price, and approved of Chamberlain's appeasement. On the other side, Welsh M.P.s still thought of Churchill as the home secretary who sent the troops in to break a strike in Tonypandy. That had been thirty years ago, but Lloyd was learning that memories could be long in politics.

At half past three Lloyd and Billy walked along the seafront in a fresh breeze and entered the Highcliff Hotel, where the meeting was to be held. They thought that a majority of the committee were against accepting Chamberlain's offer, but they could not be completely sure, and Lloyd was still worried about the result.

They went into the room and sat at the long table with the other committee members. Promptly at four the party leader came in.

Clem Attlee was a slim, quiet, unassuming man, neatly dressed, with a bald head and a mustache. He looked like a solicitor—which his father was—and people tended to underestimate him. In his dry, unemotional way he summarized, for the committee, the events of the last twenty-four hours, including Chamberlain's offer of a coalition with Labour.

Then he said: "I have two questions to ask you. The first is: Would you serve in a coalition government with Neville Chamberlain as prime minister?"

There was a resounding "No!" from the people around the table, more vehement than Lloyd had expected. He was thrilled. Chamberlain, friend of the Fascists, the betrayer of Spain, was finished. There was some justice in the world.

Lloyd also noted how subtly the unassertive Attlee had controlled the meeting. He had not opened the subject for general discussion. His question had not been: What shall we do? He had not given people the chance to express uncertainty or dither. In his understated way he had put them all up against the wall and made them choose. And Lloyd felt sure the answer he got was the one he had wanted.

Attlee said: "Then the second question is: Would you serve in a coalition under a different prime minister?"

The answer was not so vocal, but it was yes. As Lloyd looked around the table, it was clear to him that almost everyone was in favor. If there were any against, they did not bother to ask for a vote.

"In that case," said Attlee, "I shall tell Chamberlain that our party will serve in a coalition but only if he resigns and a new prime minister is appointed."

There was a murmur of agreement around the table.

Lloyd noted how cleverly Attlee had avoided asking who they thought the new prime minister should be.

Attlee said: "I shall now go and telephone Number Ten Downing Street."

He left the room.

## viii

That evening Winston Churchill was summoned to Buckingham Palace, in accordance with tradition, and the king asked him to become prime minister.

Lloyd had high hopes for Churchill, even if the man was a Conservative. Over the weekend Churchill made his dispositions. He formed a five-man War Cabinet including Clem Attlee and Arthur Greenwood, respectively leader and deputy leader of the Labour Party. Union leader Ernie Bevin became minister of labor. Clearly, Lloyd thought, Churchill intended to have a genuine cross-party government.

Lloyd packed his case ready to catch the train back to Aberowen. Once there, he expected to be quickly redeployed, probably to France. But he only needed an hour or two. He was desperate to learn the explanation of Daisy's behavior last Tuesday. Knowing he was going to see her soon increased his impatience to understand.

Meanwhile, the German army rolled across Holland and Belgium, overcoming spirited opposition with a speed that shocked Lloyd. On Sunday evening Billy spoke on the phone to a contact in the War Office, and afterward he and Lloyd borrowed an old school atlas from the boardinghouse proprietress and studied the map of northwest Europe.

Billy's forefinger drew an east-west line from Dusseldorf through Brussels to Lille. "The Germans are thrusting at the softest part of the French defenses, the northern section of the border with Belgium." His finger moved down the page. "Southern Belgium is bordered by the Ardennes forest, a huge strip of hilly, wooded terrain virtually impassable to modern motorized armies. So my friend in the War Office says." His finger moved on. "Yet farther south, the French-German border is defended by a series of heavy fortifications called the Maginot Line, stretching all the way to Switzerland." His finger returned up the page. "But there are no fortifications between Belgium and northern France."

Lloyd was puzzled. "Did no one think of this until now?"

"Of course we did. And we have a strategy to deal with it." Billy lowered his voice. "Called Plan D. It can't be a secret anymore, since we're already implementing it. The best part of the French army, plus all of the British Expeditionary Force already over there, are pouring across the border into Belgium. They will form a solid line of defense at the Dyle River. That will stop the German advance."

Lloyd was not much reassured. "So we're committing half our forces to Plan D?"

"We need to make sure it works."

"It better."

They were interrupted by the proprietress, who brought Lloyd a telegram.

It had to be from the army. He had given Colonel Ellis-Jones this address before going on leave. He was surprised he had not heard sooner. He ripped open the envelope. The cable said:

```
DO NOT RETURN ABEROWEN STOP REPORT SOUTHAMPTON
DOCKS IMMEDIATELY STOP A BIENTOT
SIGNED ELLISJONES
```

He was not going back to Tŷ Gwyn. Southampton was one of Britain's largest ports, a common embarkation point for the Continent, and it was located just a few miles along the coast from Bournemouth, an hour perhaps by train or bus.

Lloyd would not be seeing Daisy tomorrow, he realized with an ache in his heart. Perhaps he might never learn what she had wanted to tell him.

Colonel Ellis-Jones's "A BIENTOT" confirmed the obvious inference.

Lloyd was going to France.

# CHAPTER SEVEN

# 1940 (II)

**E**rik von Ulrich spent the first three days of the Battle of France in a traffic jam.

Erik and his friend Hermann Braun were part of a medical unit attached to the Second Panzer Division. They saw no action as they passed through southern Belgium, just mile after mile of hills and trees. They were in the Ardennes forest, they reckoned. They traveled on narrow roads, many not even paved, and a broken-down tank could cause a fifty-mile tailback in no time. They were stationary, stuck in queues, more than they were moving.

Hermann's freckled face was set in a grimace of anxiety, and he muttered to Erik in an undertone no one else could hear: "This is stupid!"

"You should know better than to say that—you were in the Hitler Youth," said Erik quietly. "Have faith in the Führer." But he was not angry enough to denounce his friend.

When they did move, it was painfully uncomfortable. They sat on the hard wooden floor of an army truck as it bounced over tree roots and swerved around potholes. Erik longed for battle just so that he could get out of the damn truck.

Hermann said more loudly: "What are we doing here?"

Their boss, Dr. Rainer Weiss, was sitting on a real seat beside the driver. "We are following the orders of the Führer, which are of course always correct." He said it straight-faced, but Erik felt sure he was being sarcastic. Major Weiss, a thin man with black hair and spectacles, often spoke cynically about the government and the military, but always in this enigmatic way, so that nothing could be proved against him. Anyway, the army could not afford to get rid of a good doctor at this point.

There were two other medical orderlies in the truck, both older than Erik and Hermann. One of them, Christof, had a better answer to Hermann's question. "Perhaps the French aren't expecting us to attack here, because the terrain is so difficult."

His friend Manfred said: "We will have the advantage of surprise, and will encounter light defenses."

Weiss said sarcastically: "Thanks for that lesson in tactics, you two—most enlightening." But he did not say they were wrong.

Despite all that had happened, there were still people who lacked faith in the Führer, to Erik's amazement. His own family continued to close their eyes to the triumphs of the Nazis. His father, once a man of status and power, was now a pathetic figure. Instead of rejoicing in the conquest of barbarian Poland, he just moaned about ill treatment of the Poles—which he must have heard about by listening illegally to a foreign radio station. Such behavior could get them all into trouble—including Erik, who was guilty of not reporting it to the local Nazi block supervisor.

Erik's mother was just as bad. Every now and again she disappeared with small packages of smoked fish or eggs. She said nothing in explanation, but Erik felt sure she was taking them to Frau Rothmann, whose Jewish husband was no longer allowed to practise as a doctor.

Despite that, Erik sent home a large slice of his army pay, knowing his parents would be cold and hungry if he did not. He hated their politics, but he loved them. They undoubtedly felt the same about his politics and him.

Erik's sister, Carla, had wanted to be a doctor, like Erik, and had been furious when it was made clear to her that in today's Germany this was a man's job. She was now training as a nurse, a much more appropriate role for a German girl. And she, too, was supporting their parents with her meager pay.

Erik and Hermann had wanted to join infantry units. Their idea of battle was to run at the enemy firing a rifle, and kill or be killed for the fatherland. But they were not going to be killing anyone. Both had had one year of medical school, and such training was not to be wasted; so they were made medical orderlies.

The fourth day in Belgium, Monday, May 13, was like the first three until the afternoon. Above the roar and snarl of hundreds of tank and truck engines, they began to hear another, louder sound. Aircraft were flying low over their heads and, not too far away, dropping bombs on someone. Erik's nose twitched with the smell of high explosives.

They stopped for their midafternoon break on high ground overlooking a meandering river valley. Major Weiss said the river was the Meuse, and they were west of the city of Sedan. So they had entered France. The planes of the Luftwaffe roared past them, one after another, diving toward the river a couple of miles away, bombing and strafing the scattered villages on the banks, where, presumably, there were French defensive positions. Smoke rose from countless fires among the ruined cottages and farm buildings. The barrage was relentless, and Erik almost felt pity for anyone trapped in that inferno.

This was the first action he had seen. Before long he would be in it, and perhaps some young French soldier would look from a safe vantage point and feel sorry for the Germans being maimed and killed. The thought made Erik's heart thud with excitement like a big drum in his chest.

Looking to the east, where the details of the landscape were obscured by distance, he could nevertheless see aircraft like specks, and columns of smoke rising through the air, and he realized that the battle had been joined along several miles of this river.

As he watched, the air bombardment came to an end, the planes turning and heading north, waggling their wings to say "Good luck" as they passed overhead on their way home.

Nearer to where Erik stood, on the flat plain leading to the river, the German tanks were going into action.

They were two miles from the enemy, but already the French artillery was shelling them from the town. Erik was surprised that so many gunners had survived the air bombardment. But fire flashed in the ruins, the boom of cannon was heard across the fields, and fountains of French soil spurted where the shells landed. Erik saw a tank explode with a direct hit, smoke and metal and body parts spewing out of the volcano's mouth, and he felt sick.

But the French shelling did not stop the advance. The tanks crawled on relentlessly toward the stretch of river to the east of the town, which Weiss said was called Donchery. Behind them followed the infantry, in trucks and on foot.

Hermann said: "The air attack wasn't enough. Where's our artillery? We need them to take out the big guns in the town, and give our tanks and infantry a chance to cross the river and establish a bridgehead."

Erik wanted to punch him to shut his whining mouth. They were about to go into action—they had to be positive now!

But Weiss said: "You're right, Braun—but our artillery ammunition is gridlocked in the Ardennes forest. We've only got forty-eight shells."

A red-faced major came running past, yelling: "Move out! Move out!"

Major Weiss pointed and said: "We'll set up our field dressing station over to the east, where you see that farmhouse." Erik made out a low gray roof about eight hundred yards from the river. "All right, get moving!"

They jumped into the truck and roared down the hill. When they reached level ground, they swerved left along a farm track. Erik wondered what they would do with the family that presumably lived in the building that was about to become an army hospital. Throw them out of their home, he guessed, and shoot them if they made trouble. But where would they go? They were in the middle of a battlefield.

He need not have worried: they had already left.

The building was half a mile from the worst of the fighting, Erik observed. He guessed there was no point setting up a dressing station within range of enemy guns.

"Stretcher bearers, get going," Weiss shouted. "By the time you get back here, we'll be ready."

Erik and Hermann took a rolled-up stretcher and first-aid kit from the medical supply truck and headed toward the battle. Christof and Manfred were just ahead of them, and a dozen of their comrades followed. This is it, Erik thought exultantly; this is our chance to be heroes. Who will keep his nerve under fire, and who will lose control and crawl into a hole and hide?

They ran across the fields to the river. It was a long jog, and it was going to seem longer coming back, carrying a wounded man.

They passed burned-out tanks but there were no survivors, and Erik averted his eyes from the scorched human remains smeared across the twisted metal. Shells fell around them, though not many: the river was lightly defended, and many of the guns had been taken out by the air attack. All the same, it was the first time in his life Erik had been shot at, and he felt the absurd, childish impulse to cover his eyes with his hands, but he kept running forward.

Then a shell landed right in front of them.

There was a terrific thud, and the earth shook as if a giant had stamped his foot. Christof and Manfred were hit directly, and Erik saw their bodies fly up into the air as if weightless. The blast threw Erik off his feet. As he lay on the ground, faceup, he was showered with dirt from the explosion, but he was not injured. He struggled to his feet. Right in front of him were the mangled bodies of Christof and Manfred. Christof lay like a broken doll, as if all his limbs were disjointed. Manfred's head had somehow been severed from his body and lay next to his booted feet.

Erik was paralyzed with horror. In medical school he had not had to deal with maimed and bleeding bodies. He was used to corpses in anatomy class—they had had one between two students, and he and Hermann had shared the cadaver of a shriveled old woman—and he had watched living people being cut open on the operating table. But none of that had prepared him for this.

He wanted nothing but to run away.

He turned around. His mind was blank of every thought but fear. He started to walk back the way they had come, toward the forest, away from the battle, taking long, determined strides.

Hermann saved him. He stood in front of Erik and said: "Where are you going? Don't be a fool!" Erik kept moving, and tried to walk past him. Hermann punched him in the stomach, really hard, and Erik folded over and fell to his knees.

"Don't run away!" Hermann said urgently. "You'll be shot for desertion! Pull yourself together!"

While Erik was trying to catch his breath, he came to his senses. He could not run away, he must not desert, he had to stay here, he realized. Slowly his willpower overcame his terror. Eventually he got to his feet.

Hermann looked at him warily.

"Sorry," said Erik. "I panicked. I'm all right now."

"Then pick up the stretcher and keep going."

Erik picked up the rolled stretcher, balanced it on his shoulder, turned around, and ran on.

Closer to the river, Erik and Hermann found themselves among infantry. Some were manhandling inflated rubber dinghies out of the backs of trucks and carrying them to the water's edge, while the tanks tried to cover them by firing at the French defenses. But Erik, rapidly recovering his mental powers, soon saw that it was a losing battle: the French were behind walls and inside buildings, while the German infantry were exposed on the bank of the river. As soon as they got a dinghy into the water, it came under intense machine-gun fire.

Upstream, the river turned a right-angled bend, so the infantry could not move out of range of the French without retreating a long distance.

There were already many dead and wounded men on the ground.

"Let's pick this one up," Hermann said decisively, and Erik bent to the task. They unrolled their stretcher on the ground next to a groaning infantryman. Erik gave him water from a flask, as he had learned in training. The man seemed to have numerous superficial wounds on his face and one limp arm. Erik guessed he had been hit by machine-gun fire that had luckily missed his vital areas. He saw no gush of blood, so they did not attempt to staunch his wounds. They lifted the man onto the stretcher, picked it up, and began to jog back to the dressing station.

The wounded man cried out in agony as they moved; then, when they stopped, he shouted: "Keep going, keep going!" and gritted his teeth.

Carrying a man on a stretcher was not as easy as it might seem. Erik thought his arms would fall off when they were only halfway. But he could see that the patient was in greater pain by far, and he just kept running.

Shells no longer fell around them, he noticed gratefully. The French were concentrating all their fire on the riverbank, trying to prevent the Germans from crossing.

At last Erik and Hermann reached the farmhouse with their burden. Weiss had the place organized, the rooms cleared of superfluous furniture, places marked on the floor for patients, the kitchen table set up for operations. He showed Erik and Hermann where to put the wounded man. Then he sent them back for another.

The run back to the river was easier. They were unburdened and going slightly downhill. As they approached the bank, Erik wondered fearfully whether he would panic again.

He saw with trepidation that the battle was going badly. There were several deflated vessels in midstream and many more bodies on the bank—and still no Germans on the far side.

Hermann said: "This is a catastrophe. We should have waited for our artillery!" His voice was shrill.

Erik said: "Then we would have lost the advantage of surprise, and the French would have had time to bring up reinforcements. There would have been no point in that long trek through the Ardennes."

"Well, this isn't working," said Hermann.

Deep in his heart Erik was beginning to wonder whether the Führer's plans really were infallible. The thought undermined his resolution and threatened to throw him completely off balance. Fortunately there was no more time for reflection. They stopped beside a man with most of one leg blown off. He was about their age, twenty, with pale, freckled skin and copper red hair. His right leg ended at midthigh in a ragged stump. Amazingly, he was conscious, and he stared at them as if they were angels of mercy.

Erik found the pressure point in his groin and stopped the bleeding while Hermann got out a tourniquet and applied it. Then they put him on the stretcher and began the run back.

Hermann was a loyal German, but he sometimes allowed negative feelings to get the better of him. If Erik ever had such feelings, he was careful not to voice them. That way he did not lower anyone else's morale—and he stayed out of trouble.

But he could not help thinking. It seemed the approach through the Ardennes had not given the Germans the expected walkover victory. The Meuse defenses were light but the French were fighting back fiercely. Surely, he thought, his first experience of battle was not going to destroy his faith in his Führer? The idea made him feel panicky.

He wondered whether the German forces farther east were faring any better. The First Panzer and the Tenth Panzer had been alongside Erik's division, the Second, as they approached the border, and it must be they who were attacking upstream.

His arm muscles were now in constant agony.

They arrived back at the dressing station for the second time. The place was now frantically busy, the floor crowded with men groaning and crying, bloody bandages everywhere, Weiss and his assistants moving quickly from one maimed body to the next. Erik had never imagined there could be so much suffering in one small place. Somehow, when the Führer spoke of war, Erik never thought of this kind of thing.

Then he noticed that his own patient's eyes were closed.

Major Weiss felt for a pulse, then said harshly: "Put him in the barn—and for fuck's sake don't waste time bringing me corpses!"

Erik could have cried with frustration, and with the pain in his arms, which was beginning to afflict his legs, too.

They put the body in the barn, and saw that there were already a dozen dead young men there.

This was worse than anything he had envisaged. When he had thought about battle, he had foreseen courage in the face of danger, stoicism in suffering, heroism in adversity. What he saw now was agony, screaming, blind terror, broken bodies, and a complete lack of faith in the wisdom of the mission.

They went back again to the river.

The sun was low in the sky now, and something had changed on the battlefield. The French defenders in Donchery were being shelled from the far side of the river. Erik guessed that farther upstream the First Panzers had had better luck, and had secured a bridgehead on the south bank, and now they were coming to the aid of the comrades on their flanks. Clearly *they* had not lost their ammunition in the forest.

Heartened, Erik and Hermann rescued another wounded man. When they got back to the dressing station this time, they were given tin bowls of a tasty soup. Resting for ten minutes while he drank the soup made Erik want to lie down and go to sleep for the night. It took a mighty effort to stand up and pick up his end of the stretcher and jog back to the battlefield.

Now they saw a different scene. Tanks were crossing the river on rafts. The Germans on the far side were coming under heavy fire, but they were shooting back, with the help of reinforcements from the First Panzers.

Erik saw that his side had a chance of winning their objective after all. He was heartened, and he began to feel ashamed that he had doubted the Führer.

He and Hermann kept on retrieving the wounded, hour after hour, until they forgot what it was like to be free from pain in their arms and legs. Some of their charges were unconscious; some thanked them, some cursed them; many just screamed; some lived and some died.

By eight o'clock that evening there was a German bridgehead on the far side of the river, and by ten it was secure.

The fighting came to an end at nightfall. Erik and Hermann

continued to sweep the battlefield for wounded men. They brought back the last one at midnight. Then they lay down under a tree and fell into a sleep of utter exhaustion.

Next day Erik and Hermann and the rest of the Second Panzers turned west and broke through what remained of the French defenses.

Two days later they were fifty miles away, at the river Oise, and moving fast through undefended territory.

By May 20, a week after emerging unexpectedly from the Ardennes forest, they had reached the coast of the English Channel.

Major Weiss explained their achievement to Erik and Hermann. "Our attack on Belgium was a feint, you see. Its purpose was to draw the French and British into a trap. We Panzer divisions formed the jaws of the trap, and now we have them between our teeth. Much of the French army and nearly all of the British Expeditionary Force are in Belgium, encircled by the German army. They are cut off from supplies and reinforcements, helpless—and defeated."

Erik said triumphantly: "This was the Führer's plan all along!"

"Yes," said Weiss, and as ever Erik could not tell whether he was sincere. "No one thinks like the Führer!"

## ii

Lloyd Williams was in a football stadium somewhere between Calais and Paris. With him were another thousand or more British prisoners of war. They had no shelter from the blazing June sun, but they were grateful for the warm nights as they had no blankets. There were no toilets and no water for washing.

Lloyd was digging a hole with his hands. He had organized some of the Welsh miners to make latrines at one end of the soccer pitch, and he was working alongside them to show he was willing. Other men joined in, having nothing else to do, and soon there were a hundred or so helping. When a guard strolled over to see what was going on, Lloyd explained.

"You speak good German," said the guard amiably. "What's your name?"

"Lloyd."

"I'm Dieter."

Lloyd decided to exploit this small expression of friendliness. "We could dig faster if we had tools."

"What's the hurry?"

"Better hygiene would benefit you as well as us."

Dieter shrugged and went away.

Lloyd felt awkwardly unheroic. He had seen no fighting. The Welsh Rifles had gone to France as reserves, to relieve other units in what was expected to be a long battle. But it had taken the Germans only ten days to defeat the bulk of the Allied army. Many of the defeated British troops had then been evacuated from Calais and Dunkirk, but thousands had missed the boat, and Lloyd was among them.

Presumably the Germans were now pushing south. As far as he knew, the French were still fighting, but their best troops had been annihilated in Belgium, and there was a triumphant look about the German guards, as if they knew victory was assured.

Lloyd was a prisoner of war, but how long would he remain so? At this point there must be powerful pressure on the British government to make peace. Churchill would never do so, but he was a maverick, different from all other politicians, and he could be deposed. Men such as Lord Halifax would have little difficulty signing a peace treaty with the Nazis. The same was true, Lloyd thought bitterly, of the junior Foreign Office minister Earl Fitzherbert, whom he now shamefully knew to be his father.

If peace came soon, his time as a prisoner of war could be short. He might spend all of it here, in this French arena. He would go home scrawny and sunburned, but otherwise whole.

But if the British fought on, it would be a different matter. The last war had continued more than four years. Lloyd could not bear the thought of wasting four years of his life in a prisoner-of-war camp. To avoid that, he decided, he would try to escape.

Dieter reappeared carrying half a dozen spades.

Lloyd gave them to the strongest men, and the work went faster.

At some point the prisoners would have to be moved to a permanent camp. That would be the time to make a run for it. Based on his experience in Spain, Lloyd guessed the army would not prioritize the guarding of prisoners. If one tried to get away, he might succeed, or he might be shot dead; either way, it was one less mouth to feed.

They spent the rest of the day completing the latrines. Apart from the improvement in hygiene, this project had boosted morale, and Lloyd lay awake that night, looking at the stars, trying to think of other communal activities he might organize. He decided on a grand athletics contest, a prison-camp Olympic Games.

But he did not have the chance to put this into practise, for the next morning they were marched away.

At first he was not sure of the direction they were taking, but before long they got onto a Route Napoléon two-lane road and began to go steadily east. In all probability, Lloyd thought, they were intended to walk all the way to Germany.

Once there, he knew, escape would be much more difficult. He had to seize this opportunity. And the sooner the better. He was scared— those guards had guns—but determined.

There was not much motor traffic other than the occasional German staff car, but the road was busy with people on foot, heading in the opposite direction. With their possessions in handcarts and wheelbarrows, some driving their livestock ahead of them, they were clearly refugees whose homes had been destroyed in battle. That was a heartening sign, Lloyd told himself. An escaped prisoner might hide himself among them.

The prisoners were lightly guarded. There were only ten Germans in charge of this moving column of a thousand men. The guards had one car and a motorcycle; the rest were on foot and on civilian bicycles that they must have commandeered from the locals.

All the same, escape seemed hopeless at first. There were no English-style hedgerows to provide cover, and the ditches were too shallow to hide in. A man running away would provide an easy target for a competent rifleman.

Then they entered a village. Here it was a little harder for the guards to keep an eye on everyone. Local men and women stood at the edges of the column, staring at the prisoners. A small flock of sheep got mixed up with them. There were cottages and shops beside the road. Lloyd watched hopefully for his opportunity. He needed a place to hide instantly, an open door or a passage between houses or a bush to hide behind. And he needed to be passing it at a moment when none of the guards was in sight.

In a couple of minutes he had left the village behind without spotting his opportunity.

He felt annoyed, and told himself to be patient. There would be more chances. It was a long way to Germany. On the other hand, with every day that passed the Germans would tighten their grip on conquered territory, improve their organization, impose curfews and passes and checkpoints, stop the movement of refugees. Being on the run would be easier at first, harder as time went on.

It was hot, and he took off his uniform jacket and tie. He would get rid of them as soon as he could. Close up he probably still looked like a British soldier, in his khaki trousers and shirt, but at a distance he hoped he would not be so conspicuous.

They passed through two more villages, then came to a small town. This should present some possible escape routes, Lloyd thought nervously. He realized that a part of him hoped he would not see a good opportunity, would not have to put himself in danger of those rifles. Was he getting accustomed to captivity already? It was too easy to continue marching, footsore but safe. He had to snap out of it.

The road through the town was unfortunately broad. The column kept to the middle of the street, leaving wide aisles either side that would have to be crossed before an escaper could find concealment. Some shops were closed, and a few buildings were boarded up, but Lloyd could see promising-looking alleys, cafés with open doors, a church—but he could not get to any of them unobserved.

He studied the faces of the townspeople as they stared at the passing prisoners. Were they sympathetic? Would they remember that these men had fought for France? Or would they be understandably terrified of the Germans, and refuse to put themselves in danger? Half and half, probably. Some would risk their lives to help, others would hand him over to the Germans in a heartbeat. And he would not be able to tell the difference until it was too late.

They reached the town center. I've lost half my opportunities already, he told himself. I have to act.

Up ahead he saw a crossroads. An oncoming line of traffic was waiting to turn left, its way blocked by the marching men. Lloyd saw a civilian pickup truck in the queue. Dusty and battered, it looked as if it might belong to a builder or a road mender. The back was open, but Lloyd could not see inside, for its sides were high.

He thought he might be able to pull himself up the side and scramble over the edge into the truck.

Once inside he could not be seen by anyone standing or walking on the street, nor by the guards on their bikes. But he would be plainly visible to people looking out of the upstairs windows of the buildings that lined the streets. Would they betray him?

He came closer to the truck.

He looked back. The nearest guard was two hundred yards behind.

He looked ahead. A guard on a bicycle was twenty yards in front.

He said to the man beside him: "Hold this for me, would you?" and gave him his jacket.

He drew level with the front of the truck. At the wheel was a bored-looking man in overalls and a beret with a cigarette dangling from his lip. Lloyd passed him. Then he was level with the side of the truck. There was no time to check the guards again.

Without breaking step, Lloyd put both hands on the side of the truck; heaved himself up; threw one leg over, then the other; and fell inside, hitting the bed of the truck with a crash that seemed terribly loud despite the tramp of a thousand pairs of feet. He flattened himself immediately. He lay still, listening for a clamor of shouted German, the roar of a motorcycle approaching, the crack of a rifle shot.

He heard the irregular snore of the truck's engine, the stamp and shuffle of the prisoners' feet, the background noises of a small town's traffic and people. Had he got away with it?

He looked around him, keeping his head low. In the truck with him were buckets, planks, a ladder, and a wheelbarrow. He had been hoping for a few sacks with which to cover himself, but there were none.

He heard a motorcycle. It seemed to come to a halt nearby. Then, a few inches from his head, someone spoke French with a strong German accent. "Where are you going?" A guard was talking to the truck driver, Lloyd figured with a racing heart. Would the guard try to look into the back?

He heard the driver reply, an indignant stream of fast French that Lloyd could not decipher. The German soldier almost certainly could not understand it, either. He asked the question again.

Looking up, Lloyd saw two women at a high window overlooking the street. They were staring at him, mouths open in surprise. One was pointing, her arm sticking out through the open window.

Lloyd tried to catch her eye. Lying still, he moved one hand from side to side in a gesture that meant no.

She got the message. She withdrew her arm suddenly and covered her mouth with her hand as if realizing, with horror, that her pointing could be a sentence of death.

Lloyd wanted both women to move away from the window, but that was too much to hope for, and they continued to stare.

Then the motorcycle guard seemed to decide not to pursue his inquiry, for, a moment later, the motorcycle roared away.

The sound of feet receded. The body of prisoners had passed. Was Lloyd free?

There was a crash of gears and the truck moved. Lloyd felt it turn the corner and pick up speed. He lay still, too scared to move.

He watched the tops of buildings pass by, alert in case anyone else should spot him, though he did not know what he would do if it happened. Every second was taking him away from the guards, he told himself encouragingly.

To his disappointment, the truck came to a halt quite soon. The engine was turned off; then the driver's door opened and slammed shut. Then nothing. Lloyd lay still for a while, but the driver did not return.

Lloyd looked at the sky. The sun was high: it must be after midday. The driver was probably having lunch.

The trouble was, Lloyd continued to be visible from high windows on both sides of the street. If he remained where he was, he would be noticed sooner or later. And then there was no telling what might happen.

He saw a curtain twitch in an attic, and that decided him.

He stood up and looked over the side. A man in a business suit walking along the pavement stared in curiosity but did not stop.

Lloyd scrambled over the side of the truck and dropped to the ground. He found himself outside a bar-restaurant. No doubt that was where the driver had gone. To Lloyd's horror there were two men in German army uniforms sitting at a window table with glasses of beer in their hands. By a miracle they did not look at Lloyd.

He walked quickly away.

He looked around alertly as he walked. Everyone he passed stared at him: they knew exactly what he was. One woman screamed and ran away. He realized he needed to change his khaki shirt and trousers for something more French in the next few minutes.

A young man took him by the arm. "Come with me," he said in English with a heavy accent. "I will 'elp you 'ide."

He turned down a side street. Lloyd had no reason to trust this man, but he had to make a split-second decision, and he went along.

"This way," the young man said, and steered Lloyd into a small house.

In a bare kitchen was a young woman with a baby. The young man introduced himself as Maurice, the woman as his wife, Marcelle, and the baby as Simone.

Lloyd allowed himself a moment of grateful relief. He had escaped from the Germans! He was still in danger, but he was off the streets and in a friendly house.

The stiffly correct French Lloyd had learned in school and at Cambridge had become more colloquial during his escape from Spain, and especially in the two weeks he spent picking grapes in Bordeaux. "You're very kind," he said. "Thank you."

Maurice replied in French, evidently relieved not to have to speak English. "I guess you'd like something to eat."

"Very much."

Marcelle rapidly cut several slices off a long loaf and put them on the table with a round of cheese and a wine bottle with no label. Lloyd sat down and tucked in ravenously.

"I'll give you some old clothes," said Maurice. "But also, you must try to walk differently. You were striding along looking all around you, so alert and interested, you might as well have a sign around your neck saying 'Visitor from England.' Better to shuffle with your eyes on the ground."

With his mouth full of bread and cheese, Lloyd said: "I'll remember that."

There was a small shelf of books, including French translations of Marx and Lenin. Maurice noticed Lloyd looking at them and said: "I was a Communist—until the Hitler-Stalin pact. Now—it's finished." He made a swift cutting-off gesture with his hand. "All the same, we have to defeat Fascism."

"I was in Spain," said Lloyd. "Before that, I believed in a united front of all left parties. Not anymore."

Simone cried. Marcelle lifted a large breast out of her loose dress and began to feed the baby. French women were more relaxed about this than the prudish British, Lloyd remembered.

When he had eaten, Maurice took him upstairs. From a wardrobe that had very little in it he took a pair of dark blue overalls, a light blue shirt, underwear, and socks, all worn but clean. The kindness of this evidently poor man overwhelmed Lloyd, and he had no idea how to say thank you.

"Just leave your army clothes on the floor," Maurice said. "I'll burn them."

Lloyd would have liked a wash, but there was no bathroom. He guessed it was in the backyard.

He put on the fresh clothes and studied his reflection in a mirror hanging on the wall. French blue suited him better than army khaki, but he still looked British.

He went back downstairs.

Marcelle was burping the baby. "Hat," she said.

Maurice produced a typical French beret, dark blue, and Lloyd put it on.

Then Maurice looked anxiously at Lloyd's stout black leather British army boots, dusty but unmistakably good quality. "They give you away," he said.

Lloyd did not want to give up his boots. He had a long way to walk. "Perhaps we can make them look older?" he said.

Maurice looked doubtful. "How?"

"Do you have a sharp knife?"

Maurice took a clasp knife from his pocket.

Lloyd took his boots off. He cut holes in the toecaps, then slashed the ankles. He removed the laces and re-threaded them untidily. Now they looked like something a down-and-out would wear, but they still fit well and had thick soles that would last many miles.

Maurice said: "Where will you go?"

"I have two options," Lloyd said. "I can head north, to the coast, and hope to persuade a fisherman to take me across the English Channel. Or I can go southwest, across the border into Spain." Spain was neutral, and still had British consuls in major cities. "I know the Spanish route— I've traveled it twice."

"The channel is a lot nearer than Spain," Maurice said. "But I think the Germans will close all the ports and harbors."

"Where's the front line?"

"The Germans have taken Paris."

Lloyd suffered a moment of shock. Paris had fallen already!

"The French government has moved to Bordeaux." Maurice shrugged. "But we are beaten. Nothing can save France now."

"All Europe will be Fascist," Lloyd said.

"Except for Britain. So you must go home."

Lloyd mused. North or southwest? He could not tell which would be better.

Maurice said: "I have a friend, a former Communist, who sells cattle feed to farmers. I happen to know he's delivering this afternoon to a place southwest of here. If you decide to go to Spain, he could take you twenty miles."

That helped Lloyd make up his mind. "I'll go with him," he said.

## iii

Daisy had been on a long journey that had brought her around in a circle.

When Lloyd was sent to France, she was heartbroken. She had missed her chance of telling him she loved him—she had not even kissed him!

And now there might never be another opportunity. He was reported missing in action after Dunkirk. That meant his body had not been found and identified, but neither was he registered as a prisoner of war. Most likely he was dead, blown up into unidentifiable fragments by a shell, or perhaps lying unmarked beneath the debris of a destroyed farmhouse. She cried for days.

For another month she moped about Tŷ Gwyn, hoping to hear more, but no further news came. Then she began to feel guilty. There were many women as badly off as she or worse. Some had to face the prospect of raising two or three children with no man to support the family. She had no right to feel sorry for herself just because the man with whom she had been contemplating an adulterous affair was missing.

She had to pull herself together and do something positive. Fate did not intend her to be with Lloyd, that was clear. She already had a husband, one who was risking his life every day. It was her duty, she told herself, to take care of Boy.

She returned to London. She opened up the Mayfair house, as best she could with limited servants, and made it into a pleasant home for Boy to come to when on leave.

She needed to forget Lloyd and be a good wife. Perhaps she would even get pregnant again.

Many women signed up for war work, joining the Women's Auxiliary

Air Force, or doing agricultural labor with the Women's Land Army. Others worked for no pay in the Women's Voluntary Service for Air Raid Precautions. But there was not enough for most such women to do, and *The Times* published letters to the editor complaining that air raid precautions were a waste of money.

The war in Continental Europe appeared to be over. Germany had won. Europe was Fascist from Poland to Sicily and from Hungary to Portugal. There was no fighting anywhere. Rumors said the British government had discussed peace terms.

But Churchill did not make peace with Hitler, and that summer the Battle of Britain began.

At first civilians were not much affected. Church bells were silenced, their peal reserved to warn of the expected German invasion. Daisy followed government instructions and placed buckets of sand and water on every landing in the house, for firefighting, but they were not needed. The Luftwaffe bombed harbors, hoping to cut Britain's supply lines. Then they started on air bases, trying to destroy the Royal Air Force. Boy was flying a Spitfire, engaging enemy aircraft in sky battles that were watched by openmouthed farmers in Kent and Sussex. In a rare letter home he said proudly that he had shot down three German planes. He had no leave for weeks on end, and Daisy sat alone in the house she filled with flowers for him.

At last, on the morning of Saturday, September 7, Boy showed up with a weekend pass. The weather was glorious, hot and sunny, a late spell of warmth that people called an Indian summer.

As it happened, that was the day the Luftwaffe changed their tactics.

Daisy kissed her husband and made sure there were clean shirts and fresh underwear in his dressing room.

From what other women said, she believed that fighting men on leave wanted sex, booze, and decent food, in that order.

Boy and she had not slept together since the miscarriage. This would be the first time. She felt guilty that she did not really relish the prospect. But she certainly would not refuse to do her duty.

She half-expected him to tumble her into bed the minute he arrived, but he was not that desperate. He took off his uniform, bathed and washed his hair, and dressed again in a civilian suit. Daisy ordered the cook to spare no ration coupons in the preparation of a good lunch, and Boy brought up from the cellar one of his oldest bottles of claret.

She was surprised and hurt after lunch when he said: "I'm going out for a few hours. I'll be back for dinner."

She wanted to be a good wife, but not a passive one. "This is your first leave for months!" she protested. "Where the heck are you going?"

"To look at a horse."

That was all right. "Oh, fine—I'll come with you."

"No, don't. If I show up with a woman in tow, they'll think I'm a softie and put the price up."

She could not hide her disappointment. "I always dreamed this would be something we did together—buying and breeding racehorses."

"It's not really a woman's world."

"Oh, stink on that!" she said indignantly. "I know as much about horseflesh as you do."

He looked irritated. "Perhaps you do, but I still don't want you hanging around when I'm bargaining with these blighters—and that's final."

She gave in. "As you please," she said, and she left the dining room.

Her instinct told her that he was lying. Fighting men on leave did not think about buying horses. She intended to find out what he was up to. Even heroes had to be true to their wives.

In her room she put on trousers and boots. As Boy went down the main staircase to the front door, she ran down the back stairs, through the kitchen, across the yard, and into the old stables. There she put on a leather jacket, goggles, and a crash helmet. She opened the garage door into the mews and wheeled out her motorcycle, a Triumph Tiger 100, so called because its top speed was one hundred miles per hour. She kicked it into life and drove out of the mews effortlessly.

She had taken quickly to motorcycling when petrol rationing was introduced back in September 1939. It was like bicycling, but easier. She loved the freedom and independence it gave her.

She turned into the street just in time to see Boy's cream-colored Bentley Airline disappear around the next corner.

She followed.

He drove across Trafalgar Square and through the theater district. Daisy stayed a discreet distance behind, not wanting to be conspicuous. There was still plenty of traffic in central London, where there were hundreds of cars on official business. In addition, the petrol ration for private vehicles was not unreasonably small, especially for people who only wanted to drive around town.

Boy continued east, through the financial district. There was little traffic here on a Saturday afternoon, and Daisy became more concerned about being noticed. But she was not easily recognizable, in her goggles and helmet. And Boy was paying little attention to his surroundings, driving with the window open, smoking a cigar.

He headed into Aldgate, and Daisy had a dreadful feeling she knew why.

He turned into one of the East End's less squalid streets and parked outside a pleasant eighteenth-century house. There were no stables in sight: this was not a place where racehorses were bought and sold. So much for his story.

Daisy stopped her motorcycle at the end of the street and watched. Boy got out of the car and slammed the door. He did not look around, or study the house numbers; clearly he had been here before and knew exactly where he was going. Walking with a jaunty air, cigar in his mouth, he went up to the front door and opened it with a key.

Daisy wanted to cry.

Boy disappeared into the house.

Somewhere to the east, there was an explosion.

Daisy looked in that direction and saw planes in the sky. Had the Germans chosen today to begin bombing London?

If so, she did not care. She was not going to let Boy enjoy his infidelity in peace. She drove up to the house and parked her bike behind his car. She took off her helmet and goggles, marched up to the front door of the house, and knocked.

She heard another explosion, this one closer; then the air raid sirens began their mournful song.

The door came open a crack, and she shoved it hard. A young woman in a maid's black dress cried out and staggered backward, and Daisy walked in. She slammed the door behind her. She was in the hallway of a standard middle-class London house, but it was decorated in exotic fashion with Oriental rugs, heavy curtains, and a painting of naked women in a bathhouse.

She threw open the nearest door and stepped into the front parlor. It was dimly lit, velvet drapes keeping out the sunlight. There were three people in the room. Standing up, staring at her in shock, was a woman of about forty, dressed in a loose silk wrap, but carefully made up with bright red lipstick: the mother, she assumed. Behind her, sitting on a couch, was a girl of about sixteen wearing only underwear and stockings, smoking a cigarette. Next to the girl sat Boy, his hand on her thigh above the top of the stocking. He snatched his hand away guiltily. It was a ludicrous gesture, as if taking his hand off her could make this tableau look innocent.

Daisy fought back tears. "You promised me you would give them up!" she said. She wanted to be coldly angry, like the avenging angel, but she could hear that her voice was just wounded and sad.

Boy reddened and looked panicked. "What the devil are you doing here?"

The older woman said: "Oh, fuck, it's his wife."

Her name was Pearl, Daisy recalled, and the daughter was Joanie. How dreadful that she should know the names of such women.

The maid came to the door of the room and said: "I didn't let the bitch in—she just shoved past me!"

Daisy said to Boy: "I tried so hard to make our home beautiful and welcoming for you—and yet you prefer this!"

He started to say something, but had trouble finding his words. He sputtered incoherently for a moment or two. Then a big explosion nearby shook the floor and rattled the windows.

The maid said: "Are you all deaf? There's a fucking air raid on!" No one looked at her. "I'm going down to the basement," she said, and she disappeared.

They all needed to seek shelter. But Daisy had something to say to Boy before she left. "Don't come to my bed again, ever, please. I refuse to be contaminated."

The girl on the couch—Joanie—said: "It's only a bit of fun, love. Why don't you join in? You might like it."

Pearl, the older one, looked Daisy up and down. "She's got a nice little figure."

Daisy realized they would humiliate her further if she gave them the chance. Ignoring them, she spoke to Boy. "You've made your choice," she said. "And I've made my decision." She left the room, holding her head high even though she felt debased and spurned.

She heard Boy say: "Oh, damn, what a mess."

A mess? she thought. Is that all?

She went out of the front door.

Then she looked up.

The sky was full of planes.

The sight made her shake with fear. They were high, about ten thousand feet, but all the same they seemed to block the sun. There were hundreds of them, fat bombers and waspish fighters, a fleet that seemed twenty miles wide. To the east, in the direction of the docks and Woolwich Arsenal, palls of smoke rose from the ground where the bombs were landing. The explosions ran together into a continuous tidal roar like an angry sea.

Daisy recalled that Hitler had made a speech in the German parliament, just last Wednesday, ranting about the wickedness of RAF bombing raids on Berlin, and threatening to erase British cities in retaliation. Apparently he had meant it. They were intending to flatten London.

This was already the worst day of Daisy's life. Now she realized it might be the last.

But she could not bring herself to go back into that house and share their basement shelter. She had to get away. She needed to be at home where she could cry in private.

Hurriedly, she put on helmet and goggles. She resisted an irrational but nonetheless powerful impulse to throw herself behind the nearest wall. She jumped on her motorcycle and drove away.

She did not get far.

Two streets away, a bomb landed on a house directly in her line of vision, and she braked suddenly. She saw the hole in the roof, felt the thump of the explosion, and a few seconds later saw flames inside, as if kerosene from a heater had spilled and caught fire. A moment later, a girl of about twelve came out, screaming, with her hair on fire, and ran straight at Daisy.

Daisy jumped off the bike, pulled off her leather jacket, and used it to cover the girl's head, wrapping it tightly over the hair, denying oxygen to the flames.

The screaming stopped. Daisy removed the jacket. The girl was sobbing. She was no longer in agony, but she was bald.

Daisy looked up and down the street. A man wearing a steel helmet and an Air Raid Precautions armband came running up carrying a tin case with a white first-aid cross painted on its side.

The girl looked at Daisy, opened her mouth, and screamed: "My mother's in there!"

The ARP warden said: "Calm down, love. Let's have a look at you."

Daisy left the girl with him and ran to the front door of the building. It seemed to be an old house subdivided into cheap apartments. The upper floors were burning but she was able to enter the hall. Taking a guess, she ran to the back and found herself in a kitchen. There she saw a woman unconscious on the floor and a toddler in a cot. She picked up the child and ran out again.

The girl with the burned hair yelled: "That's my sister!"

Daisy thrust the toddler into the girl's arms and ran back inside.

The unconscious woman was too heavy for her to lift. Daisy got behind her, raised her to a sitting position, took hold of her under the arms, and dragged her across the kitchen floor and through the hallway into the street.

An ambulance had arrived, a converted saloon car, its rear bodywork replaced by a canvas roof with a back opening. The ARP warden was helping the burned girl into the vehicle. The driver came running over to Daisy. Between them, they lifted the mother into the ambulance.

The driver said to Daisy: "Is there anyone else inside?"

"I don't know!"

He ran into the hall. At that moment the entire building sagged. The burning upper stories crashed through to the ground floor. The ambulance driver disappeared into an inferno.

Daisy heard herself scream.

She covered her mouth with her hand and stared into the flames, searching for him, even though she could not have helped him, and it would have been suicide to try.

The ARP warden said: "Oh, my God, Alf's been killed."

There was another explosion as a bomb landed a hundred yards along the street.

The warden said: "Now I've got no driver, and I can't leave the scene." He looked up and down the street. There were little knots of people standing outside some of the houses, but most were probably in shelters.

Daisy said: "I'll drive it. Where should I go?"

"Can you drive?"

Most British women could not drive: it was still a man's job here. "Don't ask stupid questions," Daisy said. "Where am I taking the ambulance?"

"St. Bart's. Do you know where it is?"

"Of course." St. Bartholomew's was one of the biggest hospitals in London, and Daisy had been living here for four years. "West Smithfield," she added, to make sure he believed her.

"Emergency ward is around the back."

"I'll find it." She jumped in. The engine was still running.

The warden shouted: "What's your name?"

"Daisy Fitzherbert. What's yours?"

"Nobby Clarke. Take care of my ambulance."

The car had a standard gearshift with a clutch. Daisy put it into first and drove off.

The planes continued to roar overhead, and the bombs fell

relentlessly. Daisy was desperate to get the injured people to the hospital, and St. Bart's was not much more than a mile away, but the journey was maddeningly difficult. She drove along Leadenhall Street, Poultry, and Cheapside, but several times she found the road blocked, and had to reverse away and find another route. There seemed to be at least one destroyed house in every street. Everywhere was smoke and rubble, people bleeding and crying.

With huge relief she reached the hospital and followed another ambulance to the emergency entrance. The place was frantically busy, with a dozen vehicles discharging maimed and burned patients into the care of hurrying porters with bloodstained aprons. Perhaps I've saved the mother of these children, Daisy thought. I'm not completely worthless, even if my husband doesn't want me.

The girl with no hair was still carrying her baby sister. Daisy helped them both out of the back of her ambulance.

A nurse helped Daisy lift the unconscious mother and carry her in.

But Daisy could see that the woman had stopped breathing.

She said to the nurse: "These two are her children!" She heard the edge of hysteria in her own voice. "What will happen now?"

"I'll deal with it," the nurse said briskly. "You have to go back."

"Must I?" said Daisy.

"Pull yourself together," said the nurse. "There will be a lot more dead and injured before this night is over."

"All right," said Daisy, and she got back behind the wheel and drove off.

## iv

On a warm Mediterranean afternoon in October, Lloyd Williams arrived in the sunlit French town of Perpignan, only twenty miles from the border with Spain.

He had spent the month of September in the Bordeaux area,

picking grapes for the wine harvest, just as he had in the terrible year of 1937. Now he had money in his pockets for buses and trams, and could eat in cheap restaurants instead of living on unripe vegetables he dug up in people's gardens or raw eggs stolen from hen coops. He was going back along the route he had taken when he left Spain three years ago. He had come south from Bordeaux through Toulouse and Béziers, occasionally riding freight trains, mostly begging lifts from truck drivers.

Now he was at a roadside café on the main highway running southeast from Perpignan toward the Spanish border. Still dressed in Maurice's blue overalls and beret, he carried a small canvas bag containing a rusty trowel and a mortar-spattered spirit level, evidence that he was a Spanish bricklayer making his way home. God forbid that anyone should offer him work: he had no idea how to build a wall.

He was worried about finding his way across the mountains. Three months ago, back in Picardy, he had told himself glibly that he could find the route over the Pyrenees along which his guides had led him into Spain in 1936, parts of which he had retraced in the opposite direction when he left a year later. But as the purple peaks and green passes came into distant view on the horizon, the prospect seemed more daunting. He had thought that every step of the journey must be engraved on his memory, but when he tried to recall specific paths and bridges and turning points, he found that the pictures were blurred, and the exact details slipped infuriatingly from his mind's grasp.

He finished his lunch—a peppery fish stew—then spoke quietly to a group of drivers at the next table. "I need a lift to Cerbère." It was the last village before the Spanish border. "Anyone going that way?"

They were probably all going that way: it was the only reason for being here on this southeast route. All the same they hesitated. This was Vichy France, technically an independent zone, in practise under the thumb of the Germans occupying the other half of the country. No one was in a hurry to help a traveling stranger with a foreign accent.

"I'm a mason," he said, hefting his canvas bag. "Going home to Spain. Leandro is my name."

A fat man in an undershirt said: "I can take you halfway."

"Thank you."

"Are you ready now?"

"Of course."

They went outside and got into a grimy Renault van with the name of an electrical goods store on the side. As they pulled away, the driver asked Lloyd if he was married. A series of unpleasantly personal inquiries followed, and Lloyd realized the man had a fascination with other people's sex lives. No doubt that was why he had agreed to take Lloyd: it gave him the chance to ask intrusive questions. Several of the men who had given Lloyd lifts had had some such creepy motive.

"I'm a virgin," Lloyd told him, which was true, but that only led to an interrogation about heavy petting with schoolgirls. Lloyd did have considerable experience of that, but he was not going to share it. He refused to give details while trying not to be rude, and eventually the driver despaired. "I have to turn off here," he said, and pulled over.

Lloyd thanked him for the ride and walked on.

He had learned not to march like a soldier, and had developed what he thought was a fairly realistic peasant slouch. He never carried a newspaper or a book. His hair had last been cut by a brutally incompetent barber in the poorest quarter of Toulouse. He shaved about once a week, so that he normally had a growth of stubble, which was surprisingly effective in making him look like a nobody. He had stopped washing, and acquired a ripe odor that discouraged people from talking to him.

Few working-class people had watches, in France or Spain, so the steel wristwatch with the square face that Bernie had given him as a graduation present had to go. He could not give it to one of the many French people who had helped him, for a British watch could have incriminated them, too. In the end, with great sadness, he had thrown it into a pond.

His greatest weakness was that he had no identity papers.

He had tried to buy papers from a man who looked vaguely like him, and schemed to steal them from two others, but people were cautious about such things just now, not surprisingly. His strategy was therefore to steer clear of situations in which he might be asked to identify himself. He made himself inconspicuous, he walked across fields rather than take roads when he had the choice, and he never traveled by passenger train because there were often checkpoints at stations. So far he had been lucky. One village gendarme had demanded his papers, and when he explained that they had been stolen from him after he got drunk and passed out in a bar in Marseilles, the policeman had believed him and sent him on his way.

Now, however, his luck ran out.

He was passing through poor agricultural terrain. He was in the foothills of the Pyrenees, close to the Mediterranean, and the soil was sandy. The dusty road ran through struggling smallholdings and poor villages. The landscape was sparsely populated. To his left, through the hills, he got blue glimpses of the distant sea.

The last thing he expected was the green Citroën that pulled up alongside him with three gendarmes inside.

It happened very suddenly. He heard the car approaching—the only car he had heard since the fat man dropped him off. He carried on shuffling like a tired worker going home. Either side of the road were dry fields with sparse vegetation and stunted trees. When the car stopped, he thought for a second of making a run for it across the fields. He dropped the idea when he saw the holstered pistols of the two gendarmes who jumped out of the car. They were probably not very good shots, but they might get lucky. His chances of talking his way out of this were better. These were country constables, more amiable than the hard-nosed French city police.

"Papers?" said the nearest gendarme in French.

Lloyd spread his hands in a helpless gesture. "Monsieur, I am so unfortunate. My papers were stolen in Marseilles. I am Leandro, Spanish mason, going—"

"Get in the car."

Lloyd hesitated, but it was hopeless. The odds of his getting away were now worse than before.

A gendarme took him firmly by the arm, hustled him into the backseat, and got in beside him.

His spirits sank as the car pulled away.

The gendarme next to him said: "Are you English, or what?"

"I am a Spanish mason. My name—"

The gendarme made a waving-away gesture and said: "Don't bother."

Lloyd saw that he had been wildly optimistic. He was a foreigner without papers heading for the Spanish border: they simply assumed he was an escaping British soldier. If they had any doubt, they would find proof when they ordered him to strip, for they would see the identity tag around his neck. He had not thrown it away, for without it he would automatically be shot as a spy.

And now he was stuck in a car with three armed men, and the likelihood that he would find a way to escape was zero.

They drove on, in the direction in which he had been heading, as the sun went down over the mountains on their right-hand side. There were no big towns between here and the border, so he assumed they intended to put him in a village jail for the night. Perhaps he could escape from there. Failing that, they would undoubtedly take him back to Perpignan tomorrow and hand him over to the city police. What then? Would he be interrogated? The prospect made him cold with fear. The French police would beat him up; the Germans would torture him. If he survived, he would end up in a prisoner-of-war camp, where he would remain until the end of the war, or until he died of malnutrition. And yet he was only a few miles from the border!

They drove into a small town. Could he escape between the car and the jail? He could make no plan; he did not know the terrain. There was nothing he could do but remain alert and seize any opportunity.

The car turned off the main street and into an alley behind a row of shops. Were they going to shoot him here and dump his body?

The car stopped at the back of a restaurant. The yard was littered with boxes and giant cans. Through a small window Lloyd could see a brightly lit kitchen.

The gendarme in the front passenger seat got out, then opened

Lloyd's door, on the side of the car nearest the building. Was this his chance? He would have to run around the car and along the alley. It was dusk: after the first few yards he would not be an easy target.

The gendarme reached into the car and grasped Lloyd's arm, holding him as he got out and stood up. The second one got out immediately behind Lloyd. The opportunity was not good enough.

But why had they brought him here?

They walked him into the kitchen. A chef was beating eggs in a bowl and an adolescent boy was washing up in a big sink. One of the gendarmes said: "Here's an Englishman. He calls himself Leandro."

Without pausing in his work, the chef lifted his head and bawled: "Teresa! Come here!"

Lloyd remembered another Teresa, a beautiful Spanish anarchist who had taught soldiers to read and write.

The kitchen door swung wide and she walked in.

Lloyd stared at her in astonishment. There was no possibility of mistake: he would never forget those big eyes and that mass of black hair, even though she wore the white cotton cap and apron of a waitress.

At first she did not look at him. She put a pile of plates on the counter next to the young washer-up, then turned to the gendarmes with a smile and kissed each on both cheeks, saying: "Pierre! Michel! How are you?" Then she turned to Lloyd, stared at him, and said in Spanish: "No—it's not possible. Lloyd—is it really you?"

He could only nod dumbly.

She put her arms around him, embraced him, and kissed him on both cheeks.

One of the gendarmes said: "There we are. All is well. We have to go. Good luck!" He handed Lloyd his canvas bag; then they left.

Lloyd found his tongue. "What's going on?" he said to Teresa in Spanish. "I thought I was being taken to jail!"

"They hate the Nazis, so they help us," she said.

"Who is *us*?"

"I'll explain later. Come with me." She opened a door that gave onto a staircase and led him to an upper story, where there was a sparsely furnished bedroom. "Wait here. I'll bring you something to eat."

Lloyd lay down on the bed and contemplated his extraordinary fortune. Five minutes ago he had been expecting torture and death. Now he was waiting for a beautiful woman to bring him supper.

It could change again just as quickly, he reflected.

She returned half an hour later with an omelette and fried potatoes on a thick plate. "We've been busy, but we close soon," she said. "I'll be back in a few minutes."

He ate the food quickly.

Night fell. He listened to the chatter of customers leaving and the clang of pots being put away; then Teresa reappeared with a bottle of red wine and two glasses.

Lloyd asked her why she had left Spain.

"Our people are being murdered by the thousands," she said. "For those they don't kill, they have passed the Law of Political Responsibilities, making criminals of everyone who supported the government. You can lose all your assets if you opposed Franco even by 'grave passivity.' You are innocent only if you can prove you supported him."

Lloyd thought bitterly of Chamberlain's reassurance to the House of Commons, back in March, that Franco had renounced political reprisals. What an evil liar Chamberlain had been.

Teresa went on: "Many of our comrades are in filthy prison camps."

"I don't suppose you have any idea what happened to Sergeant Lenny Griffiths, my friend?"

Teresa shook her head. "I never saw him again after Belchite."

"And you . . . ?"

"I escaped from Franco's men, came here, got a job as a waitress . . . and found there was other work for me to do."

"What work?"

"I take escaping soldiers across the mountains. That's why the gendarmes brought you to me."

Lloyd was heartened. He had been planning to do it alone, and he had been worried about finding the way. Now perhaps he would have a guide.

"I have two others waiting," she said. "A British gunner and a Canadian pilot. They are in a farmhouse in the hills."

"When are you planning to go across?"

"Tonight," she said. "Don't drink too much wine."

She went away again and returned half an hour later carrying an old, ripped brown overcoat for him. "It's cold where we're going," she explained.

They slipped out of the kitchen door and threaded their way through the small town by starlight. Leaving the houses behind, they followed a dirt track steadily uphill. After an hour they came to a small group of stone buildings. Teresa whistled, then opened the door to a barn, and two men came out.

"We always use false names," she said in English. "I am Maria and these two are Fred and Tom. Our new friend is Leandro." The men shook hands. She went on: "No talking, no smoking, and anyone who falls behind will be left. Are we ready?"

From here the path was steeper. Lloyd found himself slipping on stones. Now and again he clutched at stunted bushes of heather beside the path and pulled himself upward with their aid. The petite Teresa set a pace that soon had the three men puffing and blowing. She was carrying a flashlight, but she refused to use it while the stars were bright, saying she had to conserve the battery.

The air got colder. They waded across an icy stream, and Lloyd's feet did not get warm again afterward.

An hour later, Teresa said: "Take care to stay in the middle of the path here." Lloyd looked down and realized he was on a ridge between steep slopes. When he saw how far he could fall, he felt a little giddy, and quickly looked up and ahead at Teresa's swiftly moving silhouette. In normal circumstances he would have enjoyed every minute of walking behind a figure like that, but now he was so tired and cold he did not have the energy even to ogle.

The mountains were not uninhabited. At one point a distant dog barked; at another they heard a tinkling of eerie bells, which spooked the men until Teresa explained that mountain shepherds hung bells on their sheep so they could find their flocks.

Lloyd thought about Daisy. Was she still at Tŷ Gwyn? Or had she gone back to her husband? Lloyd hoped she had not returned to London, for London was being bombed every night, the French newspapers said. Was she alive or dead? Would he ever see her again? If he did, how would she feel about him?

They stopped every two hours to rest, drink water, and take a few mouthfuls from a bottle of wine Teresa was carrying.

It started to rain around dawn. The ground underfoot instantly became treacherous, and they all stumbled and slipped, but Teresa did not slow down. "Be glad it's not snow," she said.

Daylight revealed a landscape of scrubby vegetation in which rocky outcrops stuck up like tombstones. The rain continued, and a cold mist obscured the distance.

After a while, Lloyd realized they were walking downhill. At the next rest stop, Teresa announced: "We are now in Spain." Lloyd should have been relieved, but he just felt exhausted.

Gradually the landscape softened, rocks giving way to coarse grass and shrubs.

Suddenly Teresa dropped to the ground and lay flat.

The three men instantly did the same, not needing to be prompted. Following Teresa's gaze, Lloyd saw two men in green uniforms and peculiar hats: Spanish border guards, presumably. He realized that being in Spain did not mean he was out of trouble. If he was caught entering the country illegally, he might just be sent back. Worse, he could disappear into one of Franco's prison camps.

The border guards were walking along a mountain track toward the fugitives. Lloyd prepared himself for a fight. He would have to move fast, in order to overcome them before they could draw their guns. He wondered how good the other two men would be in a fracas.

But his trepidation was unnecessary. The two guards reached some unmarked boundary and then turned back. Teresa acted as if she had known this would happen. When the guards disappeared from sight, she stood up and the four of them walked on.

Soon afterward the mist lifted. Lloyd saw a fishing village around a sandy bay. He had been here before, when he came to Spain in 1936. He even remembered that there was a railway station.

They walked into the village. It was a sleepy place, with no signs of officialdom: no police, no town hall, no soldiers, no checkpoints. Doubtless that was why Teresa had chosen it.

They went to the station and Teresa bought tickets, flirting with the vendor as if they were old friends.

Lloyd sat on a bench on the shady platform, footsore, weary, grateful, and happy.

An hour later they caught a train to Barcelona.

### v

Daisy had never before understood the meaning of *work*.

Or *tiredness*.

Or *tragedy*.

She sat in a school classroom, drinking sweet English tea out of a cup with no saucer. She wore a steel helmet and rubber boots. It was five o'clock in the afternoon, and she was still weary from the night before.

She was part of the Aldgate district Air Raid Precautions sector. Theoretically she worked an eight-hour shift followed by eight hours on standby and eight hours off duty. In practise she worked as long as the air raid continued and there were wounded people to be driven to the hospital.

London was bombed every single night of October 1940.

Daisy always worked with one other woman, the driver's attendant, and four men, forming a first-aid party. Their headquarters was in a school, and now they were sitting at the children's desks, waiting for the planes to come and the sirens to wail and the bombs to fall.

The ambulance she drove was a converted American Buick. They also had a normal car and driver to transport what they called sitting cases—injured people who could nevertheless sit upright without assistance while being transported to hospital.

Her attendant was Naomi Avery, an attractive blond cockney who liked men and enjoyed the camaraderie of the team. Now she bantered with the post warden, Nobby Clarke, a retired policeman. "The chief warden is a man," she said. "The district warden is a man. You're a man."

"I hope so," Nobby said, and the others chuckled.

"There are plenty of women in ARP," Naomi went on. "How come none of them are officials?"

The men laughed. A bald man with a big nose called Gorgeous George said: "Here we go, women's rights again." He had a misogynist streak.

Daisy joined in. "You don't really think all you men are smarter than all of us women, do you?"

Nobby said: "Matter of fact, there are some women senior wardens."

"I've never met one," said Naomi.

"It's tradition, isn't it," Nobby said. "Women have always been homemakers."

"Like Catherine the Great of Russia," Daisy said sarcastically.

Naomi put in: "Or Queen Elizabeth of England."

"Amelia Earhart."

"Jane Austen."

"Marie Curie, the only scientist ever to win the Nobel Prize twice."

"Catherine the Great?" said Gorgeous George. "Isn't there a story about her and her horse?"

"Now, now, ladies present," said Nobby in a tone of reproof. "Anyway, I can answer Daisy's question," he went on.

Daisy, willing to be his foil, said: "Go on, then."

"I grant you that some women may be just as clever as a man," he said with the air of one who makes a remarkably generous concession. "But there is one very good reason why almost all ARP officials are men, nevertheless."

"And what would that reason be, Nobby?"

"It's very simple. Men won't take orders from a woman." He sat back with a triumphant expression, confident that he had won the argument.

The irony was that when the bombs were falling, and they were digging through the rubble to rescue the injured, they *were* equals. There was no hierarchy then. If Daisy shouted at Nobby to pick up the other end of a roof beam, he would do it without demur.

Daisy loved these men, even George. They would give their lives for her, and she for them.

She heard a low hooting sound outside. Slowly it rose in pitch until it became the tiresomely familiar siren of an air raid warning. Seconds later there was the boom of a distant explosion. The warning was often late; sometimes it sounded after the first bombs had fallen.

The phone rang and Nobby picked it up.

They all stood up. George said wearily: "Don't the Germans ever take a ruddy day off?"

Nobby put the phone down and said: "Nutley Street."

"I know where that is," said Naomi as they all hurried out. "Our M.P. lives there."

They jumped into the cars. As Daisy put the ambulance in gear and drove off, Naomi, sitting beside her, said: "Happy days."

Naomi was being ironic but, strangely, Daisy *was* happy. It was very odd, she thought as she careered around a bend. Every night she saw destruction, tragic bereavement, and horribly maimed bodies. There was a good chance she herself would die in a blazing building tonight. Yet she felt wonderful. She was working and suffering for a cause, and paradoxically that was better than pleasing herself. She was part of a group that would risk everything to help others, and it was the best feeling in the world.

Daisy did not hate the Germans for trying to kill her. She had been told by her father-in-law, Earl Fitzherbert, why they were bombing London. Until August the Luftwaffe had raided only ports and airfields. Fitz had explained, in an unusually candid moment, that the British were not so scrupulous: the government had approved bombing of targets in German cities back in May, and all through June and July the RAF had dropped bombs on women and children in their homes. The German public had been enraged by this and demanded retaliation. The Blitz was the result.

Daisy and Boy were keeping up appearances, but she locked her bedroom door when he was at home, and he made no objection. Their marriage was a sham, but they were both too busy to do anything about it. When Daisy thought about it, she felt sad, for she had lost both Boy and Lloyd now. Fortunately she hardly had time to think.

Nutley Street was on fire. The Luftwaffe dropped incendiary bombs and high explosive together. Fire did the most damage, but the high explosive helped the blaze to spread by blowing out windows and ventilating the flames.

Daisy brought the ambulance to a screeching halt and they all went to work.

People with minor injuries were helped to the nearest first-aid station. Those more seriously hurt were driven to St. Bart's or the London Hospital in Whitechapel. Daisy made one trip after another. When darkness fell, she switched on her headlights. They were masked, with only a slit of light, as part of the blackout, though it seemed a superfluous precaution when London was burning like a bonfire.

The bombing went on until dawn. In full daylight the bombers were too vulnerable to being shot down by the fighter aircraft piloted by Boy and his comrades, so the air raid petered out. As the cold gray light washed over the wreckage, Daisy and Naomi returned to Nutley Street to find there were no more victims to be taken to hospital.

They sat down wearily on the remains of a brick garden wall. Daisy took off her steel helmet. She was filthy dirty and worn out. I wonder what the girls in the Buffalo Yacht Club would think of me now, she thought; then she realized she no longer cared much what they thought. The days when their approval was all-important to her seemed a long time in the past.

Someone said: "Would you like a cup of tea, my lovely?"

She recognized the accent as Welsh. She looked up to see an

attractive middle-aged woman carrying a tray. "Oh, boy, that's what I need," she said, and helped herself. She had now grown to like this beverage. It tasted bitter but it had a remarkable restorative effect.

The woman kissed Naomi, who explained: "We're related. Her daughter, Millie, is married to my brother, Abie."

Daisy watched the woman take the tray around the little crowd of ARP wardens and firemen and neighbors. She must be a local dignitary, Daisy decided: she had an air of authority. Yet at the same time she was clearly a woman of the people, speaking to everyone with an easy warmth, making them smile. She knew Nobby and Gorgeous George, and greeted them as old friends.

She took the last cup on the tray for herself and came to sit beside Daisy. "You sound American," she said pleasantly.

Daisy nodded. "I'm married to an Englishman."

"I live in this street—but my house escaped the bombs last night. I'm the member of Parliament for Aldgate. My name is Eth Leckwith."

Daisy's heart skipped a beat. This was Lloyd's famous mother! She shook hands. "Daisy Fitzherbert."

Ethel's eyebrows went up. "Oh!" she said. "You're the Viscountess Aberowen."

Daisy blushed and lowered her voice. "They don't know that in the ARP."

"Your secret is safe with me."

Hesitantly, Daisy said: "I knew your son, Lloyd." She could not help the tears that came to her eyes when she thought of their time at Tŷ Gwyn, and the way he had looked after her when she miscarried. "He was very kind to me, once when I needed help."

"Thank you," said Ethel. "But don't talk as if he's dead."

The reproof was mild, but Daisy felt she had been dreadfully tactless. "I'm so sorry!" she said. "He's missing in action, I know. How frightfully stupid of me."

"But he's not missing any longer," Ethel said. "He escaped through Spain. He arrived home yesterday."

"Oh, my God!" Daisy's heart was racing. "Is he all right?"

"Perfectly. In fact he looks very well, despite what he's been through."

"Where . . ." Daisy swallowed. "Where is he now?"

"Why, he's here somewhere." Ethel looked around. "Lloyd?" she called.

Daisy scanned the crowd wildly. Could it be true?

A man in a ripped brown overcoat turned around and said: "Yes, Mam?"

Daisy stared at him. His face was sunburned, and he was as thin as a stick, but he looked more attractive than ever.

"Come here, my lovely," said Ethel.

Lloyd took a step forward, then saw Daisy. Suddenly his face was transformed. He smiled happily. "Hello," he said.

Daisy sprang to her feet.

Ethel said: "Lloyd, there's someone here you may remember—"

Daisy could not restrain herself. She ran to Lloyd and threw herself into his arms. She hugged him. She looked into his green eyes, then kissed his brown cheeks and his broken nose and then his mouth. "I love you, Lloyd," she said madly. "I love you, I love you, I love you."

"I love you, too, Daisy," he said.

Behind her, Daisy heard Ethel's wry voice. "You do remember, I see."


## vi

Lloyd was eating toast and jam when Daisy entered the kitchen of the house in Nutley Street. She sat at the table, looking exhausted, and took off her steel helmet. Her face was smudged and her hair was dirty with ash and dust, and Lloyd thought she looked irresistibly beautiful.

She came in most mornings when the bombing ended and the last victim had been driven to the hospital. Lloyd's mother had told her she did not need an invitation, and Daisy had taken her at her word.

Ethel poured Daisy a cup of tea and said: "Hard night, my lovely?"

Daisy nodded grimly. "One of the worst. The Peabody building on Orange Street burned down."

"Oh, no!" Lloyd was horrified. He knew the place: a big overcrowded tenement full of poor families with numerous children.

Bernie said: "That's a big building."

"It was," said Daisy. "Hundreds of people were burned and God knows how many children are orphans. Nearly all my patients died on the way to the hospital."

Lloyd reached across the little table and took her hand.

She looked up from her cup of tea. "You don't get used to it. You think you'll become hardened, but you don't." She was stricken with sadness.

Ethel put a hand on her shoulder for a moment in a gesture of compassion.

Daisy said: "And we're doing the same to families in Germany."

Ethel said: "Including my old friends Maud and Walter and their children, I presume."

"Isn't that terrible?" Daisy shook her head despairingly. "What's wrong with us?"

Lloyd said: "What's wrong with the human race?"

Bernie, ever practical, said: "I'll go over to Orange Street later and make sure everything's being done for the children."

"I'll come with you," said Ethel.

Bernie and Ethel thought alike and acted together effortlessly, often seeming to read each other's minds. Lloyd had been observing them carefully, since he got home, worrying that their marriage might have been affected by the shocking revelation that Ethel had never had a husband called Teddy Williams, and that Lloyd's father was Earl Fitzherbert. He had discussed this at length with Daisy, who now knew the whole truth. How did Bernie feel about having been lied to for twenty years? But Lloyd saw no sign that it had made any difference. In his unsentimental way Bernie adored Ethel, and to him she could do no wrong. He believed she would never do anything to hurt him, and he was right. It made Lloyd hope that he, too, might one day have such a marriage.

Daisy noticed that Lloyd was in uniform. "Where are you off to this morning?"

"I've had a summons from the War Office." He looked at the clock on the mantelpiece. "I'd better get going."

"I thought you'd already been debriefed."

"Come to my room and I'll explain while I'm putting on my tie. Bring your tea."

They went upstairs. Daisy looked around with interest, and he realized she had not been in his bedroom before. He looked at the single bed, the bookshelf of novels in German, French, and Spanish, and the writing table with the row of sharpened pencils, and wondered what she thought of it.

"What a nice little room," she said.

It was not little. It was the same size as the other bedrooms in the house. But she had different standards.

She picked up a framed photograph. It showed the family at the seaside: little Lloyd in shorts, toddling Millie in a swimsuit, young Ethel in a big floppy hat, Bernie wearing a gray suit with a white shirt open at the neck and a knotted handkerchief on his head.

"Southend," Lloyd explained. He took her cup, put it on the dressing table, and folded her into his arms. He kissed her mouth. She kissed him back with weary tenderness, stroking his cheek, letting her body slump against his.

After a minute he released her. She was really too tired to canoodle, and he had an appointment.

She took off her boots and lay down on his bed.

"The War Office have asked me to go in and see them again," he said as he tied his tie.

"But you were there for hours last time."

It was true. He had had to dredge his memory for every last detail of his time on the run in France. They wanted to know the rank and regiment of every German he had encountered. He could not remember them all, of course, but he had done his homework meticulously for the Tŷ Gwyn course and he was able to give them a great deal of information.

That was standard military intelligence debriefing. But they had also asked about his escape, the roads he had taken and who had helped him. They were even interested in Maurice and Marcelle, and reproved him for not knowing their surname. They had got very excited about Teresa, who clearly could be a major asset to future escapers.

"I'm seeing a different lot today." He glanced at a typed note on his dressing table. "At the Metropole Hotel in Northumberland Avenue. Room four twenty-four." The address was off Trafalgar Square in a neighborhood of government offices. "Apparently it's a new department dealing with British prisoners of war." He put on his peaked cap and looked in the mirror. "Am I smart enough?"

There was no answer. He looked at the bed. She had fallen asleep.

He pulled a blanket over her, kissed her forehead, and went out.

He told his mother that Daisy was asleep on his bed, and she said she would check on her later to make sure she was all right.

He took the Tube to central London.

He had told Daisy the true story of his parentage, disabusing her of the theory that he was Maud's child. She believed him readily, for she suddenly recalled Boy telling her that Fitz had an illegitimate child somewhere. "This is creepy," she had said, looking thoughtful. "The two Englishmen I've fallen for turn out to be half brothers." She had looked appraisingly at Lloyd. "You inherited your father's good looks. Boy just got his selfishness."

Lloyd and Daisy had not yet made love. One reason was that she never had a night off. Then, on the single occasion they had had a chance to be alone together, things had gone wrong.

It had been last Sunday, at Daisy's home in Mayfair. Her servants had Sunday afternoon off, and she had taken him to her bedroom in the empty house. But she had been nervous and ill at ease. She had kissed him, then turned her head aside. When he put his hands on her breasts, she had pushed them away. He had been confused: If he was not supposed to behave this way, why were they in her bedroom?

"I'm sorry," she had said at last. "I love you, but I can't do this. I can't betray my husband in his own house."

"But he betrayed you."

"At least he went somewhere else."

"All right."

She had looked at him. "Do you think I'm being silly?"

He shrugged. "After all we've been through together, this seems overly fastidious of you, yes—but, look, you feel the way you feel. What a rotter I would be if I tried to bully you into doing it when you're not ready."

She put her arms around him and hugged him hard. "I said it before," she said. "You're a grown-up."

"Don't let's spoil the whole afternoon," he said. "We'll go to the pictures."

They saw Charlie Chaplin in *The Great Dictator* and laughed their heads off; then she went back on duty.

Pleasant thoughts of Daisy occupied Lloyd all the way to Embankment station; then he walked up Northumberland Avenue to the Metropole. The hotel had been stripped of its reproduction antiques and furnished with utilitarian tables and chairs.

After a few minutes' wait Lloyd was taken to see a tall colonel with a brisk manner. "I've read your account, Lieutenant," he said. "Well done."

"Thank you, sir."

"We expect more people to follow in your footsteps, and we'd like to help them. We're especially interested in downed airmen. They're expensive to train, and we want them back so they can fly again."

Lloyd thought that was harsh. If a man survived a crash landing, should he really be asked to risk going through the whole thing again? But wounded men were sent back into battle as soon as they recovered. That was war.

The colonel said: "We're setting up a kind of underground railroad, all the way from Germany to Spain. You speak German, French, and Spanish, I see, but, more importantly, you've been at the sharp end. We'd like to second you to our department."

Lloyd had not been expecting this, and he was not sure how he felt about it. "Thank you, sir. I'm honored. But is it a desk job?"

"Not at all. We want you to go back to France."

Lloyd's heart raced. He had not thought he would have to face those perils again.

The colonel saw the dismay on his face. "You know how dangerous it is."

"Yes, sir."

In an abrupt tone the colonel said: "You can refuse if you like."

Lloyd thought of Daisy in the Blitz, and of the people burned to death in the Peabody tenement, and realized he did not even want to refuse. "If you think it's important, sir, then I will go back most willingly, of course."

"Good man," said the colonel.

Half an hour later Lloyd was dazedly walking back to the Tube station. He was now part of a department called MI9. He would return to France with false papers and large sums in cash. Already dozens of German, Dutch, Belgian, and French people in occupied territory had been recruited to the deadly dangerous task of helping British and Commonwealth airmen return home. He would be one of numerous MI9 agents expanding the network.

If he were caught, he would be tortured.

Although he was scared, he was also excited. He was going to fly to Madrid; it would be his first time up in an airplane. He would reenter France across the Pyrenees and make contact with Teresa. He would be moving in disguise among the enemy, rescuing people under the noses of the Gestapo. He would make sure that men following in his footsteps would not be as alone and friendless as he had been.

He got back to Nutley Street at eleven o'clock. There was a note from his mother: "Not a peep from Miss America." After visiting the bomb site, Ethel would have gone to the House of Commons, Bernie to County Hall. Lloyd and Daisy had the house to themselves.

He went up to his room. Daisy was still asleep. Her leather jacket and heavy-duty wool trousers were carelessly tossed on the floor. She was in his bed wearing only her underwear. This had never happened before.

He took off his jacket and tie.

A sleepy voice from the bed said: "And the rest."

He looked at her. "What?"

"Take off your clothes and get into bed."

The house was empty: no one would disturb them.

He took off his boots, trousers, shirt, and socks; then he hesitated.

"You're not going to feel cold," she said. She wriggled under the blankets, then threw a pair of silk camiknickers at him.

He had expected this to be a solemn moment of high passion, but Daisy seemed to think it should be a matter of laughter and fun. He was willing to be guided by her.

He took off his undershirt and pants and slipped into bed beside her. She was warm and languid. He felt nervous: he had never actually told her that he was a virgin.

He had always heard that the man should take the initiative, but it seemed Daisy did not know that. She kissed and caressed him; then she grasped his penis. "Oh, boy," she said. "I was hoping you'd have one of these."

After that, he stopped being nervous.

# CHAPTER EIGHT

# 1941 (I)

On a cold winter Sunday, Carla von Ulrich went with the maid, Ada, to visit Ada's son, Kurt, at the Wannsee Children's Nursing Home, by the lake on the western outskirts of Berlin. It took an hour to get there on the train. Carla made a habit of wearing her nurse's uniform on these visits, because the staff at the home talked more frankly about Kurt to a fellow professional.

In summer the lakeside would be crowded with families and children playing on the beach and paddling in the shallows, but today there were just a few walkers, well wrapped up against the chill, and one hardy swimmer with an anxious wife waiting at the waterside.

The home, which specialized in caring for severely handicapped children, was a once-grand house whose elegant reception rooms had been subdivided and painted pale green and furnished with hospital beds and cots.

Kurt was now eight years old. He could walk and feed himself about as well as a two-year-old, but he could not talk and still wore diapers. He had shown no sign of improvement for years. However, there was no doubt of his joy at seeing Ada. He beamed with happiness, burbled excitedly, and held out his arms to be picked up and hugged and kissed.

He recognized Carla, too. Whenever she saw him, she remembered the frightening drama of his birth, when she had delivered him while her brother, Erik, ran to fetch Dr. Rothmann.

They played with him for an hour or so. He liked toy trains and cars, and books with highly colored pictures. Then the time for his afternoon nap drew near, and Ada sang to him until he went to sleep.

On their way out a nurse spoke to Ada. "Frau Hempel, please come with me to the office of Herr Professor Doctor Willrich. He would like to speak to you."

Willrich was director of the home. Carla had never met him and she was not sure Ada had, either.

Ada said nervously: "Is there some problem?"

The nurse said: "I'm sure the director just wants to talk to you about Kurt's progress."

Ada said: "Fräulein von Ulrich will come with me."

The nurse did not like that idea. "Professor Willrich asked only for you."

But Ada could be stubborn when necessary. "Fräulein von Ulrich will come with me," she repeated firmly.

The nurse shrugged and said curtly: "Follow me."

They were shown into a pleasant office. This room had not been subdivided. A coal fire burned in the grate, and a bay window gave a view of the Wannsee lake. Someone was sailing, Carla saw, slicing through the wavelets before a stiff breeze. Willrich sat behind a leather-topped desk. He had a jar of tobacco and a rack of different-shaped pipes. He was about fifty, tall and heavily built. All his features seemed large: big nose, square jaw, huge ears, and a domed bald head. He looked at Ada and said: "Frau Hempel, I presume?" Ada nodded. Willrich turned to Carla. "And you are Fräulein . . . ?"

"Carla von Ulrich, Professor. I'm Kurt's godmother."

He raised his eyebrows. "A little young to be a godmother, surely?"

Ada said indignantly: "She delivered Kurt! She was only eleven, but she was better than the doctor, because he wasn't there!"

Willrich ignored that. Still looking at Carla, he said disdainfully: "And hoping to become a nurse, I see."

Carla wore a beginner's uniform, but she considered herself to be more than just hopeful. "I am a trainee nurse," she said. She did not like Willrich.

"Please sit." He opened a thin file. "Kurt is eight years old, but has reached the developmental stage of only two years."

He paused. Neither woman said anything.

"This is unsatisfactory," he said.

Ada looked at Carla. Carla did not know what he was getting at, and indicated as much with a shrug.

"There is a new treatment available for cases of this type. However, it will necessitate moving Kurt to another hospital." Willrich closed the file. He looked at Ada, and for the first time, he smiled. "I'm sure you would like Kurt to undergo a therapy that might improve his condition."

Carla did not like his smile: it seemed creepy. She said: "Could you tell us more about the treatment, Professor?"

"I'm afraid it would be beyond your understanding," he said. "Even though you are a trainee nurse."

Carla was not going to let him get away with that. "I'm sure Frau Hempel would like to know whether it would involve surgery, or drugs, or electricity, for example."

"Drugs," he said with evident reluctance.

Ada said: "Where would he have to go?"

"The hospital is in Akelberg, in Bavaria."

Ada's geography was weak, and Carla knew she had no sense of how far that was. "It's two hundred miles," she said.

"Oh, no!" said Ada. "How would I visit him?"

"By train," said Willrich impatiently.

Carla said: "It would take four or five hours. She would probably have to stay overnight. And what about the cost of the fare?"

"I cannot concern myself with such things!" said Willrich angrily. "I am a doctor, not a travel agent!"

Ada was close to tears. "If it means Kurt will get better, and learn to say a few words, and not to soil himself . . . one day we might perhaps bring him home."

"Exactly," said Willrich. "I felt sure you would not wish to deny him the chance of getting better just for your own selfish reasons."

"Is that what you're telling us?" said Carla. "That Kurt might be able to live a normal life?"

"Medicine offers no guarantees," he said. "Even a trainee nurse should know that."

Carla had learned, from her parents, to be impatient with prevarication. "I don't ask you for a guarantee," she said crisply. "I ask you for a prognosis. You must have one. Otherwise you would not be proposing the treatment."

He reddened. "The treatment is new. We hope it will improve Kurt's condition. That is what I am telling you."

"Is it experimental?"

"All medicine is experimental. All therapies work on some patients but not on others. You must listen to what I tell you: medicine offers no guarantees."

Carla wanted to oppose him just because he was so arrogant, but she realized that was not the basis on which to make a judgment. Besides, she was not sure Ada really had a choice. Doctors could go against the wishes of parents if the child's health was at risk: in effect they could do what they liked. Willrich was not asking Ada's permission—he had no real need of it. He was speaking to her only in order to avoid a fuss.

Carla said: "Can you tell Frau Hempel how long it might be before Kurt returns from Akelberg to Berlin?"

"Quite soon," said Willrich.

It was no answer at all, but Carla felt that if she pressed him he would become angry again.

Ada was looking helpless. Carla sympathized; she herself found it difficult to know what to say. They had not been given enough information. Doctors were often like this, Carla had noticed: they seemed to want to hug their knowledge to themselves. They preferred to fob patients off with platitudes, and became defensive when questioned.

Ada had tears in her eyes. "Well, if there's a chance he could get better . . ."

"That's the attitude," Willrich said.

But Ada had not finished. "What do you think, Carla?"

Willrich looked outraged at this appeal to the opinion of a mere nurse.

Carla said: "I agree with you, Ada. This opportunity must be seized, for Kurt's sake, even though it will be hard for you."

"Very sensible," said Willrich, and he got to his feet. "Thank you for coming to see me." He went to the door and opened it. Carla felt he could not get rid of them quickly enough.

They left the home and walked back to the station. As their nearly empty train pulled away, Carla picked up a leaflet that had been left on the seat. It was headed HOW TO OPPOSE THE NAZIS, and it listed ten things people could do to hasten the end of the regime, starting with slowing down their rate of work.

Carla had seen such flyers before, though not often. They were placed by some underground resistance movement.

Ada snatched it from her, crumpled it, and threw it out of the window. "You can be arrested for reading such things!" she said. She had been Carla's nanny, and sometimes she behaved as though Carla had not grown up. Carla did not mind her occasional bossiness, for she knew it came from love.

However, in this case Ada was not overreacting. People could be imprisoned not just for reading such things but even for failing to report that they had found one. Ada could be in trouble merely for throwing it out of the window. Fortunately there was no one else in the carriage to see what she had done.

Ada was still troubled by what she had been told at the home. "Do you think we did the right thing?" she said to Carla.

"I don't really know," Carla said candidly. "I think so."

"You're a nurse—you understand these things better than I do."

Carla was enjoying nursing, though she still felt frustrated that she had not been allowed to train as a doctor. Now, with so many young men in the army, the attitude toward female medical students had changed, and more women were going to medical school. Carla could have applied again for a scholarship—except that her family was so desperately poor that they depended on her meager wages. Her father had no work at all, her mother gave piano lessons, and Erik sent home as much as he could afford out of his army pay. The family had not paid Ada for years.

Ada was a naturally stoical person, and by the time they got home, she was getting over her upset. She went into the kitchen, put on her apron, and began to prepare dinner for the family, and the comfortable routine seemed to console her.

Carla was not having dinner. She had plans for the evening. She felt she was abandoning Ada to her sadness, and she was a bit guilty, but not guilty enough to sacrifice her night out.

She put on a knee-length tennis dress she had made herself by shortening the frayed hem of an old frock of her mother's. She was not going to play tennis. She was going to dance, and her aim was to look American. She put on lipstick and face powder, and combed out her hair in defiance of the government's preference for braids.

The mirror showed her a modern girl with a pretty face and a bold air. She knew that her confidence and self-possession put a lot of boys off her. Sometimes she wished she could be seductive as well as capable, a trick her mother had always been able to pull off; but it was not in her nature. She had long ago given up trying to be winsome: it just made her feel silly. Boys had to accept her as she was.

Some boys were scared of her, but others were attracted, and at parties she often ended up with a small cluster of admirers. She in turn liked boys, especially when they forgot about trying to impress people and started to talk normally. Her favorites were the ones who made her laugh. So far she had not had a serious boyfriend, though she had kissed quite a few.

To complete her outfit she put on a striped blazer she had bought from a secondhand clothing cart. She knew her parents would disapprove of her appearance, and try to make her change, saying it was dangerous to defy the Nazis' prejudices. So she needed to get out of the house without seeing them. It should be easy enough. Mother was giving a piano lesson: Carla could hear the painfully hesitant playing of her pupil. Father would be reading the newspaper in the same room, for they could not afford to heat more than one room of the house. Erik was away with the army, though he was now stationed near Berlin and due home on leave shortly.

She covered up with a conventional raincoat and put her white shoes in her pocket.

She went down to the hall, opened the front door, shouted: "Good-bye, back soon!" and hurried out.

She met Frieda at the Friedrich Strasse station. She was dressed similarly with a stripy dress under a plain tan coat, her hair hanging loose—the main difference being that Frieda's clothes were new and expensive. On the platform, two boys in Hitler Youth outfits stared at them with a mixture of disapproval and desire.

They got off the train in the northern suburb of Wedding, a working-class district that had once been a left-wing stronghold. They headed for the Pharus Hall, where in the past Communists had held their conferences. Now there was no political activity at all, of course. Nevertheless the building had become the center of the movement called Swing Kids.

Kids between fifteen and twenty-five were already gathering in the streets around the hall. Swing boys wore check jackets and carried an umbrella, to look English. They let their hair grow long to show their contempt for the military. Swing girls had heavy makeup and American sports clothes. They all thought the Hitler Youth were stupid and boring, with their folk music and community dances.

Carla thought it was ironic. When she was little, she had been teased by the other kids and called a foreigner because her mother was English; now the same children, a little older, thought English was the fashionable thing to be.

Carla and Frieda went into the hall. There was a conventional, innocent youth club there, with girls in pleated skirts and boys in short trousers playing table tennis and drinking sticky orange cordial. But the action was in the side rooms.

Frieda quickly led Carla to a large storeroom with stacked chairs around the walls. There her brother, Werner, had plugged in a record player. Fifty or sixty boys and girls were dancing the jitterbug jive. Carla recognized the tune that was playing: "Ma, He's Making Eyes at Me." She and Frieda started to dance.

Jazz records were banned because most of the best musicians were Negroes. The Nazis had to denigrate anything that was done well by non-Aryans; it threatened their theories of superiority. Unfortunately for them, Germans loved jazz just as much as everyone else. People who visited other countries brought records home, and you could buy them from American sailors in Hamburg. There was a lively black market.

Werner had lots of discs, of course. He had everything: a car, modern clothes, cigarettes, money. He was still Carla's dream boy, though he always went for girls older than she—women, really. Everyone assumed he went to bed with them. Carla was a virgin.

Werner's earnest friend Heinrich von Kessel immediately came up to them and started to dance with Frieda. He wore a black jacket and waistcoat, which looked dramatic with his longish dark hair. He was devoted to Frieda. She liked him—she enjoyed talking to clever men—but she would not go out with him because he was too old, twenty-five or twenty-six.

Soon a boy Carla did not know came and danced with her, and the evening was off to a good start.

She abandoned herself to the music: the irresistible sexual drumbeat, the suggestively crooned lyrics, the exhilarating trumpet solos, the joyous flight of the clarinet. She whirled and kicked, let her skirt flare outrageously high, fell into the arms of her partner and sprang out again.

When they had danced for an hour or so, Werner put on a slow tune. Frieda and Heinrich began dancing cheek to cheek. There was no one available whom Carla liked enough for slow dancing, so she left the room and went to get a Coke. Germany was not at war with America, so Coca-Cola syrup was imported and bottled in Germany.

To her surprise Werner followed her out, leaving someone else to put on records for a while. She was flattered that the most attractive man in the room wanted to talk to her.

She told him about Kurt being moved to Akelberg, and Werner said the same thing had happened to his brother, Axel, who was fifteen. Axel had been born with spina bifida. "Could the same treatment work for both of them?" he said with a frown.

"I doubt it, but I don't really know," Carla said.

"Why is it that medical men never explain what they're doing?" Werner said irritably.

She laughed humorlessly. "They think that if ordinary people understand medicine they won't hero-worship doctors any longer."

"Same principle as a conjurer: it's more impressive if you don't know how it's done," said Werner. "Doctors are as egocentric as anyone else."

"More so," said Carla. "As a nurse, I know."

She told him about the leaflet she had read on the train. Werner said: "How did you feel about it?"

Carla hesitated. It was dangerous to speak honestly about such things. But she had known Werner all her life, he had always been left-wing, and he was a Swing Kid. She could trust him. She said: "I'm pleased someone is opposing the Nazis. It shows that not all Germans are paralyzed by fear."

"There are lots of things you can do against the Nazis," he said quietly. "Not just wearing lipstick."

She assumed he meant she could distribute such leaflets. Could he be involved in such activity? No, he was too much of a playboy. Heinrich might be different: he was very intense.

"No, thanks," she said. "I'm too scared."

They finished their Cokes and returned to the storeroom. It was packed now, with hardly room enough to dance.

To Carla's surprise, Werner asked her for the last dance. He put on Bing Crosby singing "Only Forever." Carla was thrilled. He held her close and they swayed, rather than danced, to the slow ballad.

At the end, by tradition, someone turned off the light for a minute, so that couples could kiss. Carla was embarrassed: she had known Werner since they were children. But she had always been attracted to him, and now she turned her face up eagerly. As she had expected, he kissed her expertly, and she returned the kiss with enthusiasm. To her delight she felt his hand gently grasp her breast. She encouraged him by opening her mouth. Then the light came on and it was all over.

"Well," she said breathlessly, "that was a surprise."

He gave his most charming smile. "Perhaps I can surprise you again sometime."

## ii

Carla was passing through the hall, on her way to the kitchen for breakfast, when the phone rang. She picked up the handset. "Carla von Ulrich."

She heard Frieda's voice. "Oh, Carla, my little brother's dead!"

"What?" Carla could hardly believe it. "Frieda, I'm so sorry! Where did it happen?"

"In that hospital." Frieda was sobbing.

Carla recalled Werner telling her that Axel had been sent to the same Akelberg hospital as Kurt. "How did he die?"

"Appendicitis."

"That's terrible." Carla was sad for her friend, but also suspicious. She had had a bad feeling when Professor Willrich spoke to them a month ago about the new treatment for Kurt. Had it been more experimental than he had let on? Could it have actually been dangerous? "Do you know any more?"

"We just got a short letter. My father is enraged. He phoned the hospital but he wasn't able to speak to the senior people."

"I'll come round to your house. I'll be there in a few minutes."

"Thanks."

Carla hung up and went into the kitchen. "Axel Franck has died at that hospital in Akelberg," she said.

Her father, Walter, was looking at the morning post. "Oh!" he said. "Poor Monika." Carla recalled that Axel's mother, Monika Franck, had once been in love with Walter, according to family legend. The look of concern on Walter's face was so pained that Carla wondered if he had had a slight tendresse for Monika, despite being in love with Maud. How complicated love was.

Carla's mother, who was now Monika's best friend, said: "She must be devastated."

Walter looked down at the post again and said in a tone of surprise: "Here's a letter for Ada."

The room went quiet.

Carla stared at the white envelope as Ada took it from Walter.

Ada did not receive many letters.

Erik was home—it was the last day of his short leave—so there were four people watching as Ada opened the envelope.

Carla held her breath.

Ada drew out a typed letter on headed paper. She read the message quickly, gasped, then screamed.

"No!" said Carla. "It can't be!"

Maud jumped up and put her arms around Ada.

Walter took the letter from Ada's fingers and read it. "Oh, dear, how terribly sad," he said. "Poor little Kurt." He put the paper down on the breakfast table.

Ada began to sob. "My little boy, my dear little boy, and he died without his mother—I can't bear it!"

Carla fought back tears. She felt bewildered. "Axel *and* Kurt?" she said. "At the same time?"

She picked up the letter. It was printed with the name of the hospital and its address in Akelberg. It read:

> Dear Mrs. Hempel,
> I regret to inform you of the sad death of your son, Kurt

Walter Hempel, age eight years. He passed away on 4 April at this hospital as a result of a burst appendix. Everything possible was done for him but to no avail. Please accept my deepest condolences.

It was signed by the senior physician.

Carla looked up. Her mother was sitting next to Ada, arm around her, holding her hand as she sobbed.

Carla was grief-stricken, but more alert than Ada. She spoke to her father in a shaky voice. "There's something wrong."

"What makes you say that?"

"Look again." She handed him the letter. "Appendicitis."

"What is the significance?"

"Kurt had had his appendix removed."

"I remember," her father said. "He had an emergency operation, just after his sixth birthday."

Carla's sorrow was mixed with angry suspicion. Had Kurt been killed by a dangerous experiment that the hospital was now trying to cover up? "Why would they lie?" she said.

Erik banged his fist on the table. "Why do you say it is a lie?" he cried. "Why do you always accuse the establishment? This is obviously a mistake! Some typist has made a copying error!"

Carla was not so sure. "A typist working in a hospital is likely to know what an appendix is."

Erik said furiously: "You will seize upon even this personal tragedy as a way of attacking those in authority!"

"Be quiet, you two," said their father.

They looked at him. There was a new tone in his voice. "Erik may be right," he said. "If so, the hospital will be perfectly happy to answer questions and give further details of how Kurt and Axel died."

"Of course they will," said Erik.

Walter went on: "And if Carla is right, they will try to discourage inquiries, withhold information, and intimidate the parents of the dead children by suggesting that their questions are somehow illegitimate."

Erik looked less comfortable about that.

Half an hour ago Walter had been a shrunken man. Now somehow he seemed to fill his suit again. "We will find out as soon as we start asking questions."

Carla said: "I'm going to see Frieda."

Her mother said: "Don't you have to go to work?"

"I'm on the late shift."

Carla phoned Frieda, told her that Kurt was dead, too, and said she was coming to talk about it. She put on her coat, hat, and gloves, then wheeled her bicycle outside. She was a fast rider and it took her only a quarter of an hour to get to the Francks' villa in Schöneberg.

The butler let her in and told her the family were still in the dining room. As soon as she walked in, Frieda's father, Ludwig Franck, bellowed at her: "What did they tell you at the Wannsee children's home?"

Carla did not much like Ludwig. He was a right-wing bully and he had supported the Nazis in the early days. Perhaps he had changed his views: many businessmen had by now, though they showed little sign of the humility that ought to go with having been so wrong.

She did not answer immediately. She sat down at the table and looked at the family: Ludwig, Monika, Werner, and Frieda, and the butler hovering in the background. She collected her thoughts.

"Come on, girl, answer me!" Ludwig demanded. He had in his hand a letter that looked very like Ada's, and he was waving it angrily.

Monika put a restraining hand on her husband's arm. "Take it easy, Ludi."

"I want to know!" he said.

Carla looked at his pink face and little black mustache. He was in an agony of grief, she saw. In other circumstances she would have refused to speak to someone so rude. But he had an excuse for his bad manners, and she decided to overlook them. "The director, Professor Willrich, told us there was a new treatment for Kurt's condition."

"The same as he told us," said Ludwig. "What kind of treatment?"

"I asked him that question. He said I would not be able to understand it. I persisted, and he said it involved drugs, but he did not give any further information. May I see your letter, Herr Franck?"

Ludwig's expression said he was the one who should be asking questions, but he handed the sheet of paper to Carla.

It was exactly the same as Ada's, and Carla had a queer feeling that the typist had done several of them, just changing the names.

Franck said: "How can two boys have died of appendicitis at the same time? It's not a contagious illness."

Carla said: "Kurt certainly did not die of appendicitis, for he had no appendix. It was removed two years ago."

"Right," said Ludwig. "That's enough talk." He snatched the letter from Carla's hand. "I'm going to see someone in the government about this." He went out.

Monika followed him, and so did the butler.

Carla went over to Frieda and took her hand. "I'm so sorry," she said.

"Thank you," Frieda whispered.

Carla went to Werner. He stood up and put his arms around her. She felt a tear fall on her forehead. She was gripped by she did not know what intense emotion. Her heart was full of grief, yet she thrilled to the pressure of his body against hers, and the gentle touch of his hands.

After a long moment Werner stepped back. He said angrily: "My father has phoned the hospital twice. The second time, they told him they had no more information and hung up on him. But I'm going to find out what happened to my brother, and I won't be brushed off."

Frieda said: "Finding out won't bring him back."

"I still want to know. If necessary I'll go to Akelberg."

Carla said: "I wonder if there's anyone in Berlin who could help us."

"It would have to be someone in the government," Werner said.

Frieda said: "Heinrich's father is in the government."

Werner snapped his fingers. "The very man. He used to belong to the Centre Party, but he's a Nazi now, and something important in the Foreign Office."

Carla said: "Will Heinrich take us to see him?"

"He will if Frieda asks him," said Werner. "Heinrich will do anything for Frieda."

Carla could believe that. Heinrich had always been intense about everything he did.

"I'll phone him now," said Frieda.

She went into the hall, and Carla and Werner sat down side by side. He put his arm around her, and she leaned her head on his shoulder. She did not know whether these signs of affection were merely a side effect of the tragedy, or something more.

Frieda came back in and said: "Heinrich's father will see us right away if we go over there now."

They all got into Werner's sports car, squeezing onto the front seat. "I don't know how you keep this car going," Frieda said as he pulled away. "Even Father can't get petrol for private use."

"I tell my boss it's for official business," he said. Werner worked for an important general. "But I don't know how much longer I can get away with it."

The von Kessel family lived in the same suburb. Werner drove there in five minutes.

The house was luxurious, though smaller than the Francks'. Heinrich met them at the door and showed them into a living room with leather-bound books and an old German wood carving of an eagle.

Frieda kissed him. "Thank you for doing this," she said. "It probably wasn't easy—I know you don't get on so well with your father."

Heinrich beamed with pleasure.

His mother brought them coffee and cake. She seemed a warm, simple person. When she had served them, she left, like a maid.

Heinrich's father, Gottfried, came in. He had the same thick straight hair, but it was silver instead of black.

Heinrich said: "Father, here are Werner and Frieda Franck, whose father manufactures People's Radios."

"Ah, yes," said Gottfried. "I have seen your father in the Herrenklub."

"And this is Carla von Ulrich—I believe you know her father, too."

"We were colleagues at the German embassy in London," Gottfried said carefully. "That was in 1914." Clearly he was not so pleased to be reminded of his association with a Social Democrat. He took a piece of cake, clumsily dropped it on the rug, tried ineffectually to pick up the crumbs, then abandoned the effort and sat back.

Carla thought: What is he afraid of?

Heinrich got straight down to the purpose of the visit. "Father, I expect you've heard of Akelberg."

Carla was watching Gottfried closely. There was a split-second flash of something in his expression, but he quickly adopted a pose of indifference. "A small town in Bavaria?" he said.

"There is a hospital there," said Heinrich. "For handicapped people."

"I don't think I was aware of that."

"We think something strange is going on there, and we wondered if you might know about it."

"I certainly don't. What seems to be happening?"

Werner broke in. "My brother died there, apparently of appendicitis. Herr von Ulrich's maid's child died at the same time in the same hospital of the same illness."

"Very sad—but a coincidence, surely?"

Carla said: "My maid's child did not have an appendix. It was removed two years ago."

"I understand why you are keen to ascertain the facts," said Gottfried. "This is deeply unsatisfactory. However, the likeliest explanation would seem to be clerical error."

Werner said: "If so, we would like to know."

"Of course. Have you written to the hospital?"

Carla said: "I wrote to ask when my maid could visit her son. They never replied."

Werner said: "My father telephoned the hospital this morning. The senior physician slammed the phone down on him."

"Oh, dear. Such bad manners. But, you know, this is hardly a Foreign Office matter."

Werner leaned forward. "Herr von Kessel, is it possible that both boys were involved in a secret experiment that went wrong?"

Gottfried sat back. "Quite impossible," he said, and Carla had a feeling he was telling the truth. "That is definitely not happening." He sounded relieved.

Werner looked as if he had run out of questions, but Carla was not satisfied. She wondered why Gottfried seemed so happy about the assurance he had just given. Was it because he was concealing something worse?

She was struck by a possibility so appalling that she could hardly contemplate it.

Gottfried said: "Well, if that's all . . ."

Carla said: "You're very sure, sir, that they were not killed by an experimental therapy that went wrong?"

"Very sure."

"To know for certain that is *not* true, you must have some knowledge of what *is* being done at Akelberg."

"Not necessarily," he said, but all his tension had returned, and she knew she was on to something.

"I remember seeing a Nazi poster," she went on. It was this memory that had triggered her dreadful thought. "There was a picture of a male nurse and a mentally handicapped man. The text said something like: 'Sixty thousand reichsmarks is what this person suffering from hereditary defects costs the people's community during his lifetime. Comrade, that is your money, too!' It was an advertisement for a magazine, I think."

"I have seen some of that propaganda," Gottfried said disdainfully, as if it were nothing to do with him.

Carla stood up. "You're a Catholic, Herr von Kessel, and you brought up Heinrich in the Catholic faith."

Gottfried made a scornful noise. "Heinrich says he's an atheist now."

"But you're not. And you believe that human life is sacred."

"Yes."

"You say that the doctors at Akelberg are not testing dangerous new therapies on handicapped people, and I believe you."

"Thank you."

"But are they doing something else? Something worse?"

"No, no."

"Are they deliberately *killing* the handicapped?"

Gottfried shook his head silently.

Carla moved closer to Gottfried and lowered her voice, as if they were the only two people in the room. "As a Catholic who believes that human life is sacred, will you put your hand on your heart and tell me that mentally ill children are not being murdered at Akelberg?"

Gottfried smiled, made a reassuring gesture, and opened his mouth to speak, but no words came out.

Carla knelt on the rug in front of him. "Would you do that, please? Right now? Here in your house with you are four young Germans, your son and his three friends. Just tell us the truth. Look me in the eye and say that our government does not kill handicapped children."

The silence in the room was total. Gottfried seemed about to speak, but changed his mind. He squeezed his eyes shut, twisted his mouth into a grimace, and bowed his head. The four young people watched his facial contortions in amazement.

At last he opened his eyes. He looked at them one by one, ending with his gaze on his son.

Then he stood up and walked out of the room.

### iii

The next day, Werner said to Carla: "This is awful. We've talked of the same thing for more than twenty-four hours. We'll go mad if we don't do something else. Let's see a movie."

They went to the Kurfürstendamm, a street of theaters and shops, always called the Ku'damm. Most of the good German filmmakers had gone to Hollywood years ago, and the domestic movies were now second-rate. They saw *Three Soldiers,* set during the invasion of France.

The three soldiers were a tough Nazi sergeant, a sniveling complainer who looked a bit Jewish, and an earnest young man. The earnest one asked naïve questions like: "Do the Jews really do us any harm?" and in answer received long, stern lectures from the sergeant. When battle was joined, the sniveler admitted to being a Communist, deserted, and was blown up in an air raid. The earnest young man fought bravely, was promoted to sergeant, and became an admirer of the Führer. The script was dire but the battle scenes were exciting.

Werner held Carla's hand all the way through. She hoped he would kiss her in the dark, but he did not.

As the lights came up, he said: "Well, it was terrible, but it took my mind off things for a couple of hours."

They went outside and found his car. "Shall we go for a drive?" he said. "It could be our last chance. This car goes up on blocks next week."

He drove out to the Grunewald. On the way Carla's thoughts inevitably returned to yesterday's conversation with Gottfried von Kessel. No matter how many times she went over it in her mind, there was no way she could escape the terrible conclusion all four of them had reached at the end of it. Kurt and Axel had not been accidental victims of a dangerous medical experiment, as she had at first thought. Gottfried had denied that convincingly. But he had not been able to bring himself to deny that the government was deliberately killing the handicapped, and lying to their families about it. It was hard to believe, even of people as ruthless and brutal as the Nazis. Yet Gottfried's response had been the clearest example of guilty behavior that Carla had ever witnessed.

When they were in the forest, Werner pulled off the road and drove along a track until the car was hidden by shrubbery. Carla guessed he had brought other girls to this spot.

He turned out the lights, and they were in deep darkness. "I'm going to speak to General Dorn," he said. Dorn was his boss, an important officer in the air force. "What about you?"

"My father says there's no political opposition left, but the churches are still strong. No one who is sincere about their religious beliefs could condone what's being done."

"Are you religious?" Werner asked.

"Not really. My father is. For him, the Protestant faith is part of the German heritage he loves. Mother goes to church with him, though I suspect her theology might be a bit unorthodox. I believe in God, but I can't imagine he cares whether people are Protestant or Catholic or Muslim or Buddhist. And I like singing hymns."

Werner's voice fell to a whisper. "I can't believe in a God who allows the Nazis to murder children."

"I don't blame you."

"What is your father going to do?"

"Speak to the pastor of our church."

"Good."

They were silent for a while. He put his arm around her. "Is this all right?" he said in a half whisper.

She was tense with anticipation, and her voice seemed to fail. Her reply came out as a grunt. She tried again, and managed to say: "If it stops you feeling so sad . . . yes."

Then he kissed her.

She kissed him back eagerly. He stroked her hair, then her breasts. At this point, she knew, a lot of girls would call a halt. They said if you went any further you would lose control of yourself.

Carla decided to risk it.

She touched his cheek while he was kissing her. She caressed his throat with her fingertips, enjoying the feel of the warm skin. She put her hand under his jacket and explored his body, her hand on his shoulder blades and his ribs and his spine.

She sighed when she felt his hand on her thigh, under her skirt. As soon as he touched her between her legs, she parted her knees. Girls said a boy would think you cheap for doing that, but she could not help herself.

He touched her in just the right place. He did not try to put his hand inside her underwear, but stroked her lightly through the cotton. She heard herself making noises in her throat, quietly at first but then louder. Eventually she cried out with pleasure, burying her face in his neck to muffle the sound. Then she had to push his hand away because she felt too sensitive.

She was panting. As she began to get her breath back, she kissed his neck. He touched her cheek lovingly.

After a minute she said: "Can I do something for you?"

"Only if you want to."

She was embarrassed by how much she wanted to. "The only thing is, I've never . . ."

"I know," he said. "I'll show you."

## iv

Pastor Ochs was a portly, comfortable clergyman with a large house, a nice wife, and five children, and Carla feared he would refuse to get involved. But she underestimated him. He had already heard rumors that were troubling his conscience, and he agreed to go with Walter to the Wannsee children's home. Professor Willrich could hardly refuse a visit from an interested clergyman.

They decided to take Carla with them, because she had witnessed the interview with Ada. The director might find it more difficult to change his story in front of her.

On the train, Ochs suggested he should do the talking. "The director is probably a Nazi," he said. Most people in senior jobs nowadays were party members. "He will naturally see a former Social Democrat deputy as an enemy. I will play the role of unbiased arbitrator. That way, I believe, we may learn more."

Carla was not sure about that. She felt her father would be a more expert questioner. But Walter went along with the pastor's suggestion.

It was spring, and the weather was warmer than on Carla's last visit. There were boats on the lake. Carla decided to ask Werner to come out here for a picnic. She wanted to make the most of him before he drifted off to another girl.

Professor Willrich had a fire blazing, but a window was open, letting in a fresh breeze off the water.

The director shook hands with Pastor Ochs and Walter. He gave Carla a brief glance of recognition, then ignored her. He invited them to sit down, but Carla saw there was angry hostility behind his superficial courtesy. Clearly he did not relish being questioned. He picked up one of his pipes and played with it nervously. He was less arrogant today, confronted by two mature men rather than a couple of young women.

Ochs opened the discussion. "Herr von Ulrich and others in my congregation are concerned, Professor Willrich, about the mysterious deaths of several handicapped children known to them."

"No children have died mysteriously here," Willrich shot back. "In fact no child has died here in the last two years."

Ochs turned to Walter. "I find that very reassuring, Walter. Don't you?"

"Yes," said Walter.

Carla did not, but she kept her mouth shut for the moment.

Ochs went on unctuously: "I feel sure that you give your charges the best possible care."

"Yes." Willrich looked a little less anxious.

"But you do send children from here to other hospitals?"

"Of course, if another institution can offer a child some treatment not available here."

"And when a child is transferred, I suppose you are not necessarily kept informed about his treatment or his condition thereafter."

"Exactly!"

"Unless they come back."

Willrich said nothing.

"Have any come back?"

"No."

Ochs shrugged. "Then you cannot be expected to know what happened to them."

"Precisely."

Ochs sat back and spread his hands in a gesture of openness. "So you have nothing to hide!"

"Nothing at all."

"Some of those transferred children have died."

Willrich said nothing.

Ochs gently persisted. "That's true, isn't it?"

"I cannot answer you with any certain knowledge, Herr Pastor."

"Ah!" said Ochs. "Because even if one of those children died, you would not be notified."

"As we said before."

"Forgive me the repetition, but I simply want to establish beyond doubt that you cannot be asked to shed light on those deaths."

"Not at all."

Once again Ochs turned to Walter. "I think we're clearing matters up splendidly."

Walter nodded.

Carla wanted to say *Nothing has been cleared up!*

But Ochs was speaking again. "Approximately how many children have you transferred in, say, the last twelve months?"

"Ten," said Willrich. "Exactly." He smiled complacently. "We scientific men prefer not to deal in approximations."

"Ten patients, out of . . . ?"

"Today we have one hundred and seven children here."

"A very small proportion!" said Ochs.

Carla was getting angry. Ochs was obviously on Willrich's side! Why was her father swallowing this?

Ochs said: "And did those children suffer from one common condition, or a variety?"

"A variety." Willrich opened a folder on his desk. "Idiocy; Down's syndrome; microcephaly; hydrocephaly; malformations of limbs, head, and spinal column; and paralysis."

"These are the types of patients you were instructed to send to Akelberg."

That was a jump. It was the first mention of Akelberg, and the first suggestion that Willrich had received instructions from a higher authority. Perhaps Ochs was more subtle than he had seemed.

Willrich opened his mouth to say something, but Ochs forestalled him with another question. "Were they all to receive the same special treatment?"

Willrich smiled. "Again, I was not informed, so I cannot tell you."

"You simply complied—"

"With my instructions, yes."

Ochs smiled. "You're a judicious man. You choose your words carefully. Were the children all ages?"

"Initially the program was restricted to children under three, but later it was expanded to benefit all ages, yes."

Carla noted the mention of a "program." That had not been admitted before. She began to realize that Ochs was cleverer than he might have at first appeared.

Ochs spoke his next sentence as if confirming something already stated. "And all handicapped Jewish children were included, irrespective of their particular disability."

There was a moment of silence. Willrich looked shocked. Carla wondered how Ochs knew that about Jewish children. Perhaps he did not; he might have been guessing.

After a pause, Ochs added: "Jewish children, and those of mixed race, I should have said."

Willrich did not speak, but gave a slight nod.

Ochs went on: "It's unusual, in this day and age, for Jewish children to be given preference, isn't it?"

Willrich looked away.

The pastor stood up, and when he spoke again, his voice rang with anger. "You have told me that ten children suffering from a range of illnesses, who could not possibly all benefit from the same treatment, were sent away to a special hospital from which they never returned; and that Jews got priority. What did you think happened to them, Herr Professor Doctor Willrich? In God's name, *what did you think*?"

Willrich looked as if he would cry.

"You may say nothing, of course," Ochs said more quietly. "But one day you will be asked the same question by a higher authority, in fact by the highest of all authorities."

He stretched out his arm and pointed a condemning finger.

"And on that day, my son, you *will* answer."

With that he turned around and left the room.

Carla and Walter followed him out.

**V**

Inspector Thomas Macke smiled. Sometimes the enemies of the state did his job for him. Instead of working in secret, and hiding away where they were difficult to find, they identified themselves to him and generously provided irrefutable evidence of their crimes. They were like fish that did not require bait and a hook but simply jumped out of the river into the fisherman's basket and begged to be fried.

Pastor Ochs was one such.

Macke read his letter again. It was addressed to the justice minister, Franz Gürtner.

> Dear Minister,
> Is the government killing handicapped children? I ask you
> this question bluntly because I must have a plain answer.

What a fool! If the answer was no, this was a criminal libel; if yes, Ochs was guilty of revealing state secrets. Could he not figure that out for himself?

> After it became impossible to ignore rumors circulating
> in my congregation, I visited the Wannsee Children's
> Nursing Home and spoke to its director, Professor Willrich.
> His responses were so unsatisfactory that I became
> convinced something terrible is going on, something that is
> presumably a crime and unquestionably a sin.

The man had the nerve to write of crimes! Did it not occur to him that accusing government agencies of illegal acts was itself an illegal act? Did he imagine he was living in a degenerate liberal democracy?

Macke knew what Ochs was complaining about. The program was called Aktion T4 after its address, 4 Tiergarten Strasse. The agency was officially the Charitable Foundation for Cure and Institutional Care, though it was supervised by Hitler's personal office, the Chancellery of the Führer. Its job was to arrange the painless deaths of handicapped people who could not survive without costly care. It had done splendid work in the last couple of years, disposing of tens of thousands of useless people.

The problem was that German public opinion was not yet sophisticated enough to understand the need for such deaths, so the program had to be kept quiet.

Macke was in on the secret. He had been promoted to inspector and had at last been admitted to the Nazi Party's elite paramilitary Schutzstaffel, the SS. He had been briefed on Aktion T4 when he was assigned to the Ochs case. He felt proud: he was a real insider now.

Unfortunately, people had been careless, and there was a danger that the secret of Aktion T4 would get out.

It was Macke's job to plug the leak.

Preliminary inquiries had swiftly revealed that there were three men to be silenced: Pastor Ochs, Walter von Ulrich, and Werner Franck.

Franck was the elder son of a radio manufacturer who had been an important early supporter of the Nazis. The manufacturer himself, Ludwig Franck, had initially made furious demands for information about the death of his disabled younger son, but had quickly fallen silent after a threat to close his factories. Young Werner, a fast-rising officer in the Air Ministry, had persisted in asking troubling questions, trying to involve his influential boss, General Dorn.

The Air Ministry, said to be the largest office building in Europe, was an ultramodern edifice occupying an entire block of Wilhelm Strasse, just around the corner from Gestapo headquarters in Prinz Albrecht Strasse. Macke walked there.

In his SS uniform he was able to ignore the guards. At the reception desk he barked: "Take me to Lieutenant Werner Franck immediately."

The receptionist took him up in an elevator and along a corridor to an open door leading into a small office. The young man at the desk did not at first look up from the papers in front of him. Observing him, Macke guessed he was about twenty-two years old. Why was he not with a front-line unit, bombing England? The father had probably pulled strings, Macke thought resentfully. Werner looked like a son of privilege: tailored uniform, gold rings, and overlong hair that was distinctly unmilitary. Macke despised him already.

Werner wrote a note with a pencil, then looked up. The amiable expression on his face died quickly when he saw the SS uniform, and Macke noted with interest a flash of fear. The boy immediately tried to cover up with a show of bonhomie, standing up deferentially and smiling a welcome, but Macke was not fooled.

"Good afternoon, Inspector," said Werner. "Please be seated."

"*Heil* Hitler," said Macke.

"*Heil* Hitler. How can I help you?"

"Sit down and shut up, you foolish boy," Macke spat.

Werner struggled to hide his fear. "My goodness, what can I have done to incur such wrath?"

"Don't presume to question me. Speak when you're spoken to."

"As you wish."

"From this moment on you will ask no further questions about your brother, Axel."

Macke was surprised to see a momentary look of relief pass over Werner's face. That was puzzling. Had he been afraid of something else, something more frightening than the simple order to stop asking questions about his brother? Could Werner be involved in other subversive activities?

Probably not, Macke thought on reflection. Most likely Werner was relieved he was not being arrested and taken to the basement in Prinz Albrecht Strasse.

Werner was not yet completely cowed. He summoned the nerve to say: "Why should I not ask how my brother died?"

"I told you not to question me. Be aware that you are being treated gently only because your father has been a valued friend of the Nazi Party. Were it not for that, *you* would be in *my* office." That was a threat everyone understood.

"I'm grateful for your forbearance," Werner said, struggling to retain a shred of dignity. "But I want to know who killed my brother, and why."

"You will learn no more, regardless of what you do. But any further inquiries will be regarded as treason."

"I hardly need to make further inquiries, after this visit from you. It is now clear that my worst suspicions were right."

"I require you to drop your seditious campaign immediately."

Werner stared defiantly back but said nothing.

Macke said: "If you do not, General Dorn will be informed that there are questions about your loyalty." Werner could be in no doubt about what that meant. He would lose his cozy job here in Berlin and be dispatched to a barracks on an airstrip in northern France.

Werner looked less defiant, more thoughtful.

Macke stood up. He had spent enough time here. "Apparently General Dorn finds you a capable and intelligent assistant," he said. "If you do the right thing, you may continue in that role." He left the room.

He felt edgy and dissatisfied. He was not sure he had succeeded in crushing Werner's will. He had sensed a bedrock defiance that remained untouched.

He turned his mind to Pastor Ochs. A different approach would be required for him. Macke returned to Gestapo headquarters and collected a small team: Reinhold Wagner, Klaus Richter, and Günther Schneider. They took a black Mercedes 260D, the Gestapo's favorite car, unobtrusive because many Berlin taxis were the same model and color. In the early days, the Gestapo had been encouraged to make themselves visible and let the public see the brutal way they dealt with opposition. However, the terrorization of the German people had been accomplished long ago, and open violence was no longer necessary. Nowadays the Gestapo acted discreetly, always with a cloak of legality.

They drove to Ochs's house next to the large Protestant church in

Mitte, the central district. In the same way that Werner might think he was protected by his father, so Ochs probably imagined his church made him safe. He was about to learn otherwise.

Macke rang the bell; in the old days they would have kicked the door down, just for effect.

A maid opened the door, and he walked into a broad, well-lit hallway with polished floorboards and heavy rugs. The other three followed him in. "Where is your master?" Macke said pleasantly to the maid.

He had not threatened her, but all the same she was frightened. "In his study, sir," she said, and she pointed to a door.

Macke said to Wagner: "Get the women and children together in the next room."

Ochs opened the study door and looked into the hall, frowning. "What on earth is going on?" he said indignantly.

Macke walked directly toward him, forcing him to step back and allow Macke to enter the room. It was a small, well-appointed den, with a leather-topped desk and shelves of biblical commentaries. "Close the door," said Macke.

Reluctantly, Ochs did as he was told; then he said: "You'd better have a very good explanation for this intrusion."

"Sit down and shut up," said Macke.

Ochs was dumbfounded. Probably he had not been told to shut up since he was a boy. Clergymen were not normally insulted, even by policemen. But the Nazis ignored such enfeebling conventions.

"This is an outrage!" Ochs managed at last. Then he sat down.

Outside the room, a woman's voice was raised in protest: the wife, presumably. Ochs paled when he heard it, and rose from his chair.

Macke pushed him back down. "Stay where you are."

Ochs was a heavy man, and taller than Macke, but he did not resist.

Macke loved to see these pompous types deflated by fear.

"Who are you?" said Ochs.

Macke never told them. They could guess, of course, but it was more frightening if they did not know for sure. Afterward, in the unlikely event that anyone asked questions, the whole team would swear that they had begun by identifying themselves as police officers and showing their badges.

He went out. His men were hustling several children into the parlor. Macke told Reinhold Wagner to go into the study and keep Ochs there. Then he followed the children into the other room.

There were flowered curtains, family photographs on the mantelpiece, and a set of comfortable chairs upholstered in a checked fabric. It was a nice home and a nice family. Why could they not be loyal to the Reich and mind their own business?

The maid was by the window, hand over her mouth as if to stop herself crying out. Four children clustered around Ochs's wife, a plain, heavy-breasted woman in her thirties. She held a fifth child in her arms, a girl of about two years with blond ringlets.

Macke patted the girl's head. "And what is this one's name?" he said.

Frau Ochs was terrified. She whispered: "Lieselotte. What do you want with us?"

"Come to Uncle Thomas, little Lieselotte," said Macke, holding out his arms.

"No!" Frau Ochs cried. She clutched the child closer and turned away.

Lieselotte began to cry loudly.

Macke nodded to Klaus Richter.

Richter grabbed Frau Ochs from behind, pulling her arms back, forcing her to let go of the child. Macke took Lieselotte before she fell. The child wriggled like a fish, but he just held her tighter, as he would have held a cat. She wailed louder.

A boy of about twelve flung himself at Macke, small fists pounding ineffectually. It was about time he learned to respect authority, Macke decided. He put Lieselotte on his left hip, then, with his right hand, picked the boy up by his shirtfront and threw him across the room, making sure he landed in an upholstered chair. The boy yelled in fear and Frau Ochs screamed. The chair went over backward and the boy tumbled to the floor. He was not really hurt but he began to cry.

Macke took Lieselotte out into the hall. She screamed at the top of her voice for her mother. Macke put her down. She ran to the parlor door and banged on it, screeching in terror. She had not yet learned to turn doorknobs, Macke noted.

Leaving the child in the hallway, Macke reentered the study. Wagner was by the door, guarding it; Ochs was standing in the middle of the room, white with fear. "What are you doing to my children?" he said. "Why is Lieselotte screaming?"

"You will write a letter," Macke said.

"Yes, yes, anything," Ochs said, going to the leather-topped desk.

"Not now, later."

"All right."

Macke was enjoying this. Ochs's collapse was complete, unlike Werner's. "A letter to the justice minister," he went on.

"So that's what this is about."

"You will say you now realize there is no truth in the allegations you made in your first letter. You were misled by secret Communists. You will apologize to the minister for the trouble you have caused by your incautious actions, and assure him that you will never again speak of the matter to anyone."

"Yes, yes, I will. What are they doing to my wife?"

"Nothing. She is screaming because of what will happen to her if you fail to write the letter."

"I want to see her."

"It will be worse for her if you annoy me with stupid demands."

"Of course, I'm sorry. I beg your pardon."

The opponents of Nazism were so weak. "Write the letter this evening, and mail it in the morning."

"Yes. Should I send you a copy?"

"It will come to me anyway, you idiot. Do you think the minister himself reads your insane scribbling?"

"No, no, of course not. I see that."

Macke went to the door. "And stay away from people like Walter von Ulrich."

"I will, I promise."

Macke went out, beckoning Wagner to follow. Lieselotte was sitting on the floor screaming hysterically. Macke opened the parlor door and summoned Richter and Schneider.

They left the house.

"Sometimes violence is quite unnecessary," Macke said reflectively as they got into the car.

Wagner took the wheel and Macke gave him the address of the von Ulrich house.

"And then again, sometimes it's the simplest way," he added.

Von Ulrich lived in the neighborhood of the church. His house was a spacious old building that he evidently could not afford to maintain. The paint was peeling, the railings were rusty, and a broken window had been patched with cardboard. This was not unusual: wartime austerity meant that many houses were not kept up.

The door was opened by a maid. Macke presumed this was the woman whose handicapped child had started the whole problem—but he did not bother to inquire. There was no point in arresting girls.

Walter von Ulrich stepped into the hall from a side room.

Macke remembered him. He was the cousin of the Robert von Ulrich whose restaurant Macke and his brother had bought eight years ago. In those days he had been proud and arrogant. Now he wore a shabby suit, but his manner was still bold. "What do you want?" he said, attempting to sound as if he still had the power to demand explanations.

Macke did not intend to waste much time here. "Cuff him," he said.

Wagner stepped forward with the handcuffs.

A tall, handsome woman appeared and stood in front of von Ulrich. "Tell me who you are and what you want," she demanded. She was obviously the wife. She had the hint of a foreign accent. No surprise there.

Wagner slapped her face, hard, and she staggered back.

"Turn around and put your wrists together," Wagner said to von Ulrich. "Otherwise I'll knock her teeth down her throat."

Von Ulrich obeyed.

A pretty young woman dressed in a nurse's uniform came rushing down the stairs. "Father!" she said. "What's happening?"

Macke wondered how many more people there might be in the house. He felt a twinge of anxiety. An ordinary family could not overcome trained police officers, but a crowd of them might create enough of a fracas for von Ulrich to slip away.

However, the man himself did not want a fight. "Don't confront them!" he said to his daughter in a voice of urgency. "Stay back!"

The nurse looked terrified and did as she was told.

Macke said: "Put him in the car."

Wagner walked von Ulrich out of the door.

The wife began to sob.

The nurse said: "Where are you taking him?"

Macke went to the door. He looked at the three women: the maid, the wife, and the daughter. "All this trouble," he said, "for the sake of an eight-year-old moron. I will never understand you people."

He went out and got into the car.

They drove the short distance to Prinz Albrecht Strasse. Wagner parked at the back of the Gestapo headquarters building alongside a dozen identical black cars. They all got out.

They took von Ulrich in through a back door and down the stairs to the basement, and put him in a white-tiled room.

Macke opened a cupboard and took out three long, heavy clubs like American baseball bats. He gave one to each of his assistants.

"Beat the shit out of him," he said, and he left them to it.

## vi

Captain Volodya Peshkov, head of the Berlin section of Red Army Intelligence, met Werner Franck at the Invalids' Cemetery beside the Berlin-Spandau Ship Canal.

It was a good choice. Looking around the graveyard carefully,

Volodya was able to confirm that no one followed him or Werner in. The only other person present was an old woman in a black head scarf, and she was on her way out.

Their rendezvous was the tomb of General von Scharnhorst, a large pedestal bearing a slumbering lion made of melted-down enemy cannons. It was a sunny day in spring, and the two young spies took off their jackets as they walked among the graves of German heroes.

After the Hitler-Stalin pact almost two years ago, Soviet espionage had continued in Germany, and so had surveillance of Soviet embassy staff. Everyone saw the treaty as temporary, though no one knew how temporary. So counterintelligence agents were still tailing Volodya everywhere.

They ought to be able to tell when he was going out on a genuine secret intelligence mission, he thought, for that was when he shook them off. If he went out to buy a frankfurter for lunch, he let them shadow him. He wondered whether they were smart enough to figure that out.

"Have you seen Lili Markgraf lately?" said Werner.

She was a girl they had both dated at different times in the past. Volodya had now recruited her, and she had learned to encode and decode messages in the Red Army Intelligence cipher. Of course Volodya would not tell Werner that. "I haven't seen her for a while," he lied. "How about you?"

Werner shook his head. "Someone else has won my heart." He seemed bashful. Perhaps he was embarrassed about belying his playboy reputation. "Anyway, why did you want to see me?"

"We have received devastating information," Volodya said. "News that will change the course of history—if it is true."

Werner looked skeptical.

Volodya went on: "A source has told us that Germany will invade the Soviet Union in June." He thrilled again as he said it. It was a huge triumph for Red Army Intelligence, and a terrible threat to the USSR.

Werner pushed a lock of hair out of his eyes in a gesture that probably made girls' hearts beat faster. He said: "A reliable source?"

It was a journalist in Tokyo who was in the confidence of the German ambassador there, but was in fact a secret Communist. Everything he had said so far had turned out to be true. But Volodya could not tell Werner that. "Reliable," he said.

"So you believe it?"

Volodya hesitated. That was the problem. Stalin did not believe it. He thought it was Allied disinformation intended to sow mistrust between himself and Hitler. Stalin's skepticism about this intelligence coup had devastated Volodya's superiors, souring their jubilation. "We seek verification," he said.

Werner looked around at the trees in the graveyard coming into leaf. "I hope to God it's true," he said with sudden savagery. "It will finish the damned Nazis."

"Yes," said Volodya. "If the Red Army is prepared."

Werner was surprised. "Are you not prepared?"

Once again Volodya was not able to tell Werner the whole truth. Stalin believed the Germans would not attack before they had defeated the British, fearing a war on two fronts. While Britain continued to defy Germany, the Soviet Union was safe, he thought. In consequence the Red Army was nowhere near prepared for a German invasion.

"We *will be* prepared," Volodya said, "if you can get me verification of the invasion plan."

He could not help enjoying a moment of self-importance. His spy could be the key.

Werner said: "Unfortunately, I can't help you."

Volodya frowned. "What do you mean?"

"I can't get verification, or otherwise, of this information, nor can I get you anything else. I'm about to be fired from my job at the Air Ministry. I'll probably be posted to France—or, if your intelligence is correct, sent to invade the Soviet Union."

Volodya was horrified. Werner was his best spy. It was Werner's information that had won Volodya promotion to captain. He found he could hardly breathe. With an effort he said: "What the hell happened?"

"My brother died in a home for the handicapped, and the same thing happened to my girlfriend's godson, and we're asking too many questions."

"Why would you be demoted for that?"

"The Nazis are killing off handicapped people, but it's a secret program."

Volodya was momentarily diverted from his mission. "What? They just murder them?"

"So it seems. We don't know the details yet. But if they had nothing to hide, they wouldn't have punished me—and others—for asking questions."

"How old was your brother?"

"Fifteen."

"God! Still a child!"

"They're not going to get away with it. I refuse to shut up."

They stopped in front of the tomb of Manfred von Richthofen, the air ace. It was a huge slab, six feet high and twice as wide. On it was carved, in elegant capital letters, the single word RICHTHOFEN. Volodya always found its simplicity moving.

He tried to recover his composure. He told himself that the Soviet secret police murdered people, after all, especially anyone suspected of disloyalty. The head of the NKVD, Lavrentiy Beria, was a torturer whose favorite trick was to have his men pull a couple of pretty girls off the street for him to rape as his evening's entertainment, according to rumor. But the thought that Communists could be as bestial as Nazis was no consolation. One day, he reminded himself, the Soviets would get rid of Beria and his kind; then they could begin to build true Communism. Meanwhile, the priority was to defeat the Nazis.

They came to the canal wall and stood there, watching a barge make its slow progress along the waterway, belching oily black smoke. Volodya mulled over Werner's alarming confession. "What would happen if you stopped investigating these deaths of handicapped children?" he asked.

"I'd lose my girlfriend," Werner said. "She's as angry about it as I am."

Volodya was struck by the scary thought that Werner might reveal the truth to his girlfriend. "You certainly couldn't tell her the real reason for your change of mind," he said emphatically.

Werner looked stricken, but he did not argue.

Volodya realized that by persuading Werner to abandon his campaign he would be helping the Nazis hide their crimes. He pushed the uncomfortable thought aside. "But would you be allowed to keep your job with General Dorn if you promised to drop the matter?"

"Yes. That's what they want. But I'm not letting them murder my brother, then cover it up. They'll send me to the front line, but I won't shut up."

"What do you think they'll do to you when they realize how determined you are?"

"They'll throw me in some camp."

"And what good will that do?"

"I just can't lie down for this."

Volodya had to get Werner back on his side, but so far he had failed to get through. Werner had an answer for everything. He was a smart guy. That was why he was such a valuable spy.

"What about the others?" Volodya said.

"What others?"

"There must be thousands more handicapped adults and children. Are the Nazis going to kill them all?"

"Probably."

"You certainly won't be able to stop them, if you're in a prison camp."

For the first time, Werner did not have a comeback.

Volodya turned away from the water and surveyed the cemetery. A young man in a suit was kneeling at a small tombstone. Was he a tail? Volodya watched carefully. The man was shaking with sobs. He seemed genuine: counterintelligence agents were not good actors.

"Look at him," Volodya said to Werner.

"Why?"

"He's grieving. Which is what you're doing."

"So what?"

"Just watch."

After a minute the man got up, wiped his face with a handkerchief, and walked away.

Volodya said: "Now he's happy. That's what grieving is about. It doesn't achieve anything. It just makes you feel better."

"You think my asking questions is just to make me feel better."

Volodya turned and looked him in the eye. "I don't criticize you," he said. "You want to discover the truth, and shout it out loud. But think about it logically. The only way to end this is to bring down the regime. And the only way that's going to happen is if the Nazis are defeated by the Red Army."

"Maybe."

Werner was weakening, Volodya perceived with a surge of hope. "Maybe?" he said. "Who else is there? The British are on their knees, desperately trying to fight off the Luftwaffe. The Americans are not interested in European squabbles. Everyone else supports the Fascists." He put his hands on Werner's shoulders. "The Red Army is your only hope, my friend. If we lose, those Nazis will be murdering handicapped children—and Jews, and Communists, and homosexuals—for a thousand more blood-soaked years."

"Hell," said Werner. "You're right."

## vii

Carla and her mother went to church on Sunday. Maud was distraught about Walter's arrest and desperate to find out where he had been taken. Of course the Gestapo refused to give out any information. But Pastor Ochs's church was a fashionable one, people came in from the wealthier suburbs to attend, and the congregation included some powerful men, one or two of whom might be able to make inquiries.

Carla bowed her head and prayed that her father might not be beaten or tortured. She did not really believe in prayer but she was desperate enough to try anything.

She was glad to see the Franck family, sitting a few rows in front. She studied the back of Werner's head. He wore his hair curled a little at the neck, in contrast with most of the men, who were close-cropped. She had touched his neck and kissed his throat. He was adorable. He was easily the nicest boy who had ever kissed her. Every night before sleeping she relived that evening when they had driven to the Grunewald.

But she was not in love with him, she told herself.

Not yet.

When Pastor Ochs entered, she saw at once that he had been crushed. The change in him was horrifying. He walked slowly to the lectern, head bent and shoulders slumped, causing a few in the congregation to exchange concerned whispers. He recited the prayers without expression, then read the sermon from a book. Carla had been a nurse for two years now and she recognized in him the symptoms of depression. She guessed that he, too, had received a visit from the Gestapo.

She noticed that Frau Ochs and the five children were not in their usual places in the front pew.

As they sang the last hymn, Carla vowed that she would not give up, scared though she was. She still had allies: Frieda and Werner and Heinrich. But what could they do?

She wished she had solid proof of what the Nazis were doing. She had no doubts, herself, that they were exterminating the handicapped—this Gestapo crackdown made it obvious. But she could not convince others without concrete evidence.

How could she get it?

After the service she walked out of the church with Frieda and Werner. Drawing them away from their parents, she said: "I think we have to get evidence of what's going on."

Frieda immediately saw what she meant. "We should go to Akelberg," she said. "Visit the hospital."

Werner had proposed that, right at the start, but they had decided to begin their inquiries here in Berlin. Now Carla considered the idea afresh. "We'd need permits to travel."

"How could we manage that?"

Carla snapped her fingers. "We both belong to the Mercury Cycling Club. They can get permits for bicycle holidays." It was just the kind of thing the Nazis were keen on, healthy outdoor exercise for young people.

"Could we get inside the hospital?"

"We could try."

Werner said: "I think you should drop the whole thing."

Carla was startled. "What do you mean?"

"Pastor Ochs has obviously been scared half to death. This is a very dangerous business. You could be imprisoned, tortured. And it won't bring back Axel or Kurt."

She stared at him incredulously. "You want us to give it up?"

"You must give it up. You're talking as if Germany were a free country! You'll get yourselves killed, both of you."

"We have to take risks!" Carla said angrily.

"Leave me out of this," he said. "I've had a visit from the Gestapo, too."

Carla was immediately concerned. "Oh, Werner—what happened?"

"Just threats, so far. If I ask any more questions, I'll be sent to the front line."

"Oh, well, thank God it's not worse."

"It's bad enough."

The girls were silent for a few moments; then Frieda said what Carla was thinking. "This is more important than your job—you must see that."

"Don't tell me what I must see," Werner replied. He was superficially angry, but underneath that, Carla could tell he was in fact ashamed. "It's not your career that's at stake," he went on. "And you haven't met the Gestapo yet."

Carla was astonished. She thought she knew Werner. She would have been sure he would see this the way she did. "Actually, I have met them," she said. "They arrested my father."

Frieda was appalled. "Oh, Carla!" she said, and put her arm around Carla's shoulders.

"We can't find out where he is," Carla added.

Werner showed no sympathy. "Then you should know better than to defy them!" he said. "They would have arrested you, too, except that Inspector Macke thinks girls aren't dangerous."

Carla wanted to cry. She had been on the point of falling in love with Werner, and now he turned out to be a coward.

Frieda said: "Are you saying you won't help us?"

"Yes."

"Because you want to keep your job?"

"It's pointless—you can't beat them!"

Carla was furious with him for his cowardice and defeatism. "We can't just let this happen!"

"Open confrontation is insane. There are other ways to oppose them."

Carla said: "How, by working slowly, like those leaflets say? That won't stop them killing handicapped children!"

"Defying the government is suicidal!"

"Anything else is cowardice!"

"I refuse to be judged by two girls!" With that he stalked off.

Carla fought back tears. She could not cry in front of two hundred people standing outside the church in the sunshine. "I thought he was different," she said.

Frieda was upset, but baffled, too. "He *is* different," she said. "I've known him all my life. Something else is going on, something he's not telling us about."

Carla's mother approached. She did not notice Carla's distress, which was unusual. "Nobody knows anything!" she said despairingly. "I can't find out where your father might be."

"We'll keep trying," Carla said. "Didn't he have friends at the American embassy?"

"Acquaintances. I've asked them already, but they haven't come up with any information."

"We'll ask them again tomorrow."

"Oh, God, I suppose there are a million German wives in the same situation as me."

Carla nodded. "Let's go home, Mother."

They walked back slowly, not talking, each with her own thoughts. Carla was angry with Werner, the more so because she had badly mistaken his character. How could she have fallen for someone so weak?

They reached their street. "I shall go to the American embassy in the morning," Maud said as they approached the house. "I'll wait in the lobby all day if necessary. I'll beg them to do something. If they really want to, they can make a semiofficial inquiry about the brother-in-law of a British government minister. Oh! Why is our front door open?"

Carla's first thought was that the Gestapo had paid them a second visit. But there was no black car parked at the curb. And a key was sticking out of the lock.

Maud stepped into the hall and screamed.

Carla rushed in after her.

There was a man lying on the floor covered in blood.

Carla managed to stop herself screaming. "Who is it?" she said.

Maud knelt beside the man. "Walter," she said. "Oh, Walter, what have they done to you?"

Then Carla saw that it was her father. He was so badly injured he was almost unrecognizable. One eye was closed, his mouth was swollen into a single huge bruise, and his hair was covered with congealed blood. One arm was twisted oddly. The front of his jacket was stained with vomit.

Maud said: "Walter, speak to me, speak to me!"

He opened his ruined mouth and groaned.

Carla suppressed the hysterical grief that bubbled up inside her by shifting into professional gear. She fetched a cushion and propped up his head. She got a cup of water from the kitchen and dribbled a little on his lips. He swallowed and opened his mouth for more. When he seemed to have had enough, she went into his study and got a bottle of schnapps and gave him a few drops. He swallowed them and coughed.

"I'm going for Dr. Rothmann," Carla said. "Wash his face and give him more water. Don't try to move him."

Maud said: "Yes, yes—hurry!"

Carla wheeled her bike out of the house and pedaled away. Dr. Rothmann was not allowed to practise any longer—Jews could not be doctors—but, unofficially, he still attended poor people.

Carla pedaled furiously. How had her father got home? She guessed they had brought him in a car, and he had managed to stagger from the curbside into the house, then collapsed.

She reached the Rothmann house. Like her own home, it was in bad repair. Most of the windows had been broken by Jew-haters. Frau Rothmann opened the door. "My father has been beaten," Carla said breathlessly. "The Gestapo."

"My husband will come," said Frau Rothmann. She turned and called up the stairs. "Isaac!"

The doctor came down.

"It's Herr von Ulrich," said Frau Rothmann.

The doctor picked up a canvas shopping bag that stood near the door. Because he was banned from practising medicine, Carla guessed he could not carry anything that looked like an instrument case.

They left the house. "I'll cycle on ahead," Carla said.

When she got home, she found her mother sitting on the doorstep, weeping.

"The doctor's on his way!" Carla said.

"He is too late," said Maud. "Your father's dead."

## viii

Volodya was outside the Wertheim department store, just off the Alexander Platz, at half past two in the afternoon. He patrolled the area several times, looking for men who might be plainclothes police officers. He was sure he had not been followed here, but it was not impossible that a passing Gestapo agent might recognize him and wonder what he was up to. A busy place with crowds was the best camouflage, but it was not perfect.

Was the invasion story true? If so, Volodya would not be in Berlin much longer. He would kiss good-bye to Gerda and Sabine. He would presumably return to Red Army Intelligence headquarters in Moscow. He looked forward to spending some time with his family. His sister, Anya, had twin babies whom he had never seen. And he felt he could do with a rest. Undercover work meant continual stress: losing Gestapo shadows, holding clandestine meetings, recruiting agents, and worrying about betrayal. He would welcome a year or two at headquarters, assuming the Soviet Union survived that long. Alternatively, he might be sent on another foreign posting. He fancied Washington. He had always had a yen to see America.

He took from his pocket a ball of crumpled tissue paper and dropped it into a litter bin. At one minute to three he lit a cigarette, although he did not smoke. He dropped the lighted match carefully into the bin so that it landed in the nest of tissue paper. Then he walked away.

Seconds later, someone cried: "Fire!"

Just when everyone in the vicinity was looking at the fire in the litter bin, a taxi drew up at the entrance to the store, a regular black Mercedes 260D. A handsome young man in the uniform of an air force lieutenant jumped out. As the lieutenant was paying the driver, Volodya jumped into the cab and slammed the door.

On the floor of the cab, where the driver could not see it, was a copy of *Neues Volk*, the Nazi magazine of racial propaganda. Volodya picked it up, but did not read it.

"Some idiot has set fire to a litter bin," said the driver.

"Hotel Adlon," Volodya said, and the car pulled away.

He riffled the pages of the magazine and verified that a buff-colored envelope was concealed within.

He longed to open it, but he waited.

He got out of the cab at the hotel, but did not go inside. Instead he walked through the Brandenburg Gate and into the park. The trees were showing bright new leaves. It was a warm spring day and there were plenty of afternoon strollers.

The magazine seemed to burn the skin of Volodya's hand. He found an unobtrusive bench and sat down.

He unfolded the magazine and, behind its screen, he opened the buff-colored envelope.

He drew out a document. It was a carbon copy, typed and a bit faint, but legible. It was headed:

Directive No. 21: Case "Barbarossa"

Friedrich Barbarossa was the German emperor who had led the Third Crusade in the year 1189.

The text began: "The German Wehrmacht must be prepared, even before the completion of the war against England, to overthrow Russia in a rapid campaign."

Volodya found himself gasping for breath. This was dynamite. The Tokyo spy had been right, and Stalin wrong. And the Soviet Union was in mortal danger.

Heart pounding, Volodya looked at the end of the document. It was signed: "Adolf Hitler."

He scanned the pages, looking for a date, and found one. The invasion was scheduled for May 15, 1941.

Next to this was a penciled note in Werner Franck's handwriting: "The date has now been changed to 22 June."

"Oh, my God, he's done it," Volodya said aloud. "He's confirmed the invasion."

He put the document back into the envelope and the envelope into the magazine.

This changed everything.

He got up from the bench and walked back to the Soviet embassy to give them the news.

## ix

There was no railway station at Akelberg, so Carla and Frieda got off at the nearest stop, ten miles away, and wheeled their bicycles off the train.

They wore shorts, sweaters, and utilitarian sandals, and they had put their hair up in plaits. They looked like members of the League of German Girls, the Bund Deutscher Mädel, or BDM. Such girls often took cycling holidays. Whether they did anything other than cycle, especially during the evenings in the spartan hostels at which they stayed, was the subject of much speculation. Boys said BDM stood for "Bubi Drück Mir," "Baby, Do Me."

Carla and Frieda consulted their map, then rode out of town in the direction of Akelberg.

Carla thought about her father every hour of every day. She knew she would never get over the horror of finding him savagely beaten and dying. She had cried for days. But alongside her grief was another emotion: rage. She was not merely going to be sad. She was going to do something about it.

Maud, distraught with grief, had at first tried to persuade Carla not to go to Akelberg. "My husband is dead. My son is in the army. I don't want my daughter to put her life on the line, too!" she had wailed.

After the funeral, when horror and hysteria gave way to a calmer, more profound mourning, Carla had asked her what Walter would have wanted. Maud had thought for a long time. It was not until the next day that she answered. "He would have wanted you to carry on the fight."

It was hard for Maud to say it, but they both knew it was true.

Frieda had had no such discussion with her parents. Her mother, Monika, had once loved Walter, and was devastated by his death; nonetheless she would have been horrified if she knew what Frieda was doing. Her father, Ludi, would have locked her in the cellar. But they believed she was going bicycling. If anything, they might have suspected she was meeting some unsuitable boyfriend.

The countryside was hilly, but they were both in good shape, and an hour later they coasted down a slope into the small town of Akelberg. Carla felt apprehensive: they were entering enemy territory.

They went into a café. There was no Coca-Cola. "This isn't Berlin!" said the woman behind the counter, with as much indignation as if they had asked to be serenaded by an orchestra. Carla wondered why someone who disliked strangers would run a café.

They got glasses of Fanta, a German product, and took the opportunity to refill their water bottles.

They did not know the precise location of the hospital. They needed to ask directions, but Carla was concerned about arousing suspicion. The local Nazis might take an interest in strangers asking questions. As they were paying, Carla said: "We're supposed to meet the rest of our group at the crossroads by the hospital. Which way is that?"

The woman would not meet her eye. "There's no hospital here."

"The Akelberg Medical Institution," Carla persisted, quoting from the letterhead.

"Must be another Akelberg."

Carla thought she was lying. "How strange," she said, keeping up the pretense. "I hope we're not in the wrong place."

They wheeled their bikes along the high street. There was nothing else for it, Carla thought: she had to ask the way.

A harmless-looking old man was sitting on a bench outside a bar, enjoying the afternoon sunshine. "Where's the hospital?" Carla asked him, covering her anxiety with a cheery veneer.

"Through the town and up the hill on your left," he said. "Don't go inside, though—not many people come out!" He cackled as if he had made a joke.

The directions were a bit vague, but might suffice, Carla thought. She decided she would not draw further attention by asking again.

A woman in a head scarf took the arm of the old man. "Pay no attention to him—he doesn't know what he's saying," she said, looking worried. She jerked him to his feet and hustled him along the sidewalk. "Keep your mouth shut, you old fool," she muttered.

It seemed these people had an inkling of what was going on in their neighborhood. Fortunately their main reaction was to act surly and not get involved. Perhaps they would not be in a hurry to give information to the police or the Nazi Party.

Carla and Frieda went farther along the street and found the youth hostel. There were thousands of such places in Germany, designed to cater to exactly such people as they were pretending to be, athletic youngsters on a vigorous open-air holiday. They checked in. The facilities were primitive, with three-tiered bunk beds, but the place was cheap.

It was late afternoon when they cycled out of town. After a mile they came to a left turn. There was no signpost, but the road led uphill, so they took it.

Carla's apprehension intensified. The nearer they got, the harder it would be to seem innocent under questioning.

A mile later they saw a large house in a park. It did not seem to be walled or fenced, and the road led up to the door. Once again there were no signs.

Unconsciously, Carla had been expecting a hilltop castle of forbidding gray stone, with barred windows and ironbound oak doors. But this was a Bavarian country house, with steep overhanging roofs, wooden balconies, and a little bell tower. Surely nothing as horrible as child murder could go on here? It also seemed small, for a hospital. Then she saw that a modern extension had been added to one side, with a tall chimney.

They dismounted and leaned their bikes against the side of the building. Carla's heart was in her mouth as they walked up the steps to the entrance. Why were there no guards? Because no one would be so foolhardy as to try to investigate the place?

There was no bell or knocker, but when Carla pushed the door, it opened. She stepped inside, and Frieda followed. They found themselves in a cool hall with a stone floor and bare white walls. There were several rooms off the hall, but all the doors were closed. A middle-aged woman in spectacles was coming down a broad staircase. She wore a smart gray dress. "Yes?" she said.

"Hello," said Frieda casually.

"What are you doing? You can't come in here."

Frieda and Carla had prepared a story. "I just wanted to visit the place where my brother died," Frieda said. "He was fifteen—"

"This isn't a public facility!" the woman said indignantly.

"Yes, it is." Frieda had been brought up in a wealthy family, and was not cowed by minor functionaries.

A nurse of about nineteen appeared from a side door and stared at them. The woman in the gray dress spoke to her. "Nurse König, fetch Herr Römer immediately."

The nurse hurried away.

The woman said: "You should have written in advance."

"Did you not get my letter?" said Frieda. "I wrote to the senior physician." This was not true; Frieda was improvising.

"No such letter has been received!" Clearly the woman felt that Frieda's outrageous request could not possibly have gone unnoticed.

Carla was listening. The place was strangely quiet. She had dealt with physically and mentally handicapped people, adults and children, and they were not often silent. Even through these closed doors she should have been able to hear shouts, laughter, crying, voices raised in protest, and nonsensical ravings. But there was nothing. It was more like a morgue.

Frieda tried a new tack. "Perhaps you can tell me where my brother's grave is. I'd like to visit it."

"There are no graves. We have an incinerator." She immediately corrected herself. "A cremation facility."

Carla said: "I noticed the chimney."

Frieda said: "What happened to my brother's ashes?"

"They will be sent to you in due course."

"Don't mix them up with anyone else's, will you?"

The woman's neck reddened in a blush, and Carla guessed they did mix up the ashes, figuring that no one would know.

Nurse König reappeared, followed by a burly man in the white uniform of a male nurse. The woman said: "Ah, Römer. Please escort these girls off the premises."

"Just a minute," said Frieda. "Are you quite sure you're doing the right thing? I only wanted to see the place where my brother died."

"Quite sure."

"Then you won't mind letting me know your name."

There was a second's hesitation. "Frau Schmidt. Now please leave us."
Römer moved toward them in a menacing way.

"We're going," Frieda said frostily. "We have no intention of giving Herr Römer an excuse to molest us."

The man changed course and opened the door for them.

They went out, climbed on their bikes, and rode down the drive. Frieda said: "Do you think she believed our story?"

"Totally," said Carla. "She didn't even ask our names. If she had suspected the truth, she would have called the police right away."

"But we didn't learn much. We saw the chimney. But we didn't find anything we could call proof."

Carla felt a bit down. Getting evidence was not as easy as it sounded.

They returned to the hostel. They washed and changed and went out in search of something to eat. The only café was the one with the grumpy proprietress. They ate potato pancakes with sausage. Afterward they went to the town's bar. They ordered beers and spoke cheerfully to the other customers, but no one wanted to talk to them. This in itself was suspicious. People everywhere were wary of strangers, for anyone might be a Nazi snitch, but even so Carla wondered how many towns there were where two young girls could spend an hour in a bar without anyone even trying to flirt with them.

They returned to the hostel for an early night. Carla could not think what else to do. Tomorrow they would return home empty-handed. It seemed incredible that she should know about these awful killings yet be unable to stop them. She felt so frustrated she wanted to scream.

It occurred to her that Frau Schmidt—if that really was her name—might have further thoughts about her visitors. At the time, she had taken Carla and Frieda for what they claimed to be, but she might develop suspicions later, and call the police just to be safe. If that happened, Carla and Frieda would not be hard to find. There were just five people at the hostel tonight and they were the only girls. She listened in fear for the fatal knock on the door.

If they were questioned, they would tell part of the truth, saying that Frieda's brother and Carla's godson had died at Akelberg, and they wanted to visit their graves, or at least see the place where they died and spend a few minutes in remembrance. The local police might buy that story. But if they checked with Berlin, they would swiftly learn the connection with Walter von Ulrich and Werner Franck, two men who had been investigated by the Gestapo for asking disloyal questions about Akelberg. Then Carla and Frieda would be deep in trouble.

As they were getting ready to go to bed in the uncomfortable-looking bunks, there was a knock at the door.

Carla's heart stopped. She thought of what the Gestapo had done to her father. She knew she could not withstand torture. In two minutes she would name every Swing Kid she knew.

Frieda, who was less imaginative, said: "Don't look so scared!" and opened the door.

It was not the Gestapo but a small, pretty blond girl. It took Carla a moment to recognize her as Nurse König, out of uniform.

"I have to speak to you," she said. She was distressed, breathless and tearful.

Frieda invited her in. She sat on a bunk bed and wiped her eyes on the sleeve of her dress. Then she said: "I can't keep it inside any longer."

Carla glanced at Frieda. They were thinking the same thing. Carla said: "Keep what inside, Nurse König?"

"My name is Ilse."

"I'm Carla and this is Frieda. What's on your mind, Ilse?"

Ilse spoke in a voice so low they could hardly hear her. She said: "We kill them."

Carla could hardly breathe. She managed to say: "At the hospital?"

Ilse nodded. "The poor people who come in on the gray buses. Children, even babies, and old people, grandmothers. They're all more or less helpless. Sometimes they're horrid, dribbling and soiling themselves, but they can't help it, and some of them are really sweet and innocent. It makes no difference—we kill them all."

"How do you do it?"

"An injection of morphium-scopolamin."

Carla nodded. It was a common anesthetic, fatal in overdose. "What about the special treatments they're supposed to have?"

Ilse shook her head. "There are no special treatments."

Carla said: "Ilse, let me get this clear. Do they kill every patient that comes here?"

"Every one."

"As soon as they arrive?"

"Within a day, no more than two."

It was what Carla had suspected, but even so, the stark reality was horrifying, and she felt nauseated.

After a minute she said: "Are there any patients there now?"

"Not alive. We were giving injections this afternoon. That's why Frau Schmidt was so frightened when you walked in."

"Why don't they make it harder for strangers to get into the building?"

"They think guards and barbed wire around a hospital would make it obvious that something sinister was going on. Anyway, no one ever tried to visit before you."

"How many people died today?"

"Fifty-two."

Carla's skin crawled. "The hospital killed fifty-two people this afternoon, around the time we were there?"

"Yes."

"So they're all dead now?"

Ilse nodded.

An intention had been germinating in Carla's mind, and now she resolved to carry it out. "I want to see," she said.

Ilse looked frightened. "What do you mean?"

"I want to go inside the hospital and see those corpses."

"They're burning them already."

"Then I want to see that. Can you sneak us in?"

"Tonight?"

"Right now."

"Oh, God."

Carla said: "You don't have to do anything. You've already been brave, just by talking to us. If you don't want to do any more, it's okay. But if we're going to put a stop to this, we need proof."

"Proof?"

"Yes. Look, the government is ashamed of this project—that's why it's secret. The Nazis know that ordinary Germans won't tolerate the killing of children. But people prefer to believe it's not happening, and it's easy for them to dismiss a rumor, especially if they hear it from a young girl. So we have to prove it to them."

"I see." Ilse's pretty face took on a look of grim determination. "All right, then. I'll take you."

Carla stood up. "How do you normally get there?"

"Bicycle. It's outside."

"Then we'll all ride."

They went out. Darkness had fallen. The sky was partly cloudy, and the starlight was faint. They used their cycle lights as they rode out of town and up the hill. When they came in sight of the hospital, they switched off their lights and continued on foot, pushing their bikes. Ilse took them by a forest path that led to the rear of the building.

Carla smelled an unpleasant odor, somewhat like a car's exhaust. She sniffed.

Ilse whispered: "The incinerator."

"Oh, no!"

They hid the bikes in a shrubbery and walked silently to the back door. It was unlocked. They went in.

The corridors were bright. There were no shadowy corners: the place was lit like the hospital it pretended to be. If they met someone, they would be seen clearly. Their clothes would give them away immediately as intruders. What would they do then? Run, probably.

Ilse walked quickly along a corridor, turned a corner, and opened a door. "In here," she whispered.

They walked in.

Frieda let out a squeal of horror and covered her mouth.

Carla whispered: "Oh, my soul."

In a large, cold room were about thirty dead people, all lying faceup on tables, naked. Some were fat, some thin; some old and withered, some children, and one a baby of about a year. A few were bent and twisted, but most appeared physically normal.

Each one had a small adhesive bandage on the upper left arm, where the needle had gone in.

Carla heard Frieda crying softly.

She steeled her nerves. "Where are the others?" she whispered.

"Already gone to the furnace," Ilse replied.

They heard voices coming from behind the double door at the far end of the room.

"Back outside," Ilse said.

They stepped into the corridor. Carla closed the door all but a crack, and peeped through. She saw Herr Römer and another man push a hospital trolley through the doors.

The men did not look in Carla's direction. They were arguing about soccer. She heard Römer say: "It's only nine years ago that we won the national championship. We beat Eintracht Frankfurt two–nil."

"Yes, but half your best players were Jews, and they've all gone."

Carla realized they were talking about the Bayern Munich team.

Römer said: "The old days will come back, if only we play the right tactics."

Still arguing, the two men went to a table where a fat woman lay dead. They took her by the shoulders and knees, then unceremoniously swung her onto the trolley, grunting with the effort.

They moved the trolley to another table and put a second corpse on top of the first.

When they had three, they wheeled the trolley out.

Carla said: "I'm going to follow them."

She crossed the morgue to the double doors, and Frieda and Ilse followed her. They passed into an area that felt more industrial than medical: the walls were painted brown, the floor was concrete, and there were store cupboards and tool racks.

They looked around a corner.

They saw a large room like a garage, with harsh lighting and deep shadows. The atmosphere was warm, and there was a faint smell of cooking. In the middle of the space was a steel box large enough to hold a motorcar. A metal canopy led from the top of the box through the roof. Carla realized she was looking at a furnace.

The two men lifted a body off the trolley and shifted it to a steel conveyor belt. Römer pushed a button on the wall. The belt moved, a door opened, and the corpse passed into the furnace.

They put the next corpse on the belt.

Carla had seen enough.

She turned and motioned the others back. Frieda bumped into Ilse, who let out an involuntary cry. They all froze.

They heard Römer say: "What was that?"

"A ghost," the other replied.

Römer's voice was shaky. "Don't joke about such things!"

"Are you going to pick up the other end of this stiff, or what?"

"All right, all right."

The three girls hurried back to the morgue. Seeing the remaining bodies, Carla suffered a wave of grief about Ada's Kurt. He had lain here, with an adhesive bandage on his arm, and had been thrown onto the conveyor belt and disposed of like a bag of garbage. But you're not forgotten, Kurt, she thought.

They went out into the corridor. As they turned toward the back door, they heard footsteps and the voice of Frau Schmidt. "What is taking those two men so long?"

They hurried along the corridor and through the door. The moon was out, and the park was brightly lit. Carla could see the shrubbery where they had hidden the bikes, two hundred yards away across the grass.

Frieda came out last, and in her rush she let the door bang.

Carla thought fast. Frau Schmidt was likely to investigate the noise. The three girls might not reach the shrubbery before she opened the door. They had to hide. "This way!" Carla hissed, and she ran around the corner of the building. The others followed.

They flattened themselves against the wall. Carla heard the door open. She held her breath.

There was a long pause. Then Frau Schmidt muttered something unintelligible, and the door banged again.

Carla peeped around the corner. Frau Schmidt had gone.

The three girls ran across the lawn and retrieved their bicycles.

They pushed the bikes along the forest path and emerged onto the road. They switched on their lights, mounted up, and pedaled away. Carla felt euphoric. They had got away with it!

As they approached the town, triumph gave way to more practical considerations. What had they achieved, exactly? What would they do next?

They must tell someone what they had seen. She was not sure whom. In any event they had to convince someone. Would they be believed? The more she thought about it, the less sure she was.

When they reached the hostel and dismounted, Ilse said: "Thank goodness that's over. I've never been so scared in all my life."

"It's not over," said Carla.

"What do you mean?"

"It won't be over until we've closed that hospital, and any others like it."

"How can you do that?"

"We need you," Carla said to her. "You're the proof."

"I was afraid you were going to say that."

"Will you come with us, tomorrow, when we go back to Berlin?"

There was a long pause; then Ilse said: "Yes, I will."

## X

Volodya Peshkov was glad to be home. Moscow was at its summery best, sunny and warm. On Monday, June 30, he returned to Red Army Intelligence headquarters beside the Khodynka airfield.

Both Werner Franck and the Tokyo spy had been right: Germany had invaded the Soviet Union on June 22. Volodya and all the personnel at the Soviet embassy in Berlin had returned to Moscow, by ship and train. Volodya had been prioritized, and made it back faster than most: some were still traveling.

Volodya now realized how much Berlin had been getting him down. The Nazis were tedious in their self-righteousness and triumphalism. They were like a winning soccer team at the after-match party, getting drunker and more boring and refusing to go home. He was sick of them.

Some people might say that the USSR was similar, with its secret police, its rigid orthodoxy, and its puritan attitudes to such pleasures as abstract painting and fashion. They were wrong. Communism was a work in progress, with mistakes being made on the road to a fair society. The NKVD with its torture chambers was an aberration, a cancer in the body of Communism. One day it would be surgically removed. But probably not in wartime.

Anticipating the outbreak of war, Volodya had long ago equipped his Berlin spies with clandestine radios and codebooks. Now it was more vital than ever that the handful of brave anti-Nazis should continue to pass information to the Soviets. Before leaving he had destroyed all records of their names and addresses, which now existed only in his head.

He had found both his parents fit and well, although his father looked harassed. It was his responsibility to prepare Moscow for air raids. Volodya had gone to see his sister, Anya, her husband, Ilya Dvorkin, and the twins, now eighteen months old: Dmitriy, called Dimka, and Tatiana, called Tania. Unfortunately their father struck Volodya as being just as ratlike and contemptible as ever.

After a pleasant day at home, and a good night's sleep in his old room, he was ready to start work again.

He passed through the metal detector at the entrance to the intelligence building. The familiar corridors and staircases touched a nostalgic chord, even if they were drab and utilitarian. Walking through the building he half-expected people to come up and congratulate him: many of them must have known he had been the one to confirm Barbarossa. But no one did; perhaps they were being discreet.

He entered a large open area of typists and file clerks and spoke to the middle-aged woman receptionist. "Hello, Nika—are you still here?"

"Good morning, Captain Peshkov," she said, not as warmly as he might have hoped. "Colonel Lemitov would like to see you right away."

Like Volodya's father, Lemitov had not been important enough to suffer in the great purge of the late thirties, and now he had been promoted to fill the place of an unlucky former superior. Volodya did not know much about the purge, but he found it hard to believe that so many senior men had been disloyal enough to merit such punishment. Not that Volodya knew exactly what the punishment was. They could be in exile in Siberia, or in prison somewhere, or dead. All he knew was that they had vanished.

Nika added: "He has the big office at the end of the main corridor now."

Volodya walked through the open room, nodding and smiling at one or two acquaintances, but again he got the feeling that he was not the hero he had expected to be. He tapped on Lemitov's door, hoping the boss might shed some light.

"Come in."

Volodya entered, saluted, and closed the door behind him.

"Welcome back, Captain." Lemitov came around his desk. "Between you and me, you did a great job in Berlin. Thank you."

"I'm honored, sir," said Volodya. "But why is this between you and me?"

"Because you contradicted Stalin." He held up a hand to forestall protest. "Stalin doesn't know it was you, of course. But all the same, people around here are nervous, after the purge, of associating with anyone who takes the wrong line."

"What should I have done?" Volodya said incredulously. "Faked wrong intelligence?"

Lemitov shook his head emphatically. "You did exactly the right thing—don't get me wrong. And I've protected you. But just don't expect people around here to treat you like a champion."

"Okay," said Volodya. Things were worse than he had imagined.

"You have your own office now, at least—three doors down. You'll need to spend a day or so catching up."

Volodya took that for dismissal. "Yes, sir," he said. He saluted and left.

His office was not luxurious—a small room with no carpet—but he had it to himself. He was out of touch with the progress of the German invasion, having been busy trying to get home as fast as possible. Now he put his disappointment aside and began to read the reports of the battlefield commanders for the first week of the war.

As he did so, he became more and more desolate.

The invasion had taken the Red Army by surprise.

It seemed impossible, but the evidence covered his desk.

On June 22, when the Germans attacked, many forward units of the Red Army had had *no live ammunition.*

That was not all. Planes had been lined up neatly on airstrips with no camouflage, and the Luftwaffe had destroyed twelve hundred Soviet aircraft in the first few hours of the war. Army units had been thrown at the advancing Germans without adequate weapons, with no air cover, and lacking intelligence about enemy positions—and in consequence had been annihilated.

Worst of all, Stalin's standing order to the Red Army was that retreat was forbidden. Every unit had to fight to the last man, and officers were expected to shoot themselves to avoid capture. Troops were never allowed to regroup at a new, stronger defensive position. This meant that every defeat turned into a massacre.

Consequently the Red Army was hemorrhaging men and equipment.

The warning from the Tokyo spy, and Werner Franck's confirmation, had been ignored by Stalin. Even when the attack began, Stalin had at first insisted it was a limited act of provocation, done by German army officers without the knowledge of Hitler, who would put a stop to it as soon as he found out.

By the time it became undeniable that it was not a provocation but the largest invasion in the history of warfare, the Germans had overwhelmed the Soviets' forward positions. After a week they had pushed three hundred miles inside Soviet territory.

It was a catastrophe—but what made Volodya want to scream out loud was that it could have been avoided.

There was no doubt whose fault it was. The Soviet Union was an autocracy. Only one person made the decisions: Josef Stalin. He had been stubbornly, stupidly, disastrously wrong. And now his country was in mortal danger.

Until now Volodya had believed that Soviet Communism was the true ideology, marred only by the excesses of the secret police, the NKVD. Now he saw that the failure was at the very top. Beria and the NKVD existed only because Stalin permitted them. It was Stalin who was preventing the march to true Communism.

Late that afternoon, as Volodya was staring out of the window over the sunlit airstrip, brooding over what he had learned, he was visited by Kamen. They had been lieutenants together four years ago, fresh out of the Military Intelligence Academy, and had shared a room with two others. In those days Kamen had been the clown, making fun of everyone, daringly mocking pious Soviet orthodoxy. Now he was heavier and seemed more serious. He had grown a small black mustache like that of the foreign minister, Molotov, perhaps to make himself look more mature.

Kamen closed the door behind him and sat down. He took from his pocket a toy, a tin soldier with a key in its back. He wound up the key and placed the toy on Volodya's desk. The soldier swung his arms as if marching, and the clockwork mechanism made a loud ratcheting sound as it wound down.

In a lowered voice Kamen said: "Stalin has not been seen for two days."

Volodya realized that the clockwork soldier was there to swamp any listening device that might be hidden in his office.

He said: "What do you mean, he hasn't been seen?"

"He has not come to the Kremlin, and he is not answering the phone."

Volodya was baffled. The leader of a nation could not just disappear. "What's he doing?"

"No one knows." The soldier ran down. Kamen wound it up and set it going again. "On Saturday night, when he heard that the Soviet Western Army Group had been encircled by the Germans, he said: 'Everything's lost. I give up. Lenin founded our state and we've fucked it up.' Then he went to Kuntsevo." Stalin had a country house near the town of Kuntsevo on the outskirts of Moscow. "Yesterday he didn't show up at the Kremlin at his usual time of midday. When they phoned Kuntsevo, no one answered. Today, the same."

Volodya leaned forward. "Is he suffering"—his voice fell to a whisper—"a mental breakdown?"

Kamen made a helpless gesture. "It wouldn't be surprising. He insisted, against all the evidence, that Germany would not attack us, and now look."

Volodya nodded. It made sense. Stalin had allowed himself to be officially called Father, Teacher, Great Leader, Transformer of Nature, Great Helmsman, Genius of Mankind, the Greatest Genius of All Times and Peoples. But now it had been proved, even to him, that he had been wrong and everyone else right. Men committed suicide in such circumstances.

The crisis was even worse than Volodya had thought. Not only was the Soviet Union under attack and losing; it was also leaderless. This had to be its most perilous moment since the revolution.

But was it also an opportunity? Could it be a chance to get rid of Stalin?

The last time Stalin had appeared vulnerable was in 1924, when Lenin's Testament had said that Stalin was not fit to hold power. Since Stalin had survived that crisis, his power had seemed unassailable, even—Volodya could now see clearly—when his decisions had verged on madness: the purges, the blunders in Spain, the appointment of the sadist Beria as head of the secret police, the pact with Hitler. Was this emergency the occasion, at last, to break his hold?

Volodya hid his excitement from Kamen and everyone else. He hugged his thoughts to himself as he rode the bus home through the soft light of a summer evening. His journey was delayed by a slow-moving convoy of lorries towing antiaircraft guns—presumably being deployed by his father, who was in charge of Moscow's air raid defenses.

Could Stalin be deposed?

He wondered how many Kremlin insiders were asking themselves the same question.

He entered his parents' apartment building, the ten-story Government House, across the Moskva River from the Kremlin. They were out, but his sister was there with the twins, Dimka and Tania. The boy, Dimka, had dark eyes and hair. He held a red pencil and was scribbling messily on an old newspaper. The girl had the same intense blue-eyed stare that Grigori had—and so did Volodya, people said. She immediately showed Volodya her doll.

Also there was Zoya Vorotsyntsev, the astonishingly beautiful physicist Volodya had last seen four years earlier when he was about to leave for Spain. She and Anya had discovered a shared interest in Russian folk music: they went to recitals together, and Zoya played the *gudok,* a three-stringed fiddle. Neither could afford a phonograph, but Grigori had one, and they were listening to a record of a balalaika orchestra. Grigori was not a great music lover but he thought the record sounded jolly.

Zoya was wearing a short-sleeved summer dress the pale color of her blue eyes. When Volodya asked her the conventional question about how she was, she replied sharply: "I'm very angry."

There were lots of reasons for Russians to be angry just now. Volodya asked: "Why's that?"

"My research into nuclear physics has been canceled. All the scientists I work with have been reassigned. I myself am working on improvements to the design of bomb sights."

That seemed very reasonable to Volodya. "We are at war, after all."

"You don't understand," she said. "Listen. When uranium metal undergoes a process called fission, enormous quantities of energy are released. I mean *enormous.* We know this, and Western scientists do, too—we have read their papers in scientific journals."

"Still, the question of bomb sights seems more immediate."

Zoya said angrily: "This process, fission, could be used to create bombs that would be a hundred times more powerful than anything anyone has now. One nuclear explosion could flatten Moscow. What if the Germans make such a bomb and we don't have it? It will be as if they had rifles and we only had swords!"

Volodya said skeptically: "But is there any reason to believe that scientists in other countries are working on a fission bomb?"

"We're sure they are. The concept of fission leads automatically to the idea of a bomb. We thought of it—why shouldn't they? But there's another reason. They published all their early results in the journals— and then they stopped, suddenly, one year ago. There have been no new scientific papers on fission since this time last year."

"And you believe the politicians and generals in the West realized the military potential of the research and made it secret?"

"I can't think of another reason. And yet here in the Soviet Union we have not even begun to prospect for uranium."

"Hmm." Volodya was pretending to be doubtful, but in truth he found it all too credible. Even Stalin's greatest admirers—a group that included Volodya's father, Grigori—did not claim he understood science. And it was all too easy for an autocrat to ignore anything that made him uncomfortable.

"I've told your father," Zoya went on. "He listens to me, but no one listens to him."

"So what are you going to do?"

"What can I do? I'm going to make a damn good bomb sight for our airmen, and hope for the best."

Volodya nodded. He liked that attitude. He liked this girl. She was smart and feisty and a joy to look at. He wondered if she would go to a movie with him.

Talk of physics reminded him of Willi Frunze, who had been his friend at the Berlin Boys' Academy. According to Werner Franck, Willi was a brilliant physicist now studying in England. He might know something about the fission bomb Zoya was so exercised about. And if he was still a Communist, he might be willing to tell what he knew.

Volodya made a mental note to send a cable to the Red Army Intelligence desk in the London embassy.

His parents came in. Father was in full dress uniform, Mother in a coat and hat. They had been to one of the many interminable ceremonies the army loved: Stalin insisted such rituals continue, despite the German invasion, because they were so good for morale.

They cooed over the twins for a few minutes, but Father looked distracted. He muttered something about a phone call and went immediately to his study. Mother began to make supper.

Volodya talked to the three women in the kitchen, but he was desperate to speak to his father. He thought he could guess the subject of Father's urgent phone call: the overthrow of Stalin was being either planned or prevented right now, probably here in this building.

After a few minutes he decided to risk the old man's wrath and interrupt him. He excused himself and went to the study. But his father was just coming out. "I have to go to Kuntsevo," he said.

Volodya longed to know what was going on. "Why?" he said.

Grigori ignored the question. "I've called down for my car, but my chauffeur has gone home. You can drive me."

Volodya was thrilled. He had never been to Stalin's dacha. Now he was going there at a moment of profound crisis.

"Come on," his father said impatiently.

They shouted good-byes from the hallway and went out.

Grigori's car was a black ZIS 101-A, a Soviet copy of an American Packard, with three-speed automatic transmission. Its top speed was about eighty miles per hour. Volodya got behind the wheel and pulled away.

He drove through the Arbat, a neighborhood of craftsmen and intellectuals, and out onto the westward Mozhaisk Highway. "Have you been summoned by Comrade Stalin?" he asked his father.

"No. Stalin has been incommunicado for two days."

"That's what I heard."

"Did you? It's supposed to be secret."

"You can't keep something like that secret. What's happening now?"

"A group of us are going to Kuntsevo to see him."

Volodya asked the key question. "For what purpose?"

"Primarily to find out whether he's alive or dead."

Could he really be dead already, and no one know about it? Volodya wondered. It seemed unlikely. "And if he's alive?"

"I don't know. But whatever happens, I'd rather be there to see it than find out later."

Listening devices did not work in moving cars, Volodya knew—the microphone just picked up engine noise—so he was confident he could not be overheard. Nevertheless he felt fearful as he said the unthinkable. "Could Stalin be overthrown?"

His father answered irritably: "I told you, I don't know."

Volodya was electrified. Such a question demanded a confident negative. Anything else was a yes. His father had admitted the possibility that Stalin could be finished.

Volodya's hopes rose volcanically. "Think what that could be like!" he said joyously. "No more purges! The labor camps will be closed. Young girls will no longer be pulled off the street to be raped by the secret police." He half-expected his father to interrupt, but Grigori just listened with half-closed eyes. Volodya went on: "The stupid phrase 'Trotsky-Fascist spy' will disappear from our language. Army units who find themselves outnumbered and outgunned could retreat, instead of sacrificing themselves uselessly. Decisions will be made rationally, by groups of intelligent men working out what's best for everyone. It's the Communism you dreamed of thirty years ago!"

"Young fool," his father said contemptuously. "The last thing we want at this point is to lose our leader. We're at war and retreating! Our sole aim must be to defend the revolution—whatever it takes. We need Stalin now more than ever."

Volodya felt as if he had been slapped. It was many years since his father had called him a fool.

Was the old man right? Did the Soviet Union need Stalin? The leader had made so many disastrous decisions that Volodya did not see how the country could possibly be worse off with someone else in charge.

They reached their destination. Stalin's home was conventionally called a dacha, but it was not a country cottage. A long, low building with five tall windows each side of a grand entrance, it stood in a pine forest and was painted dull green, as if to hide it. Hundreds of armed troops guarded the gates and the double barbed-wire fence. Grigori pointed to an antiaircraft battery partly concealed by camouflage netting. "I put that there," he said.

The guard at the gate recognized Grigori, but nevertheless asked for their identification documents. Even though Grigori was a general and Volodya a captain in intelligence, they were both patted down for weapons.

Volodya drove up to the door. There were no other cars in front of the house. "We'll wait for the others," his father said.

A few moments later three more ZIS limousines drew up. Volodya recalled that ZIS stood for Zavod Imeni Stalina, Factory Called Stalin. Had the executioners arrived in cars named after their victim?

They all got out, eight middle-aged men in suits and hats, holding in their hands the future of their country. Among them Volodya recognized Foreign Minister Molotov and secret police chief Beria.

"Let's go," said Grigori.

Volodya was astonished. "I'm coming in there with you?"

Grigori reached under his seat and handed Volodya a Tokarev TT-33 pistol. "Put this in your pocket," he said. "If that prick Beria tries to arrest me, you shoot the fucker."

Volodya took it gingerly: the TT-33 had no safety catch. He slipped the gun into his jacket pocket—it was about seven inches long—and got out of the car. There were eight rounds, he recalled, in the magazine of the gun.

They all went inside. Volodya feared he would be patted down again, and his gun discovered, but there was no second check.

The house was painted dark colors and poorly lit. An officer showed the group into what looked like a small dining room. Stalin sat there in an armchair.

The most powerful man in the Eastern Hemisphere appeared

haggard and depressed. Looking up at the group entering the room he said: "Why have you come?"

Volodya gasped. Clearly he thought they were there either to arrest him or to execute him.

There was a long pause, and Volodya realized the group had not planned what to do. How could they, not even knowing whether Stalin was alive?

But what would they do now? Shoot him? There might never be another chance.

At last Molotov stepped forward. "We're asking you to come back to work," he said.

Volodya had to suppress the urge to protest.

But Stalin shook his head. "Can I live up to people's hopes? Can I lead the country to victory?"

Volodya was flabbergasted. Would he really refuse?

Stalin added: "There may be better candidates."

He was giving them a second chance to fire him!

Another member of the group spoke up, and Volodya recognized Marshal Voroshilov. "There's none more worthy," he said.

How did that help? This was hardly the time for naked flattery.

Then his father joined in, saying: "That's right!"

Were they not going to let Stalin go? How could they be so stupid?

Molotov was the first to say something sensible. "We propose to form a war cabinet called the State Defense Committee, a kind of ultra-politburo with a very small membership and sweeping powers."

Stalin quickly interposed: "Who will be its head?"

"You, Comrade Stalin!"

Volodya wanted to shout *No!*

There was another long silence.

At last Stalin spoke. "Very well," he said. "Now, who else shall we have on the committee?"

Beria stepped forward and began to propose the members.

It was all over, Volodya realized, feeling dizzy with frustration and disappointment. They had lost their chance. They could have deposed a tyrant, but they had lacked the nerve. Like the children of a violent father, they feared they could not manage without him.

In fact it was worse than that, he saw with growing despondency. Perhaps Stalin really had had a breakdown—it had certainly seemed real—but he had also made a brilliant political move. All the men who might replace him were here in this room. At the moment when his catastrophically poor judgment had been exposed for all to see, he had forced his rivals to come out and beg him to be their leader again. He had drawn a line under his appalling mistake and given himself a new start.

Stalin was not just back.

He was stronger than ever.

## xi

Who would have the courage to make a public protest about what was going on at Akelberg? Carla and Frieda had seen it with their own eyes, and they had Ilse König as a witness, but now they needed an advocate. There were no elected representatives anymore: all Reichstag deputies were Nazis. There were no real journalists, either, just scribbling sycophants. The judges were all Nazi appointees subservient to the government. Carla had never before realized how much she had been protected by politicians, newspapermen, and lawyers. Without them, she saw now, the government could do anything it liked, even kill people.

Who could they turn to? Frieda's admirer Heinrich von Kessel had a friend who was a Catholic priest. "Peter was the cleverest boy in my class," he told them. "But he wasn't the most popular. A bit upright and stiff-necked. I think he'll listen to us, though."

Carla thought it was worth a try. Her Protestant pastor had been sympathetic, until the Gestapo terrified him into silence. Perhaps the same would happen again. But she did not know what else to do.

Heinrich took Carla, Frieda, and Ilse to Peter's church in Schöneberg early on a Sunday morning in July. Heinrich was handsome in a black suit; the girls all wore their nurses' uniforms, symbols of trustworthiness. They entered by a side door and went into a small, dusty room with a few old chairs and a large wardrobe. They found Father Peter alone, praying. He must have heard them come in, but he remained on his knees for a minute before getting up and turning to greet them.

Peter was tall and thin, with regular features and a neat haircut. He was twenty-seven, Carla calculated, if he was Heinrich's contemporary. He frowned at them, not troubling to conceal his irritation at being disturbed. "I am preparing myself for Mass," he said severely. "I am pleased to see you in church, Heinrich, but you must leave me now. I will see you afterward."

"This is a spiritual emergency, Peter," said Heinrich. "Sit down. We have something important to tell you."

"It could hardly be more important than Mass."

"Yes, it could, Peter, believe me. In five minutes' time you will agree."

"Very well."

"This is my girlfriend, Frieda Franck."

Carla was surprised. Was Frieda his girlfriend now?

Frieda said: "I had a younger brother who was born with spina bifida. Earlier this year he was transferred to a hospital at Akelberg in Bavaria for special treatment. Shortly afterward we got a letter saying he had died of appendicitis."

She turned to Carla, who took up the tale. "My maid had a son born brain-damaged. He, too, was transferred to Akelberg. The maid got an identical letter on the same day."

Peter spread his hands in a so-what gesture. "I have heard this kind of thing before. It's antigovernment propaganda. The Church does not interfere in politics."

What rubbish that was, Carla thought. The Church was up to its neck in politics. But she let it pass. "My maid's son did not have an appendix," she went on. "He had had it removed two years earlier."

"Please," said Peter. "What does this prove?"

Carla felt discouraged. Peter was obviously biased against them.

Heinrich said: "Wait, Peter. You haven't heard it all. Ilse here worked at the hospital in Akelberg."

Peter looked at her expectantly.

"I was raised Catholic, Father," Ilse said.

Carla had not known that.

"I'm not a good Catholic," Ilse went on.

"God is good, not us, my daughter," said Peter piously.

Ilse said: "But I knew that what I was doing was a sin. Yet I did it, because they told me to, and I was frightened." She began to cry.

"What did you do?"

"I killed people. Oh, Father, will God forgive me?"

The priest stared at the young nurse. He could not dismiss this as propaganda: he was looking at a soul in torment. He went pale.

The others were silent. Carla held her breath.

Ilse said: "The handicapped people are brought to the hospital in gray buses. They don't have special treatment. We give them an injection, and they die. Then we cremate them." She looked up at Peter. "Will I ever be forgiven for what I have done?"

He opened his mouth to speak. His words caught in his throat, and he coughed. At last he said quietly: "How many?"

"Usually four. Buses, I mean. There are about twenty-five patients in a bus."

"A hundred people?"

"Yes. Every week."

Peter's proud composure had vanished. His face was pale gray, and his mouth hung open. "A hundred handicapped people a week?"

"Yes, Father."

"What sort of handicap?"

"All sorts, mental and physical. Some senile old people, some deformed babies, men and women, paralyzed or retarded or just helpless."

He had to keep repeating it. "And the staff of the hospital kill them all?"

Ilse sobbed. "I'm sorry. I'm sorry. I knew it was wrong."

Carla watched Peter. His supercilious air had gone. It was a remarkable transformation. After years of hearing the prosperous Catholics of this sylvan suburb confess their little sins, he had suddenly been confronted with raw evil. And he was shocked to his core.

But what would he do?

Peter stood up. He took Ilse by the hands and raised her from her seat. "Come back to the Church," he said. "Confess to your priest. God will forgive you. This much I know."

"Thank you," she whispered.

He released her hands and looked at Heinrich. "It may not be so simple for the rest of us," he said.

Then he turned his back on them and knelt to pray again.

Carla looked at Heinrich, who shrugged. They got up and left the little room, Carla with her arm around the weeping Ilse.

Carla said: "We'll stay for the service. Perhaps he'll speak to us again afterward."

The four of them walked into the nave of the church. Ilse stopped crying and became calmer. Frieda held Heinrich's arm. They took seats among the gathering congregation, prosperous men and plump women and restless children in their best clothes. People such as these would never kill the handicapped, Carla thought. Yet their government did, on their behalf. How had this happened?

She did not know what to expect of Father Peter. Clearly he had believed what they had told him, in the end. He had wanted to dismiss them as politically motivated, but Ilse's sincerity had convinced him. He had been horrified. But he had not made any promises, except that God would forgive Ilse.

Carla looked around the church. The decoration was more colorful than what she was used to in Protestant churches. There were more statues and paintings, more marble and gilding and banners and candles. Protestants and Catholics had fought wars about such trivia, she recalled. How strange it seemed, in a world where children could be murdered, that anyone should care about candles.

The service began. The priests entered in their robes, Father Peter the tallest among them. Carla could not read anything in his facial expression except stern piety.

She sat indifferent through the hymns and prayers. She had prayed for her father, and two hours later had found him cruelly beaten and dying on the floor of their home. She missed him every day, sometimes every hour. Praying had not saved him, nor would it protect those deemed useless by the government. Action was needed, not words.

Thinking of her father brought her brother, Erik, to mind. He was somewhere in Russia. He had written a letter home, jubilantly celebrating the rapid progress of the invasion, and angrily refusing to believe that Walter had been murdered by the Gestapo. Their father had obviously been released unharmed by the Gestapo and then attacked in the street by criminals or Communists or Jews, he asserted. He was living in a fantasy, beyond the reach of reason.

Was the same true of Father Peter?

Peter mounted the pulpit. Carla had not known he was due to preach a sermon. She wondered what he would say. Would he be inspired by what he had heard this morning? Would he speak of something irrelevant, the virtue of modesty or the sin of envy? Or would he close his eyes and devoutly thank God for the German army's continuing victories in Russia?

He stood tall in the pulpit and swept the church with a gaze that might have been arrogant, or proud, or defiant.

"The fifth commandment says: 'Thou shalt not kill.'"

Carla met Heinrich's eyes. What was Peter going to say?

His voice rang out between the echoing stones of the nave. "There is a place in Akelberg, Bavaria, where our government is breaking the commandment a hundred times a week!"

Carla gasped. He was doing it—he was preaching a sermon against the program! This could change everything.

"It makes no difference that the victims are handicapped, or mentally ill, or incapable of feeding themselves, or paralyzed." Peter was letting his anger show. "Helpless babies and senile old people are all God's children, and their lives are as sacred as yours and mine." His voice rose in volume. "To kill them is a mortal sin!" He lifted his right arm and made a fist, and his voice shook with emotion. "I say to you that if we do nothing about it, we sin just as much as the doctors and nurses who administer the lethal injections. If we remain silent . . ." He paused. "If we remain silent, we are murderers, too!"

## xii

Inspector Thomas Macke was furious. He had been made to look a fool in the eyes of Superintendent Kringelein and the rest of his superiors. He had assured them he had plugged the leak. The secret of Akelberg—and hospitals of the same kind in other parts of the country—was safe, he had said. He had tracked down the three troublemakers, Werner Franck, Pastor Ochs, and Walter von Ulrich, and in different ways he had silenced each of them.

And yet the secret had come out.

The man responsible was an arrogant young priest called Peter.

Father Peter was in front of Macke now, naked, strapped by wrists and ankles to a specially constructed chair. He was bleeding from the ears, nose, and mouth, and had vomit all down his chest. Electrodes were attached to his lips, his nipples, and his penis. A strap around his forehead prevented him from breaking his neck while the convulsions shook him.

A doctor sitting beside the priest checked his heart with a stethoscope and looked dubious. "He can't stand much more," he said in a matter-of-fact tone.

Father Peter's seditious sermon had been taken up elsewhere. The bishop of Münster, a much more important clergyman, had preached a similar sermon, denouncing the T4 program. The bishop had called upon Hitler to save the people from the Gestapo, cleverly implying that the Führer could not possibly know about the program, thereby offering Hitler a ready-made alibi.

His sermon had been typed out and duplicated and passed from hand to hand all over Germany.

The Gestapo had arrested every person found in possession of a copy, but to no avail. It was the only time in the history of the Third Reich that there had been a public outcry against any government action.

The clampdown was savage, but it did no good: the duplicates of the sermon continued to proliferate, more clergymen prayed for the handicapped, and there was even a protest march in Akelberg. It was out of control.

And Macke was to blame.

He bent over Peter. The priest's eyes were closed and his breathing was shallow, but he was conscious. Macke shouted in his ear: "Who told you about Akelberg?"

There was no reply.

Peter was Macke's only lead. Investigations in the town of Akelberg had turned up nothing of significance. Reinhold Wagner had been told a story about two girl cyclists who had visited the hospital, but no one knew who they were, and another story about a nurse who had resigned suddenly, writing a letter saying she was getting married in haste, but not revealing who the husband was. Neither clue led anywhere. In any case, Macke felt sure this calamity could not be the work of a gaggle of girls.

Macke nodded to the technician operating the machine. He turned a knob.

Peter screamed in agony as the electrical current coursed through his body, torturing his nerves. He shook as if in a fit, and the hair on his head stood up.

The operator turned the current off.

Macke screamed: "Give me his name!"

At last Peter opened his mouth.

Macke leaned closer.

Peter whispered: "No man."

"A woman, then! Give me the name!"

"It was an angel."

"Damn you to hell!" Macke seized the knob and turned it. "This goes on until you tell me!" he yelled, as Peter shuddered and screamed.

The door opened. A young detective looked in, turned pale, and beckoned to Macke.

The technician turned the current off, and the screaming stopped. The doctor leaned forward to check Peter's heart.

The detective said: "Excuse me, Inspector Macke, but you're wanted by Superintendent Kringelein."

"Now?" said Macke irritably.

"That's what he said, sir."

Macke looked at the doctor, who shrugged. "He's young," he said. "He'll be alive when you get back."

Macke left the room and went upstairs with the detective. Kringelein's office was on the first floor. Macke knocked and went in. "The damn priest hasn't talked yet," he said without preamble. "I need more time."

Kringelein was a slight man with spectacles, clever but weak-willed. A late convert to Nazism, he was not a member of the elite SS. He lacked the fervor of enthusiasts such as Macke. "Don't bother any further with that priest," he said. "We're no longer interested in any of the clergymen. Throw them in camps and forget them."

Macke could not believe his ears. "But these people have conspired to undermine the Führer!"

"And they have succeeded," said Kringelein. "Whereas you have failed."

Macke suspected that Kringelein was privately pleased about this.

"A decision has been made at the top," the superintendent went on. "Aktion T4 has been canceled."

Macke was flabbergasted. The Nazis never allowed their decisions to be swayed by the misgivings of the ignorant. "We didn't get where we are by kowtowing to public opinion!" he said.

"We have this time."

"Why?"

"The Führer neglected to explain his decision to me personally,"

Kringelein said sarcastically. "But I can guess. The program has attracted remarkably angry protests from a normally passive public. If we persist with it, we risk an open confrontation with churches of all denominations. That would be a bad thing. We must not weaken the unity and determination of the German people—particularly right now, when we are at war with the Soviet Union, our strongest enemy yet. So the program is canceled."

"Very good, sir," said Macke, controlling his anger. "Will there be anything else?"

"Dismissed," said Kringelein.

Macke went to the door.

"Macke."

He turned. "Yes, sir."

"Change your shirt."

"My shirt?"

"There's blood on it."

"Yes, sir. Sorry, sir."

Macke stamped down the stairs, boiling. He returned to the basement chamber. Father Peter was still alive.

Raging, he yelled again: "Who told you about Akelberg?"

There was no reply.

He turned the current up to maximum.

Father Peter screamed for a long time; then, at last, he fell into a final silence.

## xiii

The villa where the Franck family lived was set in a small park. Two hundred yards from the house, on a slight rise, was a little pagoda, open on all sides, with seats. As children Carla and Frieda had pretended it was their country house, and had played for hours pretending to have grand parties where dozens of servants waited on their glamorous guests. Later it became their favorite place to sit and talk where no one could hear them.

"The first time I sat on this bench, my feet didn't reach the floor," Carla said.

Frieda said: "I wish we could go back to those days."

It was a sultry afternoon, overcast and humid, and they both wore sleeveless dresses. They were in a somber mood. Father Peter was dead: he had committed suicide in custody, having become depressed about his crimes, according to the police. Carla wondered if he had been beaten as her father had. It seemed dreadfully likely.

There were dozens more in police cells all over Germany. Some had protested publicly about the killing of the handicapped; others had done no more than pass round copies of Bishop von Galen's sermon. She wondered if all of them would be tortured. She wondered how long she would escape such a fate.

Werner came out of the house with a tray. He carried it across the lawn to the pagoda. Cheerily he said: "How about some lemonade, girls?"

Carla looked away. "No, thank you," she said coldly. She did not understand how he could pretend to be her friend after the cowardice he had shown.

Frieda said: "Not for me."

"I hope we're still friends," Werner said, looking at Carla.

How could he say such a thing? Of course they were not friends.

Frieda said: "Father Peter is dead, Werner."

Carla added: "Probably tortured to death by the Gestapo, because he refused to accept the murder of people such as your brother. My father is dead, too, for the same reason. Lots of other people are in jail or in camps. But you kept your cushy desk job, so that's all right."

Werner looked hurt. That surprised Carla. She had expected defiance, or at least an effort at insouciance. But he seemed genuinely upset. He said: "Don't you think we each have our different ways of doing what we can?"

This was feeble. "You did nothing!" Carla said.

"Perhaps," he said sadly. "No lemonade, then?"

Neither girl answered, and he went back to the house.

Carla was indignant and angry, but she could not help also feeling regret. Before she discovered that Werner was a coward, she had been embarking on a romance with him. She had liked him a lot, ten times more than any other boy she had kissed. She was not quite heartbroken, but she was deeply disappointed.

Frieda was luckier. This thought was prompted by the sight of Heinrich coming out of the house. Frieda was glamorous and fun-loving, and Heinrich was brooding and intense, but somehow they made a good pair. "Are you in love with him?" Carla said while he was still out of earshot.

"I don't know yet," Frieda replied. "He's terribly sweet, though. I kind of adore him."

That might not be love, Carla thought, but it was well on the way.

Heinrich was bursting with news. "I had to come and tell you right away," he said. "My father told me after lunch."

"What?" said Frieda.

"The government has canceled the project. It was called Aktion T4. The killing of the handicapped. They're stopping."

Carla said: "You mean we won?"

Heinrich nodded vigorously. "My father is amazed. He says he has never known the Führer to give in to public opinion before."

Frieda said: "And we forced him to!"

"Thank God no one knows that," Heinrich said fervently.

Carla said: "They're just going to close the hospitals and end the whole program?"

"Not exactly."

"What do you mean?"

"My father says all those doctors and nurses are being transferred."

Carla frowned. "Where?"

"To Russia," said Heinrich.

# CHAPTER NINE

# 1941 (II)

The phone rang on Greg Peshkov's desk on a hot morning in July. He had finished his penultimate year at Harvard and was once again interning at the State Department for the summer, working in the information office. He was good at physics and math, and passed exams effortlessly, but he had no interest in becoming a scientist. Politics was what excited him. He picked up the phone. "Greg Peshkov."

"Morning, Mr. Peshkov. This is Tom Cranmer."

Greg's heart beat a little faster. "Thank you for returning my call. You obviously remember me."

"The Ritz-Carlton hotel, 1935. Only time I ever got my picture in the paper."

"Are you still the hotel detective?"

"I moved to retail. I'm a store detective now."

"Do you ever do any freelance work?"

"Sure. What did you have in mind?"

"I'm in my office now. I'd like to talk privately."

"You work in the Old Executive Office Building, across the street from the White House."

"How did you know that?"

"I'm a detective."

"Of course."

"I'm around the corner, at Aroma Coffee on F Street and Nineteenth."

"I can't come now." Greg looked at his watch. "In fact I have to hang up right away."

"I'll wait."

"Give me an hour."

Greg hurried down the stairs. He arrived at the main entrance just as a Rolls-Royce motorcar came silently to a stop outside. An overweight chauffeur clambered out and opened the rear door. The passenger who emerged was tall, lean, and handsome, with a full head of silver hair. He wore a perfectly cut double-breasted suit of pearl gray flannel that draped him in a style only London tailors could achieve. As he ascended the granite steps to the huge building, his fat chauffeur hurried after him, carrying his briefcase.

He was Sumner Welles, under-secretary of state, number two at the State Department, and personal friend of President Roosevelt.

The chauffeur was about to hand the briefcase to a waiting State Department usher when Greg stepped forward. "Good morning, sir," he said, and he smoothly took the briefcase from the chauffeur and held the door open. Then he followed Welles into the building.

Greg had got into the information office because he was able to show factual, well-written articles he had produced for *The Harvard Crimson*. However, he did not want to end up a press attaché. He had higher ambitions.

Greg admired Sumner Welles, who reminded him of his father. The good looks, the fine clothes, and the charm concealed a ruthless operator. Welles was determined to take over from his boss, Secretary of State Cordell Hull, and never hesitated to go behind his back and speak directly to the president—which infuriated Hull. Greg found it exciting to be close to someone who had power and was not afraid to use it. That was what he wanted for himself.

Welles had taken a shine to him. People often did take a shine to

Greg, especially when he wanted them to, but in the case of Welles there was another factor. Though Welles was married—apparently happily, to an heiress—he had a fondness for attractive young men.

Greg was heterosexual to a fault. He had a steady girl at Harvard, a Radcliffe student named Emily Hardcastle, who had promised to acquire a birth control device before September, and here in Washington he was dating Rita, the voluptuous daughter of Congressman Lawrence of Texas. He walked a tightrope with Welles. He avoided all physical contact while being amiable enough to remain in favor. Also, he stayed away from Welles any time after the cocktail hour, when the older man's inhibitions weakened and his hands began to stray.

Now, as the senior staff gathered in the office for the ten o'clock meeting, Welles said: "You can stay for this, my boy. It will be good for your education." Greg was thrilled. He wondered if the meeting would give him a chance to shine. He wanted people to notice him and be impressed.

A few minutes later Senator Dewar arrived with his son Woody. Father and son were lanky and large-headed, and wore similar dark blue single-breasted linen summer suits. However, Woody differed from his father in being artistic: his photographs for *The Harvard Crimson* had won prizes. Woody nodded to Welles's senior assistant, Bexforth Ross; they must have met before. Bexforth was an excessively self-satisfied guy who called Greg "Russkie" because of his Russian name.

Welles opened the meeting by saying: "I now have to tell you all something highly confidential that must not be repeated outside this room. The president is going to meet with the British prime minister early next month."

Greg just stopped himself from saying *Wow.*

"Good!" said Gus Dewar. "Where?"

"The plan is to rendezvous by ship somewhere in the Atlantic, for security and to reduce Churchill's travel time. The president wants me to attend, while Secretary of State Hull stays here in Washington to mind the store. He also wants you there, Gus."

"I'm honored," said Gus. "What's the agenda?"

"The British seem to have beaten off the threat of invasion, for now, but they're too weak to attack the Germans on the European continent—unless we help. Therefore Churchill will ask us to declare war on Germany. We will refuse, of course. Once we've got past that, the president wants a joint statement of aims."

"Not war aims," Gus said.

"No, because the United States is not at war and has no intention of going to war. But we are nonbelligerently allied with the British, we're supplying them with just about everything they need on unlimited credit, and when peace comes at last, we expect to have a say in how the postwar world is run."

"Will that include a strengthened League of Nations?" Gus asked. He was keen on this idea, Greg knew, and so was Welles.

"That's why I wanted to talk to you, Gus. If we want our plan implemented, we need to be prepared. We have to get FDR and Churchill to commit to it as part of their statement."

Gus said: "We both know that the president is in favor, theoretically, but he's nervous about public opinion."

An aide came in and passed a note to Bexforth, who read it and said: "Oh! My goodness."

Welles said testily: "What is it?"

"The Japanese imperial council met last week, as you know," Bexforth said. "We have some intelligence on their deliberations."

He was being vague about the source of information, but Greg knew what he meant. The Signal Intelligence Service of the U.S. Army was able to intercept and decode wireless messages from the Foreign Ministry in Tokyo to its embassies abroad. The data from these decrypts was code-named MAGIC. Greg knew about this, even though he was not supposed to—in fact there would have been a hell of a stink if the army found out he was in on the secret.

"The Japanese discussed extending their empire," Bexforth went on. They had already annexed the vast region of Manchuria, Greg knew, and had moved troops into much of the rest of China. "They do not favor the option of westward expansion, into Siberia, which would mean war with the Soviet Union."

"That's good!" said Welles. "It means the Russians can concentrate on fighting the Germans."

"Yes, sir. But the Japs are planning instead to extend southward, by taking full control of Indochina, then the Dutch East Indies."

Greg was shocked. This was hot news—and he was among the first to hear it.

Welles was indignant. "Why, that's nothing less than an imperialist war!"

Gus interposed: "Technically, Sumner, it's not war. The Japanese already have some troops in Indochina, with formal permission from the incumbent colonial power, France, as represented by the Vichy government."

"Puppets of the Nazis!"

"I did say 'technically.' And the Dutch East Indies are theoretically ruled by the Netherlands, which is now occupied by the Germans, who are perfectly happy for their Japanese allies to take over a Dutch colony."

"That's a quibble."

"It's a quibble that others will raise with us—the Japanese ambassador, for one."

"You're right, Gus, and thanks for forewarning me."

Greg was alert for an opportunity to make a contribution to the discussion. He wanted above all else to impress the senior men around him. But they all knew so much more than he did.

Welles said: "What are the Japanese after, anyway?"

Gus said: "Oil, rubber, and tin. They're securing their access to natural resources. It's hardly surprising, since we keep interfering with their supplies." The United States had embargoed exports of materials such as oil and scrap iron to Japan, in a failed attempt to discourage the Japanese from taking over ever-larger tracts of Asia.

Welles said irritably: "Our embargoes have never been applied very effectively."

"No, but the threat is obviously sufficient to panic the Japanese, who have almost no natural resources of their own."

"Clearly we need to take more effective measures," Welles snapped. "The Japanese have a lot of money in American banks. Can we freeze their assets?"

The officials around the room looked disapproving. This was a radical idea. After a moment Bexforth said: "I guess we could. That would be more effective than any embargoes. They would be unable to buy oil or any other raw materials here in the States because they couldn't pay for them."

Gus Dewar said: "The secretary of state will be concerned, as usual, to avoid any action that might lead to war."

He was right. Cordell Hull was cautious to the point of timidity, and frequently clashed with his more aggressive deputy, Welles.

"Mr. Hull has always followed that course, and very wisely," said Welles. They all knew he was insincere, but etiquette required it. "However, the United States must walk tall on the international stage. We're prudent, not cowardly. I'm going to put this idea of an asset freeze to the president."

Greg was awestruck. This was what power meant. In a heartbeat, Welles could propose something that would rock an entire nation.

Gus Dewar frowned. "Without imported oil, the Japanese economy will grind to a halt, and their military will be powerless."

"Which is good!" said Welles.

"Is it? What do you imagine Japan's military government will do, faced with such a catastrophe?"

Welles did not much like to be challenged. He said: "Why don't you tell me, Senator?"

"I don't know. But I think we should have an answer before we take the action. Desperate men are dangerous. And I do know that the United States is not ready to go to war against Japan. Our navy isn't ready and our air force isn't ready."

Greg saw his chance to speak and took it. "Mr. Under-Secretary, sir, it may help you to know that public opinion favors war with Japan, rather than appeasement, by a factor of two to one."

"Good point, Greg, thank you. Americans don't want to let Japan get away with murder."

"They don't really want war, either," said Gus. "No matter what the poll says."

Welles closed the folder on his desk. "Well, Senator, we agree about the League of Nations and disagree about Japan."

Gus stood up. "And in both cases the decision will be made by the president."

"Good of you to come in to see me."

The meeting broke up.

Greg left on a high. He had been invited into the briefing, he had learned startling news, and he had made a comment that Welles had thanked him for. It was a great start to the day.

He slipped out of the building and headed for Aroma Coffee.

He had never hired a private detective before. It felt vaguely illegal. But Cranmer was a respectable citizen. And there was nothing criminal about trying to get in contact with an old girlfriend.

At Aroma Coffee there were two girls who looked like secretaries taking a break, an older couple out shopping, and Cranmer, a broad man in a rumpled seersucker suit, dragging on a cigarette. Greg slid into the booth and asked the waitress for coffee.

"I'm trying to reconnect with Jacky Jakes," he said to Cranmer.

"The black girl?"

She had been a girl, back then, Greg thought nostalgically; sweet sixteen, though she was pretending to be older. "It's six years ago," he said to Cranmer. "She's not a girl anymore."

"It was your father who hired her for that little drama, not me."

"I don't want to ask him. But you can find her, right?"

"I expect so." Cranmer took out a little notebook and a pencil. "I guess Jacky Jakes was an assumed name?"

"Mabel Jakes is her real name."

"Actress, right?"

"Would-be. I don't know that she made it." She had had good looks and charm in abundance, but there were not many parts for black actors.

"Obviously she's not in the phone book, or you wouldn't need me."

"Could be unlisted, but more likely she can't afford a phone."

"Have you seen her since 1935?"

"Twice. First time two years ago, not far from here, on E Street. Second time, two weeks ago, two blocks away."

"Well, she sure as hell doesn't live in this swanky neighborhood, so she must work nearby. You have a photo?"

"No."

"I remember her vaguely. Pretty girl, dark skin, big smile."

Greg nodded, remembering that thousand-watt smile. "I just want her address, so I can write her a letter."

"I don't need to know what you want the information for."

"Suits me." Is it really this easy? Greg thought.

"I charge ten bucks a day, with a two-day minimum, plus expenses."

It was less than Greg had expected. He took out his billfold and gave Cranmer a twenty.

"Thanks," said the detective.

"Good luck," said Greg.

## ii

Saturday was hot, so Woody went to the beach with his brother, Chuck.

The whole Dewar family was in Washington. They had a nine-room apartment near the Ritz-Carlton hotel. Chuck was on leave from the navy, Papa was working twelve hours a day planning the summit meeting he referred to as the Atlantic Conference, and Mama was writing a new book, about the wives of presidents.

Woody and Chuck put on shorts and polo shirts, grabbed towels and sunglasses and newspapers, and caught a train to Rehoboth Beach, on the Delaware coast. The journey took a couple of hours, but this was the only place to go on a summer Saturday. There was a wide stretch of sand and a refreshing breeze off the Atlantic Ocean. And there were a thousand girls in swimsuits.

The two brothers were different. Chuck was shorter, with a compact, athletic figure. He had their mother's attractive looks and winning smile. He had been a poor student at school, but he also displayed Mama's quirky intelligence, always taking an off-center view of life. He was better than Woody at all sports except running, where Woody's long legs gave him speed, and boxing, in which Woody's long arms made him nearly impossible to hit.

At home, Chuck had not said much about the navy, no doubt because the parents were still angry with him for not going to Harvard. But alone with Woody he opened up a bit. "Hawaii is great, but I'm really disappointed to have a shore job," he said. "I joined the navy to go to sea."

"What are you doing, exactly?"

"I'm part of the signal intelligence unit. We listen to radio messages, mainly from the Imperial Japanese Navy."

"Aren't they in code?"

"Yes, but you can learn a lot even without breaking the codes. It's called traffic analysis. A sudden increase in the number of messages indicates that some action is imminent. And you learn to recognize patterns in the traffic. An amphibious landing has a distinctive configuration of signals, for example."

"That's fascinating. And I bet you're good at it."

Chuck shrugged. "I'm just a clerk, annotating and filing the transcripts. But you can't help picking up the basics."

"How's the social life in Hawaii?"

"Lots of fun. Navy bars can get pretty riotous. The Black Cat Café is the best. I have a good pal, Eddie Parry, and we go surfboarding on Waikiki Beach every chance we get. I've had some good times. But I wish I was on a ship."

They swam in the cold Atlantic, ate hot dogs for lunch, took photos of each other with Woody's camera, and studied the swimsuits until the sun began to go down. As they were leaving, picking their way through the crowd, Woody saw Joanne Rouzrokh.

He did not need to look twice. She was like no other girl on the beach, nor indeed in Delaware. There was no mistaking those high cheekbones, that scimitar nose, the luxuriant dark hair, the skin the color and smoothness of café au lait.

Without hesitation he walked straight toward her.

She looked absolutely sensational. Her black one-piece swimsuit had spaghetti straps that revealed the elegant bones of her shoulders. It was cut straight across her upper thighs, showing almost all of her long, brown legs.

He could hardly believe that he had once taken this fabulous woman in his arms and smooched her like there was no tomorrow.

She looked up at him, shading her eyes from the sun. "Woody Dewar! I didn't know you were in Washington."

That was all the invitation he needed. He knelt on the sand beside her. Just being this close made him breathe harder. "Hello, Joanne." He glanced briefly at the plump brown-eyed girl beside her. "Where's your husband?"

She burst out laughing. "Whatever made you think I was married?"

He was flustered. "I came to your apartment for a party, a couple of summers back."

"You did?"

Joanne's companion said: "I remember. I asked you your name, but you didn't answer."

Woody had no memory of her at all. "I'm sorry I was so impolite," he said. "I'm Woody Dewar, and this is my brother, Chuck."

The brown-eyed girl shook hands with both of them and said: "I'm Diana Taverner." Chuck sat beside her on the sand, which seemed to please her: Chuck was good-looking, much more handsome than Woody.

Woody went on. "Anyway, I went into the kitchen, looking for you, and a man called Bexforth Ross introduced himself to me as your fiancé. I assumed you'd be married by now. Is it an extraordinarily long engagement?"

"Don't be silly," she said with a touch of irritation, and he remembered that she did not respond well to teasing. "Bexforth told people we were engaged, because he was practically living at our apartment."

Woody was startled. Did that mean that Bexforth had been sleeping there? With Joanne? It was not uncommon, of course, but few girls admitted it.

"He was the one who talked about marriage," she went on. "I never agreed to it."

So she was single. Woody could not have been happier if he had won the lottery.

There might be a boyfriend, he warned himself. He would have to find out. But anyway, a boyfriend was not the same as a husband.

"I was at a meeting with Bexforth a few days back," Woody said. "He's a great man in the State Department."

"He'll go far, and he'll find a woman more suitable than I to be the wife of a great man in the State Department."

It seemed from her tone that she did not have warm feelings toward her former lover. Woody found that he was pleased about that, although he could not have said why.

He reclined on his elbow. The sand was hot. If she had a serious boyfriend, she would find a reason to mention him before too long, he felt sure. He said: "Speaking of the State Department, are you still working there?"

"Yes. I'm assistant to the under-secretary for Europe."

"Exciting."

"Right now it is."

Woody was looking at the line where her swimsuit crossed her thighs, and thinking that no matter how little a girl was wearing, a man was always thinking about the parts of her that were hidden. He began to get an erection, and rolled onto his front to conceal it.

Joanne saw the direction of his gaze and said: "You like my swimsuit?" She was always frank. It was one of the many things he found attractive about her.

He decided to be equally candid. "I like *you*, Joanne. I always did."

She laughed. "Don't beat about the bush, Woody—come right out with it!"

All around them, people were packing up. Diane said: "We'd better get going."

"We were just leaving," Woody said. "Shall we travel together?"

This was the moment for her to give him the polite brush-off. She could easily say *Oh, no, thanks. You guys go on ahead.* But instead she said: "Sure, why not?"

The girls pulled dresses over their swimsuits and threw their stuff into a couple of bags, and they all walked up the beach.

The train was crowded with trippers like them, sunburned and hungry and thirsty. Woody bought four Cokes at the station and produced them as the train pulled out. Joanne said: "You once bought me a Coke on a hot day in Buffalo. Do you remember?"

"During that demonstration. Of course I remember."

"We were just kids."

"Buying Cokes is a technique I use with beautiful women."

She laughed. "Is it successful?"

"It has never got me a single smooch."

She raised her bottle in a toast. "Well, keep trying."

He thought that was encouraging, so he said: "When we get back to the city, do you want to get a hamburger, or something, and maybe see a movie?"

This was the moment for her to say *No, thanks, I'm meeting my boyfriend.*

Diana said quickly: "I'd like that. How about you, Joanne?"

Joanne said: "Sure."

No boyfriend—and a date! Woody tried to hide his elation. "We could see *The Bride Came C.O.D.*," he said. "I hear it's pretty funny."

Joanne said: "Who's in it?"

"James Cagney and Bette Davis."

"I'd like to see that."

Diana said: "Me, too."

"That's settled, then," said Woody.

Chuck said: "How about you, Chuck? Would you like that? Oh, sure, I'd like it swell, but nice of you to ask, big brother."

It was not all that funny, but Diana giggled appreciatively.

Soon afterward, Joanne fell asleep with her head on Woody's shoulder.

Her dark hair tickled his neck, and he could feel her warm breath on his skin below the cuff of his short-sleeved shirt. He felt blissfully contented.

They parted company at Union Station, went home to change, and met up again at a Chinese restaurant downtown.

Over chow mein and beer they talked about Japan. Everyone was talking about Japan. "Those people have to be stopped," said Chuck. "They're Fascists."

"Maybe," said Woody.

"They're militaristic and aggressive, and the way they treat the Chinese is racialist. What else do they have to do to be Fascists?"

"I can answer that," said Joanne. "The difference is in their vision of the future. Real Fascists want to kill off all their enemies, then create a radically new type of society. The Japanese are doing all the same things in defense of traditional power groups, the military caste and the emperor. For the same reason, Spain is not really Fascist: Franco is murdering people for the sake of the Catholic Church and the old aristocracy, not to create a new world."

"Either way, the Japs must be stopped," said Diana.

"I see it differently," said Woody.

Joanne said: "Okay, Woody, how do you see it?"

She was seriously political, and would appreciate a thoughtful answer, he knew. "Japan is a trading nation, with no natural resources: no oil, no iron, just some forests. The only way they can make a living is by doing business. For example, they import raw cotton, weave it, and sell it to India and the Philippines. But in the Depression the two great economic empires—Britain and the USA—put up tariff walls to protect our own industries. That was the end of Japanese trade with the British Empire, including India, and the American zone, including the Philippines. It hit them pretty hard."

Diana said: "Does that give them the right to conquer the world?"

"No, but it makes them think that the only way to economic security is to have your own empire, as the British do, or at least to dominate your hemisphere, as the U.S. does. Then nobody else can close down your business. So they want the Far East to be their backyard."

Joanne agreed. "And the weakness of our policy is that every time we impose economic sanctions, to punish the Japanese for their aggression, it only reinforces their feeling that they've got to be self-sufficient."

"Maybe," said Chuck. "But they still have to be stopped."

Woody shrugged. He did not have an answer to that.

After dinner they went to the cinema. The movie was great. Then Woody and Chuck walked the girls back to their apartment. On the way, Woody took Joanne's hand. She smiled at him and squeezed his hand, and he took that for encouragement.

Outside the girls' building he took her in his arms. Out of the corner of his eye he saw Chuck do the same with Diana.

Joanne kissed Woody's lips briefly, almost chastely, then said: "The traditional good-night kiss."

"There was nothing traditional about it last time I kissed you," he said. He bent his head to kiss her again.

She put a forefinger on his chin and pushed him away.

Surely, he thought, that little peck was not all he was going to get?

"I was drunk that night," she said.

"I know." He saw what the problem was. She was afraid he was going to think she was easy. He said: "You're even more alluring when you're sober."

She looked thoughtful for a moment. "That was the right thing to say," she said eventually. "You win the prize." Then she kissed him again, softly, lingering, not with the urgency of passion but with a concentration that suggested tenderness.

All too soon he heard Chuck sing out: "Good night, Diana!"

Joanne broke the kiss with Woody.

Woody said in dismay: "My brother was a bit quick!"

She laughed softly. "Good night, Woody," she said; then she turned and walked to the building.

Diana was already at the door, looking distinctly disappointed.

Woody blurted out: "Can we have another date?" He sounded needy, even to himself, and he cursed his haste.

But Joanne did not seem to mind. "Call me," she said, and went inside.

Woody watched until the two girls disappeared; then he rounded on his brother. "Why didn't you kiss Diana longer?" he said crossly. "She seems really nice."

"Not my type," said Chuck.

"Really?" Woody was more mystified than annoyed. "Nice round tits, pretty face—what's not to like? I'd have kissed her, if I wasn't with Joanne."

"We all have different tastes."

They started to walk back toward their parents' apartment. "Well, what is your type, then?" Woody asked Chuck.

"There's something I should probably explain to you, before you plan any more double dates."

"Okay, what?"

Chuck stopped, forcing Woody to do the same. "You have to swear never to tell Papa and Mama."

"I swear." Woody studied his brother in the yellow light of the streetlamps. "What's the big secret?"

"I don't like girls."

"A pain in the ass, I agree, but what are you going to do?"

"I mean, I don't like to hug and kiss them."

"What? Don't be stupid."

"We're all made differently, Woody."

"Yeah, but you'd have to be some kind of pansy."

"Yes."

"Yes, what?"

"Yes, I'm some kind of pansy."

"You're such a kidder."

"I'm not kidding, Woody. I'm dead serious."

"You're *queer*?"

"That's exactly what I am. I didn't choose to be. When we were kids, and we started jerking off, you used to think about bouncy tits and hairy cunts. I never told you that I used to think about big stiff cocks."

"Chuck, this is disgusting!"

"No, it's not. It's the way some guys are made. More guys than you think—especially in the navy."

"There are pansies in the navy?"

Chuck nodded vigorously. "A lot."

"Well . . . how do you know?"

"We usually recognize one another. Like Jews always know who's Jewish. For example, the waiter in the Chinese restaurant."

"He was one?"

"Didn't you hear him say he liked my jacket?"

"Yes, but I didn't think anything of it."

"There you are."

"He was attracted to you?"

"I guess."

"Why?"

"Same reason Diana liked me, probably. Hell, I'm better looking than you."

"This is weird."

"Come on, let's go home."

They continued on their way. Woody was still reeling. "You mean there are Chinese pansies?"

Chuck laughed. "Of course!"

"I don't know. You never think of Chinese guys being that way."

"Remember, not a word to anyone, especially the parents. God knows what Papa would say."

After a while, Woody put his arm around Chuck's shoulders. "Well, what the hell," he said. "At least you're not a Republican."

### iii

Greg Peshkov sailed with Sumner Welles and President Roosevelt on a heavy cruiser, the *Augusta,* to Placentia Bay, off the coast of Newfoundland. Also in the convoy were the battleship *Arkansas,* the cruiser *Tuscaloosa,* and seventeen destroyers.

They anchored in two long lines, with a broad sea passage down the middle. At nine o'clock in the morning of Saturday, August 9, in bright sunshine, the crews of all twenty vessels mustered at the rails in their dress whites as the British battleship *Prince of Wales* arrived, escorted by three destroyers, and steamed majestically down the middle, bearing Prime Minister Churchill.

It was the most impressive show of power Greg had ever seen, and he was delighted to be part of it.

He was also worried. He hoped the Germans did not know about this rendezvous. If they found out, one U-boat could kill the two leaders of what remained of Western civilization—and Greg Peshkov.

Before leaving Washington Greg had met with the detective, Tom Cranmer, again. Cranmer had produced an address, a house in a low-rent neighborhood on the far side of Union Station. "She's a waitress at the University Women's Club near the Ritz-Carlton, which is why you saw her in that neighborhood twice," he had said as he pocketed the balance of his fee. "I guess acting didn't work out for her—but she still goes by Jacky Jakes."

Greg had written her a letter.

> Dear Jacky,
> I just want to know why you ran out on me six years ago. I thought we were so happy, but I must have been wrong. It bugs me, that's all.
>
> You act scared when you see me, but there's nothing to be afraid of. I'm not angry, just curious. I would never do anything to hurt you. You were the first girl I ever loved.
>
> Can we meet, just for a cup of coffee or something, and talk?
>
> > Very sincerely,
> > Greg Peshkov

He had added his phone number and mailed the note the day he left for Newfoundland.

The president was keen that the conference should result in a joint statement. Greg's boss, Sumner Welles, wrote a draft, but Roosevelt refused to use it, saying it was better to let Churchill produce the first draft.

Greg immediately saw that Roosevelt was a smart negotiator. Whoever produced the first draft would need, in all fairness, to put in some of what the other side wanted alongside his own demands. His statement of the other side's wishes then became an irreducible minimum, while all of his own demands were still up for negotiation. So the drafter always started at a disadvantage. Greg vowed to remember never to write the first draft.

On Saturday the president and the prime minister enjoyed a convivial lunch on board the *Augusta*. On Sunday they attended a church service on the deck of the *Prince of Wales*, with the Stars and Stripes and the Union Jack draping the altar red, white, and blue. On Monday morning, by which time they were firm friends, they got down to brass tacks.

Churchill produced a five-point plan that delighted Sumner Welles and Gus Dewar by calling for an effective international organization to assure the security of all states—in other words, a strengthened League of Nations. But they were disappointed to find that that was too much for Roosevelt. He was in favor, but he feared the isolationists, people who still believed America did not need to get involved with the troubles of the rest of the world. He was extraordinarily sensitive to public opinion, and made ceaseless efforts not to provoke opposition.

Welles and Dewar did not give up, nor did the British. They got together to seek a compromise acceptable to both leaders. Greg took notes for Welles. The group came up with a clause that called for disarmament "pending the establishment of a wider and more permanent system of general security."

They put it to the two great men, who accepted it.

Welles and Dewar were jubilant.

Greg could not see why. "It seems so little," he said. "All that effort— the leaders of two great countries brought together across thousands of miles, dozens of staffers, twenty-four ships, three days of talks—and all for a few words that don't quite say what we want."

"We move by inches, not miles," said Gus Dewar with a smile. "That's politics."

## iv

Woody and Joanne had been dating for five weeks.

Woody wanted to go out with her every night, but he held back. Nevertheless, he had seen her on four of the last seven days. Sunday they had gone to the beach; Wednesday they had dinner; Friday they saw a movie; and today, Saturday, they were spending the whole day together.

He never tired of talking to her. She was funny and intelligent and sharp-tongued. He loved the way she was so definite about everything. They jawed for hours about the things they liked and hated.

The news from Europe was bad. The Germans were still thrashing the Red Army. East of Smolensk they had wiped out the Russian Sixteenth and Twentieth Armies, taking three hundred thousand prisoners, leaving few Soviet forces between the Germans and Moscow. But bad news from afar could not dampen Woody's elation.

Joanne probably was not as crazy about him as he was about her. But she was fond of him, he could tell. They always kissed good night, and she seemed to enjoy it, though she did not show the kind of passion he knew she was capable of. Perhaps it was because they always had to kiss in public places, such as the cinema, or a doorway on the street near her building. When they were in her apartment, there was always at least one of her two roommates in the living room, and she had not yet invited him to her bedroom.

Chuck's leave had ended weeks ago, and he was back in Hawaii. Woody still did not know what to think about Chuck's confession. Sometimes he felt as shocked as if the world had turned upside down;

other times he asked himself what difference it made to anything. But he kept his promise not to tell anyone, not even Joanne.

Then Woody's father went off with the president, and his mother went to Buffalo to spend a few days with her parents. So Woody had the Washington apartment—all nine rooms—to himself for a few days. He decided he would look out for an opportunity to invite Joanne Rouzrokh there, in the hope of getting a real kiss.

They had lunch together and went to an exhibition called "Negro Art," which had been attacked by conservative writers who said there was no such thing as Negro art—despite the unmistakable genius of such people as the painter Jacob Lawrence and the sculptor Elizabeth Catlett.

As they left the exhibition, Woody said: "Would you like to have cocktails while we decide where to go for dinner?"

"No, thanks," she said in her usual decisive manner. "I'd really like a cup of tea."

"Tea?" He was not sure where you could get good tea in Washington. Then he had a brainwave. "My mother has English tea," he said. "We could go to the apartment."

"Okay."

The building was a few blocks away on Twenty-second Street NW, near L Street. They breathed easier as they stepped out of the summer heat into the air-conditioned lobby. A porter took them up in the elevator.

As they entered the apartment, Joanne said: "I see your papa around Washington all the time, but I haven't talked to your mama for years. I must congratulate her on her bestseller."

"She's not here right now," Woody said. "Come into the kitchen."

He filled the kettle from the tap and put it on the heat. Then he put his arms around Joanne and said: "Alone at last."

"Where are your parents?"

"Out of town, both of them."

"And Chuck is in Hawaii."

"Yes."

She moved away from him. "Woody, how could you do this to me?"

"Do what? I'm making you tea!"

"You've got me up here on false pretenses! I thought your parents were at home."

"I never said that."

"Why didn't you tell me they were away?"

"You didn't ask!" he said indignantly, though there was a grain of truth in her complaint. He would not have lied to her, but he had been hoping he would not have to tell her in advance that the apartment was empty.

"You got me up here to make a pass! You think I'm a cheap broad."

"I do not! It's just that we're never really private. I was hoping for a kiss, that's all."

"Don't try to kid me."

Now she really was being unjust. Yes, he hoped to go to bed with her one day, but no, he had not expected to do so today. "We'll go," he said. "We'll get tea somewhere else. The Ritz-Carlton is right down the street. All the British stay there—they must have tea."

"Oh, don't be stupid. We don't need to leave. I'm not afraid of you. I can fight you off. I'm just mad at you. I don't want a man who goes out with me because he thinks I'm easy."

"Easy?" he said, his voice rising. "Hell! I've waited six years for you to condescend to go out with me. Even now, all I'm asking for is a kiss. If you're easy, I'd hate to be in love with a girl who's difficult!"

To his astonishment, she started to laugh.

"Now what?" he said irritably.

"I'm sorry—you're right," she said. "If you wanted a girl who was easy, you would have given up on me long ago."

"Exactly!"

"After I kissed you like that when I was drunk, I thought you must have a low opinion of me. I assumed you were chasing me for a cheap thrill. I've even been worrying about that in the last few weeks. I misjudged you. I'm sorry."

He was bewildered by her rapid changes of mood, but he figured this latest phase was an improvement. "I was crazy about you even before that kiss," he said. "I guess you didn't notice."

"I hardly noticed *you.*"

"I'm pretty tall."

"It's your only attractive feature, physically."

He smiled. "I won't get swollen-headed talking to you, will I?"

"Not if I can help it."

The kettle boiled. He put tea in a china pot and poured water on top.

Joanne looked thoughtful. "You said something else a minute ago."

"What?"

"You said: 'I'd hate to be in love with a girl who's difficult.' Did you mean it?"

"Did I mean what?"

"The part about being in love."

"Oh! I didn't intend to say that." He threw caution to the wind. "But hell, yes, if you want to know the truth, I'm in love with you. I think I've loved you for years. I adore you. I want— "

She put her arms around his neck and kissed him.

This time it was the real thing, her mouth moving urgently against his, the tip of her tongue touching his lips, her body pressing against his. It was like 1935 except that she did not taste of whisky. This was the girl he loved, the real Joanne, he thought ecstatically: a woman of strong passions. And she was in his arms and kissing him for all she was worth.

She pushed her hands up inside his summer sports shirt and rubbed his chest, pressing her fingers into his ribs, grazing his nipples with her palms, grasping his shoulders, as if she wanted to sink her hands deep into his flesh. He realized that she, too, had a store of frustrated desire that was now overflowing like a busted dam, out of control. He did the same to her, stroking her sides and grasping her breasts, with a feeling of happy liberation, like a child let out of school for an unexpected holiday.

When he pressed his eager hand between her thighs, she pulled away.

But what she said surprised him. "Have you got any birth control?"

"No! I'm sorry—"

"It's okay. In fact it's good. It proves you really didn't plan to seduce me."

"I wish I had."

"Never mind. I know a woman doctor who'll fix me up on Monday. Meanwhile we'll improvise. Kiss me again."

As he did so, he felt her unbuttoning his pants.

"Oh," she said a moment later. "How nice."

"That's just what I was thinking," he whispered.

"I may need two hands, though."

"What?"

"I guess it goes with being so tall."

"I don't know what you're talking about."

"Then I'll shut up and kiss you."

A few minutes later she said: "Handkerchief."

Fortunately he had one.

He opened his eyes, a few moments before the end, and saw her looking at him. In her expression he read desire and excitement and something else that he thought might even be love.

When it was over, he felt blissfully calm. I love her, he thought, and I'm happy. How good life is. "That was wonderful," he said. "I'd like to do the same for you."

"Would you?" she said. "Really?"

"You bet."

They were still standing, there in the kitchen, leaning against the door of the refrigerator, but neither of them wanted to move. She took his hand and guided it under her summer dress and inside her cotton underwear. He felt hot skin, crisp hair, and a wet cleft. He tried to push his finger inside, but she said: "No." Grasping his fingertip, she guided it between the soft folds. He felt something small and hard, the size of a pea, just under the skin. She moved his finger in a little circle. "Yes," she said, closing her eyes. "Just like that." He watched her face adoringly as she abandoned herself to the sensation. In a minute or two she gave a little cry, and repeated it two or three times. Then she withdrew his hand and slumped against him.

After a while he said: "Your tea will be cold."

She laughed. "I love you, Woody."

"Do you really?"

"I hope you're not spooked by me saying that."

"No." He smiled. "It makes me very happy."

"I know girls aren't supposed to come right out with it, just like that. But I can't pretend to dither. Once I make up my mind, that's it."

"Yes," said Woody. "I'd noticed that."

## V

Greg Peshkov was living in his father's permanent apartment at the Ritz-Carlton. Lev came and went, stopping off for a few days between Buffalo and Los Angeles. At present Greg had the place to himself—except that the congressman's curvy daughter, Rita Lawrence, had stayed overnight, and now looked adorably tousled in a man's red silk dressing gown.

A waiter brought them breakfast, the newspapers, and a message envelope.

The joint statement by Roosevelt and Churchill had caused more of a stir than Greg expected. It was still the main news more than a week later. The press called it the Atlantic Charter. It had seemed, to Greg, to be all cautious phrases and vague commitments, but the world saw it otherwise. It was hailed as a trumpet blast for freedom, democracy, and world trade. Hitler was reported to be furious, saying it amounted to a declaration of war by the United States against Germany.

Countries that had not been at the conference nevertheless wanted to sign the charter, and Bexforth Ross had suggested the signatories should be called the United Nations.

Meanwhile the Germans were overrunning the Soviet Union. In the north they were closing in on Leningrad. In the south the retreating Russians had blown up the Dnieper Dam, the biggest hydroelectric power complex in the world and their pride and joy, in order to deny its power to the conquering Germans—a heartbreaking sacrifice. "The Red Army has slowed the invasion a bit," Greg said to Rita, reading from *The Washington Post*. "But the Germans are still advancing five miles a day. And they claim to have killed three and a half million Soviet soldiers. Is it possible?"

"Do you have any relatives in Russia?"

"As a matter of fact, I do. My father told me, one time when he was a little drunk, that he left a pregnant girl behind."

Rita made a disapproving face.

"That's him, I'm afraid," Greg said. "He's a great man, and great men don't obey the rules."

She said nothing, but he could read her expression. She disagreed with his view, but was not willing to quarrel with him about it.

"Anyway, I have a Russian half brother, illegitimate like me," Greg went on. "His name is Vladimir, but I don't know anything else about him. He may be dead by now. He's the right age to fight. He's probably one of those three and a half million." He turned the page.

When he had finished the paper, he read the message the waiter had brought.

It was from Jacky Jakes. It gave a phone number and just said *Not between 1 and 3.*

Suddenly Greg could not wait to get rid of Rita. "What time are you expected home?" he asked unsubtly.

She looked at her watch. "Oh, my gosh, I should be there before my mother starts looking for me." She had told her parents she was staying over with a girlfriend.

They got dressed together and left in two cabs.

Greg figured the phone number must be Jacky's place of work, and she would be busy between one o'clock and three. He would phone her around midmorning.

He wondered why he was so excited. After all, he was only curious.

Rita Lawrence was great-looking and very sexy, but with her and several others he had never recaptured the excitement of that first affair with Jacky. No doubt that was because he could never again be fifteen years old.

He got to the Old Executive Office Building and began his main task for the day, which was drafting a press release on advice to Americans living in North Africa, where British, Italians, and Germans fought backward and forward, mostly on a coastal strip two thousand miles long and forty miles wide.

At ten thirty he phoned the number on the message.

A woman's voice answered: "University Women's Club." Greg had never been there: men went only as guests of female members.

He said: "Is Jacky Jakes there?"

"Yes, she's expecting a call. Please hold on." She probably had to get special permission to receive a phone call at work, he reflected.

A few moments later he heard: "This is Jacky. Who's that?"

"Greg Peshkov."

"I thought so. How did you get my address?"

"I hired a private detective. Can we meet?"

"I guess we have to. But there's one condition."

"What?"

"You have to swear by all that's holy not to tell your father. Never, ever."

"Why?"

"I'll explain later."

He shrugged. "Okay."

"Do you swear?"

"Sure."

She persisted. "Say it."

"I swear it, okay?"

"All right. You can buy me lunch."

Greg frowned. "Are there any restaurants in this neighborhood that will serve a white man and a black woman together?"

"Only one that I know of—the Electric Diner."

"I've seen it." He had noticed the name, but he had never been inside: it was a cheap lunch counter used by janitors and messengers. "What time?"

"Half past eleven."

"So early?"

"What time do you think waitresses have lunch—one o'clock?"

He grinned. "You're as sassy as ever."

She hung up.

Greg finished his press release and took the typed sheets into his boss's office. Dropping the draft into the in-tray, he said: "Would it be convenient for me to take an early lunch, Mike? Around eleven thirty?"

Mike was reading *The New York Times*. "Yeah, no problem," he said without looking up.

Greg walked past the White House in the sunshine and reached the diner at eleven twenty. It was empty but for a handful of people taking a midmorning break. He sat in a booth and ordered coffee.

He wondered what Jacky would have to say. He looked forward to the solution of a puzzle that had mystified him for six years.

She arrived at eleven thirty-five, wearing a black dress and flat shoes—her waitress uniform without the apron, he presumed. Black suited her, and he remembered vividly the sheer pleasure of looking at her, with her bow-shaped mouth and her big brown eyes. She sat opposite him and ordered a salad and a Coke. Greg had more coffee; he was too tense to eat.

Her face had lost the childish plumpness he remembered. She had been sixteen when they met, so she was twenty-two now. They had been kids playing at being grown up; now they really were adults. In her face he read a story that had not been there six years ago: disappointment and suffering and hardship.

"I work the day shift," she told him. "Come in at nine, set the tables, dress the room. Wait at lunch, clear away, leave at five."

"Most waitresses work in the evening."

"I like to have evenings and weekends free."

"Still a party girl!"

"No, mostly I stay home and listen to the radio."

"I guess you have lots of boyfriends."

"All I want."

It took him a moment to realize that could mean anything.

Her lunch came. She drank her Coke and picked at the salad.

Greg said: "So why did you run out, back in 1935?"

She sighed. "I don't want to tell you this, because you're not going to like it."

"I have to know."

"I got a visit from your father."

Greg nodded. "I figured he must have something to do with it."

"He had a goon with him—Joe something."

"Joe Brekhunov. He's a thug." Greg began to feel angry. "Did he hurt you?"

"He didn't need to, Greg. I was scared to death just looking at him. I was ready to do anything your father wanted."

Greg suppressed his fury. "What did he want?"

"He said I had to leave, right then. I could write you a note but he would read it. I had to come back here to Washington. I was so sad to leave you."

Greg remembered his own anguish. "Me, too," he said. He was tempted to reach across the table and take her hand, but he was not sure she would want that.

She went on: "He said he would give me a weekly allowance just to keep away from you. He's still paying me. It's only a few bucks but it takes care of the rent. I promised—but somehow I managed to summon up the nerve to make one condition."

"What?"

"That he would never make a pass at me. If he did, I would tell you everything."

"And he agreed?"

"Yes."

"Not many people get away with threatening him."

She pushed her plate away. "Then he said if I broke my word, Joe would cut my face. Joe showed me his straight razor."

It all fell into place. "That's why you're still scared."

Her dark skin was bloodless with fear. "You bet your goddamn life."

Greg's voice fell to a whisper. "Jacky, I'm sorry."

She forced a smile. "Are you sure he was so wrong? You were fifteen. It's not a good age to get married."

"If he had said that to me, it might be different. But he decides what's going to happen and just does it, as if no one else is entitled to an opinion."

"Still, we had good times."

"You bet."

"I was your gift."

He laughed. "Best present I ever got."

"So what are you doing these days?"

"Working in the press office at the State Department for the summer."

She made a face. "Sounds boring."

"It's the opposite! It's so exciting to watch powerful men make earth-shaking decisions, just sitting there at their desks. They run the world!"

She looked skeptical, but said: "Well, it probably beats waitressing."

He began to see how far apart they had moved. "In September I'm going back to Harvard for my last year."

"I bet you're a gift to the coeds."

"There are lots of men and not many girls."

"You do all right, though, don't you?"

"I can't lie to you." He wondered whether Emily Hardcastle had kept her promise and got herself fitted with a contraceptive device.

"You'll marry one of them and have beautiful children and live in a house on the edge of a lake."

"I'd like to be something in politics, maybe secretary of state, or a senator like Woody Dewar's father."

She looked away.

Greg thought about that house on the edge of a lake. It must be her dream. He felt sad for her.

"You'll make it," she said. "I know. You have that air about you. Even when you were fifteen, you had it. You're like your father."

"What? Come on!"

She shrugged. "Think about it, Greg. You knew I didn't want to see you. But you set a private dick on me. 'He decides what's going to happen and just does it, as if no one else is entitled to an opinion.' That's what you said about him a minute ago."

Greg was dismayed. "I hope I'm not completely like him."

She gave him an appraising look. "The jury's still out."

The waitress took her plate. "Some dessert?" she said. "Peach pie's good."

Neither of them wanted dessert, so the waitress gave Greg the check.

Jacky said: "I hope I've satisfied your curiosity."

"Thank you, I appreciate it."

"Next time you see me on the street, just walk on by."

"If that's what you want."

She stood up. "Let's leave separately. I'd feel more comfortable."

"Whatever you say."

"Good luck, Greg."

"Good luck to you."

"Tip the waitress," she said, and she walked away.

# CHAPTER TEN

# 1941 (III)

In October the snow fell and melted, and the streets of Moscow were cold and wet. Volodya was searching in the store cupboard for his *valenki,* the traditional felt boots that warmed the feet of Muscovites in winter, when he was astonished to see six cases of vodka.

His parents were not great drinkers. They rarely took more than one small glass. Now and again his father went to one of Stalin's long, boozy dinners with old comrades, and staggered in through the door in the early hours of the morning as drunk as a skunk. But in this house a bottle of vodka lasted a month or more.

Volodya went into the kitchen. His parents were having breakfast, canned sardines with black bread and tea. "Father," he said, "why do we have six years' supply of vodka in the store cupboard?"

His father looked surprised.

Both men looked at Katerina, who blushed. Then she switched on the radio and turned the volume down to a low mutter. Did she suspect their apartment had concealed listening devices? Volodya wondered.

She spoke quietly but angrily. "What are you going to use for money when the Germans get here?" she said. "We won't belong to the privileged elite any longer. We'll starve unless we can buy food on the black market. I'm too damn old to sell my body. Vodka will be better than gold."

Volodya was shocked to hear his mother talking this way.

"The Germans aren't going to get here," his father said.

Volodya was not so sure. They were advancing again, closing the jaws of a pincer around Moscow. They had reached Kalinin in the north and Kaluga to the south, both cities only about a hundred miles away. Soviet casualties were unimaginably high. A month ago eight hundred thousand Red Army troops had held the line, but only ninety thousand were left, according to the estimates reaching Volodya's desk. He said to his father: "Who the hell is going to stop them?"

"Their supply lines are stretched. They're unprepared for our winter weather. We will counterattack when they're weakened."

"So why are you moving the government out of Moscow?"

The bureaucracy was in the process of being transported two thousand miles east, to the city of Kuibyshev. The citizens of the capital had been unnerved by the sight of government clerks carrying boxes of files out of their office buildings and packing them into trucks.

"That's just a precaution," Grigori said. "Stalin is still here."

"There is a solution," Volodya argued. "We have hundreds of thousands of men in Siberia. We need them here as reinforcements."

Grigori shook his head. "We can't leave the east undefended. Japan is still a threat."

"Japan is not going to attack us—we know that!" Volodya glanced at his mother. He knew he should not talk about secret intelligence in front of her, but he did anyway. "The Tokyo source that warned us— correctly—that the Germans were about to invade has now told us the Japanese will not. Surely we're not going to disbelieve him again!"

"Evaluating intelligence is never easy."

"We don't have a choice!" Volodya said angrily. "We have twelve armies in reserve—a million men. If we deploy them, Moscow might survive. If we don't, we're finished."

Grigori looked troubled. "Don't speak like that, even in private."

"Why not? I'll probably be dead soon anyway."

His mother started to cry.

His father said: "Now look what you've done."

Volodya left the room. Putting on his boots, he asked himself why he had shouted at his father and made his mother cry. He saw that it was because he now believed that Germany would defeat the Soviet Union. His mother's stash of vodka to be used as currency during a Nazi occupation had forced him to confront the reality. We're going to lose, he said to himself. The end of the Russian Revolution is in sight.

He put on his coat and hat. Then he returned to the kitchen. He kissed his mother and embraced his father.

"What's this for?" said his father. "You're only going to work."

"It's just in case we never meet again," Volodya said. Then he went out.

When he crossed the bridge into the city center, he found that all public transport had stopped. The metro was closed and there were no buses or trams.

It seemed there was nothing but bad news.

This morning's bulletin from SovInformBuro, broadcast on the radio and from black-painted loudspeaker posts on street corners, had been uncharacteristically honest. "During the night of October 14 to 15, the position on the western front became worse," it had said. "Large numbers of German tanks broke through our defenses." Everyone knew that SovInformBuro always lied, so they assumed the real situation was even worse.

The city center was clogged with refugees. They were pouring in from the west, with their possessions in handcarts, driving herds of skinny cows and filthy pigs and wet sheep through the streets, heading for the countryside east of Moscow, desperate to get as far away as possible from the advancing Germans.

Volodya tried to hitch a lift. There was not much civilian traffic in Moscow these days. Fuel was being saved for the endless military convoys driving around the Garden Ring orbital road. He was picked up by a new GAZ-64 jeep.

Looking from the open vehicle, he saw a good deal of bomb damage.

Diplomats returning from England said this was nothing by comparison with the London Blitz, but Muscovites thought it was bad enough. Volodya passed several wrecked buildings and dozens of burned-out wooden houses.

Grigori, in charge of air raid defense, had mounted antiaircraft guns on the tops of the tallest buildings, and launched barrage balloons to float below the snow clouds. His most bizarre decision had been to order the golden onion domes of the churches to be painted in camouflage green and brown. He had admitted to Volodya that this would make no difference to the accuracy—or otherwise—of the bombing but, he said, it gave citizens the feeling that they were being protected.

If the Germans won, and the Nazis ruled Moscow, then Volodya's nephew and niece, the twin children of his sister, Anya, would be brought up not as patriotic Communists but as slavish Nazis, saluting Hitler. Russia would be like France, a country in servitude, perhaps partly ruled by an obedient pro-Fascist government that would round up Jews to be sent to concentration camps. It hardly bore thinking about. Volodya wanted a future in which the Soviet Union could free itself from the malign rule of Stalin and the brutality of the secret police and begin to build true Communism.

When Volodya reached the headquarters building at the Khodynka airfield, he found the air full of grayish flakes that were not snow but ash. Red Army Intelligence was burning its records to prevent their falling into enemy hands.

Shortly after he arrived, Colonel Lemitov came into his office. "You sent a memo to London about a German physicist called Wilhelm Frunze. That was a very smart move. It turned out to be a great lead. Well done."

What does it matter? Volodya thought. The Panzers were only a hundred miles away. It was too late for spies to help. But he forced himself to concentrate. "Frunze, yes. I was at school with him in Berlin."

"London contacted him and he is willing to talk. They met at a safe house." As Lemitov talked, he fiddled with his wristwatch. It was unusual for him to fidget. He was clearly tense. Everyone was tense.

Volodya said nothing. Obviously some information had come out of the meeting; otherwise Lemitov would not be talking about it.

"London says that Frunze was wary at first, and suspected our man of belonging to the British secret police," Lemitov said with a smile. "In fact, after the initial meeting he went to Kensington Palace Gardens and knocked on the door of our embassy and demanded confirmation that our man was genuine!"

Volodya smiled. "A real amateur."

"Exactly," said Lemitov. "A disinformation decoy wouldn't do anything so stupid."

The Soviet Union was not finished yet, not quite, so Volodya had to carry on as if Willi Frunze mattered. "What did he give us, sir?"

"He says he and his fellow scientists are collaborating with the Americans to make a superbomb."

Volodya, startled, recalled what Zoya Vorotsyntsev had told him. This confirmed her worst fears.

Lemitov went on. "There's a problem with the information."

"What?"

"We've translated it, but we still can't understand a word." Lemitov handed Volodya a sheaf of typewritten sheets.

Volodya read a heading aloud. "Isotope separation by gaseous diffusion."

"You see what I mean."

"I did languages at university, not physics."

"But you once mentioned a physicist you know." Lemitov smiled. "A gorgeous blonde who declined to go to a movie with you, if I remember."

Volodya blushed. He had told Kamen about Zoya, and Kamen must have repeated the gossip. The trouble with having a spy for a boss was that he knew everything. "She's a family friend. She told me about an explosive process called fission. Do you want me to question her?"

"Unofficially and informally. I don't want to make a big thing of this until I understand it. Frunze may be a crackpot, and he could make us look foolish. Find out what the reports are about, and whether Frunze is making scientific sense. If he's genuine, can the British and Americans really make a superbomb? And the Germans, too?"

"I haven't seen Zoya for two or three months."

Lemitov shrugged. It did not really matter how well Volodya knew Zoya. In the Soviet Union, answering questions put by the authorities was never optional.

"I'll track her down."

Lemitov nodded. "Do it today." He went out.

Volodya frowned thoughtfully. Zoya was sure the Americans were making a superbomb, and she had been convincing enough to persuade Grigori to mention it to Stalin, but Stalin had scorned the idea. Now a spy in England was saying what Zoya had said. It looked as if she had been right. And Stalin had been wrong—again.

The leaders of the Soviet Union had a dangerous tendency to deny the truth of bad news. Only last week, an air reconnaissance mission had spotted German armored vehicles just eighty miles from Moscow. The General Staff had refused to believe it until the sighting had been confirmed twice. Then they had ordered the reporting air officer to be arrested and tortured by the NKVD for "provocation."

It was difficult to think long-term when the Germans were so close, but the possibility of a bomb that could flatten Moscow could not be disregarded, even at this moment of extreme peril. If the Soviets beat the Germans, they might afterward be attacked by Britain and America: something similar had happened after the 1914–18 war. Would the USSR find itself helpless against a capitalist-imperialist superbomb?

Volodya detailed his assistant, Lieutenant Belov, to find out where Zoya was.

While waiting for the address Volodya studied Frunze's reports, in the original English and in translation, memorizing what seemed to be key phrases, as he could not take the papers out of the building. At the end of an hour he understood enough to ask further questions.

Belov discovered that Zoya was not at the university nor at the nearby apartment building for scientists. However, the building administrator told him that all the younger residents had been requested to help with the construction of new inner defenses for the city, and gave him the location where Zoya was working.

Volodya put on his coat and went out.

He felt excited, but he was not sure whether that was on account of Zoya or the superbomb. Maybe both.

He was able to get an army ZIS and driver.

Passing the Kazan station—for trains to the east—he saw what looked like a full-blown riot. It seemed that people could not get into the station, let alone board the trains. Affluent men and women were struggling to reach the entrance doors with their children and pets and suitcases and trunks. Volodya was shocked to see some of them punching and kicking one another shamelessly. A few policemen looked on, helpless: it would have taken an army to impose order.

Military drivers were normally taciturn, but this one was moved to comment. "Fucking cowards," he said. "Running away, leaving us to fight the Nazis. Look at them, in their fur fucking coats."

Volodya was surprised. Criticism of the ruling elite was dangerous. Such remarks could cause a man to be denounced. Then he would spend a week or two in the basement of the NKVD's headquarters in Lubyanka Square. He might come out crippled for life.

Volodya had an unnerving sense that the rigid system of hierarchy and deference that sustained Soviet Communism was beginning to weaken and disintegrate.

They found the barricade party just where the building administrator had predicted. Volodya got out of the car, told the driver to wait, and studied the work.

A main road was strewn with antitank "hedgehogs." A hedgehog consisted of three pieces of steel railway track, each a yard long, welded together at their centers, forming an asterisk that stood on three feet and stuck three arms up. Apparently they wreaked havoc with caterpillar tracks.

Behind the hedgehog field an antitank ditch was being dug with pickaxes and shovels, and beyond that a sandbag wall was going up, with gaps for defenders to shoot through. A narrow zigzag path had been left between the obstacles so that the road could continue to be used by Muscovites until the Germans arrived.

Almost all the workers digging and building were women.

Volodya found Zoya beside a sand mountain, filling sacks with a shovel. For a minute he watched her from a distance. She wore a dirty coat, woolen mittens, and felt boots. Her blond hair was pulled back and covered with a colorless rag tied under her chin. Her face was smeared with mud, but she still looked sexy. She wielded the shovel in a steady rhythm, working efficiently. Then the supervisor blew a whistle and work stopped.

Zoya sat on a stack of sandbags and took from her coat pocket a small packet wrapped in newspaper. Volodya sat beside her and said: "You could have got exemption from this work."

"It's my city," she said. "Why wouldn't I help to defend it?"

"So you're not fleeing to the east."

"I'm not running away from the motherfucking Nazis."

Her vehemence surprised him. "Plenty of people are."

"I know. I thought you'd be long gone."

"You have a low opinion of me. You think I belong to a selfish elite."

She shrugged. "Those who are able to save themselves generally do."

"Well, you're wrong. All my family are still here in Moscow."

"Perhaps I misjudged you. Would you like a pancake?" She opened her packet to reveal four pale-colored patties wrapped in cabbage leaves. "Try one."

He accepted and took a bite. It was not very tasty. "What is it?"

"Potato peelings. You can get a bucketful free at the back door of any party canteen or officers' mess. You mince them small in the kitchen grinder, boil them until they're soft, mix them with a little flour and milk, add salt if you've got any, and fry them in lard."

"I didn't know you were so badly off," he said, feeling embarrassed. "You can always get a meal at our place, you know."

"Thank you. What brings you here?"

"A question. What is isotope separation by gaseous diffusion?"

She stared at him. "Oh, my God—what's happened?"

"Nothing has happened. I'm simply trying to evaluate some dubious information."

"Are we building a fission bomb at last?"

Her reaction told him that the information from Frunze was

probably sound. She had immediately understood the significance of what he said. "Please answer the question," Volodya said sternly. "Even though we're friends, this is official business."

"Okay. Do you know what an isotope is?"

"No."

"Some elements exist in slightly different forms. Carbon atoms, for example, always have six protons, but some have six neutrons and others have seven or eight. The different types are isotopes, called carbon-12, carbon-13, and carbon-14."

"Simple enough, even for a student of languages," Volodya said. "Why is it important?"

"Uranium has two isotopes, U-235 and U-238. In natural uranium the two are mixed up. But only U-235 is explosive."

"So we need to separate them."

"Gaseous diffusion would be one way, theoretically. When a gas is diffused through a membrane, the lighter molecules pass through faster, so the emerging gas is richer in the lower isotope. Of course I've never seen it done."

Frunze's report said that the British were building a gaseous diffusion plant in Wales, in the west of the United Kingdom. The Americans were also building one. "Would there be any other purpose for such a plant?"

"I know of no other reason for separating isotopes." She shook her head. "Figure the odds. Anyone who prioritizes this kind of process in wartime is either going crazy or building a weapon."

Volodya saw a car approach the barricade and begin to negotiate the zigzag passage. It was a KIM-10, a small two-door car designed for affluent families. It had a top speed of sixty miles per hour, but this one was so overloaded it probably would not do forty.

A man in his sixties was at the wheel, wearing a hat and a Western-style cloth coat. Beside him was a young woman in a fur hat. The backseat of the car was piled with cardboard boxes. There was a piano strapped precariously to the roof.

This was clearly a senior member of the ruling elite trying to get out of town with his wife, or mistress, and as many of his valuables as he could take—the kind of person Zoya assumed Volodya to be, which was perhaps why she had declined to go out with him. He wondered if she might be revising her opinion of him.

One of the barricade volunteers moved a hedgehog in front of the KIM-10, and Volodya saw that there was going to be trouble.

The car inched forward until its bumper touched the hedgehog. Perhaps the driver thought he could nudge it out of the way. Several more women came closer to watch. The device was designed to resist being pushed out of the way. Its legs dug into the ground, jamming, and it stuck fast. There was a sound of bending metal as the car's front bumper deformed. The driver put it in reverse and backed off.

He stuck his head out of the window and yelled: "Move that thing, right now!" He sounded as if he were used to being obeyed.

The volunteer, a chunky middle-aged woman wearing a man's checked cap, folded her arms. She shouted: "Move it yourself—deserter!"

The driver got out, red-faced with anger, and Volodya was surprised to recognize Colonel Bobrov, whom he had known in Spain. Bobrov had been famous for shooting his own men in the back of the head if they retreated. "No mercy for cowards" had been his slogan. At Belchite Volodya had personally seen him kill three International Brigade troops for retreating when they ran out of ammunition. Now Bobrov was in civilian clothes. Volodya wondered if he would shoot the woman who had blocked his way.

Bobrov walked to the front of the car and took hold of the hedgehog. It was heavier than he expected, but with an effort he was able to drag it out of the way.

As he was walking back to his car, the woman in the cap replaced the hedgehog in front of the car.

The other volunteers were now crowding around, watching the confrontation, grinning and making jokes.

Bobrov walked up to the woman, taking from his coat pocket an identification card. "I am General Bobrov!" he said. He must have been promoted since returning from Spain. "Let me pass!"

"You call yourself a soldier?" the woman sneered. "Why aren't you fighting?"

Bobrov flushed. He knew her contempt was justified. Volodya wondered if the brutal old soldier had been talked into fleeing by his younger wife.

"I call you a traitor," said the volunteer in the cap. "Trying to run away with your piano and your young tart." Then she knocked his hat off.

Volodya was flabbergasted. He had never seen such defiance of authority in the Soviet Union. Back in Berlin, before the Nazis came to power, he had been surprised by the sight of ordinary Germans fearlessly arguing with police officers, but it did not happen here.

The crowd of women cheered.

Bobrov still had short-cropped white hair all over his head. He looked at his hat as it rolled across the wet road. He took one step in pursuit, then thought better of it.

Volodya was not tempted to intervene. There was nothing he could do against the mob, and anyway he had no sympathy for Bobrov. It seemed just that Bobrov should be treated with the brutality he had always shown to others.

Another volunteer, an older woman wrapped in a filthy blanket, opened the car's trunk. "Look at all this!" she said. The trunk was full of leather luggage. She pulled out a suitcase and thumbed its catches. The lid came open, and the contents fell out: lacy underwear, linen petticoats and nightdresses, silk stockings and camisoles, all obviously made in the West, finer than anything ordinary Russian women ever saw, let alone bought. The filmy garments dropped into the filthy slush of the street and stuck there like petals on a dunghill.

Some of the women started to pick them up. Others seized more suitcases. Bobrov ran to the back of his car and started to shove the women away. This was turning very nasty, Volodya thought. Bobrov probably carried a gun, and he would draw it any second now. But then the woman in the blanket lifted a spade and hit Bobrov hard over the head. A woman who could dig a trench with a spade was no weakling, and the blow made a sickeningly loud thud as it connected. The general fell to the ground, and the woman kicked him.

The young mistress got out of the car.

The woman in the cap shouted: "Coming to help us dig?" and the others laughed.

The general's girlfriend, who looked about thirty, put her head down and walked back along the road the way the car had come. The volunteer in the checked cap shoved her, but she dodged between the hedgehogs and started to run. The volunteer ran after her. The mistress was wearing tan suede shoes with high heels, and she slipped in the wet and fell down. Her fur hat came off. She struggled to her feet and started to run again. The volunteer went after the hat, letting the mistress go.

All the suitcases now lay open around the abandoned car. The workers pulled the boxes from the backseat and turned them upside down, emptying the contents onto the road. Cutlery spilled out, china broke, and glassware smashed. Embroidered bedsheets and white towels were dragged through the slush. A dozen pretty pairs of shoes were scattered across the tarmac.

Bobrov got to his knees and tried to stand. The woman in the blanket hit him with the spade again. Bobrov collapsed on the ground. She unbuttoned Bobrov's fine wool coat and tried to pull it off him. Bobrov struggled, resisting. The woman became furious and hit Bobrov again and again until he lay still, his cropped white head covered with blood. Then she discarded her old blanket and put Bobrov's coat on.

Volodya walked across to Bobrov's unmoving body. The eyes stared lifelessly. Volodya knelt down and checked for breathing, a heartbeat, or a pulse. There was none. The man was dead.

"No mercy for cowards," Volodya said, but he closed Bobrov's eyes.

Some of the women unstrapped the piano. The instrument slid off the car roof and hit the ground with a discordant clang. They began gleefully to smash it up with picks and shovels. Others were quarreling over the scattered valuables, snatching up the cutlery, bundling the bedsheets, tearing the fine underwear as they struggled for possession. Fights broke out. A china teapot came flying through the air and just missed Zoya's head.

Volodya hurried back to her. "This is developing into a full-scale riot," he said. "I've got an army car and a driver. I'll get you out of here."

She hesitated only for a second. "Thanks," she said, and they ran to the car, jumped in, and drove away.

## ii

Erik von Ulrich's faith in the Führer was vindicated by the invasion of the Soviet Union. As the German armies raced across the vastness of Russia, sweeping the Red Army aside like chaff, Erik rejoiced in the strategic brilliance of the leader to whom he had given his allegiance.

Not that it was easy. During rainy October the countryside had been a mud bath: they called it the *rasputitsa*, the time of no roads. Erik's ambulance had plowed through a quagmire. A wave of mud built up in front of the vehicle, gradually slowing it, until he and Hermann had to get out and clear it away with shovels before they could drive any farther. It was the same for the entire German army, and the dash for Moscow had slowed to a crawl. Furthermore, the swamped roads meant that supply trucks never caught up. The army was low on ammunition, fuel, and food, and Erik's unit was dangerously short of drugs and other medical necessities.

So Erik had at first rejoiced when the frost had set in at the beginning of November. The freeze seemed a blessing, making the roads hard again and allowing the ambulance to move at normal speed. But Erik shivered in his summer coat and cotton underwear—winter uniforms had not yet arrived from Germany. Nor had the low-temperature lubricants needed to keep the engine of his ambulance operating— and the engines of all the army's trucks, tanks, and artillery. While on the road, Erik got up every two hours in the night to start his engine and run it for five minutes, the only way to keep the oil from congealing and the coolant from freezing solid. Even then he cautiously lit a fire under the vehicle every morning an hour before moving off.

Hundreds of vehicles broke down and were abandoned. The planes of the Luftwaffe, left outside all night on makeshift airfields, froze solid and refused to start, and air cover for the troops simply disappeared.

Despite all that, the Russians were retreating. They fought hard, but they were always pushed back. Erik's unit stopped continually to clear away Russian bodies, and the frozen dead stacked by the roadside made a grisly embankment. Relentlessly, remorselessly, the German army was closing in on Moscow.

Soon, Erik felt sure, he would see Panzers majestically rolling across Red Square, while swastika banners fluttered jubilantly from the towers of the Kremlin.

Meanwhile, the temperature was minus ten degrees centigrade, and falling.

Erik's field hospital unit was in a small town beside a frozen canal, surrounded by spruce forest. Erik did not know the name of the place. The Russians often destroyed everything as they retreated, but this town had survived more or less intact. It had a modern hospital, which the Germans had taken over. Dr. Weiss had briskly instructed the local doctors to send their patients home, regardless of condition.

Now Erik studied a frostbite patient, a boy of about eighteen. The skin of his face was a waxy yellow, and frozen hard to the touch. When Erik and Hermann cut away the flimsy summer uniform, they saw that the arms and legs were covered with purple blisters. The torn and broken boots had been stuffed with newspaper in a pathetic attempt to keep out the cold. When Erik took them off, he smelled the characteristic rotting stink of gangrene.

Nevertheless he thought they might yet save the boy from amputation.

They knew what to do. They were treating more men for frostbite than for combat wounds.

He filled a bathtub; then he and Hermann Braun lowered the patient into the warm water.

Erik studied the body as it thawed. He saw the black color of gangrene on one foot and the toes of the other.

When the water began to cool, they took him out, patted him dry, put him in a bed, and covered him with blankets. Then they surrounded him with hot stones wrapped in towels.

The patient was conscious and alert. He said: "Am I going to lose my foot?"

"That's up to the doctor," Erik said automatically. "We're just orderlies."

"But you see a lot of patients," he persisted. "What's your best guess?"

"I think you might be all right," Erik said. If not, he knew what would happen. On the foot less badly affected, Weiss would amputate the toes, cutting them off with a big pair of clippers like bolt cutters. The other leg would be amputated below the knee.

Weiss came a few minutes later and examined the boy's feet. "Prepare the patient for amputation," he said brusquely.

Erik was desolate. Another strong young man was going to spend the rest of his life a cripple. What a shame.

But the patient saw it differently. "Thank God," he said. "I won't have to fight anymore."

As they got the boy ready for surgery, Erik reflected that the patient was one of many who persisted in a defeatist attitude—his own family among them. He thought a lot about his late father, and felt deep rage mingled with his grief and loss. The old man would not have joined in with the majority and celebrated the triumph of the Third Reich, he thought bitterly. He would have complained about something, questioned the Führer's judgment, undermined the morale of the armed forces. Why had he had to be such a rebel? Why had he been so attached to the outdated ideology of democracy? Freedom had done nothing for Germany, whereas Fascism had saved the country!

He was angry with his father, yet hot tears came to his eyes when he thought about how he had died. Erik had at first denied that the Gestapo had killed him, but he soon realized it was probably true. They were not Sunday school teachers: they beat people who told wicked lies about the government. Father had persisted in asking whether the government was killing handicapped children. He had been foolish to listen to his English wife and his overemotional daughter. Erik loved them, which made it all the more painful to him that they were so misguided and obstinate.

While on leave in Berlin Erik had gone to see Hermann's father, the man who had first revealed the exciting Nazi philosophy to him when he and Hermann were boys. Herr Braun was in the SS now. Erik said he had met a man in a bar who claimed the government killed disabled people in special hospitals. "It is true that the handicapped are a costly drag on the forward march to the new Germany," Herr Braun had said to Erik. "The race must be purified, by repressing Jews and other degenerate types, and preventing mixed marriages that produce mongrel people. But euthanasia has never been Nazi policy. We are determined, tough, even brutal sometimes, but we do not murder people. That is a Communist lie."

Father's accusations had been wrong. Still Erik wept sometimes.

Fortunately, he was frantically busy. There was always a morning rush of patients, mostly men injured the day before. Then there was a short lull before the first new casualties of the day. When Weiss had operated on the frostbitten boy, he and Erik and Hermann took a midmorning break in the cramped staff room.

Hermann looked up from a newspaper. "In Berlin they're saying we've already won!" he exclaimed. "They ought to come here and see for themselves."

Dr. Weiss spoke with his usual cynicism. "The Führer made a most interesting speech at the Sportpalast," he said. "He spoke of the bestial inferiority of the Russians. I find that reassuring. I had the impression that the Russians were the toughest fighters we have yet come across. They have fought longer and harder than the Poles, the Belgians, the Dutch, the French, or the British. They may be underequipped and badly led and half-starved, but they come running at our machine guns, waving their obsolete rifles, as if they don't care whether they live or die. I'm glad to hear that this is no more than a sign of their bestiality. I was beginning to fear that they might be courageous and patriotic."

As always, Weiss pretended to agree with the Führer, while meaning the opposite. Hermann just looked confused, but Erik understood and was infuriated. "Whatever the Russians may be, they're losing," he said. "We're forty miles from Moscow. The Führer has been proved right."

"And he is much smarter than Napoléon," said Dr. Weiss.

"In Napoléon's time nothing could move faster than a horse," said Erik. "Today we have motor vehicles and wireless telegraphy. Modern communications have enabled us to succeed where Napoléon failed."

"Or they will have, when we take Moscow."

"Which we will do in a few days, if not hours. You can hardly doubt that!"

"Can I not? I believe some of our own generals have suggested we halt where we are and build a defense line. We could secure our positions, resupply over the winter, and go back on the offensive when the spring comes."

"That sounds to me like treacherous cowardice!" Erik said hotly.

"You are right—you must be, because that is exactly what Berlin told the generals, I understand. Headquarters people obviously have a better perspective than the men on the front line."

"We have almost wiped out the Red Army!"

"But Stalin seems to produce more armies from nowhere, like a magician. At the beginning of this campaign we thought he had two hundred divisions. Now we think he has more than three hundred. Where did he find another hundred divisions?"

"The Führer's judgment will be proved right—again."

"Of course it will, Erik."

"He has never yet been wrong!"

"A man thought he could fly, so he jumped off the top of a ten-story building, and as he fell past the fifth floor, flapping his arms uselessly in the air, he was heard to say: 'So far, so good.'"

A soldier rushed into the staff room. "There's been an accident," he said. "At the quarry north of the town. A collision, three vehicles. Some SS officers are injured."

The SS, or Schutzstaffel, had originally been Hitler's personal guard, and now formed a powerful elite. Erik admired their superb discipline, their ultrasmart uniforms, and their specially close relationship with Hitler.

"We'll send an ambulance," said Weiss.

The soldier said: "It's the Einsatzgruppe, the Special Group."

Erik had heard of the Special Groups, vaguely. They followed the army into conquered territory and rounded up troublemakers and potential saboteurs such as Communists. They were probably setting up a prison camp outside the town.

"How many hurt?" asked Weiss.

"Six or seven. They're still getting people out of the cars."

"Okay. Braun and von Ulrich, you go."

Erik was pleased. He would be glad to rub shoulders with the Führer's most fervent supporters, even happier if he could be of service to them.

The soldier handed him a message slip with directions.

Erik and Hermann gulped their tea, stubbed their cigarettes, and left the room. Erik put on a fur coat he had taken from a dead Russian officer, but left it open to show his uniform. They hurried down to the garage, and Hermann drove the ambulance out into the street. Erik read out the directions, peering through a light snowfall.

The road led out of town and snaked through the forest. They passed several buses and trucks coming the other way. The snow on the road was packed hard, and Hermann could not go fast on the glossy surface. Erik could easily imagine how there had been a collision.

It was the afternoon of the short day. At this time of year, daylight began at ten and ended at five. A gray light came through the snow clouds. The tall pine trees crowding in on either side darkened the road further. Erik felt as if he were in one of the fairy tales of the Brothers Grimm, following the path into the deep wood where evil lurked.

They looked out for a turning to the left, and found it guarded by a soldier who pointed the way. They bumped along a treacherous path between the trees until they were waved down by a second guard, who said: "Don't go faster than walking pace. That's how the crash happened."

A minute later they came upon the accident. Three damaged vehicles stood as if welded together: a bus, a jeep, and a Mercedes limousine with snow chains on the tires. Erik and Hermann jumped out of their ambulance.

The bus was empty. There were three men on the ground, perhaps the occupants of the jeep. Several soldiers gathered around the car sandwiched between the other two vehicles, apparently trying to get the people out of it.

Erik heard a volley of rifle fire, and wondered for a moment who was shooting, but he put the thought aside and concentrated on the job.

He and Hermann went from one man to the next assessing the gravity of the injuries. Of the three people on the ground one was dead, another had a broken arm, and the third appeared to be no worse than bruised. In the car, one man had bled to death, another was unconscious, and a third was screaming.

Erik gave the screamer a shot of morphine. When the drug took effect, he and Hermann were able to get the patient out of the car and into the ambulance. With him out of the way, the soldiers could begin to free the unconscious man, who was trapped by the deformed bodywork of the Mercedes. The man had a head injury that was going to kill him anyway, Erik thought, but he did not tell them that. He turned his attention to the men from the jeep. Hermann put a splint on the broken arm, and Erik walked the bruised man to the ambulance and sat him inside.

He returned to the Mercedes. "We'll have him out in five to ten minutes," said a captain. "Just hold on."

"Okay," said Erik.

He heard shooting again, and walked a little farther into the forest, curious about what the Special Group might be doing here. The snow on the ground between the trees was heavily trodden and littered with cigarette ends, apple cores, discarded newspapers, and other litter, as if a factory outing had passed this way.

He entered a clearing where lorries and buses were parked. A lot of people had been brought here. Some buses were leaving, skirting the accident; another arrived as Erik passed through. Beyond the parking lot, he came upon a hundred or so Russians of all ages, apparently prisoners, though many had suitcases, boxes, and sacks that they clutched as if guarding precious possessions. One man held a violin. A little girl with a doll caught Erik's eye, and he felt in his guts a sensation of sick foreboding.

The prisoners were being guarded by local policemen armed with truncheons. Clearly the Special Group had collaborators for whatever they were doing. The policemen looked at him, noted the German army uniform visible beneath the unbuttoned coat, and said nothing.

As he walked by, a well-dressed Russian prisoner spoke to him in German. "Sir, I am the director of the tire factory in this town. I have never believed in Communism, but only paid lip service, as all managers had to. I can help you—I know where everything is. Please take me away from here."

Erik ignored him and walked in the direction of the shooting.

He came upon the quarry. It was a large, irregular hole in the ground, its edge fringed by tall spruce trees like guardsmen in dark green uniforms laden with snow. At one end a long slope led into the pit. As he watched, a dozen prisoners began to walk down, two by two, marshaled by soldiers, into the shadowed valley.

Erik noticed three women and a boy of about eleven among them. Was their prison camp somewhere in that quarry? But they were no longer carrying luggage. Snow fell on their bare heads like a benison.

Erik spoke to an SS sergeant standing nearby. "Who are these prisoners, Sarge?"

"Communists," said the man. "From the town. Political commissars, and so on."

"What, even that little boy?"

"Jews, too," said the sergeant.

"Well, what are they, Communists or Jews?"

"What's the difference?"

"It's not the same thing."

"Balls. Most Communists are Jews. Most Jews are Communists. Don't you know anything?"

The tire factory director who had spoken to Erik seemed to be neither, he thought.

The prisoners reached the rocky floor of the quarry. Until this moment they had shuffled along like sheep in a herd, not speaking or looking around, but now they became animated, pointing at something on the ground. Peering through the snowflakes, Erik saw what looked like bodies scattered among the rocks, snow dusting their garments.

For the first time Erik noticed twelve riflemen standing on the lip of the ravine, among the trees. Twelve prisoners, twelve riflemen: he realized what was happening here, and incredulity mixed with horror rose like bile inside him.

They raised their guns and aimed at the prisoners.

"No," Erik said. "No, you can't." Nobody heard him.

A woman prisoner screamed. Erik saw her grab the eleven-year-old boy and clasp him to herself, as if her arms around him could stop bullets. She seemed to be his mother.

An officer said: "Fire."

The rifles cracked. The prisoners staggered and fell. The noise dislodged a little snow from the pines, and it fell on the riflemen, a sprinkling of pure white.

Erik saw the boy and his mother drop, still locked together in an embrace. "No," he said. "Oh, no!"

The sergeant looked at him. "What's the matter with you?" he said irritably. "Who are you, anyway?"

"Medical orderly," said Erik, without taking his eyes off the dread scene in the pit.

"What are you doing here?"

"I brought an ambulance for the officers hurt in the collision." Erik saw that another twelve prisoners were already being marched down the slope into the quarry. "Oh, God, my father was right," he moaned. "We're murdering people."

"Stop whining and fuck off back to your ambulance."

"Yes, Sergeant," said Erik.

## iii

At the end of November Volodya asked for a transfer to a fighting unit. His intelligence work no longer seemed important: the Red Army did not need spies in Berlin to discover the intentions of a German army that was already on the outskirts of Moscow. And he wanted to fight for his city.

His misgivings about the government came to seem trivial. Stalin's stupidity, the brutishness of the secret police, the way nothing in the Soviet Union worked the way it was supposed to work—all that faded away. He felt nothing but a blazing need to repel the invader who threatened to bring violence, rape, starvation, and death to his mother, his sister, the twins Dimka and Tania, and Zoya.

He was sharply aware that if everyone thought that way he would have no spies. His German informants were people who had decided that patriotism and loyalty were outweighed by the terrible wickedness of the Nazis. He was grateful to them for their courage and the stern morality that drove them. But he felt differently.

So did many of the younger men in Red Army Intelligence, and a small company of them joined a rifle battalion at the beginning of December. Volodya kissed his parents, wrote a note to Zoya saying he hoped to survive to see her again, and moved into barracks.

At long last, Stalin brought reinforcements from the east to Moscow. Thirteen Siberian divisions were deployed against the ever-nearer Germans. On their way to the front line some of them stopped briefly in Moscow, and Muscovites on the streets stared at them in their white padded coats and warm sheepskin boots, with their skis and goggles and hardy steppe ponies. They arrived in time for the Russian counterattack.

This was the Red Army's last chance. Time and time again, in the last five months, the Soviet Union had hurled hundreds of thousands of men at the invaders. Each time the Germans had paused, dealt with the attack, and continued their relentless advance. But if this attempt failed, there would be no more. The Germans would have Moscow, and when they had Moscow, they would have the USSR. And then his mother would be trading vodka for black-market milk for Dimka and Tania.

On the fourth day of December the Soviet forces moved out of the city to the north, west, and south and took up their positions for the last effort. They went without lights, to avoid alerting the enemy. They were not allowed to have fires or smoke tobacco.

That evening the front line was visited by NKVD agents. Volodya did not see his rodent-faced brother-in-law, Ilya Dvorkin, who must have been among them. A pair he did not recognize came to the bivouac where Volodya and a dozen men were cleaning their rifles. Have you heard anyone criticizing the government? they asked. What do the fellows say about Comrade Stalin? Who among your comrades questions the wisdom of the army's strategy and tactics?

Volodya was incredulous. What did it matter at this point? In the next few days Moscow would be saved or lost. Who cared if soldiers bitched about their officers? He cut the questioning short, saying that he and his men were under a rule of silence, and he had orders to shoot anyone who broke it, but—he added recklessly—he would let the secret policemen off if they left immediately.

That worked, but Volodya had no doubt that the NKVD was undermining the morale of the troops all along the line.

On Friday, December 5, in the evening, the Russian artillery thundered into action. Next morning at dawn Volodya and his battalion moved off in a blizzard. Their orders were to take a small town on the far side of a canal.

Volodya ignored orders to attack the German defenses frontally—that was the old-fashioned Russian tactic, and this was no moment to stick obstinately to wrongheaded ideas. With his company of a hundred men he went upstream and crossed the ice to the north of the town, then moved in on the Germans' flank. He could hear the crash and roar of battle off to his left, so he knew he was behind the enemy's front line.

Volodya was almost blinded by the blizzard. The occasional blaze of gunfire lit up the clouds for a moment, but at ground level visibility was only a few yards. However, he thought optimistically, that would help the Russians creep up on the Germans and take them by surprise.

It was viciously cold, down to minus thirty-five degrees centigrade in places, and while this was bad for both sides, it was worse for the Germans, who lacked cold-weather supplies.

Somewhat to his surprise Volodya found that the normally efficient Germans had not consolidated their line. There were no trenches, no antitank ditches, no dugouts. Their front was no more than a series of strongpoints. It was easy to slip through the gaps into the town and look for soft targets, barracks and canteens and ammunition dumps.

His men shot three sentries to take a soccer field in which were parked fifty tanks. Could it be so easy? Volodya wondered. Was the force that had conquered half Russia now depleted and spent?

The corpses of Soviet soldiers, killed in previous skirmishes and left to freeze where they had died, were without their boots and coats, which had presumably been taken by shivering Germans.

The streets of the town were littered with abandoned vehicles— empty trucks with open doors, snow-covered tanks with cold engines, and jeeps with their bonnet lids propped up as if to show that mechanics had tried to fix them but had given up in despair.

Crossing a main road, Volodya heard a car engine and made out, through the snowfall, a pair of headlights approaching on his left. At first he assumed it was a Soviet vehicle that had pushed through the German lines. Then he and his group were fired on, and he yelled at them to take cover. The car turned out to be a Kübelwagen, a Volkswagen jeep with the spare wheel on the hood in front. It had an air-cooled engine, which was why it had not frozen up. It rattled past them at top speed, the Germans firing from their seats.

Volodya was so surprised that he forgot to fire back. Why was a vehicle full of armed Germans driving away from the battle?

He took his company across the road. He had expected that by now they would be fighting their way from house to house, but they met little opposition. The buildings of the occupied town were locked up, shuttered, dark. Any Russians inside were hiding under their beds, if they had any sense.

More cars came along the road, and Volodya decided that officers must be fleeing the battlefield. He detailed a section with a Degtyarev

DP-28 light machine gun to take cover in a café and fire on them. He did not want them to live to kill Russians tomorrow.

Just off the main road he spotted a low brick building with bright lights behind skimpy curtains. Creeping past a sentry who could not see far in the snowstorm, he was able to peer in and discern officers inside. He guessed he was looking at a battalion headquarters.

He gave whispered instructions to his sergeants. They shot out the windows, then tossed grenades through. A few Germans came out with their hands on their heads. A minute later Volodya had taken the building.

He heard a new noise. He listened, frowning in puzzlement. More than anything else, it sounded like a football crowd. He stepped out of the headquarters building. The sound was coming from the front line, and it was growing louder.

There was a rattle of machine-gun fire; then, a hundred yards away on the main road, a truck slewed sideways and careered off the road into a brick wall, then burst into flames—hit, presumably, by the DP-28 Volodya had deployed. Two more vehicles followed immediately behind it and escaped.

Volodya ran to the café. The machine gun stood on its bipod on a dining table. This model was nicknamed Record Player because of the disc-shaped magazine that sat atop the barrel. The men were enjoying themselves. "It's like shooting pigeons in the yard, sir!" said a gunner. "Easy!" One of the men had raided the kitchen and found a big canister of ice cream, miraculously unspoiled, and they were taking turns to scoff it.

Volodya looked out through the smashed window of the café. He saw another vehicle coming, a jeep he thought, and behind it some men running. As they got nearer, he recognized German uniforms. More followed behind, dozens, perhaps hundreds. They were responsible for the football-crowd sound.

The gunner trained the barrel on the oncoming car, but Volodya put a hand on his shoulder. "Wait," he said.

He stared into the blizzard, making his eyes sting. All he could see were more vehicles and more running men, plus a few horses.

A soldier raised a rifle. "Don't shoot," Volodya said. The crowd came closer. "We can't stop this lot—we'd be overrun in a minute," he said. "Let them pass. Take cover." The men lay down. The gunner lifted the DP-28 off the table. Volodya sat on the floor and peered over the windowsill.

The noise rose to a roar. The leading men drew level with the café and passed. They were running, stumbling, and limping. Some carried rifles; most seemed to have lost their weapons; some had coats and hats, others nothing but their uniform tunics. Many were wounded. Volodya saw a man with a bandaged head fall down, crawl a few yards, and collapse. No one took any notice. A cavalryman on horseback trampled an infantryman and galloped on, heedless. Jeeps and staff cars drove dangerously through the crowd, skidding on the ice, honking madly and scattering men to both sides.

It was a rout, Volodya realized. They went by in the thousands. It was a stampede. They were on the run.

At last, the Germans were in retreat.

# CHAPTER ELEVEN

# 1941 (IV)

oody Dewar and Joanne Rouzrokh flew from Oakland, California, to Honolulu on a Boeing B-314 flying boat. The Pan Am flight took fourteen hours. Just before arriving they had a massive row.

Perhaps it was spending so long in a small space. The flying boat was one of the biggest planes in the world, but passengers sat in one of six small cabins, each of which had two facing rows of four seats. "I prefer the train," said Woody, awkwardly crossing his long legs, and Joanne had the grace not to point out that you could not go to Hawaii by train.

The trip was Woody's parents' idea. They had decided to take a vacation in Hawaii so they could see Woody's younger brother, Chuck, who was stationed there. Then they invited Woody and Joanne to join them for the second week of the holiday.

Woody and Joanne were engaged. Woody had proposed at the end of the summer, after four weeks of hot weather and passionate love in Washington. Joanne had said it was too soon, but Woody had pointed out that he had been in love with her for six years, and asked how long would be enough. She had given in. They would get married next June, as soon as Woody graduated from Harvard. Meanwhile, their engaged status entitled them to go on family holidays together.

She called him Woods, and he called her Jo.

The plane began to lose altitude as they approached Oahu, the main island. They could see forested mountains, a sparse scatter of villages in the lowlands, and a fringe of sand and surf. "I bought a new swimsuit," Joanne said. They were sitting side by side, and the roar of the four Wright Twin Cyclone fourteen-cylinder engines was too loud for her to be overheard.

Woody was reading *The Grapes of Wrath* but he put it down willingly. "I can't wait to see you in it." He meant it. She was a swimsuit manufacturer's dream, making all their products look sensational.

She glanced at him from under half-closed eyelids. "I wonder if your parents booked us adjoining rooms at the hotel." Her dark brown eyes seemed to smolder.

Their engaged status did not allow them to sleep together, at least not officially, though Woody's mother did not miss much and she might have guessed they were lovers.

Woody said: "I'll find you, wherever you are."

"You'd better."

"Don't talk like that. I'm already uncomfortable enough in this seat." She smiled contentedly.

The American naval base came into view. A lagoon shaped like a palm leaf formed a large natural harbor. Half the Pacific Fleet was here, about a hundred ships. The rows of fuel storage tanks looked like checkers on a board.

In the middle of the lagoon was an island with an airstrip. At the western end of the island, Woody saw a dozen or more seaplanes moored.

Right next to the lagoon was Hickam air base. Several hundred aircraft were parked with military precision, wingtip to wingtip, on the tarmac.

Banking for its approach, the plane flew over a beach with palm trees and gaily striped umbrellas—which Woody guessed must be Waikiki—then a small town that had to be Honolulu, the capital.

Joanne was owed some leave by the State Department, but Woody had had to skip a week of classes in order to take this vacation. "I'm kind of surprised at your father," Joanne said. "He's usually against anything that interrupts your education."

"I know," said Woody. "But you know the real reason for this trip, Jo? He thinks it could be the last time we see Chuck alive."

"Oh, my God, really?"

"He thinks there's going to be a war, and Chuck is in the navy."

"I think he's right. There will be a war."

"What makes you so sure?"

"The whole world is hostile to freedom." She pointed to the book in her lap, a bestseller called *Berlin Diary* by the radio broadcaster William Shirer. "The Nazis have Europe," she said. "The Bolsheviks have Russia. And now the Japanese are taking control of the Far East. I don't see how America can survive in such a world. We have to trade with somebody!"

"That's pretty much what my father thinks. He believes we'll go to war against Japan next year." Woody frowned thoughtfully. "What's happening in Russia?"

"The Germans don't seem quite able to take Moscow. Just before I left, there was a rumor of a massive Russian counterattack."

"Good news!"

Woody looked out. He could see Honolulu airport. The plane would splash down in a sheltered inlet alongside the runway, he presumed.

Joanne said: "I hope nothing major happens while I'm away."

"Why?"

"I want a promotion, Woods—so I don't want someone bright and promising to shine in my absence."

"Promotion? You didn't say."

"I don't have it yet, but I'm aiming for research officer."

He smiled. "How high do you want to go?"

"I'd like to be ambassador to someplace fascinating and complex, Nanking or Addis Ababa."

"Really?"

"Don't look skeptical. Frances Perkins is the first woman secretary of labor—and a damn good one."

Woody nodded. Perkins had been labor secretary from the start of Roosevelt's presidency eight years ago, and had won union support for the New Deal. An exceptional woman could aspire to almost anything nowadays. And Joanne was truly exceptional. But somehow it came as a shock to him that she was so ambitious. "But an ambassador has to live overseas," he said.

"Wouldn't it be great? Foreign culture, weird weather, exotic customs."

"But . . . how does that fit in with marriage?"

"Excuse me?" she said with asperity.

He shrugged. "It's a natural question, don't you think?"

Her expression did not change, except that her nostrils flared—a sign, he knew, that she was getting angry. "Have I asked *you* that question?" she said.

"No, but . . ."

"Well?"

"I'm just wondering, Jo—do you expect me to live wherever your career takes you?"

"I'll try to fit in with your needs, and I think you should try to fit in with mine."

"But it's not the same."

"Isn't it?" She was openly annoyed now. "This is news to me."

He wondered how the conversation had become so acrimonious so quickly. With an effort at making his tone of voice reasonable and amiable, he said: "We've talked about having children, haven't we?"

"You'll have them, as well as me."

"Not in exactly the same way."

"If children are going to make me a second-class citizen in this marriage, then we're not having any."

"That's not what I mean!"

"What the heck do you mean?"

"If you're appointed ambassador somewhere, do you expect me to drop everything and go with you?"

"I expect you to say: 'My darling, this is a wonderful opportunity for you, and I'm certainly not going to stand in your way.' Is that unreasonable?"

"Yes!" Woody was baffled and angry. "What's the point of being married, if we're not together?"

"If war breaks out, will you volunteer?"

"I guess I might."

"And the army would send you wherever they need you—Europe, the Far East."

"Well, yes."

"So you'll go where your duty takes you, and leave me at home."

"If I have to."

"But I can't do that."

"It's not the same! Why are you pretending it is?"

"Strangely enough, my career and my service to my country seem important to me—just as important as yours to you."

"You're just being perverse!"

"Well, Woods, I'm really sorry you think that, because I've been talking very seriously about our future together. Now I have to ask myself whether we even have one."

"Of course we do!" Woody could have screamed with frustration. "How did this happen? How did we get to this?"

There was a bump, and the plane splashed down in Hawaii.


## ii

Chuck Dewar was terrified that his parents would learn his secret.

Back home in Buffalo he had never had a real love affair, just a few hasty fumbles in dark alleys with boys he hardly knew. Half the reason he had joined the navy was to go places where he could be himself without his parents finding out.

Since he got to Hawaii it had been different. Here he was part of an underground community of similar people. He went to bars and restaurants and dance halls where he did not have to pretend to be heterosexual. He had had some affairs, and then he had fallen in love. A lot of people knew his secret.

And now his parents were here.

His father was invited to visit the signal intelligence unit at the naval base, known as Station HYPO. As a member of the Senate Foreign Relations Committee, Senator Dewar was let into many military secrets, and he had already been shown around signal intelligence headquarters, called Op-20-G, in Washington.

Chuck picked him up at his hotel in Honolulu in a navy car, a Packard LeBaron limousine. Papa was wearing a white straw hat. As they drove around the rim of the harbor, he whistled. "The Pacific Fleet," he said. "A beautiful sight."

Chuck agreed. "Quite something, isn't it?" he said. Ships were beautiful, especially in the U.S. Navy, where they were painted and scrubbed and shined. Chuck thought the navy was great.

"All those battleships in a perfect straight line," Gus marveled.

"We call it Battleship Row. Moored off the island are *Maryland, Tennessee, Arizona, Nevada, Oklahoma,* and *West Virginia.*" Battleships were named after states. "We also have *California* and *Pennsylvania* in harbor, but you can't see them from here."

At the main gate to the navy yard, the marine on sentry duty recognized the official car and waved them in. They drove to the submarine base and stopped in the parking lot behind headquarters, the Old Administration Building. Chuck took his father into the recently opened new wing.

Captain Vandermeier was waiting for them.

Vandermeier was Chuck's greatest fear. He had taken a dislike to Chuck, and he had guessed the secret. He was always calling Chuck a powder puff or a pantywaist. If he could, he would spill the beans.

Vandermeier was a short, stocky man with a gravelly voice and bad breath. He saluted Gus and shook hands. "Welcome, Senator. It'll be my privilege to show you the Communications Intelligence Unit of the

Fourteenth Naval District." This was the deliberately vague title for the group monitoring the radio signals of the Imperial Japanese Navy.

"Thank you, Captain," said Gus.

"A word of warning, first, sir. It's an informal group. This kind of work is often done by eccentric people, and correct naval uniform is not always worn. The officer in charge, Commander Rochefort, wears a red velvet jacket." Vandermeier gave a man-to-man grin. "You may think he looks like a goddamn homo."

Chuck tried not to wince.

Vandermeier said: "I won't say any more until we're in the secure zone."

"Very good," said Gus.

They went down the stairs and into the basement, passing through two locked doors on the way.

Station HYPO was a windowless neon-lit cellar housing thirty men. As well as the usual desks and chairs, it had oversize chart desks, racks of exotic IBM machine printers, sorters and collators, and two cots where the cryptanalysts took naps during their marathon codebreaking sessions. Some of the men wore neat uniforms but others, as Vandermeier had warned, were in scruffy civilian clothing, unshaven, and—to judge by the smell—unwashed.

"Like all navies, the Japanese have many different codes, using the simplest for less secret signals, such as weather reports, and saving the complex ones for the most highly sensitive messages," Vandermeier said. "For example, call signs identifying the sender of a message and its destination are in a primitive cipher, even when the text itself is in a high-grade cipher. They recently changed the code for call signs, but we cracked the new one in a few days."

"Very impressive," said Gus.

"We can also figure out where the signal originated, by triangulation. Given locations and the call signs, we can build up a pretty good picture of where most of the ships of the Japanese Navy are, even if we can't read the messages."

"So we know where they are, and what direction they're taking, but not what their orders are," said Gus.

"Frequently, yes."

"But if they wanted to hide from us, all they would have to do is impose radio silence."

"True," said Vandermeier. "If they go quiet, this whole operation becomes useless, and we are well and truly fucked up the ass."

A man in a smoking jacket and carpet slippers approached, and Vandermeier introduced the head of the unit. "Commander Rochefort is fluent in Japanese, as well as being a master cryptanalyst," Vandermeier said.

"We were making good progress decrypting the main Japanese cipher until a few days ago," Rochefort said. "Then the bastards changed it and undid all our work."

Gus said: "Captain Vandermeier was telling me you can learn a lot without actually reading the messages."

"Yes." Rochefort pointed to a wall chart. "Right now, most of the Japanese fleet has left home waters and is heading south."

"Ominous."

"It sure is. But tell me, Senator, what's your reading of Japanese intentions?"

"I believe they will declare war on the United States. Our oil embargo is really hurting them. The British and the Dutch are refusing to supply them, and right now they're trying to ship it from South America. They can't survive like this indefinitely."

Vandermeier said: "But what would they achieve by attacking us? A little country such as Japan can't invade the USA!"

Gus said: "Great Britain is a little country, but they achieved world domination just by ruling the seas. The Japanese don't have to conquer America. They just need to defeat us in a naval war so that they can control the Pacific, and no one can stop them trading."

"So, in your opinion, what might they be doing, heading south?"

"Their likeliest target has to be the Philippines."

Rochefort nodded agreement. "We've already reinforced our base there. But one thing bothers me: the commander of the Japanese aircraft carrier fleet hasn't received any signals for several days."

Gus frowned. "Radio silence. Has that ever happened before?"

"Yes. Aircraft carriers go quiet when they return to home waters. So we assume that's the explanation this time."

Gus nodded. "It sounds reasonable."

"Yes," said Rochefort. "I just wish I could be sure."


### iii

The Christmas lights were ablaze on Fort Street in Honolulu. It was Saturday night, December 6, and the street was thronged with sailors in white tropical uniform, each with a round white cap and a crossed black scarf, all out for a good time.

The Dewar family strolled along enjoying the atmosphere, Rosa on Chuck's arm and Gus and Woody on either side of Joanne.

Woody had patched up his quarrel with his fiancée. He apologized for making wrong assumptions about what Joanne expected in their marriage. Joanne admitted she had flown off the handle. Nothing was truly resolved, but it was enough of a rapprochement for them to tear off their clothes and jump into bed.

Afterward the quarrel seemed less important, and nothing really mattered except how much they loved each other. Then they vowed that in the future they would discuss such agreements in a loving and tolerant way. As they got dressed, Woody felt they had passed a milestone. They had had an acrimonious quarrel about a serious difference of view, but they had survived it. It could even be a good sign.

Now they were heading out for dinner, Woody carrying his camera, snapping photos of the scene as they walked along. Before they had gone far, Chuck stopped and introduced another sailor. "This is my pal Eddie Parry. Eddie, meet Senator Dewar; Mrs. Dewar; my brother, Woody; and Woody's fiancée, Miss Joanne Rouzrokh."

Rosa said: "I'm pleased to meet you, Eddie. Chuck has mentioned you several times in his letters home. Won't you join us for dinner? We're only going to eat Chinese."

Woody was surprised. It was not like his mother to invite a stranger to a family meal.

Eddie said: "Thank you, ma'am. I'd be honored." He had a Southern accent.

They went into the Heavenly Delight restaurant and sat down at a table for six. Eddie had formal manners, calling Gus "sir" and the women "ma'am," but he seemed relaxed. After they had ordered, he said: "I've heard so much about this family, I feel as if I know y'all." He had a freckled face and a big smile, and Woody could tell that everyone liked him.

Eddie asked Rosa how she liked Hawaii. "To tell you the truth, I'm a little disappointed," she said. "Honolulu is just like any small American town. I expected it to be more Asian."

"I agree," said Eddie. "It's all diners and motor courts and jazz bands."

He asked Gus if there was going to be a war. Everyone asked Gus that question. "We've tried our darnedest to reach a modus vivendi with Japan," Gus said. Woody wondered if Eddie knew what a modus vivendi was. "Secretary of State Hull had a whole series of talks with Ambassador Nomura that lasted all summer long. But we can't seem to agree."

"What's the problem?" said Eddie.

"American business needs a free trade zone in the Far East. Japan says okay, fine, we love free trade, let's have it, not just in our backyard, but all over the world. The United States can't deliver that, even if we wanted it. So Japan says that as long as other countries have their own economic zone, they need one, too."

"I still don't see why they had to invade China."

Rosa, who always tried to see the other side, said: "The Japanese want troops in China and Indochina and the Dutch East Indies to protect their interests, just as we Americans have troops in the Philippines, and the British have theirs in India, and the French in Algeria, and so on."

"When you put it that way, the Japs don't seem so unreasonable!"

Joanne said firmly: "They're not unreasonable, but they're wrong. Conquering an empire is the nineteenth-century solution. The world is changing. We're moving away from empires and closed economic zones. To give them what they want would be a backward step."

Their food arrived. "Before I forget," Gus said, "we're having breakfast tomorrow morning aboard the *Arizona*. Eight o'clock sharp."

Chuck said: "I'm not invited, but I've been detailed to get you there. I'll pick you up at seven thirty and drive you to the navy yard, then take you across the harbor in a launch."

"Fine."

Woody tucked into fried rice. "This is great," he said. "We should have Chinese food at our wedding."

Gus laughed. "I don't think so."

"Why not? It's cheap, and it tastes good."

"A wedding is more than a meal. It's an occasion. Speaking of which, Joanne, I must call your mother."

Joanne frowned. "About the wedding?"

"About the guest list."

Joanne put down her chopsticks. "Is there a problem?" Woody saw her nostrils flare, and knew there was going to be trouble.

"Not really a problem," said Gus. "I have a rather large number of friends and allies in Washington who would be offended if they were not invited to the wedding of my son. I'm going to suggest that your mother and I share the cost."

Papa was being thoughtful, Woody guessed. Because Dave had sold his business for a bargain price before he died, Joanne's mother might not have a lot of money to spare for a swanky wedding. But Joanne disliked the idea of the two parents making wedding arrangements over her head.

"Who are the friends and allies you're thinking about?" Joanne said coolly.

"Senators and congressmen, mostly. We must invite the president, but he won't come."

"Which senators and congressmen?" Joanne said.

Woody saw his mother hide a grin. She was amused at Joanne's insistence. Not many people had the nerve to push Gus up against the wall like this.

Gus began a list of names.

Joanne interrupted him. "Did you say Congressman Cobb?"

"Yes."

"He voted against the anti-lynching law!"

"Peter Cobb is a good man. But he's a Mississippi politician. We live in a democracy, Joanne; we have to represent our voters. Southerners won't support an anti-lynching law." He looked at Chuck's friend. "I hope I'm not treading on any toes here, Eddie."

"Don't mince your words on my account, sir," Eddie said. "I'm from Texas, but I feel ashamed when I think of Southern politics. I hate prejudice. A man's a man, whatever his color."

Woody glanced at Chuck. He looked so proud of Eddie he might have burst.

At that moment, Woody realized Eddie was more than just Chuck's pal.

That was weird.

There were three loving couples around the table: Papa and Mama, Woody and Joanne, and Chuck and Eddie.

He stared at Eddie. Chuck's lover, he thought.

Damn weird.

Eddie caught him staring, and smiled amiably.

Woody tore his gaze away. Thank God Papa and Mama haven't figured it out, he thought.

Unless that was why Mama had invited Eddie to join in a family dinner. Did she know? Did she even approve? No, that was beyond the bounds of possibility.

"Anyway, Cobb has no choice," Papa was saying. "And in everything else he's a liberal."

"There's nothing democratic about it," Joanne said hotly. "Cobb doesn't represent the people of the South. Only white people are allowed to vote there."

Gus said: "Nothing is perfect in this life. Cobb supported Roosevelt's New Deal."

"That doesn't mean I have to invite him to my wedding."

Woody put in: "Papa, I don't want him, either. He has blood on his hands."

"That's unfair."

"It's how we feel."

"Well, the decision is not entirely up to you. Joanne's mother will be throwing the party, and if she'll let me, I'll share the cost. I guess that gives us at least a say in the guest list."

Woody sat back. "Heck, it's our wedding."

Joanne looked at Woody. "Maybe we should have a quiet town hall wedding, with just a few friends."

Woody shrugged. "Suits me."

Gus said severely: "That would upset a lot of people."

"But not us," said Woody. "The most important person of the day is the bride. I just want her to have what she wants."

Rosa spoke up. "Listen to me, everyone," she said. "Don't let's go overboard. Gus, my darling, you may have to take Peter Cobb aside and explain to him, gently, that you are lucky enough to have an idealistic son, who is marrying a wonderful and equally idealistic girl, and they have stubbornly refused your impassioned request to invite Congressman Cobb to the wedding. You're sorry, but you cannot follow your own inclinations in this any more than Peter can follow his when voting on anti-lynching bills. He will smile and say he understands, and he has always liked you because you're as straight as a die."

Gus hesitated for a long moment, then decided to give in graciously. "I guess you're right, my dear," he said. He smiled at Joanne. "Anyway, I'd be a fool to quarrel with my delightful daughter-in-law on account of Pete Cobb."

Joanne said: "Thank you . . . Should I start calling you Papa yet?"

Woody almost gasped. It was the perfect thing to say. She was so damn smart!

Gus said: "I would really like that."

Woody thought he saw the glint of a tear in his father's eye.

Joanne said: "Then, thank you, Papa."

How about that? thought Woody. She stood up to him—and she won. What a girl!

## iv

On Sunday morning, Eddie wanted to go with Chuck to pick up the family at their hotel.

"I don't know, baby," said Chuck. "You and I are supposed to be friendly, not inseparable."

They were in bed in a motel at dawn. They had to sneak back into barracks before sunup.

"You're ashamed of me," said Eddie.

"How can you say that? I took you to dinner with my family!"

"That was your mama's idea, not yours. But your papa liked me, didn't he?"

"They all adored you. Who wouldn't? But they don't know you're a filthy homo."

"I am not a filthy homo. I'm a very clean homo."

"True."

"Please take me. I want to know them better. It's really important to me."

Chuck sighed. "Okay."

"Thank you." Eddie kissed him "Do we have time . . . ?"

Chuck grinned. "If we're quick."

Two hours later they were outside the hotel in the navy's Packard. Their four passengers appeared at seven thirty. Rosa and Joanne wore hats and gloves, Gus and Woody white linen suits. Woody had his camera.

Woody and Joanne were holding hands. "Look at my brother," Chuck murmured to Eddie. "He's so happy."

"She's a beautiful girl."

They held the doors open and the Dewars climbed into the back of the limousine. Woody and Joanne folded down the jump seats. Chuck pulled away and headed for the naval base.

It was a fine morning. On the car radio, station KGMB was playing hymns. The sun shone over the lagoon and glinted off the glass portholes and polished brass rails of a hundred ships. Chuck said: "Isn't that a pretty sight?"

They entered the base and drove to the navy yard, where a dozen ships were in floating docks and dry docks for repair, maintenance, and refueling. Chuck pulled up at the officers' landing. They all got out and looked across the lagoon at the mighty battleships standing proud in the morning light. Woody took a photo.

It was a few minutes before eight o'clock. Chuck could hear the tolling of church bells in nearby Pearl City. On the ships, the forenoon watch was being piped to breakfast, and color parties were assembling to hoist ensigns at eight precisely. A band on the deck of the *Nevada* was playing "The Star-Spangled Banner."

They walked to the jetty, where a launch was tied up ready for them. The boat was big enough to take a dozen passengers and had an inboard motor under a hatch in the stern. Eddie started the engine while Chuck handed the guests into the boat. The small motor burbled cheerfully. Chuck stood in the bows while Eddie eased the launch away from the dockside and turned toward the battleships. The prow lifted as the launch picked up speed, throwing off twin curves of foam like a seagull's wings.

Chuck heard a plane and looked up. It was coming in from the west, so low it looked as if it might be in danger of crashing. He assumed it was about to land at the naval airstrip on Ford Island.

Woody, sitting near Chuck in the bows, frowned and said: "What kind of plane is that?"

Chuck knew every aircraft of both the army and the navy, but he had trouble identifying this one. "It almost looks like a Type 97," he said. That was the carrier-based torpedo bomber of the Imperial Japanese Navy.

Woody pointed his camera.

As the plane came nearer, Chuck saw large red suns painted on its wings. "It is a Jap plane!" he said.

Eddie, steering the boat from the stern, heard him. "They must have faked it up for an exercise," he said. "A surprise drill to spoil everyone's Sunday morning."

"I guess so," said Chuck.

Then he saw a second plane behind the first.

And another.

He heard his father say anxiously: "What the heck is going on?"

The planes banked over the navy yard and passed low over the launch, their noise rising to a roar like Niagara Falls. There were about ten of them, Chuck saw; no, twenty; no, more.

They headed straight for Battleship Row.

Woody stopped taking pictures to say: "It can't be a real attack, can it?" There was fear as well as doubt in his voice.

"How could they be Japanese?" Chuck said incredulously. "Japan is nearly four thousand miles away! No plane can fly that far."

Then he remembered that the aircraft carriers of the Japanese navy had gone into radio silence. The signal intelligence unit had assumed they were in home waters, but had never been able to confirm that.

He caught his father's eye, and guessed he was remembering the same conversation.

Everything suddenly became clear, and incredulity turned to fear.

The lead plane flew low over the *Nevada,* the stern marker in Battleship Row. There was a burst of cannon fire. On deck, seamen scattered and the band left off in a ragged diminuendo of abandoned notes.

In the launch, Rosa screamed.

Eddie said: "Christ Jesus in heaven, it is an attack."

Chuck's heart pounded. The Japanese were bombing Pearl Harbor, and he was in a small boat in the middle of the lagoon. He looked at the scared faces of the others—both parents, his brother, and Eddie—and realized that all the people he loved were in the boat with him.

Long bullet-shaped torpedoes began to fall from the underbellies of the planes and splash into the tranquil waters of the lagoon.

Chuck yelled: "Turn back, Eddie!" But Eddie was already doing it, swinging the launch around in a tight arc.

As it turned, Chuck saw, over Hickam air base, another flight of aircraft with the big red discs on their wings. These were dive-bombers, and they were streaming down like birds of prey on the rows of American aircraft perfectly lined up on the runways.

How the hell many of the bastards were there? Half the Japanese air force seemed to be in the sky over Pearl.

Woody was still taking pictures.

Chuck heard a deep bang like an underground explosion, then another immediately after. He spun around. There was a flash of flame aboard the *Arizona*, and smoke began to rise from her.

The stern of the launch squatted farther into the water as Eddie opened the throttle. Chuck said unnecessarily: "Hurry, hurry!"

From one of the ships Chuck heard the insistent rhythmic hoot of a klaxon sounding general quarters, calling the crew to battle stations, and he realized that this *was* a battle, and his family was in the middle of it. A moment later on Ford Island the air raid siren began with a low moan and wailed higher in pitch until it struck its frantic top note.

There was a long series of explosions from Battleship Row as torpedoes found their targets. Eddie yelled: "Look at the *Wee Vee*!" It was what they called the *West Virginia*. "She's listing to port!"

He was right, Chuck saw. The ship had been holed on the side nearest the attacking planes. Millions of tons of water must have poured into her in a few seconds to make such a huge vessel tilt sideways.

Next to her, the same fate was overtaking the *Oklahoma*, and to his horror Chuck could see sailors slipping helplessly, sliding across the tilted deck and falling over the side into the water.

Waves from the explosions rocked the launch. Everyone clung to the sides.

Chuck saw bombs rain down on the seaplane base at the near end of Ford Island. The planes were moored close together, and the fragile aircraft were blown to pieces, fragments of wings and fuselages flying into the air like leaves in a hurricane.

Chuck's intelligence-trained mind was trying to identify aircraft types, and now he spotted a third model among the Japanese attackers, the deadly Mitsubishi "Zero," the best carrier-based fighter in the world. It had only two small bombs, but was armed with twin machine guns and a pair of 20 mm cannon. Its role in this attack must be to escort the bombers, defending them from American fighters—but all the American fighters were still on the ground, where many of them had already been destroyed. That left the Zeroes free to strafe buildings, equipment, and troops.

Or, Chuck thought fearfully, to strafe a family crossing the lagoon, desperately trying to get to shore.

At last the United States began to shoot back. On Ford Island, and on the decks of the ships that had not yet been hit, antiaircraft guns and regular machine guns came to life, adding their rattle to the cacophony of lethal noise. Antiaircraft shells burst in the sky like black flowers blossoming. Almost immediately, a machine gunner on the island scored a direct hit on a dive-bomber. The cockpit burst into flames and the plane hit the water with a mighty splash. Chuck found himself cheering savagely, shaking his fists in the air.

The listing *West Virginia* began to return to the vertical, but continued to sink, and Chuck realized that the commander must have opened the starboard seacocks, to ensure that she remained upright while she went down, giving the crew a better chance of survival. But the *Oklahoma* was not so fortunate, and they all watched in terrified awe as the great ship began to turn over. Joanne said: "Oh, God, look at the crew." The sailors were frantically scrambling up the steeply banked deck and over the starboard rail in a desperate attempt to save themselves. But they were the lucky ones, Chuck realized, as at last the mighty vessel turned turtle with a terrible crash and began to sink, for how many hundreds of men were trapped belowdecks?

"Hold on, everyone!" Chuck yelled. A huge wave created by the capsizing of the *Oklahoma* was approaching. Papa grabbed Mama and Woody held on to Joanne. The wave reached them and lifted the launch impossibly high. Chuck staggered but kept hold of the rail. The launch stayed afloat. Smaller waves followed, rocking them, but everyone was safe.

They were still a long quarter of a mile offshore, Chuck saw with consternation.

Astonishingly the *Nevada*, which had been strafed at the start, began to move off. Someone must have had the presence of mind to signal all ships to sail. If they could get out of the harbor, they could scatter and present less easy targets.

Then from Battleship Row came a bang ten times bigger than anything that had gone before. The explosion was so violent that Chuck felt the blast like a blow to his chest, though he was now almost half a mile away. A spurt of flame spewed out of the no. 2 gun turret of the *Arizona*. A split second later the forward half of the ship seemed to burst. Debris flew into the air, twisted steel girders and warped plates drifting up through the smoke with a nightmare slowness, like scraps of charred paper from a bonfire. Flames and smoke enveloped the front of the ship. The lofty mast tipped forward drunkenly.

Woody said: "What was *that*?"

"The ship's ammunition store must have gone up," Chuck said, and he realized with heartfelt grief that hundreds of his fellow seamen must have been killed in that mammoth detonation.

A column of dark red smoke rose into the air as from a funeral pyre.

There was a crash and the boat lurched as something hit it. Everyone ducked. Falling to his knees, Chuck thought it must have been a bomb, then realized it could not be, for he was still alive. When he recovered, he saw that a heavy scrap of metal debris a yard long had pierced the deck over the engine. It was a miracle it had not hit anyone.

However, the engine died.

The boat slowed and was becalmed. It wallowed in the choppy waves while Japanese planes rained hellfire on the lagoon.

Gus said tightly: "Chuck, we have to get out of here right now."

"I know." Chuck and Eddie examined the damage. They grabbed the metal scrap and tried to wrestle it out of the teak deck, but it was firmly stuck.

"We don't have time for this!" Gus said.

Woody said: "The engine is blitzed anyway, Chuck."

They were still a quarter of a mile from shore. However, the launch was equipped for an emergency such as this. Chuck unshipped a pair of oars. He took one and Eddie took the other. The boat was large for rowing, and their progress was slow.

Luckily for them there was a lull in the attack. The sky was no longer swarming with planes. Vast billows of smoke rose from the damaged ships, including a column a thousand feet high from the fatally wounded *Arizona*, but there were no new explosions. The amazingly plucky *Nevada* was now heading for the mouth of the harbor.

The water around the ships was crowded with life rafts, motor launches, and seamen swimming or clinging to floating wreckage. Drowning was not their only fear: oil from the holed ships had spread across the surface and caught fire. The cries for help of those who could not swim mingled horrifyingly with the screams of the burned.

Chuck stole a glance at his watch. He thought the attack had been going on for hours, but amazingly, it was only thirty minutes.

Just as he was thinking that, the second wave began.

This time the planes came from the east. Some of them chased the escaping *Nevada*; others targeted the navy yard, where the Dewars had boarded the launch. Almost immediately the destroyer *Shaw* in a floating dock exploded with great gouts of flame and billows of smoke. Oil spread across the water and caught fire. Then in the largest dry dock the battleship *Pennsylvania* was hit. Two destroyers in the same dry dock blew up as their ammunition stores were ignited.

Chuck and Eddie strained at the oars, sweating like racehorses.

At the navy yard, marines appeared—presumably from the nearby barracks—and broke out firefighting gear.

At last the launch reached the officers' landing. Chuck leaped out and swiftly tied up while Eddie helped the passengers out. They all ran to the car.

Chuck jumped into the driver's seat and started the engine. The car radio came on automatically, and he heard the KGMB announcer say: "All army, navy, and marine personnel report for duty immediately." Chuck had not had a chance to report to anyone, but he felt sure that his orders would be first to ensure the safety of the four civilians in his care, especially as two were women and one was a senator.

As soon as everyone was in the car, he pulled away.

The second wave of the attack seemed to be ending. Most of the Japanese planes were heading away from the harbor. All the same, Chuck drove fast: there might be a third wave.

The main gate was open. If it had been shut, he would have been tempted to crash it.

There was no other traffic.

He raced away from the harbor along Kamehameha Highway. The farther he got from Pearl Harbor, the safer his family would be, he figured.

Then he saw a lone Zero coming toward him.

It was flying low and following the highway, and after a moment he realized it was targeting the car.

The cannon were in the wings, and there was a good chance they would miss the narrow target of the car, but the machine guns were set close together, either side of the engine cowling. That was what the pilot would use if he was smart.

Chuck looked frantically at both sides of the road. There was no hiding place, nothing but cane fields.

He began to zigzag. The approaching pilot sensibly did not attempt to track him. The road was not wide, and if Chuck drove into the cane field, the car would be slowed to a walking pace. He stepped on the gas, realizing that the faster he was going, the better his chances of not being hit.

Then it was too late for forethought. The plane was so close Chuck could see the round black holes in the wings through which the cannon fired. But, as he had guessed, the pilot opened up with machine guns, and bullets spat dust from the road ahead.

Chuck moved left, to the crown of the road; then instead of continuing left, he swerved right. The pilot corrected. Bullets hit the hood. The windscreen smashed. Eddie roared with pain, and in the back one of the women screamed.

Then the Zero was gone.

The car began to zigzag of its own accord. A forward wheel must have been damaged. Chuck fought with the steering wheel, trying to stay on the road. The car slewed sideways, skidded across the tarmac, crashed into the field at the side of the road, and bumped to a stop.

Flames rose from the engine, and Chuck smelled gasoline.

"Everybody out!" Chuck yelled. "Before the fuel tank blows!" He opened his door and leaped out. He yanked open the rear door and his father jumped out, pulling his mother along. Chuck could see the others getting out on the far side. "Run!" he shouted, but it was superfluous. Eddie was already heading into the cane field, limping as though wounded. Woody was half-pulling, half-carrying Joanne, who also seemed to have been hit. His parents charged into the field, apparently unhurt. He joined them. They all ran a hundred yards, then threw themselves flat.

There was a moment of stillness. The sounds of planes had become a distant buzz. Glancing up, Chuck saw oily smoke from the harbor rising thousands of feet into the air. Above that, the last few high-level bombers were heading away to the north.

Then there was a bang that stunned his eardrums. Even with closed eyes he saw the bright flash of exploding gasoline. A wave of heat passed over him.

He lifted his head and looked back. The car was ablaze.

He jumped to his feet. "Mama! Are you okay?"

"Miraculously unhurt," she said coolly as his father helped her up.

He scanned the field and spotted the others. He ran to Eddie, who was sitting upright, clutching his thigh. "Are you hit?"

"Hurts like fuck," Eddie said. "But there's not much blood." He managed a grin. "Top of my thigh, I think, but no vital organs damaged."

"We'll get you to the hospital."

At that moment Chuck heard a terrible noise.

His brother was crying.

Woody was weeping not like a baby but like a lost child: a loud, sobbing noise of utter wretchedness.

Chuck knew immediately that it was the sound of a broken heart.

He ran to his brother. Woody was on his knees, his chest shaking, his mouth open, his eyes running with tears. There was blood all over his white linen suit, but he was not wounded. Between sobs he moaned: "No, no."

Joanne lay on the ground in front of him, faceup.

Chuck could see right away that she was dead. Her body was still and her eyes were open, staring at nothing. The front of her gaily striped cotton dress was soaked with bright red arterial blood, already darkening in patches. Chuck could not see the wound but he guessed she had taken a bullet to the shoulder that had opened her axillary artery. She would have bled to death in minutes.

He did not know what to say.

The others came and stood by him: Mama, Papa, and Eddie. Mama knelt on the ground beside Woody and put her arms around him. "My poor boy," she said, as if he were a child.

Eddie put his arm around Chuck's shoulders and gave him a discreet hug.

Papa knelt by the body. He reached out and took Woody's hand.

Woody's sobs quieted a little.

Papa said: "Close her eyes, Woody."

Woody's hand was shaking. With an effort, he steadied it.

He stretched out his fingertips to her eyelids.

Then, with infinite gentleness, he closed her eyes.

# CHAPTER TWELVE

# 1942 (I)

O n the first day of 1942 Daisy got a letter from her former fiancé, Charlie Farquharson.

When she opened it, she was at the breakfast table in the Mayfair house, alone except for the aged butler, who poured her coffee, and the fifteen-year-old maid, who brought her hot toast from the kitchen.

Charlie wrote not from Buffalo but from RAF Duxford, an air base in the east of England. Daisy had heard of the place: it was near Cambridge, where she had met both her husband, Boy Fitzherbert, and the man she loved, Lloyd Williams.

She was pleased to hear from Charlie. He had jilted her, of course, and she had hated him then, but it was a long time ago. She felt like a different person now. In 1935 she had been an American heiress called Miss Peshkov; today she was Viscountess Aberowen, an English aristocrat. All the same, she was pleased she was still in Charlie's mind. A woman would always prefer to be remembered rather than forgotten.

Charlie wrote with a heavy black pen. His handwriting was untidy, the letters large and jagged. Daisy read:

> Before anything else, I need of course to apologize
> for the way I treated you back in Buffalo. I shudder with
> mortification every time I think of it.

Good Lord, thought Daisy, he seems to have grown up.

> What snobs we all were, and how weak I was to allow my
> late mother to bully me into behaving shabbily.

Ah, she thought, his *late* mother. So the old bitch is dead. That might explain the change.

> I have joined No. 133 Eagle Squadron. We fly Hurricanes,
> but we're getting Spitfires any day now.

There were three Eagle squadrons, Royal Air Force units manned by American volunteers. Daisy was surprised: she would not have expected Charlie to go to war voluntarily. When she knew him, he had been interested in nothing but dogs and horses. He really had grown up.

> If you can find it in your heart to forgive me, or at least
> put the past behind you, I would love to see you and meet
> your husband.

The mention of a husband was a tactful way of saying he had no romantic intentions, Daisy guessed.

> I will be in London on leave next weekend. May I take the
> two of you to dinner? Do say yes.
>                           With affectionate good wishes,
>                           Charles H. B. Farquharson

Boy was not at home that weekend, but Daisy accepted for herself. She was starved of male companionship, like many women in wartime London. Lloyd had gone to Spain and disappeared. He said he was going to be a military attaché at the British embassy in Madrid. Daisy wished it might be true that he had such a safe job, but she did not believe it. When she asked why the government would send an able-bodied young officer to do a desk job in a neutral country, he had explained how important it was to discourage Spain from joining in the war on the Fascist side. But he said it with a rueful smile that told her plainly she was not to be fooled. She feared that in reality he was slipping across the border to work with the French resistance, and she had nightmares about his being captured and tortured.

She had not seen him for more than a year. His absence was like an amputation: she felt it every hour of the day. But she was glad of the chance to spend an evening out with a man, even if it was the awkward, unglamorous, overweight Charlie Farquharson.

Charlie booked a table in the Grill Room of the Savoy Hotel.

In the lobby of the hotel, as a waiter was helping her take off her mink coat, she was approached by a tall man in a well-cut dinner jacket who looked vaguely familiar. He stuck out his hand and said shyly: "Hello, Daisy. What a pleasure to see you after all these years."

When she heard his voice, she realized it was Charlie. "Good Lord!" she said. "You've changed!"

"I lost a little weight," he admitted.

"You sure did." Forty or fifty pounds, she guessed. It made him better-looking. His features now seemed craggy rather than ugly.

"But you haven't changed at all," he said, looking her up and down.

She had made an effort with her clothes. She had bought nothing new for years, because of wartime austerity, but for tonight she had exhumed an off-the-shoulder sapphire blue silk evening gown by Lanvin that she had acquired on her last prewar trip to Paris. "In a couple of months I'll be twenty-six," she said. "I can't believe I look the same as I did when I was nineteen."

He glanced down at her décolletage, blushed, and said: "Believe me, you do."

They went into the restaurant and sat down. "I was afraid you weren't coming," he said.

"My watch stopped. I'm sorry I'm late."

"Only by twenty minutes. I would have waited an hour."

A waiter asked if they would like a drink. Daisy said: "This is one of the few places in England where you can get a decent martini."

"Two of those, please," Charlie said.

"I like mine straight up with an olive."

"So do I."

She studied him, intrigued by the way he had altered. His old awkwardness had softened to a charming shyness. It was still hard to imagine him as a fighter pilot, shooting down German planes. Anyway, the Blitz on London had come to an end half a year ago, and there were no longer air battles in the skies over southern England. "What kind of flying do you do?" she said.

"Mainly daytime circus operations over northern France."

"What's a circus operation?"

"A bomber attack with a heavy escort of fighters, the main object being to lure enemy planes into an air battle in which they're outnumbered."

"I hate bombers," she said. "I lived through the Blitz."

He was surprised. "I would have thought you'd want to give the Germans a taste of their own medicine."

"Not at all." Daisy had thought about this a lot. "I could weep for all the innocent women and children who were burned and maimed in London—and it doesn't help at all to know that German women and children are suffering the same."

"I never looked at it that way."

They ordered dinner. Wartime regulations restricted them to three courses, and their meal could not cost more than five shillings. On the menu were special austerity dishes such as Mock Duck—made out of pork sausages—and Woolton Pie, which contained no meat at all.

Charlie said: "I can't tell you how good it is to hear a girl speak real American. I like English girls, and I've even dated one, but I miss American voices."

"Me, too," she said. "This is my home now, and I don't guess I'll ever go back, but I know how you feel."

"I'm sorry I missed meeting Viscount Aberowen."

"He's in the air force, like you. He's a pilot trainer. He gets home now and again—but not this weekend."

Daisy was sleeping with Boy again, on his occasional visits home. She had sworn she never would after catching him with those awful women in Aldgate. But he had put pressure on her. He said that fighting men needed consolation when they came home, and he had promised never to visit prostitutes again. She did not really believe his promises, but all the same she gave in, albeit against her inclination. After all, she told herself, I did marry him for better or worse.

However, she no longer took any pleasure in sex with him, unfortunately. She could go to bed with Boy but she could not fall back in love with him. She had to use cream for lubrication. She had tried to summon again the fond feelings she had once had for him, when she had found him an exciting young aristocrat with the world at his feet, full of fun and capable of enjoying life thoroughly. But he was not really exciting, she now realized: he was just a selfish and rather limited man with a title. When he was on top of her, all she could think about was that he might be passing her some disgusting infection.

Charlie said carefully: "I'm sure you don't want to talk too much about the Rouzrokh family . . ."

"No."

". . . but did you hear that Joanne died?"

"No!" Daisy was shocked. "How?"

"At Pearl Harbor. She was engaged to Woody Dewar, and she went with him to visit his brother, Chuck, who is stationed there. They were in a car that was strafed by a Zero—that's a Jap fighter plane—and she was hit."

"I'm so sorry. Poor Joanne. Poor Woody."

Their food came, and a bottle of wine. They ate in silence for a while. Daisy discovered that Mock Duck did not taste much like duck.

Charlie said: "Joanne was one of twenty-four hundred people killed at Pearl Harbor. We lost eight battleships and ten other vessels. Goddamn sneaky Japs."

"People here are secretly pleased, because the U.S. is in the fight now. God alone knows why Hitler was dumb enough to declare war on the States. But the British think they have a chance of winning at last, with the Russians and us on their side."

"Americans are very angry about Pearl Harbor."

"People here don't see why."

"The Japanese kept on negotiating right up until the last minute—long after they must have made the decision. That's deceitful!"

Daisy frowned. "It seems sensible to me. If agreement had been reached at the last minute, they could have called off the attack."

"But they didn't declare war!"

"Would that have made any difference? We were expecting them to attack the Philippines. Pearl Harbor would have taken us by surprise even after a declaration of war."

Charlie spread his hands in a gesture of bafflement. "Why did they have to attack us anyway?"

"We stole their money."

"Froze their assets."

"They can't see the difference. And we cut off their oil. We had them up against the wall. They were facing ruin. What were they to do?"

"They should have given in, and agreed to withdraw from China."

"Yes, they should. But if it was America that was being pushed around and told what to do by some other country, would you want us to give in?"

"Maybe not." He grinned. "I said you hadn't changed. I'd like to take that back."

"Why?"

"You never used to talk like this. In the old days you wouldn't discuss politics at all."

"If you don't take an interest, then what happens is your fault."

"I guess we've all learned that."

They ordered dessert. Daisy said: "What's going to happen to the world, Charlie? All Europe is Fascist. The Germans have conquered much of Russia. The USA is an eagle with a broken wing. Sometimes I'm glad I don't have children."

"Don't underestimate the USA. We're wounded, not crushed. Japan is cock of the walk now, but the day will come when the Japanese people shed bitter tears of regret for Pearl Harbor."

"I hope you're right."

"And the Germans aren't having things all their own way any longer. They failed to take Moscow, and they're on the retreat. Do you realize the battle of Moscow was Hitler's first real defeat?"

"Is it a defeat, or just a setback?"

"Either way, it's the worst military result he's ever had. The Bolsheviks gave the Nazis a bloody nose."

Charlie had discovered vintage port, a British taste. In London men drank it after the ladies had retired from the dinner table, a tiresome practise that Daisy had tried to abolish in her own house, without success. They had a glass each. On top of the martini and the wine, it made Daisy feel a little drunk and happy.

They reminisced about their adolescence in Buffalo, and laughed about the foolish things they and others had done. "You told us all you were going to London to dance with the king," Charlie said. "And you did!"

"I hope they were jealous."

"And how! Dot Renshaw went into spasm."

Daisy laughed happily.

"I'm glad we got back in contact," Charlie said. "I like you so much."

"I'm glad, too."

They left the restaurant and got their coats. The doorman summoned a taxi. "I'll take you home," Charlie said.

As they drove along the Strand, he put his arm around her. She was about to protest; then she thought: What the hell. She snuggled up to him.

"What a fool I am," he said. "I wish I'd married you when I had the chance."

"You would have made a better husband than Boy Fitzherbert," she said. But then she would never have met Lloyd.

She realized she had not said anything to Charlie about Lloyd.

As they turned into her street, Charlie kissed her.

It felt nice to be wrapped in a man's arms and kissing his lips, but she knew it was the booze making her feel that way, and in truth the only man she wanted to kiss was Lloyd. All the same she did not push him away until the cab came to a halt.

"How about a nightcap?" he said.

For a moment she was tempted. It was a long time since she had touched a man's hard body. But she did not really want Charlie. "No," she said. "I'm sorry, Charlie, but I love someone else."

"We don't have to go to bed together," he whispered. "But if we could just, you know, smooch awhile . . ."

She opened the door and stepped out. She felt like a heel. He was risking his life for her every day, and she would not even give him a cheap thrill. "Good night, Charlie, and good luck," she said. Before she could change her mind, she slammed the car door and went into her house.

She went straight upstairs. A few minutes later, alone in bed, she felt wretched. She had betrayed two men: Lloyd, because she had kissed Charlie; and Charlie, because she had sent him away dissatisfied.

She spent most of Sunday in bed with a hangover.

On Monday evening she got a phone call. "I'm Hank Bartlett," said a young American voice. "Friend of Charlie Farquharson, at Duxford. He talked to me about you, and I found your number in his book."

Her heart stopped. "Why are you calling me?"

"Bad news, I'm afraid," he said. "Charlie died today, shot down over Abbeville."

"No!"

"It was his first mission in his new Spitfire."

"He talked about that," she said dazedly.

"I thought you might like to know."

"Thank you, yes," she whispered.

"He just thought you were the bee's knees."

"Did he?"

"You should have heard him go on about how great you are."

"I'm sorry," she said. "I'm so sorry." Then she could no longer speak, and she hung up the phone.

## ii

Chuck Dewar looked over the shoulder of Lieutenant Bob Strong, one of the cryptanalysts. Some of them were chaotic but Strong was the tidy kind, and he had nothing on his desk but a single sheet of paper on which he had written:

YO—LO—KU—TA—WA—NA

"I can't get it," Strong said in frustration. "If the decrypt is right, it says they have struck yolokutawana. But it doesn't mean anything. There's no such word."

Chuck stared at the six Japanese syllables. He felt sure they ought to mean something to him, even though he knew only a smattering of the language. But he could not figure it out, and he got on with his work.

The atmosphere in the Old Administration Building was grim.

For weeks after the raid, Chuck and Eddie saw bloated bodies from sunken ships floating on the oily surface of Pearl Harbor. At the same time, the intelligence they were handling reported more devastating attacks by the Japanese. Only three days after Pearl Harbor, Japanese planes hit the American base at Luzon in the Philippines and destroyed the Pacific Fleet's entire stock of torpedoes. The same day in the South China Sea they sank two British battleships, the *Repulse* and the *Prince of Wales*, leaving the British helpless in the Far East.

They seemed unstoppable. Bad news just kept coming. In the first few months of the New Year Japan defeated U.S. forces in the Philippines and beat the British in Hong Kong, Singapore, and Rangoon, the capital of Burma.

Many of the place names were unfamiliar even to seamen such as Chuck and Eddie. To the American public they sounded like distant planets in a science-fiction yarn: Guam, Wake, Bataan. But everyone knew the meaning of *retreat, submit,* and *surrender.*

Chuck felt bewildered. Could Japan really beat America? He could hardly believe it.

By May the Japanese had what they wanted: an empire that gave them rubber, tin, and—most important of all—oil. Information leaking out indicated that they were ruling their empire with a brutality that would have made Stalin blush.

But there was a fly in their ointment, and it was the U.S. Navy. The thought made Chuck proud. The Japanese had hoped to destroy Pearl Harbor completely, and gain control of the Pacific Ocean, but they had failed. American aircraft carriers and heavy cruisers were still afloat. Intelligence suggested the Japanese commanders were infuriated that the Americans refused to lie down and die. After their losses at Pearl Harbor the Americans were outnumbered and outgunned, but they did not flee and hide. Instead they launched hit-and-run raids on Japanese ships, doing minor damage but boosting American morale and giving the Japanese the unshakable feeling that they had not yet won. Then, on April 25, planes launched from a carrier bombed the center of Tokyo, inflicting a terrible wound on the pride of the Japanese military. The celebrations in Hawaii were ecstatic. Chuck and Eddie got drunk that night.

But there was a showdown coming. Every man Chuck spoke to in the Old Administration Building said the Japanese would launch a major attack early in the summer to tempt American ships to come out in force for a final battle. The Japanese hoped the superior strength of their navy would be decisive, and the American Pacific Fleet would be wiped out. The only way the Americans could win was to be better prepared and have better intelligence, to move faster and be smarter.

During those months, Station HYPO worked day and night to crack JN-25b, the new code of the Imperial Japanese Navy. By May they had made progress.

The U.S. Navy had wireless intercept stations all around the Pacific Rim, from Seattle to Australia. There, men known as the On the Roof Gang sat with headsets and radio receivers listening to Japanese radio traffic. They scanned the airwaves and wrote what they heard on message pads.

The signals were in Morse code, but the dots and dashes of naval signals translated into five-digit number groups, each representing a letter, word, or phrase in a codebook. The apparently random numbers were relayed by secure cable to teleprinters in the basement of the Old Administration Building. Then the difficult part began: cracking the code.

They always started with small things. The last word of any signal was often *owari*, meaning "end." The cryptanalyst would look for other appearances of that number group in the same signal, and write "END?" above any he found.

The Japanese helped them by making an uncharacteristically careless mistake.

Delivery of the new codebooks for JN-25b was delayed to some far-flung units. So, for a fatal few weeks, the Japanese high command sent out some messages *in both codes.* Since the Americans had broken much of the original JN-25, they were able to translate the message in the old code, set the decrypt alongside the message in the new code, and figure out the meanings of the five-digit groups of the new code. For a while they progressed by leaps and bounds.

The original eight cryptanalysts were supplemented, after Pearl Harbor, by some of the musicians from the band of the sunken battleship *California.* For reasons no one understood, musicians were good at decoding.

Every signal was kept and every decrypt filed. Comparison of one with another was crucial to the work. An analyst might ask for all the signals from a particular day, or all the signals to one ship, or all the signals that mentioned Hawaii. Chuck and the other clerical staff developed ever-more-complex systems of cross-indexing to help them find whatever the analysts needed.

The unit predicted that in the first week of May the Japanese would attack Port Moresby, the Allied base in Papua. They were right, and the U.S. Navy intercepted the invasion fleet in the Coral Sea. Both sides claimed victory, but the Japanese did not take Port Moresby. And Admiral Nimitz, commander in chief of the Pacific, began to trust his codebreakers.

The Japanese did not use regular names for locations in the Pacific Ocean. Every important place had a designation consisting of two letters—in fact two characters, or kanas, of the Japanese alphabet, although the codebreakers usually used equivalents from the Roman A to Z. The men in the basement struggled to figure out the meaning of each of these two-kana designators. They made slow progress: MO was Port Moresby, AH was Oahu, but many were unknown.

In May evidence was fast building up of a major Japanese assault at a location they called AF.

The best guess of the unit was that AF meant Midway, the atoll at the western end of the fifteen-hundred-mile-long chain of islands that started at Hawaii. Midway was halfway between Los Angeles and Tokyo.

A guess was not enough, of course. Given the numerical superiority of the Japanese navy, Admiral Nimitz had to *know*.

Day by day, the men Chuck was working with built up an ominous picture of the Japanese order of battle. New planes were delivered to aircraft carriers. An "occupation force" was embarked: the Japanese were planning to hold on to whatever territory they won.

It looked as if this was the big one. But where would the attack come?

The men in the basement were particularly proud of decoding a signal from the Japanese fleet urging Tokyo: "Expedite delivery of fueling hose." They were pleased partly because of the specialized language but mainly because the signal proved that a long-range midocean maneuver was imminent.

But the American high command thought the attack might come at Hawaii, and the army feared an invasion of the West Coast of the United States. Even the team at Pearl Harbor had a nagging suspicion it could be Johnston Island, an airstrip a thousand miles south of Midway.

They had to be 100 percent certain.

Chuck had a notion how it might be done, but he hesitated to say anything. The cryptanalysts were so clever, and he was not. He had never done well in school. In third grade a classmate had called him Chucky the Chump. He had cried, and that had guaranteed that the nickname would stick. He still thought of himself as Chucky the Chump.

At lunchtime he and Eddie got sandwiches and coffee from the commissary and sat on the dockside, looking across the harbor. It was returning to normal. Most of the oil had gone, and some of the wrecks had been raised.

While they were eating, a wounded aircraft carrier appeared around Hospital Point and steamed slowly into harbor, trailing an oil slick that stretched all the way out to sea. Chuck identified the vessel as the *Yorktown*. Her hull was blackened with soot and she had a huge hole in the flight deck, presumably caused by a Japanese bomb in the Battle of the Coral Sea. Sirens and hooters sounded a congratulatory fanfare as she approached the navy yard, and tugs assembled to nudge her through the open gates of No. 1 Dry Dock.

"She needs three months' work, I hear," Eddie said. He was based in the same building as Chuck, but in the naval intelligence office upstairs, so he got to hear more gossip. "But she's putting to sea again in three days."

"How are they going to manage that?"

"They've started already. The master shipfitter flew to meet her—he's on board already, with a team. And look at the dry dock."

Chuck saw that the vacant dock was already swarming with men and equipment: he could not count the number of welding machines waiting at the quayside.

"All the same," Eddie said, "they'll just be patching her up. They'll repair the deck and make her seaworthy, and everything else will have to wait."

Something about the name of the ship bugged Chuck. He could not shake the nagging feeling. What did Yorktown mean? The siege of Yorktown was the last big battle of the War of Independence. Did that have some significance?

Captain Vandermeier walked by. "Get back to work, you two girlie boys," he said.

Eddie said under his breath: "One of these days I'm going to punch him out."

"After the war, Eddie," said Chuck.

When he returned to the basement and saw Bob Strong at his desk, Chuck realized he had solved Strong's problem.

Looking over the cryptanalyst's shoulder again, he saw the same sheet of paper with the same six Japanese syllables:

YO—LO—KU—TA—WA—NA

He tactfully tried to make it sound as if Strong himself had solved it. "But you have got it, Lieutenant!" he said.

Strong was disconcerted. "Do I?"

"It's an English name, so the Japanese have spelled it out phonetically."

"Yolokutawana is an English name?"

"Yes, sir. That's how the Japanese pronounce Yorktown."

"What?" Strong looked baffled.

For a dreadful moment, Chucky the Chump wondered if he was completely wrong.

Then Strong said: "Oh, my God, you're right! Yolokutawana—Yorktown, with a Japanese accent!" He laughed delightedly. "Thank you!" he enthused. "Well done!"

Chuck hesitated. He had another idea. Should he say what was on his mind? It was not his job to solve codes. But America was an inch away from defeat. Maybe he should take a chance. "Can I make another suggestion?" he said.

"Fire away."

"It's about the designator AF. We need definite confirmation that it's Midway, right?"

"Yup."

"Couldn't we write a message about Midway that the Japanese would want to rebroadcast in code? Then when we intercepted the broadcast, we could find out how they encode the name."

Strong looked thoughtful. "Maybe," he said. "We might have to send our message in clear, to be sure they understood it."

"We could do that. It would have to be something not very confidential—like, say: 'There is an outbreak of venereal disease on Midway, please send medicine,' or something like that."

"But why would the Japs rebroadcast that?"

"Okay, so it has to be something of military significance, but not top secret—something like the weather."

"Even weather forecasts are secret nowadays."

The cryptanalyst at the next desk put in: "How about a water shortage? If they're planning to occupy the place, that would be important information."

"Hell, this could work." Strong was getting excited. "Suppose Midway sends a message in clear to Hawaii, saying their desalination plant has broken down."

Chuck said: "And Hawaii replies, saying we're sending a water barge."

"The Japanese would be sure to rebroadcast that, if they're planning to attack Midway. They would need to make plans to ship fresh water there."

"And they would broadcast in code to avoid alerting us to their interest in Midway."

Strong stood up. "Come with me," he said to Chuck. "Let's put this to the boss, see what he thinks of the idea."

The signals were exchanged that day.

Next day, a Japanese radio signal reported a water shortage at AF.

The target was Midway.

Admiral Nimitz commenced to set a trap.


## iii


That evening, while more than a thousand workmen swarmed over the crippled aircraft carrier *Yorktown*, repairing the damage under arc lights, Chuck and Eddie went to the Band Round the Hat, a bar down a dark alley in Honolulu. It was packed, as always, with sailors and locals. Almost all the customers were men, though there were a few nurses in pairs. Chuck and Eddie liked the place because the other men were their kind. The lesbians liked it because the men did not hit on them.

There was nothing overt, of course. You could be thrown out of the navy and put in jail for homosexual acts. All the same the place was congenial. The bandleader wore makeup. The Hawaiian singer was in drag, although he was so convincing that some people did not realize he was a man. The owner was as queer as a three-dollar bill. Men could dance together. And no one would call you a wimp for ordering vermouth.

Since the death of Joanne, Chuck felt he loved Eddie even more. Of course he had always known that Eddie could be killed, in theory, but the danger had never seemed real. Now, after the attack on Pearl Harbor, Chuck never passed a day without visualizing that beautiful girl lying on the ground covered in blood, and his brother sobbing his heart out beside her. It could so easily have been Chuck kneeling next to Eddie, and feeling the same unbearable grief. Chuck and Eddie had cheated death on December 7, but they were at war now, and life was cheap. Every day together was precious because it might be the last.

Chuck was leaning on the bar with a beer in his hand, and Eddie was sitting on a high stool. They were laughing at a navy pilot called Trevor Paxman—known as Trixie—who was talking about the time he tried to have sex with a girl. "I was horrified!" Trixie said. "I thought it would be all tidy down there, and kind of sweet, like girls in paintings—but she had more hair than me!" They roared with laughter. "She was like a gorilla!" At that point Chuck saw, out of the corner of his eye, the stocky figure of Captain Vandermeier entering the bar.

Few officers went into enlisted men's bars. It was not forbidden, merely thoughtless and inconsiderate, like wearing muddy boots in the restaurant of the Ritz-Carlton. Eddie turned his back, hoping Vandermeier would not see him.

No such luck. Vandermeier came right up to them and said: "Well, well, all girls together, are we?"

Trixie turned away and melted into the crowd. Vandermeier said: "Where did he go?" He was already drunk enough to slur his words.

Chuck saw Eddie's face darken. Chuck said stiffly: "Good evening, Captain, may I buy you a beer?"

"Scotch onna rocks."

Chuck got him a drink. Vandermeier took a swallow and said: "So, I hear the action in this place is out the back—is that right?" He looked at Eddie.

"No idea," Eddie said coldly.

"Aw, come on," said Vandermeier. "Off the record." He patted Eddie's knee.

Eddie stood up abruptly and pushed his stool back. "Don't you touch me," he said.

Chuck said: "Take it easy, Eddie."

"There's no rule in the navy says I have to be pawed by this old queen!"

Vandermeier said drunkenly: "What did you call me?"

Eddie said: "If he touches me again, I swear I'll knock his ugly head off."

Chuck said: "Captain Vandermeier, sir, I know a much better place than this. Would you like to go there?"

Vandermeier looked confused. "What?"

Chuck improvised: "A smaller, quieter place—like this, but more intimate. Do you know what I mean?"

"Sounds good!" The captain drained his glass.

Chuck took Vandermeier's right arm and gestured to Eddie to take the left. They led the drunk captain outside.

Luckily, a taxi was waiting in the gloom of the alley. Chuck opened the car door.

At that point, Vandermeier kissed Eddie.

The captain threw his arms around him, pressed his lips to Eddie's, then said: "I love you."

Chuck's heart filled with fear. There was no good ending to this now.

Eddie punched Vandermeier in the stomach, hard. The captain grunted and gasped. Eddie hit him again, in the face this time. Chuck stepped between them. Before Vandermeier could fall down, Chuck bundled him into the backseat of the taxi.

He leaned through the window and gave the driver a ten-dollar bill. "Take him home, and keep the change," he said.

The taxi pulled away.

Chuck looked at Eddie. "Oh, boy," he said. "Now we're in trouble."

But Eddie Parry was never charged with the crime of assaulting an officer.

Captain Vandermeier showed up at the Old Administration Building next morning with a black eye, but he made no accusation. Chuck figured it would ruin the man's career if he admitted he had got into a fight at the Band Round the Hat. All the same everyone was talking about his bruise. Bob Strong said: "Vandermeier claims he slipped on a patch of oil in his garage, and hit his face on the lawn mower, but I think his wife socked him. Have you seen her? She looks like Jack Dempsey."

That day, the cryptanalysts in the basement told Admiral Nimitz that the Japanese would attack Midway on June 4. More specifically, the Japanese force would be one hundred and seventy-five miles north of the atoll at seven A.M.

They were almost as confident as they sounded.

Eddie was gloomy. "What can we do?" he said when he and Chuck met for lunch. He worked in naval intelligence, too, and he knew the Japanese strength as revealed by the codebreakers. "The Japs have two hundred ships at sea—practically their entire navy—and how many do we have? Thirty-five!"

Chuck was not so glum. "But their strike force is only a quarter of their strength. The rest are the occupation force, the diversion force, and the reserves."

"So? A quarter of their strength is still more than our entire Pacific Fleet!"

"The actual Japanese strike force has only four aircraft carriers."

"But we have just three." Eddie pointed with his ham sandwich at the smoke-blackened carrier in the dry dock, with workmen swarming all over her. "And that includes the broken-down *Yorktown*."

"Well, we know they're coming, and they don't know we're lying in wait."

"I sure hope that makes as much difference as Nimitz thinks."

"Yeah, so do I."

When Chuck returned to the basement, he was told that he no longer worked there. He had been reassigned—to the *Yorktown*.

"It's Vandermeier's way of punishing me," Eddie said tearfully that evening. "He thinks you'll die."

"Don't be pessimistic," Chuck said. "We might win the war."

A few days before the attack, the Japanese changed to new codebooks. The men in the basement sighed and started again from scratch, but they produced little new intelligence before the battle. Nimitz had to make do with what he already had, and hope the Japanese did not revise the whole plan at the last minute.

The Japanese expected to take Midway by surprise and overwhelm it easily. They hoped the Americans would then attack in full force in a bid to win the atoll back. At that point, the Japanese reserve fleet would pounce and wipe out the entire American fleet. Japan would rule the Pacific.

And the USA would ask for peace talks.

Nimitz planned to nip the scheme in the bud by ambushing the strike force before they could take Midway.

Chuck was now part of the ambush.

He packed his kit bag and kissed Eddie good-bye; then they went together to the dockside.

There they ran into Vandermeier.

"There was no time to repair the watertight compartments," he told them. "If she's holed, she'll go down like a lead coffin."

Chuck put a restraining hand on Eddie's shoulder and said: "How's your eye, Captain?"

Vandermeier's mouth twisted in a grimace of malice. "Good luck, faggot." He walked away.

Chuck shook hands with Eddie and went on board.

He forgot about Vandermeier instantly, for at long last he had his wish: he was at sea—and on one of the greatest ships ever made.

The *Yorktown* was the lead ship of the carrier class. She was longer than two football pitches and had a crew of more than two thousand.

She carried ninety aircraft: elderly Douglas Devastator torpedo bombers with folding wings, newer Douglas Dauntless dive-bombers, and Grumman Wildcat fighters to escort the bombers.

Almost everything was below, apart from the island structure, which stood up thirty feet from the flight deck. It contained the ship's command and communications heart, with the bridge, the radio room just below it, the chart house, and the aviators' ready room. Behind these was a huge smokestack containing three funnels in a row.

Some of the repairmen were still aboard, finishing their work, when she left the dry dock and steamed out of Pearl Harbor. Chuck thrilled to the throb of her colossal engines as she put to sea. When she reached deep water and began to rise and fall with the swell of the Pacific Ocean, he felt as if he were dancing.

Chuck was assigned to the radio room, a sensible posting that made use of his experience in handling signals.

The carrier steamed to a rendezvous northeast of Midway, her welded patches creaking like new shoes. The ship had a soda fountain, known as the Gedunk, that served freshly made ice cream. There on the first afternoon Chuck ran into Trixie Paxman, whom he had last seen at the Band Round the Hat. He was glad to have a friend aboard.

On Wednesday, June 3, the day before the predicted attack, a navy flying boat on reconnaissance west of Midway spotted a convoy of Japanese transport ships—presumably carrying the occupation force that was to take over the atoll after the battle. The news was broadcast to all U.S. ships, and Chuck in the radio room of the *Yorktown* was among the first to know. It was hard confirmation that his comrades in the basement had been right, and he felt a sense of relief that they had been vindicated. That was ironic, he realized: he would not be in such danger if they had been wrong and the Japanese were elsewhere.

He had been in the navy for a year and a half, but until now he had never gone into battle. The hastily repaired *Yorktown* was going to be the target of Japanese torpedoes and bombs. She was steaming toward people who would do everything in their power to sink her, and sink

Chuck, too. It was a weird feeling. Most of the time he was strangely calm, but every now and again he felt an impulse to dive over the side and start swimming back toward Hawaii.

That night he wrote to his parents. If he died tomorrow, he and the letter would probably go down with the ship, but he wrote it anyway. He said nothing about why he had been reassigned. It crossed his mind to confess that he was queer, but he quickly dismissed that idea. He told them he loved them and was grateful for everything they had done for him. "If I die fighting for a democratic country against a cruel military dictatorship, my life will not have been wasted," he wrote. When he read it over, it sounded a bit pompous, but he left it as it was.

It was a short night. Aircrew were piped to breakfast at one thirty A.M. Chuck went to wish Trixie Paxman good luck. In recompense for the early start, the airmen were eating steak and eggs.

Their planes were brought up from the belowdecks hangars in the ship's huge elevators, then maneuvered by hand to their parking slots on deck to be fueled and armed. A few pilots took off and went looking for the enemy. The rest sat in the briefing room, wearing their flying gear, waiting for news.

Chuck went on duty in the radio room. Just before six he picked up a signal from a reconnaissance flying boat:

MANY ENEMY PLANES HEADING MIDWAY

A few minutes later he got a partial signal:

ENEMY CARRIERS

It had started.

When the full report came in a minute later, it placed the Japanese strike force almost exactly where the cryptanalysts had forecast. Chuck felt proud—and scared.

The three American aircraft carriers—*Yorktown, Enterprise,* and *Hornet*—set a course that would bring their planes within striking distance of the Japanese ships.

On the bridge was the long-nosed Admiral Frank Fletcher, a fifty-seven-year-old veteran who had won the Navy Cross in the First World War. Carrying a signal to the bridge, Chuck heard him say: "We haven't seen a Japanese plane yet. That means they still don't know we're here."

That was all the Americans had going for them, Chuck knew: the advantage of better intelligence.

The Japanese undoubtedly hoped to catch Midway napping, in a repeat of the Pearl Harbor scenario, but it was not going to happen, thanks to the cryptanalysts. The American planes at Midway were not sitting targets parked on their runways. By the time the Japanese bombers arrived, they were all in the air and spoiling for a fight.

Tensely listening to the crackling wireless traffic from Midway and the Japanese ships, the officers and men in the radio room of the *Yorktown* had no doubt that there was a terrific air battle going on over the tiny atoll, but they did not know who was winning.

Soon afterward, American planes from Midway took the fight to the enemy and attacked the Japanese aircraft carriers.

In both battles, as far as Chuck could make out, the antiaircraft guns had the best of it. Only moderate damage was done to the base at Midway, and almost all the bombs and torpedoes aimed at the Japanese fleet missed, but in both encounters a lot of aircraft were shot down.

The score seemed even—but that bothered Chuck, for the Japanese had more in reserve.

Just before seven the *Yorktown,* the *Enterprise,* and the *Hornet* swung around to the southeast. It was a course that unfortunately took them away from the enemy, but their planes had to take off into the southeasterly wind.

Every corner of the mighty *Yorktown* trembled to the thunder of the aircraft as their engines rose to full throttle and they powered along the deck, one after another, and shot up into the air. Chuck noticed the tendency of the Wildcat to lift its right wing and wander left as it accelerated along the deck, a characteristic much complained of by pilots.

By half past eight the three carriers had sent 155 American planes to attack the enemy strike force.

The first planes arrived in the target area, with perfect timing, when the Japanese were busy refueling and rearming their own planes returning from Midway. The flight decks were littered with ammunition cases scattered in a snakes' nest of fuel hoses, all ready to blow up in an instant. There should have been carnage.

But it did not happen.

Almost all the American aircraft in the first wave were destroyed.

The Devastators were obsolete. The Wildcats that escorted them were better, but no match for the fast, maneuverable Japanese Zeroes. Those planes that survived to deliver their ordnance were decimated by devastating antiaircraft fire from the carriers.

Dropping a bomb from a moving aircraft onto a moving ship, or dropping a torpedo where it would hit a ship, was extraordinarily difficult, especially for a pilot who was under fire from above and below.

Most of the airmen gave their lives in the attempt.

And not one of them scored a hit.

No American bomb or torpedo found its target. The first three waves of attacking planes, one from each American carrier, did no damage at all to the Japanese strike force. The ammunition on their decks did not explode, and their fuel lines did not catch fire. They were unharmed.

Listening to the radio chatter, Chuck despaired.

He saw with new vividness the genius of the attack on Pearl Harbor seven months earlier. The American ships had been at anchor, static targets crowded together, relatively easy to hit. The fighter planes that might have protected them were destroyed on their airstrips. And by the time the Americans had armed and deployed their antiaircraft guns, the attack was almost over.

However, this battle was still going on, and not all the American planes had yet reached the target area. He heard an air officer on the *Enterprise* radio shout: "Attack! Attack!" and the laconic response from a pilot: "Wilco, as soon as I can find the bastards."

The good news was that the Japanese commander had not yet sent aircraft to attack the American ships. He was sticking to his plan and concentrating on Midway. He might by now have figured out that he must be under attack from carrier-borne planes, but perhaps he was not sure where the American ships were located.

Despite this advantage, the Americans were not winning.

Then the picture changed. A flight of thirty-seven Dauntless dive-bombers from the *Enterprise* sighted the Japanese. The Zeroes protecting the ships had come down almost to sea level in their dogfights with previous attackers, so the bombers found themselves fortunately above the fighters, and able to come down at them out of the sun. Just minutes later another eighteen Dauntlesses from the *Yorktown* reached the target area. One of the pilots was Trixie.

The radio exploded with excited chatter. Chuck closed his eyes and concentrated, trying to make sense of the distorted sounds. He could not identify Trixie's voice.

Then, behind the talk, he began to hear the characteristic scream of bombers diving. The attack had begun.

Suddenly, for the first time, there were cries of triumph from the pilots.

"Got you, you bastard!"

"Shit, I felt that go up!"

"Eat that, you sons of bitches!"

"Bull's-eye!"

"Look at her burn!"

The men in the radio room cheered wildly, but they were not sure what was happening.

It was over in a few minutes, but it took a long time to get a clear report. The pilots were incoherent with the joy of victory. Gradually, as they calmed down and headed back toward their ships, the picture emerged.

Trixie Paxman was among the survivors.

Most of their bombs had missed, as previously, but about ten had scored direct hits, and those few had done tremendous damage.

Three mighty Japanese aircraft carriers were burning out of control: *Kaga, Soryu,* and the flagship *Akagi.* The enemy had only one left, the *Hiryu.*

"Three out of the four!" Chuck said elatedly. "And they still haven't come anywhere near our ships!"

That soon changed.

Admiral Fletcher sent out ten Dauntlesses to scout for the surviving Japanese carrier. But it was the *Yorktown*'s radar that picked up a flight of planes, presumably from the *Hiryu,* fifty miles away and approaching. At noon Fletcher sent up twelve Wildcats to meet the attackers. The rest of the planes were also ordered up so they would not be on deck and vulnerable when the attack came. Meanwhile the *Yorktown*'s fuel lines were flooded with carbon dioxide as a fire precaution.

The attacking flight included fourteen "Vals," Aichi D3A dive-bombers, plus escorting Zeroes.

Here it comes, Chuck thought, my first action. He wanted to throw up. He swallowed hard.

Before the attackers could be seen, the *Yorktown*'s gunners opened up. The ship had four pairs of large antiaircraft guns with five-inch-diameter barrels that could send their shells several miles. Plotting the enemy's position with the aid of radar, gunnery officers sent a salvo of giant fifty-four-pound shells toward the approaching aircraft, setting the timers to explode when they reached their target.

The Wildcats got above the attackers and, according to the pilots' radio reports, shot down six bombers and three fighters.

Chuck ran to the flag bridge with a signal to say the remainder of the attack force were diving in. Admiral Fletcher said coolly: "Well, I've got my tin hat on—I can't do anything else."

Chuck looked out of the window and saw the dive-bombers screaming out of the sky toward him at an angle so steep they seemed to be falling straight down. He resisted the impulse to throw himself to the floor.

The ship made a sudden full-rudder turn to port. Anything that might throw the attacking aircraft off course was worth a try.

The *Yorktown* deck also had four "Chicago pianos"—smaller, short-range antiaircraft guns with four barrels each. Now these opened up, and so did the guns of *Yorktown*'s escort of cruisers.

As Chuck stared forward from the bridge, terrified and helpless to do anything to defend himself, a deck gunner found his range and hit a Val. The plane seemed to break into three pieces. Two fell into the sea and one crashed into the side of the ship. Then another Val blew up. Chuck cheered.

But that left six.

The *Yorktown* made a sudden turn to starboard.

The Vals braved the hail of death from the deck guns to chase after the ship.

As they got closer, the machine guns on the catwalks either side of the flight deck also opened up. Now the *Yorktown*'s guns played a lethal symphony, with deep booms from the five-inch barrels, midrange sounds from the Chicago pianos, and the urgent rattle of machine guns.

Chuck saw the first bomb.

Many Japanese bombs had a delayed fuse. Instead of exploding on impact, they went off a second or so later, the idea being that they would crash through the deck and explode deep in the interior, causing maximum devastation.

But this bomb rolled along the *Yorktown*'s deck.

Chuck watched in mesmerized horror. For a moment it looked as if it might do no harm. Then it went off with a boom and a flash of flame. The two Chicago pianos aft were destroyed in an instant. Small fires appeared on deck and in the towers.

To Chuck's amazement the men around him remained as cool as if they were attending a war game in a conference room. Admiral Fletcher issued orders even as he staggered across the shuddering deck of the flag bridge. Moments later, damage control teams were dashing across the flight deck with fire hoses, and stretcher parties were picking up the wounded and carrying them down steep companionways to dressing stations below.

There were no major fires: the carbon dioxide in the fuel lines had prevented that. And there were no bomb-loaded planes on deck to blow up.

A moment later another Val screamed down at the *Yorktown* and a bomb hit the smokestack. The explosion rocked the mighty ship. A huge pall of oily black smoke gouted from the funnels. The bomb must have damaged the engines, Chuck realized, because the ship lost speed immediately.

More bombs missed their targets, landing in the sea, sending up geysers that splashed onto the deck, where seawater mingled with the blood of the wounded.

The *Yorktown* slowed to a halt. When the crippled ship was dead in the water, the Japanese scored a third hit, and a bomb crashed through the forward elevator and exploded somewhere below.

Then, suddenly, it was over, and the surviving Vals climbed into the clear blue Pacific sky.

I'm still alive, Chuck thought.

The ship was not lost. Fire-control parties were at work before the Japanese were out of sight. Down below, the engineers said they could get the boilers going within an hour. Repair crews patched the hole in the flight deck with six-by-four planks of Douglas fir.

But the radio gear had been destroyed, so Admiral Fletcher was deaf and blind. With his personal staff he transferred to the cruiser *Astoria*, and he handed over tactical command to Spruance on the *Enterprise*.

Under his breath, Chuck said: "Fuck you, Vandermeier—I survived."

He spoke too soon.

The engines throbbed back to life. Now under the command of Captain Buckmaster, the *Yorktown* began once again to cut through the Pacific waves. Some of her planes had already taken refuge on the *Enterprise*, but others were still in the air, so she turned into the wind, and they began to touch down and refuel. As she had no working radio, Chuck and his colleagues became a semaphore team to communicate with other ships using old-fashioned flags.

At half past two, the radar of a cruiser escorting the *Yorktown* revealed planes coming in low from the west—an attack flight from the

*Hiryu,* presumably. The cruiser signaled the news to the carrier. Buckmaster sent up twelve Wildcats to intercept.

The Wildcats must have been unable to stop the attack, for ten torpedo bombers appeared, skimming the waves, heading straight for the *Yorktown.*

Chuck could see the planes clearly. They were Nakajima B5Ns, called Kates by the Americans. Each carried a torpedo slung under its fuselage, the weapon almost half the length of the entire plane.

The four heavy cruisers escorting the carrier shelled the sea around her, throwing up a screen of foamy water, but the Japanese pilots were not so easily deterred, and they flew straight through the spray.

Chuck saw the first plane drop its torpedo. The long bomb splashed into the water, pointed at the *Yorktown.*

The plane flashed past the ship so close that Chuck saw the pilot's face. He was wearing a white-and-red headband as well as his flight helmet. He shook a triumphant fist at the crew on deck. Then he was gone.

More planes roared by. Torpedoes were slow, and ships could sometimes dodge them, but the crippled *Yorktown* was too cumbersome to zigzag. There was a tremendous bang, shaking the ship: torpedoes were several times more powerful than regular bombs. It felt to Chuck as if she had been struck on the port stern. Another explosion followed close behind, and this one actually lifted the ship, throwing half the crew to the deck. Immediately afterward, the mighty engines faltered.

Once again the damage parties were at work before the attacking planes were out of sight. But this time the men could not cope. Chuck joined the teams manning the pumps, and saw that the steel hull of the great ship was ripped like a tin can. A Niagara of seawater poured through the gash. Within minutes Chuck could feel that the deck had tilted. The *Yorktown* was listing to port.

The pumps could not cope with the inward rush of water, especially as the ship's watertight compartments had been damaged at the Coral Sea and not fixed during her rush repairs.

How long could it be before she capsized?

At three o'clock Chuck heard the order: "Abandon ship!"

Sailors dropped ropes over the high edge of the sloping deck. On the hangar deck, by jerking a few strings crewmen released thousands of life jackets from overhead stowage to fall like rain. The escort vessels moved closer and launched their boats. The crew of the *Yorktown* took off their shoes and swarmed over the side. For some reason, they put their shoes on the deck in neat lines, hundreds of pairs, like some ritual sacrifice. Wounded men were lowered on stretchers to waiting whaleboats. Chuck found himself in the water, swimming as fast as he could to get away from the *Yorktown* before she turned over. A wave took him by surprise and washed away his cap. He was glad he was in the warm Pacific: the Atlantic might have killed him with cold while he was waiting to be rescued.

He was picked up by a lifeboat. The boat continued to retrieve men from the sea. Dozens of other boats were doing the same. Many of the crew climbed down from the main deck, which was lower than the flight deck. The *Yorktown* somehow managed to stay afloat.

When all the crew were safe, they were taken aboard the escorting vessels.

Chuck stood on deck, looking across the water as the sun went down behind the slowly sinking *Yorktown.* It occurred to him that during the whole day he had not seen a Japanese ship. The entire battle had been fought by aircraft. He wondered if this was the first of a new kind of naval battle. If so, aircraft carriers would be the key vessels in the future. Nothing else would count for much.

Trixie Paxman appeared beside him. Chuck was so pleased to see him alive that he hugged him.

Trixie told Chuck that the last flight of Dauntless dive-bombers, from the *Enterprise* and the *Yorktown,* had set alight the *Hiryu,* the surviving Japanese carrier, and destroyed her.

"So all four Japanese carriers are out of action," Chuck said.

"That's right. We got them all, and lost only one of our own."

"So," said Chuck, "does that mean we won?"

"Yes," said Trixie. "I guess it does."

## V

After the Battle of Midway it was clear that the Pacific war would be won by planes launched from ships. Both Japan and the United States began crash programs to build aircraft carriers as fast as possible.

During 1943 and 1944, Japan produced seven of these huge, costly vessels.

In the same period, the United States produced ninety.

# CHAPTER THIRTEEN

# 1942 (II)

Nursing Sister Carla von Ulrich wheeled a cart into the supply room and closed the door behind her.

She had to work quickly. What she was about to do would get her sent to a concentration camp if she were caught.

She took a selection of wound dressings from a cupboard, plus a roll of bandage and a jar of antiseptic cream. Then she unlocked the drug cabinet. She took morphine for pain relief, sulfonamide for infections, and aspirin for fever. She added a new hypodermic syringe, still in its box.

She had already falsified the register, over a period of weeks, to look as if what she was stealing had been used legitimately. She had rigged the register before taking the stuff, rather than afterward, so that any spot check would reveal a surplus, suggesting mere carelessness, instead of a deficit, which indicated theft.

She had done all this twice before, but she felt no less frightened.

As she wheeled the cart out of the store, she hoped she looked innocent: a nurse bringing medical necessities to a patient's bedside.

She walked into the ward. To her dismay she saw Dr. Ernst there, sitting beside a bed, taking a patient's pulse.

All the doctors should have been at lunch.

It was now too late to change her mind. Trying to assume an air of confidence that was the opposite of what she felt, she held her head high and walked through the ward, pushing her cart.

Dr. Ernst glanced up at her and smiled.

Berthold Ernst was the nurses' dreamboat. A talented surgeon with a warm bedside manner, he was tall, handsome, and single. He had romanced most of the attractive nurses, and had slept with many of them, if hospital gossip could be credited.

She nodded to him and went briskly past.

She pushed the trolley out of the ward, then suddenly turned into the nurses' cloakroom.

Her outdoor coat was on a hook. Beneath it was a basketwork shopping bag containing an old silk scarf, a cabbage, and a box of sanitary towels in a brown paper bag. Carla removed the contents, then swiftly transferred the medical supplies from the trolley to the bag. She covered the supplies with the scarf, a blue-and-gold geometric design that her mother must have bought in the twenties. Then she put the cabbage and the sanitary towels on top, hung the bag on a hook, and arranged her coat to cover it.

I got away with it, she thought. She realized she was trembling a little. She took a deep breath, got herself under control, opened the door—and saw Dr. Ernst standing just outside.

Had he been following her? Was he about to accuse her of stealing? His manner was not hostile; in fact he looked friendly. Perhaps she had got away with it.

She said: "Good afternoon, Doctor. Can I help you with something?"

He smiled. "How are you, Sister? Is everything going well?"

"Perfectly, I think." Guilt made her add ingratiatingly: "But it is you, Doctor, who must say whether things are going well."

"Oh, I have no complaints," he said dismissively.

Carla thought: So what is this about? Is he toying with me, sadistically delaying the moment when he makes his accusation?

She said nothing, but stood waiting, trying not to shake with anxiety.

He looked down at the cart. "Why did you take that into the cloakroom?"

"I wanted something," she said, improvising desperately. "Something from my raincoat." She tried to suppress the frightened tremor in her voice. "A handkerchief, from my pocket." Stop gabbling, she told herself. He's a doctor, not a Gestapo agent. But he scared her all the same.

He looked amused, as if he enjoyed her nervousness. "And the trolley?"

"I'm returning it to its place."

"Tidiness is essential. You're a very good nurse . . . Fräulein von Ulrich . . . or is it Frau?"

"Fräulein."

"We should talk some more."

The way he smiled told her this was not about stealing medical supplies. He was about to ask her to go out with him. She would be the envy of dozens of nurses if she said yes.

But she had no interest in him. Perhaps it was because she had loved one dashing Lothario, Werner Franck, and he had turned out to be a self-centered coward. She guessed that Berthold Ernst was similar.

However, she did not want to risk annoying him, so she just smiled and said nothing.

"Do you like Wagner?" he said.

She could see where this was going. "I have no time for music," she said firmly. "I take care of my elderly mother." In fact Maud was fifty-one and enjoyed robust good health.

"I have two tickets for a recital tomorrow evening. They're playing the *Siegfried Idyll.*"

"A chamber piece!" she said. "Unusual." Most of Wagner's work was on a grand scale.

He looked pleased. "You know about music, I see."

She wished she had not said it. She had just encouraged him. "My family is musical—my mother gives piano lessons."

"Then you must come. I'm sure someone else could take care of your mother for an evening."

"It's really not possible," Carla said. "But thank you very much for the invitation." She saw anger in his eyes: he was not used to rejection. She turned and started to push the cart away.

"Another time, perhaps?" he called after her.

"You're very kind," she replied, without slowing her pace.

She was afraid he would come after her, but her ambiguous reply to his last question seemed to have mollified him. When she looked back over her shoulder, he had gone.

She stowed the trolley and breathed easier.

She returned to her duties. She checked on all the patients in her ward and wrote her reports. Then it was time to hand over to the evening shift.

She put on her raincoat and slung her bag over her arm. Now she had to walk out of the building with stolen property, and her fear mounted again.

Frieda Franck was going at the same time, and they left together. Frieda had no idea Carla was carrying contraband. They walked in June sunshine to the tram stop. Carla wore a coat mainly to keep her uniform clean.

She thought she was giving a convincing impression of normality until Frieda said: "Are you worried about something?"

"No, why?"

"You seem nervous."

"I'm fine." To change the subject, she pointed at a poster. "Look at that."

The government had opened an exhibition in Berlin's Lustgarten, the park in front of the cathedral. "The Soviet Paradise" was the ironic title of a show about life under Communism, portraying Bolshevism as a Jewish trick and the Russians as subhuman Slavs. But even today the Nazis did not have everything their own way, and someone had gone around Berlin pasting up a spoof poster that read:

Permanent Installation
## The NAZI PARADISE
### War Hunger Lies Gestapo
*How much longer?*

There was one such poster stuck to the tram shelter, and it warmed Carla's heart. "Who puts these things up?" she said.

Frieda shrugged.

Carla said: "Whoever they are, they're brave. They would be killed if caught." Then she remembered what was in her bag. She, too, could be killed if caught.

Frieda just said: "I'm sure."

Now it was Frieda who seemed a little jumpy. Could she be one of those who put up the posters? Probably not. Maybe her boyfriend, Heinrich, was. He was the intense, moralistic type who would do that sort of thing. "How's Heinrich?" said Carla.

"He wants to get married."

"Don't you?"

Frieda lowered her voice. "I don't want to have children." This was a seditious remark: young women were supposed to produce children gladly for the Führer. Frieda nodded at the illegal poster. "I wouldn't like to bring a child into this paradise."

"I guess I wouldn't, either," said Carla. Maybe that was why she had turned down Dr. Ernst.

A tram arrived and they got on. Carla perched the basket on her lap nonchalantly, as if it contained nothing more sinister than cabbage. She scanned the other passengers. She was relieved to see no uniforms.

Frieda said: "Come home with me. Let's have a jazz night. We can play Werner's records."

"I'd love to, but I can't," Carla said. "I've got a call to pay. Remember the Rothmann family?"

Frieda looked around warily. Rothmann might or might not be a Jewish name. But no one was near enough to hear them. "Of course—he used to be our doctor."

"He's not supposed to practise anymore. Eva Rothmann went to London before the war and married a Scottish soldier. But the parents can't get out of Germany, of course. Their son, Rudi, was a violin maker—quite brilliant, apparently—but he lost his job, and now he repairs instruments and tunes pianos." He came to the von Ulrich house four times a year to tune the Steinway grand. "Anyway, I said I'd go round there this evening and see them."

"Oh," said Frieda. It was the long drawn-out *oh* of someone who has just seen the light.

"Oh, what?" said Carla.

"Now I understand why you're clutching that basket as if it contained the Holy Grail."

Carla was thunderstruck. Frieda had guessed her secret! "How did you know?"

"You said he's not *supposed* to practise. That suggests he does."

Carla saw that she had given Dr. Rothmann away. She should have said that he was not *allowed* to practise. Fortunately it was only to Frieda that she had betrayed him. She said: "What is he to do? They come to his door and beg him to help them. He can't turn sick people away! It's not as if he makes any money—all his patients are Jews and other poor folk who pay him with a few potatoes or an egg."

"You don't have to defend him to me," said Frieda. "I think he's brave. And you're heroic, stealing supplies from the hospital to give to him. Is this the first time?"

Carla shook her head. "Third. But I feel such a fool for letting you find out."

"You're not a fool. It's just that I know you too well."

The tram approached Carla's stop. "Wish me luck," she said, and she got off.

When she entered her house, she heard hesitant notes on the piano upstairs. Maud had a pupil. Carla was glad. It would cheer her mother up as well as provide a little money.

Carla took off her raincoat, then went into the kitchen and greeted Ada. When Maud had announced that she could no longer pay Ada's wages, Ada had asked if she could stay on anyway. Now she had a job cleaning an office in the evening, and she did housework for the von Ulrich family in exchange for her room and board.

Carla kicked off her shoes under the table and rubbed her feet together to ease their ache. Ada made her a cup of grain coffee.

Maud came into the kitchen, eyes sparkling. "A new pupil!" she said. She showed Carla a handful of banknotes. "And he wants a lesson every day!" She had left him practising scales, and his novice fingering sounded in the background like a cat walking along the keyboard.

"That's great," said Carla. "Who is he?"

"A Nazi, of course. But we need the money."

"What's his name?"

"Joachim Koch. He's quite young and shy. If you meet him, for goodness' sake bite your tongue and be polite."

"Of course."

Maud disappeared.

Carla drank her coffee gratefully. She had got used to the taste of burned acorns, as most people had.

She chatted idly to Ada for a few minutes. Ada had once been plump, but now she was thin. Few people were fat in today's Germany, but there was something wrong with Ada. The death of her handicapped son, Kurt, had hit her hard. She had a lethargic air. She did her job competently, but then she sat staring out of the window for hours, her expression blank. Carla was fond of her, and felt her anguish, but did not know what to do to help her.

The sound of the piano ceased and, a little later, Carla heard two voices in the hallway, her mother's and a man's. She assumed Maud was seeing Herr Koch out, and she was horrified, a moment later, when her mother entered the kitchen, closely followed by a man in an immaculate lieutenant's uniform.

"This is my daughter," Maud said cheerfully. "Carla, this is Lieutenant Koch, a new pupil."

Koch was an attractive, shy-looking man in his twenties. He had a fair mustache, and reminded Carla of pictures of her father when young.

Carla's heart raced with fear. The basket containing the stolen medical supplies was on the kitchen chair next to her. Would she accidentally betray herself to Lieutenant Koch, as she had to Frieda?

She could hardly speak. "I—I—I am pleased to make your acquaintance," she said.

Maud looked at her with curiosity, surprised at her nervousness. All Maud wanted was for Carla to be nice to the new pupil in the hope that he would continue his studies. She saw no harm in bringing an army officer into the kitchen. She had no idea that Carla had stolen medicines in her shopping basket.

Koch made a formal bow and said: "The pleasure is mine."

"And Ada is our maid."

Ada shot him a hostile look, but he did not see it: maids were beneath his notice. He put his weight on one leg and stood lopsided, trying to seem at ease but giving the opposite impression.

He acted younger than he looked. There was an innocence about him that suggested an overprotected child. All the same he was a danger.

Changing his stance, he rested his hands on the back of the chair on which Carla had put her basket. "I see you are a nurse," he said to her.

"Yes." Carla tried to think calmly. Did Koch have any idea who the von Ulrichs were? He might be too young to know what a Social Democrat was. The party had been illegal for nine years. Perhaps the infamy of the von Ulrich family had faded away with the death of Walter. At any rate, Koch seemed to take them for a respectable German family who were poor simply because they had lost the man who had supported them, a situation in which many well-bred women found themselves.

There was no reason he should look in the basket.

Carla made herself speak pleasantly to him. "How are you getting on with the piano?"

"I believe I am making rapid progress!" He glanced at Maud. "So my teacher tells me."

Maud said: "He shows evidence of talent, even at this early stage." She always said that, to encourage them to pay for a second lesson, but it seemed to Carla that she was being more charming than usual. She was entitled to flirt, of course; she had been a widow for more than a year. But she could not possibly have romantic feelings for someone half her age.

"However, I have decided not to tell my friends until I have mastered the instrument," Koch added. "Then I will astonish them with my skill."

"Won't that be fun?" said Maud. "Please sit down, Lieutenant, if you have a few minutes to spare." She pointed to the chair on which Carla's basket stood.

Carla reached out to grab the basket, but Koch beat her to it. He picked it up, saying: "Allow me." He glanced inside. Seeing the cabbage, he said: "Your supper, I presume?"

Carla said: "Yes." Her voice came out as a squeak.

He sat on the chair and placed the basket on the floor by his feet, on the side away from Carla. "I always fancied I might be musical. Now I have decided it is time to find out." He crossed his legs, then uncrossed them.

Carla wondered why he was so fidgety. He had nothing to fear. The thought crossed her mind that his unease might be sexual. He was alone with three single women. What was going through his mind?

Ada put a cup of coffee in front of him. He took out cigarettes. He smoked like a teenager, as if he were trying it out. Ada gave him an ashtray.

Maud said: "Lieutenant Koch works at the Ministry of War on Bendler Strasse."

"Indeed!" That was the headquarters of the Supreme Staff. It was just as well Koch was telling no one there about learning the piano. All the greatest secrets of the German military were in that building. Even if Koch himself was ignorant, some of his colleagues might remember that Walter von Ulrich had been an anti-Nazi. And that would be the end of his lessons with Frau von Ulrich.

"It is a great privilege to work there," said Koch.

Maud said: "My son is in Russia. We're terribly worried about him."

"That is natural in a mother, of course," Koch said. "But please do not be pessimistic! The recent Russian counteroffensive has been decisively beaten back."

That was rubbish. The propaganda machine could not conceal the fact that the Russians had won the battle of Moscow and pushed the German line back a hundred miles.

Koch went on: "We are now in a position to resume our advance."

"Are you sure?" Maud looked anxious. Carla felt the same. They were both tortured by fear of what might happen to Erik.

Koch tried a superior smile. "Believe me, Frau von Ulrich, I am certain. Of course I cannot reveal all that I know. However, I can assure you that a very aggressive new operation is being planned."

"I am sure our troops have everything they need—enough food, and so on." She put a hand on Koch's arm. "All the same, I worry. I shouldn't say that, I know, but I feel I can trust you, Lieutenant."

"Of course."

"I haven't heard from my son for months. I don't know if he's dead or alive."

Koch reached into his pocket and took out a pencil and a small notebook. "I can certainly find out for you," he said.

"Could you?" said Maud, wide-eyed.

Carla thought this might be her reason for flirting.

Koch said: "Oh, yes. I am on the General Staff, you know—albeit in a humble role." He tried to look modest. "I can inquire about . . ."

"Erik."

"Erik von Ulrich."

"That would be wonderful. He's a medical orderly. He was studying to be a doctor, but he was impatient to fight for the Führer."

It was true. Erik had been a gung-ho Nazi—although his last few letters home had taken a more subdued tone.

Koch wrote down the name.

Maud said: "You're a wonderful man, Lieutenant Koch."

"It is nothing."

"I'm so glad we're about to counterattack on the eastern front. But you mustn't tell me when the attack will begin. Though I'm desperate to know."

Maud was fishing for information. Carla could not imagine why. She had no use for it.

Koch lowered his voice, as if there might be a spy outside the open kitchen window. "It will be very soon," he said. He looked around at the three women. Carla saw that he was basking in their attention. Perhaps it was unusual for him to have women hanging on his words. Prolonging the moment, he said: "Case Blue will begin very soon."

Maud flashed her eyes at him. "Case Blue—how tremendously thrilling!" she said in the tone a woman might use if a man offered to take her to the Ritz in Paris for a week.

He whispered: "The twenty-eighth of June."

Maud put her hand on her heart. "So soon! That's marvelous news."

"I should not have said anything."

Maud put her hand over his. "I'm so glad you did, though. You've made me feel so much better."

He stared at her hand. Carla realized he was not used to being touched by women. He looked up from her hand to her eyes. She smiled warmly—so warmly that Carla could hardly believe it was 100 percent fake.

Maud withdrew her hand. Koch stubbed out his cigarette and stood up. "I must go," he said.

Thank God, Carla thought.

He bowed to her. "A pleasure to meet you, Fräulein."

"Good-bye, Lieutenant," she replied neutrally.

Maud saw him to the door, saying: "Same time tomorrow, then."

When she came back into the kitchen, she said: "What a find—a foolish boy who works for the General Staff!"

Carla said: "I don't understand why you're so excited."

Ada said: "He's very handsome."

Maud said: "He gave us secret information!"

"What good is it to us?" Carla asked. "We're not spies."

"We know the date of the next offensive—surely we can find a way to pass it to the Russians?"

"I don't know how."

"We're supposed to be surrounded by spies."

"That's just propaganda. Everything that goes wrong is blamed on subversion by Jewish-Bolshevik secret agents, instead of Nazi bungling."

"All the same, there must be some real spies."

"How would we get in touch with them?"

Mother looked thoughtful. "I'd speak to Frieda."

"What makes you say that?"

"Intuition."

Carla recalled the moment at the bus stop, when she had wondered aloud who put up the anti-Nazi posters, and Frieda had gone quiet. Carla's intuition agreed with her mother's.

But that was not the only problem. "Even if we could, do we want to betray our country?"

Maud was emphatic. "We have to defeat the Nazis."

"I hate the Nazis more than anyone, but I'm still German."

"I know what you mean. I don't like the idea of turning traitor, even though I was born English. But we aren't going to get rid of the Nazis unless we lose the war."

"But suppose we could give the Russians information that would ensure we lost a battle. Erik might die in that battle! Your son—my brother! We might be the cause of his death."

Maud opened her mouth to answer, but found she could not speak. Instead she began to cry. Carla stood up and put her arms around her.

After a minute, Maud whispered: "He might die anyway. He might die fighting for Nazism. Better he should be killed losing a battle than winning it."

Carla was not sure about that.

She released her mother. "Anyway, I wish you'd warn me before bringing someone like that into the kitchen," she said. She picked up her basket from the floor. "It's a good thing Lieutenant Koch didn't look any further into this."

"Why, what have you got in there?"

"Medicines stolen from the hospital for Dr. Rothmann."

Maud smiled proudly through her tears. "That's my girl."

"I nearly died when he picked up the bag."

"I'm sorry."

"You couldn't know. But I'm going to get rid of the stuff right now."

"Good idea."

Carla put her raincoat back on over her uniform and went out.

She walked quickly to the street where the Rothmanns lived. Their house was not as big as the von Ulrich place, but it was a well-proportioned town dwelling with pleasant rooms. However, the windows were now boarded up and there was a crude sign on the front door that said: SURGERY CLOSED.

The Rothmanns had once been prosperous. Dr. Rothmann had had a flourishing practise with many wealthy patients. He had also treated poor people at cheaper prices. Now only the poor were left.

Carla went around the back, as the patients did.

She knew immediately that something was wrong. The back door was open, and when she stepped into the kitchen, she saw a guitar with a broken neck lying on the tiled floor. The room was empty, but she could hear sounds from elsewhere in the house.

She crossed the kitchen and entered the hall. There were two main rooms on the ground floor. They had been the waiting room and the consulting room. Now the waiting room was disguised as a family sitting room, and the surgery had become Rudi's workshop, with a bench and woodworking tools, and usually half a dozen mandolins, violins, and cellos in various states of repair. All medical equipment was stashed out of sight in locked cupboards.

But not anymore, she saw when she walked in.

The cupboards had been opened and their contents thrown out. The floor was littered with smashed glass and assorted pills, powders, and liquids. In the debris Carla saw a stethoscope and a blood pressure gauge. Parts of several instruments were strewn around, evidently having been thrown on the floor and stamped upon.

Carla was shocked and disgusted. All that waste!

Then she looked into the other room. Rudi Rothmann lay in a corner.

He was twenty-two years old, a tall man with an athletic build. His eyes were closed, and he was moaning in agony.

His mother, Hannelore, knelt beside him. Once a handsome blonde, Hannelore was now gray and gaunt.

"What happened?" said Carla, fearing the answer.

"The police," said Hannelore. "They accused my husband of treating Aryan patients. They have taken him away. Rudi tried to stop them smashing the place up. They have . . ." She choked up.

Carla put down her basket and knelt beside Hannelore. "What have they done?"

Hannelore recovered the power of speech. "They broke his hands," she whispered.

Carla saw it at once. Rudi's hands were red and horribly twisted. The police seemed to have broken his fingers one by one. No wonder he was moaning. She was sickened. But she saw horror every day, and she knew how to suppress her personal feelings and give practical help. "He needs morphine," she said.

Hannelore indicated the mess on the floor. "If we had any, it's gone."

Carla felt a spasm of pure rage. Even the hospitals were short of supplies—and yet the police had wasted precious drugs in an orgy of destruction. "I brought you morphine." She took from her basket a vial of clear fluid and the new syringe. Swiftly, she took the syringe from its box and charged it with the drug. Then she injected Rudi.

The effect was almost instant. The moaning stopped. He opened his eyes and looked at Carla. "You angel," he said. Then he closed his eyes and seemed to sleep.

"We must try to set his fingers," Carla said. "So that the bones heal straight." She touched Rudi's left hand. There was no reaction. She grasped the hand and lifted it. Still he did not stir.

"I've never set bones," said Hannelore. "Though I've seen it done often enough."

"Same here," said Carla. "But we'd better try. I'll do his left hand. You do the right. We must finish before the drug wears off. God knows he'll be in enough pain."

"All right," said Hannelore.

Carla paused a moment longer. Her mother was right. They had to do anything they could to end this Nazi regime, even if it meant betraying their own country. She was no longer in any doubt.

"Let's get it done," Carla said.

Gently, carefully, the two women began to straighten Rudi's broken hands.

## ii

Thomas Macke went to the Tannenberg Bar every Friday afternoon.

It was not much of a place. On one wall was a framed photograph of the proprietor, Fritz, in a First World War uniform, twenty-five years younger and without a beer belly. He claimed to have killed nine Russians at the Battle of Tannenberg. There were a few tables and chairs, but the regulars all sat at the bar. A menu in a leather cover was almost entirely fantasy: the only dishes served were sausages with potatoes or sausages without potatoes.

But the place stood across the street from the Kreuzberg police station, so it was a cop bar. That meant it was free to break all the rules. Gambling was open, street girls gave blow jobs in the bathroom, and the food inspectors of the Berlin city government never entered the kitchen. It opened when Fritz got up and closed when the last drinker went home.

Macke had been a lowly police officer at the Kreuzberg station years ago, before the Nazis took over and men such as he were suddenly given a break. Some of his former colleagues still drank at the Tannenberg, and he could be sure of seeing a familiar face or two. He still liked to talk to old friends, even though he had risen so far above them, becoming an inspector and a member of the SS.

"You've done well, Thomas. I'll give you that," said Bernhardt Engel, who had been a sergeant over Macke in 1932 and was still a sergeant.

"Good luck to you, son." He raised to his lips the stein of beer that Macke had bought him.

"I won't argue with you," Macke replied. "Though I will say, Superintendent Kringelein is a lot worse to work for than you were."

"I was too soft on you boys," Bernhardt admitted.

Another old comrade, Franz Edel, laughed scornfully. "I wouldn't say soft!"

Glancing out of the window, Macke saw a motorcycle pull up outside, driven by a young man in the light blue belted jacket of an air force officer. He looked familiar: Macke had seen him somewhere before. He had overlong red-blond hair flopping onto a patrician forehead. He crossed the pavement and came into the Tannenberg.

Macke remembered the name. He was Werner Franck, spoiled son of the radio manufacturer Ludi Franck.

Werner came to the bar and asked for a pack of Kamel cigarettes. How predictable, Macke thought, that the playboy should smoke American-style cigarettes, even if they were a German imitation.

Werner paid, opened the pack, took out a cigarette, and asked Fritz for a light. Turning to leave, cigarette in his mouth tilted at a rakish angle, he caught Macke's eye and, after a moment's thought, said: "Inspector Macke."

The men in the bar all stared at Macke to see what he would say.

He nodded casually. "How are you, young Werner?"

"Very well, sir, thank you."

Macke was pleased, but surprised, by the respectful tone. He recalled Werner as an arrogant whippersnapper with insufficient respect for authority.

"I'm just back from a visit to the eastern front with General Dorn," Werner added.

Macke sensed the cops in the bar become alert to the conversation. A man who had been to the eastern front merited respect. Macke could not help feeling pleased that they were all impressed that he moved in such elevated circles.

Werner offered Macke the cigarette pack, and Macke took one. "A beer," Werner said to Fritz. Turning back to Macke, he said: "May I buy you a drink, Inspector?"

"The same, thank you."

Fritz filled two steins. Werner raised his glass to Macke and said: "I want to thank you."

That was another surprise. "For what?" said Macke.

His friends were all listening intently.

Werner said: "A year ago you gave me a good telling-off."

"You didn't seem grateful at the time."

"And for that I apologize. But I thought very hard about what you said to me, and eventually I realized you were right. I had allowed personal emotion to cloud my judgment. You set me straight. I'll never forget that."

Macke was touched. He had disliked Werner, and had spoken harshly to him, but the young man had taken his words to heart and changed his ways. It gave Macke a warm glow to feel that he had made such a difference in a young man's life.

Werner went on: "In fact I thought of you the other day. General Dorn was talking about catching spies, and asking if we could track them down by their radio signals. I'm afraid I couldn't tell him much."

"You should have asked me," said Macke. "It's my specialty."

"Is that so?"

"Come and sit down."

They carried their drinks to a grubby table.

"These men are all police officers," Macke said. "But still, one should not talk publicly about such matters."

"Of course." Werner lowered his voice. "But I know I may confide in you. You see, some of the battlefield commanders told Dorn they believe the enemy often knows our intentions in advance."

"Ah!" said Macke. "I feared as much."

"What can I tell Dorn about radio signal detection?"

"The correct term is goniometry." Macke collected his thoughts. This was an opportunity to impress an influential general, albeit indirectly. He needed to be clear, and emphasize the importance of what he was doing without exaggerating its success. He imagined General Dorn saying casually to the Führer: "There's a very good man in the Gestapo—name of Macke—only an inspector, at the moment, but most impressive . . ."

"We have an instrument that tells us the direction from which the signal is coming," he began. "If we take three readings from widely separated locations, we can draw three lines on the map. Where they intersect is the address of the transmitter."

"That's fantastic!"

Macke raised a cautionary hand. "In theory," he said. "In practise, it's more difficult. The pianist—that's what we call the radio operator— does not usually stay in the location long enough for us to find him. A careful pianist never broadcasts from the same place twice. And our instrument is housed in a van with a conspicuous aerial on its roof, so they can see us coming."

"But you have had some success."

"Oh, yes. But perhaps you should come out in the van with us one evening. Then you could see the whole process for yourself—and make a firsthand report to General Dorn."

"That's a good idea," said Werner.

### iii

Moscow in June was sunny and warm. At lunchtime Volodya waited for Zoya at a fountain in the Alexander Gardens behind the Kremlin. Hundreds of people strolled by, many in pairs, enjoying the weather. Life was hard, and the water in the fountain had been turned off to save power, but the sky was blue, the trees were in leaf, and the German army was a hundred miles away.

Volodya was full of pride every time he thought back to the Battle of Moscow. The dreaded German army, master of blitzkrieg attack, had been at the gates of the city—and had been thrown back. Russian soldiers had fought like lions to save their capital.

Unfortunately the Russian counterattack had petered out in March. It had won back much territory, and made Muscovites feel safer, but the Germans had licked their wounds and were now preparing to try again.

And Stalin was still in charge.

Volodya spotted Zoya walking through the crowd toward him. She was wearing a red-and-white checked dress. There was a spring in her step, and her pale blond hair seemed to bounce with her stride. Every man stared at her.

Volodya had dated some beautiful women, but he was surprised to find himself courting Zoya. For years she had treated him with cool indifference, and talked to him about nothing but nuclear physics. Then one day, to his astonishment, she had asked him to go to a movie.

It was shortly after the riot in which General Bobrov had been killed. Her attitude to him had changed that day—he was not sure he understood why; somehow the shared experience had created an intimacy. Anyway, they had gone to see *George's Dinky Jazz Band*, a knockabout comedy starring an English banjolele player called George Formby. It was a popular movie, and had been running for months in Moscow. The plot was about as unrealistic as could be: unknown to George, his instrument was sending messages to German U-boats. It was so silly that they had both laughed their socks off.

Since then they had been dating regularly.

Today they were to have lunch with his father. He had arranged to meet her beforehand at the fountain in order to have a few minutes alone with her.

Zoya gave him her thousand-candlepower smile and stood on tiptoe to kiss him. She was tall, but he was taller. He relished the kiss. Her lips were soft and moist on his. It was over too soon.

Volodya was not completely sure of her yet. They were still "walking out," as the older generation termed it. They kissed a lot, but they had not yet gone to bed together. They were not too young: he was twenty-seven, she twenty-eight. All the same, Volodya sensed that Zoya was not going to sleep with him until she was ready.

Half of him did not believe he would ever spend a night with this dream girl. She seemed too blond, too intelligent, too tall, too self-possessed, too sexy ever to give herself to a man. Surely he would never be allowed to watch her take off her clothes, to gaze at her naked body, to touch her all over, to lie on top of her . . . ?

They walked through the long, narrow park. On one side was a busy road. All along the other side, the towers of the Kremlin loomed over a high wall. "To look at it, you'd think our leaders in there were being held prisoner by the Russian people," Volodya said.

"Yes," Zoya agreed. "Instead of the other way round."

He looked behind them, but no one had heard. All the same it was foolhardy to talk like that. "No wonder my father thinks you're dangerous."

"I used to think you were like your father."

"I wish I was. He's a hero. He stormed the Winter Palace! I don't suppose I'll ever change the course of history."

"Oh, I know, but he's so narrow-minded and conservative. You're not like that."

Volodya thought he was pretty much like his father, but he was not going to argue.

"Are you free this evening?" she said. "I'd like to cook for you."

"You bet!" She had never invited him to her place.

"I've got a piece of steak."

"Great!" Good beef was a treat even in Volodya's privileged home.

"And the Kovalevs are out of town."

That was even better news. Like many Muscovites, Zoya lived in someone else's apartment. She had two rooms and shared the kitchen and bathroom with another scientist, Dr. Kovalev, and his wife and child. But the Kovalevs had gone away, so Zoya and Volodya would have the place to themselves. His pulse quickened. "Should I bring my toothbrush?" he said.

She gave him an enigmatic smile and did not answer the question.

They left the park and crossed the road to a restaurant. Many were closed, but the city center was full of offices whose workers had to eat lunch somewhere, and a few cafés and bars survived.

Grigori Peshkov was at a pavement table. There were better

restaurants inside the Kremlin, but he liked to be seen in places used by ordinary Russians. He wanted to show that he was not above the common people just because he wore a general's uniform. All the same, he had chosen a table well away from the rest, so that he could not be overheard.

He disapproved of Zoya, but he was not immune to her enchantment, and he stood up and kissed her on both cheeks.

They ordered potato pancakes and beer. The only alternatives were pickled herrings and vodka.

"Today I am not going to speak to you about nuclear physics, General," said Zoya. "Please take my word for it that I still believe everything I said last time we talked about the subject. I don't want to bore you."

"That's a relief," he said.

She laughed, showing white teeth. "Instead you can tell me how much longer we will be at war."

Volodya shook his head in mock despair. She always had to challenge his father. If she had not been a beautiful young woman, Grigori would have had her arrested long ago.

"The Nazis are beaten, but they won't admit it," Grigori said.

Zoya said: "Everyone in Moscow is wondering what will happen this summer—but you two probably know."

Volodya said: "If I did, I certainly could not tell my girlfriend, no matter how crazy I am about her." Apart from anything else, it could get her shot, he thought, but he did not say it.

The potato pancakes came and they began to eat. As always, Zoya tucked in hungrily. Volodya loved the relish with which she attacked food. But he did not much like the pancakes. "These potatoes taste suspiciously like turnips," he said.

His father shot him a disapproving look.

"Not that I'm complaining," Volodya added hastily.

When they had finished, Zoya went to the ladies' room. As soon as she was out of earshot, Volodya said: "We think the German summer offensive is imminent."

"I agree," said his father.

"Are we ready?"

"Of course," said Grigori, but he looked anxious.

"They will attack in the south. They want the oilfields of the Caucasus."

Grigori shook his head. "They will come back to Moscow. It's all that matters."

"Stalingrad is equally symbolic. It bears the name of our leader."

"Fuck symbolism. If they take Moscow, the war is over. If they don't, they haven't won, no matter what else they gain."

"You're just guessing," Volodya said with irritation.

"So are you."

"On the contrary, I have evidence." He looked around, but there was no one nearby. "The offensive is code-named Case Blue. It will start on the twenty-eighth of June." He had learned that much from Werner Franck's network of spies in Berlin. "And we found partial details in the briefcase of a German officer who crash-landed a reconnaissance plane near Kharkov."

"Officers on reconnaissance do not carry battle plans in briefcases," Grigori said. "Comrade Stalin thinks that was a ruse to deceive us, and I agree. The Germans want us to weaken our central front by sending forces south to deal with what will turn out to be no more than a diversion."

This was the problem with intelligence, Volodya thought with frustration. Even when you had the information, stubborn old men would believe what they wanted.

He saw Zoya coming back, all eyes on her as she walked across the plaza. "What would convince you?" he said to his father before she arrived.

"More evidence."

"Such as?"

Grigori thought for a moment, taking the question seriously. "Get me the battle plan."

Volodya sighed. Werner Franck had not yet succeeded in obtaining the document. "If I get it, will Stalin reconsider?"

"If you get it, I'll ask him to."

"It's a deal," said Volodya.

He was being rash. He had no idea how he was going achieve this. Werner, Heinrich, Lili, and the others already took horrendous risks. Yet he would have to put even more pressure on them.

Zoya reached their table and Grigori stood up. They were going in three different directions, so they said good-bye.

"I'll see you tonight," Zoya said to Volodya.

He kissed her. "I'll be there at seven."

"Bring your toothbrush," she said.

He walked away a happy man.

## iv

A girl knows when her best friend has a secret. She may not know what the secret is, but she knows it is there, like an unidentifiable piece of furniture under a dust sheet. She realizes, from guarded and unforthcoming answers to innocent questions, that her friend is seeing someone she shouldn't; she just doesn't know the name, although she may guess that the forbidden lover is a married man, or a dark-skinned foreigner, or another woman. She admires that necklace, and knows from her friend's muted reaction that it has shameful associations, though it may not be until years later that she discovers it was stolen from a senile grandmother's jewel box.

So Carla thought when she reflected on Frieda.

Frieda had a secret, and it was connected with resistance to the Nazis. She might be deeply, criminally involved: perhaps she went through her brother Werner's briefcase every night, copied secret papers, and handed the copies to a Russian spy. More likely it was not so dramatic: she probably helped print and distribute those illegal posters and leaflets that criticized the government.

So Carla was going to tell Frieda about Joachim Koch. However, she did not immediately get a chance. Carla and Frieda were nurses in different departments of a large hospital, and had different rotas, so they did not necessarily meet every day.

Meanwhile, Joachim came to the house daily for lessons. He made no more indiscreet revelations, but Maud continued to flirt with him. "You do realize that I'm almost forty years old?" Carla heard her say one day, although she was in fact fifty-one. Joachim was completely infatuated. Maud was enjoying the power she still had to fascinate an attractive young man, albeit a very naïve one. The thought crossed Carla's mind that her mother might be developing deeper feelings for this boy with a fair mustache who looked a bit like the young Walter, but that seemed ridiculous.

Joachim was desperate to please her, and soon brought news of her son. Erik was alive and well. "His unit is in the Ukraine," Joachim said. "That's all I can tell you."

"I wish he could get leave to come home," Maud said wistfully.

The young officer hesitated.

She said: "A mother worries so much. If I could just see him, even for only a day, it would be such a comfort to me."

"I *might* be able to arrange that."

Maud pretended to be astonished. "Really? You're that powerful?"

"I'm not sure. I could try."

"Thank you for even trying." She kissed his hand.

It was a week before Carla saw Frieda again. When she did, she told her all about Joachim Koch. She told the story as if simply retelling an interesting piece of news, but she felt sure Frieda would not regard it in that innocent light. "Just imagine," she said. "He told us the code name of the operation and the date of the attack!" She waited to see how Frieda would respond.

"He could be executed for that," Frieda said.

"If we knew someone who could get in touch with Moscow, we might turn the course of the war," Carla went on, as if still talking about the gravity of Joachim's crime.

"Perhaps," said Frieda.

That proved it. Frieda's normal reaction to such a story would include expressions of surprise, lively interest, and further questions. Today she offered nothing but neutral phrases and noncommittal grunts. Carla went home and told her mother that her intuition had been correct.

Next day at the hospital, Frieda appeared in Carla's ward looking frantic. "I have to talk to you urgently," she said.

Carla was changing a dressing for a young woman who had been badly burned in a munitions factory explosion. "Go to the cloakroom," she said. "I'll be there as soon as I can."

Five minutes later she found Frieda in the little room, smoking by an open window. "What is it?" she said.

Frieda put out the cigarette. "It's about your Lieutenant Koch."

"I thought so."

"You have to find out more from him."

"I *have* to? What are you talking about?"

"He has access to the entire battle plan for Case Blue. We know something about it, but Moscow needs the details."

Frieda was making a bewildering set of assumptions, but Carla went along with it. "I can ask him . . ."

"No. You have to *make* him bring you the battle plan."

"I'm not sure that's possible. He's not completely stupid. Don't you think—"

Frieda was not even listening. "Then you have to photograph it," she interrupted. She produced from the pocket of her uniform a stainless-steel box about the size of a pack of cigarettes but longer and narrower. "This is a miniature camera specially designed for photographing documents." Carla noticed the name *Minox* on the side. "You'll get eleven pictures on one film. Here are three films." She brought out three cassettes, the shape of dumbbells but small enough to fit into the little camera. "This is how you load the film." Frieda demonstrated. "To take a picture, you look through this window. If you're not sure, read this manual."

Carla had never known Frieda to be so domineering. "I really need to think about this."

"There's no time. This is your raincoat, isn't it?"

"Yes, but—"

Frieda stuffed the camera, films, and booklet into the pockets of the coat. She seemed relieved they were out of her hands. "I've got to go." She went to the door.

"But, Frieda!"

At last Frieda stopped and looked directly at Carla. "What?"

"Well . . . You're not behaving like a friend."

"This is more important."

"You've backed me into a corner."

"You created this situation when you told me about Joachim Koch. Don't pretend you didn't expect me to do something with the information."

It was true. Carla had triggered this emergency herself. But she had not envisaged things turning out this way. "What if he says no?"

"Then you'll probably be living under the Nazis the rest of your life." Frieda went out.

"Hell," said Carla.

She stood alone in the cloakroom, thinking. She could not even get rid of the little camera without risk. It was in her raincoat, and she could hardly throw it into a hospital rubbish bin. She would have to leave the building with it in her pocket, and try to find a place where she could dispose of it secretly.

But did she want to?

It seemed unlikely that Koch, naïve though he was, could be talked into smuggling a copy of a battle plan out of the War Ministry and bringing it to show his inamorata. However, if anyone could persuade him, Maud could.

But Carla was scared. There would be no mercy for her if she was caught. She would be arrested and tortured. She thought of Rudi Rothmann, moaning in the agony of broken bones. She recalled her father after they released him, so brutally beaten that he had died. Her crime would be worse than theirs, her punishment correspondingly bestial. She would be executed, of course—but not for a long time.

She told herself she was willing to risk that.

What she could not accept was the danger that she would help kill her brother.

He was there, on the eastern front; Joachim had confirmed it. He would be involved in Case Blue. If Carla enabled the Russians to win that battle, Erik could die as a result. She could not bear that.

She went back to her work. She was distracted and made mistakes, but fortunately the doctors did not notice and the patients could not tell. When at last her shift ended, she hurried away. The camera was burning a hole in her pocket but she did not see a safe place to dump it.

She wondered where Frieda had got it. Frieda had plenty of money, and could easily have bought it, though she would have had to come up with a story about why she needed such a thing. More likely she could have got it from the Russians before they closed their embassy a year ago.

The camera was still in Carla's coat pocket when she arrived home.

There was no sound from the piano upstairs; Joachim was having his lesson later today. Her mother was sitting at the kitchen table. When Carla walked in, Maud beamed and said: "Look who's here!"

It was Erik.

Carla stared at him. He was painfully thin, but apparently uninjured. His uniform was grimy and ripped, but he had washed his face and hands. He stood up and put his arms around her.

She hugged him hard, careless of dirtying her spotless uniform. "You're safe," she said. There was so little flesh on him that she could feel his bones, his ribs and hips and shoulders and spine, through the thin material.

"Safe for the moment," he said.

She released her hold. "How are you?"

"Better than most."

"You weren't wearing this flimsy uniform in the Russian winter?"

"I stole a coat from a dead Russian."

She sat down at the table. Ada was there, too. Erik said: "You were right. About the Nazis, I mean. You were right."

She was pleased, but not sure exactly what he meant. "In what way?"

"They murder people. You told me that. Father told me, too, and Mother. I'm sorry I didn't believe you. I'm sorry, Ada, that I didn't believe they killed your poor little Kurt. I know better now."

This was a big reversal. Carla said: "What changed your mind?"

"I saw them doing it, in Russia. They round up all the important people in town, because they must be Communists. And they get the Jews, too. Not just men, but women and children. And old people too frail to do anyone any harm." Tears were streaming down his face now. "Our regular soldiers don't do it—there are special groups. They take the prisoners out of town. Sometimes there's a quarry, or some other kind of pit. Or they make the younger ones dig a great hole. Then . . ."

He choked up, but Carla had to hear him say it. "Then what?"

"They do them twelve at a time. Six pairs. Sometimes the husbands and wives hold hands as they walk down the slope. The mothers carry the babies. The riflemen wait until the prisoners are in the right spot. Then they shoot." Erik wiped his tears with his dirty uniform sleeve. "Bang," he said.

There was a long silence in the kitchen. Ada was crying. Carla was aghast. Only Maud was stony-faced.

Eventually Erik blew his nose, then took out cigarettes. "I was surprised to get leave and a ticket home," he said.

Carla said: "When do you have to go back?"

"Tomorrow. I have only twenty-four hours here. All the same I'm the envy of all my comrades. They'd give anything for a day at home. Dr. Weiss said I must have friends in high places."

"You do," said Maud. "Joachim Koch, a young lieutenant who works at the War Ministry and comes to me for piano lessons. I asked him to arrange leave for you." She glanced at her watch. "He'll be here in a few minutes. He has grown fond of me—he's in need of a mother figure, I think."

Mother, hell, Carla thought. There was nothing maternal about Maud's relationship with Joachim.

Maud went on: "He's very innocent. He told us there's going to be a new offensive on the eastern front starting on the twenty-eighth of June. He even mentioned the code name: Case Blue."

Erik said: "He's going to get himself shot."

Carla said: "Joachim is not the only one who might be shot. I told someone what I learned. Now I've been asked to persuade Joachim, somehow, to get me the battle plan."

"Good God!" Erik was rocked. "This is serious espionage—you're in more danger than I am on the eastern front!"

"Don't worry. I can't imagine Joachim would do it," Carla said.

"Don't be so sure," said Maud.

They all looked at her.

"He might do it for me," she said. "If I asked him the right way."

Erik said: "He's *that* naïve?"

She looked defiant. "He's in love with me."

"Oh." Erik was embarrassed at the idea of his mother being involved in a romance.

Carla said: "All the same, we can't do it."

Erik said: "Why not?"

"Because if the Russians win the battle you might die!"

"I'll probably die anyway."

Carla heard her own voice rise in pitch agitatedly. "But we'd be helping the Russians kill you!"

"I still want you to do it," Erik said fiercely. He looked down at the checkered oilcloth on the kitchen table, but what he was seeing was a thousand miles away.

Carla felt torn. If he *wanted* her to . . . She said: "But why?"

"I think of those people walking down the slope into the quarry, holding hands." His own hands on the table grasped each other hard enough to bruise. "I'll risk my life, if we can put a stop to that. I *want* to risk my life—I'll feel better about myself, and my country, if I do. Please, Carla, if you can, send the Russians that battle plan."

Still she hesitated. "Are you sure?"

"I'm begging you."

"Then I will," said Carla.

**V**

Thomas Macke told his men—Wagner, Richter, and Schneider—to be on their best behavior. "Werner Franck is only a lieutenant, but he works for General Dorn. I want him to have the best possible impression of our team and our work. No swearing, no jokes, no eating, and no rough stuff unless it's really necessary. If we catch a Communist spy, you can give him a good kicking. But if we fail, I don't want you to pick on someone else just for fun." Normally he would turn a blind eye to that sort of thing. It all helped to keep people in fear of the displeasure of the Nazis. But Franck might be squeamish.

Werner turned up punctually at Gestapo headquarters in Prinz Albrecht Strasse on his motorcycle. They all got into the surveillance van with the revolving aerial on the roof. With so much radio equipment inside it was cramped. Richter took the wheel and they drove around the city in the early evening, the favored time for spies to send messages to the enemy.

"Why is that, I wonder?" said Werner.

"Most spies have a regular job," Macke explained. "It's part of their cover story. So they go to an office or a factory in the daytime."

"Of course," said Werner. "I never thought of that."

Macke was worried they might not pick up anything at all tonight. He was terrified that he would get the blame for the reverses the German army was suffering in Russia. He had done his best, but there were no prizes for effort in the Third Reich.

It sometimes happened that the unit picked up no signals. On other occasions there would be two or three, and Macke would have to choose which to follow up on and which to ignore. He felt sure there was more than one spy network in the city, and they probably did not know of each other's existence. He was trying to do an impossible job with inadequate tools.

They were near the Potsdamer Platz when they heard a signal. Macke recognized the characteristic sound. "That's a pianist," he said with relief. At least he could prove to Werner that the equipment worked.

Someone was broadcasting five-digit numbers, one after the other. "Soviet intelligence uses a code in which pairs of numbers stand for letters," Macke explained to Werner. "So, for example, 11 might stand for A. Transmitting them in groups of five is just a convention."

The radio operator, an electrical engineer named Mann, read off a set of coordinates, and Wagner drew a line on a map with a pencil and rule. Richter put the van in gear and set off again.

The pianist continued to broadcast, his beeps sounding loud in the van. Macke hated the man, whoever he was. "Bastard Communist swine," he said. "One day he'll be in our basement, begging me to let him die so the pain will come to an end."

Werner looked pale. He was not used to police work, Macke thought.

After a moment the young man pulled himself together. "The way you describe the Soviet code, it sounds as if it might not be too difficult to break," he said thoughtfully.

"Correct!" Macke was pleased that Werner caught on so fast. "But I was simplifying. They have refinements. After encoding the message as a series of numbers, the pianist then writes a key word underneath it repeatedly—it might be *Kurfürstendamm*, say—and encodes that. Then he subtracts the second numbers from the first and broadcasts the result."

"Almost impossible to decipher if you don't know the key word!"

"Exactly."

They stopped again near the burned-out Reichstag building and drew another line on the map. The two met in Friedrichshain, to the east of the city center.

Macke told the driver to swing northeast, taking them nearer to the likely spot while giving them a third line from a different angle. "Experience shows that it's best to take three bearings," Macke told Werner. "The equipment is only approximate, and the extra measurement reduces error."

"Do you always catch him?" said Werner.

"By no means. In most cases we don't. Often we're just not quick enough. He may change frequency halfway through, so that we lose him. Sometimes he breaks off in midtransmission and resumes at another location. He may have lookouts who see us coming and warn him to flee."

"A lot of snags."

"But we catch them, sooner or later."

Richter stopped the van and Mann took the third bearing. The three pencil lines on Wagner's map met to form a small triangle near the East Station. The pianist was somewhere between the railway line and the canal.

Macke gave Richter the location and added: "Quick as you can."

Werner was perspiring, Macke noticed. Perhaps it was rather hot in the van. And the young lieutenant was not accustomed to action. He was learning what life was like in the Gestapo. All the better, Macke thought.

Richter headed south on Warschauer Strasse, crossed the railway, then turned into a cheap industrial neighborhood of warehouses, yards, and small factories. There was a group of soldiers toting kit bags outside a back entrance to the station, no doubt embarking for the eastern front. And a fellow countryman somewhere in this neighborhood is doing his best to betray them, Macke thought angrily.

Wagner pointed down a narrow street leading away from the station. "He's in the first few hundred yards, but could be either side," he said. "If we take the van any closer, he'll see us."

"All right, men, you know the drill," Macke said. "Wagner and Richter take the left-hand side. Schneider and I will take the right." They all picked up long-handled sledgehammers. "Come with me, Franck."

There were few people on the street—a man in a worker's cap walking briskly toward the railway station, an older woman in shabby clothes probably on her way to clean offices—and they hurried quickly past, not wanting to attract the attention of the Gestapo.

Macke's team entered each building, one man leapfrogging his partner. Most businesses were closed for the day, so they had to rouse a janitor. If he took more than a minute to come to the door, they knocked it down. Once inside they raced through the building checking every room.

The pianist was not in the first block.

The first building on the right-hand side of the next block had a fading sign that said: FASHION FURS. It was a two-story factory that stretched along the side street. It looked disused, but the front door was steel and the windows were barred: a fur coat factory naturally had heavy security.

Macke led Werner down the side street, looking for a way in. The adjacent building was bomb-damaged and derelict. The rubble had been cleared from the street and there was a hand-painted sign saying: DANGER—NO ENTRY. The remains of a name board identified it as a furniture warehouse.

They stepped over a pile of stones and splintered timbers, going as fast as they could but forced to tread carefully. A surviving wall concealed the rear of the building. Macke went behind it and found a hole through to the factory next door.

He had a strong feeling the pianist was in here.

He stepped through the hole, and Werner followed.

They found themselves in an empty office. There was an old steel desk with no chair, and a file cabinet opposite. The calendar pinned to the wall was for 1939, probably the last year during which Berliners could afford such frivolities as fur coats.

Macke heard a footstep on the floor above.

He drew his gun.

Werner was unarmed.

They opened the door and stepped into a corridor.

Macke noted several open doors, a staircase up, and a door under the staircase that might lead to a basement.

Macke crept along the corridor toward the foot of the stairs, then noticed that Werner was checking the door to the basement.

"I thought I heard a noise from below," Werner said. He turned the handle but the door had a flimsy lock. He stepped back and raised his right foot.

Macke said: "No—"

"Yes—I hear them!" Werner said, and he kicked the door open.

The crash resounded throughout the empty factory.

Werner burst through the door and disappeared. A light came on, showing a stone staircase. "Don't move!" Werner yelled. "You are under arrest!"

Macke went down the stairs after him.

He reached the basement. Werner stood at the foot of the stairs, looking baffled.

The room was empty.

Suspended from the ceiling were rails on which coats had probably been hung. An enormous roll of brown paper stood on end in one corner, probably intended for wrapping. But there was no radio and no spy tapping messages to Moscow.

"You fucking idiot," Macke said to Werner.

He turned and ran back up the stairs. Werner ran after him. They traversed the hallway and went up to the next floor.

There were rows of workbenches under a glass roof. At one time the place must have been full of women working at sewing machines. Now there was nobody.

A glass door led to a fire escape, but the door was locked. Macke looked out and saw nobody.

He put his gun away. Breathing hard, he leaned on a workbench.

On the floor he noticed a couple of cigarette ends, one with lipstick on it. They did not look very old. "They were here," he said to Werner, pointing at the floor. "Two of them. Your shout warned them, and they escaped."

"I was a fool," Werner said. "I'm sorry, but I'm not used to this kind of thing."

Macke went to the corner window. Along the street he saw a young man and woman walking briskly away. The man was carrying a tan leather suitcase. As he watched, they disappeared into the railway station. "Shit," he said.

"I don't think they were spies," Werner said. He pointed to something on the floor, and Macke saw a crumpled condom. "Used, but empty," Werner said. "I think we caught them in the act."

"I hope you're right," said Macke.

## vi

The day Joachim Koch promised to bring the battle plan, Carla did not go to work.

She probably could have done her usual morning shift and been home in time—but "probably" was not enough. There was always a risk that there might be a major fire or a road accident obliging her to work after the end of her shift to deal with an inrush of injured people. So she stayed home all day.

In the end Maud had not had to ask Joachim to bring the plan. He had said he needed to cancel his lesson; then, unable to resist the temptation to boast, he had explained that he had to carry a copy of the plan across town. "Come for your lesson on the way," Maud had said, and he had agreed.

Lunch was strained. Carla and Maud ate a thin soup made with a ham bone and dried peas. Carla did not ask what Maud had done, or promised to do, to persuade Koch. Perhaps she had told him he was making marvelous progress on the piano but could not afford to miss a lesson. She might have asked whether he was so junior that he was monitored every minute: such a remark would sting him, for he pretended constantly to be more important than he was, and it might easily provoke him into showing up just to prove her wrong. However, the ploy most likely to have succeeded was the one Carla did not want to think about: sex. Her mother flirted outrageously with Koch, and he responded with slavish devotion. Carla suspected that this was the irresistible temptation that had made Joachim ignore the voice in his head saying: "Don't be so damn stupid."

Or perhaps not. He might see sense. He could show up this

afternoon, not with a carbon copy in his bag, but with a Gestapo squad and a set of handcuffs.

Carla loaded a film cassette into the Minox camera, then put the camera and the two remaining cassettes in the top drawer of a low kitchen cupboard, under some towels. The cupboard stood next to the window, where the light was bright. She would photograph the document on the cupboard top.

She did not know how the exposed film would reach Moscow, but Frieda had assured her it would, and Carla imagined a traveling salesman—in pharmaceuticals, perhaps, or German-language Bibles— who had permission to sell his wares in Switzerland and could discreetly pass the film to someone from the Soviet embassy in Bern.

The afternoon was long. Maud went to her room to rest. Ada did laundry. Carla sat in the dining room, which they rarely used nowadays, and tried to read, but she could not concentrate. The newspaper was all lies. She needed to cram for her next nursing exam, but the medical terms in her textbook swam before her eyes. She was reading an old copy of *All Quiet on the Western Front*, a German bestseller about the First World War, now banned because it was too honest about the hardships of soldiers, but she found herself holding the book in her hand and gazing out of the window at the June sunlight beating down on the dusty city.

At last he came. Carla heard a footstep on the path and jumped up to look out. There was no Gestapo squad, just Joachim Koch in his pressed uniform and shiny boots, his movie-star face as full of eager anticipation as that of a child arriving for a birthday party. He had his canvas bag over his shoulder as usual. Had he kept his promise? Did that bag hold a copy of the battle plan for Case Blue?

He rang the bell.

Carla and Maud had premeditated every move from now on. In accordance with their plan, Carla did not answer the door. A few moments later she saw her mother walk across the hall wearing a purple silk dressing gown and high-heeled slippers—almost like a prostitute, Carla thought with shame and embarrassment. She heard the front door open, then close again. From the hall there was a whisper of silk and a murmured endearment that suggested an embrace. Then the purple robe and the field gray uniform passed the dining room door and disappeared upstairs.

Maud's first priority was to make sure he had the document. She was to look at it, say something admiring, then put it down. She would lead Joachim to the piano. Then she would find some pretext—Carla tried not to think what—for taking the young man through the double doors that led from the drawing room into the neighboring study, a smaller, more intimate room with red velvet curtains and a big, sagging old couch. As soon as they were there, Maud would give the signal.

Because it was hard to know in advance the exact choreography of their movements, there were several possible signals, all of which meant the same thing. The simplest was that she would slam the door loud enough to be heard throughout the house. Alternatively, she would use the bell-push beside the fireplace that sounded a ring in the kitchen, part of the obsolete system for summoning servants. But any other noise would do, they had decided: in desperation she would knock the marble bust of Goethe to the floor or "accidentally" smash a vase.

Carla stepped out of the dining room and stood in the hall, looking up the stairs. There was no sound.

She looked into the kitchen. Ada was washing the iron pot in which she had made the soup, scrubbing with an energy that was undoubtedly fueled by tension. Carla gave her what she hoped was an encouraging smile. Carla and Maud would have liked to keep this whole affair secret from Ada, not because they did not trust her—quite the contrary; her hostility to the Nazis was fanatical—but because the knowledge made her complicit in treachery, and liable to the most extreme punishment. However, they lived too much together for secrecy to be possible, and Ada knew everything.

Carla faintly heard Maud give a tinkling laugh. She knew that sound. It struck an artificial note, and indicated that she was straining her powers of fascination to the limit.

Did Joachim have the document, or not?

A minute or two later Carla heard the piano. It was undoubtedly Joachim playing. The tune was a simple children's song about a cat in the snow: *"ABC, die Katze lief im Schnee."* Carla's father had sung it to her a hundred times. She felt a lump in her throat now when she thought of that. How dare the Nazis play such songs when they had made orphans of so many children?

The song stopped abruptly in the middle. Something had happened. Carla strained to hear—voices, footsteps, anything—but there was nothing.

A minute went by, then another.

Something had gone wrong—but what?

She looked through the kitchen doorway at Ada, who stopped scrubbing to spread her hands in a gesture that signified *I have no idea.*

Carla had to find out.

She went quietly up the stairs, treading noiselessly on the threadbare carpet.

She stood outside the drawing room. Still she could hear nothing: no piano music, no movement, no voices.

She opened the door as quietly as possible.

She peeped in. She could see no one. She stepped inside and looked all around. The room was empty.

There was no sign of Joachim's canvas bag.

She looked at the double door that led to the study. One of the two doors stood half open.

Carla tiptoed across the room. There was no carpet here, just polished wood blocks, and her footsteps were not completely silent, but she had to take the risk.

As she got nearer, she heard whispers.

She reached the doorway. She flattened herself against the wall, then risked a look inside.

They were standing up, embracing, kissing. Joachim had his back to the door and to Carla: no doubt Maud had taken care to move him into that position. As Carla watched, Maud broke the kiss, looked over his shoulder, and caught Carla's eye. She took her hand away from Joachim's neck and made an urgent pointing gesture.

Carla saw the canvas bag on a chair.

She understood immediately what had gone wrong. When Maud had inveigled Joachim into the study, he had not obliged them by leaving his bag in the drawing room, but had nervously taken it with him.

Now Carla had to retrieve it.

Heart thudding, she stepped into the room.

Maud murmured: "Oh, yes, keep doing that, my sweet boy."

Joachim groaned: "I love you, my darling."

Carla took two paces forward, picked up the canvas bag, turned around, and stepped silently out of the room.

The bag was light.

She walked quickly across the drawing room and ran down the stairs, breathing hard.

In the kitchen she put the bag on the table and unbuckled its straps. Inside were today's edition of the Berlin newspaper *Der Angriff*, a fresh pack of Kamel cigarettes, and a plain buff-colored cardboard folder. With trembling hands she took out the folder and opened it. It contained a carbon copy of a document.

The first page was headed:

DIRECTIVE NO. 41

On the last page was a dotted line for a signature. Nothing was penned there, no doubt because this was a copy, but the name typed beside the line was Adolf Hitler.

In between was the plan for Case Blue.

Exultation rose in her heart, mingled with the tension she already felt and the terrible dread of discovery.

She put the document on the low cupboard next to the kitchen window. She jerked open the drawer and took out the Minox camera and the two spare films. She positioned the document carefully, then began to photograph it page by page.

It did not take long. There were just ten pages. She did not even have to reload film. She was done. She had stolen the battle plan.

*That was for you, Father.*

She put the camera back in the drawer, closed the drawer, slipped the document into the cardboard folder, put the folder back in the canvas bag, and closed the bag, fastening the straps.

Moving as quietly as she could, she carried the bag back upstairs.

As she crept into the drawing room, she heard her mother's voice. Maud was speaking clearly and emphatically, as if she wanted to be overheard, and Carla immediately sensed a warning. "Please don't worry," she was saying. "It's because you were so excited. We were both excited."

Joachim's voice came in reply, low and embarrassed. "I feel a fool," he said. "You only touched me, and it was all over."

Carla could guess what had happened. She had no experience of it, but girls talked, and nurses' conversations were brutally detailed. Joachim must have ejaculated prematurely. Frieda had told her that Heinrich had done the same, several times, when they were first together, and had been mortified with embarrassment, though he had soon got over it. It was a sign of nervousness, she said.

The fact that Maud and Joachim's embraces were over so early created a difficulty for Carla. Joachim would be more alert now, no longer blind and deaf to everything going on around him.

All the same, Maud must be doing her best to keep his back to the doorway. If Carla could just slip in for a second and replace the bag on the chair without being seen by Joachim, they could still get away with it.

Heart pounding, Carla crossed the drawing room and paused at the open door.

Maud said reassuringly: "It happens often—the body becomes impatient. It's nothing."

Carla put her head around the door.

The two of them were still standing in the same place, still close together. Maud looked past Joachim and saw Carla. She put her hand on Joachim's cheek, keeping his gaze away from Carla, and said: "Kiss me again, and tell me you don't hate me for this little accident."

Carla stepped inside.

Joachim said: "I need a cigarette."

As he turned around, Carla stepped back outside.

She waited by the door. Did he have cigarettes in his pocket, or would he look for the new pack in his bag?

The answer came a second later. "Where's my bag?" he said.

Carla's heart stopped.

Maud's voice came clearly. "You left it in the drawing room."

"No, I didn't."

Carla crossed the room, dropped the bag on a chair, and stepped outside. Then she paused on the landing, listening.

She heard them move from the study to the drawing room.

Maud said: "There it is. I told you so."

"I did not leave it there," he said stubbornly. "I vowed I would not let it out of my sight. But I did—when I was kissing you."

"My darling, you're upset about what happened between us. Try to relax."

"Someone must have come into the room, while I was distracted . . ."

"How absurd."

"I don't think so."

"Let's sit at the piano, side by side, the way you like to," she said, but she was beginning to sound desperate.

"Who else is in this house?"

Guessing what would happen next, Carla ran down the stairs and into the kitchen. Ada stared at her in alarm, but there was no time to explain.

She heard Joachim's boots on the stairs.

A moment later he was in the kitchen. He had the canvas bag in his hand. His face was angry. He looked at Carla and Ada. "One of you has been looking inside this bag!" he said.

Carla spoke as calmly as she could. "I don't know why you should think that, Joachim," she said.

Maud appeared behind Joachim and came past him into the kitchen. "Let's have coffee, please, Ada," she said brightly. "Joachim, do sit down, please."

He ignored her and scrutinized the kitchen. His eye lit upon the top of the low cupboard by the window. Carla saw, to her horror, that although she had put the camera away, she had left the two spare film cassettes out.

"Those are eight-millimeter film cassettes, aren't they?" Joachim said. "Have you got a miniature camera?"

Suddenly he did not seem such a little boy.

"Is that what those things are?" said Maud. "I've been wondering. They were left behind by another pupil, a Gestapo officer in fact."

It was a clever improvisation, but Joachim was not buying it. "And did he also leave behind his camera, I wonder?" he said. He pulled open the drawer.

The neat little stainless-steel camera lay there on a white towel, guilty as a bloodstain.

Joachim looked shocked. Perhaps he had not really believed he was the victim of treachery, but had been blustering to compensate for his sexual failure, and now he was facing the truth for the first time. Whatever the reason, he was momentarily stunned. Still holding the knob of the drawer, he stared at the camera as if hypnotized. In that short moment Carla saw that a young man's dream of love had been defiled, and his rage was going to be terrible.

At last he raised his eyes. He looked at the three women around him, and his gaze rested on Maud. "You have done this," he said. "You tricked me. But you will be punished." He picked up the camera and films and put them in his pocket. "You are under arrest, Frau von Ulrich." He took a step forward and grabbed her arm. "I am taking you to Gestapo headquarters."

Maud jerked her arm free of his grasp and took a step back.

Joachim drew back his arm and punched her with all his might. He was tall, strong, and young. The blow landed on her face and knocked her down.

Joachim stood over her. "You made a fool of me!" he screeched. "You lied, and I believed you!" He was hysterical now. "We will both be tortured by the Gestapo, and we both deserve it!" He began to kick her where she lay. She tried to roll away, but came up against the cooker. His right boot thudded into her ribs, her thigh, her belly.

Ada rushed at him and scratched his face with her nails. He batted her away with a swipe. Then he kicked Maud in the head.

Carla moved.

She knew that people recovered from all kinds of trauma to the body, but a head injury often did irreparable damage. However, the reasoning was barely conscious. She acted without forethought. She picked up from the kitchen table the iron soup pot that Ada had so energetically scrubbed clean. Holding it by its long handle, she raised it high, then brought it down with all her might on top of Joachim's head.

He staggered, stunned.

She hit him again, even harder.

He slumped to the floor, unconscious. Maud moved out of the way of his falling body, and sat upright against the wall, holding her chest.

Carla raised the pot again.

Maud screamed: "No! Stop!"

Carla put the pot down on the kitchen table.

Joachim moved, trying to rise.

Ada seized the pot and hit him again, furiously. Carla tried to grab her arm but she was in a mad rage. She battered the unconscious man's head again and again until she was exhausted, and then she dropped the pot to the floor with a clang.

Maud struggled to her knees and stared at Joachim. His eyes were wide and staring. His nose was twisted sideways. His skull seemed to be out of shape. Blood came from his ear. He did not appear to be breathing.

Carla knelt beside him, put her fingertips to his neck, and felt for a pulse. There was none. "He's dead," she said. "We've killed him. Oh, my God."

Maud said: "You poor, stupid boy." She was crying.

Ada, panting with effort, said: "What do we do now?"

Carla realized they had to get rid of the body.

Maud struggled to her feet with difficulty. The left side of her face was swelling. "Dear God, it hurts," she said, holding her side. Carla guessed she had a cracked rib.

Looking down at Joachim, Ada said: "We could hide him in the attic."

Carla said: "Yes, until the neighbors start to complain about the smell."

"Then we'll bury him in the back garden."

"And what will people think when they see three women digging a hole six feet long in the yard of a Berlin town house? That we are prospecting for gold?"

"We could dig at night."

"Would that seem less suspicious?"

Ada scratched her head.

Carla said: "We have to take the body somewhere and dump it. A park, or a canal."

"But how will we carry it?" said Ada.

"He doesn't weigh much," said Maud sadly. "So slim and strong."

Carla said: "It's not the weight that's the problem. Ada and I can carry him. But somehow we have to do it without arousing suspicion."

Maud said: "I wish we had a car."

Carla shook her head. "No one can get petrol anyway."

They were silent. Outside, dusk was falling. Ada got a towel and wrapped it around Joachim's head, to prevent his blood staining the floor. Maud cried silently, the tears rolling down a face twisted in anguish. Carla wanted to sympathize but first she had to solve this problem.

"We could put him in a box," she said.

Ada said: "The only box that size is a coffin."

"How about a piece of furniture? A sideboard?"

"Too heavy." Ada looked thoughtful. "But the wardrobe in my room is not so weighty."

Carla nodded. A maid was assumed not to have many clothes, nor to need mahogany furniture, she realized with a touch of embarrassment, so Ada's room had a narrow hanging cupboard made of flimsy deal wood. "Let's get it," she said.

Ada had originally lived in the basement, but that was now an air raid shelter, and her room was upstairs. Carla and Ada went up. Ada opened her cupboard and pulled all the clothes off the rail. There were not many: two sets of uniforms, a few dresses, one winter coat, all old. She laid them neatly on the single bed.

Carla tilted the wardrobe and took its weight; then Ada picked up the other end. It was not heavy, but it was awkward, and it took them some time to manhandle it out of the door and down the stairs.

At last they laid it on its back in the hall. Carla opened the door. Now it looked like a coffin with a hinged lid.

Carla went back into the kitchen and bent over the body. She took the camera and films from Joachim's pocket, and replaced them in the kitchen drawer.

Carla took his arms, Ada took his legs, and they lifted the body. They carried it out of the kitchen into the hall and lowered it into the wardrobe. Ada rearranged the towel about the head, though the bleeding had stopped.

Should they take off his uniform? Carla wondered. It would make the body harder to identify—but it would give her two problems of disposal instead of one. She decided against.

She picked up the canvas bag and dropped it into the wardrobe with the corpse.

She closed the wardrobe door and turned the key, to make sure it did not fall open by accident. She put the key in the pocket of her dress.

She went into the dining room and looked out through the window. "It's getting dark," she said. "That's good."

Maud said: "What will people think?"

"That we're moving a piece of furniture—selling it, perhaps, to get money for food."

"Two women, moving a wardrobe?"

"Women do this sort of thing all the time, now that so many men are in the army or dead. It's not as if we could get a removal van—they can't buy petrol."

"Why would you be doing it in the half dark?"

Carla let her frustration show. "I don't know, Mother. If we're asked, I'll have to make something up. But the body can't stay here."

"They'll know he's been murdered, when they find the body. They'll examine the injuries."

Carla, too, was worried about that. "Nothing we can do."

"They may try to investigate where he went today."

"He said he had not told anyone about his piano lessons. He wanted to astonish his friends with his skill. With luck, no one knows he came here." And without luck, Carla thought, we're all dead.

"What will they guess to be the motive for the murder?"

"Will they find traces of semen in his underwear?"

Maud looked away, embarrassed. "Yes."

"Then they will imagine a sexual encounter, perhaps with another man, that ended in a quarrel."

"I hope you're right."

Carla was not at all sure, but she could not think of anything they could do about it. "The canal," she said. The body would float, and be found sooner or later, and there would be a murder investigation. They would just have to hope it did not lead to them.

Carla opened the front door.

She stood at the front of the wardrobe on its left, and Ada positioned herself at the back on the right. They bent down.

Ada, who undoubtedly had more experience of heavy lifting than her employers, said: "Tilt it sideways and get your hands under it."

Carla did as she said.

"Now lift your end a little."

Carla did so.

Ada got her hands underneath her end and said: "Bend your knees. Take the weight. Straighten up."

They raised the wardrobe to hip height. Ada bent down and got her shoulder underneath. Carla did the same.

The two women straightened up.

The weight tilted to Carla as they went down the steps from the front door, but she could bear it. When they reached the street, she turned toward the canal, a few blocks away.

It was now full dark, with no moon but a few stars shedding a faint light. With the blackout, there was a good chance no one would see them tip the wardrobe into the water. The disadvantage was that Carla could hardly see where she was going. She was terrified she would stumble and fall, and the wardrobe would smash to splinters, revealing the murdered man inside.

An ambulance drove by, its headlights covered by slit masks. It was probably hurrying to a road accident. There were many during the blackout. That meant there would be police cars in the vicinity.

Carla recalled a sensational murder case from the beginning of the blackout. A man had killed his wife, forced her body into a packing case, and carried it across town on the seat of his bicycle in the dark before dropping it in the Havel River. Would the police remember the case and suspect anyone transporting a large object?

As she thought that, a police car drove by. A cop stared out at the two women with their wardrobe, but the car did not stop.

The burden seemed to get heavier. It was a warm night, and soon Carla was running with perspiration. The wood hurt her shoulder, and she wished she had thought of putting a folded handkerchief inside her blouse as a cushion.

They turned a corner and came upon the accident.

An eight-wheeler articulated truck carrying timber had collided head-on with a Mercedes saloon car, which had been badly crushed. The police car and the ambulance were shining their headlights onto the wreckage. In a little pool of faint light, a group of men gathered around the car. The crash must have happened in the last few minutes, for there were still people inside the car. An ambulance man was leaning in at the back door, probably examining the injuries to see whether the passengers could be moved.

Carla was momentarily terrified. Guilt froze her and she stopped in her tracks. But no one had noticed her and Ada and the wardrobe, and after a moment she realized she just needed to steal away, double back, and take a different route to the canal.

She began to turn, but just then an alert policeman shone a flashlight her way.

She was tempted to drop the wardrobe and run, but she held her nerve.

The cop said: "What are you up to?"

"Moving a wardrobe, officer," she said. Recovering her presence of mind, she faked a grisly curiosity to cover her guilty nervousness. "What happened here?" she said. For good measure she added: "Is anyone dead?"

Professionals disliked this kind of vampire inquisitiveness, she knew—she was a professional herself. As she expected, the policeman reacted dismissively. "None of your business," he said. "Just keep out of the way." He turned back and shone his light into the crashed car.

The pavement on this side of the street was clear. Carla made a snap decision and walked straight on. She and Ada carried the wardrobe containing the dead man toward the wreckage.

She kept her eyes on the little knot of emergency workers in the small circle of light. They were intensely focused on their task and no one looked up as Carla passed the car.

It seemed to take forever to pass along the length of the eight-wheel trailer. Then, when at last she drew level with the back end, she had a flash of inspiration.

She stopped.

Ada hissed: "What is it?"

"This way." Carla stepped into the road at the back of the truck. "Put the wardrobe down," she hissed. "No noise."

They placed the wardrobe gently on the pavement.

Ada whispered: "Are we leaving it here?"

Carla drew the key from her pocket and unlocked the wardrobe door. She looked up: as far as she could tell, the men were still gathered around the car, twenty feet away on the other side of the truck.

She opened the wardrobe door.

Joachim Koch stared up sightlessly, his head wrapped in a bloody towel.

"Tip him out," Carla said. "By the wheels."

They tilted the wardrobe, and the body rolled out, coming to rest up against the tires.

Carla retrieved the bloody towel and threw it into the wardrobe. She left the canvas bag lying beside the corpse; she was glad to get rid of it. She closed and locked the wardrobe door; then they picked it up and walked away.

It was easy to carry now.

When they were fifty yards away in the dark, Carla heard a distant voice say: "My God, there's another casualty—looks like a pedestrian was run over!"

Carla and Ada turned a corner, and relief washed over Carla like a tidal wave. She had got rid of the corpse. If only she could get home without attracting further attention—and without anyone looking inside the wardrobe and seeing the bloody towel—she would be safe. There would be no murder investigation. Joachim had become a pedestrian killed in a blackout accident. If he had really been dragged along the cobbled street by the wheels of the truck, he might have received injuries similar to those caused by the heavy base of Ada's soup pot. Perhaps a skilled autopsy doctor could tell the difference—but no one would consider an autopsy necessary.

Carla thought about dumping the wardrobe, and decided against. Even without the towel it had bloodstains inside, and might spark a police investigation on its own. They had to take it home and scrub it clean.

They got home without meeting anyone else.

They put the wardrobe down in the hall. Ada took out the towel, put it in the kitchen sink, and ran the cold tap. Carla felt a mixture of elation and sadness. She had stolen the Nazis' battle plan, but she had killed a young man who was more foolish than wicked. She would think about that for many days, perhaps years, before she could be sure how she felt about it. For now she was just too tired.

She told her mother what they had done. Maud's left cheek was so puffed up that her eye was almost closed. She was pressing her left side as if to ease a pain. She looked terrible.

Carla said: "You were terribly brave, Mother. I admire you so much for what you did today."

Maud said wearily: "I don't feel admirable. I'm so ashamed. I despise myself."

"Because you didn't love him?" said Carla.

"No," said Maud. "Because I did."

# CHAPTER FOURTEEN

# 1942 (III)

Greg Peshkov graduated from Harvard summa cum laude, the highest honor. He could have gone on effortlessly to take a doctorate in physics, his major, and thus have avoided military service. But he did not want to be a scientist. His ambition was to wield a different kind of power. And, after the war was over, a military record would be a huge plus for a rising young politician. So he joined the army.

On the other hand, he did not want actually to have to fight.

He followed the European war with heightened interest at the same time as he pressured everyone he knew in Washington—which was a lot of people—to get him a desk job at War Department headquarters.

The German summer offensive had started on June 28, and they had swiftly pushed east, meeting relatively light opposition, until they reached the city of Stalingrad, formerly called Tsaritsyn, where they were halted by fierce Russian resistance. Now they were stalled, with overstretched supply lines, and it was looking more and more as if the Red Army had drawn them into a trap.

Greg had not long been in basic training when he was summoned to the colonel's office. "The Army Corps of Engineers needs a bright young officer in Washington," the colonel said. "You've interned in Washington, but all the same you wouldn't have been my first choice—you can't even keep your goddamn uniform clean; look at you—but the job requires a knowledge of physics, and the field is kind of limited."

Greg said: "Thank you, sir."

"Try that kind of sarcasm on your new boss and you'll regret it. You're going to be an assistant to a Colonel Groves. I was at West Point with him. He's the biggest son of a bitch I ever met, in the army or out. Good luck."

Greg called Mike Penfold in the State Department press office and found out that until recently Leslie Groves had been chief of construction for the entire U.S. Army, and had been responsible for the military's new Washington headquarters, the vast five-sided building they were beginning to call the Pentagon. But he had been moved to a new project that no one knew much about. Some said he had offended his superiors so often that he had been effectively demoted, others that his new role was even more important but top secret. They all agreed he was egotistical, arrogant, and ruthless.

"Does *everybody* hate him?" Greg asked.

"Oh, no," Mike said. "Only those who have met him."

Lieutenant Greg Peshkov was full of trepidation when he arrived at Groves's office in the striking new War Department Building, a pale tan art deco palace on Twenty-first Street and Virginia Avenue. Right away he learned that he was part of a group called the Manhattan Engineer District. This deliberately uninformative name camouflaged a team who were trying to invent a new kind of bomb using uranium as an explosive.

Greg was intrigued. He knew there was incalculable energy locked up in uranium's lighter isotope, U-235, and he had read several papers on the subject in scientific journals. But news of the research had dried up a couple of years ago, and now Greg knew why.

He learned that President Roosevelt felt the project was moving too slowly, and Groves had been appointed to crack the whip.

Greg arrived six days after Groves had been reassigned. His first task for Groves was to help him pin stars to the collar of his khaki shirt: he had just been promoted to brigadier general. "It's mainly to impress all these civilian scientists we have to work with," Groves growled. "I have a meeting in the secretary of war's office in ten minutes. You'd better come with me. It'll serve you for a briefing."

Groves was heavy. An inch under six feet tall, he had to weigh two hundred and fifty pounds, maybe three hundred. He wore his uniform pants high, and his belly bulged under his webbing belt. He had chestnut-colored hair that might have curled if it had been grown long enough. He had a narrow forehead, fat cheeks, and a jowly chin. His small mustache was all but invisible. He was an unattractive man in every way, and Greg was not looking forward to working for him.

Groves and his entourage, including Greg, left the building and walked down Virginia Avenue to the National Mall. On the way, Groves said to Greg: "When they gave me this job, they told me it could win the war. I don't know if that's true, but my plan is to act as if it is. You'd better do the same."

"Yes, sir," said Greg.

The secretary of war had not yet moved into the unfinished Pentagon, and War Department headquarters were still in the old Munitions Building, a long, low, out-of-date "temporary" structure on Constitution Avenue.

Secretary of War Henry Stimson was a Republican, brought in by the president to keep that party from undermining the war effort by making trouble in Congress. At seventy-five Stimson was an elder statesman, a dapper old man with a white mustache, but the light of intelligence still gleamed in his gray eyes.

The meeting was a full-dress performance, and the room was full of bigwigs, including Army Chief of Staff George Marshall. Greg felt nervous, and he thought admiringly that Groves was remarkably calm for someone who had been a mere colonel yesterday.

Groves began by outlining how he intended to impose order on the hundreds of civilian scientists and dozens of physics laboratories involved in the Manhattan Project. He made no attempt to defer to the high-ranking men who might well have thought they were in charge.

He outlined his plans without troubling to use such mollifying phrases as "with your permission" and "if you agree." Greg wondered whether the man was trying to get himself fired.

Greg learned so much new information that he wanted to take notes, but no one else did, and he guessed it would not look right.

When Groves had done, one of the group said: "I believe supplies of uranium are crucial to the project. Do we have enough?"

Groves answered: "There are twelve hundred fifty tons of pitchblende—that's the ore that contains uranium oxide—in a yard on Staten Island."

"Then we'd better acquire some of that," said the questioner.

"I bought it all on Friday, sir."

"Friday? The day after you were appointed?"

"Correct."

The secretary of war smothered a smile. Greg's surprise at Groves's arrogance began to turn to admiration of his nerve.

A man in admiral's uniform said: "What about the priority rating of this project? You need to clear the decks with the War Production Board."

"I saw Donald Nelson on Saturday, sir," said Groves. Nelson was the civilian head of the board. "I asked him to raise our rating."

"What did he say?"

"He said no."

"That's a problem."

"Not any longer. I told him I would have to recommend to the president that the Manhattan Project be abandoned because the War Production Board was unwilling to cooperate. Then he gave us a triple-A."

"Good," said the secretary of war.

Greg was impressed again. Groves was a real pistol.

Stimson said: "Now, you'll be supervised by a committee that will report to me. Nine members have been suggested—"

"Hell, no," said Groves.

The secretary of war said: "What did you say?"

Surely, Greg thought, Groves has gone too far this time.

Groves said: "I can't report to a committee of nine, Mr. Secretary. I'll never get 'em off my back."

Stimson grinned. He was too old a hand to get offended by this kind of talk, it seemed. He said mildly: "What number would you suggest, General?"

Greg could see that Groves wanted to say *None,* but what came out was: "Three would be perfect."

"All right," said the secretary of war, to Greg's amazement. "Anything else?"

"We're going to need a large site, something like sixty thousand acres, for a uranium enrichment plant and associated facilities. There's a suitable area in Oak Ridge, Tennessee. It's a ridge valley, so that if there should be an accident the explosion will be contained."

"An accident?" said the admiral. "Is that likely?"

Groves did not hide his feeling that this was a dumb question. "We're making an experimental bomb, for Christ's sake," he said. "A bomb so powerful that it promises to flatten a medium-size city with one detonation. We'd be pretty goddamn dumb if we ignored the possibility of accidents."

The admiral looked as if he wanted to protest, but Stimson intervened, saying: "Carry on, General."

"Land is cheap in Tennessee," Groves said. "So is electricity—and our plant will use huge quantities of power."

"So you're proposing to buy this land."

"I'm proposing to view it today." Groves looked at his watch. "In fact I need to leave now to catch my train to Knoxville." He stood up. "If you will excuse me, gentlemen, I don't want to lose any time."

The other men in the room were flabbergasted. Even Stimson looked startled. No one in Washington dreamed of leaving a secretary's office before he indicated he was through. It was a major breach of etiquette. But Groves seemed not to care.

And he got away with it. "Very well," said Stimson. "Don't let us hold you up."

"Thank you, sir," said Groves, and he left the room.

Greg hurried out after him.

## ii

The most attractive civilian secretary in the New War Office Building was Margaret Cowdry. She had big dark eyes and a wide, sensual mouth. When you saw her sitting behind her typewriter, and she glanced up at you and smiled, you felt as if you were already making love to her.

Her father had turned baking into a mass-production industry: "Cowdry's Cookies crumble just like Ma's!" She had no need to work, but she was doing her bit for the war effort. Before inviting her to lunch Greg made sure she knew that he, too, was the child of a millionaire. An heiress usually preferred to date a rich boy: she could feel confident he was not after her money.

It was October and cold. Margaret wore a stylish navy blue coat with padded shoulders and a nipped-in waist. Her matching beret had a military look.

They went to the Ritz-Carlton, but when they got to the dining room, Greg saw his father having lunch with Gladys Angelus. He did not want to make it a foursome. When he explained this to Margaret, she said: "No problem. We'll have lunch at the University Women's Club around the corner. I'm a member there."

Greg had never been there, but he had a feeling he knew something about it. For a moment he chased the thought around his memory, but it eluded him, so he put it out of his mind.

At the club Margaret removed her coat to reveal a royal blue cashmere dress that clung to her alluringly. She kept on her hat and gloves, as all respectable women did when eating out.

As always, Greg loved the sensation of walking into a place with a beautiful woman on his arm. In the dining room of the University Women's Club there was only a handful of men, but they all envied him. Although he might not admit it to anyone else, he enjoyed this as much as sleeping with women.

He ordered a bottle of wine. Margaret mixed hers with mineral water, French-style, saying: "I don't want to spend the afternoon correcting my typing mistakes."

He told her about General Groves. "He's a real go-getter. In some ways he's a badly dressed version of my father."

"Everyone hates him," Margaret said.

Greg nodded. "He rubs people the wrong way."

"Is your father like that?"

"Sometimes, but mostly he uses charm."

"Mine's the same! Maybe all successful men are that way."

The meal went quickly. Service in Washington restaurants had speeded up. The nation was at war and men had urgent work to do.

A waitress brought them the dessert menu. Greg glanced at her and was startled to recognize Jacky Jakes. "Hello, Jacky!" he said.

"Hi, Greg," she replied, familiarity overlaying nervousness. "How have you been?"

Greg recalled the detective telling him that she worked at the University Women's Club. That was the memory that had eluded him before. "I'm just fine," he said. "How about you?"

"Real good."

"Everything going on just the same?" He was wondering if his father was still paying her an allowance.

"Pretty much."

Greg guessed that some lawyer was paying out the money and Lev had forgotten all about it. "That's good," he said.

Jacky remembered her job. "Can I offer you some dessert today?"

"Yes, thank you."

Margaret asked for fruit salad and Greg had ice cream.

When Jacky had gone, Margaret said: "She's very pretty," then looked expectant.

"I guess," he said.

"No wedding ring."

Greg sighed. Women were so perceptive. "You're wondering how come I'm friendly with a pretty black waitress who isn't married," he said. "I might as well tell you the truth. I had an affair with her when I was fifteen. I hope you're not shocked."

"Of course I am," she said. "I'm morally outraged." She was neither serious nor joking, but something in between. She was not really scandalized, he felt sure, but perhaps she did not want to give him the impression that she was easygoing about sex—not on their first lunch date, anyway.

Jacky brought the desserts and asked if they wanted coffee. They did not have time—the army did not believe in long lunch hours—and Margaret asked for the check. "Guests aren't allowed to pay here," she explained.

When Jacky had gone, Margaret said: "What's nice is that you're so fond of her."

"Am I?" Greg was surprised. "I have fond memories, I guess. I wouldn't mind being fifteen again."

"And yet she's scared of you."

"She is not!"

"Terrified."

"I don't think so."

"Take my word. Men are blind, but a woman sees these things."

Greg looked hard at Jacky when she brought the bill, and he realized that Margaret was right. Jacky was still scared. Every time she saw Greg, she was reminded of Joe Brekhunov and his straight razor.

It made Greg angry. The girl had a right to live in peace.

He was going to have to do something about this.

Margaret, who was as sharp as a tack, said: "I think you know why she's scared."

"My father frightened her off. He was worried I might marry her."

"Is your father scary?"

"He does like to get his own way."

"My father's the same," she said. "Sweet as cherry pie, until you cross him. Then he turns mean."

"I'm so glad you understand."

They returned to work. Greg felt angry all afternoon. Somehow his father's curse still lay like a blight over Jacky's life. But what could he do?

What would his father do? That was a good way to look at it. Lev would be completely single-minded about getting his way, and would not care whom he hurt in the process. General Groves would be similar. I can be like that, Greg thought; I'm my father's son.

The beginning of a plan began to form in his mind.

He spent the afternoon reading and summarizing an interim report from the University of Chicago Metallurgical Laboratory. The scientists there included Leo Szilard, the man who first conceived of the nuclear chain reaction. Szilard was a Hungarian Jew who had studied at the University of Berlin—until the fatal year of 1933. The research team in Chicago was led by Enrico Fermi, the Italian physicist. Fermi, whose wife was Jewish, had left Italy when Mussolini published his *Manifesto of Race.*

Greg wondered whether the Fascists realized that their racism had brought such a windfall of brilliant scientists to their enemies.

He understood the physics perfectly well. The theory of Fermi and Szilard was that when a neutron struck a uranium atom, the collision could produce two neutrons. Those two neutrons could then collide with further uranium atoms to make four, then eight, and so on. Szilard had called this a chain reaction a brilliant insight.

That way, a ton of uranium could produce as much energy as three million tons of coal—in theory.

In practise, it had never been done.

Fermi and his team were building a pile of uranium at Stagg Field, a disused football stadium belonging to the University of Chicago. To prevent the stuff exploding spontaneously, they buried the uranium in graphite, which absorbed the neutrons and killed the chain reaction. Their aim was to bring the radioactivity up, very gradually, to the level at which more was being created than absorbed—which would prove that a chain reaction was a reality—then close it down, fast, before it blew up the pile, the stadium, the campus of the university, and quite possibly the city of Chicago.

So far they had not succeeded.

Greg wrote a favorable précis of the report, asked Margaret Cowdry to type it right away, then took it in to Groves.

The general read the first paragraph and said: "Will it work?"

"Well, sir—"

"You're the goddamn scientist. Will it work?"

"Yes, sir, it will work," Greg said.

"Good," said Groves, and threw the summary in his wastepaper bin.

Greg returned to his desk and sat for a while, staring at the representation of the Periodic Table of the Elements on the wall opposite his desk. He was pretty sure the nuclear pile would work. He was more worried about how to force his father to withdraw the threat to Jacky.

Earlier, he had thought about handling the problem as Lev would have done. Now he began to think about practical details. He needed to take a dramatic stand.

His plan began to take shape.

But did he have the guts to confront his father?

At five he left for the day.

On the way home he stopped at a barbershop and bought a straight razor, the folding kind where the blade slid into the handle. The barber said: "You'll find it better than a safety razor, with your beard."

Greg was not going to shave with it.

His home was his father's permanent suite at the Ritz-Carlton. When Greg arrived, Lev and Gladys were having cocktails.

He remembered meeting Gladys for the first time in this room seven years ago, sitting on the same yellow silk couch. She was an even bigger star now. Lev had put her in a series of shamelessly gung-ho war movies in which she defied sneering Nazis, outwitted sadistic Japanese, and nursed square-jawed American pilots back to health. She was not quite as beautiful as she had been at twenty, Greg observed. The skin of her face did not have the same perfect smoothness; her hair did not seem so luxuriant; and she was wearing a brassiere, which she would undoubtedly have scorned before. But she still had dark blue eyes that seemed to issue an irresistible invitation.

Greg accepted a martini and sat down. Was he really going to defy his father? He had not done it in the seven years since he had first shaken Gladys's hand. Perhaps it was time.

I'll do it just the way he would, Greg thought.

He sipped his drink and set it down on a side table with spidery legs. Speaking conversationally, he said to Gladys: "When I was fifteen, my father introduced me to an actress called Jacky Jakes."

Lev's eyes widened.

"I don't think I know her," said Gladys.

Greg took the razor from his pocket, but did not open it. He held it in his hand as if feeling its weight. "I fell in love with her."

Lev said: "Why are you dragging this ancient history up now?"

Gladys sensed the tension and looked anxious.

Greg went on: "Father was afraid I might want to marry her."

Lev laughed mockingly. "That cheap tart?"

"Was she a cheap tart?" Greg said. "I thought she was an actress." He looked at Gladys.

Gladys flushed at the implied insult.

Greg said: "Father paid her a visit, and took with him a colleague, Joe Brekhunov. Have you met him, Gladys?"

"I don't believe so."

"Lucky you. Joe has a razor like this." Greg snapped the razor open, showing the gleaming sharp blade.

Gladys gasped.

Lev said: "I don't know what game you think you're playing—"

"Just a minute," Greg said. "Gladys wants to hear the rest of the story." He smiled at her. She looked terrified. He said: "My father told Jacky that if she ever saw me again, Joe would cut her face with his razor."

He jerked the knife, just a little, and Gladys gave a small scream.

"The hell with this," Lev said, and took a step toward Greg. Greg raised the hand holding the razor. Lev stopped.

Greg did not know whether he would be able to cut his father. But Lev did not know, either.

"Jacky lives right here in Washington," Greg said.

His father said crudely: "Are you fucking her again?"

"No. I'm not fucking anyone, though I have plans for Margaret Cowdry."

"The cookie heiress?"

"Why, do you want Joe to threaten her, too?"

"Don't be stupid."

"Jacky is a waitress now—she never got the movie part she was hoping for. I run into her on the street sometimes. Today she served me in a restaurant. Every time she sees my face, she thinks Joe is going to come after her."

"She's out of her mind," Lev said. "I'd forgotten all about her until five minutes ago."

"Can I tell her that?" Greg said. "I think by now she's entitled to her peace of mind."

"Tell her whatever the hell you like. For me she doesn't exist."

"That's great," said Greg. "She'll be pleased to hear it."

"Now put that damn blade away."

"One more thing. A warning."

Lev looked angry. "You're warning *me*?"

"If anything bad happens to Jacky—anything at all . . ." Greg moved the razor side to side, just a little.

Lev said scornfully: "Don't tell me you're going to cut Joe Brekhunov."

"No."

Lev showed a hint of fear. "You'd cut me?"

Greg shook his head.

Angrily, Lev said: "What, then, for Christ's sake?"

Greg looked at Gladys.

She took a second to catch his drift. Then she jerked back in her silk-upholstered chair, put both hands on her cheeks as if to protect them, and gave another little scream, louder this time.

Lev said to Greg: "You little asshole."

Greg folded the razor and stood up. "It's how you would have handled it, Father," he said.

Then he went out.

He slammed the door and leaned against the wall, breathing as hard as if he had been running. He had never felt so scared in his life. Yet he also felt triumphant. He had stood up to the old man, used his own tactics back on him, even scared him a little.

He walked to the elevator, pocketing the razor. His breathing eased. He looked back along the hotel corridor, half-expecting his father to come running after him. But the door of the suite remained closed, and Greg boarded the elevator and went down to the lobby.

He entered the hotel bar and ordered a dry martini.

## iii

On Sunday Greg decided to visit Jacky.

He wanted to tell her the good news. He remembered the address—the only piece of information he had ever paid a private detective for. Unless she had moved, she lived just the other side of Union Station. He had promised her he would not go there, but now he could explain to her that such caution was no longer necessary.

He went by cab. Crossing town, he told himself he would be glad to draw a line at last under his affair with Jacky. He had a soft spot for his first lover, but he did not want to be involved in her life in any way. It would be a relief to get her off his conscience. Then, next time he ran into her, she would not look scared to death. They could say hello, chat for a while, and walk on.

The cab took him to a poor neighborhood of one-story homes with low chain-link fences around small yards. He wondered how Jacky lived these days. What did she do during those evenings she was so keen to have to herself? No doubt she saw movies with her girlfriends. Did she go to Washington Redskins football games, or follow the Nats baseball team? When he had asked her about boyfriends, she had been enigmatic. Perhaps she was married and could not afford a ring. By his calculation she was twenty-four. If she was looking for Mr. Right, she should have found him by now. But she had never mentioned a husband, nor had the detective.

He paid off the taxi outside a small, neat house with flower pots in a concrete front yard—more domesticated than he had expected. As soon as he opened the gate, he heard a dog bark. That made sense: a woman living alone might feel safer with a dog. He stepped onto the porch and rang the doorbell. The barking got louder. It sounded like a big dog, but that could be deceptive, Greg knew.

No one came to the door.

When the dog paused for breath, Greg heard the distinctive silence of an empty house.

There was a wooden bench on the stoop. He sat and waited a few minutes. No one came, and no helpful neighbor appeared to tell him whether Jacky was away for a few minutes, all day, or two weeks.

He walked a few blocks, bought the Sunday edition of *The Washington Post,* and returned to the bench to read it. The dog continued to bark intermittently, knowing he was still there. It was the first of November, and he was glad he had worn his olive green uniform greatcoat and cap: the weather was wintry. Midterm elections would be held on Tuesday, and the *Post* was predicting that the Democrats would take a beating because of Pearl Harbor. That incident had transformed America, and it came as a surprise to Greg to realize that it had happened less than a year ago. Now American men of his own age were dying on an island no one had ever heard of called Guadalcanal.

He heard the gate click, and looked up.

At first Jacky did not notice him, and he had a moment to study her. She looked dowdily respectable in a dark coat and a plain felt hat, and she carried a book with a black cover. If he had not known her better, Greg would have thought she was coming home from church.

With her was a little boy. He wore a tweed coat and a cap, and he was holding her hand.

The boy saw Greg first, and said: "Look, Mommy, there's a soldier!"

Jacky looked at Greg, and her hand flew to her mouth.

Greg stood up as they mounted the steps to the stoop. A child! She had kept that secret. It explained why she needed to be home in the evenings. He had never thought of it.

"I told you never to come here," she said as she put the key in the lock.

"I wanted to tell you that you need not be afraid of my father anymore. I didn't know you had a son."

She and the boy stepped into the house. Greg stood expectantly at the door. A German shepherd growled at him, then looked up at Jacky for guidance. Jacky glared at Greg, evidently thinking about slamming the door in his face, but after a moment she gave an exasperated sigh and turned away, leaving it open.

Greg walked in and offered his left fist to the dog. It sniffed warily and gave him provisional approval. He followed Jacky into a small kitchen.

"It's All Saints' Day," Greg said. He was not religious, but at his boarding school he had been forced to learn all the Christian festivals. "Is that why you went to church?"

"We go every Sunday," she replied.

"This is a day of surprises," Greg murmured.

She took off the boy's coat, sat him at the table, and gave him a cup of orange juice. Greg sat opposite and said: "What's your name?"

"Georgy." He said it quietly, but with confidence: he was not shy. Greg studied him. He was as pretty as his mother, with the same bow-shaped mouth, but his skin was lighter than hers, more like coffee with cream, and he had green eyes, unusual in a Negro face. He reminded Greg a little of his half sister, Daisy. Meanwhile Georgy looked at Greg with an intense gaze that was almost intimidating.

Greg said: "How old are you, Georgy?"

He looked at his mother for help. She gave Greg a strange look and said: "He's six."

"Six!" said Greg. "You're quite a big boy, aren't you? Why . . . ?"

A bizarre thought crossed his mind, and he fell silent. Georgy had been born six years ago. Greg and Jacky had been lovers seven years ago. His heart seemed to falter.

He stared at Jacky. "Surely not," he said.

She nodded.

"He was born in 1936," said Greg.

"May," she said. "Eight and a half months after I left that apartment in Buffalo."

"Does my father know?"

"Heck, no. That would have given him even more power over me."

Her hostility had vanished, and now she just looked vulnerable. In her eyes he saw a plea, though he was not sure what she was pleading for.

He looked at Georgy with new eyes: the light skin, the green eyes, the odd resemblance to Daisy. Are you mine? he thought. Can it be true?

But he knew it was.

His heart filled with a strange emotion. Suddenly Georgy seemed terribly vulnerable, a helpless child in a cruel world, and Greg needed to take care of him, make sure he came to no harm. He had an impulse to take the boy in his arms, but he realized that might scare him, so he held back.

Georgy put down his orange juice. He got off his chair and came around the table to stand close to Greg. With a remarkably direct look, he said: "Who are you?"

Trust a kid to ask the toughest question of all, Greg thought. What the hell was he going to say? The truth was too much for a six-year-old to take. I'm just a former friend of your mother's, he thought; I was just passing the door, thought I'd say hello. Nobody special. May see you again, most likely not.

He looked at Jacky, and saw that pleading expression intensified. He realized what was on her mind: she was desperately afraid he was going to reject Georgy.

"I tell you what," Greg said, and he lifted Georgy onto his knees. "Why don't you call me Uncle Greg?"

## iv

Greg stood shivering in the spectators' gallery of an unheated squash court. Here, under the west stand of the disused stadium on the edge of the University of Chicago campus, Fermi and Szilard had built their atomic pile. Greg was impressed and scared.

The pile was a cube of gray bricks reaching the ceiling of the court, standing just shy of the end wall, which still bore the polka-dot marks of hundreds of squash balls. The pile had cost a million dollars, and it could blow up the entire city.

Graphite was the material of which pencil leads were made, and it gave off a filthy dust that covered the floor and walls. Everyone who had been in the room awhile was as black-faced as a coal miner. No one had a clean lab coat.

Graphite was not the explosive material—on the contrary, it was there to suppress radioactivity. But some of the bricks in the stack were drilled with narrow holes stuffed with uranium oxide, and this was the material that radiated the neutrons. Running through the pile were ten channels for control rods. These were thirteen-foot strips of cadmium, a metal that absorbed neutrons even more hungrily than graphite. Right now the rods were keeping everything calm. When they were withdrawn from the pile, the fun would start.

The uranium was already throwing off its deadly radiation, but the graphite and the cadmium were soaking it up. Radiation was measured by counters that clicked menacingly and a cylindrical pen recorder that was mercifully silent. The array of controls and meters near Greg in the gallery gave off the only heat in the place.

Greg visited on Wednesday, December 2, a bitterly cold, windy day in Chicago. Today for the first time the pile was supposed to go critical. Greg was there to observe the experiment on behalf of his boss, General Groves. He hinted jovially to anyone who asked that Groves feared an explosion and had deputed Greg to take the risk for him. In fact Greg had a more sinister mission. He was making an initial assessment of the scientists with a view to deciding who might be a security risk.

Security on the Manhattan Project was a nightmare. The top scientists were foreigners. Most of the rest were left-wingers, either Communists themselves or liberals who had Communist friends. If everyone suspicious was fired, there would be hardly any scientists left. So Greg was trying to figure out which ones were the worst risks.

Enrico Fermi was about forty. A small, balding man with a long nose, he smiled engagingly while supervising this terrifying experiment. He was smartly dressed in a suit with a waistcoat. It was midmorning when he ordered the trial to begin.

He instructed a technician to withdraw all but one of the control rods from the pile. Greg said: "What, all at once?" It seemed frighteningly precipitate.

The scientist standing next to him, Barney McHugh, said: "We took it this far last night. It worked fine."

"I'm glad to hear it," said Greg.

McHugh, bearded and podgy, was low down on Greg's list of suspects. He was American, with no interest in politics. The only black mark against him was a foreign wife: she was British—never a good sign, but not in itself evidence of treachery.

Greg had assumed there would be some sophisticated mechanism for moving the rods in and out, but it was simpler than that. The technician just put a ladder up against the pile, climbed halfway up it, and pulled out the rods by hand.

Speaking conversationally, McHugh said: "We were originally going to do this in the Argonne Forest."

"Where's that?"

"Twenty miles southwest of Chicago. Pretty isolated. Fewer casualties."

Greg shivered. "So why did you change your minds and decide to do it right here on Fifty-seventh Street?"

"The builders we hired went on strike, so we had to build the damn thing ourselves, and we couldn't be that far away from the laboratories."

"So you took the risk of killing everyone in Chicago."

"We don't think that will happen."

Greg had not thought so, either, but he did not feel so sure now, standing a few feet away from the pile.

Fermi was checking his monitors against a forecast he had prepared of radiation levels at every stage of the experiment. Apparently the initial stage went according to plan, for he now ordered the last rod to be pulled halfway out.

There were some safety measures. A weighted rod hung poised to be dropped into the pile automatically if the radiation rose too high. In case that did not work, a similar rod was tied to the gallery railing with a rope, and a young physicist, looking as if he felt a bit silly, stood holding an axe, ready to cut the rope in an emergency. Finally three more scientists called the suicide squad were positioned near the ceiling, standing on the platform of the elevator used during construction, holding large jugs of cadmium sulfate solution, which they would throw onto the pile, as if dousing a bonfire.

Greg knew that neutron generation multiplied in thousandths of a second. However, Fermi argued that some neutrons took longer, perhaps several seconds. If Fermi was right, there would be no problem. But if he was wrong, the squad with the jugs and the physicist with the axe would be vaporized before they could blink.

Greg heard the clicking become more rapid. He looked anxiously at Fermi, who was doing calculations with a slide rule. Fermi looked pleased. Anyway, Greg thought, if things go wrong, it will probably happen so fast that we'll never know anything about it.

The rate of clicking leveled off. Fermi smiled and gave the order for the rod to be pulled out another six inches.

More scientists were arriving, climbing the stairs to the gallery in their heavyweight Chicago-winter clothing, coats and hats and scarves and gloves. Greg was appalled at the lack of security. No one was checking credentials: any one of these men could have been a spy for the Japanese.

Among them Greg recognized the great Szilard, tall and heavy, with a round face and thick curly hair. Leo Szilard was an idealist who had imagined nuclear power liberating the human race from toil. It was with a heavy heart that he had joined the team designing the atom bomb.

Another six inches, another increase in the pace of the clicking.

Greg looked at his watch. It was eleven thirty.

Suddenly there was a loud crash. Everyone jumped. McHugh said: "Fuck."

Greg said: "What happened?"

"Oh, I see," said McHugh. "The radiation level activated the safety mechanism and released the emergency control rod, that's all."

Fermi announced: "I'm hungry. Let's go to lunch." In his Italian accent it came out "I'm hungary. Les go to luncha."

How could they think about food? But no one argued. "You never know how long an experiment is going to take," said McHugh. "Could be all day. Best to eat when you can." Greg could have screamed.

All the control rods were reinserted into the pile and locked into position, and everyone left.

Most of them went to a campus canteen. Greg got a grilled cheese sandwich and sat next to a solemn physicist called Wilhelm Frunze. Most scientists were badly dressed but Frunze was notably so, in a green suit with tan suede trimmings: buttonholes, collar lining, elbow patches, pocket flaps. This guy was high on Greg's suspect list. He was German, though he had left in the mid-1930s and gone to London. He was an anti-Nazi but not a Communist: his politics were Social Democrat. He was married to an American girl, an artist. Talking to him over lunch, Greg found no reason for suspicion: he seemed to love living in America and to be interested in little but his work. But with foreigners you could never be quite sure where their ultimate loyalty lay.

After lunch he stood in the derelict stadium, looking at thousands of empty stands, and thought about Georgy. He had told no one he had a son—not even Margaret Cowdry, with whom he was now enjoying delightfully carnal relations—but he longed to tell his mother. He felt proud, for no reason—he had made no contribution to bringing Georgy into the world apart from making love to Jacky, probably about the easiest thing he had ever done. Most of all he felt excited. He was at the beginning of some kind of adventure. Georgy was going to grow, and learn, and change, and one day become a man, and Greg would be there, watching and marveling.

The scientists reassembled at two o'clock. Now there were about forty people crowded into the gallery with the monitoring equipment. The experiment was carefully reset in the position at which they had left off, Fermi checking his instruments constantly.

Then he said: "This time, withdraw the rod twelve inches."

The clicks became rapid. Greg waited for the increase to level off, as it had before, but it did not. Instead the clicking became faster and faster until it was a continuous roar.

The radiation level was above the maximum of the counters, Greg realized when he noticed that everyone's attention had switched to the pen recorder. Its scale was adjustable. As the level rose, the scale was changed, then changed again, and again.

Fermi raised a hand. They all went silent. "The pile has gone critical," he said. He smiled—and did nothing.

Greg wanted to scream *So turn the fucker off!* But Fermi remained silent and still, watching the pen, and such was his authority that no one challenged him. The chain reaction was happening, but it was under control. He let it run for a minute, then another.

McHugh muttered: "Jesus Christ."

Greg did not want to die. He wanted to be a senator. He wanted to sleep with Margaret Cowdry again. He wanted to see Georgy go to college. I haven't had half a life yet, he thought.

At last Fermi ordered the control rods to be pushed in.

The noise of the counters reverted to a clicking that gradually slowed and stopped.

Greg breathed normally.

McHugh was jubilant. "We proved it!" he said. "The chain reaction is real!"

"And it's controllable, more importantly," said Greg.

"Yes, I suppose that is more important, from the practical point of view."

Greg smiled. Scientists were like this, he knew from Harvard: for them theory was reality, and the world a rather inaccurate model.

Someone produced a bottle of Italian wine in a straw basket and some paper cups. The scientists all drank a tiny share. This was another reason Greg was not a scientist: they had no idea how to party.

Someone asked Fermi to sign the basket. He did so; then all the others signed it.

The technicians shut down the monitors. Everyone began to drift away. Greg stayed, observing. After a while he found himself alone in the gallery with Fermi and Szilard. He watched as the two intellectual giants shook hands. Szilard was a big, round-faced man; Fermi was elfin. For a moment Greg was inappropriately reminded of Laurel and Hardy.

Then he heard Szilard speak. "My friend," he said, "I think this will go down as a black day in the history of mankind."

Greg thought: Now what the hell did he mean by that?

## V

Greg wanted his parents to accept Georgy.

It would not be easy. No doubt it would be unnerving for them to be told they had a grandson who had been concealed from them for six years. They might be angry. On top of that, they might look down on Jacky. They had no right to take a moralistic attitude, he thought wryly: they themselves had an illegitimate child—himself. But people were not rational.

He was not sure how much difference it would make that Georgy was black. Greg's parents were laid-back about race, and never talked viciously about niggers or kikes as some people of their generation did, but they might change when they learned there was a Negro in the family.

His father would be the more difficult one, he guessed, so he spoke to his mother first.

He got a few days' leave at Christmas and went home to her place in Buffalo. Marga had a large apartment in the best building in town. She lived mostly alone, but she had a cook, two maids, and a chauffeur. She had a safe full of jewelry and a dress closet the size of a two-car garage. But she did not have a husband.

Lev was in town, but traditionally he took Olga out on Christmas Eve. He was still married to her, technically, though he had not spent a night at her house for years. As far as Greg knew, Olga and Lev hated one another, but for some reason they met once a year.

That evening, Greg and his mother had dinner together in the apartment. He put on a tuxedo to please her. "I love to see my men dressed up," she often said. They had fish soup, roast chicken, and Greg's boyhood favorite, peach pie.

"I have some news for you, Mother," he said nervously as the maid poured coffee. He feared she would be angry. He was not frightened for himself, but for Georgy, and he wondered if this was what parenthood was about—worrying about someone else more than you worried about yourself.

"Good news?" she said.

She had become heavier in recent years, but she was still glamorous at forty-six. If there was any gray in her dark hair, it had been carefully camouflaged by her hairdresser. Tonight she wore a simple black dress and a diamond choker.

"Very good news, but I guess a little surprising, so please don't fly off the handle."

She raised a black eyebrow but said nothing.

He reached inside his dinner jacket and took out a photograph. It showed Georgy on a red bicycle with a ribbon around the handlebars. The rear wheel of the bike had a pair of stabilizing wheels so that it would not fall over. The expression on the boy's face was ecstatic. Greg was kneeling beside him, looking proud.

He handed the picture to his mother.

She studied it thoughtfully. After a minute she said: "I'm assuming you gave this little boy a bicycle for Christmas."

"That's right."

She looked up. "Are you telling me you have a child?"

Greg nodded. "His name is Georgy."

"Are you married?"

"No."

She threw down the photo. "For God's sake!" she said angrily. "What is the matter with you Peshkov men?"

Greg was dismayed. "I don't know what you mean!"

"Another illegitimate child! Another woman bringing him up alone!"

He realized that she saw Jacky as a younger version of herself. "Mother, I was fifteen . . ."

"Why can't you be normal?" she stormed. "For the love of Jesus Christ, what's wrong with having a regular family?"

Greg looked down. "There's nothing wrong with it."

He felt ashamed. Until this moment he had seen himself as a passive player in this drama, even a victim. Everything that had happened had been done to him by his father and Jacky. But his mother did not view it that way, and now he saw that she was right. He had not thought twice about sleeping with Jacky, he had not questioned her when she had said airily that there was no need to worry about contraception, and he had not confronted his father when Jacky left. He had been very young, yes, but if he was old enough to fuck her, he was old enough to take responsibility for the consequences.

His mother was still raging. "Don't you remember how you used to carry on? 'Where is my daddy? Why doesn't he sleep here? Why can't we go with him to Daisy's house?' And then later, the fights you had at school when the boys called you a bastard. And you were so angry to be refused membership of that goddamn yacht club."

"Of course I remember."

She banged a beringed fist on the table, causing crystal glasses to shake. "Then how can you put another little boy through the same torture?"

"I didn't know he existed until two months ago. Father scared the mother away."

"Who is she?"

"Her name is Jacky Jakes. She's a waitress." He took out another photo.

His mother sighed. "A pretty Negress." She was calming down.

"She was hoping to be an actress, but I guess she gave that up when Georgy came along."

Marga nodded. "A baby will ruin your career faster than a dose of the clap."

Mother assumed that an actress had to sleep with the right people to progress, Greg noted. How the hell would she know? But then, she had been a nightclub singer when his father met her . . .

He did not want to go down that road.

She said: "What did you give her for Christmas?"

"Medical insurance."

"Good choice. Better than a fluffy bear."

Greg heard a step in the hall. His father was home. Hastily, he said: "Mother, will you meet Jacky? Will you accept Georgy as your grandson?"

Her hand went to her mouth. "Oh, my God, I'm a grandmother." She did not know whether to be shocked or pleased.

Greg leaned forward. "I don't want Father to reject him. Please!"

Before she could reply, Lev came into the room.

Marga said: "Hello, darling, how was your evening?"

He sat at the table, looking grumpy. "Well, I've had my shortcomings explained to me in full detail, so I guess I had a great time."

"You poor thing. Did you get enough to eat? I can make you an omelette in a minute."

"The food was fine."

The photographs were on the table, but Lev had not noticed them yet.

The maid came in and said: "Would you like coffee, Mr. Peshkov?"

"No, thank you."

Marga said: "Bring the vodka, in case Mr. Peshkov would like a drink later."

"Yes, ma'am."

Greg noticed how solicitous Marga was about Lev's comfort and pleasure. He guessed that was why Lev was here, not at Olga's, for the night.

The maid brought a bottle and three small glasses on a silver tray. Lev still drank vodka the Russian way, warm and neat.

Greg said: "Father, you know Jacky Jakes—"

"Her again?" Lev said irritably.

"Yes, because there's something you don't know about her."

That got his attention. He hated to think other people knew things he did not. "What?"

"She has a child." He pushed the photographs across the polished table.

"Is it yours?"

"He's six years old. What do you think?"

"She kept this pretty damned quiet."

"She was scared of you."

"What did she think I might do, cook the baby and eat it?"

"I don't know, Father—you're the expert at scaring people."

Lev gave him a hard look. "You're learning, though."

He was talking about the scene with the razor. Maybe I am learning to scare people, Greg thought.

Lev said: "Why are you showing me these photos?"

"I thought you might like to know that you have a grandson."

"By a goddamn two-bit actress who was hoping to snag herself a rich man!"

Marga said: "Darling! Please remember that I was a two-bit nightclub singer hoping to snag myself a rich man."

He looked furious. For a moment he glared at Marga. Then his expression changed. "You know what?" he said. "You're right. Who am I to judge Jacky Jakes?"

Greg and Marga stared at him, astonished at this sudden humility.

He said: "I'm just like her. I was a two-kopek hoodlum from the slums of St. Petersburg until I married Olga Vyalov, my boss's daughter."

Greg caught his mother's eye, and she gave an almost imperceptible shrug that simply said *You never can tell.*

Lev looked again at the photo. "Apart from the color, this kid looks like my brother, Grigori. There's a surprise. Until now I thought all these picaninnies looked the same."

Greg could hardly breathe. "Will you see him, Father? Will you come with me and meet your grandson?"

"Hell, yes." Lev uncorked the bottle, poured vodka into three glasses, and passed them round. "What's the boy's name, anyway?"

"Georgy."

Lev raised his glass. "So here's to Georgy."

They all drank.

# CHAPTER FIFTEEN

# 1943 (I)

Lloyd Williams walked along a narrow uphill path at the tail end of a line of desperate fugitives.

He breathed easily. He was used to this. He had now crossed the Pyrenees several times. He wore rope-soled espadrilles that gave his feet a better grip on the rocky ground. He had a heavy coat on top of his blue overalls. The sun was hot now but later, when the party reached higher altitudes and the sun went down, the temperature would drop below freezing.

Ahead of him were two sturdy ponies, three local people, and eight weary, bedraggled escapers, all loaded with packs. There were three American airmen, the surviving crew of a B-24 Liberator bomber that had crash-landed in Belgium. Two more were British officers who had escaped from the Oflag 65 prisoner-of-war camp in Strasbourg. The others were a Czech Communist, a Jewish woman with a violin, and a mysterious Englishman called Watermill who was probably some kind of spy.

They had all come a long way and suffered many hardships. This was the last leg of their journey, and the most dangerous. If captured now, they would all be tortured until they betrayed the brave men and women who had helped them en route.

Leading the party was Teresa. The climb was hard work for people who were not used to it, but they had to keep up a brisk pace to minimize their exposure, and Lloyd had found that the refugees were less likely to fall behind when they were led by a small, ravishingly pretty woman.

The path leveled and broadened into a small clearing. Suddenly a loud voice rang out. Speaking French with a German accent, it shouted: "Halt!"

The column came to an abrupt halt.

Two German soldiers emerged from behind a rock. They carried standard Mauser bolt-action rifles, each holding five rounds of ammunition.

Reflexively Lloyd touched the overcoat pocket that contained his loaded 9 mm Luger pistol.

Escaping from mainland Europe had become harder, and Lloyd's job had grown even more dangerous. At the end of last year the Germans had occupied the southern half of France, contemptuously ignoring the Vichy French government like the flimsy sham it had always been. A forbidden zone ten miles deep was declared all along the frontier with Spain. Lloyd and his party were in that zone now.

Teresa addressed the soldiers in French. "Good morning, gentlemen. Is everything all right?" Lloyd knew her well, and he could hear the tremor of fear in her voice, but he hoped it was too faint for the sentries to notice.

Among the French police there were many Fascists and a few Communists, but all of them were lazy, and none wanted to chase refugees across the icy passes of the Pyrenees. However, the Germans did. German troops had moved into border towns and begun to patrol the hill paths and mule trails Lloyd and Teresa used. The occupiers were not crack troops; those were fighting in Russia, where they had recently surrendered Stalingrad after a long and murderous struggle. Many of the Germans in France were old men, boys, and the walking wounded. But that seemed to make them more determined to prove themselves. Unlike the French, they rarely turned a blind eye.

Now the older of the two soldiers, cadaverously thin with a gray mustache, said to Teresa: "Where are you going?"

"To the village of Lamont. We have groceries for you and your comrades."

This particular German unit had moved into a remote hill village, kicking out the local inhabitants. Then they had realized how difficult it was to supply troops in that location. It had been a stroke of genius on Teresa's part to undertake to carry food to them—at a healthy profit—and thereby get permission to enter the prohibited zone.

The thin soldier looked suspiciously at the men with their backpacks. "All this is for German soldiers?"

"I hope so," Teresa said. "There's no one else up here to sell it to." She took a piece of paper from her pocket. "Here's the order, signed by your Sergeant Eisenstein."

The man read it carefully and handed it back. Then he looked at Lieutenant Colonel Will Donelly, a beefy American pilot. "Is he French?"

Lloyd put his hand on the gun in his pocket.

The appearance of the fugitives was a problem. In this part of the world the local people, French and Spanish, were usually small and dark. And everyone was thin. Both Lloyd and Teresa fitted that description, as did the Czech and the violinist. But the British were pale and fair-haired, and the Americans were huge.

Teresa said: "Guillaume was born in Normandy. All that butter."

The younger of the two soldiers, a pale boy with glasses, smiled at Teresa. She was easy to smile at. "Do you have wine?" he said.

"Of course."

The two sentries brightened visibly.

Teresa said: "Would you like some right now?"

The older man said: "It's thirsty in the sun."

Lloyd opened a pannier on one of the ponies, took out four bottles of Roussillon white wine, and handed them over. The Germans took two each. Suddenly everyone was smiling and shaking hands. The older sentry said: "Carry on, friends."

The fugitives went on. Lloyd had not really expected trouble, but you could never be sure, and he was relieved to have got past the sentry post.

It took them two more hours to reach Lamont. A dirt-poor hamlet with a handful of crude houses and some empty sheep pens, it stood on the edge of a small upland plain where the new spring grass was just beginning to show. Lloyd pitied the people who had lived here. They had had so little, and even that had been taken from them.

The party walked into the center of the village and gratefully unshouldered their burdens. They were surrounded by German soldiers.

This was the most dangerous moment, Lloyd thought.

Sergeant Eisenstein was in charge of a platoon of fifteen or twenty men. Everyone helped to unload the supplies: bread, sausage, fresh fish, condensed milk, canned food. The soldiers were pleased to get supplies and glad to see new faces. They merrily attempted to engage their benefactors in conversation.

The fugitives had to say as little as possible. This was the moment when they could so easily betray themselves by a slip. Some Germans spoke French well enough to detect an English or American accent. Even those who had passable accents, such as Teresa and Lloyd, could give themselves away with a grammatical error. It was so easy to say "*sur le table*" instead of "*sur la table*," but it was a mistake no French person would ever make.

To compensate, the two genuine Frenchmen in the party went out of their way to be voluble. Any time a soldier began to talk to a fugitive, someone would jump into the conversation.

Teresa presented the sergeant with a bill, and he took a long time to check the numbers, then count out the money.

At last they were able to take their leave, with empty backpacks and lighter hearts.

They walked back down the mountain half a mile; then they split up. Teresa went on down with the Frenchmen and the horses. Lloyd and the fugitives turned onto an upward path.

The German sentries at the clearing would probably be too drunk by now to notice that fewer people were coming down than went up. But if they asked questions, Teresa would say some of the party had started a card game with the soldiers, and would be following later.

Then there would be a change of shift and the Germans would lose track.

Lloyd made his group walk for two hours; then he allowed them a ten-minute break. They had all been given bottles of water and packets of dried figs for energy. They were discouraged from bringing anything else: Lloyd knew from experience that treasured books, silverware, ornaments, and gramophone records would become too heavy and be thrown into a snow-filled ravine long before the footsore travelers crested the pass.

This was the hard part. From now on it would only get darker and colder and rockier.

Just before the snow line, he instructed them to refill their water bottles at a clear cold stream.

When night fell, they kept going. It was dangerous to let people sleep: they might freeze to death. They were tired, and they slipped and stumbled on the icy rocks. Inevitably their pace slowed. Lloyd could not let the line spread: stragglers might lose their way, and there were precipitate ravines for the careless to fall into. But he had never lost anyone, yet.

Many of the fugitives were officers, and this was the point where they would sometimes challenge Lloyd, arguing when he ordered them to keep going. Lloyd had been promoted to major to give him more authority.

In the middle of the night, when their morale was at rock bottom, Lloyd announced: "You are now in neutral Spain!" and they raised a ragged cheer. In truth he did not know exactly where the border was, and always made the announcement when they seemed most in need of a boost.

Their spirits lifted again when dawn broke. They still had some way to go, but the route now led downhill, and their cold limbs gradually thawed.

At sunrise they skirted a small town with a dust-colored church at the top of a hill. Just beyond, they reached a large barn beside the road. Inside was a green Ford flatbed truck with a grimy canvas cover. The lorry was large enough to carry the whole party. At the wheel was Captain Silva, a middle-aged Englishman of Spanish descent who worked with Lloyd.

Also there, to Lloyd's surprise, was Major Lowther, who had been in charge of the intelligence course at Tŷ Gwyn, and had been snootily disapproving—or perhaps just envious—of Lloyd's friendship with Daisy.

Lloyd knew that Lowthie had been posted to the British embassy in Madrid, and guessed he worked for MI6, the Secret Intelligence Service, but he would not have expected to see him this far from the capital.

Lowther wore an expensive white flannel suit that was crumpled and grubby. He stood beside the truck looking proprietorial. "I'll take over from here, Williams," he said. He looked at the fugitives. "Which one of you is Watermill?"

Watermill could have been a real name or a code.

The mysterious Englishman stepped forward and shook hands.

"I'm Major Lowther. I'm taking you straight to Madrid." Turning back to Lloyd he said: "I'm afraid your party will have to make your way to the nearest railway station."

"Just a minute," said Lloyd. "That truck belongs to my organization." He had purchased it with his budget from MI9, the department that helped escaping prisoners. "And the driver works for me."

"Can't be helped," Lowther said briskly. "Watermill has priority."

The Secret Intelligence Service always thought they had priority. "I don't agree," Lloyd said. "I see no reason why we can't all go to Barcelona in the truck, as planned. Then you can take Watermill on to Madrid by train."

"I didn't ask for your opinion, laddie. Just do as you're told."

Watermill himself interjected, in a reasonable tone: "I'm perfectly happy to share the truck."

"Leave this to me, please," Lowther told him.

Lloyd said: "All these people have just walked across the Pyrenees. They're exhausted."

"Then they'd better have a rest before going on."

Lloyd shook his head. "Too dangerous. The town on the hill has a sympathetic mayor—that's why we rendezvous here. But farther down the valley their politics are different. The Gestapo are everywhere—you know that—and most of the Spanish police are on their side, not ours. My group will be in serious danger of arrest for entering the country illegally. And you know how difficult it is to get people out of Franco's jails even when they're innocent."

"I'm not going to waste my time arguing with you. I outrank you."

"No, you don't."

"What?"

"I'm a major. So don't call me 'laddie' ever again, unless you want a punch on the nose."

"My mission is urgent!"

"So why didn't you bring your own vehicle?"

"Because this one was available!"

"But it wasn't."

Will Donelly, the big American, stepped forward. "I'm with Major Williams," he drawled. "He's just saved my life. You, Major Lowther, haven't done shit."

"That's got nothing to do with it," said Lowther.

"Well, the situation here seems pretty clear," Donelly said. "The truck is under the authority of Major Williams. Major Lowther wants it, but he can't have it. End of story."

Lowther said: "You keep out of this."

"I happen to be a lieutenant colonel, so I guess I outrank you both."

"But this isn't under your jurisdiction."

"Nor yours, evidently." Donelly turned to Lloyd. "Should we get going?"

"I insist!" spluttered Lowther.

Donelly turned back to him. "Major Lowther," he said. "Shut the fuck up. And that's an order."

Lloyd said: "All right, everybody—climb aboard."

Lowther glared furiously at Lloyd. "I'll get you for this, you little Welsh bastard," he said.

## ii

The daffodils were out in London on the day Daisy and Boy went for their medical.

The visit to the doctor was Daisy's idea. She was fed up with Boy blaming her for not getting pregnant. He constantly compared her to his brother Andy's wife, May, who now had three children. "There must be something wrong with you," he had said aggressively.

"I got pregnant once before." She winced at the remembered pain of her miscarriage; then she recalled how Lloyd had taken care of her, and she felt a different kind of pain.

Boy said: "Something could have happened since then to make you infertile."

"Or you."

"What do you mean?"

"There might just as easily be something wrong with you."

"Don't be absurd."

"Tell you what. I'll make a deal." The thought flashed through her mind that she was negotiating rather as her father, Lev, might have done. "I'll go for an examination—if you will."

That had surprised him, and he had hesitated, then said: "All right. You go first. If they say there's nothing wrong with you, I'll go."

"No," she said. "You go first."

"Why?"

"Because I don't trust you to keep your promises."

"All right, then, we'll go together."

Daisy was not sure why she was bothering. She did not love Boy— had not loved him for a long time. She was in love with Lloyd Williams, still in Spain on a mission he could not say much about. But she was married to Boy. He had been unfaithful to her, of course, with numerous women. But she had committed adultery, too, albeit with only one man. She had no moral ground to stand on, and in consequence she was paralyzed. She just felt that if she did her duty as a wife she might retain the last shreds of her self-respect.

The doctor's office was in Harley Street, not far from their house though in a less expensive neighborhood. Daisy found the examination unpleasant. The doctor was a man, and he was grumpy about her being ten minutes late. He asked her a lot of questions about her general health, her menstrual periods, and what he called her "relations" with her husband, not looking at her but making notes with a fountain pen. Then he put a series of cold metal instruments up her vagina. "I do this every day, so you don't need to worry," he said; then he gave her a grin that told her the opposite.

When she came out of the doctor's office, she half-expected Boy to renege on their deal and refuse to take his turn. He looked sour about it, but he went in.

While she was waiting, Daisy reread a letter from her half brother, Greg. He had discovered he had a child, from an affair he had with a black girl when he was fifteen. To Daisy's astonishment the playboy Greg was excited about his son and keen to be part of the child's life, albeit as an uncle rather than a father. Even more surprising, Lev had met the child and announced that he was smart.

It was ironic, she thought, that Greg had a son even though he had never wanted one, and Boy had no son even though he longed for one so badly.

Boy came out of the doctor's office an hour later. The doctor promised to give them their results in a week. They left at twelve noon.

"I need a drink after that," Boy said.

"So do I," said Daisy.

They looked up and down the street of identical row houses. "This neighborhood is a bloody desert. Not a pub in sight."

"I'm not going to a pub," said Daisy. "I want a martini, and they don't know how to make them in pubs." She spoke from experience. She had asked for a dry martini at the King's Head in Chelsea and had been served a glass of disgustingly warm vermouth. "Take me to Claridge's hotel, please. It's only five minutes' walk."

"Now that's a damn good idea."

The bar at Claridge's was full of people they knew. There were austerity rules about the meals restaurants could sell, but Claridge's had found a loophole: there were no restrictions on giving food away, so they offered a free buffet, charging only their usual high prices for drinks.

Daisy and Boy sat in art deco splendor and sipped perfect cocktails, and Daisy began to feel better.

"The doctor asked me if I'd had mumps," Boy said.

"But you have." It was mainly a childhood illness, but Boy had caught it a couple of years back. He had been briefly billeted at a vicarage in East Anglia, and had picked up the infection from the vicar's three small sons. It had been very painful. "Did he say why?"

"No. You know what these chaps are like. Never tell you a bloody thing."

It occurred to Daisy that she was not as happy-go-lucky as she had once been. In the old days she would never have brooded about her marriage this way. She had always liked what Scarlett O'Hara said in *Gone With the Wind*: "I'll think about that tomorrow." Not anymore. Perhaps she was growing up.

Boy was ordering a second cocktail when Daisy looked toward the door and saw the Marquis of Lowther walking in, dressed in a creased and stained uniform.

Daisy disliked him. Ever since he had guessed at her relationship with Lloyd, he had treated her with oily familiarity, as if they shared a secret that made them intimates.

Now he sat at their table uninvited, dropping cigar ash on his khaki trousers, and asked for a Manhattan.

Daisy knew at once that he was up to no good. There was a look of malignant relish in his eye that could not be explained merely as anticipation of a good cocktail.

Boy said: "I haven't seen you for a year or so, Lowthie. Where have you been?"

"Madrid," Lowthie said. "Can't say much about it. Hush-hush, you know. How about you?"

"I spend a lot of time training pilots, though I've flown a few missions lately, now that we've stepped up the bombing of Germany."

"Jolly good thing, too. Give the Germans a taste of their own medicine."

"You may say that, but there's a lot of muttering among the pilots."

"Really—why?"

"Because all this stuff about military targets is absolute rubbish. There's no point in bombing German factories, because they just rebuild them. So we're targeting large areas of dense working-class housing. They can't replace the workers so fast."

Lowther looked shocked. "That would mean it's our policy to kill civilians."

"Exactly."

"But the government assures us—"

"The government lies," Boy said. "And the bomber crews know it. Many of them don't give a damn, of course, but some feel bad. They believe that if we're doing the right thing, then we should say so, and if we're doing the wrong thing, we should stop."

Lowther looked uneasy. "I'm not sure we should be talking like this here."

"You're probably right," Boy said.

The second round of cocktails came. Lowther turned to Daisy. "And what about the little woman?" he said. "You must have some war work. The devil finds mischief for idle hands, according to the proverb."

Daisy replied in a neutral matter-of-fact tone. "Now that the Blitz is over, they don't need women ambulance drivers, so I'm working with the American Red Cross. We have an office in Pall Mall. We do what we can to help American servicemen over here."

"Men lonely for a bit of feminine company, eh?"

"Mostly they're just homesick. They like to hear an American accent."

Lowthie leered. "I expect you're very good at consoling them."

"I do what I can."

"I bet you do."

Boy said: "Look here, Lowthie, are you a bit drunk? Because this sort of talk is awfully bad form, you know."

Lowther's expression turned spiteful. "Oh, come on, Boy, don't tell me you don't know. What are you, blind?"

Daisy said: "Take me home, please, Boy."

He ignored her and spoke to Lowther. "What the devil do you mean?"

"Ask her about Lloyd Williams."

Boy said: "Who the hell is Lloyd Williams?"

Daisy said: "I'm going home alone, if you won't take me."

"Do you know a Lloyd Williams, Daisy?"

He's your brother, Daisy thought, and she felt a powerful impulse to reveal the secret, and knock him sideways, but she resisted the temptation. "You know him," she said. "He was up at Cambridge with you. He took us to a music hall in the East End, years ago."

"Oh!" said Boy, remembering. Then, puzzled, he said to Lowther: "Him?" It was difficult for Boy to see someone such as Lloyd as a rival. With growing incredulity he added: "A man who can't even afford his own dress clothes?"

Lowther said: "Three years ago he was on my intelligence course down at Tŷ Gwyn while Daisy was living there. You were risking your life in a Hawker Hurricane over France at the time, I seem to remember. She was dallying with that Welsh weasel—in your family's house!"

Boy was getting red in the face. "If you're making this up, Lowthie, by God I'll thrash you."

"Ask your wife!" said Lowther with a confident grin.

Boy turned to Daisy.

She had not slept with Lloyd at Tŷ Gwyn. She had slept with him in his own bed at his mother's house during the Blitz. But she could not explain that to Boy in front of Lowther, and anyway it was a detail. The accusation of adultery was true, and she was not going to deny it. The secret was out. All she wanted now was to retain some semblance of dignity.

She said: "I will tell you everything you want to know, Boy—but not in front of this leering slob."

Boy raised his voice in astonishment. "So you don't deny it?"

The people at the next table looked around, seemed embarrassed, and returned their attention to their drinks.

Daisy raised her own voice. "I refused to be cross-examined in the bar of Claridge's hotel."

"You admit it, then?" he shouted.

The room went quiet.

Daisy stood up. "I don't admit or deny anything here. I'll tell you everything in private at home, which is where civilized couples discuss such matters."

"My God, you did it. You slept with him!" Boy roared.

Even the waiters had paused in their work and were standing still, watching the row.

Daisy walked to the door.

Boy yelled: "You slut!"

Daisy was not going to exit on that line. She turned around. "You know about sluts, of course. I had the misfortune to meet two of yours, remember?" She looked around the room. "Joanie and Pearl," she said contemptuously. "How many wives would put up with that?" She went out before he could reply.

She stepped into a waiting taxi. As it pulled away, she saw Boy emerge from the hotel and get into the next cab in line.

She gave the driver her address.

In a way she felt relieved that the truth was out. But she also felt terribly sad. Something had ended, she knew.

The house was only a quarter of a mile away. As she arrived, Boy's taxi pulled up behind hers.

He followed her into the hall.

She could not stay here with him, she realized. That was over. She would never again share his home or his bed. "Bring me a suitcase, please," she said to the butler.

"Very good, my lady."

She looked around. It was an eighteenth-century town house of perfect proportions, with an elegantly curving staircase, but she was not really sorry to leave it.

Boy said: "Where are you going?"

"To a hotel, I suppose. Probably not Claridge's."

"To meet your lover!"

"No, he's overseas. But, yes, I do love him. I'm sorry, Boy. You have no right to judge me—your offenses are worse—but I judge myself."

"That's it," he said. "I'm going to divorce you."

Those were the words she had been waiting for, she realized. Now they had been said, and everything was over. Her new life began from this moment.

She sighed. "Thank God," she said.

### iii

Daisy rented an apartment in Piccadilly. It had a large American-style bathroom with a shower. There were two separate toilets, one for guests—a ridiculous extravagance in the eyes of most English people.

Fortunately money was not an issue for Daisy. Her grandfather Vyalov had left her rich, and she had had control of her own fortune since she was twenty-one. And it was all in American dollars.

New furniture was difficult to buy, so she shopped for antiques, of which there were plenty for sale cheap. She hung modern paintings for a gay, youthful look. She hired an elderly laundress and a girl to clean, and found it was easy to manage the place without a butler or a cook, especially when you did not have a husband to mollycoddle.

The servants at the Mayfair house packed all her clothes and sent them to her in a pantechnicon. Daisy and the laundress spent an afternoon opening the boxes and putting everything away tidily.

She had been both humiliated and liberated. On balance, she thought she was better off. The wound of rejection would heal, but she would be free of Boy forever.

After a week she wondered what had been the results of the medical examination. The doctor would have reported to Boy, of course, as the husband. She did not want to ask him, and anyway it did not seem important any longer, so she forgot about it.

She enjoyed making a new home. For a couple of weeks she was too busy to socialize. When she had fixed up the apartment, she decided to see all the friends she had been ignoring.

She had a lot of friends in London. She had been there seven years. For the last four years Boy had been away more than he was home, and she had gone to parties and balls on her own, so being without a husband would not make much difference to her life, she figured. No doubt she would be crossed off the Fitzherbert family's invitation lists, but they were not the only people in London society.

She bought crates of whisky, gin, and champagne, scouring London for what little was available legitimately and buying the rest on the black market. Then she sent out invitations to a flat-warming party.

The responses came back with ominous promptness, and they were all declines.

In tears, she phoned Eva Murray. "Why won't anyone come to my party?" she wailed.

Eva was at her door ten minutes later.

She arrived with three children and a nanny. Jamie was six, Anna four, and baby Karen two.

Daisy showed her around the apartment, then ordered tea while Jamie turned the couch into a tank, using his sisters as crew.

Speaking English with a mixture of German, American, and Scots accents, Eva said: "Daisy, dear, this isn't Rome."

"I know. Are you sure you're comfortable?"

Eva was heavily pregnant with her fourth child. "Would you mind if I put my feet up?"

"Of course not." Daisy fetched a cushion.

"London society is respectable," Eva went on. "Don't imagine I approve of it. I have been excluded often, and poor Jimmy is snubbed sometimes for having married a half-Jewish German."

"That's awful."

"I wouldn't wish it on anyone, whatever the reason."

"Sometimes I hate the British."

"You're forgetting what Americans are like. Don't you remember telling me that all the girls in Buffalo were snobs?"

Daisy laughed. "What a long time ago it seems."

"You've left your husband," Eva said. "And you did so in undeniably spectacular fashion, hurling insults at him in the bar of Claridge's hotel."

"And I'd only had one martini!"

Eva grinned. "How I wish I'd been there!"

"I kind of wish I hadn't."

"Needless to say, everyone in London society has talked about little else for the last three weeks."

"I guess I should have anticipated that."

"Now, I'm afraid, anyone who appears at your party will be seen as approving of adultery and divorce. Even I wouldn't like my mother-in-law to know I'd come here and had tea with you."

"But it's so unfair—Boy was unfaithful first!"

"And you thought women were treated equally?"

Daisy remembered that Eva had a great deal more to worry about than snobbery. Her family were still in Nazi Germany. Fitz had made inquiries through the Swiss embassy and learned that her doctor father was now in a concentration camp, and her brother, a violin maker, had been beaten up by the police, his hands smashed. "When I think about your troubles, I'm ashamed of myself for complaining," Daisy said.

"Don't be. But cancel the party."

Daisy did.

But it made her miserable. Her work for the Red Cross filled her days, but in the evenings she had nowhere to go and nothing to do. She went to the movies twice a week. She tried to read *Moby-Dick* but found it tedious. One Sunday she went to church. St. James's, the Wren church opposite her apartment building in Piccadilly, had been bombed, so she went to St. Martin-in-the-Fields. Boy was not there, but Fitz and Bea were, and Daisy spent the service looking at the back of Fitz's head, reflecting that she had fallen in love with two of this man's sons. Boy had his mother's looks and his father's single-minded selfishness. Lloyd had Fitz's good looks and Ethel's big heart. Why did it take me so long to see that? she wondered.

The church was full of people she knew, and after the service none of them spoke to her. She was lonely and almost friendless in a foreign country in the middle of a war.

One evening she took a taxi to Aldgate and knocked at the Leckwith house. When Ethel opened the door, Daisy said: "I've come to ask for your son's hand in marriage." Ethel let out a peal of laughter and hugged her.

She had brought a gift, an American tin of ham she had got from a USAF navigator. Such things were luxuries to British families on rations. She sat in the kitchen with Ethel and Bernie, listening to dance tunes on the radio. They all sang along with "Underneath the Arches" by Flanagan and Allen. "Bud Flanagan was born right here in the East End," Bernie said proudly. "Real name Chaim Reuben Weintrop."

The Leckwiths were excited about the Beveridge Report, a government paper that had become a bestseller. "Commissioned under a Conservative prime minister and written by a Liberal economist," said Bernie. "Yet it proposes what the Labour Party has always wanted! You know you're winning, in politics, when your opponents steal your ideas."

Ethel said: "The idea is that everyone of working age should pay a weekly insurance premium, then get benefits when they are sick, unemployed, retired, or widowed."

"A simple proposal, but it will transform our country," Bernie said enthusiastically. "Cradle to grave, no one will ever be destitute again."

Daisy said: "Has the government accepted it?"

"No," said Ethel. "Clem Attlee pressed Churchill very hard, but Churchill won't endorse the report. The Treasury thinks it will cost too much."

Bernie said: "We'll have to win an election before we can implement it."

Ethel and Bernie's daughter, Millie, dropped in. "I can't stay long," she said. "Abie's watching the children for half an hour." She had lost her job—women were not buying expensive gowns now, even if they could afford them—but fortunately her husband's leather business was flourishing, and they had two babies, Lennie and Pammie.

They drank cocoa and talked about the young man they all adored. They had little real news of Lloyd. Every six or eight months Ethel received a letter on the headed paper of the British embassy in Madrid, saying he was safe and well and doing his bit to defeat Fascism. He had been promoted to major. He had never written to Daisy, for fear Boy might see the letters, but he could now. Daisy gave Ethel the address of her new flat, and took down Lloyd's address, which was a British Forces Post Office number.

They had no idea when he might come home on leave.

Daisy told them about her half brother, Greg, and his son, Georgy. She knew that the Leckwiths of all people would not be censorious, and would be able to rejoice in such news.

She also told the story of Eva's family in Berlin. Bernie was Jewish, and tears came to his eyes when he heard about Rudi's broken hands. "They should have fought the bastard Fascists on the street, when they had the chance," he said. "That's what we did."

Millie said: "I've still got the scars on my back, where the police pushed us through Gardiner's plate-glass window. I used to be ashamed of them—Abie never saw my back until we'd been married six months, but he says they make him proud of me."

"It wasn't pretty, the fighting in Cable Street," said Bernie. "But we put a stop to their bloody nonsense." He took off his glasses and wiped his eyes with his handkerchief.

Ethel put her arm around his shoulders. "I told people to stay home that day," she said. "I was wrong, and you were right."

He smiled ruefully. "Doesn't happen often."

"But it was the Public Order Act, brought in after Cable Street, that finished the British Fascists," Ethel said. "Parliament banned the wearing of political uniforms in public. That finished them. If they couldn't strut up and down in their black shirts, they were nothing. The Conservatives did that—credit where credit's due."

Always a political family, the Leckwiths were planning the postwar reform of Britain by the Labour Party. Their leader, the quietly brilliant Clement Attlee, was now deputy prime minister under Churchill, and union hero Ernie Bevin was minister of labour. Their vision made Daisy feel excited about the future.

Millie left and Bernie went to bed. When they were alone, Ethel said to Daisy: "Do you really want to marry my Lloyd?"

"More than anything in the world. Do you think it will be all right?"

"I do. Why not?"

"Because we come from such different backgrounds. You're all such good people. You live for public service."

"Except for our Millie. She's like Bernie's brother—she wants to make money."

"Even she has scars on her back from Cable Street."

"True."

"Lloyd is like you. Political work isn't something extra he does, like a hobby—it's the center of his life. And I'm a selfish millionaire."

"I think there are two kinds of marriage," Ethel said thoughtfully. "One is a comfortable partnership, where two people share the same hopes and fears, raise children as a team, and give each other comfort and help." She was talking about herself and Bernie, Daisy realized. "The other is a wild passion, madness and joy and sex, possibly with someone completely unsuitable, maybe someone you don't admire or don't even really like." She was thinking about her affair with Fitz, Daisy felt sure. She held her breath: she knew Ethel was now telling her the raw truth. "I've been lucky. I've had both," Ethel said. "And here's my advice to you. If you get the chance of the mad kind of love, grab it with both hands, and to hell with the consequences."

"Wow," said Daisy.

She left a few minutes later. She felt privileged that Ethel had given her a glimpse into her soul. But when she got back to her empty apartment, she felt depressed. She made a cocktail and poured it away. She put the kettle on and took it off again. The radio went off the air. She lay between cold sheets and wished Lloyd were there.

She compared Lloyd's family with her own. Both had troubled histories, but Ethel had forged a strong, supportive family out of unfavorable materials, which Daisy's own mother had been unable to do—though that was more Lev's fault than Olga's. Ethel was a remarkable woman, and Lloyd had many of her qualities.

Where was he now, and what was he doing? Whatever the answer, he was sure to be in danger. Would he be killed now, when at last she was free to love him without restraint and, eventually, to marry him? What would she do if he died? Her own life would be at an end, she felt: no husband, no lover, no friends, no country. In the early hours of the morning she cried herself to sleep.

Next day she slept late. At midday she was drinking coffee in her little dining room, dressed in a black silk wrap, when her fifteen-year-old maid came in and said: "Major Williams is here, my lady."

"What?" she screeched. "He can't be!"

Then he came through the door with his kit bag over his shoulder.

He looked tired and had several days' growth of beard, and he had evidently slept in his uniform.

She threw her arms around him and kissed his bristly face. He kissed her back, inhibited somewhat by being unable to stop grinning. "I must stink," he said between kisses. "I haven't changed my clothes for a week."

"You smell like a cheese factory," she said. "I love it." She pulled him into her bedroom and started to take his clothes off.

"I'll take a quick shower," he said.

"No," she said. She pushed him back on the bed. "I'm in too much of a hurry." Her longing for him was frantic. And the truth was that she relished the strong smell. It should have repelled her, but it had the opposite effect. It was him, the man she had thought might be dead, and he was filling her nostrils and her lungs. She could have wept with joy.

Taking off his trousers would require removing his boots, and she could see that would be complicated, so she did not bother. She just unbuttoned his fly. She threw off her black silk robe and hiked her nightdress up to her waist, all the time staring with happy lust at the white penis sticking up out of the rough khaki cloth. Then she straddled him, easing herself down, and leaned forward and kissed him. "Oh, God," she said. "I can't tell you how much I've been longing for you."

She lay on him, not moving much, kissing him again and again. He held her face in his hands and stared at her. "This is real, isn't it?" he said. "Not just another happy dream?"

"It's real," she said.

"Good. I wouldn't like to wake up now."

"I want to stay like this forever."

"Nice idea, but I can't keep still much longer." He began to move under her.

"If you do that, I'll come," she said.

And she did.

Afterward they lay on her bed for a long time, talking.

He had two weeks' leave. "Live here," she said. "You can visit your parents every day, but I want you at night."

"I wouldn't like you to get a bad reputation."

"That ship has sailed. I've already been shunned by London society."

"I know." He had telephoned Ethel from Waterloo station, and she had told him about Daisy's separation from Boy and given him the address of the flat.

"We must do something about contraception," he said. "I'll get some rubber johnnies. But you might want to get fixed up with a device. What do you think?"

"You want to make sure I don't get pregnant?" she said.

There was a note of sadness in her voice, she realized, and he heard it. "Don't get me wrong," he said. He raised himself on his elbow. "I'm illegitimate. I was told lies about my parentage, and when I found out the truth, it was a terrible shock." His voice shook a little with emotion. "I'll never put my children through that. Never."

"We wouldn't have to lie to them."

"Would we tell them that we're not married? That in fact you're married to someone else?"

"I don't see why not."

"Think how they would be teased at school."

She was not convinced, but clearly the issue was a profound one for him. "So, what's your plan?" she said.

"I want us to have children. But not until we're married. To each other."

"I get that," she said. "So . . ."

"We have to wait."

Men were slow to pick up hints. "I'm not much of a girl for tradition," she said. "But, still, there are some things . . ."

At last he saw what she was getting at. "Oh! Okay. Just a minute." He knelt upright on the bed. "Daisy, dear—"

She burst out laughing. He looked comical, in full uniform with his limp dick hanging out of his fly. "Can I take a photo of you like that?" she said.

He looked down and saw what she meant. "Oh, sorry."

"No—don't you dare put it away! Stay just as you are, and say what you were going to say."

He grinned. "Daisy, dear, will you be my wife?"

"In a heartbeat," she said.

They lay down again, embracing.

Soon the novelty of his odor wore off. They got into the shower together. She soaped him all over, taking merry pleasure in his embarrassment when she washed his most intimate places. She put shampoo on his hair and scrubbed his grimy feet with a brush.

When he was clean, he insisted on washing her, but he had only got as far as her breasts when they had to make love again. They did it standing in the shower with the hot water coursing down their bodies. Clearly he had momentarily forgotten his aversion to illegitimate pregnancy, and she did not care.

Afterward he stood at her mirror, shaving. She wrapped a large towel around herself and sat on the lid of the toilet, watching him. He asked: "How long will it take you to get divorced?"

"I don't know. I'd better speak to Boy."

"Not today, though. I want you to myself all day."

"When will you go to see your parents?"

"Tomorrow, maybe."

"Then I'll go to Boy at the same time. I want to get this over as soon as possible."

"Good," he said. "That's settled, then."

## iv

Daisy felt strange going into the house where she had lived with Boy. A month ago it had been hers. She had been free to come and go as she wished, and enter any room without asking permission. The servants had obeyed her every order without question. Now she was a stranger in the same house. She kept her hat and gloves on, and she had to follow the old butler as he led her to the morning room.

Boy did not shake hands or kiss her cheek. He looked full of righteous indignation.

"I haven't hired a lawyer yet," Daisy said as she sat down. "I wanted to talk to you personally first. I'm hoping we can do this without hating one another. After all, there are no children to fight over, and we both have plenty of money."

"You betrayed me!" he said.

Daisy sighed. Clearly it was not going to go the way she had hoped. "We both committed adultery," she said. "You first."

"I've been humiliated. Everyone in London knows!"

"I did try to stop you making a fool of yourself in Claridge's—but you were too busy humiliating me! I hope you've thrashed the loathsome marquis."

"How could I? He did me a favor."

"He might have done you a bigger favor by having a quiet word at the club."

"I don't understand how you could fall for such a low-class oik as Williams. I've found out a few things about him. His mother was a housemaid!"

"She's probably the most impressive woman I've ever met."

"I hope you realize that no one really knows who his father is."

That was about as ironic as you could get, Daisy thought. "I know who his father is," she said.

"Who?"

"I'm certainly not telling you."

"There you are, then."

"This isn't getting us anywhere, is it?"

"No."

"Perhaps I should just have a lawyer write to you." She stood up. "I loved you once, Boy," she said sadly. "You were fun. I'm sorry I wasn't enough for you. I wish you happiness. I hope you marry someone who suits you better, and that she gives you lots of sons. I would be happy for you if that came about."

"Well, it won't," he said.

She had turned toward the door, but now she looked back. "Why do you say that?"

"I got the report from that doctor we went to."

She had forgotten about the medical. It had seemed irrelevant after they split. "What did he say?"

"There's nothing wrong with you—you can have a whole litter of pups. But I can't father children. Mumps in adult men sometimes causes infertility, and I copped it." He laughed bitterly. "All those bloody Germans shooting at me for years, and I've been downed by a vicar's three little brats."

She felt sad for him. "Oh, Boy, I'm really sorry to hear that."

"Well, you're going to be sorrier, because I'm not divorcing you."

She suddenly felt cold. "What do you mean? Why not?"

"Why should I bother? I don't want to marry again. I can't have children. Andy's son will inherit."

"But I want to marry Lloyd!"

"Why should I care about that? Why should he have children if I can't?"

Daisy was devastated. Would happiness be snatched away from

her just when it seemed to be within her reach? "Boy, you can't mean this!"

"I've never been more serious in my life."

Her voice was anguished. "But Lloyd wants children of his own!"

"He should have thought of that before he f-f-fucked another man's wife."

"Very well, then," she said defiantly. "I'll divorce you."

"On what grounds?"

"Adultery, of course."

"But you have no evidence." She was about to say that that shouldn't be a problem when he grinned maliciously and added: "And I'll take care you don't get any."

He could do that, if he was discreet about his liaisons, she realized with growing horror. "But you threw me out!" she said.

"I shall tell the judge you're welcome to come home anytime."

She tried to stop herself crying. "I never thought you'd hate me this much," she said miserably.

"Didn't you?" said Boy. "Well, now you bloody well know."

## V

Lloyd Williams went to Boy Fitzherbert's house in Mayfair at midmorning, when Boy would be sober, and told the butler he was Major Williams, a distant relative. He thought a man-to-man conversation was worth a try. Surely Boy did not really want to dedicate the rest of his life to revenge? Lloyd was in uniform, hoping to appeal to Boy as one fighting man to another. Good sense must surely prevail.

He was shown into the morning room, where Boy sat reading the paper and smoking a cigar. It took Boy a moment to recognize him. "You!" he said when comprehension dawned. "You can piss off right away."

"I've come to ask you to give Daisy a divorce," Lloyd said.

"Get out." Boy got to his feet.

Lloyd said: "I can see that you're toying with the idea of taking a swing at me, so in fairness I should tell you that it won't be as easy as you imagine. I'm a bit smaller than you, but I box at welterweight, and I've won quite a lot of contests."

"I'm not going to soil my hands on you."

"Good decision. But will you reconsider the divorce?"

"Absolutely not."

"There's something you don't know," Lloyd said. "I wonder if it might change your mind."

"I doubt it," Boy said. "But go on, now that you're here, give it a shot." He sat down, but did not offer Lloyd a chair.

Be it on your own head, Lloyd thought.

He took from his pocket a faded sepia photograph. "If you'd be so kind, glance at this picture of me." He put it on the side table next to Boy's ashtray.

Boy picked it up. "This isn't you. It looks like you, but the uniform is Victorian. It must be your father."

"My grandfather, in fact. Turn it over."

Boy read the inscription on the back. "Earl Fitzherbert?" he said scornfully.

"Yes. The previous earl, your grandfather—and mine. Daisy found that photo at Tŷ Gwyn." Lloyd took a deep breath. "You told Daisy that no one knows who my father is. Well, I can tell you. It's Earl Fitzherbert. You and I are brothers." He waited for Boy's response.

Boy laughed. "Ridiculous!"

"My reaction, exactly, when I was first told."

"Well, I must say, you have surprised me. I would have thought you could come up with something better than this absurd fantasy."

Lloyd had been hoping the revelation would shock Boy into a different frame of mind, but so far it was not working. Nevertheless he continued to reason. "Come on, Boy—how unlikely is it? Doesn't it happen all the time in great houses? Maids are pretty, young noblemen are randy, and nature takes its course. When a baby is born, the matter is hushed up. Please don't pretend you had no idea such things could occur."

"No doubt it's common enough." Boy's confidence was shaken, but still he blustered. "However, lots of people pretend they have connections with the aristocracy."

"Oh, please," Lloyd said disparagingly. "I don't want connections with the aristocracy. I'm not a draper's assistant with daydreams of grandeur. I come from a distinguished family of socialist politicians. My maternal grandfather was one of the founders of the South Wales Miners' Federation. The last thing I need is a wrong-side-of-the-blanket link with a Tory peer. It's highly embarrassing to me."

Boy laughed again, but with less conviction. "*You're* embarrassed! Talk about inverted snobbery."

"Inverted? I'm more likely to become prime minister than you are." Lloyd realized they had got into a pissing contest, which was not what he wanted. "Never mind that," he said. "I'm trying to persuade you that you can't spend the rest of your life taking revenge on me—if only because we're brothers."

"I still don't believe it," Boy said, putting the photo down on the side table and picking up his cigar.

"Nor did I, at first." Lloyd kept trying: his whole future was at stake. "Then it was pointed out to me that my mother was working at Tŷ Gwyn when she fell pregnant, that she had always been evasive about my father's identity, and that shortly before I was born she somehow acquired the funds to buy a three-bedroom house in London. I confronted her with my suspicions and she admitted the truth."

"This is laughable."

"But you know it's true, don't you?"

"I know no such thing."

"You do, though. For the sake of our brotherhood, won't you do the decent thing?"

"Certainly not."

Lloyd saw that he was not going to win. He felt downcast. Boy had the power to blight Lloyd's life, and he was determined to use it.

He picked up the photograph and put it back in his pocket. "You'll ask our father about this. You won't be able to restrain yourself. You'll have to find out."

Boy made a scornful noise.

Lloyd went to the door. "I believe he will tell you the truth. Good-bye, Boy."

He went out and closed the door behind him.

# CHAPTER SIXTEEN

# 1943 (II)

Colonel Albert Beck got a Russian bullet in his right lung at Kharkov in March 1943. He was lucky: a field surgeon put in a chest drain and reinflated the lung, saving his life, just. Weakened by blood loss and the almost inevitable infection, Beck was put on a train home and ended up in Carla's hospital in Berlin.

He was a tough, wiry man in his early forties, prematurely bald, with a protruding jaw like the prow of a Viking longboat. The first time he spoke to Carla, he was drugged and feverish and wildly indiscreet. "We're losing the war," he said.

She was immediately alert. A discontented officer was a potential source of information. She said lightly: "The newspapers say we're shortening the line on the eastern front."

He laughed scornfully. "That means we're retreating."

She continued to draw him out. "And Italy looks bad." The Italian dictator Benito Mussolini—Hitler's greatest ally—had fallen.

"Remember 1939, and 1940?" Beck said nostalgically. "One brilliant lightning victory after another. Those were the days."

Clearly he was not ideological, perhaps not even political. He was a normal patriotic soldier who had stopped kidding himself.

Carla led him on. "It can't be true that the army is short of everything from bullets to underpants." This kind of mildly risky talk was not unusual in Berlin nowadays.

"Of course we are." Beck was radically disinhibited but quite articulate. "Germany simply can't produce as many guns and tanks as the Soviet Union, Great Britain, and the United States combined— especially when we're being bombed constantly. And no matter how many Russians we kill, the Red Army seems to have an inexhaustible supply of new recruits."

"What do you think will happen?"

"The Nazis will never admit defeat, of course. So more people will die. Millions more, just because they're too proud to yield. Insanity. Insanity." He drifted off to sleep.

You had to be sick—or crazy—to voice such thoughts, but Carla believed that more and more people were thinking that way. Despite relentless government propaganda it was becoming clear that Hitler was losing the war.

There had been no police investigation of the death of Joachim Koch. It had been reported in the newspaper as a road accident. Carla had got over the initial shock, but every now and again the realization hit her that she had killed a man, and she would relive his death in her imagination. It made her shake and she had to sit down. This had happened only once when she was on duty, fortunately, and she had passed that off as a faint due to hunger—highly plausible in wartime Berlin. Her mother was worse. It was strange that Maud had loved Joachim, weak and foolish as he was, but there was no explaining love. Carla herself had completely misjudged Werner Franck, thinking he was strong and brave, only to learn that he was selfish and weak.

She talked to Beck a lot before he was discharged, probing to find out what kind of man he was. Once recovered, he never again spoke indiscreetly about the war. She learned that he was a career soldier, his wife was dead, and his married daughter lived in Buenos Aires. His father had been a Berlin city councilor; he did not say for which party, so clearly it was not the Nazis or any of their allies. He never said anything bad about Hitler, but he never said anything good, either, nor did he speak disparagingly of Jews or Communists. These days that in itself was close to insubordination.

His lung would heal, but he would never again be strong enough for active service, and he told her he was being posted to the General Staff. He could become a diamond mine of vital secrets. She would be risking her life if she tried to recruit him—but she had to try.

She knew he would not remember their first conversation. "You were very candid," Carla told him in a low voice. There was no one nearby. "You said we were losing the war."

His eyes flashed fear. He was no longer a woozy patient in a hospital gown with stubble on his cheeks. He was washed and shaved, sitting upright in dark blue pajamas buttoned to the throat. "I suppose you're going to report me to the Gestapo," he said. "I don't think a man should be held to account for what he says when he's sick and raving."

"You weren't raving," she said. "You were very clear. But I'm not going to report you to anyone."

"No?"

"Because you are right."

He was surprised. "Now I should report *you*."

"If you do, I'll say that you insulted Hitler in your delirium, and when I threatened to report it, you made up a story about me in self-defense."

"If I denounce you, you'll denounce me," he said. "Stalemate."

"But you're not going to denounce me," she said. "I know that, because I know you. I've nursed you. You're a good man. You joined the army for love of your country, but you hate the war and you hate the Nazis." She was 99 percent sure of this.

"It's very dangerous to talk like that."

"I know."

"So this isn't just a casual conversation."

"Correct. You said that millions of people are going to die just because the Nazis are too proud to surrender."

"Did I?"

"You can help save some of those millions."

"How?"

Carla paused. This was where she put her life on the line. "Any information you have, I can pass it to the appropriate quarters." She held her breath. If she was wrong about Beck, she was dead.

She read amazement in his look. He could hardly imagine that this briskly efficient young nurse was a spy. But he believed her, she could see that. He said: "I think I understand you."

She handed him a green hospital file folder, empty.

He took it. "What's this for?" he said.

"You're a soldier—you understand camouflage."

He nodded. "You're risking your life," he said, and she saw something like admiration in his eyes.

"So are you, now."

"Yes," said Colonel Beck. "But I'm used to it."

## ii

Early in the morning, Thomas Macke took young Werner Franck to the Plötzensee Prison in the western suburb of Charlottenburg. "You should see this," he said. "Then you can tell General Dorn how effective we are."

He parked in the Königsdamm and led Werner to the rear of the main prison. They entered a room twenty-five feet long and about half as wide. Waiting there was a man dressed in a tailcoat, a top hat, and white gloves. Werner frowned at the peculiar costume. "This is Herr Reichhart," said Macke. "The executioner."

Werner swallowed. "So we're going to witness an execution?"

"Yes."

With a casual air that might have been faked, Werner said: "Why the fancy dress outfit?"

Macke shrugged. "Tradition."

A black curtain divided the room in two. Macke drew it back to show eight hooks attached to an iron girder that ran across the ceiling.

Werner said: "For hanging?"

Macke nodded.

There was also a wooden table with straps for holding someone down. At one end of the table was a high device of distinctive shape. On the floor was a heavy basket.

The young lieutenant was pale. "A guillotine," he said.

"Exactly," said Macke. He looked at his watch. "We shan't be kept waiting long."

More men filed into the room. Several nodded in a familiar way to Macke. Speaking quietly into Werner's ear, Macke said: "Regulations demand that the judges, the court officers, the prison governor, and the chaplain all attend."

Werner swallowed. He was not liking this, Macke could see.

He was not meant to. Macke's motive in bringing him here had nothing to do with impressing General Dorn. Macke was worried about Werner. There was something about him that did not ring true.

Werner worked for Dorn; that was not in question. He had accompanied Dorn on a visit to Gestapo headquarters, and subsequently Dorn had written a note saying that the Berlin counterespionage effort was most impressive, and mentioning Macke by name. For weeks afterward Macke had walked around in a miasma of warm pride.

But Macke could not forget Werner's behavior on that evening, nearly a year ago now, when they had almost caught a spy in a disused fur coat factory near the East Station. Werner had panicked—or had he? Accidentally or otherwise, he had given the pianist enough warning to get away. Macke could not shake the suspicion that the panic had been an act, and Werner had in fact been coolly and deliberately sounding the alarm.

Macke did not quite have the nerve to arrest and torture Werner. It could be done, of course, but Dorn might well kick up a fuss, and then Macke would be questioned. His boss, Superintendent Kringelein, who did not much like him, would ask what hard evidence he had against Werner—and he had none.

But this ought to reveal the truth.

The door opened again, and two prison guards entered either side of a young woman called Lili Markgraf.

He heard Werner gasp. "What's the matter?" Macke said.

Werner said: "You didn't tell me it was going to be a girl."

"Do you know her?"

"No."

Lili was twenty-two, Macke knew, though she looked younger. Her fair hair had been cut this morning, and it was now as short as a man's. She was limping, and walked bent over as if she had an abdominal injury. She wore a plain blue dress of heavy cotton with no collar, just a round neckline. Her eyes were red with crying. The guards held her arms firmly, not taking any chances.

"This woman was denounced by a relative who found a codebook hidden in her room," Macke said. "The five-digit Russian code."

"Why is she walking like that?"

"The effects of interrogation. But we didn't get anything from her."

Werner's face was impassive. "What a shame," he said. "She might have led us to other spies."

Macke saw no sign that he was faking. "She knew her associate only as Heinrich—no last name—and he may have used a pseudonym anyway. I find we rarely profit by arresting women—they don't know enough."

"But at least you have her codebook."

"For what it's worth. They change the key word regularly, so we still face a challenge in decrypting their signals."

"Pity."

One of the men cleared his throat and spoke loudly enough for everyone to hear. He said he was the president of the court, then read out the death sentence.

The guards walked Lili to the wooden table. They gave her the chance of lying on it voluntarily, but she took a step backward, so they picked her up forcibly. She did not struggle. They laid her facedown and strapped her in.

The chaplain began a prayer.

Lili began to plead. "No, no," she said, without raising her voice. "No, please, let me go. Let me go." She spoke coherently, as if she were merely asking someone for a favor.

The man in the top hat looked at the president, who shook his head and said: "Not yet. The prayer must be finished."

Lili's voice rose in pitch and urgency. "I don't want to die! I'm afraid to die! Don't do this to me, please!"

The executioner looked again at the court president. This time the president just ignored him.

Macke studied Werner. He looked sick, but so did everybody else in the room. As a test, this was not really working. Werner's reaction showed that he was sensitive, not that he was a traitor. Macke might have to think of something else.

Lili began to scream.

Even Macke felt impatient.

The pastor hurried through the rest of the prayer.

When he said "Amen," she stopped screaming, as if she knew it was all over.

The president gave the nod.

The executioner moved a lever, and the weighted blade fell.

It made a whispering sound as it sliced through Lili's pale neck. Her head with its short-cropped hair fell forward and there was a gush of blood. The head hit the basket with a loud thump that seemed to resound in the room.

Absurdly, Macke wondered if the head felt any pain.

### iii

Carla bumped into Colonel Beck in the hospital corridor. He was in uniform. She looked at him in sudden fear. Ever since he was discharged, she had lived every day in fear that he had betrayed her, and that the Gestapo were on their way.

But he smiled and said: "I came back for a checkup with Dr. Ernst."

Was that all? Had he forgotten their conversation? Was he pretending to have forgotten it? Was there a black Gestapo Mercedes waiting outside?

Beck was carrying a green hospital file folder.

A cancer specialist in a white coat approached. As he went by, Carla said brightly to Beck: "How are things?"

"I'm as fit as I'm ever going to be. I'll never lead a battalion into battle again, but aside from athletics I can lead a normal life."

"I'm glad to hear that."

People kept walking by. Carla feared Beck would never get the chance to say anything to her privately.

But he remained unruffled. "I'd just like to thank you for your kindness and professionalism."

"You're welcome."

"Good-bye, Sister."

"Good-bye, Colonel."

When Beck left, Carla was holding the file folder.

She walked briskly to the nurses' cloakroom. It was empty. She stood with her heel firmly wedged against the door so no one could come in.

Inside the folder was a large envelope made of the cheap buff-colored paper used in offices everywhere. Carla opened the envelope. It contained several typewritten sheets. She looked at the first without removing it from the envelope. It was headed:

Operational Order No. 6

Code Zitadelle

It was the battle plan for the summer offensive on the eastern front. Her heart raced. This was gold dust.

She had to pass the envelope to Frieda. Unfortunately Frieda was not working at the hospital today: it was her day off. Carla considered leaving the hospital right away, in the middle of her shift, and going to Frieda's house, but she swiftly rejected that idea. Better to behave normally, not to attract attention.

She slipped the envelope into the shoulder bag hanging on her coat hook. She covered it with the blue-and-gold silk scarf that she always carried for hiding things. She stood still for a few moments, letting her breathing return to normal. Then she went back to the ward.

She worked the rest of her shift as best she could; then she put on her coat, left the hospital, and walked to the station. Passing a bomb site, she saw graffiti on the remains of the building. A defiant patriot had written: "Our walls might break, but not our hearts." But someone else had ironically quoted Hitler's 1933 election slogan: "Give me four years, and you will not recognize Germany."

She bought a ticket to the Zoo.

On the train she felt like an alien. All the other passengers were loyal Germans, and she was the one with secrets in her bag to betray to Moscow. She did not like the feeling. No one looked at her, but that only made her think they were all deliberately avoiding her eye. She could hardly wait to hand over the envelope to Frieda.

The Zoo Station was on the edge of the Tiergarten. The trees were dwarfed now by a huge flak tower. One of three in Berlin, this square concrete block was more than a hundred feet high. At the corners of the roof were four giant 128 mm antiaircraft guns weighing twenty-five tons each. The raw concrete was painted green in a hopelessly optimistic attempt to make the monstrosity less of an eyesore in the park.

Ugly though it was, Berliners loved it. When the bombs were falling, its thunder reassured them that someone was shooting back.

Still in a state of high tension, Carla walked from the station to Frieda's house. It was midafternoon, so the Franck parents would probably be out, Ludi at his factory and Monika seeing a friend, possibly Carla's mother. Werner's motorcycle was parked on the drive.

The manservant opened the door. "Miss Frieda is out, but she won't be long," he said. "She went to KaDeWe to buy gloves. Mr. Werner is in bed with a heavy cold."

"I'll wait for Frieda in her room, as usual."

Carla took off her coat and went upstairs, still carrying her bag. In

Frieda's room she kicked off her shoes and lay on the bed to read the battle plan for Operation Zitadelle. She was as stressed as an overwound clock, but she would feel better when she had given the purloined document to someone else.

From the next room she heard the sound of sobbing.

She was surprised. That was Werner's room. Carla found it hard to imagine the suave playboy in tears.

But the sound definitely came from a man, and he seemed to be trying and failing to suppress his grief.

Against her will, Carla felt pity. She told herself that some feisty woman had thrown Werner over, probably for very good reasons. But she could not help responding to the real distress she was hearing.

She got off the bed, put the battle plan back in her bag, and stepped outside.

She listened at Werner's door. She could hear it even more clearly. She was too softhearted to ignore it. She opened the door and went in.

Werner was sitting on the edge of the bed, head in hands. When he heard the door, he looked up, startled. His face was red with emotion and wet with tears. His tie was pulled down and his collar undone. He looked at Carla with misery in his eyes. He was bowled over, devastated, and too wretched to care who knew it.

Carla could not pretend to be heartless. "What is it?" she said.

"I can't do this anymore," he said.

She closed the door behind her. "What happened?"

"They cut off Lili Markgraf's head—and I had to watch."

Carla stared, openmouthed. "What on earth are you talking about?"

"She was twenty-two." He took a handkerchief from his pocket and wiped his face. "You're already in danger, but if I tell you this, it will be a lot worse."

Her mind was full of amazing surmises. "I think I can guess, but tell me," she said.

He nodded. "You'll figure it out soon anyway. Lili helped Heinrich broadcast to Moscow. It's much quicker if someone reads you the code groups. And the faster you go, the less likely you are to be caught. But

Lili's cousin stayed at the apartment for a few days and found her codebooks. Nazi bitch."

His words confirmed her astonishing suspicions. "You know about the spying?"

He looked at her with an ironic smile. "I'm in charge of it."

"Good God!"

"That's why I had to drop the whole business of the murdered children. Moscow ordered me to. And they were right. If I'd lost my job at the Air Ministry, I would have had no access to secret papers, nor to other people who could bring me secrets."

She needed to sit down. She perched on the edge of the bed beside him. "Why didn't you tell me?"

"We work on the assumption that everyone talks under torture. Knowing nothing, you can't betray others. Poor Lili was tortured, but she only knew Volodya, who's back in Moscow now, and Heinrich, and she never knew Heinrich's second name or anything else about him."

Carla was chilled to the bone. *Everyone talks under torture.*

Werner finished: "I'm sorry I've told you, but after seeing me like this, you were on the point of guessing it all anyway."

"So I've completely misjudged you."

"Not your fault. I deliberately misled you."

"I feel a fool just the same. I've despised you for two years."

"All the while I was desperate to explain to you."

She put her arm around him.

He took her other hand and kissed it. "Can you forgive me?"

She was not sure how she felt, but she did not want to reject him when he was so down, so she said: "Yes, of course."

"Poor Lili," he said. His voice fell to a whisper. "She had been so badly beaten, she could hardly walk to the guillotine. Yet she begged for life, right up to the end."

"How come you were there?"

"I've befriended a Gestapo man, Inspector Thomas Macke. He took me."

"Macke? I remember him—he arrested my father." She vividly

recalled a round-faced man with a small black mustache, and she experienced again her rage at the arrogant power Macke had to take her father away, and her grief when he died of the injuries he suffered at Macke's hands.

"I think he suspects me, and taking me to the execution was a test. Perhaps he thought I might lose my self-control and try to intervene. Anyway, I think I passed the test."

"But if you were arrested . . ."

Werner nodded. "Everyone talks under torture."

"And you know everything."

"Every agent, every code . . . The only thing I don't know is where they broadcast from. I leave it up to them to pick the locations, and they don't tell me."

They held hands in silence. After a while, Carla said: "I came to give it to Frieda, but I might as well give it to you."

"Give what?"

"The battle plan for Operation Zitadelle."

Werner was electrified. "But I've been trying to put my hands on that for weeks! Where did you get it?"

"From an officer on the General Staff. Perhaps I shouldn't say his name."

"Quite right, don't tell me. But is it authentic?"

"You'd better take a look." She went to Frieda's room and returned with the buff envelope. It had never occurred to her that the document might not be genuine. "It looks all right to me, but what do I know?"

He took out the typewritten sheets. After a minute he said: "This is the real thing. Fantastic!"

"I'm so glad."

He stood up. "I have to take this to Heinrich right away. We must get this encrypted and broadcast tonight."

Carla felt disappointed that their moment of intimacy was over so soon, though she could not have said what she had been expecting. She followed him through the door. She picked up her bag from Frieda's room and went downstairs.

With his hand on the front door, Werner said: "I'm so glad we're friends again."

"Me, too."

"Do you think we'll be able to forget this period of estrangement?"

She did not know what he was trying to say. Did he want to be her lover again—or was he telling her that was out of the question? "I think we can put it behind us," she said neutrally.

"Good." He bent and kissed her lips very quickly. Then he opened the door.

They left the house together, and he climbed on his motorcycle.

Carla walked down the driveway to the street and headed for the station. A moment later, Werner drove past her with a honk and a wave.

Now that she was alone, she could begin to think about his revelation. How did she feel? For two years she had hated him. But in that time she had not had a serious boyfriend. Had she remained in love with him all along? At a minimum she had retained, in her heart of hearts, a fondness for him despite everything. Today, when she heard him in such distress, her hostility had melted away. Now she felt a glow of affection.

Did she love him still?

She did not know.

## iv

Macke sat in the rear seat of the black Mercedes with Werner beside him. Around Macke's neck was a bag like a school satchel, except that he wore it in front instead of behind. It was small enough to be covered by a buttoned overcoat. A thin wire ran from the bag to a small earphone. "It's the latest thing," Macke said. "As you get closer to the broadcaster, the sound gets louder."

Werner said: "More discreet than a van with a big aerial on its roof."

"We have to use both—the van to discover the general area, and this to pinpoint the exact location."

Macke was in trouble. Operation Zitadelle had been a catastrophe. Even before the offensive opened, the Red Army had attacked the airfields where the Luftwaffe were assembling. Zitadelle had been called off after a week, but even that was too late to prevent irreparable damage to the German army.

Germany's leaders were always quick to blame Jewish-Bolshevik conspirators whenever things went wrong, but in this case they were right. The Red Army had appeared to know the entire battle plan in advance. And that, according to Superintendent Kringelein, was Thomas Macke's fault. He was head of counterespionage for the city of Berlin. His career was on the line. He faced dismissal and worse.

His only hope now was a tremendous coup, a massive operation to round up the spies who were undermining the German war effort. So tonight he had set a trap for Werner Franck.

If Franck turned out to be innocent, he did not know what he would do.

In the front seat of the car, a walkie-talkie crackled. Macke's pulse quickened. The driver picked up the handset. "Wagner here." He started the engine. "We're on our way," he said. "Over and out."

It had started.

Macke asked him: "Where are we headed?"

"Kreuzberg." It was a densely populated low-rent neighborhood south of the city center.

As they pulled away, the air raid siren sounded.

That was an unwelcome complication. Macke looked out of the window. The searchlights came on, waving like giant wands. Macke supposed they must have found planes sometimes, but he had never seen it happen. When the sirens ceased their howling, he could hear the thunder of approaching bombers. In the early years of the war, a British bombing mission had consisted of a few dozen aircraft—which was bad enough—but now they were sending hundreds at a time. The noise was terrifying even before they dropped their bombs.

Werner said: "I suppose we'd better call off our mission tonight."

"Hell, no," said Macke.

The roar of the planes grew.

Flares and small incendiary bombs began to fall as the car approached Kreuzberg. The neighborhood was a typical target for the RAF's current strategy of killing as many civilian factory workers as possible. With staggering hypocrisy Churchill and Attlee were claiming they attacked only military targets, and civilian casualties were a regrettable side effect. Berliners knew better.

Wagner drove as fast as he could along streets lit fitfully by flames. There were no people around apart from air raid officials: everyone else was legally obliged to take shelter. The only other vehicles were ambulances, fire engines, and police cars.

Macke covertly studied Werner. The boy was edgy, never quite still, staring out of the window anxiously, tapping his foot in unconscious tension.

Macke had not confided his suspicions to anyone but his immediate team. It was going to be difficult for him if he had to admit that he had demonstrated Gestapo operations to someone whom he now thought was a spy. He could end up under interrogation in his own basement torture chamber. He was not going to do it until he was sure. The only way he might get away with it would be if at the same time he could present his superiors with a captured spy.

But then, if his suspicion turned out to be true, he would arrest not just Werner but his family and friends, and announce the destruction of a massive spy ring. That would transform the picture. He might even be promoted.

As the raid progressed, the type of bombs changed, and Macke heard the profound thudding sound of high explosive. Once the target was illuminated, the RAF liked to drop a mixture of large oil bombs to start fires and high explosive to ventilate the flames and hamper the emergency services. It was cruel, but Macke knew that the Luftwaffe's bombing pattern was similar.

The sound in Macke's earphone started up as they drove cautiously along a street of five-story tenements. The area was taking a terrific pounding and several buildings were newly demolished. Werner said shakily: "We're in the middle of the target area, for Christ's sake."

Macke did not care: tonight was already life or death to him. "All the better," he said. "The pianist will imagine he doesn't need to worry about the Gestapo, in the middle of an air raid."

Wagner stopped the car next to a burning church and pointed along a side street. "Down there," he said.

Macke and Werner jumped out.

Macke walked quickly along the street with Werner beside him and Wagner behind. Werner said: "Are you sure it's a spy? Could it be anything else?"

"Broadcasting a radio signal?" Macke said. "What else could it be?"

Macke could still hear his earphone, but only just, for the air raid was cacophonous: the planes, the bombs, the antiaircraft guns, the crash of falling buildings, and the roar of huge fires.

They passed a stable where horses were neighing in terror, the signal growing ever stronger. Werner was glancing from side to side anxiously. If he was a spy, he would now be fearing that one of his colleagues was about to be arrested by the Gestapo—and wondering what the hell he could do about it. Would he repeat the trick he used last time, or think of some new way of giving a warning? If he was not a spy, this whole farce was a waste of time.

Macke took out the earpiece and handed it to Werner. "Listen," he said, continuing to walk.

Werner nodded. "Getting stronger," he said. The look in his eyes was almost frantic. He handed the earpiece back.

I believe I've got you, Macke thought triumphantly.

There was a thunderous crash as a bomb landed in a building they had just passed. They turned to see flames already licking up beyond the smashed windows of a bakery. Wagner said: "Christ, that was close."

They came to a school, a low brick building in an asphalt yard. "In there, I think," said Macke.

The three men walked up a short flight of stone steps to the entrance. The door was not locked. They went in.

They were at one end of a broad corridor. At its far end was a large door that probably led to the school hall. "Straight ahead," said Macke.

He drew his gun, a 9 mm Luger pistol.

Werner was not armed.

There was a crash, a thud, and the roar of an explosion, all terrifyingly close. All the windows in the corridor smashed, and shards of glass rained on the tiled floor. A bomb must have landed in the playground.

Werner shouted: "Clear out, everyone! The building is about to collapse."

There was no danger of the building collapsing, Macke could see. This was Werner's ruse for giving the alarm to the pianist.

Werner broke into a run, but instead of heading back the way they had come, he went on down the corridor toward the hall.

To warn his friends, Macke thought.

Wagner drew his gun, but Macke said: "No! Don't shoot!"

Werner reached the end of the corridor and flung open the door to the hall. "Run, everyone!" he yelled. Then he fell silent and stood still.

Inside the hall Macke's colleague Mann, the electrical engineer, was tapping out nonsense on a suitcase radio.

Beside him stood Schneider and Richter, both holding drawn guns.

Macke smiled triumphantly. Werner had fallen straight into his trap.

Wagner walked forward and put his gun to Werner's head.

Macke said: "You're under arrest, you subhuman Bolshevik."

Werner acted fast. He jerked his head away from Wagner's gun, seized Wagner's arm, and pulled him into the hall. For a moment Wagner shielded Werner from the guns in the hall. Then he thrust Wagner away from him, causing Wagner to stumble and fall. In the next moment he stepped out of the hall and slammed the door.

For a few seconds it was just Macke and Werner in the corridor.

Werner walked toward Macke.

Macke pointed his Luger. "Stop, or I'll shoot."

"No, you won't." Werner came closer. "You need to interrogate me, and find out who the others are."

Macke pointed his gun at Werner's legs. "I can interrogate you with a bullet in your knee," he said, and he fired.

The shot missed.

Werner lunged and knocked Macke's gun hand aside. Macke dropped the weapon. As he stooped to retrieve it, Werner ran past.

Macke picked up the gun.

Werner reached the school door. Macke took careful aim at his legs and fired.

His first three shots missed, and Werner went through the door.

Macke fired one more shot through the still-open door, and Werner cried out and fell down.

Macke ran along the corridor. Behind him, he heard the others coming out of the school hall.

Then the roof opened with a crash, there was another noise like a thud, and liquid fire splashed like a fountain. Macke screamed in terror, then in agony as his clothes caught alight. He fell to the ground; then there was silence, then darkness.

## V

The doctors were triaging patients in the hospital lobby. Those merely bruised and cut were sent into the outpatients' waiting area, where the most junior nurses cleaned their cuts and consoled them with aspirins. The serious cases were given emergency treatment right there in the lobby, then sent to specialists upstairs. The dead were taken into the yard and laid on the cold ground until someone claimed them.

Dr. Ernst examined a screaming burn victim and prescribed morphine. "Then get his clothes off and put some gel on those burns," he said, and moved on to the next one.

Carla loaded a syringe while Frieda cut the patient's blackened clothes away. He had severe burns all down his right side, but the left was not so bad. Carla found an intact patch of skin and flesh on his left thigh. She was about to inject the patient when she looked at his face and froze.

She knew that fat round countenance with the mustache like a dirt mark under the nose. Two years ago he had come into the hall of her house and arrested her father. Next time she saw her father, he had been dying. This was Inspector Thomas Macke of the Gestapo.

You killed my father, she thought.

Now I can kill you.

It would be simple. She would give him four times the maximum dose of morphine. No one would notice, especially on a night like tonight. He would fall unconscious immediately and die in a few minutes. A doctor who was almost asleep on his feet would assume his heart had failed. No one would doubt the diagnosis, and no one would ask skeptical questions. He would be one of thousands killed in a massive air raid. Rest in peace.

She knew that Werner feared Macke might be on to him. Any day now Werner could be arrested. *Everyone talks under torture.* Werner would give away Frieda, and Heinrich, and others—and Carla. She could save them all, now, in a minute.

But she hesitated.

She asked herself why. Macke was a torturer and a killer. He deserved to die a thousand deaths.

Carla had killed Joachim, or at least helped to kill him. But that had been a fight. Joachim had been kicking Carla's mother to death when she hit him over the head with a soup cauldron. This was different.

Macke was a patient.

Carla was not very religious, but she did believe that some things were sacred. She was a nurse, and patients put their trust in her. She knew that Macke would torture and kill her without hesitation—but she was not like Macke; she was not that kind. This was nothing to do with him: it was about her.

If she killed a patient, she felt, she would have to leave the profession and never again dare to care for sick people. She would be like a banker who steals money, or a politician who takes bribes, or a priest who feels up the young girls who come to him for first communion classes. She would have betrayed herself.

Frieda said: "What are you waiting for? I can't gel him until he calms down."

Carla stuck the needle in Thomas Macke, and he stopped screaming.

Frieda started to put gel on his burned skin.

"This one's only concussed," Dr. Ernst was saying of another patient. "But he's got a bullet in his backside." He raised his voice to talk to the patient. "How did you get shot? Bullets are about the only things the RAF isn't throwing at us tonight."

Carla turned to look. The patient was lying on his front. His trousers had been cut off, showing his rear. He had white skin and fine, fair hair on the small of his back. He was woozy, but he muttered something.

Ernst said: "Policeman's gun went off by accident, did you say?"

The patient spoke more clearly. "Yes."

"I'm going to take the bullet out. It will hurt, but we're short of morphine, and there are worse cases than you."

"Go ahead."

Carla swabbed the wound. Ernst picked up a long, narrow pair of forceps. "Bite the pillow," he said.

He inserted the forceps into the wound. A muffled cry of pain came from the patient.

Dr. Ernst said: "Try not to tense your muscles. It makes it worse."

Carla thought that was a stupid thing to say. No one could relax their muscles while a wound was being probed.

The patient roared: "Ah, shit!"

"I've got it," Dr. Ernst said. "Try to keep still!"

The patient lay still, and Ernst drew the slug out and dropped it into a tray.

Carla wiped the blood from the hole and slapped a dressing on the wound.

The patient rolled over.

"No," Carla said. "You must lie on your—"

She stopped. The patient was Werner.

"Carla?" he said.

"It's me," she said happily. "Putting a bandage on your bum."

"I love you," he said.

She threw her arms around him in the most unprofessional way possible and said: "Oh, my dearest, I love you, too."

## vi

Thomas Macke came around slowly. At first he was in a dreamlike state. Then he became more aware, and realized he was in a hospital and drugged. He knew why, too: his skin hurt intensely, especially down his right side. He was able to figure out that the drugs must be reducing the pain but not completely eliminating it.

Slowly he remembered how he had come here. He had been bombed. He would be dead if he had not been running away from the blast, chasing a fugitive. Those behind him were certainly dead: Mann, Schneider, Richter, and young Wagner. His whole team.

But he had caught Werner.

Or had he? He had shot Werner, and Werner had fallen; then the bomb had dropped. Macke had survived, so Werner might have, too.

Macke was now the only man living who knew that Werner was a spy. He had to speak to his boss, Superintendent Kringelein. He tried to sit upright, but found he did not have the strength to move. He decided to call a nurse, but when he opened his mouth, no sound came out. The effort exhausted him and he went back to sleep.

The next time he awoke, he sensed it was night. The place was quiet, no one moving. He opened his eyes to see a face hovering over him.

It was Werner.

"You're leaving here now," Werner said.

Macke tried to call for help, but found he could not speak.

"You're going to a new place," Werner said. "You won't be a torturer anymore—in fact you'll be the one who gets tortured there."

Macke opened his mouth to scream.

A pillow descended on his face. It was pressed firmly over his mouth and nose. He found he could not breathe. He tried to struggle, but there was no strength in his limbs. He tried to gasp for air, but there was no air. He started to panic. He managed to move his head from side to side, but the pillow was pressed down more firmly. At last he made a noise, but it was only a whimper in his throat.

The universe became a disc of light that shrank slowly until it was a pinpoint.

Then it went out.

# CHAPTER SEVENTEEN

# 1943 ( III )

ill you marry me?" said Volodya Peshkov, and held his breath.

"No," said Zoya Vorotsyntsev. "But thank you."

She was remarkably matter-of-fact about everything, but this was unusually brisk even for her.

They were in bed at the lavish Hotel Moskva, and they had just made love. Zoya had come twice. Her preferred type of sex was cunnilingus. She liked to recline on a pile of pillows while he knelt worshipfully between her legs. He was a willing acolyte, and she returned the favor with enthusiasm.

They had been a couple for more than a year, and everything seemed to be going wonderfully well. Her refusal baffled him.

He said: "Do you love me?"

"Yes. I adore you. Thank you for loving me enough to propose marriage."

That was a bit better. "So why won't you accept?"

"I don't want to bring children into a world at war," she said.

"Okay, I can understand that."

"Ask me again when we've won."

"By then I may not want to marry you."

"If that's how inconstant you are, it's a good thing I refused you today."

"Sorry. For a moment there, I forgot that you don't understand teasing."

"I have to pee." She got off the bed and walked naked across the hotel room. Volodya could hardly believe he was allowed to see this. She had the body of a fashion model or a movie star. Her skin was milk white and her hair pale blond—all of it. She sat on the toilet without closing the bathroom door, and he listened to her peeing. Her lack of modesty was a perpetual delight.

He was supposed to be working.

The Moscow intelligence community was thrown into disarray every time Allied leaders visited, and Volodya's normal routine had been disrupted again for the Foreign Ministers' Conference that had opened on October 18.

The visitors were the American secretary of state, Cordell Hull, and the British foreign secretary, Anthony Eden. They had a harebrained scheme for a four-power pact including China. Stalin thought it was all nonsense and did not understand why they were wasting time on it. The American, Hull, was seventy-two years old and coughing blood—his doctor had come to Moscow with him—but he was no less forceful for that, and he was insistent on the pact.

There was so much to do during the conference that the NKVD—the secret police—were forced to cooperate with their hated rivals in Red Army Intelligence, Volodya's outfit. Microphones had to be concealed in hotel rooms—there was one in here, only Volodya had disconnected it. The visiting ministers and all their aides had to be kept under minute-by-minute surveillance. Their luggage had to be clandestinely opened and searched. Their phone calls had to be tape-recorded and transcribed and translated into Russian and read and summarized. Most of the people they met, including waiters and chambermaids, were NKVD agents, but anyone else they happened to speak to, in the hotel lobby or on the street, had to be checked out, perhaps arrested and imprisoned and interrogated under torture. It was a lot of work.

Volodya was riding high. His spies in Berlin were producing remarkable intelligence. They had given him the battle plan for the Germans' main summer offensive, Zitadelle, and the Red Army had inflicted a tremendous defeat.

Zoya was happy, too. The Soviet Union had resumed nuclear research, and Zoya was part of the team trying to design a nuclear bomb. They were a long way behind the West, because of the delay caused by Stalin's skepticism, but in compensation they were getting invaluable help from Communist spies in England and America, including Volodya's old school friend Willi Frunze.

She came back to bed. Volodya said: "When we first met, you didn't seem to like me much."

"I didn't like men," she replied. "I still don't. Most of them are drunks and bullies and fools. It took me a while to figure out that you were different."

"Thanks, I think," he said. "But are men really so bad?"

"Look around you," she said. "Look at our country."

He reached over her and turned on the bedside radio. Even though he had disconnected the listening device behind the headboard, you couldn't be too careful. When the radio had warmed up, a military band played a march. Satisfied that he could not be overheard, Volodya said: "You're thinking of Stalin and Beria. But they won't always be around."

"Do you know how my father fell from favor?" she said.

"No. My parents never mentioned it."

"There's a reason for that."

"Go on."

"According to my mother, there was an election at my father's factory for a deputy to attend the Moscow Soviet. A Menshevik candidate stood against the Bolshevik, and my father went to a meeting to hear him speak. He did not support the Menshevik, nor vote for him, but everyone who went to that meeting was sacked, and a few weeks later my father was arrested and taken to the Lubyanka."

She meant the NKVD headquarters and prison in Lubyanka Square.

She went on: "My mother went to your father and begged him to help. He immediately went with her to the Lubyanka. They saved my father, but they saw twelve other workers shot."

"That's terrible," Volodya said. "But it was Stalin—"

"No. This was 1920. Stalin was just a Red Army commander fighting in the Soviet-Polish War. Lenin was leader."

"This happened under Lenin?"

"Yes. So, you see, it's not just Stalin and Beria."

Volodya's view of Communist history was badly shaken. "What is it, then?"

The door opened.

Volodya reached for his gun in the bedside table drawer.

But the person who came in was a girl wearing a fur coat and, as far as he could see, nothing else.

"Sorry, Volodya," she said. "I didn't know you had company."

Zoya said: "Who the fuck is she?"

Volodya said: "Natasha, how did you open my door?"

"You gave me a passkey. It opens every door in the hotel."

"Well, you might have knocked!"

"Sorry. I just came to tell you the bad news."

"What?"

"I went into Woody Dewar's room, just as you told me. But I didn't succeed."

"What did you do?"

"This." Natasha opened her coat to show her naked body. She had a voluptuous figure and a luxuriant bush of dark pubic hair.

"All right, I get the picture. Close your coat," said Volodya. "What did he say?"

She switched to English. "He just said: 'No.' I said: 'What do you mean, no?' He said: 'It's the opposite of yes.' Then he just held the door wide open until I went out."

"Bugger," said Volodya. "I'll have to think of something else."

Chuck Dewar knew there was going to be trouble when Captain Vandermeier came into the enemy land section in the middle of the afternoon, red-faced from a beery lunch.

The intelligence unit at Pearl Harbor had expanded. Formerly called Station HYPO, it now had the grand title of Joint Intelligence Center, Pacific Ocean Area, or JICPOA.

Vandermeier had a marine sergeant in tow. "Hey, you two powder puffs," Vandermeier said. "You got a customer complaint here."

As the operation had grown, everyone began to specialize, and Chuck and Eddie had become experts at mapping the territory where American forces were about to land as they fought their way island by island across the Pacific.

Vandermeier said: "This is Sergeant Donegan." The marine was very tall and looked as hard as a rifle. Chuck guessed that the sexually troubled Vandermeier was smitten.

Chuck stood up: "Good to meet you, Sergeant. I'm Chief Petty Officer Dewar."

Chuck and Eddie had both been promoted. As thousands of conscripts poured into the U.S. military, there was a shortage of officers, and prewar enlisted men who knew the ropes rose fast. Chuck and Eddie were now permitted to live off base. They had rented a small apartment together.

Chuck put out his hand, but Donegan did not shake it.

Chuck sat down again. He slightly outranked a sergeant, and he was not going to be polite to one who was rude. "Something I can do for you, Captain Vandermeier?"

There were many ways a captain could torment petty officers in the navy, and Vandermeier knew them all. He adjusted rotas so that Chuck and Eddie never had the same day off. He marked their reports "adequate," knowing full well that anything less than "excellent" was in fact a black mark. He sent confusing messages to the pay office, so that Chuck and Eddie were paid late or got less than they should have, and had to spend hours straightening things out. He was a royal pain. And now he had thought up some new mischief.

Donegan pulled from his pocket a grubby sheet of paper and unfolded it. "Is this your work?" he said aggressively.

Chuck took the paper. It was a map of New Georgia, a group in the Solomon Islands. "Let me check," he said. It was his work, and he knew it, but he was playing for time.

He went to a filing cabinet and pulled open a drawer. He took out the file for New Georgia and shut the drawer with his knee. He returned to his desk, sat down, and opened the file. It contained a duplicate of Donegan's map. "Yes," Chuck said. "That's my work."

"Well, I'm here to tell you it's shit," said Donegan.

"Is it?"

"Look, right here. You show the jungle coming down to the sea. In fact there's a beach a quarter of a mile wide."

"I'm sorry to hear that."

"Sorry!" Donegan had drunk about the same amount of beer as Vandermeier, and he was spoiling for a fight. "Fifty of my men died on that beach."

Vandermeier belched and said: "How could you make a mistake like that, Dewar?"

Chuck was shaken. If he was responsible for an error that had killed fifty men, he deserved to be shouted at. "This is what we had to work on," he said. The file contained an inaccurate map of the islands that might have been Victorian, and a more recent naval chart that showed sea depths but almost no terrain features. There were no on-the-spot reports and no wireless decrypts. The only other item in the file was a blurred black-and-white aerial reconnaissance photograph. Putting his finger on the relevant spot in the photo, Chuck said: "It sure looks as if the trees come all the way to the waterline. Is there a tide? If not, the sand might have been covered with algae when the photograph was taken. Algae can bloom suddenly, and die off just as fast."

Donegan said: "You wouldn't be so goddamn casual about it if you had to fight over the terrain."

Maybe that was true, Chuck thought. Donegan was aggressive and rude, and he was being egged on by the malicious Vandermeier, but that did not mean he was wrong.

Vandermeier said: "Yeah, Dewar. Maybe you and your nancy-boy friend should go with the marines on their next assault. See how your maps are used in action."

Chuck was trying to think of a smart retort when it occurred to him to take the suggestion seriously. Maybe he ought to see some action. It *was* easy to be blasé behind a desk. Donegan's complaint deserved to be taken seriously.

On the other hand, it would mean risking his life.

Chuck looked Vandermeier in the eye. "That sounds like a good idea, Captain," he said. "I'd like to volunteer for that duty."

Donegan looked startled, as if he were beginning to think he might have misjudged the situation.

Eddie spoke for the first time. "So would I. I'll go, too."

"Good," said Vandermeier. "You'll come back wiser—or not at all."

### iii

Volodya could not get Woody Dewar drunk.

In the bar of the Hotel Moskva he thrust a glass of vodka in front of the young American and said in schoolboy English: "You'll like this—it's the very best."

"Thank you very much," said Woody. "I appreciate it." And he left the glass untouched.

Woody was tall and gangly and seemed straightforward to the point of naïveté, which was why Volodya had targeted him.

Speaking through the interpreter, Woody said: "Is Peshkov a common Russian name?"

"Not especially," Volodya replied in Russian.

"I'm from Buffalo, where there is a well-known businessman called Lev Peshkov. I wonder if you're related."

Volodya was startled. His father's brother was called Lev Peshkov and had gone to Buffalo before the First World War. But caution made him prevaricate. "I must ask my father," he said.

"I was at Harvard with Lev Peshkov's son, Greg. He could be your cousin."

"Possibly." Volodya glanced nervously at the police spies around the table. Woody did not understand that any connection with someone in America could bring down suspicion on a Soviet citizen. "You know, Woody, in this country it's considered an insult to refuse to drink."

Woody smiled pleasantly. "Not in America," he said.

Volodya picked up his own glass and looked around the table at the assorted secret policemen pretending to be civil servants and diplomats. "A toast!" he said. "To friendship between the United States and the Soviet Union!"

The others raised their glasses high. Woody did the same. "Friendship!" they all echoed.

Everyone drank except Woody, who put his glass down untasted.

Volodya began to suspect that he was not as naïve as he seemed.

Woody leaned across the table. "Volodya, you need to understand that I don't know any secrets. I'm too junior."

"So am I," said Volodya. It was far from the truth.

Woody said: "What I'm trying to explain is that you can just ask me questions. If I know the answers, I'll tell you. I can do that, because anything I know can't possibly be secret. So you don't need to get me drunk or send prostitutes to my room. You can just ask me."

It was some kind of trick, Volodya decided. No one could be so innocent. But he decided to humor Woody. Why not? "All right," he said. "I need to know what you're after. Not you personally, of course. Your delegation, and Secretary Hull, and President Roosevelt. What do you want from this conference?"

"We want you to back the Four-Power Pact."

It was the standard answer, but Volodya decided to persist. "This is what we don't understand." He was being candid now, perhaps more than he should have, but instinct was telling him to take the risk of opening up a little. "Who cares about a pact with China? We need to defeat the Nazis in Europe. We want you to help us do that."

"And we will."

"So you say. But you said you would invade Europe this summer."

"Well, we did invade Italy."

"It's not enough."

"France next year. We've promised that."

"So why do you need the pact?"

"Well." Woody paused, collecting his thoughts. "We have to show the American people how it's in their interests to invade Europe."

"Why?"

"Why what?"

"Why do you need to explain this to the public? Roosevelt is president, isn't he? He should just do it!"

"Next year is election year. He wants to get reelected."

"So?"

"American people won't vote for him if they think he's involved them unnecessarily in the war in Europe. So he wants to put it to them as part of his overall plan for world peace. If we have the Four-Power Pact, showing that we're serious about the United Nations organization, then American voters are more likely to accept that the invasion of France is a step on the road to a more peaceful world."

"This is amazing," Volodya said. "He's the president, yet he has to make excuses all the time for what he does!"

"Something like that," Woody said. "We call it democracy."

Volodya had a sneaking suspicion that this incredible story might actually be the truth. "So the pact is necessary to persuade American voters to support the invasion of Europe."

"Exactly."

"Then why do we need China?" Stalin was particularly scornful of the Allies' insistence that China should be included in the pact.

"China is a weak ally."

"So ignore China."

"If the Chinese are left out, they will become discouraged, and may fight less enthusiastically against the Japanese."

"So?"

"So we will have to bolster our forces in the Pacific theater, and that will take away from our strength in Europe."

That alarmed Volodya. The Soviet Union did not want Allied forces diverted from Europe to the Pacific. "So you are making a friendly gesture to China simply in order to conserve more forces for the invasion of Europe."

"Yes."

"You make it seem simple."

"It is," said Woody.

## iv

In the early hours of the morning on November 1, Chuck and Eddie ate a steak breakfast with the U.S. Marine Third Division just off the South Sea island of Bougainville.

The island was about 125 miles long. It had two Japanese naval air bases, one in the north and one in the south. The marines were getting ready to land halfway along the lightly defended west coast. Their object was to establish a beachhead and win enough territory to build an airstrip from which to launch attacks on the Japanese bases.

Chuck was on deck at twenty-six minutes past seven when marines in helmets and backpacks began to swarm down the rope nets hanging over the sides of the ship and jump into high-sided landing craft. With them were a small number of war dogs, Doberman pinschers that made tireless sentries.

As the boats approached land, Chuck could already see a flaw in the map he had prepared. Tall waves crashed onto a steeply sloping beach. As he watched, a boat turned sideways to the waves and capsized. The marines swam for shore.

"We have to show surf conditions," Chuck said to Eddie, who was standing beside him on the deck.

"How do we find them out?"

"Reconnaissance aircraft will have to fly low enough for whitecaps to register on their photographs."

"They can't risk coming that low when there are enemy air bases so close."

Eddie was right. But there had to be a solution. Chuck filed it away as the first question to be considered as a result of this mission.

For this landing they had benefited from more information than usual. As well as the normal unreliable maps and hard-to-decipher aerial photographs, they had a report from a reconnaissance team landed by submarine six weeks earlier. The team had identified twelve beaches suitable for landing along a four-mile stretch of coast. But they had not warned of the surf. Perhaps it was not so high that day.

In other respects Chuck's map was right, so far. There was a sandy beach about a hundred yards wide, then a tangle of palm trees and other vegetation. Just beyond the brush line, according to the map, there should be a swamp.

The coast was not completely undefended. Chuck heard the roar of artillery fire, and a shell landed in the shallows. It did no harm, but the gunner's aim would improve. The marines were galvanized with a new urgency as they leaped from the landing craft to the beach and ran for the brush line.

Chuck was glad he had decided to come. He had never been careless or slack about his maps, but it was salutary to see firsthand how correct mapping could save men's lives, and how the smallest errors could be deadly. Even before they embarked, he and Eddie had become a lot more demanding. They asked for blurred photographs to be taken again, they interrogated reconnaissance parties by phone, and they cabled all over the world for better charts.

He was glad for another reason. He was at sea, which he loved. He was on a ship with seven hundred young men, and he relished the camaraderie, the jokes, the songs, and the intimacy of crowded berths and shared showers. "It's like being a straight guy in a girls' boarding school," he said to Eddie one evening.

"Except that that never happens, and this does," Eddie said. He felt the same as Chuck. They loved each other, but they did not mind looking at naked sailors.

Now all seven hundred marines were getting off the ship and onto land as fast as they could. The same was happening at eight other locations along this stretch of coast. As soon as a landing craft emptied out, it lost no time in turning around and coming back for more, but the process still seemed desperately slow.

The Japanese artillery gunner, hidden somewhere in the jungle, found his range at last, and to Chuck's shock a well-aimed shell exploded in a knot of marines, sending men and rifles and body parts flying through the air to litter the beach and stain the sand red.

Chuck was staring in horror at the carnage when he heard the roar of a plane, and looked up to see a Japanese Zero flying low, following the coast. The red suns painted on the wings struck fear into his heart. Last time he saw that sight had been at the Battle of Midway.

The Zero strafed the beach. Marines who were in the process of disembarking from landing craft were caught defenseless. Some threw themselves flat in the shallows, some tried to get behind the hull of the boat, some ran for the jungle. For a few seconds blood spurted and men fell.

Then the plane was gone, leaving the beach scattered with American dead.

Chuck heard it open up a moment later, strafing the next beach.

It would be back.

There were supposed to be U.S. planes in attendance, but he could not see any. Air support was never where you wanted it to be, which was directly above your head.

When all the marines were ashore, alive and dead, the boats transported medics and stretcher parties to the beach. Then they began landing supplies: ammunition, drinking water, food, drugs, and dressings. On the return trip the landing craft brought the wounded back to the ship.

Chuck and Eddie, as nonessential personnel, went ashore with the supplies.

The boat skippers had got used to the swell now, and their craft held a stable position, with its ramp on the sand and the waves breaking on its stern, while the boxes were unloaded and Chuck and Eddie jumped into the surf to wade to shore.

They reached the waterline together.

As they did so, a machine gun opened up.

It seemed to be in the jungle about four hundred yards along the beach. Had it been there all along, the gunner biding his time, or had it just been moved into position from another location? Eddie and Chuck bent double and ran for the tree line.

A sailor with a crate of ammunition on his shoulder gave a shout of pain and fell, dropping the box.

Then Eddie cried out.

Chuck ran on two paces before he could stop. When he turned, Eddie was rolling on the sand clutching his knee, yelling: "Ah, fuck!"

Chuck came back and knelt beside him. "It's okay, I'm here!" he shouted. Eddie's eyes were closed, but he was alive, and Chuck could see no wounds other than the knee.

He glanced up. The boat that had brought them was still close to shore, being unloaded. He could get Eddie back to the ship in minutes. But the machine gun was still firing.

He got into a crouching position. "This is going to hurt," he said. "Yell as much as you like."

He got his right arm under Eddie's shoulder, then slid his left under Eddie's thighs. He took the weight and straightened up. Eddie screamed with pain as his smashed leg swung free. "Hang in there, buddy," Chuck said. He turned toward the water.

He felt sudden, unbearably sharp pains in his legs, his back, and finally his head. In the next fraction of a second he thought he must not drop Eddie. A moment later he knew he was going to. There was a flash of light behind his eyes that rendered him blind.

And then the world came to an end.

## V

On her day off, Carla worked at the Jewish Hospital.

Dr. Rothmann had persuaded her. He had been released from the camp—no one knew why, except the Nazis, and they did not tell anyone. He had lost one eye and he walked with a limp, but he was alive, and capable of practising medicine.

The hospital was in the northern working-class district of Wedding, but there was nothing proletarian about the architecture. It had been built before the First World War, when Berlin's Jews had been prosperous and proud. There were seven elegant buildings set in a large garden. The different departments were linked by tunnels, so that patients and staff could move from one to another without braving the weather.

It was a miracle there was still a Jewish hospital. Very few Jews were left in Berlin. They had been rounded up in their thousands and sent away in special trains. No one knew where they had gone or what happened to them. There were incredible rumors about extermination camps.

The few Jews still in Berlin could not be treated, if they were sick, by Aryan doctors and nurses. So, by the tangled logic of Nazi racism, the hospital was allowed to remain. It was mainly staffed by Jews and other unfortunate people who did not count as properly Aryan: Slavs from eastern Europe, people of mixed ancestry, and those married to Jews. But there were not enough nurses, so Carla helped out.

The hospital was harassed constantly by the Gestapo; critically short of supplies, especially drugs; understaffed; and almost completely without funds.

Carla was breaking the law as she took the temperature of an eleven-year-old boy whose foot had been crushed in an air raid. It was also a crime for her to smuggle medicines out of her everyday hospital and bring them here. But she wanted to prove, if only to herself, that not everyone had given in to the Nazis.

As she finished her ward round, she saw Werner outside the door, in his air force uniform.

For several days he and Carla had lived in fear, wondering whether anyone had survived the bombing of the school and lived to condemn Werner, but it was now clear they had all died, and no one else knew of Macke's suspicions. They had got away with it, again.

Werner had recovered quickly from his bullet wound.

And they were lovers. Werner had moved into the von Ulrichs' large, half-empty house, and he slept with Carla every night. Their parents made no objection; everyone felt they could die any day, and people should take what joy they could from a life of hardship and suffering.

But Werner looked more solemn than usual as he waved to Carla through the glass panel in the door to the ward. She beckoned him inside and kissed him. "I love you," she said. She never tired of saying it.

He was always happy to say: "I love you, too."

"What are you doing here?" she said. "Did you just want a kiss?"

"I've got bad news. I've been posted to the eastern front."

"Oh, no!" Tears came to her eyes.

"It's really a miracle I've avoided it this long. But General Dorn can't keep me any longer. Half our army consists of old men and schoolboys, and I'm a fit twenty-four-year-old officer."

She whispered: "Please don't die."

"I'll do my best."

Still whispering, she said: "But what will happen to the network? You know everything. Who else could run it?"

He looked at her without speaking.

She realized what was in his mind. "Oh, no—not me!"

"You're the best person. Frieda's a follower, not a leader. You've shown the ability to recruit new people and motivate them. You've never been in trouble with the police and you have no record of political activity. No one knows the role you played in opposing Aktion T4. As far as the authorities are concerned, you are a blameless nurse."

"But, Werner, I'm scared!"

"You don't have to do it. But no one else can."

Just then they heard a commotion.

The neighboring ward was for mental patients, and it was not unusual to hear shouting and even screaming, but this seemed different. A cultured voice was raised in anger. Then they heard a second voice, this one with a Berlin accent and the insistent, bullying tone that outsiders said was typical of Berliners.

Carla stepped into the corridor, and Werner followed.

Dr. Rothmann, wearing a yellow star on his jacket, was arguing with a man in SS uniform. Behind them, the double doors to the psychiatric ward, normally locked, were wide open. The patients were leaving. Two more policemen and a couple of nurses were herding a ragged line of men and women, most in pajamas, some walking upright and apparently normal, others shambling and mumbling as they followed one another down the staircase.

Carla was immediately reminded of Ada's son, Kurt, and Werner's brother, Axel, and the so-called hospital in Akelberg. She did not know where these patients were going, but she was quite sure they would be killed there.

Dr. Rothmann was saying indignantly: "These people are sick! They need treatment!"

The SS officer replied: "They're not sick, they're lunatics, and we're taking them where lunatics belong."

"To a hospital?"

"You will be informed in due course."

"That's not good enough."

Carla knew she should not intervene. If they found out she was not Jewish, she would be in deep trouble. She did not look particularly Aryan or otherwise, with dark hair and green eyes. If she kept quiet, probably they would not bother her. But if she protested about what the SS were doing, she would be arrested and questioned, and then it would come out that she was working illegally. So she clamped her teeth together.

The officer raised his voice. "Hurry up—get those cretins in the bus."

Rothmann persisted. "I must be informed where they are going. They are my patients."

They were not really his patients—he was not a psychiatrist.

The SS man said: "If you're so concerned about them, you can go with them."

Dr. Rothmann paled. He would almost certainly be going to his death.

Carla thought of his wife, Hannelore; his son, Rudi; and his daughter in England, Eva, and she felt sick with fear.

The officer grinned. "Suddenly not so concerned?" he jeered.

Rothmann straightened up. "On the contrary," he said. "I accept your offer. I swore an oath, many years ago, to do all I can to help sick people. I'm not going to break my oath now. I hope to die at peace with my conscience." He limped down the stairs.

An old woman went by wearing nothing but a robe open at the front, showing her nakedness.

Carla could not remain silent. "It's November out there!" she cried. "They have no outdoor clothing!"

The officer gave her a hard look. "They'll be all right on the bus."

"I'll get some warm clothing." Carla turned to Werner. "Come and help me. Grab blankets from anywhere."

The two of them ran around the emptying psychiatric ward, pulling blankets off beds and out of the cupboards. Each carrying a pile, they hurried down the stairs.

The garden of the hospital was frozen earth. Outside the main door was a gray bus, its engine idling, its driver smoking at the wheel. Carla saw that he was wearing a heavy coat plus a hat and gloves, which told her that the bus was not heated.

A small group of Gestapo and SS men stood in a knot, watching the proceedings.

The last few patients were climbing aboard. Carla and Werner boarded the bus and began to distribute the blankets.

Dr. Rothmann was standing at the back. "Carla," he said. "You . . . you'll tell my Hannelore how it was. I have to go with the patients. I have no choice."

"Of course." Her voice was choked.

"I may be able to protect these people."

Carla nodded, though she did not really believe it.

"In any event, I cannot abandon them."

"I'll tell her."

"And say that I love her."

Carla could no longer stop the tears.

Rothmann said: "Tell her that was the last thing I said. I love her."

Carla nodded.

Werner took her arm. "Let's go."

They got off the bus.

An SS man said to Werner: "You, in the air force uniform, what the hell do you think you're doing?"

Werner was so angry that Carla was frightened he would start a fight. But he spoke calmly. "Giving blankets to old people who are cold," he said. "Is that against the law now?"

"You should be fighting on the eastern front."

"I'm going there tomorrow. How about you?"

"Take care what you say."

"If you would be kind enough to arrest me before I go, you might save my life."

The man turned away.

The gears of the bus crashed and its engine note rose. Carla and Werner turned to look. At every window was a face, and they were all different: babbling, drooling, laughing hysterically, distracted, or distorted with spiritual distress—all insane. Psychiatric patients being taken away by the SS. The mad leading the mad.

The bus pulled away.

## vi

"I might have liked Russia, if I'd been allowed to see it," Woody said to his father.

"I feel the same."

"I didn't even get any decent photographs."

They were sitting in the grand lobby of the Hotel Moskva, near the entrance to the subway station. Their bags were packed and they were on their way home.

Woody said: "I have to tell Greg Peshkov that I met a Volodya Peshkov. Though Volodya was not so pleased about it. I guess anyone with connections in the West might fall under suspicion."

"You bet your socks."

"Anyway, we got what we came for—that's the main thing. The allies are committed to the United Nations organization."

"Yes," said Gus with satisfaction. "Stalin took some persuading, but he saw sense in the end. You helped with that, I think, by your straight-talking to Peshkov."

"You've fought for this all your life, Papa."

"I don't mind admitting that this is a pretty good moment."

A worrying thought crossed Woody's mind. "You're not going to retire now, are you?"

Gus laughed. "No. We've won agreement in principle, but the job has only just begun."

Cordell Hull had already left Moscow, but some of his aides were still there, and now one of them approached the Dewars. Woody knew him, a young man called Ray Baker. "I have a message for you, Senator," he said. He seemed nervous.

"Well, you just caught me in time—I'm about to leave," said Gus. "What is it?"

"It's about your son Charles—Chuck."

Gus went pale and said: "What is the message, Ray?"

The young man was having trouble speaking. "Sir, it's bad news. He's been in a battle in the Solomon Islands."

"Is he wounded?"

"No, sir, it's worse."

"Oh, Christ," said Gus, and he began to cry.

Woody had never seen his father cry.

"I'm sorry, sir," said Ray. "The message is that he's dead."

# CHAPTER EIGHTEEN

# 1944

Woody stood in front of the mirror in his bedroom at his parents' Washington apartment. He was wearing the uniform of a second lieutenant in the 510th Parachute Regiment of the United States Army.

He had had the suit made by a good Washington tailor, but it did not look good on him. Khaki made his complexion sallow, and the badges and flashes on the tunic jacket just seemed untidy.

He could probably have avoided the draft, but he had decided not to. Part of him wanted to continue to work with his father, who was helping President Roosevelt plan a new global order that would avoid any more world wars. They had won a triumph in Moscow, but Stalin was inconstant, and seemed to relish creating difficulties. At the Tehran Conference in December, the Soviet leader had revived the halfway-house idea of regional councils, and Roosevelt had had to talk him out of it. Clearly the United Nations organization was going to require tireless vigilance.

But Gus could do that without Woody. And Woody was feeling worse and worse about letting other men fight the war for him.

He was looking as good as he ever would in the uniform, so he went into the drawing room to show his mother.

Rosa had a visitor, a young man in navy whites, and after a moment Woody recognized the freckled good looks of Eddie Parry. He was sitting on the couch with Rosa, holding a walking stick. He got to his feet with difficulty to shake Woody's hand.

Mama had a sad face. She said: "Eddie was telling me about the day Chuck died."

Eddie sat down again, and Woody sat opposite. "I'd like to hear about that," Woody said.

"It doesn't take long to tell," Eddie began. "We were on the beach at Bougainville for about five seconds when a machine gun opened up from somewhere in the swamp. We ran for cover, but I got a couple of bullets in my knee. Chuck should have gone on to the tree line. That's the drill—you leave the wounded to be picked up by the medics. Of course, Chuck disobeyed that rule. He stopped and came back for me."

Eddie paused. There was a cup of coffee on the small table beside him, and he took a gulp.

"He picked me up in his arms," he went on. "Darn fool. Made himself a target. But I guess he wanted to get me back in the landing craft. Those boats have high sides, and they're made of steel. We would have been safe, and I could have gotten medical attention right away on the ship. But he shouldn't have done it. Soon as he stood upright, he got hit by a spray of bullets—legs, back, and head. I think he must have died before he hit the sand. Anyway, by the time I was able to lift my head and look at him, he just wasn't there anymore."

Woody saw that his mother was controlling herself with difficulty. He was afraid that if she cried, he would too.

"I lay on that beach beside his body for an hour," Eddie said. "I held his hand all the time. Then they brought a stretcher for me. I didn't want to go. I knew I'd never see him again." He buried his face in his hands. "I loved him so much," he said.

Rosa put her arm around his big shoulders and hugged him. He laid his head on her chest and sobbed like a child. She stroked his hair. "There, there," she said. "There, there."

Woody realized that his mother knew what Chuck and Eddie were.

After a minute Eddie began to pull himself together. He looked at Woody. "You know what this is like," he said.

He was talking about the death of Joanne. "Yes, I do," Woody said. "It's the worst thing in the world—but it hurts a little less every day."

"I sure hope so."

"Are you still in Hawaii?"

"Yes. Chuck and I work in the enemy land unit. Used to work." He swallowed. "Chuck decided we needed to get a better feel for how our maps were used in action. That's why we went to Bougainville with the marines."

"You must be doing a good job," Woody said. "We seem to be beating the Japs in the Pacific."

"Inch by inch," Eddie said. He glanced at Woody's uniform. "Where are you stationed?"

"I've been at Fort Benning, in Georgia, doing parachute training," Woody said. "Now I'm on my way to London. I leave tomorrow."

He caught his mother's eye. Suddenly she looked older. He realized her face was lined. Her fiftieth birthday had passed with no big fuss. However, he guessed that talking about Chuck's death while her other son stood there in army uniform had struck her a hard blow.

Eddie did not pick that up. "People say we'll invade France this year," he said.

"I assume that's why my training was accelerated," Woody said.

"You should see some action."

Rosa muffled a sob.

Woody said: "I hope I'll be as brave as my brother."

Eddie said: "I hope you never find out."

ii

Greg Peshkov took dark-eyed Margaret Cowdry to an afternoon symphony concert. Margaret had a wide, generous mouth that loved kissing. But Greg had something else on his mind.

He was following Barney McHugh.

So was an FBI agent called Bill Bicks.

Barney McHugh was a brilliant young physicist. He was on leave from the U.S. Army's secret laboratory at Los Alamos, New Mexico, and had brought his British wife to Washington to see the sights.

The FBI had found out in advance that McHugh was coming to the concert, and Special Agent Bicks had managed to get Greg two seats a few rows behind McHugh's. A concert hall, with hundreds of strangers crowding together to come in and go out, was the perfect location for a clandestine rendezvous, and Greg wanted to know what McHugh might be up to.

It was a pity they had met before. Greg had talked to McHugh in Chicago on the day the nuclear pile was tested. It had been a year and a half ago, but McHugh might remember. So Greg had to make sure McHugh did not see him.

When Greg and Margaret arrived, McHugh's seats were empty. Either side were two ordinary-looking couples, a middle-aged man in a cheap gray chalk-stripe suit and his dowdy wife on the left, and two elderly ladies on the right. Greg hoped McHugh was going to show up. If the guy was a spy, Greg wanted to nail him.

They were going to hear Tchaikovsky's first symphony. "So, you like classical music," said Margaret chattily as the orchestra tuned up. She had no idea of the real reason she had been brought here. She knew that Greg was working in weapons research, which was secret, but like almost all Americans she had no inkling of the nuclear bomb. "I thought you only listened to jazz," she said.

"I love Russian composers—they're so dramatic," Greg told her. "I expect it's in my blood."

"I was raised listening to classical. My father likes to have a small orchestra at dinner parties." Margaret's family were rich enough to make Greg feel a pauper by comparison. But he still had not met her parents, and he suspected they would disapprove of the illegitimate son of a famous Hollywood womanizer. "What are you looking at?" she said.

"Nothing." The McHughs had arrived. "What's your perfume?"

"Chichi by Renoir."

"I love it."

The McHughs looked happy, a bright and prosperous young couple on holiday. Greg wondered if they were late because they had been making love in their hotel room.

Barney McHugh sat next to the man in the gray chalk stripe. Greg knew it was a cheap suit by the unnatural stiffness of the padded shoulders. The man did not look at the newcomers. The McHughs started to do a crossword, their heads leaning together intimately as they studied the newspaper Barney was holding. A few minutes later the conductor appeared.

The opening piece was by Saint-Saëns. German and Austrian composers had declined in popularity since war broke out, and concertgoers were discovering alternatives. There was a revival of Sibelius.

McHugh was probably a Communist. Greg knew this because J. Robert Oppenheimer had told him. Oppenheimer, a leading theoretical physicist from the University of California, was director of the Los Alamos laboratory and scientific leader of the entire Manhattan Project. He had strong Communist ties, though he insisted he had never joined the party.

Special Agent Bicks had said to Greg: "Why does the army have to have all these pinkos? Whatever it is you're trying to achieve out there in the desert, aren't there enough bright young conservative scientists in America to do it?"

"No, there aren't," Greg had told him. "If there were, we would have hired them."

Communists were sometimes more loyal to their cause than to their country, and might think it right to share the secrets of nuclear research with the Soviet Union. This would not be like giving information to the enemy. The Soviets were America's allies against the Nazis—in fact they had done more of the fighting than all the other allies put together. All the same it was dangerous. Information intended for Moscow might find its way to Berlin. And anyone who thought about the postwar world for more than a minute could guess that the USA and the USSR might not always be friends.

The FBI thought Oppenheimer was a security risk and kept trying to persuade Greg's boss, General Groves, to fire him. But Oppenheimer was the outstanding scientist of his generation, so the general insisted on keeping him.

In an attempt to prove his loyalty, Oppenheimer had named McHugh as a possible Communist, and that was why Greg was tailing him.

The FBI was skeptical. "Oppenheimer is blowing smoke up your ass," Bicks had said.

Greg said: "I can't believe it. I've known him for a year now."

"He's a fucking Communist, like his wife and his brother and his sister-in-law."

"He's working nineteen hours a day to build better weapons for American soldiers—what kind of traitor does that?"

Greg hoped McHugh did turn out to be a spy, for that would lift suspicion from Oppenheimer, bolster General Groves's credibility, and boost Greg's own status, too.

He watched McHugh constantly throughout the first half of the concert, not wanting to take his eyes off. The physicist did not look at the people either side of him. He seemed absorbed in the music, and only moved his gaze from the stage to look lovingly at Mrs. McHugh, who was a pale English rose. Had Oppenheimer simply been wrong about McHugh? Or, more subtly, was Oppenheimer's accusation a distraction to divert suspicion away from himself?

Bicks was watching, too, Greg knew. He was upstairs in the dress circle. Perhaps he had seen something.

During the intermission, Greg followed the McHughs out and stood in the same line for coffee. Neither the dowdy couple nor the two old ladies were anywhere nearby.

Greg felt thwarted. He did not know what to conclude. Were his suspicions unfounded? Or was it simply that this visit by the McHughs was innocent?

As he and Margaret were returning to their seats, Bill Bicks came up beside him. The agent was middle-aged, a little overweight, and losing his hair. He wore a light gray suit that had sweat stains under the armpits. He said in a low voice: "You were right."

"How do you know?"

"That guy sitting next to McHugh."

"In a gray striped suit?"

"Yeah. He's Nikolai Yenkov, a cultural attaché at the Soviet embassy."

Greg said: "Good God!"

Margaret turned around. "What?"

"Nothing," Greg said.

Bicks moved away.

"You've got something on your mind," she said as they took their seats. "I don't believe you heard a single bar of the Saint-Saëns."

"Just thinking about work."

"Tell me it's not another woman, and I'll forget it."

"It's not another woman."

In the second half he began to feel anxious. He had seen no contact between McHugh and Yenkov. They did not speak, and Greg saw nothing pass from one to the other: no file, no envelope, no roll of film.

The symphony came to an end and the conductor took his bows. The audience began to file out. Greg's spy hunt was a washout.

In the lobby, Margaret went to the ladies' room. While Greg was waiting, Bicks approached him.

"Nothing," Greg said.

"Me, neither."

"Maybe it's a coincidence, McHugh sitting by Yenkov."

"There are no coincidences."

"Perhaps there was a snag. A wrong code word, say."

Bicks shook his head. "They passed something. We just didn't see it."

Mrs. McHugh also went to the ladies' room and, like Greg, McHugh waited nearby. Greg studied him from behind a pillar. He had no briefcase, no raincoat under which to conceal a package or a file. But all the same, something about him was wrong. What was it?

Then Greg realized. "The newspaper!" he said.

"What?"

"When Barney came in, he was carrying a newspaper. They did the crossword while waiting for the show. Now he doesn't have it!"

"Either he threw it away—or he passed it to Yenkov, with something concealed inside."

"Yenkov and his wife have left already."

"They may still be outside."

Bicks and Greg ran for the door.

Bicks shoved his way through the crowd still filing out of the exits. Greg stayed close behind. They reached the sidewalk outside and looked both ways. Greg could not see Yenkov, but Bicks had sharp eyes. "Across the street!" he cried.

The attaché and his dowdy wife were standing at the curb, and a black limousine was approaching them slowly.

Yenkov was holding a folded newspaper.

Greg and Bicks ran across the road.

The limousine stopped.

Greg was faster than Bicks and reached the far sidewalk first.

Yenkov had not noticed them. Unhurriedly, he opened the car door, then stepped back to let his wife get in.

Greg threw himself at Yenkov. They both fell to the ground. Mrs. Yenkov screamed.

Greg scrambled to his feet. The chauffeur had got out of the car and was coming around it, but Bicks yelled: "FBI!" and held up his badge.

Yenkov had dropped the newspaper. Now he reached for it. But Greg was faster. He picked it up, stepped back, and opened it.

Inside was a sheaf of papers. The top one was a diagram. Greg recognized it immediately. It showed the working of an implosion trigger for a plutonium bomb. "Jesus Christ," he said. "This is the very latest stuff!"

Yenkov jumped into the car, slammed the door, and locked it from the inside.

The chauffeur got back in and drove away.

## iii

It was Saturday night, and Daisy's apartment in Piccadilly was heaving. There had to be a hundred people there, she thought, feeling pleased.

She had become the leader of a social group based on the American Red Cross in London. Every Saturday she gave a party for American servicemen, and invited nurses from St. Bart's Hospital to meet them. RAF pilots came, too. They drank her unlimited Scotch and gin, and danced to Glenn Miller records on her gramophone. Conscious that it might be the last party the men ever attended, she did everything she could to make them happy—except kiss them, but the nurses did plenty of that.

Daisy never drank liquor at her own parties. She had too much to think about. Couples were always locking themselves in the toilet, and having to be dragged out because the room was needed for its regular purpose. If a really important general got drunk, he had to be seen safely home. She often ran out of ice—she could not make her British staff understand how much ice a party needed.

For a while after she split up with Boy Fitzherbert, her only friends had been the Leckwith family. Lloyd's mother, Ethel, had never judged her. Although Ethel was the height of respectability now, she had mistakes in her past, and that made her more understanding. Daisy still went to Ethel's house in Aldgate every Wednesday evening, and drank cocoa around the radio. It was her favorite night of the week.

She had now been socially rejected twice, once in Buffalo and again in London, and the depressing thought occurred to her that it might be her fault. Perhaps she did not really belong in those prissy high-society groups, with their strict rules of conduct. She was a fool to be attracted to them.

The trouble was that she loved parties and picnics and sporting events and any gathering where people dressed up and had fun.

However, she now knew she did not need British aristocrats or old-money Americans to have fun. She had created her own society, and it was a lot more exciting than theirs. Some of the people who had refused to speak to her after she left Boy now hinted heavily that they would like an invitation to one of her famous Saturday nights. And many guests came to her apartment to let their hair down after an excruciatingly grand dinner in a palatial Mayfair residence.

Tonight was the best party so far, for Lloyd was home on leave.

He was openly living with her at the flat. She did not care what people thought: her reputation in respectable circles was already so bad that no further damage could be done. Anyway, the urgency of wartime love had driven many people to break the rules in similar ways. Domestic staff could sometimes be as rigid as duchesses about such things, but all Daisy's employees adored her, so she and Lloyd did not even pretend to be occupying separate bedrooms.

She loved sleeping with him. He was not as experienced as Boy, but he made up for that in enthusiasm—and he was eager to learn. Every night was a voyage of exploration in a double bed.

As they looked at their guests talking and laughing, drinking and smoking, dancing and smooching, Lloyd smiled at her and said: "Happy?"

"Almost," she said.

"Almost?"

She sighed. "I want to have children, Lloyd. I don't care that we're not married. Well, I do care, of course, but I still want a baby."

His face darkened. "You know how I feel about illegitimacy."

"Yes, you explained it to me. But I want some part of you to cherish if you die."

"I'll do my best to stay alive."

"I know." But if her suspicion was correct, and he was working undercover in occupied territory, he could be executed, as German spies were executed in Britain. He would be gone, and she would have nothing left. "It's the same for a million women, I realize that, but I can't face the thought of life without you. I think I'll die."

"If I could make Boy divorce you, I would."

"Well, this is no kind of talk for a party." She looked across the room. "What do you know? I believe that's Woody Dewar!"

Woody was wearing a lieutenant's uniform. She went over and greeted him. It was strange to see him again after nine years—though he did not look much different, just older.

"There are thousands of American soldiers here now," Daisy said as they foxtrotted to "Pennsylvania Six-Five Thousand." "We must be about to invade France. What else?"

"The top brass certainly don't share their plans with greenhorn lieutenants," Woody said. "But like you I can't think of any other reason why I'm here. We can't leave the Russians to bear the brunt of the fighting much longer."

"When do you think it will happen?"

"Offensives always begin in the summer. Late May or early June is everyone's best guess."

"That soon!"

"But no one knows where."

"Dover-to-Calais is the shortest sea crossing," Daisy said.

"And for that reason the German defenses are concentrated around Calais. So maybe we'll try to surprise them—say, by landing on the south coast, near Marseilles."

"Perhaps then it will be over at last."

"I doubt it. Once we have a bridgehead, we still have to conquer France, then Germany. There's a long road ahead."

"Oh, dear." Woody seemed to need cheering up. And Daisy knew just the girl to do it. Isabel Hernandez was a Rhodes scholar doing a master's in history at St. Hilda's College, Oxford. She was gorgeous, but the boys called her a ball-buster because she was so fiercely intellectual. However, Woody would be oblivious to that. "Come over here," she called to Isabel. "Woody, this is my friend Bella. She's from San Francisco. Bella, meet Woody Dewar from Buffalo."

They shook hands. Bella was tall, with thick dark hair and olive skin just like Joanne Rouzrokh's. Woody smiled at her and said: "What are you doing here in London?" Daisy left them.

She served supper at midnight. When she could get American supplies, it was ham and eggs; otherwise, cheese sandwiches. It provided a lull when people could talk, a bit like the intermission at the theater. She noticed that Woody Dewar was still with Bella Hernandez, and they seemed to be deep in conversation. She made sure everyone had what they needed, then sat in a corner with Lloyd.

"I've decided what I'd like to do after the war, if I'm still alive," he said. "As well as marry you, that is."

"What?"

"I'm going to try for Parliament."

Daisy was thrilled. "Lloyd, that's wonderful!" She put her arms around his neck and kissed him.

"It's too early for congratulations. I've put my name down for Hoxton, the constituency next to Mam's. But the local Labour Party may not pick me. And if they do, I may not win. Hoxton has a strong Liberal M.P. at the moment."

"I want to help you," she said. "I could be your right-hand woman. I'll write your speeches—I bet I'd be good at that."

"I'd love you to help me."

"Then it's settled!"

The older guests left after supper, but the music continued and the drink never ran out, so the party became even more uninhibited. Woody was now slow-dancing with Bella: Daisy wondered if this was his first romance since Joanne.

The petting got heavier, and people began disappearing into the two bedrooms. They could not lock the doors—Daisy took the keys out—so there were sometimes several couples in the same room, but no one seemed to mind. Daisy had once found two people in the broom cupboard, fast asleep in each other's arms.

At one o'clock her husband arrived.

She had not invited Boy, but he showed up in the company of a couple of American pilots, and Daisy shrugged and let him in. He was amiably squiffy, and danced with several nurses, then politely asked her.

Was he just drunk, she wondered, or had he softened toward her? And if so, might he reconsider the divorce?

She consented, and they did the jitterbug. Most of the guests had no idea they were a separated husband and wife, but those who knew were amazed.

"I read in the papers that you bought another racehorse," she said, making small talk.

"Lucky Laddie," he said. "Cost me eight thousand guineas—a record price."

"I hope he's worth it." She loved horses, and she had thought they would buy and train racehorses together, but he had not wanted to share that enthusiasm with his wife. It had been one of the frustrations of her marriage.

He read her mind. "I disappointed you, didn't I?" he said.

"Yes."

"And you disappointed me."

That was a new thought to her. After a minute's reflection she said: "By not turning a blind eye to your infidelities?"

"Exactly." He was drunk enough to be honest.

She saw her opportunity. "How long do you think we should punish one another?"

"Punish?" he said. "Who's punishing anyone?"

"We're punishing each other by staying married. We should get divorced, as sensible people do."

"Perhaps you're right," he said. "But this time on a Saturday night is not the best moment to discuss it."

Her hopes rose. "Why don't I come and see you?" she said. "When we're both fresh—and sober."

He hesitated. "All right."

She pressed her advantage eagerly. "How about tomorrow?"

"All right."

"I'll see you after church. Say, twelve noon?"

"All right," said Boy.


## iv

As Woody was walking Bella home through Hyde Park, to a friend's flat in South Kensington, she kissed him.

He had not done this since Joanne died. At first he froze. He liked Bella a lot: she was the smartest girl he had met since Joanne. And the way she had clung to him while they were slow-dancing had let him know he could kiss her if he wanted to. All the same he had been holding back. He kept thinking about Joanne.

Then Bella took the initiative.

She opened her mouth and he tasted her tongue, but that only made him think of Joanne kissing him that way. It was only two and a half years since she died.

His brain was forming words of polite rejection when his body took over. He was suddenly consumed with desire. He began to kiss her back hungrily.

She responded eagerly to his access of passion. She took both his hands and put them on her breasts, which were large and soft. He groaned helplessly.

It was dark and he could hardly see but he realized, by half-smothered sounds coming from the surrounding vegetation, that there were numerous couples doing similar things nearby.

She pressed her body against his, and he knew she could feel his erection. He was so excited he felt he would ejaculate any second. She seemed as madly aroused as he was. He felt her unbuttoning his pants with frantic fingers. Her hands were cool on his hot penis. She eased it out of his clothing; then, to his surprise and delight, she knelt down. As soon as her lips closed over the head, he spurted uncontrollably into her mouth. She sucked and licked feverishly as he did so.

When the climax was over, she continued to kiss it until it softened. Then she gently put it away and stood up.

"That was exciting," she whispered. "Thank you."

He had been about to thank her. Instead he put his arms around her and pulled her close. He felt so grateful to her that he could have wept. He had not realized how badly he needed a woman's affection tonight. Some kind of shadow had been lifted from him. "I can't tell you . . . " he began, but he could not find words to explain how much it meant to him.

"Then don't," she said. "I know, anyway. I could feel it."

They walked to her building. At the door he said: "Can we—"

She put a finger on his lips to silence him. "Go and win the war," she said.

Then she went inside.

**V**

When Daisy went to a Sunday service, which was not often, she now avoided the elite churches of the West End, whose congregations had snubbed her, and instead caught the Tube to Aldgate and attended the Calvary Gospel Hall. The doctrinal differences were wide, but they did not matter to her. The singing was better in the East End.

She and Lloyd arrived separately. People in Aldgate knew who she was, and they liked having a rogue aristocrat sitting on one of their cheap seats, but it would have been pushing their tolerance too far for a married-and-separated woman to walk in on the arm of her paramour. Ethel's brother Billy had said: "Jesus did not condemn the adulteress, but he did tell her to sin no more."

During the service she thought about Boy. Had he really meant last night's conciliatory words, or were they just the softness of the drunken moment? Boy had even shaken hands with Lloyd as he left. Surely that meant forgiveness? But she told herself not to let her hopes rise. Boy was the most completely self-absorbed person she had ever known, worse than his father or her brother Greg.

After church Daisy often went to Eth Leckwith's house for Sunday dinner, but today she left Lloyd to his family and hurried away.

She returned to the West End and knocked on the door of her husband's house in Mayfair. The butler showed her into the morning room.

Boy came in shouting. "What the hell is this?" he roared, and he threw a newspaper at her.

She had seen him in this mood plenty of times, and she was not afraid of him. Only once had he raised a hand to strike her. She had seized a heavy candlestick and threatened to bop him. It did not happen again.

Though not scared, she was disappointed. He had been in such a good mood last night. But perhaps he might still listen to reason.

"What has happened to displease you?" she said calmly.

"Look at that bloody paper."

She bent and picked it up. It was today's edition of the *Sunday Mirror*, a popular left-wing tabloid. On the front page was a photograph of Boy's new horse, Lucky Laddie, and the headline:

### LUCKY LADDIE—
#### Worth 28
#### Coal Miners

The story of Boy's record-breaking purchase had appeared in yesterday's press, but today the *Mirror* had an outraged opinion piece, pointing out that the price of the horse, £8,400, was exactly twenty-eight times the £300 standard compensation paid to the widow of a miner who died in a pit accident.

And the Fitzherbert family wealth came from coal mines.

Boy said: "My father is furious. He was hoping to be foreign secretary in the postwar government. This has probably ruined his chances."

Daisy said in exasperation: "Boy, kindly explain why this is my fault?"

"Look who wrote the damned thing!"

Daisy looked.

### By Billy Williams
*Member of Parliament for Aberowen*

Boy said: "Your boyfriend's uncle!"

"Do you imagine he consults me before writing his articles?"

He wagged a finger. "For some reason, that family hates us!"

"They think it's unfair that you should make so much money from coal, when the miners themselves get such a raw deal. There is a war on, you know."

"You live on inherited money," he said. "And I didn't see much sign of wartime austerity at your Piccadilly apartment last night."

"You're right," she said. "But I gave a party for the troops. You spent a fortune on a horse."

"It's my money!"

"But you got it from coal."

"You've spent so much time in bed with that Williams bastard that you've become a bloody Bolshevik."

"And that's one more thing that's driving us apart. Boy, do you really want to stay married to me? You could find someone who suits you. Half the girls in London would love to be Viscountess Aberowen."

"I won't do anything for that damned Williams family. Anyway, I heard last night that your boyfriend wants to be a member of Parliament."

"He'll make a great one."

"Not with you in tow. He won't even get elected. He's a bloody socialist. You're an ex-Fascist."

"I've thought about this. I know it's a bit of a problem—"

"Problem? It's an insuperable barrier. Wait till the papers get that story! You'll be crucified the way I've been today."

"I suppose you'll give the story to the *Daily Mail*."

"I won't need to—his opponents will do that. You mark my words. With you by his side, Lloyd Williams doesn't stand a bloody chance."

For the first five days of June, Lieutenant Woody Dewar and his platoon of paratroopers, plus a thousand or so others, were isolated at an airfield somewhere northwest of London. An aircraft hangar had been converted into a giant dormitory with hundreds of cots in long rows. There were movies and jazz records to entertain them while they waited.

Their objective was Normandy. By means of elaborate deception plans, the Allies had tried to convince the German High Command that the target would be two hundred miles northeast, at Calais. If the Germans had been fooled, the invasion force would meet relatively light resistance, at least for the first few hours.

The paratroopers were to be the first wave, in the middle of the night. The second wave would be the main force of one hundred and thirty thousand men, aboard a fleet of five thousand vessels, landing on the beaches of Normandy at dawn. By then, the paratroopers should have already destroyed inland strongpoints and taken control of key transport links.

Woody's platoon had to capture a bridge across a river in a small town called Eglise-des-Soeurs, ten miles inland. When they had done so, they had to keep control of the bridge, blocking any German units that might be sent to reinforce the beach, until the main invasion force caught up with them. At all costs they must prevent the Germans from blowing up the bridge.

While they waited for the green light, Ace Webber ran a marathon poker game, winning a thousand dollars and losing it again. Lefty Cameron obsessively cleaned and oiled his lightweight M1 semiautomatic carbine, the paratrooper model with a folding stock. Lonnie Callaghan and Tony Bonanio, who did not like one another, went to Mass together every day. Sneaky Pete Schneider sharpened the commando knife he had bought in London until he could have shaved with it. Patrick Timothy, who looked like Clark Gable and had a similar mustache, played a ukulele, the same tune over and over again, driving everybody crazy. Sergeant Defoe wrote long letters to his wife, then tore them up and started again. Mack Trulove and Smoking Joe Morgan cropped and shaved each other's hair, believing that would make it easier for the medics to deal with head injuries.

Most of them had nicknames. Woody had discovered that his own was Scotch.

D-day was set for Sunday, June 4, then postponed because of bad weather.

On Monday, June 5, in the evening, the colonel made a speech. "Men!" he shouted. "Tonight is the night we invade France!"

They roared their approval. Woody thought it was ironic. They were safe and warm here, but they could hardly wait to get over there, jump out of airplanes, and land in the arms of enemy troops who wanted to kill them.

They were given a special meal, all they could eat: steak, pork, chicken, fries, ice cream. Woody did not want any. He had more idea than the other men of what was ahead of him, and he did not want to do it on a full stomach. He got coffee and a donut. The coffee was American, fragrant and delicious, unlike the frightful brew served up by the British, when they had any coffee at all.

He took off his boots and lay down on his cot. He thought about Bella Hernandez, her lopsided smile and her soft breasts.

Next thing he knew, a hooter was sounding.

For a moment, Woody thought he was waking from a bad dream in which he was going into battle to kill people. Then he realized it was true.

They all put on their jumpsuits and assembled their equipment. They had too much. Some of it was essential: a carbine with 150 rounds of .30 ammunition; antitank grenades; a small bomb known as a Gammon grenade; K rations; water purifying tablets; a first-aid kit with morphine. Other things they might have done without: an entrenching tool, a shaving kit, a French phrase book. They were so overloaded that the smaller men struggled to walk to the planes lined up on the runway in the dark.

Their transport aircraft were C-47 Skytrains. To Woody's surprise, he saw by the dim lights that they had all been painted with distinctive black-and-white stripes. The pilot of his aircraft, a bad-tempered Midwesterner called Captain Bonner, said: "That's to prevent us being shot down by our own goddamn side."

Before boarding, the men were weighed. Callaghan and Bonanio both had disassembled bazookas packed in bags that dangled from their legs, adding eighty pounds to their weight. As the total mounted, Captain Bonner became angry. "You're overloading me!" he snarled at Woody. "I won't get this motherfucker off the ground!"

"Not my decision, Captain," Woody said. "Talk to the colonel."

Sergeant Defoe boarded first and went to the front of the plane, taking a seat beside the open arch leading to the flight deck. He would be the last to jump. Any man who developed a last-minute reluctance to leap into the night would be helped along with a good shove from Defoe.

Callaghan and Bonanio, carrying the leg bags holding their bazookas as well as everything else, had to be helped up the steps. Woody as platoon commander boarded last. He would be first out, and first on the ground.

The interior was a tube with a row of simple metal seats on either side. The men had trouble fastening seat belts around their equipment, and some did not bother. The door closed and the engines roared into life.

Woody felt excited as well as scared. Against all reason, he felt eager for the battle to come. To his surprise he found himself impatient to get down on the ground, meet the enemy, and fire his weapons. He wanted the waiting to be over.

He wondered if he would ever see Bella Hernandez again.

He thought he could feel the plane straining as it lumbered down the runway. Painfully, it picked up speed. It seemed to rumble along on the ground forever. Woody found himself wondering how long the damn runway was anyhow. Then at last it lifted. There was little sensation of flying, and he thought the plane must be remaining just a few feet above the ground. Then he looked out. He was sitting by the rearmost of the seven windows, next to the door, and he could see the shrouded lights of the base dropping away. They were airborne.

The sky was overcast, but the clouds were faintly luminous, presumably because the moon had risen beyond them. There was a blue light at the tip of each wing, and Woody could see as his plane moved into formation with others, forming a giant V shape.

The cabin was so noisy that men had to shout into one another's ears to be heard, and conversation soon ceased. They all shifted in their hard seats, trying in vain to get comfortable. Some closed their eyes, but Woody doubted that anyone actually slept.

They were flying low, not much above a thousand feet, and occasionally Woody saw the dull pewter gleam of rivers and lakes. At one point he glimpsed a crowd of people, hundreds of faces all staring up at the planes roaring overhead. Woody knew that more than a thousand aircraft were flying over southern England at the same time, and he realized it must be a remarkable sight. It occurred to him that those people were watching history being made, and he was part of it.

After half an hour they crossed the English beach resorts and were over the sea. For a moment the moon shone through a break in the clouds, and Woody saw the ships. He could hardly believe what he was looking at. It was a floating town, vessels of all sizes sailing in ragged rows like assorted houses in city streets, thousands of them, as far as the eye could see. Before he could call the attention of his comrades to the remarkable sight, the clouds covered the moon again and the vision was gone like a dream.

The planes headed right in a long curve, aiming to hit France to the west of the drop area and then follow the coastline eastward, checking position by terrain features to ensure the paratroopers landed where they should.

The Channel Islands, British though closer to France, had been occupied by Germany at the end of the Battle of France in 1940, and now, as the armada overflew the islands, German antiaircraft guns opened fire. At such a low altitude the Skytrains were terribly vulnerable. Woody realized he could be killed even before he reached the battlefield. He would hate to die pointlessly.

Captain Bonner zigzagged to avoid the flak. Woody was glad he did, but the effect on the men was unfortunate. They all felt airsick, Woody included. Patrick Timothy was the first to succumb, and vomited on the floor. The foul smell made the others feel worse. Sneaky Pete threw up next, then several men all at once. They had stuffed themselves with steak and ice cream, all of which now came back up. The stink was appalling and the floor became disgustingly slippery.

The flight path straightened as they left the islands behind. A few minutes later the French coast appeared. The plane banked and turned left. The copilot got up from his seat and spoke in the ear of Sergeant Defoe, who turned to the platoon and held up ten fingers. Ten minutes to drop.

The plane slowed from its cruising speed of 160 mph to the approximate speed for a parachute jump, about 100 mph.

Suddenly they entered fog. It was heavy enough to blot out the blue light at the tip of the wing. Woody's heart raced. For planes flying in close formation this was very dangerous. How tragic it would be to die in a plane crash, not even in combat. But Bonner could do nothing but fly straight and level and hope for the best. Any change of direction would cause a collision.

The plane left the fog bank as suddenly as it had entered it. To either side, the other planes were still miraculously in formation.

Almost immediately, antiaircraft fire broke out, the flak exploding in deadly blossoms among the serried planes. In these circumstances, Woody knew, the pilot's orders were to maintain speed and fly straight to the target zone. But Bonner defied orders and broke formation. The roar of the engines went to full throttle. He began to zigzag again. The nose of the plane dipped as he tried for more speed. Looking out of the window, Woody saw that many other pilots had been equally undisciplined. They could not control the urge to save their own lives.

The red light went on over the door: four minutes to go.

Woody felt certain the crew had put the light on too soon, desperate to dump their troops and fly to safety. But they had the charts and he could not argue.

He got to his feet. "Stand up and hook!" he yelled. Most of the men could not hear him, but they knew what he was saying. They got up, and each man clipped his static line to the overhead cable, so that he could not be thrown through the door accidentally. The door opened, and the wind roared in. The plane was still going too fast. Jumping at this speed was unpleasant, but that was not the main problem. They would land farther apart, and it would take Woody much longer to find his men on the ground. His approach to his objective would be delayed. He would begin his mission behind schedule. He cursed Bonner.

The pilot continued to bank one way, then the other, dodging flak. The men struggled to keep their footing on a floor that was slimy with vomit.

Woody looked out of the open door. Bonner had lost height while trying to gain speed, and the plane was now at about five hundred feet—too low. There might not be enough time for the parachutes to open fully before the men hit the ground. He hesitated, then beckoned his sergeant forward.

Defoe stood beside him and looked down, then shook his head. He put his mouth to Woody's ear and shouted: "Half our men will break their ankles if we jump at this height. The bazooka carriers will kill themselves."

Woody made a decision.

"Make sure no one jumps!" he yelled at Defoe.

Then he unhooked his static line and went forward, pushing through the double row of standing men, to the flight deck. There were three crew. Yelling at the top of his voice, Woody said: "Climb! Climb!"

Bonner yelled: "Get back there and jump!"

"No one is going to jump at this altitude!" Woody leaned over and pointed at the altimeter, which showed 480 feet. "It's suicide!"

"Get off the flight deck, Lieutenant. That's an order."

Woody was outranked, but he stood his ground. "Not until you gain height."

"We'll be past your target zone if you don't jump now!"

Woody lost his temper. "Climb, you dumb fuck! Climb!"

Bonner looked furious, but Woody did not move. He knew the pilot would not want to return home with a full plane. He would face a military inquiry into what had gone wrong. Bonner had disobeyed too many orders tonight for that. With a curse, he jerked the control lever back. The nose went up immediately, and the aircraft began to gain height and lose speed.

"Satisfied?" Bonner snarled.

"Hell, no." Woody was not going to go aft now and give Bonner the chance to reverse the maneuver. "We jump at a thousand feet."

Bonner went to full throttle. Woody kept his eyes on the altimeter.

When it touched one thousand, he went aft. He pushed through his men, reached the door, looked out, gave the men the thumbs-up, and jumped.

His chute opened immediately. He dropped fast through the air while it spread its dome; then his fall was arrested. Seconds later he hit water. He suffered a split second of panic, fearing that the cowardly Bonner had dropped them all in the sea. Then his feet touched solid ground, or at least soft mud, and he understood that he had come down in a flooded field.

The silk of the parachute fell around him. He struggled out of its folds and unfastened his harness.

Standing in two feet of water, he looked around. This was either a water meadow or, more likely, a field that had been flooded by the Germans to impede an invasion force. He saw no one, enemy or friend, and no animals, either, but the light was poor.

He checked his watch—it was three forty A.M.—then looked at his compass and oriented himself.

Next he took his M1 carbine out of its case and unfolded the stock. He snapped a fifteen-round magazine into the slot, then worked the slide to chamber a round. Finally he rotated the safety lever into the disengaged position.

He reached into a pocket and took out a small tin object like a child's toy. When pressed, it made a distinctive clicking sound. It had been issued to everyone so that they could recognize each other in the dark without resorting to giveaway English passwords.

When he was ready, he looked around again.

Experimentally, he pressed the click twice. After a moment, an answering click came from directly ahead.

He splashed through the water. He smelled vomit. In a low voice he said: "Who's there?"

"Patrick Timothy."

"Lieutenant Dewar here. Follow me."

Timothy had been second to jump, so Woody figured if he continued in the same direction he had a good chance of finding the others.

Fifty yards along he bumped into Mack and Smoking Joe, who had found one another.

They emerged from the water onto a narrow road, and found their first casualties. Lonnie and Tony, with their bazookas in leg bags, had both landed too hard. "I think Lonnie's dead," said Tony. Woody checked: he was right. Lonnie was not breathing. He looked as if he had broken his neck. Tony himself could not move, and Woody thought the man's leg was broken. He gave him a shot of morphine, then dragged him off the road into the next field. Tony would have to wait there for the medics.

Woody ordered Mack and Smoking Joe to hide Lonnie's body, for fear it might lead the Germans to Tony.

He tried to see the landscape around him, straining to recognize something that corresponded to his map. The task seemed impossible, especially in the dark. How was he going to lead these men to the objective if he did not know where he was? The only thing of which he could be reasonably sure was that they had not landed where they were supposed to.

He heard a strange noise, and a moment later he saw a light.

He motioned for the others to duck down.

The paratroopers were not supposed to use flashlights, and French people were subject to a curfew, so the person approaching was probably a German soldier.

In the dim light Woody saw a bicycle.

He stood up and aimed his carbine. He thought of shooting the rider immediately, but could not bring himself to do it. Instead he shouted: "Halt! *Arretez!*"

The cycle stopped. "Hello, Lieut," said the rider, and Woody recognized the voice of Ace Webber.

Woody lowered his weapon. "Where did you get the bike?" he said incredulously.

"Outside a farmhouse," Ace said laconically.

Woody led the group the way Ace had come, figuring that the others were more likely to be in that direction than any other. He looked anxiously for terrain features to match his map, but it was too dark. He felt useless and stupid. He was the officer. He had to solve such problems.

He picked up more of his platoon on the road; then they came to a windmill. Woody decided he could not blunder around any longer, so he went to the mill house and hammered on the door.

An upstairs window opened, and a man said in French: "Who is it?"

"The Americans," Woody said. "*Vive la France!*"

"What do you want?"

"To set you free," Woody said in schoolboy French. "But first I need some help with my map."

The miller laughed and said: "I'm coming down."

A minute later Woody was in the kitchen, spreading his silk map over the table under a bright light. The miller showed him where he was. It was not as bad as Woody had feared. Despite Captain Bonner's panic, they were only four miles northeast of Eglise-des-Soeurs. The miller traced the best route on the map.

A girl of about thirteen crept into the room in a nightdress. "Maman says you're American," she said to Woody.

"That's right, mademoiselle," he said.

"Do you know Gladys Angelus?"

Woody laughed. "As it happens, I did meet her once, at the apartment of a friend's father."

"Is she really, really beautiful?"

"Even more beautiful than she looks in the movies."

"I knew it!"

The miller offered him wine. "No, thanks," said Woody. "Maybe after we've won." The miller kissed him on both cheeks.

Woody went back outside and led his platoon away, heading in the direction of Eglise-des-Soeurs. Including himself, nine of the original eighteen were now together. They had suffered two casualties, Lonnie dead and Tony wounded, and seven more had not yet appeared. His orders were not to spend too much time trying to find everyone. As soon as he had enough men to do the job, he was to proceed to the target.

One of the missing seven showed up right away. Sneaky Pete emerged from a ditch and joined the group with a casual "Hi, gang," as if it was the most natural thing in the world.

"What were you doing in there?" Woody asked him.

"I thought you were German," Pete said. "I was hiding."

Woody had seen the pale gleam of parachute silk in the ditch. Pete must have been hiding there since he landed. He had obviously suffered panic, and curled up in a ball. But Woody pretended to accept his story.

The one Woody really wanted to find was Sergeant Defoe. He was an experienced soldier, and Woody had been planning to rely heavily on him. But he was nowhere to be seen.

They were approaching a crossroads when they heard noises. Woody identified the sound of an engine idling, and two or three voices in conversation. He ordered everyone down on their hands and knees, and the platoon advanced crawling.

Up ahead, he saw that a motorcycle rider had stopped to talk to two men on foot. All three were in uniform. They were speaking German. There was a building at the crossroads, perhaps a small tavern or a bakery.

He decided to wait. Perhaps they would leave. He wanted his group to move silently and unobserved for as long as possible.

After five minutes he ran out of patience. He turned around. "Patrick Timothy!" he hissed.

Someone else said: "Pukey Pat! Scotch wants you."

Timothy crawled forward. He still smelled of vomit, and now it had become his name.

Woody had seen Timothy play baseball, and knew he could throw hard and accurately. "Hit that motorcycle with a grenade," Woody said.

Timothy took a grenade from his pack, pulled the pin, and lobbed it.

There was a clang. One of the men said in German: "What was that?" Then the grenade detonated.

There were two explosions. The first knocked all three Germans to the ground. The second was the motorcycle's fuel tank blowing up, and it sent a starburst of flame that burned the men, leaving a stink of scorched flesh.

"Stay where you are!" Woody shouted to his platoon. He watched the building. Was there anyone inside? During the next five minutes, no one opened a window or a door. Either the place was empty, or the occupants were hiding under their beds.

Woody got to his feet and waved the platoon on. He felt strange as he stepped over the grisly bodies of the three Germans. He had ordered their deaths—men who had mothers and fathers, wives or girlfriends, perhaps sons and daughters. Now each man was an ugly mess of blood and burned flesh. Woody should have felt triumphant. It was his first encounter with the enemy, and he had vanquished them. But he just felt a bit sick.

Past the crossroads, he set a brisk pace, and ordered no talking or smoking. To keep up his strength he ate a bar of D-ration chocolate, which was a bit like builder's putty with sugar added.

After half an hour he heard a car and ordered everyone to hide in the fields. The vehicle was traveling fast, with its headlights on. It was probably German, but the Allies were sending over jeeps by glider, along with antitank guns and other artillery, so it was just possible this was a friendly vehicle. He lay under a hedge and watched it go by.

It went too fast for him to identify it. He wondered whether he should have ordered the platoon to shoot it up. No, he thought, on balance they did better to focus on their mission.

They passed through three hamlets that Woody was able to identify on his map. Dogs barked occasionally but no one came to investigate. Doubtless the French had learned to mind their own business under enemy occupation. It was eerie, creeping along foreign roads in the dark, armed to the teeth, passing quiet houses where people slept unconscious of the deadly firepower outside their windows.

At last they came to the outskirts of Eglise-des-Soeurs. Woody ordered a short rest. They entered a little stand of trees and sat on the ground. They drank from their canteens and ate rations. Woody still would not permit smoking: the glow of a cigarette could be seen from surprisingly far.

The road they were on should lead straight to the bridge, he reckoned. There was no hard information about how the bridge was guarded. Since the Allies had decided it was important, he assumed the Germans thought the same; therefore some security was likely, but it might be anything from one man with a rifle to a whole platoon. Woody could not plan the assault until he saw the target.

After ten minutes he moved them on. The men did not have to be nagged about silence now: they sensed the danger. They trod quietly along the street, past houses and churches and shops, keeping to the sides, peering into the gloomy night, jumping at the least sound. A sudden loud cough from an open bedroom window almost caused Woody to fire his carbine.

Eglise-des-Soeurs was a large village rather than a small town, and Woody saw the silver glint of the river sooner than he expected. He raised a hand for them all to halt. The main street led gently downhill at a slight angle to the bridge, so he had a good view. The waterway was about a hundred feet wide, and the bridge had a single curved span. It must be an old structure, he guessed, because it was so narrow that two cars could not have passed.

The bad news was that there was a pillbox at each end, twin concrete domes with horizontal shooting slits. A pair of sentries patrolled the bridge between the pillboxes. They stood one at each end. The nearer one was speaking through a firing slit, presumably chatting to whomever was inside. Then they both walked to the middle, where they looked over the parapet at the black water flowing beneath. They did not appear very tense, so Woody deduced they had not yet learned that the invasion had begun. On the other hand they were not slacking. They were awake and moving and looking about them with some degree of alertness.

Woody could not guess how many men were inside, nor how they were armed. Were there machine guns behind those slits, or just rifles? It would make a big difference.

Woody wished he had some experience of battle. How was he supposed to deal with this situation? He guessed there must be thousands of men like him, new junior officers who just had to make it up as they went along. If only Sergeant Defoe were here.

The easy way to neutralize a pillbox was to sneak up and put a grenade through one of the slits. A good man could probably crawl to the nearer one unobserved. But Woody needed to take out both at the same time—otherwise the attack on the first would forewarn the occupants of the second.

How could he reach the farther pillbox without being seen by the patrolling sentries?

He sensed his men getting restless. They did not like to think their leader might be unsure what to do next.

"Sneaky Pete," he said. "You'll crawl up to that nearest pillbox and put a grenade through the slit."

Pete looked terrified, but he said: "Yes, sir."

Next, Woody named the two best shots in the platoon. "Smoking Joe and Mack," he said. "Choose one each of the sentries. As soon as Pete deploys his grenade, take the sentries out."

The two men nodded and hefted their weapons.

In the absence of Defoe, he decided to make Ace Webber his deputy. He named four others and said: "Go with Ace. As soon as the shooting starts, run like hell across the bridge and storm the pillbox on the other side. If you're quick enough, you'll catch them napping."

"Yes, sir," said Ace. "The bastards won't know what's hit them." His aggression was masking fear, Woody guessed.

"Everyone not in Ace's group, follow me into the near pillbox."

Woody felt bad about giving Ace and those with him the more dangerous assignment, and himself the relative safety of the nearer pillbox, but it had been drummed into him that an officer must not risk his life unnecessarily, for then he might leave his men leaderless.

They walked toward the bridge, Pete in the lead. This was a dangerous moment. Ten men going along a street together could not remain unnoticed for long even at night. Anyone looking carefully in their direction would sense movement.

If the alarm was raised too soon, Sneaky Pete might not get to the pillbox, and then the platoon would lose the advantage of surprise.

It was a long walk.

Pete reached a corner and stopped. Woody guessed he was waiting for the near sentry to leave his post outside the pillbox and walk to the middle.

The two sharpshooters found cover and settled in.

Woody dropped to one knee and signaled the others to do likewise. They all watched the sentry.

The man took a long pull on his cigarette, dropped it, trod on the end to put it out, and blew a long cloud of smoke. Then he eased himself upright, settled his rifle strap on his shoulder, and started walking.

The sentry on the far side did the same.

Pete ran the next block and came to the end of the street. He got down on his hands and knees and crawled rapidly across the road. He reached the pillbox and stood up.

No one had noticed. The two sentries were still approaching one another.

Peter took out a grenade and pulled the pin. Then he waited a few seconds. Woody guessed he did not want the men inside to have time to throw the grenade out again.

Pete reached around the curve of the dome and gently dropped the grenade inside.

Joe's and Mack's carbines barked. The nearer sentry fell, but the farther one was unhurt. To his credit he did not turn and run, but courageously went down on one knee and unslung his rifle. He was too slow, though: the carbines spoke again, almost simultaneously, and he fell without firing.

Then Pete's grenade exploded inside the nearer pillbox with a muffled thump.

Woody was already running full pelt, and the men were close behind him. Within seconds he reached the bridge.

The pillbox had a low wooden door. Woody flung it open and stepped inside. Three men in German uniforms were dead on the floor.

He moved to a firing slit and looked out. Ace and his four men were haring across the short bridge, shooting at the farther pillbox as they ran. The bridge was only a hundred feet long, but that proved to be fifty feet too much. As they reached the middle, a machine gun opened up. The Americans were trapped in a narrow corridor with no cover. The machine gun clacked insanely and in seconds all five of them had fallen. The gun continued to rake them for several seconds, to be certain they were dead—and, in the process, making sure of the two German sentries, too.

When it stopped, they were all still.

Silence fell.

Beside Woody, Lefty Cameron said: "Jesus Christ Almighty."

Woody could have wept. He had sent ten men to their deaths, five Americans and five Germans, yet he had failed to achieve his objective. The enemy still held the far end of the bridge and could stop Allied forces crossing it.

He had four men left. If they tried again, and ran across the bridge together, they would all be killed. He needed a new plan.

He studied the townscape. What could he do? He wished he had a tank.

He had to act fast. There might well be enemy troops elsewhere in the town. They would have been alerted by the gunfire. They would respond soon. He could deal with them if he had both pillboxes. Otherwise he would be in trouble.

If his men could not cross the bridge, he thought desperately, perhaps they could swim the river. He decided to take a quick look at the bank. "Mack and Smoking Joe," he said. "Fire at the other pillbox. See if you can get a bullet through the slit. Keep them busy while I scout around."

The carbines opened up and he went out through the door.

He was able to shelter behind the near pillbox while he looked over the parapet at the upstream bank. Then he had to scuttle across the road to see the other edge. However, no fire came from the enemy position.

There was no river wall. Instead an earth slope went down to the water. It looked the same on the far bank, he thought, though there was not enough light to be sure. A good swimmer might get across. Under the span of the arch he would not be easy to see from the enemy position. Then he could repeat on the far side what Sneaky Pete had done this side, and grenade the pillbox.

Looking at the structure of the bridge, he had a better idea. Below the level of the parapet was a stone ledge a foot wide. A man with steady nerves could crawl across, all the time remaining out of sight.

He returned to the captured pillbox. The smallest man was Lefty Cameron. He was also feisty, not the type to get the shakes. "Lefty," said Woody. "There's a hidden ledge that runs across the outside of the bridge below the parapet. Probably used by workmen doing repairs. I want you to crawl across and grenade the other pillbox."

"You bet," said Lefty.

It was a gutsy response from someone who had just seen five comrades killed.

Woody turned to Mack and Smoking Joe and said: "Give him cover." They began to shoot.

Lefty said: "What if I fall in?"

"It's only fifteen or twenty feet above the water at most," Woody said. "You'll be fine."

"Okay," said Lefty. He went to the door. "I can't swim, though," he said. Then he was gone.

Woody saw him dart across the road. He looked over the parapet, then straddled it and eased down the other side until he was lost to view.

"Okay," he said to the others. "Hold your fire. He's on his way."

They all stared out. Nothing moved. It was dawn, Woody realized: the town was coming more clearly into view. But none of the inhabitants showed themselves: they knew better. Perhaps German troops were mobilizing in some neighboring street, but he could hear nothing. He realized he was listening for a splash, fearful that Lefty would fall in the river.

A dog came trotting across the bridge, a medium-size mongrel with a curled tail that stuck up jauntily. It sniffed the dead bodies with curiosity, then moved on purposefully, as if it had an important rendezvous elsewhere. Woody watched it pass the far pillbox and continue into the other side of the town.

Dawn meant the main force was now landing on the beaches. Someone had said it was the largest amphibious attack in the history of warfare. He wondered what kind of resistance they were meeting. There was no one more vulnerable than an infantryman loaded with gear splashing through the shallows, the flat beach ahead of him offering a clear field of fire to gunners in the dunes. Woody felt grateful for this concrete pillbox.

Lefty was taking a long time. Had he fallen in the water quietly? Could something else have gone wrong?

Then Woody saw him, a slim khaki form bellying over the parapet of the bridge at the far end. Woody held his breath. Lefty dropped to his knees, crawled to the pillbox, and came upright with his back flat against the curved concrete. With his left hand he drew out a grenade. He pulled the pin, waited a couple of seconds, then reached around and threw the grenade through the slit.

Woody heard the boom of the explosion and saw a flash of lurid light from the firing slits. Lefty raised his arms above his head like a champion.

"Get back under cover, asshole," Woody said, though Lefty could not hear him. There could be a German soldier hiding in a nearby building waiting to avenge the deaths of his friends.

But no shot rang out, and after a brief victory dance Lefty went inside the pillbox, and Woody breathed easier.

However, he was not yet fully secure. At this point a sudden sally by a couple of dozen Germans could win the bridge back. Then it would all have been in vain.

He forced himself to wait another minute to see if any enemy troops showed themselves. Still nothing moved. It was beginning to look as if there were no Germans in Eglise-des-Soeurs other than those manning the bridge: they were probably relieved every twelve hours from a barracks a few miles away.

"Smoking Joe," he said. "Get rid of the dead Germans. Throw them in the river."

Joe dragged the three bodies out of the pillbox and disposed of them, then did the same with the two sentries.

"Pete and Mack," Woody said. "Go over to the other pillbox and join Lefty. Make sure the three of you stay alert. We haven't killed all the Germans in France yet. If you see enemy troops approaching your position, don't hesitate, don't negotiate, just shoot them."

The two men left the pillbox and walked briskly across the bridge to the far end.

There were now three Americans in the far pillbox. If the Germans tried to retake the bridge, they would have a hard time of it, especially in the growing light.

Woody realized that the dead Americans on the bridge would forewarn any approaching enemy forces that the pillboxes had been captured. Otherwise he might retain an element of surprise.

That meant he had to get rid of the American corpses too.

He told the others what he was going to do, then stepped outside.

The morning air tasted fresh and clean.

He walked to the middle of the bridge. He checked each body for a pulse, but there was no doubt: they were all dead.

One by one, he picked up his comrades and dropped them over the parapet.

The last one was Ace Webber. As he hit the water, Woody said: "Rest in peace, buddies." He stood still for a minute with his head bent and his eyes closed.

When he turned around, the sun was coming up.

## vii

The great fear of Allied planners was that the Germans would rapidly reinforce their troops in Normandy, and mount a powerful counterattack that would drive the invaders back into the sea, in a repeat of the Dunkirk disaster.

Lloyd Williams was one of the people trying to make sure that did not happen.

His job helping escaped prisoners get home had low priority after the invasion, and he was now working with the French Resistance.

At the end of May the BBC broadcast coded messages that triggered a campaign of sabotage in German-occupied France. During the first few days of June hundreds of telephone lines were cut, usually in hard-to-find places. Fuel depots were set on fire, roads were blocked by trees, and tires were slashed.

Lloyd was assisting the railwaymen, who were strongly Communist and called themselves Résistance-Fer. For years they had maddened the Nazis with their sly subversion. German troop trains somehow got diverted down obscure branch lines and sent many miles out of their way. Engines broke down unaccountably and carriages were derailed. It was so bad that the occupiers brought railwaymen from Germany to run the system. But the disruption got worse. In the spring of 1944 the railwaymen began to damage their own network. They blew up tracks and sabotaged the heavy lifting cranes required for moving crashed trains.

The Nazis did not take this lying down. Hundreds of railwaymen were executed, and thousands deported to camps. But the campaign escalated, and by D-day rail traffic in some parts of France had come to a halt.

Now, on D-day plus one, Lloyd lay at the summit of an embankment beside the main line to Rouen, capital city of Normandy, at a point where the track entered a tunnel. From his vantage point he could see approaching trains a mile away.

With Lloyd were two others, code-named Legionnaire and Cigare. Legionnaire was leader of the resistance in this neighborhood. Cigare was a railwayman. Lloyd had brought the dynamite. Supplying weaponry was the main role played by the British in the French Resistance.

The three men were half hidden by long grass dotted with wildflowers. It was the kind of place to bring a girl on a fine day such as this, Lloyd thought. Daisy would like it.

A train appeared in the distance. Cigare scrutinized it as it came nearer. He was about sixty, wiry and small, with the lined face of a heavy smoker. When the train was still a quarter of a mile away, he shook his head in negation. This was not the one they were waiting for. The engine passed them, puffing smoke, and entered the tunnel. It was hauling four passenger coaches, all full, carrying a mixture of civilians and uniformed men. Lloyd had more important prey in his sights.

Legionnaire looked at his watch. He had dark skin and a black mustache, and Lloyd guessed he might have a North African somewhere in his ancestry. Now he was jumpy. They were exposed here, in the open air and in daylight. The longer they stayed, the higher the chance they would be spotted. "How much longer?" he said worriedly.

Cigare shrugged. "We'll see."

Lloyd said in French: "You can leave now, if you wish. Everything is set."

Legionnaire did not reply. He was not going to miss the action. For the sake of his prestige and authority he had to be able to say: "I was there."

Cigare tensed, peering into the distance, the skin around his eyes creasing with the effort. "So," he said cryptically. He raised himself to his knees.

Lloyd could hardly see the train, let alone identify it, but Cigare was alert. It was moving a lot faster than the previous one, Lloyd could tell. As it came closer, he observed that it was longer, too: twenty-four carriages or more, he thought.

"This is it," said Cigare.

Lloyd's pulse quickened. If Cigare was right, this was a German troop train carrying more than a thousand officers and men to the Normandy battlefield—perhaps the first of many such trains. It was Lloyd's job to make sure neither this train nor any following passed through the tunnel.

Then he saw something else. A plane was tracking the train. As he watched, the aircraft matched course with the train and began to lose height.

The plane was British.

Lloyd recognized it as a Hawker Typhoon, nicknamed a Tiffy, a one-man fighter-bomber. Tiffies were often given the dangerous mission of penetrating deep behind enemy lines to harass communications. There was a brave man at the controls, Lloyd thought.

But this formed no part of Lloyd's plan. He did not want the train to be wrecked before it reached the tunnel.

"Shit," he said.

The Tiffy fired a machine-gun burst at the carriages.

Legionnaire said: "But what is this?"

Lloyd replied in English: "Fucked if I know."

He could see now that the engine was hauling a mixture of passenger coaches and cattle trucks. However, the cattle trucks probably also contained men.

The plane, traveling faster, strafed the carriages as it overhauled the train. It had four belt-fed 20 mm cannon, and they made a fearsome rattling sound that could be heard over the roar of the plane's engine and the energetic puffing of the train. Lloyd could not help feeling sorry for the trapped soldiers, unable to get out of the way of the lethal hail of bullets. He wondered why the pilot did not fire his rockets. They were highly destructive against trains and cars, though difficult to fire accurately. Perhaps they had been used up in an earlier encounter.

Some of the Germans bravely put their heads out of the windows and fired pistols and rifles at the plane, with no effect.

But Lloyd now saw a light antiaircraft battery emplaced on a flatbed car immediately behind the engine. Two gunners were hastily deploying the big gun. It swiveled on its base and the barrel lifted to aim at the British plane.

The pilot did not appear to have seen it, for he held his course, rounds from his cannon tearing through the roofs of the carriages as he overhauled them.

The big gun fired and missed.

Lloyd wondered if he knew the flyer. There were only about five thousand pilots on active service in the UK at any one time. Quite a lot of them had been to Daisy's parties. Lloyd thought of Hubert St. John, a brilliant Cambridge graduate with whom he had been reminiscing about student days a few weeks ago; of Dennis Chaucer, a West Indian from Trinidad who complained bitterly about tasteless English food, especially the mashed potatoes that seemed to be served with every meal; and of Brian Mantel, an amiable Australian he had brought across the Pyrenees on his last trip. The brave man in the Tiffy could easily be someone Lloyd had met.

The antiaircraft gun fired again, and missed again.

Either the pilot still had not seen the gun, or he felt it could not hit him, for he took no evasive action, but continued to fly dangerously low and wreak carnage on the troop train.

The engine was just a few seconds from the tunnel when the plane was hit.

Flame flared from the plane's engine, and black smoke billowed. Too late, the pilot veered away from the railway track.

The train entered the tunnel, and the carriages flashed past Lloyd's position. He saw that every one was packed full with dozens, hundreds of German soldiers.

The Tiffy flew directly at Lloyd. For a moment he thought it would crash where he lay. He was already flat on the ground, but he stupidly put his hands over his head, as if that could protect him.

The Tiffy roared by a hundred feet above him.

Then Legionnaire pressed the plunger of the detonator.

There was a roar like thunder inside the tunnel as the track blew up, followed by a terrible screeching of tortured steel as the train crashed.

At first the carriages full of soldiers continued to flash by, but a second later their charge was arrested. The ends of two linked carriages rose in the air, forming an inverted V. Lloyd heard the men inside screaming. All the carriages came off the rails and tumbled like dropped matchsticks around the dark O of the tunnel's mouth. Iron crumpled like paper, and broken glass rained on the three saboteurs watching from the top of the embankment. They were in danger of being killed by their own explosion, and without a word they all leaped to their feet and ran.

By the time they had reached a safe distance, it was all over. Smoke was billowing out of the tunnel: in the unlikely event that any men in there had survived the crash, they would burn to death.

Lloyd's plan was a success. Not only had he killed hundreds of enemy troops and wrecked a train, he had also blocked a main railway line. Crashes in tunnels took weeks to clear. He had made it much more difficult for the Germans to reinforce their defenses in Normandy.

He was horrified.

He had seen death and destruction in Spain, but nothing like this. And he had caused it.

There was another crash, and when he looked in the direction of the sound, he saw that the Tiffy had hit the ground. It was burning, but the fuselage had not broken up. The pilot might be alive.

He ran toward the plane, and Cigare and Legionnaire followed.

The downed aircraft lay on its belly. One wing had snapped in half.

Smoke came from the single engine. The Perspex dome was blackened by soot and Lloyd could not see the pilot.

He stepped on the wing and unfastened the hood catch. Cigare did the same on the other side. Together, they slid the dome back on its rails.

The pilot was unconscious. He wore a helmet and goggles, and an oxygen mask over his nose and mouth. Lloyd could not tell whether it was someone he knew.

He wondered where the oxygen tank was, and whether it had yet burst.

Legionnaire had a similar thought. "We have to get him out before the plane blows up," he said.

Lloyd reached inside and unfastened the safety harness. Then he put his hands under the pilot's arms and pulled. The man was completely limp. Lloyd had no way of knowing what his injuries might be. He was not even sure the man was alive.

He dragged the pilot out of the cockpit, then got him over his shoulder in a fireman's lift and carried him a safe distance from the burning wreckage. As gently as he could, he laid the man on the ground faceup.

He heard a noise that was a cross between a whoosh and a thump, and looked back to see that the whole plane was ablaze.

He bent over the pilot and carefully removed the goggles and the oxygen mask, revealing a face that was shockingly familiar.

The pilot was Boy Fitzherbert.

And he was breathing.

Lloyd wiped blood from Boy's nose and mouth.

Boy opened his eyes. At first there seemed to be no intelligence behind them. Then, after a minute, his expression altered and he said: "You."

"We blew up the train," Lloyd said.

Boy seemed unable to move anything but his eyes and mouth. "Small world," he said.

"Isn't it?"

Cigare said: "Who is he?"

Lloyd hesitated, then said: "My brother."

"My God."

Boy's eyes closed.

Lloyd said to Legionnaire: "We have to bring a doctor."

Legionnaire shook his head. "We must get out of here. The Germans will be coming to investigate the train crash within minutes."

Lloyd knew he was right. "We'll have to take him with us."

Boy opened his eyes and said: "Williams."

"What is it, Boy?"

Boy seemed to grin. "You can marry the bitch now," he said.

Then he died.

## viii

Daisy cried when she heard. Boy had been a rotter, and treated her badly, but she had loved him once, and he had taught her a lot about sex; she felt sad that he had been killed.

His brother, Andy, was now a viscount and heir to the earldom; Andy's wife, May, was a viscountess; and Daisy's name, according to the elaborate rules of the aristocracy, was the Dowager Viscountess Aberowen—until she married Lloyd, when she would be relieved to become plain Mrs. Williams.

However, that might be a long time coming, even now. Over the summer, hopes of a quick end to the war came to nothing. A plot by German army officers to kill Hitler on July 20 failed. The German army was in full retreat on the eastern front, and the Allies took Paris in August, but Hitler was determined to fight on to the terrible end. Daisy had no idea when she would see Lloyd, let alone marry him.

One Wednesday in September, when she went to spend the evening in Aldgate, she was greeted by a jubilant Eth Leckwith. "Great news!" Ethel said when Daisy walked into the kitchen. "Lloyd has been selected as prospective parliamentary candidate for Hoxton!"

Lloyd's sister, Millie, was there with her two children, Lennie and Pammie. "Isn't it wonderful?" she said. "He'll be prime minister, I bet."

"Yes," said Daisy, and she sat down heavily.

"Well, I can see you're not happy about that," said Ethel. "As my friend Mildred would say, it went down like a cup of cold sick. What's the matter?"

"It's just that having me as a wife isn't going to help him get elected." It was because she loved him so much that she felt so bad. How could she blight his prospects? But how could she give him up? When she thought like this, her heart felt heavy and life seemed desolate.

"Because you're an heiress?" said Ethel.

"Not just that. Before Boy died, he told me Lloyd would never get elected with an ex-Fascist as his wife." She looked at Ethel, who always told the truth, even when it hurt. "He was right, wasn't he?"

"Not entirely," Ethel said. She put the kettle on for tea, then sat opposite Daisy at the kitchen table. "I'm not going to say it doesn't matter. But I don't think you should despair."

You're just like me, Daisy thought. You say what you think. No wonder he loves me: I'm a younger version of his mother!

Millie said: "Love conquers all, doesn't it?" She noticed that four-year-old Lennie was hitting two-year-old Pammie with a wooden soldier. "Don't bash your sister!" she said. Turning back to Daisy, she went on: "And my brother loves you to bits. I don't think he's ever loved anyone else, to tell you the truth."

"I know," said Daisy. She wanted to cry. "But he's determined to change the world, and I can't bear the thought that I'm standing in his way."

Ethel took the crying two-year-old onto her knee, and the toddler calmed down immediately. "I'll tell you what to do," she said to Daisy. "Be prepared for questions, and expect hostility, but don't dodge the issue and don't hide your past."

"What should I say?"

"You might say you were fooled by Fascism, as millions of others were, but you drove an ambulance in the Blitz, and you hope you've paid your dues. Work out the exact words with Lloyd. Be confident, be your irresistibly charming self, and don't let it get you down."

"Will it work?"

Ethel hesitated. "I don't know," she said after a pause. "I really don't. But you have to try."

"It would be awful if he had to give up what he loves most for my sake. Something like that could destroy a marriage."

Daisy was half hoping Ethel would deny this, but she did not. "I don't know," she said again.

# CHAPTER NINETEEN

# 1945 (I)

**W**oody Dewar got used to the crutches quickly.

He was wounded at the end of 1944, in Belgium, in the Battle of the Bulge. The Allies pushing toward the German border had been surprised by a powerful counterattack. Woody and others of the 101st Airborne Division had held out at a vital crossroads town called Bastogne. When the Germans sent a formal letter demanding surrender, General McAuliffe sent back a one-word message that became famous: "Nuts!"

Woody's right leg was smashed up by machine-gun bullets on Christmas Day. It hurt like hell. Even worse, it was a month before he got out of the besieged town and into a real hospital.

His bones would mend, and he might even lose the limp, but his leg would never again be strong enough for parachuting.

The Battle of the Bulge was the last offensive of Hitler's army in the west. After that they would never counterattack again.

Woody returned to civilian life, which meant he could live at his parents' apartment in Washington and enjoy being fussed over by his mother. When the plaster cast came off, he went back to work at his father's office.

On Thursday, April 12, 1945, he was in the Capitol building, the home of the Senate and the House of Representatives, hobbling slowly through the basement, talking to his father about refugees. "We think about twenty-one million people in Europe have been driven from their homes," said Gus. "The United Nations Relief and Rehabilitation Administration is ready to help them."

"I guess that will start any day now," said Woody. "The Red Army is almost in Berlin."

"And the U.S. Army is only fifty miles away."

"How much longer can Hitler hold out?"

"A sane man would have surrendered by now."

Woody lowered his voice. "Somebody told me the Russians found what seems to have been an extermination camp. The Nazis killed hundreds of people a day there. A place called Auschwitz, in Poland."

Gus nodded grimly. "It's true. The public don't know yet, but they'll find out sooner or later."

"Someone should be put on trial for that."

"The UN War Crimes Commission has been at work for a couple of years now, making lists of war criminals and collecting evidence. Someone will be put on trial, provided we can keep the United Nations going after the war."

"Of course we can," Woody said indignantly. "Roosevelt campaigned on that basis last year, and he won the election. The United Nations conference opens in San Francisco in a couple of weeks." San Francisco had a special significance for Woody, because Bella Hernandez lived there, but he had not yet told his father about her. "The American people want to see international cooperation, so that we never have another war like this one. Who could be against that?"

"You'd be surprised. Look, most Republicans are decent men who simply have a view of the world that is different from ours. But there is a hard core of fucking nutcases."

Woody was startled. His father rarely swore.

"The types who planned an insurrection against Roosevelt in the thirties," Gus went on. "Businessmen like Henry Ford, who thought

Hitler was a good strong anti-Communist leader. They sign up for right-wing groups such as America First."

Woody could not remember him speaking this angrily before.

"If these fools have their way, there will be a third world war even worse than the first two," Gus said. "I've lost a son to war, and if I ever have a grandson, I don't want to lose him, too."

Woody suffered a stab of grief: Joanne would have given Gus grandchildren, if she had lived.

Right now Woody was not even dating, so grandchildren were a distant prospect—unless he could track down Bella in San Francisco . . .

"We can't do anything about complete idiots," Gus went on. "But perhaps we can deal with Senator Vandenberg."

Arthur Vandenberg was a Republican from Michigan, a conservative, and an opponent of Roosevelt's New Deal. He was on the Senate Foreign Relations Committee with Gus.

"He's our greatest danger," Gus said. "He may be self-important and vain, but he commands respect. The president has been wooing him, and he's come around to our point of view, but he could backslide."

"Why would he do that?"

"He's strongly anti-Communist."

"Nothing wrong with that. We are, too."

"Yes, but Arthur is kind of rigid about it. He'll get riled if we do anything he thinks is kowtowing to Moscow."

"Such as?"

"God knows what kind of compromises we might have to make in San Francisco. We've already agreed to admit Belorussia and the Ukraine as separate states, which is just a way of giving Moscow three votes in the General Assembly. We have to keep the Soviets on board—but if we go too far, Arthur could turn against the whole United Nations project. Then the Senate may refuse to ratify it, exactly the way they rejected the League of Nations in 1919."

"So our job in San Francisco is to keep the Soviets happy without offending Senator Vandenberg."

"Exactly."

They heard running footsteps, an unusual sound in the dignified hallways of the Capitol. They both looked around. Woody was surprised to see the vice president, Harry Truman, running through the hallway. He was dressed normally, in a gray double-breasted suit and a polka-dot tie, though he had no hat. He seemed to have lost his normal escort of aides and Secret Service guards. He was running steadily, breathing hard, not looking at anyone, going somewhere in a terrific hurry.

Woody and Gus watched in astonishment. So did everyone else.

When Truman disappeared around a corner, Woody said: "What the heck . . . ?"

Gus said: "I think the president must have died."


## ii

Volodya Peshkov entered Germany in a ten-wheeler Studebaker US6 army truck. Made in South Bend, Indiana, the truck had been carried by rail to Baltimore, shipped across the Atlantic and around the Cape of Good Hope to the Persian Gulf, then sent by train from Persia to central Russia. Volodya knew it was one of two hundred thousand Studebaker trucks given to the Red Army by the American government. The Russians liked them: they were tough and reliable. The men said the letters "USA" stenciled on the side stood for *Ubit Sukina syna Adolf,* which meant "Kill that son of a bitch Adolf."

They also liked the food the Americans were sending, especially the cans of compressed meat called Spam, strangely bright pink in color but gloriously fatty.

Volodya had been posted to Germany because the intelligence he was getting from spies in Berlin was now not as up-to-date as information that could be gained by interviewing German prisoners of war. His fluent German made him a first-class frontline interrogator.

When he crossed the border, he had seen a Soviet government poster that said: RED ARMY SOLDIER: YOU ARE NOW ON GERMAN SOIL. THE

HOUR OF REVENGE HAS STRUCK! It was among the milder pieces of propaganda. The Kremlin had been whipping up hatred of Germans for some time, believing it would make soldiers fight harder. Political commissars had calculated—or said they had—the number of men killed in battle, the number of houses torched, the number of civilians murdered for being Communists or Slavs or Jews, in every village and town overrun by the German army. Many frontline soldiers could quote the figures for their own neighborhoods, and were eager to do the same kind of damage in Germany.

The Red Army had reached the river Oder, which snaked north-south across Prussia, the last barrier before Berlin. A million Soviet soldiers were within fifty miles of the capital, poised to strike. Volodya was with the 5th Shock Army. Waiting for the fighting to begin, he was studying the army newspaper, *Red Star*.

What he read horrified him.

The hate propaganda went further than anything he had read before. "If you have not killed at least one German a day, you have wasted that day," he read. "If you are waiting for the fighting, kill a German before combat. If you kill one German, kill another—there is nothing more amusing for us than a heap of German corpses. Kill the German—this is your old mother's prayer. Kill the German—this is what your children beseech you to do. Kill the German—this is the cry of your Russian earth. Do not waver. Do not let up. Kill."

It was a bit sickening, Volodya thought. But worse was implied. The writer made light of looting: "German women are only losing fur coats and silver spoons that were stolen in the first place." And there was a sidelong joke about rape: "Soviet soldiers do not refuse the compliments of German women."

Soldiers were not the most civilized of men in the first place. The way the invading Germans had behaved in 1941 had enraged all Russians. The government was fueling their wrath with talk of revenge. And now the army newspaper was making it clear they could do anything they liked to the defeated Germans.

It was a recipe for Armageddon.

Erik von Ulrich was consumed by a yearning that the war should be over.

With his friend Hermann Braun and their boss Dr. Weiss, Erik set up a field hospital in a small Protestant church; then they sat in the nave with nothing to do but wait for the horse-drawn ambulances to arrive loaded with horribly torn and burned men.

The German army had reinforced Seelow Heights, overlooking the Oder River where it passed closest to Berlin. Erik's aid station was in a village a mile back from the line.

Dr. Weiss, who had a friend in army intelligence, said there were 110,000 Germans defending Berlin against a million Soviets. With his usual sarcasm he said: "But our morale is high, and Adolf Hitler is the greatest genius in military history, so we are certain to win."

There was no hope, but German soldiers were still fighting fiercely. Erik believed this was because of the stories filtering back about how the Red Army behaved. Prisoners were killed, homes were looted and wrecked, women were raped and nailed to barn doors. The Germans believed they were defending their own families from Communist brutality. The Kremlin's hate propaganda was backfiring.

Erik was looking forward to defeat. He longed for the killing to stop. He just wanted to go home.

He would have his wish soon—or he would be dead.

Sleeping on a wooden pew, Erik was awakened at three o'clock in the morning on Monday, April 16, by the Russian guns. He had heard artillery bombardments before, but this was ten times as loud as anything in his experience. For the men on the front line it must have been literally deafening.

The wounded started to arrive at dawn, and the team went wearily to work, amputating limbs, setting broken bones, extracting bullets, and cleaning and bandaging wounds. They were short of everything from drugs to clean water, and they gave morphine only to those who were screaming in agony.

Men who could still walk and hold a gun were sent back to the line.

The German defenders held out longer than Dr. Weiss expected. At the end of the first day they were still in position, and as darkness fell, the rush of wounded slowed. The medical unit got some sleep that night.

Early on the next day Werner Franck was brought in, his right wrist horribly crushed.

He was a captain now. He had been in charge of a section of the line with thirty 88 mm flak guns. "We only had eight shells for each gun," he said while Dr. Weiss's clever fingers worked slowly and meticulously to set his smashed bones. "Our orders were to fire seven at the Russian tanks, then use the eighth to destroy our own gun so that it could not be used by the Reds." He had been standing by an 88 when it suffered a direct hit from the Soviet artillery and turned over on him. "I was lucky it was only my hand," he said. "It might have been my damn head."

When his wrist had been taped up, he said to Erik: "Have you heard from Carla?"

Erik knew that his sister and Werner were now a couple. "I haven't had any letters for weeks."

"Nor me. I hear things are pretty grim in Berlin. I hope she's all right."

"I worry, too," said Erik.

Surprisingly, the Germans held the Seelow Heights for another day and night.

The dressing station got no warning that the line had collapsed. They were triaging a fresh cartload of wounded when seven or eight Soviet soldiers crashed into the church. One fired a machine-gun burst at the vaulted ceiling and Erik threw himself to the ground, as did everyone else capable of moving.

Seeing that no one was armed, the Russians relaxed. They went around the room taking watches and rings from those who had them. Then they left.

Erik wondered what would happen next. This was the first time he had been trapped behind enemy lines. Should they abandon the field hospital and try to catch up with their retreating army? Or were their patients safer here?

Dr. Weiss was decisive. "Carry on with your work, everyone," he said.

A few minutes later a Soviet soldier came in with a comrade over his shoulder. Pointing his gun at Weiss, he spoke a rapid stream of Russian. He was in a panic, and his friend was covered in blood.

Weiss replied calmly. In halting Russian he said: "No need for the gun. Put your friend on this table."

The soldier did so, and the team went to work. The soldier kept his rifle pointed at the doctor.

Later in the day, the German patients were marched or carried out and put into the back of a truck, which drove away east. Erik watched Werner Franck disappear, a prisoner of war. As a boy, Erik had often been told the story of his uncle Robert, who had been imprisoned by the Russians during the First World War, and had walked home from Siberia, a journey of four thousand miles. Erik wondered now where Werner would end up.

More wounded Russians were brought in, and the Germans took care of them as they would have for their own men.

Later, as Erik fell into an exhausted sleep, he realized that now he, too, was a prisoner of war.

### iv

As the Allied armies closed in on Berlin, the victorious countries began squabbling among themselves at the United Nations conference in San Francisco. Woody would have found it depressing, except that he was more interested in trying to reconnect with Bella Hernandez.

She had been on his mind all through the D-day invasion and the fighting in France, his time in the hospital, and his convalescence. A year ago she had been at the end of her period at Oxford University and planning to do a doctorate at Berkeley, right here in San Francisco. She would probably be living at her parents' home in Pacific Heights, unless she had an apartment near the campus.

Unfortunately, he was having trouble getting a message to her.

His letters were not answered. When he called the number listed in the phone book, a middle-aged woman who he suspected was Bella's mother said with icy courtesy: "She's not at home right now. May I give her a message?" Bella never called back.

She probably had a serious boyfriend. If so he wanted her to tell him. But perhaps her mother was intercepting her mail and not passing on messages.

He should probably give up. He might be making a fool of himself. But that was not his way. He recalled his long, stubborn courtship of Joanne. There seems to be a pattern here, he thought; is it something about me?

Meanwhile, every morning he went with his father to the penthouse at the top of the Fairmont Hotel, where Secretary of State Edward Stettinius held a briefing for the American team at the conference. Stettinius had taken over from Cordell Hull, who was in the hospital. The USA also had a new president, Harry Truman, who had been sworn in on the death of the great Franklin D. Roosevelt. It was a pity, Gus Dewar observed, that at such a crucial moment in world history the United States should be led by two inexperienced newcomers.

Things had begun badly. President Truman had clumsily offended Soviet foreign minister Molotov at a preconference meeting at the White House. Consequently Molotov arrived in San Francisco in a foul mood. He announced he was going home unless the conference agreed immediately to admit Belorussia, Ukraine, and Poland.

No one wanted the USSR to pull out. Without the Soviets, the United Nations were not the United Nations. Most of the American delegation were in favor of compromising with the Communists, but the bow-tied Senator Vandenberg prissily insisted that nothing should be done under pressure from Moscow.

One morning when Woody had a couple of hours to spare, he went to Bella's parents' house.

The swanky neighborhood where they lived was not far from the

Fairmont Hotel on Nob Hill, but Woody was still walking with a cane, so he took a taxi. Their home was a yellow-painted Victorian mansion on Gough Street. The woman who came to the door was too well dressed to be a maid. She gave him a lopsided smile just like Bella's: she had to be the mother. He said politely: "Good morning, ma'am. I'm Woody Dewar. I met Bella Hernandez in London last year and I'd sure like to see her again, if I may."

The smile disappeared. She gave him a long look and said: "So you're him."

Woody had no idea what she was talking about.

"I'm Caroline Hernandez, Isabel's mother," she said. "You'd better come in."

"Thank you."

She did not offer to shake hands, and she was clearly hostile, though there was no clue as to why. However, he was inside the house.

Mrs. Hernandez led Woody into a large, pleasant parlor with a breathtaking ocean view. She pointed to a chair, indicating that he should sit down with a gesture that was barely polite. She sat opposite him and gave him another hard look. "How much time did you spend with Bella in England?" she asked.

"Just a few hours. But I've been thinking about her ever since."

There was another pregnant pause; then she said: "When she went to Oxford, Bella was engaged to be married to Victor Rolandson, a splendid young man she has known most of her life. The Rolandsons are old friends of my husband's and mine—or, at least, they were, until Bella came home and broke off the engagement abruptly."

Woody's heart leaped with hope.

"She would only say she had realized she did not love Victor. I guessed she'd met someone else, and now I know who."

Woody said: "I had no idea she was engaged."

"She was wearing a diamond ring that was pretty hard to miss. Your poor powers of observation have caused a tragedy."

"I'm very sorry," Woody said. Then he told himself to stop being a pussy. "Or rather, I'm not," he said. "I'm very glad she's broken off her engagement, because I think she's absolutely wonderful and I want her for myself."

Mrs. Hernandez did not like that. "You're mighty fresh, young man."

Woody suddenly felt resentful of her condescension. "Mrs. Hernandez, you used the word *tragedy* just now. My fiancée, Joanne, died in my arms at Pearl Harbor. My brother, Chuck, was killed by machine-gun fire on the beach at Bougainville. On D-day I sent Ace Webber and four other young Americans to their deaths for the sake of a bridge in a one-horse town called Eglise-des-Soeurs. I know what tragedy is, ma'am, and it's not a broken engagement."

She was taken aback. He guessed young people did not often stand up to her. She did not reply, but looked a little pale. After a moment she got up and left the room without explanation. Woody was not sure what she expected him to do, but he had not yet seen Bella so he sat tight.

Five minutes later, Bella came in.

Woody stood up, his pulse quickening. Just the sight of her made him smile. She wore a plain pale yellow dress that set off her lustrous dark hair and coffee skin. She would always look good in dramatically simple clothing, he guessed, just like Joanne. He wanted to put his arms around her and crush her soft body to his own, but he waited for a sign from her.

She looked anxious and uncomfortable. "What are you doing here?" she said.

"I came looking for you."

"Why?"

"Because I can't get you out of my mind."

"We don't even know each other."

"Let's put that right, starting today. Will you have dinner with me?"

"I don't know."

He crossed the room to where she stood.

She was startled to see him using the walking stick. "What happened to you?"

"My knee got shot up in France. It's getting better, slowly."

"I'm so sorry."

"Bella, I think you're wonderful. I believe you like me. We're both free of commitments. What's worrying you?"

She gave that lopsided grin that he liked so much. "I guess I'm embarrassed. About what I did, that night in London."

"Is that all?"

"It was a lot, for a first date."

"That kind of thing went on all the time. Not to me, necessarily, but I heard about it. You thought I was going to die."

She nodded. "I've never done anything like that, not even with Victor. I don't know what came over me. And in a public park! I feel like a whore."

"I know exactly what you are," Woody said. "You're a smart, beautiful woman with a big heart. So why don't we forget that mad moment in London, and start getting to know one another like the respectable well-brought-up young people that we are?"

She began to soften. "Can we, really?"

"You bet."

"Okay."

"I'll pick you up at seven?"

"Okay."

That was an exit line, but he hesitated. "I can't tell you how glad I am that I found you again," he said.

She looked him in the eye for the first time. "Oh, Woody, so am I," she said. "So glad!" Then she put her arms around his waist and hugged him.

It was what he had been longing for. He embraced her and put his face into her wonderful hair. They stayed like that for a long minute.

At last she pulled away. "I'll see you at seven," she said.

"You bet."

He left the house in a cloud of happiness.

He went from there straight to a meeting of the steering committee in the Veterans Building next to the opera house. There were forty-six members around the long table, with aides such as Gus Dewar sitting behind them. Woody was an aide to an aide, and sat up against the wall.

The Soviet foreign minister, Molotov, made the first speech. He was not impressive to look at, Woody reflected. With his receding hair, neat mustache, and glasses, he looked like a store clerk, which was what his father had been. But he had survived a long time in Bolshevik politics. A friend of Stalin's since before the revolution, he was the architect of the Nazi-Soviet pact of 1939. He was a hard worker, and was nicknamed Stone Arse because of the long hours he spent at his desk.

He proposed that Belorussia and Ukraine be admitted as original members of the United Nations. These two Soviet republics had borne the brunt of the Nazi invasion, he pointed out, and each had contributed more than a million men to the Red Army. It had been argued that they were not fully independent of Moscow, but the same argument could be applied to Canada and Australia, dominions of the British Empire that had each been given separate membership.

The vote was unanimous. It had all been fixed up in advance, Woody knew. The Latin American countries had threatened to dissent unless Hitler-supporting Argentina was admitted, and that concession had been granted to secure their votes.

Then came a bombshell. The Czech foreign minister, Jan Masaryk, stood up. He was a famous liberal and anti-Nazi who had been on the cover of *Time* magazine in 1944. He proposed that Poland should also be admitted to the UN.

The Americans were refusing to admit Poland until Stalin permitted elections there, and Masaryk as a democrat should have supported that stand, especially as he, too, was trying to create a democracy with Stalin looking over his shoulder. Molotov must have put terrific pressure on Masaryk to get him to betray his ideals in this way. And, indeed, when Masaryk sat down, he wore the expression of one who has eaten something disgusting.

Gus Dewar also looked grim. The prearranged compromises over Belorussia, Ukraine, and Argentina should have ensured that this session went smoothly. But now Molotov had thrown them a curve ball.

Senator Vandenberg, sitting with the American contingent, was outraged. He took out a pen and notepad and began writing furiously.

After a minute he tore the sheet off, beckoned Woody, gave him the note, and said: "Take that to the secretary of state."

Woody went to the table, leaned over Stettinius's shoulder, put the note in front of him, and said: "From Senator Vandenberg, sir."

"Thank you."

Woody returned to his chair up against the wall. My part in history, he thought. He had glanced at the note as he handed it over. Vandenberg had drafted a short, passionate speech rejecting the Czech proposal. Would Stettinius follow the senator's lead?

If Molotov got his way over Poland, then Vandenberg might sabotage the United Nations in the Senate. But if Stettinius took Vandenberg's line now, Molotov might walk out and go home, which would kill off the UN just as effectively.

Woody held his breath.

Stettinius stood up with Vandenberg's note in his hand. "We've just honored our Yalta engagements in behalf of Russia," he said. He meant the commitment made by the USA to support Belorussia and Ukraine. "There are other Yalta obligations which equally require allegiance." He was using the words Vandenberg had written. "One calls for a new and representative Polish provisional government."

There was a murmur of shock around the room. Stettinius was going up against Molotov. Woody glanced at Vandenberg. He was purring.

"Until that happens," Stettinius went on, "the conference cannot, in good conscience, recognize the Lublin government." He looked directly at Molotov and quoted Vandenberg's exact words. "It would be a sordid exhibition of bad faith."

Molotov looked incandescent.

The British foreign secretary, Anthony Eden, unfolded his lanky figure and stood up to support Stettinius. His tone was faultlessly courteous, but his words were scathing. "My government has no way of knowing whether the Polish people support their provisional government," he said, "because our Soviet allies refuse to let British observers into Poland."

Woody sensed the meeting turning against Molotov. The Russian clearly had the same impression. He was conferring with his aides loudly enough for Woody to hear the fury in his voice. But would he walk out?

The Belgian foreign minister, bald and podgy with a double chin, proposed a compromise, a motion expressing the hope that the new Polish government might be organized in time to be represented here in San Francisco before the end of the conference.

Everyone looked at Molotov. He was being offered a face-saver. But would he accept it?

He still looked angry. However, he gave a slight but unmistakable nod of assent.

And the crisis was over.

Well, Woody thought, two victories in one day. Things are looking up.

## V

Carla went out to queue for water.

There had been no water in the taps for two days. Luckily, Berlin's housewives had discovered that every few blocks there were old-fashioned street pumps, long disused, connected to underground wells. They were rusty and creaky but, amazingly, they still worked. So every morning now the women stood in line, holding their buckets and jugs.

The air raids had stopped, presumably because the enemy was on the point of entering the city. But it was still dangerous to be on the street, because the Red Army's artillery was shelling. Carla was not sure why they bothered. Much of the city had gone. Whole blocks and even larger areas had been completely flattened. All utilities were cut off. No trains or buses ran. Thousands were homeless, perhaps millions. The city was one huge refugee camp. But the shelling went on. Most people spent all day in their cellars or in public air raid shelters, but they had to come out for water.

On the radio, shortly before the electricity went off permanently, the

BBC had announced that the Sachsenhausen concentration camp had been liberated by the Red Army. Sachsenhausen was north of Berlin, so clearly the Soviets, coming from the east, were encircling the city instead of marching straight in. Carla's mother, Maud, deduced that the Russians wanted to keep out the American, British, French, and Canadian forces rapidly approaching from the west. She had quoted Lenin: "Who controls Berlin, controls Germany; and who controls Germany, controls Europe."

Yet the German army had not given up. Outnumbered, outgunned, short of ammunition and fuel, and half-starved, they slogged on. Again and again their leaders hurled them at overwhelming enemy forces, and again and again they obeyed orders, fought with spirit and courage, and died in their hundreds of thousands. Among them were the two men Carla loved: her brother, Erik, and her boyfriend, Werner. She had no idea where they were fighting or even whether they were alive.

Carla had wound up the spy ring. The fighting was deteriorating into chaos. Battle plans meant little. Secret intelligence from Berlin was of small value to the conquering Soviets. It was no longer worth the risk. The spies had burned their codebooks and hidden their radio transmitters in the rubble of bombed buildings. They had agreed never to speak of their work. They had been brave, they had shortened the war, and they had saved lives, but it was too much to expect the defeated German people to see things that way. Their courage would remain forever secret.

While Carla waited her turn at the tap, a Hitler Youth tank-hunting squad went past, heading east, toward the fighting. There were two men in their fifties and a dozen teenage boys, all on bicycles. Strapped to the front of each bicycle were two of the new one-shot antitank weapons called *Panzerfäuste.* The uniforms were too large for the boys, and their oversize helmets would have looked comical if their plight had not been so pathetic. They were off to fight the Red Army.

They were going to die.

Carla looked away as they passed: she did not want to remember their faces.

As she was filling her bucket, the woman behind her in line, Frau Reichs, spoke to her quietly, so that no one else could hear: "You're a friend of the doctor's wife, aren't you?"

Carla tensed. Frau Reichs was obviously talking about Hannelore Rothmann. The doctor had disappeared along with the mental patients from the Jewish Hospital. Hannelore's son, Rudi, had thrown away his yellow star and joined those Jews living clandestinely, called U-boats in Berlin slang. But Hannelore, not herself Jewish, was still at the old house.

For twelve years a question such as the one just asked—are you a friend of a Jew's wife?—had been an accusation. What was it today? Carla did not know. Frau Reichs was only a nodding acquaintance: she could not be trusted.

Carla turned off the tap. "Dr. Rothmann was our family physician when I was a child," she said guardedly. "Why?"

The other woman took her place at the standpipe and began to fill a large can that had once held cooking oil. "Frau Rothmann has been taken away," she said. "I thought you'd like to know."

It was commonplace. People were "taken away" all the time. But when it happened to someone close to you, it came as a blow to the heart.

There was no point in trying to find out what had happened to them—in fact it was downright dangerous: people who inquired about disappearances tended to disappear themselves. All the same, Carla had to ask. "Do you know where they took her?"

This time there was an answer. "The Schul Strasse transit camp." Carla felt hopeful. "It's in the old Jewish Hospital, in Wedding. Do you know it?"

"Yes, I do." Carla sometimes worked at the hospital, unofficially and illegally, so she knew that the government had taken over one of the hospital buildings, the pathology lab, and surrounded it with barbed wire.

"I hope she's all right," said the other woman. "She was good to me when my Steffi was ill." She turned off the tap and walked away with her can of water.

Carla hurried away in the opposite direction, heading for home.

She had to do something about Hannelore. It had always been nearly impossible to get anyone out of a camp, but now that everything was breaking down, perhaps there might be a way.

She took the bucket into the house and gave it to Ada.

Maud had gone to queue for food rations. Carla changed into her nurse's uniform, thinking it might help. She explained to Ada where she was going and left again.

She had to walk to Wedding. It was two or three miles. She wondered if it was worth it. Even if she found Hannelore, she probably would not be able to help her. But then she thought of Eva in London and Rudi in hiding somewhere here in Berlin: how terrible it would be if they lost their mother in the last hours of the war. She had to try.

The military police were on the streets, stopping people and demanding papers. They worked in threes, forming summary courts, and were mainly interested in men of fighting age. They did not bother Carla in her nurse's uniform.

It was strange that in this blasted cityscape the apple and cherry trees were gorgeous with white and pink blossoms, and that in the quiet moments between explosions she could hear the birds singing as optimistically as they did every spring.

To her horror she saw several men hanged from lampposts, some in uniform. Most of the bodies had a card hanging around the neck saying COWARD or DESERTER. These had been found guilty by those three-man street courts, she knew. Was there not already enough killing to satisfy the Nazis? It made her want to weep.

She was forced to take shelter from artillery bombardments three times. On the last occasion, when she was only a few hundred yards from the hospital, the Soviets and the Germans seemed to be fighting only a few streets away. The shooting was so heavy that Carla was tempted to turn back. Hannelore was probably doomed, and might already be dead: Why should Carla add her own life to the toll? But she went on anyway.

It was evening when she reached her destination. The hospital was in Iranische Strasse, on the corner of Schul Strasse. The trees lining the streets were in new leaf. The laboratory building, which had been turned into a transit camp, was guarded. Carla considered going up to the guard and explaining her mission, but it seemed an unpromising strategy. She wondered if she might slip inside from the tunnel system.

She went into the main building. The hospital was functioning. All the patients had been moved into the basements and tunnels. The staff were working by the light of oil lamps. Carla could tell by the smell that the toilets were not flushing. Water was being carried in buckets from an old well in the garden.

Surprisingly, soldiers were bringing wounded comrades in for help. Suddenly they did not care that the doctors and nurses might be Jewish.

She followed a tunnel under the garden to the basement of the laboratory. As she expected, the door was guarded. However, the young Gestapo man looked at her uniform and waved her through without questioning her. Perhaps he no longer saw any point in his job.

She was inside the camp now. She wondered whether it would be as easy to get out.

The smell here was worse, and she soon saw why. The basement was overcrowded. Hundreds of people were packed into four storerooms. They sat or lay on the floor, the lucky ones having a wall to lean against. They were dirty, smelly, and exhausted, and they looked at her with dull uninterested gazes.

She found Hannelore after a few minutes.

The doctor's wife had never been beautiful, but she had once been a statuesque woman with a strong face. Now she was gaunt, like most people, and her hair was gray and lifeless. She was hollow-cheeked and lined with strain.

She was talking to an adolescent who was at the age when a girl can seem too voluptuous for her years, having womanly breasts and hips but the face of a child. The girl was sitting on the floor, crying, and Hannelore was kneeling beside her, holding her hand and speaking in a low, soothing voice.

When Hannelore saw Carla, she stood up, saying: "Good God! Why are you in here?"

"I thought maybe if I tell them you're not Jewish, they might let you go."

"That was brave."

"Your husband saved many lives. Someone ought to save yours."

For a moment, Carla thought Hannelore was going to cry. Her face seemed about to crumple. Then she blinked and shook her head. "This is Rebecca Rosen," she said in a controlled voice. "Her parents were killed by a shell today."

Carla said: "I'm so sorry, Rebecca."

The girl did not speak.

Carla said: "How old are you, Rebecca?"

"Nearly fourteen."

"You're going to have to be a grown-up now."

"Why didn't I die, too?" Rebecca said. "I was right beside them. I should have died. Now I'm all alone."

"You're not alone," Carla said briskly. "We're with you." She turned back to Hannelore. "Who's in charge here?"

"His name is Walter Dobberke."

"I'm going to tell him he must let you go."

"He's left for the day. And his second-in-command is a sergeant with the brains of a warthog. But look, here comes Gisela. She's Dobberke's mistress."

The young woman walking into the room was pretty, with long fair hair and creamy skin. No one looked at her. She wore a defiant expression.

Hannelore said: "She has sex with him on the bed in the electrocardiogram room upstairs. She gets extra food in exchange. No one will speak to her except me. I just don't think we can judge people for the compromises they make. We are living in hell, after all."

Carla was not so sure. She would not befriend a Jewish girl who slept with a Nazi.

Gisela met Hannelore's eye and came over. "He's had new orders," she said, speaking so quietly that Carla had to strain to hear her. Then she hesitated.

Hannelore said: "Well? What are the orders?"

Gisela's voice fell to a whisper. "To shoot everyone here."

Carla felt a cold hand grasp her heart. All these people—including Hannelore and young Rebecca.

"Walter doesn't want to do it," Gisela said. "He's not a bad man, really."

Hannelore spoke with fatalistic calm. "When is he supposed to kill us?"

"Immediately. But he wants to destroy the records first. Hans-Peter and Martin are putting the files into the furnace right now. It's a long job, so we have a few hours left. Maybe the Red Army will get here in time to save us."

"And maybe they won't," Hannelore said crisply. "Is there any way we can persuade him to disobey his orders? For God's sake, the war is almost over!"

"I used to be able to talk him into anything," Gisela said sadly. "But he's getting tired of me now. You know what men are like."

"But he should be thinking of his own future. Any day now the Allies will be in charge here. They will punish Nazi crimes."

Gisela said: "If we're all dead, who's going to accuse him?"

"I will," said Carla.

The other two stared at her, not speaking.

Carla realized that even though she was not Jewish, she, too, would be shot, to prevent her bearing witness.

Casting about for ideas, she said: "Perhaps, if Dobberke spared us, it would help him with the Allies."

"That's a thought," said Hannelore. "We could all sign a declaration saying that he saved our lives."

Carla looked inquiringly at Gisela. Her expression was dubious, but she said: "He might do it."

Hannelore looked around. "There's Hilde," she said. "She acts as a secretary for Dobberke." She called the woman over and explained the plan.

"I'll type out release documents for everyone," Hilde said. "We'll ask him to sign them before we give him the declaration."

There were no guards within the basement area, just at the ground-floor door and the tunnel, so the prisoners could move around freely inside. Hilde went into the room that served as Dobberke's underground office. She typed the declaration first. Hannelore and Carla went around the basement explaining the plan and getting everyone to sign. Meanwhile Hilde typed the release documents.

By the time they finished, it was the middle of the night. There was no more they could do until Dobberke showed up in the morning.

Carla lay on the floor next to Rebecca Rosen. There was nowhere else to sleep.

After a while Rebecca began to cry quietly.

Carla was not sure what to do. She wanted to give comfort, but no words came. What did you say to a child who had just seen both her parents killed? The muffled weeping continued. In the end Carla rolled over and put her arms around Rebecca.

She knew immediately that she had done the right thing. Rebecca cuddled up to her, head on her breast. Carla patted her back as if she were a baby. Slowly the sobs eased and eventually Rebecca fell asleep.

Carla did not sleep. She spent the night making imaginary speeches to the camp commandant. Sometimes she appealed to his better nature, sometimes she threatened him with Allied justice, sometimes she argued from his own self-interest.

She tried not to think about the process of being shot. Erik had explained to her how the Nazis executed people twelve at a time in Russia. She supposed they would have an efficient system here, too. It was hard to imagine. Perhaps that was just as well.

She could probably escape shooting if she left the camp right now, or first thing in the morning. She was not an inmate, nor a Jew, and her papers were perfectly in order. She could go out the way she came in, dressed in her nurse's uniform. But that would mean abandoning both Hannelore and Rebecca. She could not bring herself to do that, no matter how badly she longed to get out of here.

The fighting in the streets outside continued until the small hours; then there was a short pause. It began again at dawn. Now it was close enough for her to hear machine-gun fire as well as artillery.

Early in the morning the guards brought an urn of watery soup and a sack of bread, all discarded parts of stale loaves. Carla drank the soup and ate the bread and then, reluctantly, used the toilet, which was unspeakably dirty.

With Hannelore, Gisela, and Hilde she went up to the ground floor to wait for Dobberke. The shelling had resumed, and they were in danger every second, but they wanted to confront him the moment he arrived.

He did not appear at his usual hour. He was normally punctual, Hilde said. Perhaps he had been delayed by the fighting in the streets. He might have been killed, of course. Carla hoped not. His second-in-command, Sergeant Ehrenstein, was too stupid to argue with.

When Dobberke was an hour late, Carla began to lose hope.

After another hour, he arrived.

"What's this?" he said when he saw the four women waiting in the hall. "A mothers' meeting?"

Hannelore replied: "All the prisoners have signed a declaration saying you saved their lives. It may save *your* life, if you accept our terms."

"Don't be ridiculous," he said.

Carla spoke up. "According to the BBC, the United Nations has a list of the names of Nazi officers who have taken part in mass murders. In a week's time you could be on trial. Wouldn't you like to have a signed declaration that you spared people?"

"Listening to the BBC is a crime," he said.

"Though not as serious as murder."

Hilde had a file folder in her hand. She said: "I have typed release orders for all the prisoners here. If you sign them, you can have the declaration."

"I could just take it from you."

"No one will believe in your innocence if we're all dead."

Dobberke was angered by the situation he found himself in, but not confident enough just to walk away. "I could shoot the four of you for insolence," he said.

Carla spoke impatiently. "This is what defeat is like," she said. "Get used to it."

His face darkened with anger, and she realized she had gone too far. She wished she could take back her words. She stared at Dobberke's furious expression, trying not to let her fear show.

At that moment a shell landed outside the building. The doors rattled and a window smashed. They all ducked instinctively, but no one was hurt.

When they straightened up, Dobberke's face had changed. Rage was replaced by something like disgusted resignation. Carla's heartbeat quickened. Had he given up?

Sergeant Ehrenstein ran in. "No one hurt, sir," he reported.

"Very good, Sergeant."

Ehrenstein was about to go out again when Dobberke called him back. "This camp is now closed," Dobberke said.

Carla held her breath.

"Closed, sir?" There was aggression as well as surprise in the sergeant's voice.

"New orders. Tell the men to go . . ." Dobberke hesitated. "Tell them to report to the railway bunker at Friedrich Strasse station."

Carla knew Dobberke was making this up, and Ehrenstein seemed to suspect it, too. "When, sir?"

"Immediately."

"Immediately." Ehrenstein paused, as if the word *immediately* required further elucidation.

Dobberke stared him out.

"Very good, sir," said the sergeant. "I'll tell the men." He went out.

Carla felt a surge of triumph, but told herself she was not yet free.

Dobberke said to Hilde: "Show me the declaration."

Hilde opened her folder. There were a dozen sheets, all with the same wording typed at the top, the rest of the space covered with signatures. She handed them over.

Dobberke folded the papers and stuffed them in his pocket.

Hilde placed the release orders in front of him. "Sign these, please."

"You don't need release orders," Dobberke said. "And I don't have time to sign my name hundreds of times."

Carla said: "The police are on the streets. They're hanging people from the lampposts. We need papers."

He patted his pocket. "They'll hang me if they find this declaration." He went to the door.

Gisela cried: "Take me with you, Walter!"

He turned to her. "Take you?" he said. "What would my wife say?" He went out and slammed the door.

Gisela burst into tears.

Carla went to the door, opened it, and watched Dobberke stride away. There were no other Gestapo men in sight: they had already obeyed his orders and abandoned the camp.

The commandant reached the street and broke into a run.

He left the gate open.

Hannelore was standing beside Carla, looking out with incredulity.

"We're free, I think," said Carla.

"We must tell the others."

Hilde said: "I'll tell them." She went down the basement stairs.

Carla and Hannelore walked fearfully along the path that led from the laboratory entrance to the open gate. There they hesitated and looked at one another.

Hannelore said: "We're frightened of freedom."

Behind them a girlish voice said: "Carla, don't go without me!" It was Rebecca, running down the path, her breasts bouncing under a grubby blouse.

Carla sighed. I've acquired a child, she thought. I don't feel ready to be a mother. But what can I do?

"Come on, then," she said. "But be ready to run." She realized she did not need to worry about Rebecca's agility: the girl could undoubtedly run faster than either Carla or Hannelore.

They crossed the hospital garden to the main gate. There they paused and looked up and down Iranische Strasse. It seemed quiet. They crossed the road and ran to the corner. As Carla looked along Schul Strasse, she heard a burst of machine-gun fire and saw that farther up the street there was a firefight. She saw German troops retreating toward her and Red Army soldiers coming after them.

She looked around. There was nowhere to hide except behind trees, and that was hardly any protection at all.

A shell landed in the middle of the road fifty yards away and exploded. Carla felt the blast, but she was not hurt.

Without conferring, all three women ran back inside the hospital grounds.

They returned to the laboratory building. Some of the other prisoners were standing just inside the barbed wire, as if not quite daring to come out.

Carla said to them: "The basement stinks, but right now it's the safest place." She went inside the building and down the stairs, and most of the others followed.

She wondered how long she would have to stay here. The German army must give up, but when? Somehow she could not imagine Hitler agreeing to surrender under any circumstances. The man's whole life had been based on arrogantly shouting that he was the boss. How could such a man admit that he had been wrong, stupid, and wicked? That he had murdered millions and caused his country to be bombed to ruins? That he would go down in history as the most evil man who had ever lived? He could not. He would go mad, or die of shame, or put a pistol in his mouth and pull the trigger.

But how long would it take? Another day? Another week? Longer?

There was a shout from upstairs. "They're here! The Russians are here!"

Then Carla heard heavy boots clattering down the steps. Where had the Russians got such good boots? From the Americans?

Then they were in the room, four, six, eight, nine men with dirty faces, carrying submachine guns with drum magazines, ready to kill as quick as look at you. They seemed to take up a lot of room. People shrank away from them, even though they were the liberators.

The soldiers took in their surroundings. They saw that they were in no danger from the emaciated prisoners, mainly female. They lowered their guns. Some moved into the adjoining rooms.

A tall soldier pulled up his left sleeve. He was wearing six or seven wristwatches. He shouted something in Russian, pointing at the watches with the stock of his gun. Carla thought she knew what he was saying, but she could hardly believe it. The man then grabbed an elderly woman, took her hand, and pointed to her wedding ring.

Hannelore said: "Are they going to rob us of what little the Nazis didn't steal?"

They were. The tall soldier looked frustrated and tried to pull off the woman's ring. When she realized what he wanted, she took it off herself and gave it to him.

The Russian took it, nodded, then pointed all around the room.

Hannelore stepped forward. "These people are prisoners!" she said in German. "Jews, and families of Jews, persecuted by the Nazis!"

Whether he understood her or not, he took no notice, but just pointed insistently at the watches on his arm.

Those few who had any valuables that had not been stolen or traded for food handed them over.

Liberation by the Red Army was not going to be the happy event many people had been looking forward to.

But there was worse to come.

The tall soldier pointed at Rebecca.

She cringed away from him and tried to hide behind Carla.

A second man, small with fair hair, grabbed Rebecca and pulled her away. Rebecca screamed, and the small man grinned as if he liked the sound.

Carla had a dreadful feeling she knew what was going to happen next.

The short man held Rebecca firmly while the tall man squeezed her breasts roughly, then said something that made them both laugh.

There were cries of protest from the people all around.

The tall man leveled his gun. Carla was terrified he would fire. He would kill and wound dozens of people if he pulled the trigger of a submachine gun in a crowded room.

Everyone else realized the danger, and they went quiet.

The two soldiers backed toward the door, taking Rebecca with them. She yelled and struggled, but she could not break the small soldier's grip.

When they reached the door, Carla stepped forward and cried: "Wait!"

Something in her voice made them stop.

"She's too young," Carla said. "Only thirteen!" She did not know whether they understood her. She held up two hands, showing ten fingers, then one hand showing three. "Thirteen!"

The tall soldier seemed to understand her. He grinned and said in German: "*Frau ist Frau.*" A woman is a woman.

Carla found herself saying: "You need a real woman." She walked slowly forward. "Take me, instead." She tried to smile seductively. "I'm not a child. I know what to do." She came close, close enough to smell the rank odor of a man who had not bathed for months. Trying to conceal her distaste, she lowered her voice and said: "I understand what a man wants." She touched her own breast suggestively. "Forget the child."

The tall soldier looked again at Rebecca. Her eyes were red with weeping and her nose was running, which helpfully made her look more like a child, less like a woman.

He looked back at Carla.

She said: "There's a bed upstairs. Shall I show you where?"

Again she was not sure he understood the words, but she took him by the hand and he followed her up the steps to the ground floor.

The fair one let go of Rebecca and came after.

Now that she had succeeded, Carla regretted her bravado. She wanted to break away from the Russians and run. But they would probably shoot her down, then go back to Rebecca. Carla thought of the devastated child who had lost both parents yesterday. To be raped the next day would surely destroy her spirit forever. Carla had to save her.

I will not be smashed by this, Carla thought. I can live through it. I will be myself again afterward.

She led them to the electrocardiogram room. She felt cold, as if her heart were freezing and her thoughts becoming sluggish. Next to the bed was a can of the grease used by the doctors to improve the conductivity of the terminals. She pulled off her underpants, then took a large dab of grease and pushed it into her vagina. That might save her from bleeding.

She had to keep her act up. She turned back to the two soldiers. To her horror, three more followed them into the room. She tried to smile, but she could not.

She lay on her back and parted her legs.

The tall one knelt between her knees. He ripped open her uniform blouse to expose her breasts. She could see that he was manipulating himself, making his penis erect. He lay on top and entered her. She told herself this had no connection with what she and Werner had done together.

She turned her head to the side, but the soldier grasped her chin and turned her face back, making her look at him as he thrust inside her. She closed her eyes. She felt him kissing her, trying to force his tongue into her mouth. His breath smelled like rotting meat. When she clamped her mouth shut, he punched her face. She cried out and opened her bruised lips to him. She tried to think how much worse this would have been for a thirteen-year-old virgin.

The soldier grunted and ejaculated inside her. She tried not to let her disgust show on her face.

He climbed off, and the fair-haired one took his place.

Carla tried to close down her mind, to make her body into something detached, a machine, an object that had nothing to do with her. This one did not want to kiss her, but he sucked her breasts and bit her nipples, and when she cried out in pain, he seemed pleased and did it harder.

Time passed, and he ejaculated.

Then another one got on top.

She realized that when this was over, she would not be able to bathe or shower, for there was no running water in the city. That thought pushed her over the top. Their fluids would be inside her, their smell would be on her skin, their saliva in her mouth, and she would have no effective way to wash. Somehow that was worse than everything else. Her courage failed her, and she started to cry.

The third soldier satisfied himself; then the fourth lay on her.

# CHAPTER TWENTY

# 1945 (II)

dolf Hitler killed himself on Monday, April 30, 1945, in his bunker in Berlin. Exactly a week later in London, at twenty to eight in the evening, the Ministry of Information announced that Germany had surrendered. A holiday was declared for the following day, Tuesday, May 8.

Daisy sat at the window of her apartment in Piccadilly, watching the celebrations. The street was thronged with people, making it almost impassable to cars and buses. The girls would kiss any man in uniform, and thousands of lucky servicemen were taking full advantage. By early afternoon many people were drunk. Through the open window Daisy could hear distant singing, and guessed that the crowd outside Buckingham Palace was doing "Land of Hope and Glory." She shared their happiness, but Lloyd was somewhere in France or Germany, and he was the only soldier she wanted to kiss. She prayed he had not been killed in the last few hours of the war.

Lloyd's sister, Millie, showed up with her two children. Millie's husband, Abe Avery, was also with the army somewhere. She and the children had come to the West End to join in the celebrations, and they took a break from the crowds at Daisy's place. The Leckwith home in Aldgate had long been a place of refuge for Daisy, and she was glad to have a chance to reciprocate. She made tea for Millie—her staff were out there celebrating—and poured orange juice for the children. Lennie was five now and Pammie three.

Since Abe had been conscripted, Millie had been running his leather wholesaling business. His sister, Naomi Avery, was the bookkeeper, but Millie did the selling. "It's going to change now," Millie said. "For the past five years the demand has been for tough hides for boots and shoes. Now we're going to need softer leathers, calf and pigskin, for handbags and briefcases. When the luxury market comes back, there'll be decent money to be made at last."

Daisy recalled that her father had the same way of thinking as Millie. Lev, too, was always looking ahead, searching out the opportunities.

Eva Murray appeared next, with her four children in tow. Jamie, aged eight, organized a game of hide-and-seek, and the apartment became like a kindergarten. Eva's husband, Jimmy, now a colonel, was also somewhere in France or Germany, and Eva was suffering the same agonies of anxiety as Daisy and Millie.

"We'll hear from them, any day now," Millie said. "And then it will really be all over."

Eva was also desperate for news of her family in Berlin. However, she thought it might be weeks or months before anyone could learn the fates of individual Germans in the postwar chaos. "I wonder whether my children will ever know my parents," she said sadly.

At five o'clock Daisy made a pitcher of martinis. Millie went into the kitchen and, with characteristic speed and efficiency, produced a plate of sardines on toast to eat with the drinks. Eth and Bernie arrived just as Daisy was making a second round.

Bernie told Daisy that Lennie could read already, and Pammie could sing the national anthem. Ethel said: "Typical grandfather, thinks there have never been bright children before," but Daisy could tell that in her heart she was just as proud of them.

Feeling relaxed and happy halfway down her second martini, she looked around at the disparate group gathered in her home. They had paid her the compliment of coming to her door without an invitation, knowing they would be welcomed. They belonged to her, and she to them. They were, she realized, her family.

She felt very blessed.

## ii

Woody Dewar sat outside Leo Shapiro's office, looking through a sheaf of photographs. They were the pictures he had taken at Pearl Harbor, in the hour before Joanne died. The film had stayed in his camera for months, but eventually he had developed it and printed the pictures. Looking at them had made him so sad that he had put them in a drawer in his bedroom at the Washington apartment and left them there.

But this was a time for change.

He would never forget Joanne, but he was in love again, at last. He adored Bella and she felt the same. When they parted, at the Oakland train station outside San Francisco, he had told her that he loved her, and she had said: "I love you, too." He was going to ask her to marry him. He would have done so already but it seemed too soon—less than three months—and he did not want to give her hostile parents a pretext for objecting.

Also, he needed to make a decision about his future.

He did not want to go into politics.

This was going to shock his parents, he knew. They had always assumed he would follow in his father's footsteps and end up as the third Senator Dewar. He had gone along with this assumption unthinkingly. But in the war, and especially while in hospital, he had asked himself what he *really* wanted to do, if he survived, and the answer was not politics.

This was a good time to leave. His father had achieved his life's ambition. The Senate had debated the United Nations. It was at a similar point in history that the old League of Nations had foundered, a painful memory for Gus Dewar. But Senator Vandenberg had spoken passionately in favor, speaking of "the dearest dream of mankind," and the UN Charter had been ratified by eighty-nine votes to two. The job was done. Woody would not be letting his father down by quitting now.

He hoped Gus would see it that way, too.

Shapiro opened his office door and beckoned. Woody stood up and went in.

Shapiro was younger than Woody had expected, somewhere in his thirties. He was Washington bureau chief for the National Press Agency. He sat behind his desk and said: "What can I do for Senator Dewar's son?"

"I'd like to show you some photographs, if I may."

"All right."

Woody spread his pictures on Shapiro's desk.

"Is this Pearl Harbor?" Shapiro said.

"Yes. December seventh, nineteen forty-one."

"My God."

Woody was looking at them upside down, but still they brought tears to his eyes. There was Joanne, looking so beautiful, and Chuck, grinning happily to be with his family and Eddie. Then the planes coming over, the bombs and torpedoes dropping from their bellies, the black-smoke explosions on the ships, and the sailors scrambling over the sides, dropping into the sea, swimming for their lives.

"This is your father," Shapiro said. "And your mother. I recognize them."

"And my fiancée, who died a few minutes later. My brother, who was killed at Bougainville. And my brother's best friend."

"These are fantastic photographs! How much do you want for them?"

"I don't want money," Woody said.

Shapiro looked up in surprise.

Woody said: "I want a job."

## iii

Fifteen days after VE Day, Winston Churchill called a general election.

The Leckwith family were taken by surprise. Like most people, Ethel and Bernie had thought Churchill would wait until the Japanese surrendered. The Labour leader, Clement Attlee, had suggested an election in October. Churchill wrong-footed them all.

Major Lloyd Williams was released from the army to stand as Labour candidate for Hoxton, in the East End of London. He was full of eager enthusiasm for the future envisioned by his party. Fascism had been vanquished, and now British people could create a society that combined freedom with welfare. Labour had a well-thought-out plan for avoiding the catastrophes of the last twenty years: universal comprehensive unemployment insurance to help families through hard times, economic planning to prevent another Depression, and the United Nations organization to keep the peace.

"You don't stand a chance," said his stepfather, Bernie, in the kitchen of the house in Aldgate on Monday, June 4. Bernie's pessimism was the more convincing for being so uncharacteristic. "They'll vote Tory because Churchill won the war," he went on gloomily. "It was the same with Lloyd George in 1918."

Lloyd was about to reply, but Daisy got in first. "The war wasn't won by the free market and capitalist enterprise," she said indignantly. "It was people working together and sharing the burdens, everybody doing his bit. That's socialism!"

Lloyd loved her most when she was passionate, but he was more deliberate. "We already have measures that the old Tories would have condemned as Bolshevism: government control of railways, mines, and shipping, for example, all brought in by Churchill. And Ernie Bevin has been in charge of economic planning all through the war."

Bernie shook his head knowingly, an old-man gesture that irritated Lloyd. "People vote with their hearts, not brains," he said. "They'll want to show their gratitude."

"Well, no point sitting here arguing with you," Lloyd said. "I'm going to argue with voters instead."

He and Daisy took a bus a few stops north to the Black Lion pub in Shoreditch, where they met up with a canvassing team from the Hoxton Constituency Labour Party. In fact canvassing was not about arguing with voters, Lloyd knew. Its main purpose was to identify supporters, so that on election day the party machine could make sure they all went to the polling station. Firm Labour supporters were noted; firm supporters of other parties were crossed off. Only people who had not yet made up their minds were worth more than a few seconds: they were offered the chance to speak to the candidate.

Lloyd got some negative reactions. "Major, eh?" one woman said. "My Alf is a corporal. He says the officers nearly lost us the war."

There were also accusations of nepotism. "Aren't you the son of the M.P. for Aldgate? What is this, a hereditary monarchy?"

He remembered his mother's advice. "You never win a vote by proving the constituent a fool. Be charming, be modest, and don't lose your temper. If a voter is hostile and rude, thank him for his time and go away. You'll leave him thinking maybe he misjudged you."

Working-class voters were strongly Labour. A lot of people told Lloyd that Attlee and Bevin had done a good job during the war. The waverers were mostly middle-class. When people said that Churchill had won the war, Lloyd quoted Attlee's gentle put-down: "It wasn't a one-man government, and it wasn't a one-man war."

Churchill had described Attlee as a modest man with much to be modest about. Attlee's wit was less brutal, and for that reason more effective—at least, Lloyd thought so.

A couple of constituents mentioned the sitting M.P. for Hoxton, a Liberal, and said they would vote for him because he had helped them solve some problem. Members of Parliament were often called upon by constituents who felt they were being treated unjustly by the government, an employer, or a neighbor. It was time-consuming work but it won votes.

Overall, Lloyd could not tell which way public opinion was leaning.

Only one constituent mentioned Daisy. The man came to the door with his mouth full of food. Lloyd said: "Good evening, Mr. Perkinson, I understand you wanted to ask me something."

"Your fiancée was a Fascist," the man said, chewing.

Lloyd guessed he had been reading the *Daily Mail,* which had run a spiteful story about Lloyd and Daisy under the headline THE SOCIALIST AND THE VISCOUNTESS.

Lloyd nodded. "She was briefly fooled by Fascism, like many others."

"How can a socialist marry a Fascist?"

Lloyd looked around, spotted Daisy, and beckoned her. "Mr. Perkinson here is asking me about my fiancée being an ex-Fascist."

"Pleased to meet you, Mr. Perkinson." Daisy shook the man's hand. "I quite understand your concern. My first husband was a Fascist in the thirties, and I supported him."

Perkinson nodded. He probably believed a wife should take her views from her husband.

"How foolish we were," Daisy went on. "But, when the war came, my first husband joined the RAF and fought against the Nazis as bravely as anyone."

"Is that a fact?"

"Last year he was flying a Typhoon over France, strafing a German troop train, when he was shot down and killed. So I'm a war widow."

Perkinson swallowed his food. "I'm sorry to hear that, of course."

But Daisy had not finished. "For myself, I lived in London throughout the war. I drove an ambulance all through the Blitz."

"Very brave of you, I'm sure."

"Well, I just hope you think that my late husband and I both paid our dues."

"I don't know about that," Perkinson said sulkily.

"We won't take up any more of your time," said Lloyd. "Thank you for explaining your views to me. Good evening."

As they walked away, Daisy said: "I don't think we won him around."

"You never do," Lloyd said. "But he's seen both sides of the story now, which might make him a bit less vociferous about it, later this evening, when he talks about us in the pub."

"Hmm."

Lloyd sensed he had failed to reassure Daisy.

Canvassing finished early, for tonight the first of the radio election broadcasts would be aired on the BBC, and all party workers would be listening. Churchill had the privilege of making the first one.

On the bus home, Daisy said: "I'm worried. I'm an election liability to you."

"No candidate is perfect," Lloyd said. "It's how you deal with your weaknesses that matters."

"I don't want to be your weakness. Perhaps I should stay out of the way."

"On the contrary, I want everyone to know all about you from the start. If you are a liability, I will get out of politics."

"No, no! I'd hate to think I made you give up your ambitions."

"It won't come to that," he said, but once again he could see that he had not succeeded in assuaging her anxiety.

Back in Nutley Street, the Leckwith family sat around the radio in the kitchen. Daisy held Lloyd's hand. "I came here a lot while you were away," she said. "We used to listen to swing music and talk about you."

The thought made Lloyd feel very lucky.

Churchill came on. The familiar rasp was stirring. For five grim years that voice had given people strength and hope and courage. Lloyd felt despairing: even he was tempted to vote for this man.

"My friends," the prime minister said. "I must tell you that a socialist policy is abhorrent to the British ideas of freedom."

Well, that was routine knockabout stuff. All new ideas were condemned as foreign imports. But what would Churchill offer people? Labour had a plan, but what did the Conservatives propose?

"Socialism is inseparably interwoven with totalitarianism," Churchill said.

Lloyd's mother, Ethel, said: "Surely he's not going to pretend we're like the Nazis?"

"I think he is, though," Bernie said. "He'll say we've defeated the enemy abroad, now we must defeat the enemy in our midst. Standard conservative tactic."

"People won't believe that," Ethel said.

Lloyd said: "Hush!"

Churchill said: "A socialist state, once thoroughly completed in all its details and its aspects, could not afford to suffer opposition."

"This is outrageous," said Ethel.

"But I will go farther," said Churchill. "I declare to you, from the bottom of my heart, that no socialist system can be established without a political police."

"Political police?" Ethel said indignantly. "Where is he getting this stuff from?"

Bernie said: "This is good, in a way. He can't find anything to criticize in our manifesto. Therefore he's attacking us for things we aren't actually proposing to do. Bloody liar."

Lloyd shouted: "Listen!"

Churchill said: "They would have to fall back on some form of Gestapo."

Suddenly they were all on their feet, shouting protests. The prime minister was drowned out. "Bastard!" Bernie yelled, shaking his fist at the Marconi radio set. "Bastard, bastard!"

When they had quietened down, Ethel said: "Is that going to be their campaign? Just lies about us?"

"It bloody well is," said Bernie.

Lloyd said: "But will people believe it?"

## iv

In southern New Mexico, not far from El Paso, there is a desert called Jornada del Muerto, the Voyage of the Dead. All day long the cruel sun beats down on needle-thorn mesquite and sword-leafed yucca plants. The inhabitants are scorpions and rattlesnakes and fire ants and tarantula spiders. Here the men of the Manhattan Project tested the most dreadful weapon the human race had ever devised.

Greg Peshkov was with the scientists watching from ten thousand yards away. He had two hopes: first, that the bomb would work, and second, that ten thousand yards was far enough.

The countdown started at nine minutes past five in the morning, Mountain War Time, on Monday, July 16. It was dawn, and there were streaks of gold in the sky to the east.

The test was code-named Trinity. When Greg had asked why, the senior scientist, the pointy-eared Jewish New Yorker J. Robert Oppenheimer, had quoted a poem by John Donne: "Batter my heart, three-person'd God."

"Oppie" was the cleverest person Greg had ever met. The most brilliant physicist of his generation, he also spoke six languages. He had read Karl Marx's *Capital* in the original German. The kind of thing he did for fun was learn Sanskrit. Greg liked and admired him. Most physicists were geeks, but Oppie, like Greg himself, was an exception: tall, handsome, charming, and a real lady-killer.

In the middle of the desert, Oppie had instructed the Army Corps of Engineers to build a one-hundred-foot tower of steel struts in concrete footings. On top was an oak platform. The bomb had been winched up to the platform on Saturday.

The scientists never used the word *bomb*. They called it "the gadget." At its heart was a ball of plutonium, a metal that did not exist in nature but was created as a by-product in nuclear piles. The ball weighed ten pounds and contained all the plutonium in the world. Someone had calculated that it was worth a billion dollars.

Thirty-two detonators on the surface of the ball would go off simultaneously, creating such powerful inward pressure that the plutonium would become more dense and go critical.

No one really knew what would happen next.

The scientists were running a betting pool, a dollar a ticket, on the force of the explosion measured in equivalent tons of TNT. Edward Teller bet 45,000 tons. Oppie bet 300 tons. The official forecast was 20,000 tons. The night before, Enrico Fermi had offered to take side bets on whether the blast would wipe out the entire state of New Mexico. General Groves had not found it funny.

The scientists had had a perfectly serious discussion about whether the explosion would ignite the atmosphere of the entire earth, and destroy the planet, but they had come to the conclusion that it would not. If they were wrong, Greg just hoped it would happen fast.

The trial had originally been scheduled for July 4. However, every time they tested a component, it failed, so the big day had been postponed several times. Back at Los Alamos, on Saturday, a mock-up they called the Chinese Copy had refused to ignite. In the betting pool, Norman Ramsey had picked zero, gambling that the bomb would be a dud.

Today detonation had been scheduled for two A.M., but at that time there had been a thunderstorm—in the desert! Rain would bring the radioactive fallout down on the heads of the watching scientists, so the blast was postponed.

The storm had ended at dawn.

Greg was at a bunker called S-10000, which was the control room. Like most of the scientists, he was standing outside for a better view. Hope and fear struggled for mastery of his heart. If the bomb was a dud, the efforts of hundreds of people—plus about two billion dollars— would have gone for nothing. And if the bomb was not a dud, they might all be killed in the next few minutes.

Beside him was Wilhelm Frunze, a young German scientist he had first met in Chicago. "What would have happened, Will, if lightning had struck the bomb?"

Frunze shrugged. "No one knows."

A green Verey rocket shot into the sky, startling Greg.

"Five-minute warning," Frunze said.

Security had been haphazard. Santa Fe, the nearest town to Los Alamos, was crawling with well-dressed FBI agents. Leaning nonchalantly against walls in their tweed jackets and neckties, they were obvious to local residents, who wore blue jeans and cowboy boots.

The bureau was also illegally tapping the phones of hundreds of people involved in the Manhattan Project. This bewildered Greg. How could the nation's premier law enforcement agency systematically commit criminal acts?

Nevertheless, army security and the FBI had identified some spies and quietly removed them from the project, including Barney McHugh. But had they found them all? Greg did not know. Groves had been forced to take risks. If he had fired everyone the FBI asked him to, there would not have been enough scientists left to build the bomb.

Unfortunately, most scientists were radicals, socialists, and liberals. There was hardly a conservative among them. And they believed that the truths discovered by science were for humankind to share, and should never be kept secret in the service of one regime or country. So while the American government was keeping this huge project top secret, the scientists held discussion groups about sharing nuclear technology with all the nations of the world. Oppie himself was suspect: the only reason he was not in the Communist Party was that he never joined clubs.

Right now Oppie was lying on the ground next to his kid brother, Frank, also an outstanding physicist, also a Communist. They both held pieces of welding glass through which to observe the explosion. Greg and Frunze had similar pieces of glass. Some of the scientists were wearing sunglasses.

Another rocket went off. "One minute," said Frunze.

Greg heard Oppie say: "Lord, these affairs are hard on the heart."

He wondered if those would be Oppie's last words.

Greg and Frunze lay on the sandy earth near Oppie and Frank. They all held their visors of welding glass in front of their eyes and gazed toward the test site.

Facing death, Greg thought about his mother, his father, and his sister, Daisy, in London. He wondered how much they would miss him. He thought, with mild regret, of Margaret Cowdry, who had dumped him for a guy who was willing to marry her. But most of all he thought of Jacky Jakes and Georgy, now nine years old. He passionately wanted to watch Georgy grow up. He realized Georgy was the main reason he was hoping to stay alive. Stealthily, the child had crept into his soul and stolen his love. The strength of this feeling surprised Greg.

A gong chimed, a strangely inappropriate sound in the desert.

"Ten seconds."

Greg suffered an impulse to get up and run away. Silly though it was—how far could he get in ten seconds?—he had to force himself to lie still.

The bomb went off at five twenty-nine and forty-five seconds.

First there was an awesome flash, impossibly bright, the fiercest glare Greg had ever seen, stronger than the sun.

Then a weird dome of fire seemed to come out of the ground. With terrifying speed it grew monstrously high. It reached the level of the mountains and continued to rise, rapidly dwarfing the peaks.

Greg whispered: "Jesus . . ."

The dome morphed into a square. The light was still brighter than noonday, and the distant mountains were so vividly illuminated that Greg could see every fold and crevice and rock.

Then the shape changed again. A pillar appeared below, seeming to push miles into the sky, like the fist of God. The cloud of boiling fire above the pillar spread like an umbrella, until the whole thing looked like a mushroom seven miles tall. The colors in the cloud were hellish orange, green, and purple.

Greg was hit by a wave of heat as if the Almighty had opened a giant oven. At the same moment the bang of the explosion reached his ears like the crack of doom. But that was only the beginning. A noise like supernaturally loud thunder rolled over the desert, drowning all other sound.

The blazing cloud began to diminish but the thunder went on and on, impossibly sustained, until Greg wondered if this was the sound of the end of the world.

At last it faded away, and the mushroom cloud began to disperse.

Greg heard Frank Oppenheimer say: "It worked."

Oppie said: "Yes, it worked."

The two brothers shook hands.

And the world is still here, Greg thought.

But it has been forever changed.

## V

Lloyd Williams and Daisy went to Hoxton Town Hall on the morning of July 26 to watch the votes being counted.

If Lloyd lost, Daisy was going to break off the engagement.

He fervently denied that she was a political liability, but she knew better. Lloyd's political enemies made a point of calling her "Lady Aberowen." Voters reacted to her American accent by looking indignant, as if she had no right to take part in British politics. Even Labour Party members treated her differently, asking if she would prefer coffee when they were all drinking tea.

As Lloyd had forecast, she was often able to overcome people's initial hostility by being natural and charming, and helping the other women wash up the teacups. But was that enough? The election results would give the only definite answer.

She was not going to marry him if it meant his giving up his life's work. He said he was willing to do it, but it was a hopeless foundation for marriage. Daisy shuddered with horror as she imagined him doing some other job, working at a bank or in the civil service, miserably unhappy and trying to pretend it was not her fault. It did not bear thinking about.

Unfortunately, everyone thought the Conservatives were going to win the election.

Some things had gone Labour's way in the campaign. Churchill's "Gestapo" speech had backfired. Even Conservatives had been dismayed. Clement Attlee, broadcasting the following evening for Labour, had been coolly ironic. "When I listened to the prime minister's speech last night, in which he gave such a travesty of the policy of the Labour Party, I realized at once what was his object. He wanted the voters to understand how great was the difference between Winston Churchill, the great leader in war of a united nation, and Mr. Churchill, the party leader of the Conservatives. He feared lest those who had accepted his leadership in war might be tempted out of gratitude to follow him further. I thank him for having disillusioned them so thoroughly."

Attlee's magisterial disdain had made Churchill seem a rabble-rouser. People had had too much of bloodred passion, Daisy thought; they would surely prefer temperate common sense in peacetime.

A Gallup poll taken the day before voting showed Labour winning, but no one believed it. The idea that you could forecast the result by asking a small number of electors seemed a bit unlikely. The *News Chronicle,* which had published the poll, was predicting a tie.

All the other papers said the Conservatives would win.

Daisy had never before taken any interest in the mechanics of democracy, but her fate was in the balance now, and she watched, mesmerized, as the voting papers were taken out of the boxes, sorted, counted, bundled, and counted again. The man in charge was called the returning officer, as if he had been away for a while. He was in fact the town clerk. Observers from each of the parties monitored the proceedings to make sure there was no carelessness or dishonesty. The process was long, and Daisy felt tortured by suspense.

At half past ten they heard the first result from elsewhere. Harold Macmillan, a protégé of Churchill's and a wartime cabinet minister, had lost Stockton-on-Tees to Labour. Fifteen minutes later there was news of a huge swing to Labour in Birmingham. No radios were allowed into the hall, so Daisy and Lloyd were relying on rumors filtering in from outside, and Daisy was not sure what to believe.

It was midday when the returning officer called the candidates and their agents into a corner of the room, to give them the result before making the announcement publicly. Daisy wanted to go with Lloyd but she was not permitted.

The man spoke quietly to all of them. As well as Lloyd and the sitting M.P., there was a Conservative and a Communist. Daisy studied their faces, but could not guess who had won. They all went up onto the platform, and the room fell silent. Daisy felt nauseated.

"I, Michael Charles Davies, being the duly appointed returning officer for the parliamentary constituency of Hoxton . . ."

Daisy stood with the Labour Party observers and stared at Lloyd. Was she about to lose him? The thought squeezed her heart and made her breathless with fear. In her life she had twice chosen a man who was disastrously wrong. Charlie Farquharson had been the opposite of her father, nice but weak. Boy Fitzherbert had been much like her father, willful and selfish. Now, at last, she had found Lloyd, who was both strong and kind. She had not picked him for his social status or for what he could do for her, but simply because he was an extraordinarily good man. He was gentle, he was smart, he was trustworthy, and he adored her. It had taken her a long time to realize that he was what she was looking for. How foolish she had been.

The returning officer read out the number of votes cast for each candidate. They were listed alphabetically, so Williams came last. Daisy was so anxious that she could not keep the numbers in her head. "Reginald Sidney Blenkinsop, five thousand four hundred and twenty-seven . . ."

When Lloyd's vote was read out, the Labour Party people all around Daisy burst out cheering. It took her a moment to realize that meant he had won. Then she saw his solemn expression turn into a broad grin. Daisy began to clap and cheer louder than anyone. He had won! And she did not have to leave him! She felt as if her life had been saved.

"I therefore declare that Lloyd Williams is duly elected member of Parliament for Hoxton."

Lloyd was a member of Parliament. Daisy watched proudly as he stepped forward and made an acceptance speech. There was a formula for such speeches, she realized, and he tediously thanked the returning officer and his staff, then thanked his losing opponents for a fair fight. She was impatient to hug him. He finished with a few sentences about the task that lay ahead, of rebuilding war-torn Britain and creating a fairer society. He stood down to more applause.

Coming off the stage, he walked straight to Daisy, put his arms around her, and kissed her.

She said: "Well done, my darling." Then she found she could no longer speak.

After a while they went outside and caught a bus to Labour Party headquarters at Transport House. There they learned that Labour had already won 106 seats.

It was a landslide.

Every pundit had been wrong, and everyone's expectations were confounded. When all the results were in, Labour had 393 seats, the Conservatives 210. The Liberals had twelve and the Communists one— Stepney. Labour had an overwhelming majority.

At seven o'clock in the evening Winston Churchill, Britain's great war leader, went to Buckingham Palace and resigned as prime minister.

Daisy thought of one of Churchill's jibes about Attlee: "An empty car drew up and Clem got out." The man he called a nonentity had thrashed him.

At half past seven Clement Attlee went to the palace in his own car, driven by his wife, Violet, and King George VI asked him to become prime minister.

In the house in Nutley Street, after they had all listened to the news on the radio, Lloyd turned to Daisy and said: "Well, that's that. Can we get married now?"

"Yes," said Daisy. "As quick as you like."


## vi

Volodya and Zoya's wedding reception was held in one of the smaller banqueting halls in the Kremlin.

The war with Germany was over, but the Soviet Union was still battered and impoverished, and a lavish celebration would have been frowned upon. Zoya had a new dress, but Volodya wore his uniform. However, there was plenty to eat, and the vodka flowed freely.

Volodya's nephew and niece were there, the twin children of his sister, Anya, and her unpleasant husband, Ilya Dvorkin. They were not yet six years old. Dimka, the dark-haired boy, sat quietly reading a book, while blue-eyed Tania was running around the room crashing into tables and annoying the guests, in a reversal of the expected behavior of boys and girls.

Zoya looked so desirable in pink that Volodya would have liked to leave right away and take her to bed. That was out of the question, of course. His father's circle of friends included some of the most senior generals and politicians in the country, and many of them had come to toast the happy couple. Grigori was hinting that one extremely distinguished guest might arrive later; Volodya hoped it was not the depraved NKVD boss Beria.

Volodya's happiness did not quite let him forget the horrors he had seen and the profound misgivings he had developed about Soviet Communism. The unspeakable brutality of the secret police, the blunders of Stalin that had cost millions of lives, and the propaganda that had encouraged the Red Army to behave like crazed beasts in Germany had all caused him to doubt the most fundamental things he had been brought up to believe. He wondered uneasily what kind of country Dimka and Tania would grow up in. But today was not the day to think about that.

The Soviet elite were in a good mood. They had won the war and defeated Germany. Their old enemy Japan was being crushed by the USA. The insane honor code of Japan's leaders made it difficult for them to surrender, but it was only a matter of time now. Tragically, while they clung to their pride, more Japanese and American troops would die, and more Japanese women and children would be bombed out of their homes, but the end result would be the same. Sadly, it seemed there was nothing the Americans could do to hasten the process and prevent unnecessary deaths.

Volodya's father, drunk and happy, made a speech. "The Red Army has occupied Poland," he said. "Never again will that country be used as a springboard for a German invasion of Russia."

All the old comrades cheered and thumped the tables.

"In Western Europe, Communist parties are being endorsed by the masses as never before. In the Paris municipal elections last March, the Communist Party won the largest share of the vote. I congratulate our French comrades."

They cheered again.

"As I look around the world today, I see that the Russian Revolution, in which so many brave men fought and died . . ." He trailed off as drunken tears came to his eyes. A hush descended on the room. He recovered himself. "I see that the revolution has never been as secure as it is today!"

They raised their glasses. "The revolution! The revolution!" Everyone drank.

The doors flew open, and Comrade Stalin walked in.

Everyone stood up.

His hair was gray, and he looked tired. He was about sixty-five, and he had been ill: there were rumors that he had suffered a series of strokes or minor heart attacks. But his mood today was ebullient. "I have come to kiss the bride!" he said.

He walked up to Zoya and put his hands on her shoulders. She was a good three inches taller than he, but she managed to stoop discreetly. He kissed her on both cheeks, allowing his gray-mustached mouth to linger just long enough to make Volodya feel resentful. Then he stepped back and said: "How about a drink for me?"

Several people hastened to get him a glass of vodka. Grigori insisted on giving Stalin his chair in the center of the head table. The buzz of conversation resumed, but it was subdued: they were thrilled he was here, but now they had to be careful of every word and every move. This man could have a person killed with a snap of his fingers, and he frequently had.

More vodka was brought, the band began to play Russian folk dances, and slowly people relaxed. Volodya, Zoya, Grigori, and Katerina did a four-person dance called a *kadril,* which was intended to be comic and always made people laugh. After that more couples danced, and the men started to do the *barynya,* in which they had to squat and kick up their legs, which caused many of them to fall over. Volodya kept checking on Stalin out of the corner of his eye—as did everyone else in the room—and he seemed to be enjoying himself, tapping his glass on the table in time with the balalaikas.

Zoya and Katerina were dancing a troika with Zoya's boss, Vasili, a senior physicist working on the bomb project, and Volodya was sitting out, when the atmosphere changed.

An aide in a civilian suit came in, hurried around the edge of the room, and went right up to Stalin. Without ceremony, he leaned over the leader's shoulder and spoke to him quietly but urgently.

Stalin at first looked puzzled, and asked a sharp question, then another. Then his face changed. He went pale, and seemed to stare at the dancers without seeing them.

Volodya said under his breath: "What the hell has happened?"

The dancers had not yet noticed, but those sitting at the head table looked frightened.

After a moment Stalin stood up. Those around him deferentially did the same. Volodya saw that his father was still dancing. People had been shot for less.

But Stalin had no eyes for the wedding guests. With the aide at his side he left the table. He walked toward the door, crossing the dance floor. Terrified revelers jumped out of his way. One couple fell over. Stalin did not seem to notice. The band ground to a halt. Saying nothing, looking at nobody, Stalin left the room.

Some of the generals followed him out, looking scared.

Another aide appeared, then two more. They all sought out their bosses and spoke to them. A young man in a tweed jacket went up to Vasili. Zoya seemed to know the man, and listened intently to him. She looked shocked.

Vasili and the aide left the room. Volodya went to Zoya and said: "For God's sake, what's going on?"

Her voice was shaky. "The Americans have dropped a nuclear bomb on Japan." Her beautifully pale face seemed even whiter than normal. "At first the Japanese government couldn't figure out what had happened. It took them hours to realize what it was."

"Are we sure?"

"It flattened five square miles of buildings. They estimate that seventy-five thousand people were killed instantly."

"How many bombs?"

"One."

"One bomb?"

"Yes."

"Good God. No wonder Stalin turned pale."

They both stood silent. The news was spreading around the room visibly. Some people sat stunned; others got up and left, heading for their offices, their telephones, their desks, and their staffs.

"This changes everything," Volodya said.

"Including our honeymoon plans," said Zoya. "My leave is sure to be canceled."

"We thought the Soviet Union was safe."

"Your father has just made a speech about how the revolution has never been so secure."

"Now nothing is secure."

"No," said Zoya. "Not until we have a bomb of our own."

## vii

Jacky Jakes and Georgy were in Buffalo, staying at Marga's apartment for the first time. Greg and Lev were there, too, and on Victory in Japan Day—Wednesday, August 15—they all went to Humboldt Park. The paths were crowded with jubilant couples and there were hundreds of children splashing in the pond.

Greg was happy and proud. The bomb had worked. The two devices dropped on Hiroshima and Nagasaki had wreaked sickening devastation, but they had brought the war to a quick end and saved thousands of American lives. Greg had played a role in that. Because of what they had all done, Georgy was going to grow up in a free world.

"He's nine," Greg said to Jacky. They were sitting on a bench, talking, while Lev and Marga took Georgy to buy ice cream.

"I can hardly believe it."

"What will he be, I wonder?"

Jacky said fiercely: "He's not going to do something stupid like acting or playing the goddamn trumpet. He's got brains."

"Would you like him to be a college professor, like your father?"

"Yes."

"In that case"—Greg had been leading up to this, and was nervous about how Jacky might react—"he ought to go to a good school."

"What did you have in mind?"

"How about boarding school? He could go where I went."

"He'd be the only black pupil."

"Not necessarily. When I was there, we had a colored guy, an Indian from Delhi called Kamal."

"Just one."

"Yes."

"Was he teased?"

"Sure. We called him Camel. But the boys got used to him, and he made some friends."

"What happened to him, do you know?"

"He became a pharmacist. I hear he already owns two drugstores in New York."

Jacky nodded. Greg could tell that she was not opposed to this plan. She came from a cultured family. Although she herself had rebelled and dropped out, she believed in the value of education. "What about the school fees?"

"I could ask my father."

"Would he pay?"

"Look at them." Greg pointed along the path. Lev, Marga, and Georgy were returning from the ice-cream vendor's cart. Lev and Georgy were walking side by side, eating ice-cream cones, holding hands. "My conservative father, holding the hand of a colored child in a public park. Trust me, he'll pay the school fees."

"Georgy doesn't really fit anywhere," Jacky said, looking troubled. "He's a black boy with a white daddy."

"I know."

"People in your mother's apartment building think I'm the maid— did you know that?"

"Yes."

"I've been careful not to set them straight. If they thought Negroes were in the building as guests, there might be trouble."

Greg sighed. "I'm sorry, but you're right."

"Life is going to be tough for Georgy."

"I know," said Greg. "But he's got us."

Jacky gave him a rare smile. "Yeah," she said. "That's something."

# PART THREE

## THE
## COLD PEACE

# CHAPTER TWENTY-ONE

# 1945 ( III )

After the wedding Volodya and Zoya moved into an apartment of their own. Few Russian newlyweds were so lucky. For four years the industrial might of the Soviet Union had been directed to making weapons. Hardly any homes had been built, and many had been destroyed. But Volodya was a major in Red Army Intelligence, as well as the son of a general, and he was able to pull strings.

It was a compact space: a living room with a dining table, a bedroom so small the bed almost filled it, a kitchen that was crowded with two people in it, a cramped toilet with a washbasin and shower, and a tiny hall with a closet for their clothes. When the radio was on in the living room, they could hear it all over the flat.

They quickly made it their own. Zoya bought a bright yellow coverlet for the bed. Volodya's mother produced a set of crockery that she had bought in 1940, in anticipation of his wedding, and saved all through the war. Volodya hung a picture on the wall, a graduation photograph of his class at the Military Intelligence Academy.

They made love more now. Being alone made a difference Volodya had not anticipated. He had never felt particularly inhibited when sleeping with Zoya at his parents' place, or in the apartment she used to share, but now he realized it had an influence. You had to keep your voice down, you listened in case the bed squeaked, and there was always the possibility, albeit remote, that somebody would walk in on you. Other people's homes were never completely private.

They often woke early, made love, then lay kissing and talking for an hour before getting dressed for work. Lying with his head on her thighs on one such morning, the smell of sex in his nostrils, Volodya said: "Do you want some tea?"

"Yes, please." She stretched luxuriously, reclining on the pillows.

Volodya put on a robe and crossed the tiny hallway to the little kitchen, where he lit the gas under the samovar. He was displeased to see the pots and dishes from last night's dinner stacked in the sink. "Zoya!" he said. "This kitchen's in a mess!"

She could hear him easily in the small apartment. "I know," she said.

He went back to the bedroom. "Why didn't you clean up last night?"

"Why didn't you?"

It had not occurred to him that it might be his responsibility. But he said: "I had a report to write."

"And I was tired."

The suggestion that it was his fault irritated him. "I hate a filthy kitchen."

"So do I."

Why was she being so obtuse? "If you don't like it, clean it!"

"Let's do it together, right away." She sprang out of bed. She pushed past him with a sexy smile and went into the kitchen.

Volodya followed.

She said: "You wash. I'll dry." She took a clean towel from a drawer.

She was still naked. He could not help but smile. Her body was long and slim, and her skin was white. She had flat breasts and pointed nipples, and the hair of her groin was fine and blond. One of the joys of being married to her was her habit of moving around the apartment in the nude. He could stare at her body for as long as he liked. She seemed to enjoy it. If she caught his eye, she showed no embarrassment, but just smiled.

He rolled up the sleeves of his robe and began to wash the dishes, passing them to Zoya to dry. Washing up was not a very manly activity— Volodya had never seen his father do it—but Zoya seemed to think such chores should be shared. It was an eccentric idea. Did Zoya have a highly developed sense of fairness in marriage? Or was he being emasculated?

He thought he heard something outside. He glanced into the hall: the apartment door was only three or four steps from the kitchen sink. He could see nothing out of the ordinary.

Then the door was smashed open.

Zoya screamed.

Volodya picked up the carving knife he had just washed. He stepped past Zoya and stood in the kitchen doorway. A uniformed policeman holding a sledgehammer was just outside the ruined door.

Volodya was filled with fear and rage. He said: "What the fuck is this?"

The policeman stepped back, and a small, thin man with a face like a rodent entered the flat. It was Volodya's brother-in-law, Ilya Dvorkin, an agent of the secret police. He was wearing leather gloves.

"Ilya!" said Volodya. "You stupid weasel."

"Speak respectfully," said Ilya.

Volodya was baffled as well as angry. The secret police did not normally arrest the staff of Red Army Intelligence, and vice versa. Otherwise it would have been gang warfare. "Why the hell have you busted my door? I would have opened it!"

Two more agents stepped into the hall and stood behind Ilya. They wore their trademark leather coats, despite the mild late-summer weather.

Volodya was fearful. What was going on?

Ilya said in a shaky voice: "Put the knife down, Volodya."

"No need to be afraid," said Volodya. "I was just washing up." He handed the knife to Zoya, standing behind him. "Please step into the living room. We can talk while Zoya gets dressed."

"Do you imagine this is a social call?" Ilya said indignantly.

"Whatever kind of call it is, I'm sure you don't want the embarrassment of seeing my wife naked."

"I am here on official police business!"

"Then why did they send my brother-in-law?"

Ilya lowered his voice. "Don't you understand that it would be much worse for you if someone else had come?"

This looked like bad trouble. Volodya struggled to keep up the façade of bravado. "Exactly what do you and these other assholes want?"

"Comrade Beria has taken over the direction of the nuclear physics program."

Volodya knew that. Stalin had set up a new committee to direct the work and made Beria chairman. Beria knew nothing about physics and was completely unqualified to organize a scientific research project. But Stalin trusted him. It was the usual problem of Soviet government: incompetent but loyal people were promoted into jobs they could not cope with.

Volodya said: "And Comrade Beria needs my wife in her laboratory, developing the bomb. Have you come to drive her to work?"

"The Americans created their nuclear bomb before the Soviets."

"Indeed. Could they perhaps have given research physics higher priority than we did?"

"It is not possible that capitalist science should be superior to Communist science!"

"This is a truism." Volodya was puzzled. Where was this heading? "So what do you conclude?"

"There must have been sabotage."

That was exactly the kind of ludicrous fantasy the secret police would dream up. "What kind of sabotage?"

"Some of the scientists deliberately delayed the development of the Soviet bomb."

Volodya began to understand, and he felt afraid. But he continued to respond belligerently: it was always a mistake to show weakness with these people. "Why the hell would they do that?"

"Because they are traitors—and your wife is one!"

"You'd better not be serious, you piece of shit—"

"I am here to arrest your wife."

"What?" Volodya was flabbergasted. "This is insane!"

"It is the view of my organization."

"There is no evidence."

"For evidence, go to Hiroshima!"

Zoya spoke for the first time since she had screamed. "I'll have to go with them, Volodya. Don't get yourself arrested, too."

Volodya pointed a finger at Ilya. "You are in so much fucking trouble."

"I'm carrying out my orders."

"Step out of the way. My wife is going into the bedroom to get dressed."

"No time for that," said Ilya. "She must come as she is."

"Don't be ridiculous."

Ilya put his nose in the air. "A respectable Soviet citizen would not walk around the apartment with no clothes on."

Volodya wondered briefly how his sister felt being married to this creep. "You, the secret police, morally disapprove of nudity?"

"Her nakedness is evidence of her degradation. We will take her as she is."

"No, you fucking won't."

"Stand aside."

"You stand aside. She's going to get dressed." Volodya stepped into the hall and stood in front of the three agents, holding his arms out so that Zoya could pass behind him.

As she moved, Ilya reached past Volodya and grabbed her arm.

Volodya punched him in the face, twice. Ilya cried out and staggered back. The two men in leather coats stepped forward. Volodya aimed a punch at one, but the man dodged it. Then each man took one of Volodya's arms. He struggled, but they were strong and seemed to have done this before. They slammed him against the wall.

While they held him, Ilya punched him in the face with leather-gloved fists, twice, three times, four, then in the stomach, again and again until Volodya puked blood. Zoya tried to intervene, but Ilya punched her, too, and she screamed and fell back.

Volodya's bathrobe came open in front. Ilya kicked him in the balls, then kicked his knees. Volodya sagged, unable to stand, but the two men in leather coats held him up, and Ilya punched him some more.

At last Ilya turned away, rubbing his knuckles. The other two released Volodya, and he crumpled to the floor. He could hardly breathe and felt unable to move, but he was conscious. Out of the corner of his eye he saw the two heavies grab Zoya and march her naked out of the apartment. Ilya followed.

As the minutes went by, the pain changed from sharp agony to deep, dull ache, and Volodya's breathing began to return to normal.

Motion eventually returned to his limbs, and he dragged himself upright. He made it to the phone and dialed his father's number, hoping the old man had not yet left for work. He was relieved to hear his father's voice. "They've arrested Zoya," he said.

"Fucking bastards," Grigori said. "Who was it?"

"It was Ilya."

"What?"

"Make some calls," Volodya said. "See if you can find out what the fuck is going on. I have to wash off the blood."

"What blood?"

Volodya hung up.

It was only a couple of steps to the bathroom. He dropped his bloodstained robe and got into the shower. The warm water brought some relief to his bruised body. Ilya was mean but not strong, and he had not broken any bones.

Volodya turned off the water. He looked in the bathroom mirror. His face was covered with cuts and bruises.

He did not bother to dry himself. With considerable effort, he got dressed in his Red Army uniform. He wanted the symbol of authority.

His father arrived as he was trying to tie the laces of his boots. "What the fucking hell happened here?" Grigori roared.

Volodya said: "They were looking for a fight, and I was foolish enough to give them one."

His father was unsympathetic at first. "I'd have expected you to know better."

"They insisted on taking her away naked."

"Fucking creeps."

"Did you find out anything?"

"Not yet. I talked to a couple of people. No one knows anything." Grigori looked worried. "Either someone has made a really stupid mistake . . . or for some reason they're very sure of themselves."

"Drive me to my office. Lemitov is going to be mad as hell. He won't let them get away with this. If they are allowed to do it to me, they'll do it to all of Red Army Intelligence."

Grigori's car and driver were waiting outside. They drove to the Khodynka airfield. Grigori stayed in the car while Volodya limped into Red Army Intelligence headquarters. He went straight to the office of his boss, Colonel Lemitov.

He tapped on the door, walked in, and said: "The fucking secret police have arrested my wife."

"I know," said Lemitov.

"You know?"

"I okayed it."

Volodya's jaw dropped. "What the fuck?"

"Sit down."

"What is going on?"

"Sit down and shut up, and I'll tell you."

Volodya eased himself painfully into a chair.

Lemitov said: "We have to have a nuclear bomb, and fast. At the moment, Stalin is playing it tough with the Americans, because we're fairly sure they don't have a big enough arsenal of nuclear weapons to wipe us out. But they're building a stockpile, and at some point they will use them—unless we are in a position to retaliate."

This made no sense. "My wife can't design the bomb while the secret police are punching her in the face. This is insane."

"Shut the fuck up. Our problem is that there are several possible designs. The Americans took five years to figure out which would work. We don't have that much time. We have to steal their research."

"We'll still need Russian physicists to copy the design—and for that they have to be in their laboratories, not locked in the basement of the Lubyanka."

"You know a man called Wilhelm Frunze."

"I was at school with him. The Berlin Boys' Academy."

"He gave us valuable information about British nuclear research. Then he moved to the States, where he worked on the nuclear bomb project. The Washington staff of the NKVD contacted him, scared him by their incompetence, and fucked up the relationship. We need to win him back."

"What has all this got to do with me?"

"He trusts you."

"I don't know that. I haven't seen him for twelve years."

"We want you to go to America and talk to him."

"But why did you arrest Zoya?"

"To make sure you come back."

## ii

Volodya told himself he knew how to do this. In Berlin, before the war, he had shaken off Gestapo tails, met with potential spies, recruited them, and made them into reliable sources of secret intelligence. It was never easy—especially the part where he had to talk someone into turning traitor—but he was an expert.

However, this was America.

The Western countries he had visited, Germany and Spain in the thirties and forties, were nothing like this.

He was overwhelmed. All his life he had been told that Hollywood movies gave an exaggerated impression of prosperity, and that in reality most Americans lived in poverty. But it was clear to Volodya, from the day he arrived in the USA, that the movies hardly exaggerated at all. And poor people were hard to find.

New York was jammed with cars, many driven by people who clearly were not important government officials: youngsters, men in work clothes, even women out shopping. And everybody was so well dressed! All the men appeared to be wearing their best suits. The women's calves were clad in sheer stockings. Everyone seemed to have new shoes.

He had to keep reminding himself of the bad side of America. There was poverty, somewhere. Negroes were persecuted, and in the South they could not vote. There was a lot of crime—Americans themselves said that it was rampant—although, strangely, Volodya did not actually see any evidence of it, and he felt quite safe walking the streets.

He spent a few days exploring New York. He worked on his English, which was not good, but it hardly mattered: the city was full of people who spoke broken English with heavy accents. He got to know the faces of some of the FBI agents assigned to tail him, and identified several convenient locations where he would be able to lose them.

One sunny morning he left the Soviet consulate in New York, hatless and wearing only gray slacks and a blue shirt, as if he were going to run a few errands. A young man in a dark suit and tie followed him.

He went to the Saks Fifth Avenue department store and bought underwear and a shirt with a small brown checked pattern. Whoever was tailing him had to think he was probably just shopping.

The NKVD chief at the consulate had announced that a Soviet team would shadow Volodya throughout his American visit, to make sure of his good behavior. He could barely contain his rage at the organization that had imprisoned Zoya, and he had to repress the urge to take the man by the throat and strangle him. But he had remained calm. He had pointed out sarcastically that in order to fulfill his mission he would have to evade FBI surveillance, and in doing so he might inadvertently also lose his NKVD tail, but he wished them luck. Most days he shook them off in five minutes.

So the young man tailing him was almost certainly an FBI agent. His crisply conservative clothes corroborated that.

Carrying his purchases in a paper bag, Volodya left the store by a side entrance and hailed a cab. He left the FBI man at the curb waving his arm. When the cab had turned two corners, Volodya threw the driver a bill and jumped out. He darted into a subway station, left again by a different entrance, and waited in the doorway of an office building for five minutes.

The young man in the dark suit was nowhere to be seen.

Volodya walked to Penn Station.

There he double-checked that he was not being followed, then bought his ticket. With nothing but that and his paper bag he boarded a train.

The journey to Albuquerque took three days.

The train sped through mile after endless mile of rich farmland, mighty factories belching smoke, and great cities with skyscrapers pointing arrogantly at the heavens. The Soviet Union was bigger, but apart from the Ukraine it was mostly pine forests and frozen steppes. He had never imagined wealth on this scale.

And wealth was not all. For several days something had been nagging at the back of Volodya's mind, something strange about life in America. Eventually he realized what it was: no one asked for his papers. After he had passed through immigration control in New York, he had not shown his passport again. In this country, it seemed, anyone could walk into a railway station or a bus terminus and buy a ticket to any place without having to get permission or explain the purpose of the trip to an official. It gave him a dangerously exhilarating sense of freedom. He could go anywhere!

America's wealth also heightened Volodya's sense of the danger his country faced. The Germans had almost destroyed the Soviet Union, and this country was three times as populous and ten times as rich. The thought that Russians might become underlings, frightened into subservience, softened Volodya's doubts about Communism, despite what the NKVD had done to him and his wife. If he had children, he did not want them to grow up in a world tyrannized by America.

He traveled via Pittsburgh and Chicago and attracted no attention en route. His clothes were American, and his accent was not noticed for the simple reason that he spoke to no one. He bought sandwiches and coffee by pointing and paying. He flicked through newspapers and magazines that other travelers left behind, looking at the pictures and trying to work out the meanings of the headlines.

The last part of the journey took him through a desert landscape of desolate beauty, with distant snowy peaks stained red by the sunset, which probably explained why they were called the Blood of Christ Mountains.

He went to the toilet, where he changed his underwear and put on the new shirt he had bought in Saks.

He expected the FBI or army security to be watching the train station in Albuquerque, and sure enough he spotted a young man whose check jacket—too warm for the climate of New Mexico in September—did not quite conceal the bulge of a gun in a shoulder holster. However, the agent was undoubtedly interested in long-distance travelers who might be arriving from New York or Washington. Volodya, with no hat or jacket and no luggage, looked like a local man coming back from a short trip. He was not followed as he walked to the bus station and boarded a Greyhound for Santa Fe.

He reached his destination late in the afternoon. He noted two FBI men at the Santa Fe bus station, and they scrutinized him. However, they could not tail everyone who got off the bus, and once again his casual appearance caused them to dismiss him.

Doing his best to look as if he knew where he was going, he strolled along the streets. The low flat-roofed pueblo-style houses and squat churches baking in the sun reminded him of Spain. The storefront buildings overhung the sidewalks, creating pleasantly shady arcades.

He avoided La Fonda, the big hotel on the town square next to the cathedral, and checked into the St. Francis. He paid cash and gave his name as Robert Pender, which might have been American or one of several European nationalities. "My suitcase will be delivered later," he said to the pretty girl behind the reception desk. "If I'm out when it comes, can you make sure it gets sent up to my room?"

"Oh, sure, that won't be a problem," she said.

"Thank you," he said; then he added a phrase he had heard several times on the train: "I sure appreciate it."

"If I'm not here, someone else will deal with the bag, so long as it has your name on it."

"It does." He had no luggage, but she would never realize that.

She looked at his entry in the book. "So, Mr. Pender, you're from New York."

There was a touch of skepticism in her voice, no doubt because he did not sound like a New Yorker. "I'm from Switzerland originally," he explained, naming a neutral country.

"That accounts for the accent. I haven't met a Switzerland person before. What's it like there?"

Volodya had never been to Switzerland, but he had seen photographs. "It snows a lot," he said.

"Well, enjoy our New Mexico weather!"

"I will."

Five minutes later he went out again.

Some of the scientists lived at the Los Alamos laboratory, he had learned from his colleagues in the Soviet embassy, but it was a shantytown with few civilized comforts, and they preferred to rent houses and apartments nearby if they could. Willi Frunze could afford it easily: he was married to a successful artist who drew a syndicated cartoon strip called *Slack Alice*. His wife, also called Alice, could work anywhere, so they had a place in the historic downtown neighborhood.

The New York office of the NKVD had provided this information. They had researched Frunze carefully, and Volodya had his address and phone number and a description of his car, a prewar Plymouth convertible with whitewall tires.

The Frunzes' building had an art gallery on the ground floor. The apartment upstairs had a large north-facing window that would appeal to an artist. A Plymouth convertible was parked outside.

Volodya preferred not to go in: the place might be bugged.

The Frunzes were an affluent childless couple, and he guessed they would not stay at home listening to the radio on a Friday night. He decided to wait around and see if they came out.

He spent some time in the art gallery, looking at the paintings for sale. He liked clear, vivid pictures and would not have wanted to own any of these messy daubs. He found a coffee shop down the block and got a window seat from which he could just see the Frunzes' door. He left there after an hour, bought a newspaper, and stood at a bus stop pretending to read it.

The long wait permitted him to establish that no one was watching the Frunze apartment. That meant that the FBI and army security had not tagged Frunze as a high risk. He was a foreigner, but so were many of the scientists, and presumably nothing else was known against him.

This was a downtown commercial district, not a residential neighborhood, and there were plenty of people on the streets, but all the same after a couple of hours Volodya began to worry that someone might notice him hanging around.

Then the Frunzes came out.

Frunze was heavier than he had been twelve years ago— there was no shortage of food in America. His hairline was beginning to recede, although he was only thirty. He still had that solemn look. He wore a sports shirt and khaki pants, a common American combination.

His wife was not so conservatively dressed. Her fair hair was pinned up under a beret, and she wore a shapeless cotton dress in an indistinct brown color, but she had an assortment of bangles on both wrists, and numerous rings. Artists had dressed like that in Germany before Hitler, Volodya remembered.

The couple set off along the street, and Volodya followed.

He wondered what the wife's politics were, and what difference her presence would make in the difficult conversation he was about to have. Frunze had been a staunch Social Democrat back in Germany, so it was not likely his wife would be a conservative, a speculation that was borne out by her appearance. On the other hand, she probably did not know he had given secrets to the Soviets in London. She was an unknown quantity.

He would prefer to deal with Frunze alone, and he considered leaving them and trying again tomorrow. But the hotel receptionist had noticed his foreign accent, so by the morning he might have an FBI tail.

He could deal with that, he thought, though not as easily in this small town as in New York or Berlin. And tomorrow was Saturday, so the Frunzes would probably spend the day together. How long might Volodya have to wait before catching Frunze alone?

There was never an easy way to do this. On balance he decided to go ahead tonight.

The Frunzes went into a diner.

Volodya walked past the place and glanced through the window. It was an inexpensive restaurant with booths. He thought of going in and sitting down with them, but he decided to let them eat first. They would be in a good mood when full of food.

He waited half an hour, watching the door from a distance. Then, full of trepidation, he went in.

They were finishing their dinner. As he crossed the restaurant, Frunze glanced up, then looked away, not recognizing him.

He slid into the booth next to Alice and spoke quietly in German. "Hello, Willi, don't you remember me from school?"

Frunze looked hard at him for several seconds; then his face broke into a smile. "Peshkov? Volodya Peshkov? Is it really you?"

A wave of relief washed over Volodya. Frunze was still friendly. There was no barrier of hostility to overcome. "It's really me," Volodya said. He offered his hand and they shook. Turning to Alice, he said in English: "I am very bad speaking your language. Sorry."

"Don't bother to try," she replied in fluent German. "My family were immigrants from Bavaria."

Frunze said in amazement: "I've been thinking about you lately, because I know another guy with the same surname—Greg Peshkov."

"Really? My father had a brother called Lev who came to America in about 1915."

"No, Lieutenant Peshkov is much younger. Anyway, what are you doing here?"

Volodya smiled. "I came to see you." Before Frunze could ask why, he said: "Last time I saw you, you were secretary of the Neukölln Social Democratic Party." This was his second step. Having established a friendly footing, he was reminding Frunze of his youthful idealism.

"That experience convinced me that democratic socialism doesn't work," Frunze said. "Against the Nazis we were completely impotent. It took the Soviet Union to stop them."

That was true, and Volodya was pleased Frunze realized it, but, more importantly, the comment showed that Frunze's political ideas had not been softened by life in affluent America.

Alice said: "We were planning to have a couple of drinks at a bar around the corner. A lot of the scientists go there on a Friday night. Would you like to join us?"

The last thing Volodya wanted was to be seen in public with the Frunzes. "I don't know," he said. In fact he had been too long with them in this restaurant. It was time for step three: reminding Frunze of his terrible guilt. He leaned forward and lowered his voice. "Willi, did you know the Americans were going to drop nuclear bombs on Japan?"

There was a long pause. Volodya held his breath. He was gambling that Frunze would be racked by remorse.

For a moment he feared he had gone too far. Frunze looked as if he might burst into tears.

Then the scientist took a deep breath and got control of himself. "No, I didn't know," he said. "None of us did."

Alice interjected angrily: "We assumed the American military would give *some* demonstration of the power of the bomb, as a threat to make the Japanese surrender earlier." So she had known about the bomb beforehand, Volodya noted. He was not surprised. Men found it hard to keep such things from their wives. "So we expected a detonation sometime, somewhere," she went on. "But we imagined they would destroy an uninhabited island, or maybe a military facility with a lot of weapons and very few people."

"That might have been justifiable," Frunze said. "But . . ." His voice fell to a whisper. "Nobody thought they would drop it on a city and kill eighty thousand men, women, and children."

Volodya nodded. "I thought you might feel this way." He had been hoping for it with all his heart.

Frunze said: "Who wouldn't?"

"Let me ask you an even more important question." This was step four. "Will they do it again?"

"I don't know," Frunze said. "They might. Christ forgive us all, they might."

Volodya concealed his satisfaction. He had made Frunze feel responsible for future use of nuclear weapons, as well as past.

Volodya nodded. "That's what we think."

Alice said sharply: "Who's *we*?"

She was shrewd, and probably more worldly-wise than her husband. She would be hard to fool, and Volodya decided not to try. He had to risk leveling with her. "A fair question," he said. "And I didn't come all this way to deceive an old friend. I'm a major in Red Army Intelligence."

They stared at him. The possibility must have crossed their minds already, but they were surprised by the stark admission.

"I have something I need to say to you," Volodya went on. "Something hugely important. Is there somewhere we can go to talk privately?"

They both looked uncertain. Frunze said: "Our apartment?"

"It has probably been bugged by the FBI."

Frunze had some experience of clandestine work, but Alice was shocked. "You think so?" she said incredulously.

"Yes. Could we drive out of town?"

Frunze said: "There's a place we go sometimes, around this time of the evening, to watch the sunset."

"Perfect. Go to your car, sit in, and wait for me. I'll be a minute behind you."

Frunze paid the check and left with Alice, and Volodya followed. During the short walk he established that no one was tailing him. He reached the Plymouth and got in. They sat three across the front seat, American-style. Frunze drove out of town.

They followed a dirt road to the top of a low hill. Frunze stopped the car. Volodya motioned for them all to get out, and led them a hundred yards away, just in case the car was bugged, too.

They looked across the landscape of stony soil and low bushes toward the setting sun, and Volodya took step five. "We think the next nuclear bomb will be dropped somewhere in the Soviet Union."

Frunze nodded. "God forbid, but you're probably right."

"And there's absolutely nothing we can do about it," Volodya went on, pressing home his point relentlessly. "There are no precautions we can take, no barriers we can erect, no way we can protect our people. There is no defense against the nuclear bomb—the bomb that you made, Willi."

"I know it," said Frunze miserably. Clearly he felt it would be his fault if the USSR was attacked with nuclear weapons.

Step six. "The only protection would be our own nuclear bomb."

Frunze did not want to believe that. "It's not a defense," he said.

"But it's a deterrent."

"It might be," he conceded.

Alice said: "We don't want these bombs to spread."

"Nor do I," said Volodya. "But the only sure way to stop the Americans flattening Moscow the way they flattened Hiroshima is for the Soviet Union to have a nuclear bomb of its own, and threaten retaliation."

Alice said: "He's right, Willi. Hell, we all know it."

She was the tough one, Volodya saw.

Volodya made his voice light for step seven. "How many bombs do the Americans have right now?"

This was a crucial moment. If Frunze answered this question, he would have crossed a line. So far the conversation had been general. Now Volodya was requesting secret information.

Frunze hesitated for a long moment. Finally he glanced at Alice.

Volodya saw her give an almost imperceptible nod.

Frunze said: "Only one."

Volodya concealed his triumph. Frunze had betrayed trust. It was the difficult first move. A second secret would come more easily.

Frunze added: "But they'll have more soon."

"It's a race, and if we lose, we die," Volodya said urgently. "We have to build at least one bomb of our own before they have enough to wipe us out."

"Can you do that?"

That gave Volodya the cue for step eight. "We need help."

He saw Frunze's face harden, and guessed he was remembering whatever it was that had made him refuse to cooperate with the NKVD.

Alice said to Volodya: "What if we say we can't help you? That it's too dangerous?"

Volodya followed his instinct. He held up his hands in a gesture of surrender. "I go home and report failure," he said. "I can't make you do anything you don't want to do. I wouldn't want to pressure you or coerce you in any way."

Alice said: "No threats?"

That confirmed Volodya's guess that the NKVD had tried to bully Frunze. They tried to bully everyone: it was all they knew. "I'm not even trying to persuade you," Volodya said to Frunze. "I'm laying out the facts. The rest is up to you. If you want to help, I'm here as your contact. If you see things differently, that's the end of it. You're both smart people. I couldn't fool you even if I wanted to."

Again they looked at each other. He hoped they were thinking how different he was from the last Soviet agent who had approached them.

The moment stretched out agonizingly.

It was Alice who spoke at last. "What kind of help do you need?"

That was not a yes, but it was better than rejection, and it led logically to step nine. "My wife is one of the physicists on the team," he said, hoping this would humanize him at a moment when they might be in danger of seeing him as manipulative. "She tells me there are several routes to a nuclear bomb, and we don't have time to try them all. We can save years if we know what worked for you."

"That makes sense," Willi said.

Step ten, the big one. "We have to know what type of bomb was dropped on Japan."

Frunze's expression was agonized. He looked at his wife. This time she did not give him the nod, but neither did she shake her head. She seemed as torn as he did.

Frunze sighed. "Two kinds," he said.

Volodya was thrilled and startled. "Two different designs?"

Frunze nodded. "For Hiroshima they used a uranium device with a gun ignition. We called it Little Boy. For Nagasaki, Fat Man, a plutonium bomb with an implosion trigger."

Volodya could hardly breathe. This was red-hot data. "Which is better?"

"They both worked, obviously, but Fat Man is easier to make."

"Why?"

"It takes years to produce enough U-235 for a bomb. Plutonium is quicker, once you have a nuclear pile."

"So the USSR should copy Fat Man."

"Definitely."

"There is one more thing you could do to help save Russia from destruction," Volodya said.

"What?"

Volodya looked him in the eye. "Get me the design drawings," he said.

Willi paled. "I'm an American citizen," he said. "You're asking me to commit treason. The penalty is death. I could go to the electric chair."

So could your wife, Volodya thought; she's complicit. Thank God you haven't thought of that.

He said: "I've asked a lot of people to put their lives at risk in the last few years. People like yourselves, Germans who hated the Nazis, men and women who took terrible risks to send us information that helped us win the war. And I have to say to you what I said to them: a lot more people will be killed if you don't do it." He fell silent. That was his best shot. He had nothing more to offer.

Frunze looked at his wife.

Alice said: "You made the bomb, Willi."

Frunze said to Volodya: "I'll think about it."

## iii

Two days later he handed over the plans.

Volodya took them to Moscow.

Zoya was released from jail. She was not as angry about her imprisonment as he was. "They did it to protect the revolution," she said. "And I wasn't hurt. It was like staying in a really bad hotel."

On her first day at home, after they made love, he said: "I have something to show you, something I brought back from America." He rolled off the bed, opened a drawer, and took out a book. "It's called the Sears Roebuck Catalogue," he said. He sat beside her on the bed and opened the book. "Look at this."

The catalogue fell open at a page of women's dresses. The models were impossibly slender, but the fabrics were bright and cheerful, stripes and checks and solid colors, some with ruffles, pleats, and belts. "That's attractive," Zoya said, putting her finger on one. "Is two dollars ninety-eight a lot of money?"

"Not really," Volodya said. "The average wage is about fifty dollars a week. Rent is about a third of that."

"Really?" Zoya was amazed. "So most people could easily afford these dresses?"

"That's right. Maybe not peasants. On the other hand, these catalogues were invented for farmers who lived a hundred miles from the nearest store."

"How does it work?"

"You pick what you want from the book and send them the money. Then a couple of weeks later the mailman brings you whatever you ordered."

"It must be like being a tsar." Zoya took the book from him and turned the page. "Oh! Here are some more." The next page showed jacket-and-skirt combinations for four dollars and ninety-eight cents. "These are elegant, too," she said.

"Keep turning the pages," Volodya said.

Zoya was astonished to see page after page of women's coats, hats, shoes, underwear, pajamas, and stockings. "People can have *any* of these?" she said.

"That's right."

"But there's more choice on one of these pages than there is in the average Russian shop!"

"Yes."

She carried on slowly leafing through the book. There was a similar range of clothing for men, and again for children. Zoya put her finger on a heavy woolen winter coat for boys that cost fifteen dollars. "At that price, I suppose every boy in America has one."

"They probably do."

After the clothes came furniture. You could buy a bed for twenty-five dollars. Everything was cheap if you had fifty dollars a week. And it went on and on. There were hundreds of things that could not be bought for any money in the Soviet Union: toys and games, beauty products, guitars, elegant chairs, power tools, novels in colorful jackets, Christmas decorations, and electric toasters.

There was even a tractor. "Do you think," Zoya said, "that any farmer in America who wants a tractor can have one *right away*?"

"Only if he has the money," said Volodya.

"He doesn't have to put his name down on a list and wait for a few years?"

"No."

Zoya closed the book and looked at him solemnly. "If people can have all this," she said, "why would they want to be Communist?"

"Good question," said Volodya.

# CHAPTER TWENTY-TWO

# 1946

The children of Berlin had a new game called Komm, Frau—Come, Woman. It was one of a dozen games in which boys chased girls, but it had a new twist, Carla noticed. The boys would team up and target one of the girls. When they caught her, they would shout: "*Komm, Frau!*" and throw her to the ground. Then they would hold her down while one of their number lay on top of her and simulated sexual intercourse. Children of seven and eight, who ought not to know what rape was, played this game because they had seen what Red Army soldiers did to German women. Every Russian knew that one phrase of the German language: "*Komm, Frau.*"

What was it about the Russians? Carla had never met anyone who had been raped by a French, British, American, or Canadian soldier, though she supposed it must happen. By contrast, every woman she knew between fifteen and fifty-five had been raped by at least one Soviet soldier: her mother, Maud; her friend Frieda; Frieda's mother, Monika; Ada, the maid; all of them.

Yet they were lucky, for they were still alive. Some women, abused by dozens of men, hour after hour, had died. Carla had heard of a girl who had been bitten to death.

Only Rebecca Rosen had escaped. After Carla had protected her, the day the Jewish Hospital was liberated, Rebecca moved into the von Ulrich town house. It was in the Soviet zone, but she had nowhere else to go. She hid for months like a criminal in the attic, coming down only late at night when the bestial Russians had fallen into drunken sleep. Carla spent a couple of hours up there with her when she could, and they played card games and told each other their life stories. Carla wanted to be like an older sister, but Rebecca treated her like a mother.

Then Carla found she was going to be a mother for real.

Maud and Monika were in their fifties, and too old to have babies, mercifully, and Ada was lucky, but both Carla and Frieda were pregnant by their rapists.

Frieda had an abortion.

It was illegal, and a Nazi law that threatened the death penalty was still in force. So Frieda went to an elderly "midwife" who did it for five cigarettes. Frieda contracted a severe infection, and would have died but that Carla was able to steal scarce penicillin from the hospital.

Carla decided to have her baby.

Her feelings about it swung violently from one extreme to another. When suffering morning sickness she raged against the beasts who had violated her body and left her with this burden. At other times she found herself sitting with her hands on her belly, staring into space and thinking dreamily about baby clothes. Then she would wonder if the baby's face would remind her of one of the men, and cause her to hate her own child. But surely it would have some von Ulrich features, too? She felt anxious and frightened.

She was eight months pregnant in January 1946. Like most Germans she was also cold, hungry, and destitute. When her pregnancy became obvious, she had to give up nursing and join the millions of unemployed. Food rations were issued every ten days. The daily amount, for those without special privileges, was fifteen hundred calories. It still had to be paid for, of course. And even for customers with cash and ration cards, sometimes there was simply no food to buy.

Carla had considered asking the Soviets for special treatment because of her wartime work as a spy. But Heinrich had tried that and suffered a frightening experience. Red Army Intelligence had expected him to continue to spy for them, and asked him to infiltrate the U.S. military. When he said he would rather not, they became nasty and threatened to send him to a labor camp. He got out of it by saying he spoke no English, therefore was no use to them. But Carla was well warned, and decided it was safest to keep quiet.

Today Carla and Maud were happy because they had sold a chest of drawers. It was a Jugendstil piece in burled light oak that Walter's parents had bought when they got married in 1889. Carla, Maud, and Ada had loaded it onto a borrowed handcart.

There were still no men in their house. Erik and Werner were among millions of German soldiers who had disappeared. Perhaps they were dead. Colonel Beck had told Carla that almost three million Germans had died in battle on the eastern front, and more had died as prisoners of the Soviets—killed by hunger, cold, and disease. But another two million were still alive and working in labor camps in the Soviet Union. Some had come back: they had either escaped from their guards or had been released because they were too ill to work, and they had joined the thousands of displaced persons on the tramp all over Europe, trying to find their way home. Carla and Maud had written letters and sent them care of the Red Army, but no replies had ever come.

Carla felt torn about the prospect of Werner's return. She still loved him, and hoped desperately that he was alive and well, but she dreaded meeting him when she was pregnant with a rapist's baby. Although it was not her fault, she felt irrationally ashamed.

So the three women pushed the handcart through the streets. They left Rebecca behind. The Red Army orgy of rape and looting had passed its nightmare peak, and Rebecca no longer lived in the attic, but it was still not safe for a pretty girl to walk the streets.

Huge photographs of Lenin and Stalin now hung over Unter den Linden, once the promenade of Germany's fashionable elite. Most Berlin roads had been cleared, and the rubble of destroyed buildings stood in stacks every few hundred yards, ready to be reused, perhaps, if ever Germans were able to rebuild their country. Acres of houses had been flattened, often entire city blocks. It would take years to deal with the wreckage. There were thousands of bodies rotting in the ruins, and the sickly-sweet smell of decaying human flesh had been in the air all summer. Now it smelled only after rain.

Meanwhile, the city had been divided into four zones: Russian, American, British, and French. Many of the buildings still standing had been commandeered by the occupying troops. Berliners lived where they could, often seeking inadequate shelter in the surviving rooms of half-demolished houses. The city had running water again, and electric power came on fitfully, but it was hard to find fuel for heating and cooking. The chest of drawers might be almost as valuable chopped up for firewood.

They took it to Wedding, in the French zone, where they sold it to a charming Parisian colonel for a carton of Gitanes. The occupation currency had become worthless, because the Soviets printed too much of it, so everything was bought and sold for cigarettes.

Now they were returning triumphant, Maud and Ada steering the empty cart while Carla walked alongside. She ached all over from pushing the cart, but they were rich: a whole carton of cigarettes would go a long way.

Night fell and the temperature dropped to freezing. Their route home took them briefly into the British sector. Carla sometimes wondered whether the British might help her mother if they knew the hardship she was suffering. On the other hand, Maud had been a German citizen for twenty-six years. Her brother, Earl Fitzherbert, was wealthy and influential, but he had refused to support her after her marriage to Walter von Ulrich, and he was a stubborn man: it was not likely he would change his attitude.

They came across a small crowd, thirty or forty ragged people, outside a house that had been taken over by the occupying power. Stopping to find out what they were staring at, the three women saw a party going on inside. Through the windows they could observe brightly lit rooms, laughing men and women holding drinks, and waitresses moving through the throng with trays of food. Carla looked around her. The crowd was mostly women and children—there were not many men left in Berlin, or indeed in Germany—and they were all staring longingly at the windows, like rejected sinners outside the gates of paradise. It was a pathetic sight.

"This is obscene," said Maud, and she marched up the path to the door of the house.

A British sentry stood in her way and said: "*Nein, nein,*" probably the only German he knew.

Maud addressed him in the crisp upper-class English she had spoken as a girl. "I must see your commanding officer immediately."

Carla admired her mother's nerve and poise, as always.

The sentry looked doubtfully at Maud's threadbare coat, but after a moment he tapped on the door. It opened, and a face looked out. "English lady wants the CO," said the sentry.

A moment later the door opened again and two people looked out. They might have been caricatures of a British officer and his wife: he in his mess kit with a black bow tie, she in a long dress and pearls.

"Good evening," Maud said. "I'm frightfully sorry to disturb your party."

They stared at her, astonished to be spoken to that way by a woman in rags.

Maud went on: "I just thought you should see what you're doing to these wretched people outside."

The couple looked at the crowd.

Maud said: "You might draw the curtains, for pity's sake."

After a moment the woman said: "Oh, dear, George, have we been terribly unkind?"

"Unintentionally, perhaps," the man said gruffly.

"Could we possibly make amends by sending some food out to them?"

"Yes," Maud said quickly. "That would be a kindness as well as an apology."

The officer looked dubious. It was probably against some kind of regulation to give canapés to starving Germans.

The woman pleaded: "George, darling, may we?"

"Oh, very well," said her husband.

The woman turned back to Maud. "Thank you for alerting us. We really didn't mean to do this."

"You're welcome," Maud said, and she retreated down the path.

A few minutes later, guests began to emerge from the house with plates of sandwiches and cakes, which they offered to the starving crowd. Carla grinned. Her mother's impudence had paid off. She took a large piece of fruitcake, which she wolfed in a few starved bites. It contained more sugar than she had eaten in the past six months.

The curtains were drawn, the guests returned to the house, and the crowd dispersed. Maud and Ada grasped the handles of the cart and recommenced pushing it home. "Well done, Mother," said Carla. "A carton of Gitanes *and* a free meal, all in one afternoon!"

Apart from the Soviets, few of the occupying soldiers were cruel to Germans, Carla reflected. She found it surprising. American GIs gave out chocolate bars. Even the French, whose own children had gone hungry under German occupation, often showed kindness. After all the misery we Germans have inflicted on our neighbors, Carla thought, it's astonishing they don't hate us more. On the other hand, what with the Nazis, the Red Army, and the air raids, perhaps they think we've been punished enough.

It was late when they got home. They left the cart with the neighbors who had loaned it, giving them half a pack of Gitanes as payment. They entered their house, which was luckily still intact. There was no glass in most of the windows, and the stonework was pocked with craters, but the place had not suffered structural damage, and it still kept the weather out.

All the same, the four women now lived in the kitchen, sleeping there on mattresses they dragged in from the hall at night. It was hard enough to warm that one room, and they certainly did not have fuel to heat the rest of the house. The kitchen stove had burned coal, in the old days, but that was now virtually unobtainable. However, they had found the stove would burn many other things: books, newspapers, broken furniture, even net curtains.

They slept in pairs, Carla with Rebecca and Maud with Ada. Rebecca often cried herself to sleep in Carla's arms, as she had the night after her parents were killed.

The long walk had exhausted Carla, and she immediately lay down. Ada built up the fire in the stove with old news magazines Rebecca had brought down from the attic. Maud added water to the remains of the lunchtime bean soup and reheated it for their supper.

Sitting up to drink her soup, Carla suffered a sharp abdominal pain. This was not a result of pushing the handcart, she realized. It was something else. She checked the date and counted back to the date of the liberation of the Jewish Hospital.

"Mother," she said fearfully, "I think the baby's coming."

"It's too soon!" Maud said.

"I'm thirty-six weeks pregnant, and I'm getting cramps."

"Then we'd better get ready."

Maud went upstairs to fetch towels.

Ada brought a wooden chair from the dining room. She had a useful length of twisted steel from a bomb site that served her as a sledgehammer. She smashed the chair into manageable pieces, then built up the fire in the stove.

Carla put her hands on her distended belly. "You might have waited for warmer weather, Baby," she said.

Soon she was in too much pain to notice the cold. She had not known anything could hurt this much.

Nor that it could go on so long. She was in labor all night. Maud and Ada took turns holding her hand while she moaned and cried. Rebecca looked on, white-faced and scared.

The gray light of morning was filtering through the newspaper taped over the glassless kitchen window when at last the baby's head emerged. Carla was overwhelmed by a feeling of relief like nothing she had ever experienced, even though the pain did not immediately cease.

After one more agonizing push, Maud took the baby from between her legs.

"A boy," she said.

She blew on his face, and he opened his mouth and cried.

She gave the baby to Carla, and propped her upright on the mattress with some cushions from the drawing room.

He had lots of dark hair all over his head.

Maud tied off the cord with a piece of cotton, then cut it. Carla unbuttoned her blouse and put the baby to her breast.

She was worried she might have no milk. Her breasts should have swollen and leaked toward the end of her pregnancy, but they had not, perhaps because the baby was early, perhaps because the mother was undernourished. But, after a few moments of sucking, she felt a strange pain, and the milk began to flow.

Soon he fell asleep.

Ada brought a bowl of warm water and a rag, and gently washed the baby's face and head, then the rest of him.

Rebecca whispered: "He's so beautiful."

Carla said: "Mother, shall we call him Walter?"

She had not intended to be dramatic, but Maud fell apart. Her face crumpled and she bent double, racked by terrible sobs. She recovered herself sufficiently to say, "I'm sorry." Then she was convulsed by grief again. "Oh, Walter, my Walter," she wept.

Eventually her crying subsided. "I'm sorry," she said again. "I didn't mean to make a fuss." She wiped her face with her sleeve. "I just wish your father could see the baby, that's all. It's so unfair."

Ada surprised them both by quoting the book of Job: "'The Lord giveth and the Lord taketh away,'" she said. "'Blessed be the name of the Lord.'"

Carla did not believe in God—no holy being worthy of the name could have allowed the Nazi death camps to happen—but all the same she found comfort in the quotation. It was about accepting everything in human life, including the pain of birth and the sorrow of death. Maud seemed to appreciate it, too, and she became calmer.

Carla looked adoringly at baby Walter. She would care for him and feed him and keep him warm, she vowed, no matter what difficulties stood in the way. He was the most wonderful child that had ever been born, and she would love and cherish him forever.

He woke up, and Carla gave him her nipple again. He sucked

contentedly, making small smacking noises with his mouth, while four women watched him. For a little while, in the warm, dim-lit kitchen, there was no other sound.

## ii

The first speech made by a new member of Parliament is called a maiden speech, and is usually dull. Certain things have to be said, stock phrases are used, and the convention is that the subject must not be controversial. Colleagues and opponents alike congratulate the newcomer, the traditions are observed, and the ice is broken.

Lloyd Williams made his first *real* speech a few months later, during the debate on the national insurance bill. That was more scary.

In preparing it he had two orators in mind. His grandfather Dai Williams used the language and rhythms of the Bible, not just in chapel but also—perhaps especially—when speaking of the hardship and injustice of the life of a coal miner. He relished short words rich in meaning: *toil, sin, greed.* He spoke of the hearth and the pit and the grave.

Churchill did the same, but had humor that Dai Williams lacked. His long, majestic sentences often ended with an unexpected image or a reversal of meaning. Having been editor of the government newspaper the *British Gazette* during the General Strike of 1926, he had warned trade unionists: "Make your minds perfectly clear: if ever you let loose upon us again a general strike, we will loose upon you another *British Gazette.*" A speech needed such surprises, Lloyd believed; they were like the raisins in a bun.

But when he stood up to speak, he found that his carefully wrought sentences suddenly seemed unreal. His audience clearly felt the same, and he could sense that the fifty or sixty M.P.s in the chamber were only half listening. He suffered a moment of panic: How could he be boring about a subject that mattered so profoundly to the people he represented?

On the government front bench he could see his mother, now minister for schools, and his uncle Billy, minister for coal. Billy Williams had started work down the pit at the age of thirteen, Lloyd knew. Ethel had been the same age when she began scrubbing the floors of Tŷ Gwyn. This debate was not about fine phrases; it was about their lives.

After a minute he abandoned his script and spoke extempore. He recalled instead the misery of working-class families made penniless by unemployment or disability, scenes he had witnessed firsthand in the East End of London and the South Wales coalfield. His voice betrayed the emotion he felt, somewhat to his embarrassment, but he plowed on. He sensed his audience beginning to pay attention. He spoke of his grandfather and others who had started the Labour movement with the dream of comprehensive employment insurance to banish forever the fear of destitution. When he sat down, there was a roar of approval.

In the visitors' gallery his wife, Daisy, smiled proudly and gave him a thumbs-up sign.

He listened to the rest of the debate in a glow of satisfaction. He felt he had passed his first real test as an M.P.

Afterward, in the lobby, he was approached by a Labour whip, one of the people responsible for making sure M.P.s voted the right way. After congratulating Lloyd on his speech, the whip said: "How would you like to be a parliamentary private secretary?"

Lloyd was thrilled. Each minister and secretary of state had at least one PPS. In truth a PPS was often little more than a bag-carrier, but the job was the usual first step on the way to a ministerial appointment. "I'd be honored," Lloyd said. "Who would I be working for?"

"Ernie Bevin."

Lloyd could hardly believe his luck. Bevin was foreign secretary and the closest colleague of Prime Minister Attlee. The intimate relationship between the two men was a case of the attraction of opposites. Attlee was middle-class: the son of a lawyer, an Oxford graduate, an officer in the First World War. Bevin was the illegitimate child of a housemaid, never knew his father, started work at the age of eleven, and founded the mammoth Transport and General Workers' Union. They were physical opposites, too: Attlee slim and dapper, quiet, solemn; Bevin a huge man, tall and strong and overweight, with a loud laugh. The foreign secretary referred to the prime minister as "little Clem." All the same they were staunch allies.

Bevin was a hero to Lloyd and to millions of ordinary British people. "There's nothing I'd like more," Lloyd said. "But hasn't Bevin already got a PPS?"

"He needs two," the whip said. "Go to the Foreign Office tomorrow morning at nine and you can get started."

"Thank you!"

Lloyd hurried along the oak-paneled corridor, heading for his mother's office. He had arranged to meet Daisy there after the debate. "Mam!" he said as he entered. "I've been made PPS to Ernie Bevin!"

Then he saw that Ethel was not alone. Earl Fitzherbert was with her.

Fitz stared at Lloyd with a mixture of surprise and distaste.

Even in his shock Lloyd noticed that his father was wearing a perfectly cut light gray suit with a double-breasted waistcoat.

He looked back at his mother. She was quite calm. This encounter was not a surprise to her. She must have contrived it.

The earl came to the same conclusion. "What the devil is this, Ethel?"

Lloyd stared at the man whose blood ran in his veins. Even in this embarrassing situation, Fitz was poised and dignified. He was handsome, despite the drooping eyelid that resulted from the Battle of the Somme. He leaned on a walking stick, another consequence of the Somme. A few months short of sixty years old, he was immaculately groomed, his gray hair neatly trimmed, his silver tie tightly knotted, his black shoes shining. Lloyd, too, always liked to look well turned out. That's where I get it from, he thought.

Ethel went and stood close to the earl. Lloyd knew his mother well enough to understand this move. She frequently used her charm when she wanted to persuade a man. All the same, Lloyd did not like to see her being so warm to one who had exploited her, then let her down.

"I was so sorry when I heard about the death of Boy," she said to Fitz. "Nothing is as precious to us as our children, is it?"

"I must go," Fitz said.

Until this moment, Lloyd had met Fitz only in passing. He had never before spent this much time with him or heard him speak this number of words. Despite feeling uncomfortable, Lloyd was fascinated. Grumpy though he was right now, Fitz had a kind of allure.

"Please, Fitz," said Ethel. "You have a son whom you have never acknowledged—a son you should be proud of."

"You shouldn't do this, Ethel," said Fitz. "A man is entitled to forget the mistakes of his youth."

Lloyd cringed with embarrassment, but his mother pressed on. "Why should you want to forget? I know he was a mistake, but look at him now—a member of Parliament who has just made a thrilling speech and been appointed PPS to the foreign secretary."

Fitz pointedly did not look at Lloyd.

Ethel said: "You want to pretend that our affair was a meaningless dalliance, but you know the truth. Yes, we were young and foolish, and randy, too—me as much as you—but we loved each other. We *really* loved each other, Fitz. You should admit it. Don't you know that if you deny the truth about yourself you lose your soul?"

Fitz's face was no longer merely impassive, Lloyd saw. He was struggling to maintain control. Lloyd understood that his mother had put her finger on the real problem. It was not so much that Fitz was ashamed of having an illegitimate son. But he was too proud to accept that he had loved a housemaid. He probably loved Ethel more than his wife, Lloyd guessed. And that upset all his most fundamental beliefs about the social hierarchy.

Lloyd spoke for the first time. "I was with Boy at the end, sir. He died bravely."

For the first time, Fitz looked at him. "My son doesn't require your approval," he said.

Lloyd felt as if he had been slapped.

Even Ethel was shocked. "Fitz!" she said. "How can you be so mean?"

At that point Daisy came in.

"Hello, Fitz!" she said gaily. "You probably thought you'd got rid of me, but now you're my father-in-law again. Isn't that amusing?"

Ethel said: "I'm just trying to persuade Fitz to shake Lloyd's hand."

Fitz said: "I try to avoid shaking hands with socialists."

Ethel was fighting a losing battle, but she would not give up. "See how much of yourself there is in him! He resembles you, dresses like you, shares your interest in politics—he'll probably end up foreign secretary, which you always wanted to be!"

Fitz's expression darkened further. "It is now most unlikely that I shall ever be foreign secretary." He went to the door. "And it would not please me in the least if that great office of state were to be held by my Bolshevik bastard!" With that he walked out.

Ethel burst into tears.

Daisy put her arm around Lloyd. "I'm so sorry," she said.

"Don't worry," Lloyd said. "I'm not shocked or disappointed." This was not true, but he did not want to appear pathetic. "I was rejected by him a long time ago." He looked at Daisy with adoration. "I'm lucky to have plenty of other people who love me."

Ethel said tearfully: "It's my fault. I shouldn't have asked him to come here. I might have known it would turn out badly."

"Never mind," said Daisy. "I have some good news."

Lloyd smiled at her. "What's that?"

She looked at Ethel. "Are you ready for this?"

"I think so."

"Come on," said Lloyd. "What is it?"

Daisy said: "We're going to have a baby."

## iii

Carla's brother, Erik, came home that summer, near to death. He had contracted tuberculosis in a Soviet labor camp, and they had released him when he became too ill to work. He had been sleeping rough for weeks, traveling on freight trains and begging lifts on lorries. He arrived at the von Ulrich house barefoot and wearing filthy clothes. His face was like a skull.

However, he did not die. It might have been being with people who loved him, or the warmer weather as winter turned into spring, or perhaps just rest, but he coughed less and regained enough energy to do some work around the house, boarding up smashed windows, repairing roof tiles, unblocking pipes.

Fortunately, at the beginning of the year Frieda Franck had struck gold.

Ludwig Franck had been killed in the air raid that destroyed his factory, and for a while Frieda and her mother had been as destitute as everyone else. But she got a job as a nurse in the American zone, and soon afterward, she explained to Carla, a little group of American doctors had asked her to sell their surplus food and cigarettes on the black market in exchange for a cut of the proceeds. Thereafter she turned up at Carla's house once a week with a little basket of supplies: warm clothing, candles, flashlight batteries, matches, soap, and food— bacon, chocolate, apples, rice, canned peaches. Maud divided the food into portions and gave Carla double. Carla accepted without hesitation, not for her own sake, but to help her feed baby Walli.

Without Frieda's illicit groceries, Walli might not have made it.

He was changing fast. The dark hair with which he had been born had now gone, and instead he had fine, fair hair. At six months he had Maud's wonderful green eyes. As his face took shape, Carla noticed a fold of flesh in the outer corners of his eyes that gave him a slant-eyed look, and she wondered if his father had been a Siberian. She could not remember all the men who had raped her. Most of the time she had closed her eyes.

She no longer hated them. It was strange, but she was so happy to have Walli that she could hardly bring herself to regret what had happened.

Rebecca was fascinated by Walli. Now just fifteen, she was old enough to have the beginnings of maternal feelings, and she eagerly helped Carla bathe and dress the baby. She played with him constantly, and he gurgled with delight when he saw her.

As soon as Erik felt well enough, he joined the Communist Party.

Carla was baffled. After what he had suffered at the hands of the

Soviets, how could he? But she found that he talked about Communism in the same way he had talked about Nazism a decade earlier. She just hoped that this time his disillusionment would not be so long coming.

The Allies were keen for democracy to return to Germany, and city elections were scheduled for Berlin later in 1946.

Carla felt sure the city would not return to normal until its own people took control, so she decided to stand for the Social Democratic Party. But Berliners quickly discovered that the Soviet occupiers had a curious notion of what democracy meant.

The Soviets had been shocked by the results of elections in Austria last November. The Austrian Communists had expected to run neck and neck with the socialists, but had won only four seats out of 165. It seemed that voters blamed Communism for the brutality of the Red Army. The Kremlin, unused to genuine elections, had not anticipated that.

To avoid a similar result in Germany, the Soviets proposed a merger between the Communists and the Social Democrats in what they called a united front. The Social Democrats refused, despite heavy pressure. In East Germany the Russians started arresting Social Democrats, just as the Nazis had in 1933. There the merger was forced through. But the Berlin elections were supervised by the four Allies, and the Social Democrats survived.

Once the weather warmed up, Carla was able to take her turn queuing for food. She carried Walli with her wrapped in a pillowcase—she had no baby clothes. Standing in line for potatoes one morning, a few blocks from home, she was surprised to see an American jeep pull up with Frieda in the passenger seat. The balding, middle-aged driver kissed her on the lips, and she jumped out. She was wearing a sleeveless blue dress and new shoes. She walked quickly away, heading for the von Ulrich house, carrying her little basket.

Carla saw everything in a flash. Frieda was not trading on the black market, and there was no syndicate of doctors. She was the paid mistress of an American officer.

It was not unusual. Thousands of pretty German girls had been faced with the choice: see your family starve, or sleep with a generous officer. French women had done the same under German occupation; officers' wives back here in Germany had spoken bitterly about it.

All the same, Carla was horrified. She believed that Frieda loved Heinrich. They were planning to get married as soon as life returned to some semblance of normality. Carla felt sick at heart.

She reached the head of the line and bought her ration of potatoes, then hurried home.

She found Frieda upstairs in the drawing room. Erik had cleaned up the room and put newspaper in the windows, the next best thing to glass. The curtains had long ago been recycled as bed linen, but most of the chairs had survived so far, their upholstery faded and worn. The grand piano was still there, miraculously. A Russian officer had discovered it and announced that he would return next day with a crane to lift it out through the window, but he had never come back.

Frieda immediately took Walli from Carla and began to sing to him. "*A, B, C, die Katze lief im Schnee.*" The women who had not yet had children, Rebecca and Frieda, could hardly get enough of Walli, Carla observed. Those who had had children of their own, Maud and Ada, adored him but dealt with him in a briskly practical way.

Frieda opened the lid of the piano and encouraged Walli to bang on the keys as she sang. The instrument had not been played for years: Maud had not touched it since the death of her last pupil, Joachim Koch.

After a few minutes Frieda said to Carla: "You're a bit solemn. What is it?"

"I know how you get the food you bring us," Carla said. "You're not a black marketeer, are you?"

"Of course I am," Frieda said. "What are you talking about?"

"I saw you this morning, getting out of a jeep."

"Colonel Hicks gave me a lift."

"He kissed you on the lips."

Frieda looked away. "I knew I should have got out earlier. I could have walked from the American zone."

"Frieda, what about Heinrich?"

"He'll never know! I'll be more careful, I swear."

"Do you still love him?"

"Of course! We're going to get married."

"Then why . . . ?"

"I've had enough of hard times! I want to put on pretty clothes and go to nightclubs and dance."

"No, you don't," Carla said confidently. "You can't lie to me, Frieda—we've been friends too long. Tell me the truth."

"The truth?"

"Yes, please."

"You're sure?"

"I'm sure."

"I did it for Walli."

Carla gasped with shock. That had never occurred to her, but it made sense. She could believe Frieda would make such a sacrifice for her and her baby.

But she felt dreadful. This made her responsible for Frieda's prostituting herself. "This is terrible!" Carla said. "You shouldn't have done it—we would have managed somehow."

Frieda sprang up from the piano stool with the baby still in her arms. "No, you wouldn't!" she blazed.

Walli was frightened, and cried. Carla took him and rocked him, patting his back.

"You wouldn't have managed," Frieda said more quietly.

"How do you know?"

"All last winter, babies were brought into the hospital naked, wrapped in newspapers, dead of hunger and cold. I could hardly bear to look at them."

"Oh, God." Carla held Walli tight.

"They turn a peculiar bluish color when they freeze to death."

"Stop it."

"I have to tell you. Otherwise you won't understand what I did. Walli would have been one of those blue frozen babies."

"I know," Carla whispered. "I know."

"Percy Hicks is a kind man. He has a frumpy wife back in Boston and I'm the sexiest thing he's ever seen. He's nice and quick about intercourse and always uses a condom."

"You should stop," Carla said.

"You don't mean that."

"No, I don't," Carla confessed. "And that's the worst part. I feel so guilty. I am guilty."

"You're not. It's my choice. German women have to make hard choices. We're paying for the easy choices German men made fifteen years ago. Men such as my father, who thought Hitler would be good for business, and Heinrich's father, who voted for the Enabling Act. The sins of the fathers are visited on the daughters."

There was a loud knock at the front door. A moment later they heard scampering steps as Rebecca hurried upstairs to hide, just in case it was the Red Army.

Then Ada's voice said: "Oh! Sir! Good morning!" She sounded surprised and a bit worried, though not scared. Carla wondered who would induce that particular mixture of reactions in the maid.

There was a heavy masculine tread on the stairs; then Werner walked in.

He was dirty and ragged and thin as a rail, but there was a broad smile on his handsome face. "It's me!" he said ebulliently. "I'm back!"

Then he saw the baby. His jaw dropped and the happy smile disappeared. "Oh," he said. "What . . . who . . . whose baby is that?"

"Mine, my darling," said Carla. "Let me explain."

"Explain?" he said angrily. "What explanation is necessary? You've had someone else's baby!" He turned to go.

Frieda said: "Werner! In this room are two women who love you. Don't walk out without listening to us. You don't understand."

"I think I understand everything."

"Carla was raped."

He went pale. "Raped? Who by?"

Carla said: "I never knew their names."

"Names?" Werner swallowed. "There . . . there was more than one?"

"Five Red Army soldiers."

His voice fell to a whisper. "Five?"

Carla nodded.

"But . . . couldn't you . . . I mean . . ."

Frieda said: "I was raped, too, Werner. And so was Mother."

"Dear God, what has been going on here?"

"Hell," said Frieda.

Werner sat down heavily in a worn leather chair. "I thought hell was where I've been," he said. He buried his face in his hands.

Carla crossed the room, still holding Walli, and stood in front of Werner's chair. "Look at me, Werner," she said. "Please."

He looked up, his face twisted with emotion.

"Hell is over," she said.

"Is it?"

"Yes," she said firmly. "Life is hard, but the Nazis have gone, the war is finished, Hitler is dead, and the Red Army rapists have been brought under control, more or less. The nightmare has ended. And we're both alive, and together."

He reached out and took her hand. "You're right."

"We've got Walli, and in a minute you'll meet a fifteen-year-old girl called Rebecca who has somehow become my child. We have to make a new family out of what the war has left us, just as we have to build new houses with the rubble in the streets."

He nodded acceptance.

"I need your love," she said. "So do Rebecca and Walli."

He stood up slowly. She looked at him expectantly. He said nothing, but after a long moment, he put his arms around her and the baby, gently embracing them both.

## iv

Under wartime regulations still in force, the British government had a right to open a coal mine anywhere, regardless of the wishes of the owner of the land. Compensation was paid only for loss of earnings on farmland or commercial property.

Billy Williams, as minister for coal, authorized an open-cast mine on the grounds of Tŷ Gwyn, the palatial residence of Earl Fitzherbert on the outskirts of Aberowen.

No compensation was payable, as the land was not commercial.

There was uproar on the Conservative benches in the House of Commons. "Your slag heap will be right under the bedroom windows of the countess!" said one indignant Tory.

Billy Williams smiled. "The earl's slag heap has been under my mother's window for fifty years," he said.

Lloyd Williams and Ethel both traveled to Aberowen with Billy the day before the engineers began to dig the hole. Lloyd was reluctant to leave Daisy, who was due to give birth in two weeks, but it was a historic moment, and he wanted to be there.

Both his grandparents were now in their late seventies. Granda was almost blind despite his pebble-lensed glasses, and Grandmam was bent-backed. "This is nice," Grandmam said when they all sat around the old kitchen table. "Both my children here." She served stewed beef with mashed turnips and thick slices of homemade bread spread with the butcher's fat called dripping. She poured large mugs of sweetened milky tea to go with it.

Lloyd had eaten like this frequently as a child, but now he found it coarse. He knew that even in hard times French and Spanish women managed to serve up tasty dishes delicately flavored with garlic and garnished with herbs. He was ashamed of his fastidiousness, and pretended to eat and drink with relish.

"Pity about the gardens at Tŷ Gwyn," Grandmam said tactlessly.

Billy was stung. "What do you mean? Britain needs the coal."

"But people love those gardens. Beautiful, they are. I've been there at least once every year since I was a girl. Shame it is to see them go."

"There's a perfectly good recreation ground right in the middle of Aberowen!"

"It's not the same," said Grandmam imperturbably.

Granda said: "Women will never understand politics."

"No," said Grandmam. "I don't suppose we will."

Lloyd caught his mother's eye. She smiled and said nothing.

Billy and Lloyd shared the second bedroom, and Ethel made up a bed on the kitchen floor. "I slept in this room every night of my life until I went in the army," Billy said as they lay down. "And I looked out the window every morning at that fucking slag heap."

"Keep your voice down, Uncle Billy," Lloyd said. "You don't want your mother to hear you swear."

"Aye, you're right," said Billy.

Next morning after breakfast they all walked up the hill to the big house. It was a mild morning, and for a change there was no rain. The ridge of mountains at the skyline was softened with summer grass. As Tŷ Gwyn came into view, Lloyd could not help seeing it more as a beautiful building than as a symbol of oppression. It was both, of course; nothing was simple in politics.

The great iron gates stood open. The Williams family passed onto the grounds. A crowd had gathered already: the contractor's men with their machinery, a hundred or so miners and their families, Earl Fitzherbert with his son Andrew, a handful of reporters with notebooks, and a film crew.

The gardens were breathtaking. The avenue of ancient chestnut trees was in full leaf, there were swans on the lake, and the flower beds blazed with color. Lloyd guessed the earl had made sure the place looked its best. He wanted to brand the Labour government as wreckers in the eyes of the world.

Lloyd found himself sympathizing with Fitz.

The mayor of Aberowen was giving an interview. "The people of this town are against the open-cast mine," he said. Lloyd was surprised; the town council was Labour, and it must have gone against the grain for them to oppose the government. "For more than a hundred years, the beauty of these gardens has refreshed the souls of people who live in a grim industrial landscape," the mayor went on. Switching from prepared speech to personal reminiscence, he added: "I proposed to my wife under that cedar tree."

He was interrupted by a loud clanking sound like the footsteps of an iron giant. Turning to look back along the drive, Lloyd saw a huge machine approaching. It looked like the biggest crane in the world. It had an enormous boom ninety feet long and a bucket into which a lorry could easily fit. Most astonishing of all, it moved along on rotating steel shoes that made the earth shake every time they hit the ground.

Billy said proudly to Lloyd: "That's a walking monighan dragline excavator. Picks up six tons of earth at a time."

The camera rolled as the monstrous machine stomped up the drive.

Lloyd had only one misgiving about the Labour Party. There was a streak of puritan authoritarianism in many socialists. His grandfather had it, and so did Billy. They were not comfortable with sensual pleasures. Sacrifice and self-denial suited them better. They dismissed the ravishing beauty of these gardens as irrelevant. They were wrong.

Ethel was not that way, nor was Lloyd. Perhaps the killjoy strain had been bred out of their line. He hoped so.

Fitz gave an interview on the pink gravel path while the digger driver maneuvered his machine into position. "The minister for coal has told you that when the mine is exhausted, the garden will be subject to what he calls an effective restoration program," he said. "I say to you that that promise is worthless. It has taken more than a century for my grandfather and my father and me to bring the garden to its present pitch of beauty and harmony. It would take another hundred years to restore it."

The boom of the excavator was lowered until it stood at a forty-five-degree angle over the shrubbery and flower beds of the west garden. The bucket was positioned over the croquet lawn. There was a long moment of waiting. The crowd fell silent. Billy said loudly: "Get on with it, for God's sake."

An engineer in a bowler hat blew a whistle.

The bucket was dropped to the earth with a massive thud. Its steel teeth dug into the flat green lawn. The dragrope tautened, there was a loud creak of straining machinery, and then the bucket began to move back. As it was dragged across the ground, it dug up a bed of huge yellow sunflowers, the rose garden, a shrubbery of summersweet and bottlebrush buckeye, and a small magnolia tree. At the end of its travel the bucket was full of earth, flowers, and plants.

The bucket was then lifted to a height of twenty feet, dribbling loose earth and blossoms.

The boom swung sideways. It was taller than the house, Lloyd saw. He almost thought the bucket would smash the upstairs windows, but the operator was skilled, and stopped it just in time. The dragrope slackened, the bucket tilted, and six tons of garden fell to the ground a few feet from the entrance.

The bucket was returned to its original position, and the process was repeated.

Lloyd looked at Fitz and saw that he was crying.

CHAPTER TWENTY-THREE

# 1947

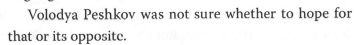

At the beginning of 1947 it seemed possible that all Europe might go Communist.

Volodya Peshkov was not sure whether to hope for that or its opposite.

The Red Army dominated Eastern Europe, and Communists were winning elections in the west. Communists had gained respect for their role in resisting the Nazis. Five million people had voted Communist in the first French postwar election, making the Communists the most popular party. In Italy a Communist-socialist alliance won 40 percent of the vote. In Czechoslovakia the Communists on their own won 38 percent and led the democratically elected government.

It was different in Austria and Germany, where voters had been robbed and raped by the Red Army. In the Berlin city elections, the Social Democrats won 63 of 130 seats, the Communists only 26. However, Germany was ruined and starving, and the Kremlin still hoped that the people might turn to Communism in desperation, just as they had turned to Nazism in the Depression.

Britain was the great disappointment. Only one Communist had been sent to Parliament in the postwar election there. And the Labour government was delivering everything Communism promised: welfare, free health care, education for all, even a five-day week for coal miners.

But in the rest of Europe, capitalism was failing to lift people out of the postwar slump.

And the weather was on Stalin's side, Volodya thought as the layers of snow grew thick on the onion domes. The winter of 1946–47 was the coldest in Europe for more than a century. Snow fell in St.-Tropez. British roads and railways became impassable, and industry ground to a halt—something that had never happened in the war. In France, food rations fell below wartime levels. The United Nations organization calculated that one hundred million Europeans were living on fifteen hundred calories a day—the level at which health begins to suffer from malnutrition. As the engines of production ran slower and slower, people began to feel they had nothing to lose, and revolution came to seem the only way out.

Once the USSR had nuclear weapons, no other country would be able to stand in its way. Volodya's wife, Zoya, and her colleagues had built a nuclear pile, at Laboratory No. 2 of the Academy of Sciences, a deliberately vague name for the powerhouse of Soviet nuclear research. The pile had gone critical on Christmas Day, six months after the birth of their son, Konstantin, who was at the time sleeping in the laboratory's crèche. If the experiment went wrong, Zoya had whispered to Volodya, it would do little Kotya no good to be a mile or two away: all central Moscow would be flattened.

Volodya's conflicting feelings about the future took on a new intensity with the birth of his son. He wanted Kotya to grow up a citizen of a proud and powerful country. The Soviet Union deserved to dominate Europe, he felt. It was the Red Army that had defeated the Nazis, in four cruel years of total warfare; the other Allies had stood on the sidelines, fighting minor wars, joining in only for the last eleven months. All their casualties put together were only a fraction of those suffered by the Soviet people.

But then he would think of what Communism meant: arbitrary

purges, torture in the basements of the secret police, conquering soldiers urged on to excesses of bestiality, the whole vast country forced to obey the wayward decisions of a tyrant more powerful than a tsar. Did Volodya really want to extend that brutal system to the rest of the continent?

He remembered walking into Penn Station in New York and buying a ticket to Albuquerque, without asking anyone's permission or showing any papers, and the exhilarating sense of total freedom that had given him. He had long ago burned the Sears Roebuck Catalogue, but it lived in his memory, with its hundreds of pages of good things available for everyone to have. Russian people believed that stories of Western freedom and prosperity were just propaganda, but Volodya knew better. A part of him longed for Communism to be defeated.

The future of Germany, and therefore of Europe, was to be decided at the Conference of Foreign Ministers held in Moscow in March 1947.

Volodya, now a colonel, was in charge of the intelligence team assigned to the conference. Meetings were held in an ornate room at Aviation Industry House, conveniently close to the Hotel Moskva. As always, the delegates and their interpreters sat around a table, with their aides on several rows of chairs behind them. The Soviet foreign minister, Vyacheslav Molotov, Old Stone Arse, demanded that Germany pay ten billion dollars to the USSR in war reparations. The Americans and British protested that this would be a deathblow to Germany's sickly economy. That was probably what Stalin wanted.

Volodya renewed his acquaintance with Woody Dewar, who was now a news photographer assigned to cover the conference. He was married, too, and showed Volodya a photo of a striking dark-haired woman holding a baby. Sitting in the back of a ZIS-110B limousine, returning from a formal photo session at the Kremlin, Woody said to Volodya: "You realize that Germany doesn't have the money to pay your reparations, don't you?"

Volodya's English had improved, and they could manage without an interpreter. He said: "Then how are they feeding their people and rebuilding their cities?"

"With handouts from us, of course," said Woody. "We're spending a fortune in aid. Any reparations the Germans paid you would be, in reality, our money."

"Is that so wrong? The United States prospered in the war. My country was devastated. Maybe you should pay."

"American voters don't think so."

"American voters may be wrong."

Woody shrugged. "True—but it's their money."

There it was again, Volodya thought: the deference to public opinion. He had remarked it before in Woody's conversation. Americans talked about voters the way Russians talked about Stalin: they had to be obeyed, right or wrong.

Woody wound down the window. "You don't mind if I take a cityscape, do you? The light is wonderful." His camera clicked.

He knew he was supposed to take only approved shots. However, there was nothing sensitive on the street, just some women shoveling snow. All the same, Volodya said: "Please don't." He leaned past Woody and wound up the window. "Official photos only."

He was about to ask for the film out of Woody's camera when Woody said: "Do you remember me mentioning my friend Greg Peshkov, with the same surname as you?"

Volodya certainly did. Willi Frunze had said something similar. It was probably the same man. "No, I don't remember," Volodya lied. He wanted nothing to do with a possible relative in the West. Such connections brought suspicion and trouble to Russians.

"He's on the American delegation. You should talk to him. See if you're related."

"I will," said Volodya, resolving to avoid the man at all costs.

He decided not to insist on taking Woody's film. It was not worth the fuss for a harmless street scene.

At the next day's conference the American secretary of state, George Marshall, proposed that the four Allies should abolish the separate sectors of Germany and unify the country, so that it could once again become the beating economic heart of Europe, mining and manufacturing and buying and selling.

That was the last thing the Soviets wanted.

Molotov refused to discuss unification until the question of reparations had been settled.

The conference was stalemated.

And that, Volodya thought, was exactly where Stalin wanted it.

## ii

The world of international diplomacy was a small one, Greg Peshkov reflected. One of the young aides in the British delegation at the Moscow conference was Lloyd Williams, the husband of Greg's half sister, Daisy. At first Greg did not like the look of Lloyd, who was dressed like a prissy English gentleman, but he turned out to be a regular guy. "Molotov is a prick," Lloyd said in the bar of the Hotel Moskva over a couple of vodka martinis.

"So what are we going to do about him?"

"I don't know, but Britain can't live with these delays. The occupation of Germany is costing money we can't afford, and the hard winter has turned the problem into a crisis."

"You know what?" said Greg, thinking aloud. "If the Soviets won't play ball, we should just go ahead without them."

"How could we do that?"

"What do we want?" Greg counted points on his fingers. "We want to unify Germany and hold elections."

"So do we."

"We want to scrap the worthless reichsmark and introduce a new currency, so that Germans can start to do business again."

"Yes."

"And we want to save the country from Communism."

"Also British policy."

"We can't do it in the east because the Soviets won't come to the party. So fuck them! We control three-quarters of Germany—let's do it in our zone, and let the eastern part of the country go to blazes."

Lloyd looked thoughtful. "Is this something you've discussed with your boss?"

"Hell, no. I'm just running off at the mouth. But listen, why not?"

"I might suggest it to Ernie Bevin."

"And I'll put it to George Marshall." Greg sipped his drink. "Vodka is the only thing the Russians do well," he said. "So, how's my sister?"

"She's expecting our second baby."

"What is Daisy like as a mother?"

Lloyd laughed. "You think she's probably terrible."

Greg shrugged. "I never saw her as the domestic type."

"She's patient, calm, and organized."

"She didn't hire six nurses to do all the work?"

"Just one, so that she can come out with me in the evenings, usually to political meetings."

"Wow, she's changed."

"Not completely. She still loves parties. What about you—still single?"

"There's a girl called Nelly Fordham that I'm pretty serious about. And I guess you know that I have a godson."

"Yes," said Lloyd. "Daisy told me all about him. Georgy."

Greg felt sure, from the slightly embarrassed look on Lloyd's face, that he knew Georgy was Greg's child. "I'm very fond of him."

"That's great."

A member of the Russian delegation came up to the bar, and Greg caught his eye. There was something very familiar about him. He was in his thirties, handsome apart from a brutally short military haircut, and he had a slightly intimidating blue-eyed gaze. He nodded in a friendly way, and Greg said: "Have we met before?"

"Perhaps," the Russian said. "I was at school in Germany—the Berlin Boys' Academy."

Greg shook his head. "Ever been to the States?"

"No."

Lloyd said: "This is the guy with the same surname as you, Volodya Peshkov."

Greg introduced himself. "We might be related. My father, Lev

Peshkov, emigrated in 1914, leaving behind a pregnant girlfriend, who then married his older brother, Grigori Peshkov. Could we be half brothers?"

Volodya's manner altered immediately. "Definitely not," he said. "Excuse me." He left the bar without buying a drink.

"That was abrupt," Greg said to Lloyd.

"It was," said Lloyd.

"He looked kind of shocked."

"It must have been something you said."

## iii

It could not be true, Volodya told himself.

Greg claimed that Grigori had married a girl who was already pregnant by Lev. If that was the case, the man Volodya had always called Father was not his father but his uncle.

Perhaps it was a coincidence. Or the American could just be stirring up trouble.

All the same Volodya was reeling with shock.

He returned home at his usual time. He and Zoya were rising fast and had been given an apartment in Government House, the luxury block where his parents lived. Grigori and Katerina came to the apartment at Kotya's suppertime, as they did most evenings. Katerina bathed her grandson; then Grigori sang to him and told him Russian fairy tales. Kotya was nine months old and not yet talking, but he seemed to like bedtime stories just the same.

Volodya followed the evening routine as if sleepwalking. He tried to behave normally, but he found he could hardly speak to either of his parents. He did not believe Greg's story, but he could not stop thinking about it.

When Kotya was asleep, and the grandparents were about to leave, Grigori said to Volodya: "Have I got a boil on my nose?"

"No."

"Then why have you been staring at me all evening?"

Volodya decided to tell the truth. "I met a man called Greg Peshkov. He's part of the American delegation. He thinks we're related."

"It's possible." Grigori's tone was light, as if it did not much matter, but Volodya saw that his neck had reddened, a giveaway sign of suppressed emotion in his father. "I last saw my brother in 1919. Since then I haven't heard from him."

"Greg's father is called Lev, and Lev had a brother called Grigori."

"Then Greg could be your cousin."

"He said brother."

Grigori's blush deepened and he said nothing.

Zoya put in: "How could that be?"

Volodya said: "According to this American Peshkov, Lev had a pregnant girlfriend in St. Petersburg who married his brother."

Grigori said: "Ridiculous!"

Volodya looked at Katerina. "You haven't said anything, Mother."

There was a long pause. That in itself was significant. What did they have to think about, if there was no truth in Greg's story? A weird coldness descended on Volodya like a freezing fog.

At last his mother said: "I was a flighty girl." She looked at Zoya. "Not sensible, like your wife." She sighed deeply. "Grigori Peshkov fell in love with me, more or less at first sight, poor idiot." She smiled fondly at her husband. "But his brother, Lev, had fancy clothes, cigarettes, money for vodka, gangster friends. I liked Lev better. More fool me."

Volodya said amazedly: "So it's true?" Part of him still hoped desperately for a denial.

"Lev did what such men always do," Katerina said. "He made me pregnant, then left me."

"So Lev is my father." Volodya looked at Grigori. "And you're just my uncle!" He felt as if he might fall over. The ground under his feet had shifted. It was like an earthquake.

Zoya stood beside Volodya's chair and put her hand on his shoulder, as if to calm him, or perhaps restrain him.

Katerina went on: "And Grigori did what men such as Grigori always do: he took care of me. He loved me, he married me, and he provided for me and my children." Sitting on the couch next to Grigori, she took his hand. "I didn't want him, and I certainly didn't deserve him, but God gave him to me anyway."

Grigori said: "I have dreaded this day. Ever since you were born, I have dreaded it."

Volodya said: "Then why did you keep the secret? Why didn't you just speak the truth?"

Grigori was choked up, and spoke with difficulty. "I couldn't bear to tell you that I wasn't your father," he managed to say. "I loved you too much."

Katerina said: "Let me tell you something, my beloved son. Listen to me, now, and I don't care if you never listen to your mother again, but hear this. Forget the stranger in America who once seduced a foolish girl. Look at the man sitting in front of you with tears in his eyes."

Volodya looked at Grigori and saw a pleading expression that tugged at his heart.

Katerina went on: "This man has fed you and clothed you and loved you unfailingly for three decades. If the word *father* means anything at all, this is your father."

"Yes," Volodya said. "I know that."

### iv

Lloyd Williams got on well with Ernie Bevin. They had a lot in common, despite the age difference. During the four-day train journey across snowy Europe, Lloyd had confided that he, like Bevin, was the illegitimate son of a housemaid. They were both passionate anti-Communists: Lloyd because of his experiences in Spain, Bevin because he had seen Communist tactics in the trade union movement. "They're slaves to the Kremlin and tyrants over everyone else," Bevin said, and Lloyd knew exactly what he meant.

Lloyd had not warmed to Greg Peshkov, who always looked as if he had dressed in a rush: shirtsleeves unbuttoned, coat collar twisted, shoelaces untied. Greg was shrewd, and Lloyd tried to like him, but he felt that underneath Greg's casual charm there was a core of ruthlessness. Daisy had said that Lev Peshkov was a gangster, and Lloyd could imagine that Greg had the same instincts.

However, Bevin jumped at Greg's idea for Germany. "Was he speaking for Marshall, do you suppose?" said the portly foreign secretary in his broad West Country accent.

"He said not," Lloyd replied. "Do you think it could work?"

"I think it's the best idea I've heard in three bloody weeks in bloody Moscow. If he's serious, arrange an informal lunch, just Marshall and this youngster with you and me."

"I'll do it right away."

"But tell nobody. We don't want the Soviets to get a whisper of this. They'll accuse us of conspiring against them, and they'll be right."

They met the following day at no. 10 Spasopeskovskaya Square, the American ambassador's residence, an extravagant neoclassical mansion built before the revolution. Marshall was tall and lean, every inch a soldier; Bevin rotund, nearsighted, a cigarette frequently dangling from his lips; but they clicked immediately. Both were plain-speaking men. Bevin had once been accused of ungentlemanly speech by Stalin himself, a distinction of which the foreign secretary was very proud. Beneath the painted ceilings and chandeliers they got down to the task of reviving Germany without the help of the USSR.

They agreed rapidly on the principles: the new currency; the unification of the British, American, and—if possible—French zones; the demilitarization of West Germany; elections; and a new transatlantic military alliance. Then Bevin said bluntly: "None of this will work, you know."

Marshall was taken aback. "Then I fail to understand why we're discussing it," he said sharply.

"Europe's in a slump. This scheme will fail if people are starving. The best protection against Communism is prosperity. Stalin knows that—which is why he wants to keep Germany impoverished."

"I agree."

"Which means we've got to rebuild. But we can't do it with our bare hands. We need tractors, lathes, excavators, rolling stock—all of which we can't afford."

Marshall saw where he was going. "Americans aren't willing to give Europeans any more handouts."

"Fair enough. But there must be a way the USA can lend us the money we need to buy equipment from you."

There was a silence.

Marshall hated to waste words, but this was a long pause even by his standards.

Then at last he spoke. "It makes sense," he said. "I'll see what I can do."

The conference lasted six weeks, and when they all went home again, nothing had been decided.

**v**

Eva Williams was a year old when she got her back teeth. The others had come fairly easily, but these hurt. There was not much Lloyd and Daisy could do for her. She was miserable, she could not sleep, she would not let them sleep, and they were miserable, too.

Daisy had a lot of money, but they lived unostentatiously. They had bought a pleasant row house in Hoxton, where their neighbors were a shopkeeper and a builder. They got a small family car, a new Morris Eight with a top speed of almost sixty miles per hour. Daisy still bought pretty clothes, but Lloyd had just three suits: evening dress, a chalk stripe for the House of Commons, and tweeds for constituency work on the weekends.

Lloyd was in his pajamas late one evening, trying to rock the grizzling Evie to sleep, and at the same time leafing through *Life* magazine. He noticed a striking photograph taken in Moscow. It showed a Russian woman, wearing a head scarf and a coat tied with string like a parcel, her old face deeply lined, shoveling snow on the street.

Something about the way the light struck her gave her a look of timelessness, as if she had been there for a thousand years. He looked for the photographer's name and found it was Woody Dewar, whom he had met at the conference.

The phone rang. He picked it up and heard the voice of Ernie Bevin. "Turn your wireless on," Bevin said. "Marshall's made a speech." He hung up without waiting for a reply.

Lloyd went downstairs to the living room, still carrying Evie, and switched on the radio. The show was called *American Commentary*. The BBC's Washington correspondent, Leonard Miall, was reporting from Harvard University in Cambridge, Massachusetts. "The secretary of state told alumni that the rebuilding of Europe is going to take a longer time, and require a greater effort, than was originally foreseen," said Miall.

That was promising, Lloyd thought with excitement. "Hush, Evie, please," he said, and for once she quietened.

Then Lloyd heard the low, reasonable voice of George C. Marshall. "Europe's requirements, for the next three or four years, of foreign food and other essential products—principally from America—are so much greater than her present ability to pay that she must have substantial additional help . . . or face economic, social, and political deterioration of a very grave character."

Lloyd was electrified. "Substantial additional help" was what Bevin had asked for.

"The remedy lies in breaking the vicious circle and restoring the confidence of the European people in the economic future," Marshall said. "The United States should do whatever it is able to assist in the return of normal economic health in the world."

"He's done it!" Lloyd said triumphantly to his uncomprehending baby daughter. "He's told America they have to give us aid! But how much? And how, and when?"

The voice changed, and the reporter said: "The secretary of state did not outline a detailed plan for aid to Europe, but said it was up to the Europeans to draft the program."

"Does that mean we have carte blanche?" Lloyd eagerly asked Evie.

Marshall's voice returned to say: "The initiative, I think, must come from Europe."

The report ended, and the phone rang again. "Did you hear that?" said Bevin.

"What does it mean?"

"Don't ask!" said Bevin. "If you ask questions, you'll get answers you don't want."

"All right," Lloyd said, baffled.

"Never mind what he meant. The question is, what do we do? The initiative must come from Europe, he said. That means me and you."

"What can I do?"

"Pack a bag," said Bevin. "We're going to Paris."

# CHAPTER TWENTY-FOUR

# 1948

Volodya was in Prague as part of a Red Army delegation holding talks with the Czech military. They were staying in art deco splendor at the Imperial Hotel.

It was snowing.

He missed Zoya and little Kotya. His son was two years old and learning new words at bewildering speed. The child was changing so fast that he seemed different every day. And Zoya was pregnant again. Volodya resented having to spend two weeks apart from his family. Most of the men in the group saw the trip as a chance to get away from their wives, drink too much vodka, and maybe fool around with loose women. Volodya just wanted to go home.

The military talks were genuine, but Volodya's part in them was a cover for his real assignment, which was to report on the activities in Prague of the ham-fisted Soviet secret police, perennial rivals of Red Army Intelligence.

Volodya had little enthusiasm for his work nowadays. Everything he had once believed in had been undermined. He no longer had faith in Stalin, Communism, or the essential goodness of the Russian people. Even his father was not his father. He would have defected to the West if he could have found a way of getting Zoya and Kotya out with him.

However, he did have his heart in his mission here in Prague. It was a rare chance to do something he believed in.

Two weeks before, the Czech Communist Party had taken full control of the government, ousting their coalition partners. Foreign Minister Jan Masaryk, a war hero and democratic anti-Communist, had become a prisoner on the top floor of his official residence, the Czernin Palace. The Soviet secret police had undoubtedly been behind the coup. In fact Volodya's brother-in-law, Colonel Ilya Dvorkin, was also in Prague, staying at the same hotel, and had almost certainly been involved.

Volodya's boss, General Lemitov, saw the coup as a public relations catastrophe for the USSR. Masaryk had constituted proof, to the world, that east European countries could be free and independent in the shadow of the USSR. He had enabled Czechoslovakia to have a Communist government friendly to the Soviet Union and at the same time wear the costume of bourgeois democracy. This had been the perfect arrangement, for it gave the USSR everything it wanted while reassuring the Americans. But that equilibrium had been upset.

However, Ilya was crowing. "The bourgeois parties have been smashed!" he said to Volodya in the hotel bar one night.

"Did you see what happened in the American Senate?" Volodya said mildly. "Vandenberg, the old isolationist, made an eighty-minute speech in favor of the Marshall Plan, and he was cheered to the rafters."

George Marshall's vague ideas had become a plan. This was mainly thanks to the ratlike cunning of British foreign secretary Ernie Bevin. In Volodya's opinion, Bevin was the most dangerous kind of anti-Communist: a working-class Social Democrat. Despite his bulk he moved fast. With lightning speed he had organized a conference in Paris that had given a resounding collective European welcome to George Marshall's Harvard speech.

Volodya knew, from spies in the British Foreign Office, that Bevin was determined to bring Germany into the Marshall Plan and keep the USSR out. And Stalin had fallen straight into Bevin's trap, by commanding the east European countries to repudiate Marshall Aid.

Now the Soviet secret police seemed to be doing all they could to assist the passage of the bill through Congress. "The Senate was all set to reject Marshall," Volodya said to Ilya. "American taxpayers don't want to foot the bill. But the coup here in Prague has persuaded them that they have to, because European capitalism is in danger of collapse."

Ilya said indignantly: "The bourgeois Czech parties wanted to take the American bribe."

"We should have let them," said Volodya. "It might have been the quickest way to sabotage the whole scheme. Congress would then have rejected the Marshall Plan—they don't want to give money to Communists."

"The Marshall Plan is an imperialist trick!"

"Yes, it is," said Volodya. "And I'm afraid it's working. Our wartime allies are forming an anti-Soviet bloc."

"People who obstruct the forward march of Communism must be dealt with appropriately."

"Indeed they must." It was amazing how consistently people such as Ilya made the wrong political judgments.

"And I must go to bed."

It was only ten, but Volodya went, too. He lay awake thinking about Zoya and Kotya and wishing he could kiss them both good night.

His thoughts drifted to his mission. He had met Jan Masaryk, the symbol of Czech independence, two days earlier, at a ceremony at the grave of his father, Thomas Masaryk, the founder and first president of Czechoslovakia. Dressed in a coat with a fur collar, head bared to the falling snow, the second Masaryk had seemed beaten and depressed.

If he could be persuaded to stay on as foreign minister, some compromise might be possible, Volodya mused. Czechoslovakia could have a thoroughly Communist domestic government, but in its international relations it might be neutral, or at least minimally anti-American. Masaryk had both the diplomatic skills and the international credibility to walk that tightrope.

Volodya decided he would suggest it to Lemitov tomorrow.

He slept fitfully and woke before six o'clock with a mental alarm ringing in his imagination. It was something about last night's conversation with Ilya. Volodya ran over it again in his mind. When Ilya had said "people who obstruct the forward march of Communism," he had been talking about Masaryk, and when a secret policeman said someone had to be "dealt with appropriately," he always meant "killed."

Then Ilya had gone to bed early, which suggested an early start this morning.

I'm a fool, Volodya thought. The signs were there and it took me all night to read them.

He leaped out of bed. Perhaps he was not too late.

He dressed quickly and put on a heavy overcoat, scarf, and hat. There were no taxis outside the hotel—it was too early. He could have called a Red Army car, but by the time a driver was awakened and the car brought, it would have taken the best part of an hour.

He set out to walk. The Czernin Palace was only a mile or two away. He headed west out of Prague's gracious city center, crossed the Charles Bridge, and hurried uphill toward the castle.

Masaryk was not expecting him, nor was the foreign minister obliged to give audience to a Red Army colonel. But Volodya felt sure Masaryk would be curious enough to see him.

He walked fast through the snow and reached the Czernin Palace at six forty-five. It was a huge baroque building with a grandiose row of Corinthian half columns on the three upper stories. The place was lightly guarded, he found to his surprise. A sentry pointed to the front door. Volodya walked unchallenged through an ornate hall.

He had expected to find the usual secret police moron behind a reception desk, but there was no one. This was a bad sign, and he was filled with foreboding.

The hall led to an inner courtyard. Glancing through a window, he saw what looked like a man sleeping in the snow. Perhaps he had fallen there drunk: if so, he was in danger of freezing to death.

Volodya tried the door and found it open.

He ran across the quadrangle. A man in blue silk pajamas lay facedown on the ground. There was no snow covering him, so he could not have been there many minutes. Volodya knelt beside him. The man was quite still and did not appear to be breathing.

Volodya looked up. Rows of identical windows like soldiers on parade looked into this courtyard. All were closed tightly against the freezing weather—except one, high above the man in pajamas, that stood wide open.

As if someone had been thrown out of it.

Volodya turned the lifeless head and looked at the man's face.

It was Jan Masaryk.

## ii

Three days later in Washington, the Joint Chiefs of Staff presented to President Truman an emergency war plan to meet a Soviet invasion of Western Europe.

The danger of a third world war was a hot topic in the press. "We just *won* the war," Jacky Jakes said to Greg Peshkov. "How come we're about to have another?"

"That's what I keep asking myself," said Greg.

They were sitting on a park bench while Greg took a breather from throwing a football with Georgy.

"I'm glad he's too young to fight," Jacky said.

"Me, too."

They both looked at their son, standing talking to a blond girl about his age. The laces of his Keds were undone and his shirt was untucked. He was twelve years old and growing up. He had a few soft black hairs on his upper lip, and he seemed three inches taller than last week.

"We've been bringing our troops home as fast as we can," Greg said. "So have the British and the French. But the Red Army stayed put. Result: they now have three times as many soldiers in Germany as we do."

"Americans don't want another war."

"You can say that again. And Truman hopes to win the presidential election in November, so he's going to do everything he can to avoid war. But it may happen anyway."

"You're getting out of the army soon. What are you going to do?"

There was a quaver in her voice that made him suspect the question was not as casual as she pretended. He looked at her face, but her expression was unreadable. He answered: "Assuming America is not at war, I'm going to run for Congress in 1950. My father has agreed to finance my campaign. I'll start as soon as the presidential election is over."

She looked away. "Which party?" She asked the question mechanically.

He wondered if he had said something to upset her. "Republican, of course."

"What about marriage?"

Greg was taken aback. "Why do you ask that?"

She was looking hard at him now. "Are you getting married?" she persisted.

"As it happens, I am. Her name is Nelly Fordham."

"I thought so. How old is she?"

"Twenty-two. What do you mean, you thought so?"

"A politician needs a wife."

"I love her!"

"Sure you do. Is her family in politics?"

"Her father is a Washington lawyer."

"Good choice."

Greg felt annoyed. "You're being very cynical."

"I know you, Greg. Good Lord, I fucked you when you weren't much older than Georgy is now. You can fool everyone except your mother and me."

She was perceptive, as always. His mother had also been critical of his engagement. They were right: it was a career move. But Nelly was pretty and charming and she adored Greg, so what was so wrong? "I'm meeting her for lunch near here in a few minutes," he said.

Jacky said: "Does Nelly know about Georgy?"

"No. And we must keep it that way."

"You're right. Having an illegitimate child is bad enough; a black one could ruin your career."

"I know."

"Almost as bad as a black wife."

Greg was so surprised that he came right out with it. "Did you think I was going to marry *you*?"

She looked sour. "Hell, no, Greg. If I was given a choice between you and the Acid Bath Murderer, I'd ask for time to think about it."

She was lying, he knew. For a moment he contemplated the idea of marrying Jacky. Interracial marriages were unusual, and attracted a good deal of hostility from blacks as well as whites, but some people did it and put up with the consequences. He had never met a girl he liked as much as Jacky, not even Margaret Cowdry, whom he had dated for a couple of years, until she got fed up waiting for him to propose. Jacky was sharp-tongued, but he liked that, maybe because his mother was the same. There was something deeply attractive about the idea of the three of them being together all the time. Georgy would learn to call him Dad. They could buy a house in a neighborhood where people were broad-minded, someplace that had a lot of students and young professors, maybe Georgetown.

Then he saw Georgy's blond friend being called away by her parents, a cross white mother wagging a finger in admonition, and he realized that marrying Jacky was the worst idea in the world.

Georgy returned to where Greg and Jacky sat. "How's school?" Greg asked him.

"I like it better than I used to," the boy said. "Math is getting more interesting."

"I was good at math," Greg said.

Jacky said: "Now there's a coincidence."

Greg stood up. "I have to go." He squeezed Georgy's shoulder. "Keep working on the math, buddy."

"Sure," said Georgy.

Greg waved at Jacky and left.

She had been thinking about marriage at the same time as he, no doubt. She knew that coming out of the army was a decisive moment for him. It forced him to think about his future. She could not really have thought he would marry her, but all the same she must have harbored a secret fantasy. Now he had shattered it. Well, that was too bad. Even if she had been white, he would not have married her. He was fond of her, and he loved the kid, but he had his whole life ahead of him, and he wanted a wife who would bring him connections and support. Nelly's father was a powerful man in Republican politics.

He walked to the Napoli, an Italian restaurant a few blocks from the park. Nelly was already there, her copper red curls escaping from under a little green hat. "You look great!" he said. "I hope I'm not late." He sat down.

Nelly's face was stony. "I saw you in the park," she said.

Greg thought: Oh, shit.

"I was a little early, so I sat for a while," she said. "You didn't notice me. Then I started to feel like a snoop, so I left."

"So you saw my godson?" he said with forced cheerfulness.

"Is that who he is? You're a surprising choice for a godfather. You never even go to church."

"I'm good to the kid!"

"What's his name?"

"Georgy Jakes."

"You've never mentioned him before."

"Haven't I?"

"How old is he?"

"Twelve."

"So you were sixteen when he was born. That's young to be a godfather."

"I guess it is."

"What does his mother do for a living?"

"She's a waitress. Years ago she was an actress. Her stage name was Jacky Jakes. I met her when she was under contract to my father's studio." That was more or less true, Greg thought uncomfortably.

"And his father?"

Greg shook his head. "Jacky is single." A waiter approached. Greg said: "How about a cocktail?" Perhaps it might ease the tension. "Two martinis," he said to the waiter.

"Right away, sir."

As soon as the waiter had left, Nelly said: "You're the boy's father, aren't you?"

"Godfather."

Her voice became contemptuous. "Oh, stop it."

"What makes you so sure?"

"He may be black, but he looks like you. He can't keep his shoelaces tied or his shirt tucked in, and neither can you. And he was charming the pants off that little blond girl he was talking to. Of course he's yours."

Greg gave in. He sighed and said: "I was going to tell you."

"When?"

"I was waiting for the right moment."

"Before you proposed would have been a good time."

"I'm sorry." He was embarrassed, but not really contrite: he thought she was making an unnecessary fuss.

The waiter brought menus and they both looked at them. "The spaghetti Bolognese is great," said Greg.

"I'm going to get a salad."

Their martinis arrived. Greg raised his glass and said: "To forgiveness in marriage."

Nelly did not pick up her drink. "I can't marry you," she said.

"Honey, come on, don't overreact. I've apologized."

She shook her head. "You don't get it, do you?"

"What don't I get?"

"That woman sitting on the park bench with you—she loves you."

"Does she?" Greg would have denied it yesterday, but after today's conversation he was not sure.

"Of course she does. Why hasn't she married? She's pretty enough. By now she could have found a man willing to take on a stepson, if she'd really been trying. But she's in love with you, you rotter."

"I'm not so sure."

"And the boy adores you, too."

"I'm his favorite uncle."

"Except that you're not." She pushed her glass across the table. "You have my drink."

"Honey, please relax."

"I'm leaving." She stood up.

Greg was not used to girls walking out on him. He found it unnerving. Was he losing his allure?

"I want to marry you!" he said. He sounded desperate even to himself.

"You can't marry me, Greg," she said. She slipped the diamond ring off her finger and put it down on the red-checked tablecloth. "You already have a family."

She walked out of the restaurant.


### iii

The world crisis came to a head in June, and Carla and her family were at the center of it.

The Marshall Plan had been signed into law by President Truman, and the first shipments of aid were arriving in Europe, to the fury of the Kremlin.

On Friday, June 18, the Western Allies alerted Germans that they would make an important announcement at eight o'clock that evening. Carla's family gathered around the radio in the kitchen, tuned to Radio Frankfurt, and waited anxiously. The war had been over for three years, yet still they did not know what the future held: capitalism or Communism, unity or fragmentation, freedom or subjugation, prosperity or destitution.

Werner sat beside Carla with Walli, now two and a half, on his knee. They had married quietly a year ago. Carla was working as a nurse again. She was also a Berlin city councilor for the Social Democrats. So was Frieda's husband, Heinrich.

In East Germany the Russians had banned the Social Democratic

Party, but Berlin was an oasis in the Soviet sector, ruled by a council of the four main Allies called the Kommandatura, which had vetoed the ban. As a result, the Social Democrats had won, and the Communists had come a poor third after the conservative Christian Democrats. The Russians were incensed and did everything they could to obstruct the elected council. Carla found it frustrating, but she could not give up the hope of independence from the Soviets.

Werner had managed to start a small business. He had searched through the ruins of his father's factory and scavenged a small hoard of electrical supplies and radio parts. Germans could not afford to buy new radios, but everyone wanted their old ones repaired. Werner had found some engineers formerly employed at the factory and set them to work fixing broken wireless sets. He was the manager and salesman, going to houses and apartment buildings, knocking on doors, drumming up business.

Maud, also at the kitchen table this evening, worked as an interpreter for the Americans. She was one of the best, and often translated at meetings of the Kommandatura.

Carla's brother, Erik, was wearing the uniform of a policeman. Having joined the Communist Party—to the dismay of his family—he had got a job as a police officer in the new East German force organized by the Russian occupiers. Erik said the Western Allies were trying to split Germany in two. "You Social Democrats are secessionists," he said, quoting the Communist line in the same way he had parroted Nazi propaganda.

"The Western Allies haven't divided anything," Carla retorted. "They've opened the borders between their zones. Why don't the Soviets do the same? Then we would be one country again." He seemed not to hear her.

Rebecca was almost seventeen. Carla and Werner had legally adopted her. She was doing well at school and good at languages.

Carla was pregnant again, though she had not told Werner. She was thrilled. He had an adopted daughter and a stepson, but now he would have a child of his own as well. She knew he would be delighted when she told him. She was waiting a little longer to be sure.

But she yearned to know in what kind of country her three children were going to live.

An American officer called Robert Lochner came on the air. He had been raised in Germany and spoke the language effortlessly. Beginning at seven o'clock on Monday morning, he explained, West Germany would have a new currency, the deutsche mark.

Carla was not surprised. The reichsmark was worth less every day. Most people were paid in reichsmarks, if they had a job at all, and the currency could be used for basics such as food rations and bus fares, but everyone preferred to get groceries or cigarettes. Werner charged people in reichsmarks in his business but offered overnight service for five cigarettes and delivery anywhere in the city for three eggs.

Carla knew from Maud that the new currency had been discussed at the Kommandatura. The Russians had demanded plates so that they could print it. But they had debased the old currency by printing too much, and there was no point in a new currency if the same thing was going to happen. Consequently the West refused and the Soviets sulked.

Now the West had decided to go ahead without the cooperation of the Soviets. Carla was pleased, for the new currency would be good for Germany, but she felt apprehensive about the Soviet reaction.

People in West Germany could exchange sixty inflated old reichsmarks for three deutsche marks and ninety new pennies, said Lochner.

Then he said that none of this would apply in Berlin, at least at first, whereupon there was a collective groan in the kitchen.

Carla went to bed wondering what the Soviets would do. She lay beside Werner, part of her brain listening in case Walli, in the next room, should cry. The Soviet occupiers had been getting angrier for the last few months. A journalist called Dieter Friede had been kidnapped in the American zone by the Soviet secret police, then held captive; the Soviets at first denied all knowledge, then said they had arrested him as a spy. Three students had been expelled from university for criticizing the Russians in a magazine. Worst of all, a Soviet fighter aircraft buzzed a British European Airways passenger plane landing at Gatow airport and clipped its wing, causing both planes to crash and killing four BEA crew, ten passengers, and the Soviet pilot. When the Russians got angry, someone else always suffered.

Next morning the Soviets announced it would be a crime to import deutsche marks into East Germany. This included Berlin, the statement said, "which is part of the Soviet zone." The Americans immediately denounced this phrase and affirmed that Berlin was an international city, but the temperature was rising, and Carla remained anxious.

On Monday, West Germany got the new currency.

On Tuesday, a Red Army courier came to Carla's house and summoned her to city hall.

She had been summoned this way before, but all the same she was fearful as she left home. There was nothing to stop the Soviets imprisoning her. The Communists had all the same arbitrary powers the Nazis had assumed. They were even using the old concentration camps.

The famous Red City Hall had been damaged by bombing, and the city government was based in the New City Hall in Parochial Strasse. Both buildings were in the Mitte district, where Carla lived, which was in the Soviet zone.

When she got there, she found that Acting Mayor Louise Schroeder and others had also been called for a meeting with the Soviet liaison officer, Major Otshkin. He informed them that the East German currency was to be reformed, and in future only the new ostmark would be legal in the Soviet zone.

Acting Mayor Schroeder immediately saw the crucial point. "Are you telling us that this will apply in all sectors of Berlin?"

"Yes."

Frau Schroeder was not easily intimidated. "Under the city constitution, the Soviet occupying power cannot make such a rule for the other sectors," she said firmly. "The other Allies must be consulted."

"They will not object." He handed over a sheet of paper. "This is Marshal Sokolovsky's decree. You will bring it before the city council tomorrow."

Later that evening, as Carla got into bed with Werner, she said: "You can see what the Soviet tactic is. If the city council were to pass the decree, it would be difficult for the democratically minded Western Allies to overturn it."

"But the council won't pass it. The Communists are a minority, and no one else will want the ostmark."

"No. Which is why I'm wondering what Marshal Sokolovsky has up his sleeve."

The next morning's newspapers announced that from Friday there would be two competing currencies in Berlin, the ostmark and the deutsche mark. It turned out that the Americans had secretly flown in 250 million in the new currency in wooden boxes marked "Clay" and "Bird Dog," which were now stashed all over Berlin.

During the day Carla began to hear rumors from West Germany. The new money had brought about a miracle there. Overnight, more goods had appeared in shop windows: baskets of cherries and neatly tied bundles of carrots from the surrounding countryside, butter and eggs and pastries, and long-hoarded luxuries such as new shoes, handbags, and even stockings at four deutsche marks the pair. People had been waiting until they could sell things for real money.

That afternoon Carla set off for city hall to attend the council meeting scheduled for four o'clock. As she drew near, she saw dozens of Red Army trucks parked in the streets around the building, their drivers lounging around, smoking. They were mostly American vehicles that must have been given to the USSR as Lend-Lease aid during the war. She got an inkling of their purpose when she began to hear the sound of an unruly mob. What the Soviet governor had up his sleeve, she suspected, was a truncheon.

In front of city hall, red flags fluttered above a crowd of several thousand, most of them wearing Communist Party badges. Loudspeaker trucks blared angry speeches, and the crowd chanted: "Down with the secessionists."

Carla did not see how she was going to reach the building. A handful of policemen looked on uninterestedly, making no attempt to help councilors get through. It reminded Carla painfully of the attitude of police on the day the Brownshirts had trashed her mother's office, fifteen years ago. She was quite sure the Communist councilors were already inside, and that if Social Democrats did not get into the building, the minority would pass the decree and claim it to be valid.

She took a deep breath and began to push through the crowd.

For a few steps she made progress unnoticed. Then someone recognized her. "American whore!" he yelled, pointing at her. She pressed on determinedly. Someone else spat at her, and a gob of saliva smeared her dress. She kept going, but she felt panicky. She was surrounded by people who hated her, something she had never experienced, and it made her want to run away. She was shoved, but managed to keep her feet. A hand grasped her dress, and she pulled free with a tearing sound. She wanted to scream. What would they do, rip all her clothes off?

Someone else was fighting his way through the crowd behind her, she realized, and she looked back and saw Heinrich von Kessel, Frieda's husband. He drew level with her and they barreled on together. Heinrich was more aggressive, stamping on toes and vigorously elbowing everyone within range. Together they moved faster, and at last reached the door and went in.

But their ordeal was not over. There were Communist demonstrators inside, too, hundreds of them. They had to fight through the corridors. In the meeting hall the demonstrators were everywhere—not just in the visitors' gallery but on the floor of the chamber. Their behavior here was just as aggressive as outside.

Some Social Democrats were here, and others arrived after Carla. Somehow most of the sixty-three had been able to fight their way through the mob. She was relieved. The enemy had not managed to scare them off.

When the speaker of the assembly called for order, a Communist assemblyman standing on a bench urged the demonstrators to stay. When he saw Carla, he yelled: "Traitors stay outside!"

It was all grimly reminiscent of 1933: bullying, intimidation, and democracy being undermined by rowdyism. Carla was in despair.

Glancing up to the gallery, she was appalled to see her brother, Erik, among the yelling mob. "You're German!" she screamed at him. "You lived under the Nazis. Have you learned *nothing*?"

He seemed not to hear her.

Frau Schroeder stood on the platform, calling for calm. She was jeered and booed by the demonstrators. Raising her voice to a shout, she said: "If the city council cannot hold an orderly debate in this building, I will move the meeting to the American sector."

There was renewed abuse, but the twenty-six Communist councilors saw that this move would not suit their purpose. If the council met outside the Soviet zone once, it might do so again, and even move permanently out of the range of Communist intimidation. After a short discussion, one of them stood up and told the demonstrators to leave. They filed out, singing "The Internationale."

"It's obvious whose command they're under," Heinrich said.

At last there was quiet. Frau Schroeder explained the Soviet demand, and said that it could not apply outside the Soviet sector of Berlin unless it was ratified by the other Allies.

A Communist deputy made a speech accusing her of taking orders directly from New York.

Accusations and abuse raged to and fro. Eventually they voted. The Communists unanimously backed the Soviet decree—after accusing others of being controlled from outside. Everyone else voted against, and the motion was defeated. Berlin had refused to be bullied. Carla felt wearily triumphant.

However, it was not yet over.

By the time they left, it was seven o'clock in the evening. Most of the mob had disappeared, but there was a thuggish hard core still hanging around the entrance. An elderly woman councilor was kicked and punched as she left. The police looked on with indifference.

Carla and Heinrich left by a side door with a few friends, hoping to depart unobserved, but a Communist on a bicycle was monitoring the exit. He rode off quickly.

As the councilors hurried away, he returned at the head of a small gang. Someone tripped Carla, and she fell to the ground. She was kicked painfully once, twice, three times. Terrified, she covered her belly with her hands. She was almost three months pregnant—the stage at which most miscarriages occurred, she knew. Will Werner's baby die, she thought desperately, kicked to death on a Berlin street by Communist thugs?

Then they disappeared.

The councilors picked themselves up. No one was badly injured. They moved off together, fearful of a recurrence, but it seemed the Communists had roughed up enough people for one day.

Carla got home at eight o'clock. There was no sign of Erik.

Werner was shocked to see her bruises and torn dress. "What happened?" he said. "Are you all right?"

She burst into tears.

"You're hurt," Werner said. "Should we go to the hospital?"

She shook her head vigorously. "It's not that," she said. "I'm just bruised. I've had worse." She slumped in a chair. "Christ, I'm tired."

"Who did this?" he asked angrily.

"The usual people," she said. "They call themselves Communists instead of Nazis, but they're the same type. It's 1933 all over again."

Werner put his arms around her.

She could not be consoled. "The bullies and the thugs have been in power for so long!" she sobbed. "Will it ever end?"

## iv

That night the Soviet news agency put out an announcement. From six o'clock in the morning, all passenger and freight transport in and out of West Berlin—trains, cars, and canal barges—would be stopped. No supplies of any kind would get through: no food, no milk, no medicines, no coal. Because the electricity generating stations would therefore be shut down, they were switching off the supply of electricity—to western sectors only.

The city was under siege.

Lloyd Williams was at British military headquarters. There was a short parliamentary recess, and Ernie Bevin had gone on holiday to Sandbanks, on the south coast of England, but he was worried enough to send Lloyd to Berlin to observe the introduction of the new currency and keep him informed.

Daisy had not accompanied Lloyd. Their new baby, Davey, was only six months old, and anyway Daisy and Eva Murray were organizing a birth-control clinic for women in Hoxton that was about to open its doors.

Lloyd was desperately afraid that this crisis would lead to war. He had fought in two wars, and he never wanted to see a third. He had two small children who he hoped would grow up in a peaceful world. He was married to the prettiest, sexiest, most lovable woman on the planet and he wanted to spend many long decades with her.

General Clay, the workaholic American military governor, ordered his staff to plan an armored convoy that would barrel down the autobahn from Helmstedt, in the west, straight through Soviet territory to Berlin, sweeping all before it.

Lloyd heard about this plan at the same time as the British governor, Sir Brian Robertson, and heard him say in his clipped soldierly tones: "If Clay does that, it will be war."

But nothing else made any sense. The Americans came up with other suggestions, Lloyd heard, talking to Clay's younger aides. The secretary of the army, Kenneth Royall, wanted to halt the currency reform. Clay told him it had gone too far to be reversed. Next, Royall proposed evacuating all Americans. Clay told him that was exactly what the Soviets wanted.

Sir Brian wanted to supply the city by air. Most people thought that was impossible. Someone calculated that Berlin required four thousand tons of fuel and food per day. Were there enough airplanes in the *world* to move that much stuff? No one knew. Nevertheless, Sir Brian ordered the Royal Air Force to make a start.

On Friday afternoon Sir Brian went to see Clay, and Lloyd was invited to be part of the entourage. Sir Brian said to Clay: "The Russians might block the autobahn ahead of your convoy, and wait and see if you have the nerve to attack them, but I don't think they'll shoot planes down."

"I don't see how we can deliver enough supplies by air," Clay said again.

"Nor do I," said Sir Brian. "But we're going to do it until we think of something better."

Clay picked up the phone. "Get me General LeMay in Wiesbaden," he said. After a minute he said: "Curtis, have you got any planes there that can carry coal?"

There was a pause.

"Coal," said Clay more loudly.

Another pause.

"Yes, that is what I said—coal."

A moment later, Clay looked up at Sir Brian. "He says the U.S. Air Force can deliver anything."

The British returned to their headquarters.

On Saturday, Lloyd got an army driver and went into the Soviet zone on a personal mission. He drove to the address at which he had visited the von Ulrich family fifteen years ago.

He knew that Maud was still living there. His mother and Maud had resumed correspondence at the end of the war. Maud's letters put a brave face on what was undoubtedly severe hardship. She did not ask for help, and anyway there was nothing Ethel could do for her— rationing was still in force in Britain.

The place looked very different. In 1933 it had been a fine town house, a little run-down but still gracious. Now it looked like a dump. Most of the windows had boards or paper instead of glass. There were bullet holes in the stonework, and the garden wall had collapsed. The woodwork had not been painted for many years.

Lloyd sat in the car for a few moments, looking at the house. Last time he came here, he had been eighteen, and Hitler had only just become chancellor of Germany. The young Lloyd had not dreamed of the horrors the world was going to see. Neither he nor anyone else had suspected how close Fascism would come to triumphing over all Europe, and how much they would have to sacrifice to defeat it. He felt a bit like the von Ulrich house looked, battered and bombed and shot at but still standing.

He walked up the path and knocked.

He recognized the maid who opened the door. "Hello, Ada, do you remember me?" he said in German. "I'm Lloyd Williams."

The house was better inside than out. Ada showed him up to the drawing room, where there were flowers in a glass tumbler on the piano. A brightly patterned blanket had been thrown over the sofa, no doubt to hide holes in the upholstery. The newspapers in the windows let in a surprising amount of light.

A two-year-old boy walked into the room and inspected him with frank curiosity. He was dressed in clothes that were evidently homemade, and he had an Oriental look. "Who are you?" he said.

"My name is Lloyd. Who are you?"

"Walli," he said. He ran out again, and Lloyd heard him say to someone outside: "That man talks funny!"

So much for my German accent, Lloyd thought.

Then he heard the voice of a middle-aged woman. "Don't make such remarks! It's impolite."

"Sorry, Grandma."

Next moment Maud walked in.

Her appearance shocked Lloyd. She was in her midfifties, but looked seventy. Her hair was gray, her face was gaunt, and her blue silk dress was threadbare. She kissed his cheek with shrunken lips. "Lloyd Williams, what a joy to see you!"

She's my aunt, Lloyd thought with a rather queer feeling. But she did not know that: Ethel had kept the secret.

Maud was followed by Carla, who was unrecognizable, and her husband. Lloyd had met Carla as a precocious eleven-year-old; now, he calculated, she was twenty-six. Although she looked half-starved—most Germans did—she was pretty, and had a confident air that surprised Lloyd. Something about the way she stood made him think she might be pregnant. He knew from Maud's letters that Carla had married Werner, who had been a handsome charmer back in 1933 and was still the same.

They spent an hour catching up. The family had been through unimaginable horror, and said so frankly, yet Lloyd still had a sense that they were editing out the worst details. He told them about Daisy, Evie, and Davey. During the conversation a teenage girl came in and asked Carla if she could go to her friend's house.

"This is our daughter, Rebecca," Carla said to Lloyd.

She was about sixteen, so Lloyd supposed she must be adopted.

"Have you done your homework?" Carla asked the girl.

"I'll do it tomorrow morning."

"Do it now, please," Carla said firmly.

"Oh, Mother!"

"No argument," said Carla. She turned back to Lloyd, and Rebecca stomped out.

They talked about the crisis. Carla was deeply involved, as a city councilor. She was pessimistic about the future of Berlin. She thought the Russians would simply starve the population until the West gave in and handed the city over to total Soviet control.

"Let me show you something that may make you feel differently," Lloyd said. "Will you come with me in the car?"

Maud stayed behind with Walli, but Carla and Werner went with Lloyd. He told the driver to take them to Tempelhof, the airport in the American zone. When they arrived, he led them to a high window from which they could look down on the runway.

There on the tarmac were a dozen C-47 Skytrain aircraft lined up nose to tail, some with the American star, some with the RAF roundel. Their cargo doors were open, and a truck stood at each one. German porters and American airmen were unloading the aircraft. There were sacks of flour, big drums of kerosene, cartons of medical supplies, and wooden crates containing thousands of bottles of milk.

While they watched, empty aircraft were taking off and more were coming in to land.

"This is amazing," said Carla, her eyes glistening. "I've never seen anything like it."

"There has never *been* anything like it," Lloyd replied.

She said: "But can the British and Americans keep it up?"

"I think we have to."

"But for how long?"

"As long as it takes," said Lloyd firmly.

And they did.

# CHAPTER TWENTY-FIVE

# 1949

Almost halfway through the twentieth century, on August 29, 1949, Volodya Peshkov was on the Ustyurt Plateau, east of the Caspian Sea in Kazakhstan. It was a stony desert in the deep south of the USSR, where nomads herded goats in much the same way as they had in biblical times. Volodya was in a military truck that bounced uncomfortably along a rough track. Dawn was breaking over a landscape of rock, sand, and low thorny bushes. A bony camel, alone beside the road, stared malevolently at the truck as it passed.

In the dim distance, Volodya saw the bomb tower, lit by a battery of spotlights.

Zoya and the other scientists had built their first nuclear bomb according to the design Volodya had got from Willi Frunze in Santa Fe. It was a plutonium device with an implosion trigger. There were other designs, but this one had worked twice before, once in New Mexico and once at Nagasaki.

So it should work today.

The test was code-named RDS-1, but they called it First Lightning.

Volodya's truck pulled up at the foot of the tower. Looking up, he saw a clutch of scientists on the platform, doing something with a snake's nest of cables that led to detonators on the skin of the bomb. A figure in blue overalls stepped back, and there was a toss of blond hair: Zoya. Volodya felt a flush of pride. My wife, he thought, top physicist *and* mother of two.

She conferred with two men, the three heads close together, arguing. Volodya hoped nothing was wrong.

This was the bomb that would save Stalin.

Everything else had gone wrong for the Soviet Union. Western Europe had turned decisively democratic, scared off Communism by bully-boy Kremlin tactics and bought off by Marshall Plan bribes. The USSR had not even been able to take control of Berlin: when the airlift had gone on relentlessly day after day for almost a year, the Soviet Union had given up and reopened the roads and railways. In Eastern Europe, Stalin had retained control only by brute force. Truman had been reelected president, and considered himself leader of the world. The Americans had stockpiled nuclear weapons, and had stationed B-29 bombers in Britain, ready to turn the Soviet Union into a radioactive wasteland.

But everything would change today.

If the bomb exploded as it should, the USSR and the USA would be equals again. When the Soviet Union could threaten America with nuclear devastation, American domination of the world would be over.

Volodya no longer knew whether that would be good or bad.

If it did not explode, both Zoya and Volodya would probably be purged, sent to labor camps in Siberia or just shot. Volodya had already talked to his parents, and they had promised to take care of Kotya and Galina.

As they would if Volodya and Zoya were killed by the test.

In the strengthening light Volodya saw, at various distances around the tower, an odd variety of buildings: houses of brick and wood, a bridge over nothing, and the entrance to some kind of underground structure. Presumably the army wanted to measure the effect of the blast. Looking more carefully he saw trucks, tanks, and obsolete aircraft, placed for the same purpose, he imagined. The scientists were also going to assess the impact of the bomb on living creatures: there were horses, cattle, sheep, and dogs in kennels.

The confab on the platform ended with a decision. The three scientists nodded and resumed their work.

A few minutes later Zoya came down and greeted her husband.

"Is everything all right?" he said.

"We think so," Zoya replied.

"You *think* so?"

She shrugged. "We've never done this before, obviously."

They got into the truck and drove, across country that was already a wasteland, to the distant control bunker.

The other scientists were close behind.

At the bunker they all put on welders' goggles as the countdown ticked away.

At sixty seconds, Zoya held Volodya's hand.

At ten seconds, he smiled at her and said: "I love you."

At one second, he held his breath.

Then it was as if the sun had suddenly risen. A light stronger than noon flooded the desert. In the direction of the bomb tower, a ball of fire grew impossibly high, reaching for the moon. Volodya was startled by the lurid colors in the fireball: green, purple, and orange.

The ball turned into a mushroom whose umbrella kept rising. At last the sound arrived, a bang as if the largest artillery piece in the Red Army had been fired a foot away, followed by rolling thunder that reminded Volodya of the terrible bombardment of the Seelow Heights.

At last the cloud began to disperse and the noise faded.

There was a long moment of stunned silence.

Someone said: "My God, I didn't expect *that*."

Volodya embraced his wife. "You did it," he said.

She looked solemn. "I know," she said. "But *what* did we do?"

"You saved Communism," said Volodya.

## ii

"The Russian bomb was based on Fat Man, the one we dropped on Nagasaki," said Special Agent Bill Bicks. "Someone gave them the plans."

"How do you know?" Greg asked him.

"From a defector."

They were sitting in Bicks's carpeted office in the Washington headquarters of the FBI at nine o'clock in the morning. Bicks had his jacket off. His shirt was stained in the armpits with sweat, though the building was comfortably air-conditioned.

"According to this guy," Bicks went on, "a Red Army Intelligence colonel got the plans from one of the scientists on the Manhattan Project team."

"Did he say who?"

"He doesn't know which scientist. That's why I called you in. We need to find the traitor."

"The FBI checked them all out at the time."

"And most of them were security risks! There was nothing we could do. But you knew them personally."

"Who was the Red Army colonel?"

"I was coming to that. You know him. His name is Vladimir Peshkov."

"My half brother!"

"Yes."

"If I were you, I'd suspect me." Greg said it with a laugh, but he was very uneasy.

"Oh, we did, believe me," Bicks said. "You've been subjected to the most thorough investigation I have seen in twenty years with the bureau."

Greg gave him a skeptical look. "No kidding."

"Your kid's doing well in school, isn't he?"

Greg was shocked. Who could have told the FBI about Georgy? "You mean my godson?" he said.

"Greg, I said *thorough*. We know he's your son."

Greg was annoyed, but he suppressed the feeling. He had probed the personal secrets of numerous suspects during his time in army security. He had no right to object.

"You're clean," Bicks went on.

"I'm relieved to hear it."

"Anyway, our defector insisted the plans came from a scientist, rather than any of the normal army personnel working on the project."

Greg said thoughtfully: "When I met Volodya in Moscow, he told me he had never been to the United States."

"He lied," said Bicks. "He came here in September 1945. He spent a week in New York. Then we lost him for eight days. He resurfaced briefly, then went home."

"Eight days?"

"Yeah. We're embarrassed."

"It's enough time to go to Santa Fe, stay a couple of days, and come back."

"Right." Bicks leaned forward across his desk. "But think. If the scientist had already been recruited as a spy, why wasn't he contacted by his regular controller? Why bring someone from Moscow to talk to him?"

"You think the traitor was recruited on this two-day visit? It seems too quick."

"Possibly he had worked for them before but lapsed. Either way, we're guessing the Soviets needed to send *someone who the scientist already knew.* That means there ought to be a connection between Volodya and one of the scientists." Bicks gestured at a side table covered with tan file folders. "The answer is in there somewhere. Those are our files on every one of the scientists who had access to those plans."

"What do you want me to do?"

"Go through them."

"Isn't that your job?"

"We've already done it. We didn't find anything. We're hoping you'll spot something we've missed. I'll sit here and keep you company, do some paperwork."

"It's a long job."

"You've got all day."

Greg frowned. Did they know . . . ?

Bicks said confidently: "You have no plans for the rest of the day."

Greg shrugged. "Got any coffee?"

He had coffee and donuts, then more coffee, then a sandwich at lunchtime, then a banana midafternoon. He read every known detail about the lives of the scientists, their wives and families: childhood, education, career, love and marriage, achievements and eccentricities and sins.

He was eating the last bite of banana when he said: "Jesus fucking Christ."

"What?" said Bicks.

"Willi Frunze went to the Berlin Boys' Academy." Greg slapped the file triumphantly down on the desk.

"And . . . ?"

"So did Volodya—he told me."

Bicks thumped his desk in excitement. "School friends! That's it! We've got the bastard!"

"It's not proof," said Greg.

"Oh, don't worry. He'll confess."

"How can you be sure?"

"Those scientists believe that knowledge should be shared with everyone, not kept secret. He'll try to justify himself by arguing that he did it for the good of humanity."

"Maybe he did."

"He'll go to the electric chair all the same," said Bicks.

Greg was suddenly chilled. Willi Frunze had seemed a nice guy. "Will he?"

"You bet your ass. He's going to fry."

Bicks was right. Willi Frunze was found guilty of treason and sentenced to death, and he died in the electric chair.

So did his wife.

## iii

Daisy watched her husband tie his white bow tie and slip into the tailcoat of his perfectly fitting dress suit. "You look like a million dollars," she said, and she meant it. He should have been a movie star.

She remembered him thirteen years earlier, wearing borrowed clothes at the Trinity Ball, and she felt a pleasant frisson of nostalgia. He had looked pretty good then, she recalled, even though his suit was two sizes too big.

They were staying in her father's permanent suite at the Ritz-Carlton hotel in Washington. Lloyd was now a junior minister in the British Foreign Office, and he had come here on a diplomatic visit. Lloyd's parents, Ethel and Bernie, were thrilled to be looking after two grandchildren for a week.

Tonight Daisy and Lloyd were going to a ball at the White House.

She was wearing a drop-dead dress by Christian Dior, pink satin with a dramatically spreading skirt made of endless folds of flaring tulle. After the years of wartime austerity she was delighted to be able to buy gowns in Paris again.

She thought of the Yacht Club Ball of 1935 in Buffalo, the event that she imagined, at the time, had ruined her life. The White House was obviously a lot more prestigious, but she knew that nothing that happened tonight could ruin her life. She reflected on that while Lloyd helped her put on her mother's necklace of rose-colored diamonds with matching earrings. At the age of nineteen she had desperately wanted high-status people to accept her. Now she could hardly imagine worrying about such a thing. As long as Lloyd said she looked fabulous, she did not care what anyone else thought. The only other person whose approval she might seek was her mother-in-law, Eth Leckwith, who had little social status and had certainly never worn a Paris gown.

Did every woman look back and think how foolish she had been when young? Daisy thought again about Ethel, who had certainly behaved foolishly—getting pregnant by her married employer—but never spoke regretfully about it. Maybe that was the right attitude.

Daisy contemplated her own mistakes: becoming engaged to Charlie Farquharson, rejecting Lloyd, marrying Boy Fitzherbert. She was not quite able to look back and think about the good that had come of those choices. It was really not until she had been decisively rejected by high society, and had found consolation at Ethel's kitchen in Aldgate, that her life had taken a turn for the better. She had stopped yearning for social status and had learned what real friendship was, and she had been happy ever since.

Now that she no longer cared, she enjoyed parties even more.

"Ready?" said Lloyd.

She was ready. She put on the matching evening coat that Dior had made to go with the dress. They went down in the elevator, left the hotel, and stepped into the waiting limousine.

## iv

Carla persuaded her mother to play the piano on Christmas Eve.

Maud had not played for years. Perhaps it saddened her by bringing back memories of Walter: they had always played and sung together, and she had often told the children how she had tried, and failed, to teach him to play ragtime. But she no longer told that story, and Carla suspected that nowadays the piano made Maud think of Joachim Koch, the young officer who had come to her for piano lessons, whom she had deceived and seduced, and whom Carla and Ada had killed in the kitchen. Carla herself was not able to shut out the recollection of that nightmare evening, especially getting rid of the body. She did not regret it—they had done the right thing—but, all the same, she would have preferred to forget it.

However, Maud at last agreed to play "Silent Night" for them all to sing along. Werner, Ada, Erik, and the three children, Rebecca, Walli, and the new baby, Lili, gathered around the old Steinway in the drawing room. Carla put a candle on the piano, and studied the faces of her family in its moving shadows as they sang the familiar German carol.

Walli, in Werner's arms, would be four years old in a few weeks' time, and he tried to sing along, alertly guessing the words and the melody. He had the Oriental eyes of his rapist father; Carla had decided that her revenge would be to raise a son who treated women with tenderness and respect.

Erik sang the words of the hymn sincerely. He supported the Soviet regime as blindly as he had supported the Nazis. Carla had at first been baffled and infuriated, but now she saw a sad logic to it. Erik was one of those inadequate people who were so scared by life that they preferred to live under harsh authority, to be told what to do and what to think by a government that allowed no dissent. They were foolish and dangerous, but there were an awful lot of them.

Carla gazed fondly at her husband, still handsome at thirty. She recalled kissing him, and more, in the front of his sexy car, parked in the Grunewald, when she was nineteen. She still liked kissing him.

When she thought over the time that had passed since then, she had a thousand regrets, but the biggest was her father's death. She missed him constantly and still cried when she remembered him lying in the hall, beaten so cruelly that he did not live until the doctor arrived.

But everyone had to die, and Father had given his life for the sake of a better world. If more Germans had had his courage, the Nazis would not have triumphed. She wanted to do all the things he had done: to raise her children well, to make a difference to her country's politics, to love and be loved. Most of all, when she died, she wanted her children to be able to say, as she said of her father, that her life had meant something, and that the world was a better place for it.

The carol came to an end; Maud held the final chord; and little Walli leaned forward and blew the candle out.

# ACKNOWLEDGMENTS

My principal history adviser for the Century Trilogy is Richard Overy. I am grateful also to historians Evan Mawdsley, Tim Rees, Matthias Reiss, and Richard Toye for reading the typescript of *Winter of the World* and making corrections.

As always I had invaluable help from my editors and agents, especially Amy Berkower, Leslie Gelbman, Phyllis Grann, Neil Nyren, Susan Opie, and Jeremy Treviathan.

I met my agent Al Zuckerman in about 1975 and he has been my most critical and inspiring reader ever since.

Several friends made helpful comments. Nigel Dean has an eye for detail like no one else. Chris Manners and Tony McWalter were as sharply perceptive as ever. Angela Spizig and Annemarie Behnke saved me from numerous errors in the German sections.

We always thank our families, and so we should. Barbara Follett, Emanuele Follett, Jann Turner, and Kim Turner read the first draft and made useful criticisms, as well as giving me the matchless gift of their love.

# ABOUT THE AUTHOR

**Ken Follett** burst into the book world with *Eye of the Needle*, an award-winning thriller and international bestseller. After several more successful thrillers, he surprised everyone with *The Pillars of the Earth* and its long-awaited sequel, *World Without End*, a national and international bestseller. Follett's new, magnificent historical epic, the Century Trilogy, opened with the bestselling *Fall of Giants*. He lives in England with his wife, Barbara.

CONNECT ONLINE

www.ken-follett.com

# ABOUT THE AUTHOR

KEN FOLLETT burst into the book world with *Eye of the Needle*, an award-winning thriller and international bestseller. After several more successful thrillers, he surprised everyone with *The Pillars of the Earth* and its long-awaited sequel, *World Without End*, a national and international bestseller. Follett's new, magnificent historical epic, the Century Trilogy, opened with the bestselling *Fall of Giants*. He lives in England with his wife, Barbara.

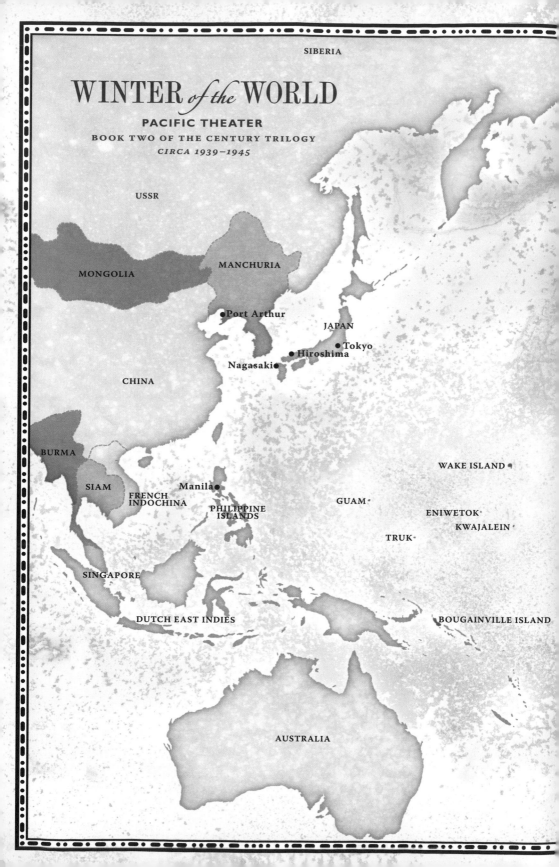

# WINTER *of the* WORLD

## PACIFIC THEATER

### BOOK TWO OF THE CENTURY TRILOGY

*CIRCA 1939–1945*

SIBERIA

USSR

MONGOLIA

MANCHURIA

● Port Arthur

JAPAN

● Tokyo
● Hiroshima

Nagasaki ●

CHINA

BURMA

SIAM

FRENCH
INDOCHINA

Manila ●

PHILIPPINE
ISLANDS

GUAM

WAKE ISLAND

ENIWETOK

KWAJALEIN

TRUK

SINGAPORE

DUTCH EAST INDIES

BOUGAINVILLE ISLAND

AUSTRALIA

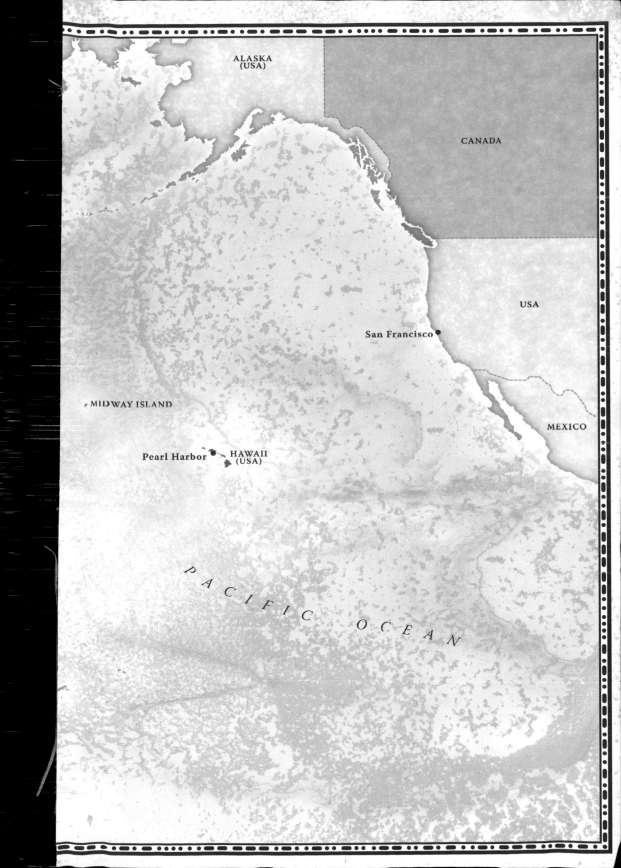

★ BOOK THREE OF ★
THE CENTURY TRILOGY

EDGE OF
ETERNITY

FALL 2014

Dutton, A member of Penguin Group (USA) Inc.